I0819218

BY ALISON WEIR

FICTION

Six Tudor Queens:
Katharine Parr, The Sixth Wife
Katheryn Howard, The Scandalous Queen
Anna of Kleve, The Princess in the Portrait
Jane Seymour, The Haunted Queen
Anne Boleyn, A King's Obsession
Katherine of Aragon: The True Queen

The King's Pleasure
The Last White Rose
The Marriage Game
A Dangerous Inheritance
Captive Queen
The Lady Elizabeth
Innocent Traitor
The Passionate Tudor
The Cardinal

NONFICTION

England's Medieval Queens:
Queens of the Crusades
Queens of the Conquest
Queens of the Age of Chivalry
Queens at War

The Lost Tudor Princess: The Life of Lady Margaret Douglas
Elizabeth of York: A Tudor Queen and Her World
Mary Boleyn: The Mistress of Kings
The Lady in the Tower: The Fall of Anne Boleyn
Mistress of the Monarchy: The Life of Katherine Swynford, Duchess of Lancaster
Queen Isabella: Treachery, Adultery, and Murder in Medieval England
Mary Queen of Scots and the Murder of Lord Darnley
Henry VIII: The King and His Court
Eleanor of Aquitaine: A Life
The Life of Elizabeth I
The Children of Henry VIII
The Wars of the Roses
The Princes in the Tower
The Six Wives of Henry VIII

THE BOLEYN SECRET

THE BOLEYN SECRET

A NOVEL

Alison Weir

BALLANTINE BOOKS
NEW YORK

Ballantine Books
An imprint of Random House
A division of Penguin Random House LLC
1745 Broadway, New York, NY 10019
randomhousebooks.com
penguinrandomhouse.com

Copyright © 2026 by Alison Weir

Penguin Random House values and supports copyright. Copyright fuels creativity, encourages diverse voices, promotes free speech, and creates a vibrant culture. Thank you for buying an authorized edition of this book and for complying with copyright laws by not reproducing, scanning, or distributing any part of it in any form without permission. You are supporting writers and allowing Penguin Random House to continue to publish books for every reader. Please note that no part of this book may be used or reproduced in any manner for the purpose of training artificial intelligence technologies or systems.

BALLANTINE BOOKS & colophon are registered trademarks of Penguin Random House LLC.

Published in the United Kingdom by Headline Review, an imprint of the Headline Publishing Group, a Hachette company, London.

Hardcover ISBN 978-0-593-97473-5
Ebook ISBN 978-0-593-97474-2

Printed in the United States of America

2nd Printing

First U.S. Edition

BOOK TEAM: Production editor: Luke Epplin • Managing editor: Pamela Alders • Production manager: Sarah Feightner • Proofreaders: Pam Feinstein, Rebecca Maines, Adele Starrs

Book design by Kim Henze Walker

The authorized representative in the EU for product safety and compliance is Penguin Random House Ireland, Morrison Chambers, 32 Nassau Street, Dublin D02 YH68, Ireland. https://eu-contact.penguin.ie

To Siobhan and Roger,
to mark their marriage

Katherine Carey's Family

ANNE
c. 1475–1556
m.
SIR JOHN SHELTON
c. 1472–1539
(issue)

THOMAS BOLEYN m. ELIZABETH
Earl of Wiltshire and Ormond
1477–1539

ELIZABETH
d. 1538
dr. of Thomas Howard, 2nd Duke of Norfolk

MARY
c. 1498–1543
m.
1 WILLIAM CAREY
1496?–1528
2 WILLIAM STAFFORD
1512?–56
(issue, d. young)

KATHERINE CAREY
1524–69

HENRY CAREY
Lord Hunsdon
1525–96
M. ANNE MORGAN
(issue)

SIR WILLIAM BOLEYN
1451?–1505
m.
MARGARET
1454-1465?–1539/40
dr. of Thomas Butler, Earl of Ormond

JAMES
1493?–1561
m.
ELIZABETH WOOD

ANNE
c. 1501–36
m.
HENRY VIII
King of England
1491–1547

ELIZABETH I
Queen of England
1533–1603

GEORGE
1503?–36
Viscount Rochford
m.
JANE PARKER

MARGARET
1489–1541

m.

1 JAMES IV
King of Scots
1473–1513

2 ARCHIBALD DOUGLAS
Earl of Angus
c. 1489–1557

HENRY VIII
1491–1547

m.

1 KATHERINE OF ARAGON
1485–1536

2 ANNE BOLEYN
c. 1501–36

3 JANE SEYMOUR
c. 1508–37

4 ANNA OF CLEVES
1515–57

5 KATHERYN HOWARD
1521?–42

6 KATHARINE PARR
1512–48

JAMES V
King of Scots
1512–42

MARGARET DOUGLAS
1515–78
m.
MATTHEW STEWART
Earl of Lennox
1516–71

MARY
Queen of Scots
1542–87

m.

HENRY STEWART
Lord Darnley
1546–67

JAMES VI & I
1566–1625

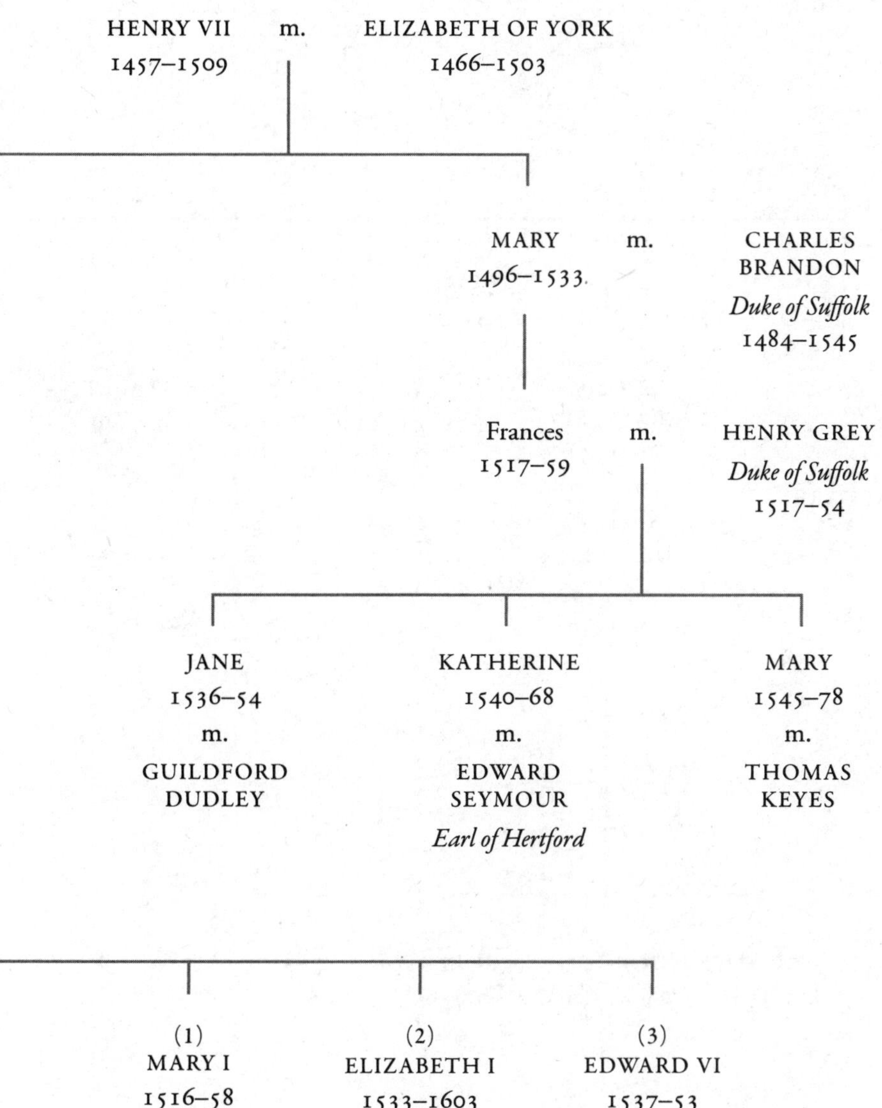
HENRY VII
1457–1509
m.
ELIZABETH OF YORK
1466–1503
MARY
1496–1533
m.
CHARLES BRANDON
Duke of Suffolk
1484–1545
Frances
1517–59
m.
HENRY GREY
Duke of Suffolk
1517–54
JANE
1536–54
m.
GUILDFORD DUDLEY
KATHERINE
1540–68
m.
EDWARD SEYMOUR
Earl of Hertford
MARY
1545–78
m.
THOMAS KEYES
(1)
MARY I
1516–58
(2)
ELIZABETH I
1533–1603
(3)
EDWARD VI
1537–53

The Knollys Family

MARY
b. 1542

WILLIAM
b. 1545

MAUD
b. 1548

HENRY
b. 1541
m.
MARGARET CAVE

LETTICE (LAETITIA)
b. 1543
m.
WALTER DEVEREUX
Lord Hereford
b. 1539

EDWARD
b. 1546

ELIZABETH
b. 1549

PENELOPE
b. 1563

DOROTHY
b. 1564

ROBERT
b. 1565

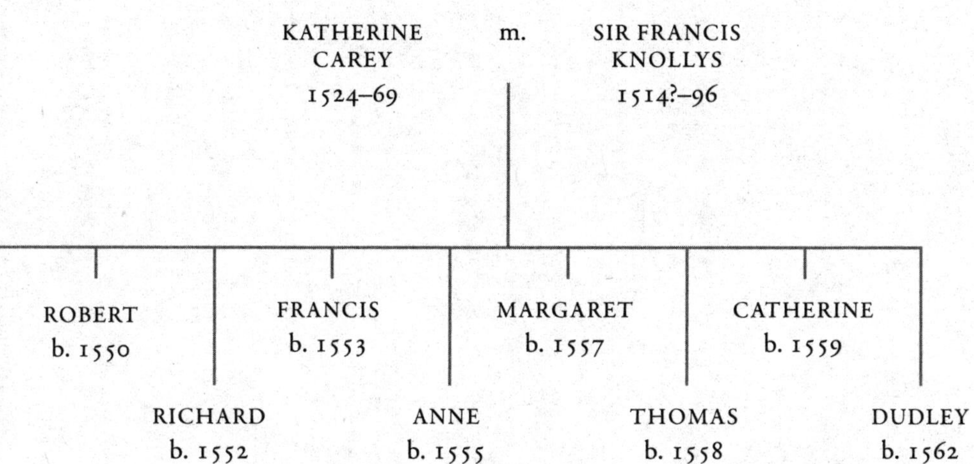
KATHERINE CAREY 1524–69
m.
SIR FRANCIS KNOLLYS 1514?–96
ROBERT b. 1550
RICHARD b. 1552
FRANCIS b. 1553
ANNE b. 1555
MARGARET b. 1557
THOMAS b. 1558
CATHERINE b. 1559
DUDLEY b. 1562

PART ONE

Suspicions

1536–43

Chapter 1

1536

KATE WAS AT THE PALACE OF GREENWICH, RETURNING FROM the gardens with the Princess Elizabeth trying to wriggle out of her hand when she saw Lady Bryan hastening in her direction. The child should have gone back to her household at Hatfield days ago, after celebrating Easter with her royal parents, but no instructions had been received.

"Kate! Kate," Lady Bryan cried. "You have been summoned to London!"

"London?" Kate echoed.

"Yes, child." Elizabeth's plump lady mistress paused to catch her breath, squinting in the May sunshine. "A messenger from the King has arrived with an escort. You are to be conveyed to the Tower."

Kate felt faint. "The Tower? What have I done wrong?"

"Nothing, my dear. I'm sorry, I did not mean to alarm you. You are to attend on the Queen, your aunt."

Their eyes met. Everyone except the little Princess knew that Kate's aunt, Queen Anne, had been arrested and imprisoned in that grim fortress. Just a few days ago, when walking in the gardens at Greenwich, Kate herself had looked up and witnessed a terrible scene between the King and Queen. They had been standing in a window, she with her daughter in her arms, and quarrelling bitterly. It had been the talk of the court, and soon afterward the Queen had been taken away.

No one, however, had any idea of what might happen to Anne now, for never before had a queen been accused of treason. The royal household was holding its collective breath and there had been much gossip and speculation, although Lady Bryan had sternly ensured that none of it was in Elizabeth's hearing. Not yet three, the child was as sharp as nails and little escaped her.

Kate was astonished. "Did my aunt ask for me?"

"I have no idea," Lady Bryan said, picking up Elizabeth and steering Kate back toward the palace. Elizabeth struggled in her arms, shaking her long red curls, her pointed face screwed up in protest. "Hush, my Lady Princess. You shall have a sugar comfit when we get back." The child quietened instantly, but all conversation had to cease.

The King's groom, very smart in his green and white, was courtesy personified as he greeted Kate and bade her gather her livery things.

"How long will I be staying at the Tower?" she asked, an eye on Elizabeth's retreating back as she was borne away to the nursery.

"I do not know, Mistress Kate, so I advise taking enough clothes for a week or so. Please be quick. We can still catch the tide upriver."

No one seemed to know anything, Kate thought, frowning as she sped upstairs to her chamber. She opened her traveling chest, packed her three best gowns and several changes of body linen, two books—would she have leisure for reading?—and the little silver casket containing her few jewels. She would have taken her lute, yet feared that music, which she loved, might not be appropriate in the circumstances. Then she threw her cloak over her arm and ran downstairs.

"My chest is ready," she told the groom.

When it had been loaded, she followed him to the palace jetty, climbed into the barge, and was carried away, waving back at Lady Bryan, who had watched her departure with a worried countenance. What awaited her at the end of her journey? And when would she be back?

As the barge glided along the Thames, Kate had time to reflect on this strange summons. *Had* it come from her aunt? It was Queen Anne who, two and a half years ago, had appointed her as a companion for the newborn Princess Elizabeth, a young cousin to keep her daily company in her large household of servants. Kate had been nine then, and she had been glad to leave the tense atmosphere of Hever Castle for the palace at Hatfield where the royal nursery had been established. Hever was Grandfather's house, where Mother, Kate, and her little brother, Henry, had lived since Father's death from the sweating sickness when Kate was four. But Grandfather and Mother had not got on for as long as Kate could remember. She hated seeing her plump, comely, sweet-natured mother being bullied by Grandfather, who made it plain that he didn't want them under his roof. And Grandmother, who was daughter to the Duke of Norfolk, had held aloof. The grandparents didn't get on well, and Grandmother was often at court, leaving the steward to run the household.

Kate had shed many tears for the loss of her father—or rather, its consequences. She had rarely seen him, for he had spent most of his time at court serving the King, and she could not remember him well, yet his death had rocked her world. Until then, she and Harry, who was just a year her junior, had been living with their mother at the beautiful royal palace of Beaulieu in Essex, of which Father had been appointed keeper. It was a paradise for children, a place to play boisterous games in the gardens or hide-and-seek in the vast chambers. She had a treasured memory of her father, resplendent in a doublet with yellow satin sleeves, picking her up and spinning her around in his arms as she shrieked with delight. She remembered him sitting her on his knee and showing her the pictures in an exquisitely illuminated book. Those had been happy times; she had felt loved and cherished. And then everything had come to an end.

Even now, as a great girl of twelve, Kate sometimes found herself weeping at the memory of what she had lost. For after Father's death, Mother had been left destitute and they had had no roof over their heads, so they had sought refuge at Hever Castle, the Boleyn family's home in Kent. Shifting in her cushioned seat, as the barge continued its journey along the Thames, Kate shuddered, remembering Grandfather shouting and Mother crying wildly. He had said that there was no place for them at Hever and that they must leave at once.

"I'll not have you under my roof!" he had spat at Mother, as if she had done something terrible.

Mother had dragged Kate and Harry up to the court to collect Father's belongings, then she had sought out her sister, Anne, and begged for her help. At that time, Aunt Anne had been the King's sweetheart, and he was doing his best to put away his old wife, Queen Katherine (for whom Kate was named), so that he could marry her. It was a source of great pride to the whole Boleyn family, especially Grandfather and Uncle George, that the King wanted to make Anne his queen. Anne had always been eager to advance or assist her kinsfolk. She had gone to the King, as Mother later told Kate, and he had ordered Grandfather to take them in and support them. And horrid Grandfather had had no choice!

But their lives at Hever had been miserable, for it was constantly being made clear to them that they were there on sufferance. Grandfather was often away at court, where he was a very important man, but his servants followed his lead and treated Mother with contempt. Kate could not understand why, for surely a father should love his daughter, as her father had loved her. What had Mother done to deserve such treatment?

"Why is Grandfather so horrible to you?" she had asked one day, when they were making daisy chains in the meadow and Harry was rampaging about on his hobby horse.

Mother's face had grown pink. She seemed to be struggling to find something to say. "I am not like your aunt Anne and your uncle George," she said. "They are ambitious to get on in the world. I am a disappointment to him."

Kate was rather glad that Mother was not like Uncle George, who was loud and full of himself; she could sense a dark streak in him. She didn't much like his wife, Aunt Jane, who seemed sly and calculating.

She sought to comfort her mother. "But you were married to Father, and he was close to the King."

"Indeed, I was, but he left me in a poor case. All his wealth is being held in trust until Harry comes of age."

"But that's not your fault?" Kate had been indignant.

"No." Mother sighed. "But Grandfather feels that I have let the family down and am not deserving of his love."

It had made no sense. Kate had refrained from pressing further, yet she'd been left with the feeling that Mother had done something wrong and that there was some dark secret in her past. Being widowed and poor did not explain Grandfather's cruelty. She had hoped that one day she would find out the truth. But even now, she was no wiser.

KATE REMEMBERED THE wild elation that had swept through the Boleyns when Aunt Anne finally became queen. They had all gone to London to play prominent parts in her coronation—all except for Mother. She had never been summoned to court and had never been present at state occasions or involved in her sister's life. This continued to puzzle Kate. Yet she had not let it bother her too much, for without Mother, she and Harry would have been left at Hever to the tender mercies of Grandfather and, when he was away at court, Great-Grandmother Butler, who was inclined to be a little strange.

Kate had long wished that Mother would marry again, but she was old enough to know that men wanted rich brides, and Mother had nothing. Suitors would not be beating a path to the castle drawbridge. Yet that did not stop her from dreaming. She could see her mother at the church door with a handsome man who looked very much like Father, and herself as bridesmaid, wearing a gorgeous gown.

But after the Princess Elizabeth had been born in September 1533, Kate escaped the oppressive atmosphere at Hever. How, living there in obscurity, she had been chosen for the coveted post of companion to the heir to the throne was a mystery to her, but Grandfather—seemingly pleased with her for once—told her briskly that she should embrace her great good fortune and not ask silly questions. She felt a pang at the thought of leaving her mother behind, yet she was eager to be at Hatfield in time for Christmas. There, she had quickly fallen in love with her baby cousin and felt herself very fortunate indeed.

Mother's letters depressed her, though. When Father died, Harry, his heir, had become a ward of the Crown because he was a minor. Two years later, the King had granted his wardship to Aunt Anne, who arranged for him to have a good education that would befit him to rise high in the world. Mother wrote to Kate that she was not happy about this because she had had no choice in the matter, but she knew it was for Harry's good. It especially galled her that Anne had the use of the revenues from Father's estate, which left Mother in worse penury than before. Kate had sighed as she read the letter. She prayed there would not be bad blood between the sisters; Mother was jealous enough of Anne as it was.

But soon afterward, things had improved for her. Mysteriously, she came into some money. Kate had no idea how, and did not like to ask, for she was more sure than ever now that Mother was keeping a secret. She expected to hear that she had left Hever for a house of her own, but Mother stayed on, in bondage, as she put it. She said she was keeping the money so that Kate would have a fine dowry one day, which would increase her chances of making a good marriage. Kate felt bad about that; she would have preferred Mother to use the money to improve her circumstances. Yet Mother remained adamant. "They have deprived me of doing the best for my son," she wrote. "They shall not prevent me from doing the best for my daughter."

Kate understood how she felt. Mother was not for nothing a Boleyn; she came from a family that prized educated women, and she had ensured that Kate was well taught. Until she went to Hatfield, Kate had shared Harry's tutor. Then, in Elizabeth's household, she had been provided with a tutor of her own, at the King's expense. She had learned Latin and French and even some Italian, for she excelled at languages. She now wrote in an elegant Italic hand, she knew all about the Greek and Roman myths, and she could draw, too. She often drew pictures for Elizabeth, humorous sketches that made the little girl squeal with laughter.

HOW SHE WISHED she were back in the nursery now. Reclining on the rough cushions in the cabin, Kate longed for the comforts of Greenwich or Hatfield. She loved her life in Elizabeth's household. Her little cousin, for all her imperious, wayward ways and bossy nature, was enchanting, a creature formed—everyone said—to make a special mark in the world. She would be a great queen one day, or even an empress. The suitors would be queuing up!

Kate loved Elizabeth's quicksilver mind, her rampant curiosity, and her fierce independence. Yet this demanding little Princess could also be affectionate and thoughtful, and there was no doubting that she loved her big cousin. She was always trailing along behind Kate or demanding that she play with her or read her a story; and she would climb on Kate's lap and cover her face with kisses. They looked alike, the pair of them, with their long red hair and long noses, and there was something similar about their eyes. But it was Elizabeth who had the greater spirit. Yes, Kate was missing Elizabeth already.

She could not stop wondering why she had been sent for. Was it the King who had commanded it? Or had Aunt Anne requested it? Kate would have preferred both of them to leave her in peace. She had seen King Henry several times when he came to visit Elizabeth and found him quite terrifying. He was a big man who dressed dazzlingly and dominated the house with his presence. He exuded power and authority, but he had piggy eyes, a cruel little mouth, and an evil sense of humor. Kate always shrank away from him, and yet there was something familiar about him, although she could not put her finger on it. He had sometimes noticed her, looked her up and down, and then chucked her under the chin.

"What a pretty little maid you are," he'd said once, to her intense mortification. And yet, she had to admit that he was a loving father to Elizabeth, taking an interest in her progress and clearly enjoying her babyish prattle.

Kate just wanted him to leave her alone.

Queen Anne came less often. She sent exquisite items of clothing and other fripperies for Elizabeth, yet Kate wondered if she was disappointed in having a princess when the King had wanted a son, and could not love her daughter. Everyone knew that his Grace desperately needed a male heir to succeed him, yet so far, the Queen had presented him with just the one girl. All her other children had been lost. Some of the servants muttered that it was a judgment of God on the King for putting away Queen Katherine; others speculated that Queen Anne would go the way of her predecessor.

Kate felt sorry for her aunt. She was eternally grateful to her for placing her in Elizabeth's household. She could not, however, like her, not after the way she had treated Mother. It was because of Aunt Anne that Mother was now living beyond the sea. Kate missed her. She had not seen her in a long while.

She had never forgotten the day, back in 1533, when Mother brought William Stafford to Hever, on a day when Grandfather was away. William was tall, handsome, strong, and fit, as became a soldier, and he knew how to befriend children. Kate and Harry soon ended up shrieking with laughter as he chased them around the garden pretending to be a dragon. He clearly adored Mother. Even at nine years old, Kate could tell that they were in love. The knowledge thrilled her.

Soon afterward, she had joined Elizabeth's household and was rarely home at Hever. Just once, about six months later, did she see William Stafford again, when she visited her mother during one of Grandfather's long absences. She warmed to Will again, to his kind eyes and winning smile, and was overjoyed to see her mother looking so happy. She found herself praying that Mother might marry Master Stafford.

What she had not known that day was that they had already wed in secret. Mother told Kate and Harry about that weeks later, in the summer, after she had briefly visited the court and come home very distressed. With tears in her eyes, she also said that she had to go away for what might be a long time.

"But why?" they had wanted to know.

"Because the King and Queen do not approve of my marriage. Your aunt has banished me from court."

Kate could not understand why Aunt Anne did not like William Stafford, who was even now putting a loving arm around Mother and dabbing away her tears with his kerchief. It was a complete mystery.

"I fear that I am not of sufficient rank or wealth to marry the Queen's sister," he said gently.

"It's not so much that," Mother said bitterly, "as that I did not ask *her* permission. She thinks she's head of the family now and has the right to say yea or nay. So she flounced off in a fury and complained to the King. She made him banish me—as if I had done something wrong, when all I did was fall in love with a wonderful man who will take care of me, and you children." She squeezed Will's hand. They had already learned to call him Will; Kate never called him "Stepfather." She had not had much chance anyway, for within a week, he and Mother had sailed for Calais, where he was a soldier in the garrison, the port being an English outpost; and Kate went back to Hatfield, feeling very miserable.

THE TOWER LOOMED ahead. Kate began to feel nervous, wondering how she would be received by the aunt who had been so unkind to Mother. Kate had seen Queen Anne since the rift, when she visited Hatfield, but Anne had behaved as if she wasn't there.

Her misgivings deepened as the walls of London appeared in the distance. Rising above them, she could see the great keep of the Tower. She shivered, knowing she would be walking into a house of gloom, for Aunt Anne must be terrified at the prospect of what might happen to her. Was her aunt in a dungeon? She didn't like to ask her escort. What treason had she been accused of? And was she innocent or guilty? More importantly, what happened to queens who were found guilty of treason?

As the King's groom helped her to alight at the Water Gate and they climbed the slippery steps, Kate was struck by how massive and forbidding a fortress the Tower was. She wanted nothing more than to go back to Greenwich, away from this horrible place. And yet, here they were, being escorted by yeomen warders through the outer ward to a stone stair that led up to a walkway along the walls.

She ascended the steps and passed through a doorway. To her astonishment, she found herself walking through vaulted rooms of great splendor, one adorned with wall paintings of angels and, in another, a high throne on a pedestal. Then they passed along another walkway and the groom knocked at the door. It was opened by a burly, well-dressed man with pudgy features and kind eyes.

"Sir William Kingston?" the groom asked. "I have here Mistress Carey." He turned to Kate. "Mistress, Sir William is the Constable of the Tower. Make your curtsey."

Kate bobbed as the Constable smiled gravely at her. "Welcome, Mistress Carey. I hope your journey was not too choppy. I fear this will be a mournful posting for you, but the Queen requested your presence, and that of three of her maids-of-honor. You are to wait on her at her trial tomorrow."

Kate was astounded. That she, a simple girl of twelve, was to witness the trial about which everyone had been speculating and hear the evidence firsthand seemed incredible. And yet, she did not want to be there. She wanted no part in this.

It was a relief to find that her aunt was not lodged in a dungeon, but in the sumptuous Queen's apartments. She was shown through to the walled garden below them, where she found Anne seated on a stone bench with two older ladies, one of whom she recognized as her great-aunt, Lady Boleyn, Grandfather's sister-in-law, a stern woman she barely knew.

Anne looked haunted; her sallow skin was pale and there were shadows under her dark eyes.

"Kate," she said, extending a hand, her eyes glittering with tears.

Kate knelt on the grass and kissed her hand.

"Be seated," her aunt bade her. "I am so glad to see you. I have been tormented by those creatures who were set to spy on me, women I did not like." She cast an icy glare in the direction of her two companions. "But now, God be praised, I am allowed to have about me those I love."

Kate perched on the end of the bench, relieved that her aunt had greeted her so warmly. The lady she did not know was regarding her with some compassion.

"You are very young, child," she said.

"Lady Kingston, my niece is twelve, old enough to serve as a maid-of-honor and even to be married!" Anne retorted. "And she is my blood kin, my sister Mary's daughter."

"Even so, Anne, she is of too tender years to attend the trial, considering the circumstances," Lady Boleyn said primly.

Anne bristled visibly and grasped Kate's hand. "Kate, I want you to know now that I am innocent of all the vile charges laid against me. I have never betrayed the King. Whatever you hear tomorrow, do not believe it, for it is all lies. And anyway, I think his Grace is doing this to prove me. It will all blow over, for they can offer no proofs against me."

Brave words, Kate thought. And yet there was a brittleness about her aunt, as if she was struggling to hide the fear she must be feeling.

Lady Kingston rose. "Mistress Carey, you are to sleep in the maidens' chamber. I will take you there now."

"I will see you at supper," Anne said.

AS KATE UNPACKED, storing her traveling chest beside one of the four beds in the beamed, lattice-windowed bedchamber, and hanging up her cloak on the peg on the wall beside her pallet bed, she wondered why Lady Boleyn thought her too young to attend the trial. What were the vile charges Anne had mentioned? And what did the King think she had done to betray him? Fall in love with another?

Kate was aware that married people were supposed to stay faithful, but she knew there were those who strayed. Elizabeth's servants loved to gossip, and she had come to understand that there was something unmentionable that married people did with each other, which they were not supposed to do with anyone else. It was all to do with making babies, and of course you should not have a baby unless you were married. She had asked some of the Princess's maids what that unmentionable something was, but they had just blushed and giggled and told her that there would be time enough to find out when she was older.

Her reverie was interrupted by the arrival of three young ladies, who had come from the court: Mary Norris, Mary Zouche, and Nan Cobham, whom Anne favored. Like Kate, they did not want to be here in the Tower and made no bones about saying so.

"And we are to attend her Grace at her trial tomorrow," Mary Norris said fearfully. "I'm terrified that it will not be a happy outcome."

"Why do you say that?" asked Kate.

"The word at court is that she is accused of adultery with several men."

"And worse!" Mary Zouche added.

"I don't know what adultery is," Kate said.

"It's being unfaithful to your husband," Nan Cobham told her. "It's becoming the mistress of another man."

Kate asked her what a mistress was. She had heard the word before, used to describe Aunt Anne before her marriage to the King.

"It can be one of two things. A lady who is courted from afar by a suitor who serves her. Or one who has a carnal relationship with a man outside marriage."

"What's a carnal relationship?"

Nan blushed. "It is when they join their bodies during bed sport. It's what men and women do to make babies. Didn't you know that, sweet innocent?"

"I knew there was something they did, but not that." Certain things were beginning to make sense, but still Kate was a little shocked. "How do they join their bodies?"

Nan giggled and lowered her voice. "The man puts his member inside the woman and spurts out the seed that makes a baby."

Kate knew what a male member was. She had seen her brother's when they were little. She wondered how on earth he could do that with it but decided that she would prefer not to know. She had heard enough already and was certain that she would die of embarrassment if any man tried to do that to her. And surely Aunt Anne would never have allowed anyone but the King inside her?

"She says she is innocent," she declared.

"Then let us hope that she clears herself."

SUPPER, SERVED IN the Queen's dining chamber, was a dismal affair. Anne was tense, saying little, and the older ladies looked on disapprovingly as the young ones attempted to make jests to cheer her.

Anne caught Kate looking up at the gilded ceilings and the richly molded friezes that adorned the walls.

"These are the rooms that I stayed in before my coronation," she said. "They were refurbished for me at great expense by Master Cromwell. He helped to raise me up, and now he is determined to destroy me!"

Master Cromwell, Kate knew, was the King's chief minister, who seemed—if you listened to what people said—to rule all.

"But why, Madam?" she asked.

"Because he fears my power! And he knows that I would destroy him if I could. So he made up all these lies about me. But the truth will out tomorrow. I am putting my trust in God and English justice."

Kate could see, from the faces of the older ladies, that they were not as confident of a just outcome as Anne seemed to be. Again, she shivered.

Chapter 2

1536

IN THE MORNING, THE FOUR MAIDS-OF-HONOR DONNED THE black gowns and hoods deemed suitable by Lady Kingston for the solemnity of a trial. They found Anne in the great chamber, elegantly dressed in a black velvet gown and a small cap sporting a black-and-white feather. Kate thought she seemed calm.

"Remember, I am innocent!" she declared.

When Sir William Kingston came to tell them that it was time, Kate and her companions, with Lady Kingston and Lady Boleyn, walked behind the Queen as Sir William escorted her across the Inmost Ward of the Tower to the lofty King's Hall opposite. Beside Anne walked the Gentleman Jailer, with his ceremonial axe turned away from her. A crowd had gathered, standing silently to watch the extraordinary spectacle of a queen being put on trial.

They waited in the porch until an usher summoned Anne into the court. No one spoke, but she held herself as tense as a bowstring.

When Kate entered the ancient hall, she drew in her breath. It was packed almost to the rafters with people, most of them crammed onto the tiered benches on either side. In the center, there was a raised platform, on which had been placed a velvet-upholstered chair behind a bar. Facing it, on the dais at the far end, sat Kate's great-uncle, the Duke of Norfolk, beneath a rich cloth of estate bearing the royal arms, for as Lord High Steward, he was representing the King. Beside him sat the peers who were to judge the Queen.

Anne made an entry as if she were going to a great triumph, carrying herself with calm dignity as she was led to the bar. She curtseyed to her judges, resting her gaze on them all, without any sign of fear. Even when she spied Grandfather among them, Kate didn't see her flinch. Kate was appalled to see him there and thought her aunt's composure wonderful. There was no hint of the nervousness she had shown earlier. By contrast, the man whom Mary Norris whispered was Master Cromwell looked tense, as well he might, for if the Queen went free, there might be dire consequences for him.

Anne seated herself on the chair on the platform. She seemed unmoved by the thousands of eyes staring at her. Kate and the other young ladies were shown to a bench at the side, where they had a good view of the proceedings. Kate watched as a yeoman warder carried in the Queen's crown on a cushion and placed it on a small table next to her.

The indictment was read out. The Queen was accused of procuring Uncle George, her own brother, and four other men to defile her and have carnal knowledge of her, which they had done often; furthermore, she and these men were supposed to have conspired the death of the King, for she had said to them that she had never loved the King in her heart, and had told every one of them that she loved them more than the others.

"And this," thundered the Attorney General, "was to the slander of the issue that was born to the King and her—and it is treason under the law."

Kate had worked out what "defile" and "carnal knowledge" meant. The Attorney General had made them sound shameful. Looking around at the faces of those in court, she could see flushed cheeks or outrage. Yet Anne's face betrayed no embarrassment. Her expression said more than words; no one looking at her could have thought her guilty. As each charge was put to her, she raised her hand and pleaded, "Not guilty."

The Attorney General was having none of it. "Admit it—you cohabited with your brother and the other accused."

"I did not," Anne said firmly.

"There was a promise between you and Sir Henry Norris to marry after the King's death, which you hoped for." Kate turned to look at Norris's daughter, Mary, who was silently shaking her head.

"He is too loyal to the King to have stooped so low," she whispered, earning herself a thunderous look from Master Cromwell.

On and on went the charges, most of them petty and quite ridiculous, Kate thought. Whoever had drawn them up didn't know Aunt Anne very well or had a short memory. It was part of Boleyn family lore that Anne had refused to become the King's mistress before he proposed marriage to her, and that she had kept herself chaste for him for the best part of seven years—Kate now understood what that meant. Was she therefore likely to have taken a succession of lovers after her marriage?

It was noticeable that little was being made of the more serious charge, that of plotting the King's death. Kate wondered if that had been made up, because the other girls were whispering that the proofs seemed unbelievably shaky. In promising to marry Sir Henry Norris (which Anne denied), it did not necessarily follow that she wanted the King assassinated. She could have been talking about what might happen if she was widowed. But Kate was beginning to understand that it was treason even to imagine the King's death, which was a rather scary thought.

Anne answered all the charges calmly, counteracting them firmly and rationally. She was adamant that she had never been false to the King. It surely seemed obvious to everyone present that she was innocent. Kate prayed that the lords would see sense and declare her not guilty. When they were asked for their verdict, she watched them conferring with each other, murmuring, frowning, and nodding.

But what if they were too frightened of the King and Master Cromwell to give the right judgment? Kate felt a tremor of fear. Her heart burned with anger at the King for putting his poor wife through this terrible ordeal. Yet Anne was sitting there, impassive, watching the lords' faces.

Next to Kate, Lady Boleyn was trembling. "If she falls, we all fall," she muttered. "The Boleyns will be finished."

Kate shuddered. She had not thought of that. She had expected that, when this was over, she would go back to Elizabeth's household. But what if she was not allowed? What if she had to go back to Hever and Grandfather, who was looking decidedly grim-faced. How must it feel to have to pass judgment on your own child? Surely he could have refused to do so?

It seemed that the lords had finished their discussions. Norfolk's heir, the Earl of Surrey, Kate's cousin, stood up.

"Have you reached a verdict?" his father asked.

Kate held her breath.

"Guilty!" Surrey replied, as Kate felt horror and disbelief flood through her. Beside her, Lady Boleyn burst into tears.

One by one, the peers rose. All, to a man, said, "Guilty," even Grandfather; Kate watched aghast as he cast his vote, his face taut. Excited murmurs rippled along the spectator benches.

"Prisoner at the bar, stand," called an usher.

Anne got to her feet, as unmoved as a stone.

"Anne, Queen of England, you must now resign your crown into the hands of the lords."

Choking back tears, Kate saw her aunt pick it up reverently and give it to the Duke of Suffolk.

"I am innocent of having offended against the King," she said in a loud voice.

A hush descended on the court as Norfolk stood to pronounce sentence. Tears were running down his cheeks as he addressed Anne; they were running down Kate's, too, and she was seized with such a horrible sense of dread that she wanted to cover her ears.

The Duke cleared his throat. His expression was grave. "Because you have offended against our sovereign the King's Grace in committing treason against his person, the law of the realm is this, that you have deserved death, and your judgment is this: that you shall be burned here within the Tower of London on the green, or have your head cut off, according to the King's pleasure."

A woman screamed from the gallery.

Kate was so horror-struck at Norfolk's sentence that she thought she would faint. She had had no idea that it would come to this, for no one had discussed what might happen to Anne, who had been adamant that she'd be safe because she was innocent. But the thought of her being burned to death was dreadful, while having her head cut off was almost as bad. Kate felt hot fury against the King, in whose name this travesty of justice was being handed down. How could a man allow such tortures to be meted out to a lady he had loved, the mother of his child? And what of that child? How was this to be explained to Elizabeth, that her father had had her mother killed?

The court had erupted in a buzz of voices, but Anne remained standing, still and composed, at the bar. Silence fell as she raised her eyes to Heaven and began speaking. "O Father, O Creator, Thou who art the way, the life, and the truth, know whether I have deserved this death." She turned to her judges. "My lords, I will not say your sentence is unjust, nor presume that my reasoning can prevail against your convictions. I am willing to believe that you have sufficient reasons for what you have done; but they cannot be those which have been produced in court, for I am clear of all the offenses which you have laid to my charge. I have always been a faithful wife to the King, though I confess I have had jealous fancies and suspicions of him, which I had not discretion enough to conceal. But God knows, and is my witness, that I have not sinned against him in any other way. Do not think I say this in the hope of prolonging my life, for He who saves us from death has taught me how to die, and He will strengthen my faith. As for those men who are also unjustly condemned, I would gladly suffer many deaths to deliver them, but since I see it pleases the King, I shall willingly accompany them in death, being assured that I shall lead an endless life with them in peace and joy, where I will pray to God for the King and for you, my lords. I ask only for a short time for the quietening of my conscience."

Kate could not credit that someone condemned to such a terrible fate could speak so eloquently—let alone speak at all. She herself was shaking uncontrollably and could hardly stand when the court rose and it was time to depart. The other young ladies were dabbing their eyes with their kerchiefs and Lady Boleyn was crying openly. Yet when Anne had curtseyed to the peers, they all composed themselves and followed her as Sir William Kingston escorted her from the hall. This time, the Gentleman Jailer's axe was turned toward her, to show that she had been condemned to death.

WHEN THEY RETURNED to the Queen's lodgings, Anne sank down on her bed and sat there trembling, as Kate looked on helplessly, having no idea of how to comfort her. It was Lady Kingston who went to her and put an arm around her.

"God help me!" Anne cried, her teeth chattering. "How will I bear the heat of the flames and the scorching of my flesh? Can you imagine the agony and horror of being burned to death?"

"It will not come to that, I am sure," Lady Boleyn soothed, although she did not sound convinced. "The King will show mercy."

"He wants to be rid of me and marry that wench Seymour!" Anne flared.

"But I am sure he will not condemn you to the flames," Lady Kingston said.

"No, but he will have my head cut off!" Anne wailed hysterically, and nothing anyone could say or do would calm her. All the brave composure she had shown at her trial had left her. She was like a cornered animal, cowering in uncontrollable fear.

ANNE WAS ONLY slightly calmer when Sir William Kingston brought her news of the condemnation of her brother, Lord Rochford, who was to suffer what Sir William called a traitor's death.

"But because he is a nobleman, it will doubtless be commuted to beheading," he added. That sounded dreadful enough to Kate. She had little affection for her uncle on account of his barbed tongue and the unkind way he teased her, but she was certain he did not deserve to die, and so cruelly.

"Did he deny the charges?" Anne was desperate to know. Lady Kingston signaled that Kate and the other young ladies should make themselves scarce.

"These are not matters for innocent ears," she said. Unwillingly, they all withdrew to the dining chamber and—at Mary Zouche's suggestion—got out the playing cards, although no one felt like entering into the game, and Kate was still in shock after hearing that terrible sentence.

In the evening, as they sat with Anne at supper, which none of them could face, they were joined by Mrs. Orchard, the Queen's old nurse.

"He won't let them kill you," she said, holding Anne to her ample bosom as if she were a child again. "When it comes to it, you'll get a reprieve, you'll see."

Anne began sobbing. "Yes. I pray you are right."

"Something strange happened at your brother's trial," Mrs. Orchard told her.

Anne sat up. "What?"

Lady Kingston threw the nurse a warning glance. "Little pitchers . . ."

Again, Kate and her companions were sent out. Since they could not face going to bed and the night terrors that would surely follow, they gathered in their chamber and took out their embroidery, chatting mournfully as they worked. At one point, Nan took up her lute and began to play a poignant tune. Kate longed to ask if she could have a turn, but didn't like to. It was gone one by the time they doused the candles and retired. Kate barely slept at all that night, and when she did, her dreams were of her aunt's face surrounded by flames.

THE NEXT DAY, Kingston went see the King, and everyone's hopes rose, especially when he told Anne that although the condemned men were to die the next day, no instructions had been sent, or any date set, for her own execution.

"Sir William, have you been told how—how I am to die?" she faltered.

"No, Madam. Today I mean to discover the King's pleasure concerning you, in regard to your comfort and what is to be done with you."

"I pray he will put me out of this misery. It's not knowing what will happen that torments me the most. If I know my fate, I can prepare myself to face it."

Kate could only admire her aunt's bravery. She was sure that, were she in her place, she would have been a gibbering wreck.

ANNE EMERGED FROM her presence chamber that afternoon looking composed as she bade farewell to Archbishop Cranmer. When he had gone, she ordered supper and invited her ladies and Sir William Kingston to join her.

"It is to be the sword," she said, as if it was good news. "The King offered me the kinder death if I would agree to the annulment of our marriage." Her lip trembled. "I agreed, of course. It is for the best."

Kingston bowed his head. "His Grace, out of pity, has sent for an expert executioner, the Sword of Calais."

Anne shuddered. There was a long silence.

"What of the Princess Elizabeth?" Lady Boleyn asked.

Anne made an effort. "She will be declared baseborn and removed from the succession," she said, swallowing. "I had no choice, you understand? It will be done tomorrow. And it will be better for her to grow up knowing that her mother was beheaded rather than burned!"

Kate felt the tears welling. That poor, innocent child. What had she ever done to deserve such ignominy?

"On what grounds is your marriage to be annulled?" Lady Kingston asked. "I'm no theologian, but I do know that if people marry in good faith, in ignorance of any impediment, their children are deemed legitimate."

Kate saw Anne glance briefly her way, then give a barely perceptible shake of her head. "I am not at liberty to discuss that."

Kate stared at her, convinced that this had something to do with her in some way.

"Why?" she dared to ask.

"Because the King wishes it!" Anne said sharply. Then suddenly, as so often, her mood changed, and she smiled. "I do not believe that his Grace really intends to put me to death. He just wants to be free of me, and now that he is, I believe that he will send me to a nunnery and that my life will be spared."

The older ladies were regarding her with pity in their eyes.

"The gentlemen are all to die tomorrow, Madam," Kingston said gently.

Anne looked as if she had been winded, while Mary Norris gasped and began weeping. Kate saw her aunt clench her hands. "I do hope that those poor gentlemen will not suffer traitors' deaths," Anne said.

Kate laid down her knife. She could not swallow the meat in her mouth, let alone face any more food. In a day or so, hours maybe, she would be called upon to witness her aunt being done to death. It was the thing she had been dreading ever since the trial. Mercifully, it would not be the fire—that she could not have borne—but the sword would be terrible enough. There would be blood, lots of it. She felt sick at the thought.

Perhaps she would be excused such a duty on account of her age. And yet it was important that her aunt have someone of her blood, someone who loved her, with her at the last. Mother would have wanted it. Mother had fallen out with Anne, but she would not have been so rancorous as to deny her that final comfort. If she were here, bygones would certainly have been bygones. But she was not here—Heaven knew how much news had filtered through to Calais—and so Kate herself must stand in her place.

IT SEEMED THAT cruelty upon cruelty was being heaped upon the Queen. The following morning, she was made to witness the executions of her brother and her so-called lovers. She did not want to—she was weeping when Kate and the others dressed her—but orders were orders, as Kingston told her when he came to escort her to the viewing place.

When she returned, less than an hour later, Lady Kingston was supporting her, for she could barely walk and was shaking convulsively. Her face was ravaged by tears and grief.

"She could not look," Lady Kingston told them. "It was a pitiful sight, but my husband said that they all died very charitably." She sat Anne down in the chair by the fire. Kate could have wept for her. She almost wept for herself, looking at how distraught Anne was. That would be her very soon—but when?

Kingston stepped forward and faced Anne. "It is my heavy duty, Madam, to inform you that you are to die tomorrow morning."

As Kate's heart began thumping loudly, she was amazed to see her aunt's face lighten.

"This is joyful news to me!" Anne sobbed. "I long only to keep company with my brother and those other gentlemen in Heaven."

Kate could bear it no longer. Slipping out of the room, hoping no one had noticed, she fled to the privy in the thickness of the wall and was violently sick. Wiping her mouth on one of the clean cloths piled up on the floor, she hastened to the maidens' chamber and lay down, sobbing her heart out.

And that was where Mary Norris found her. Mary herself was weeping, for her father had died on the block this morning, and she was inconsolable. She lay down next to Kate and put her arms around her, craving comfort. They lay there, shoulders heaving, crying uncontrollably for a long while until they were drained. Kate was briefly aware of Lady Kingston looking in on them, then going away. After that, she knew no more until late afternoon, when she awoke to find Mary gone.

HAVING WASHED HER face, tidied her hair, and smoothed her gown, she went shamefacedly to the presence chamber, where she found Anne sitting by the hearth, staring into space, her prayer book open on her lap, while her ladies worked silently at their needlework around the table.

Anne reached out a hand to her. "There you are, Kate. Are you feeling better now? I fear this is all too much for one of your tender years. You should be at Greenwich, playing with Elizabeth." Her voice broke. "I shall never see my child again," she whispered.

She turned again to Kate, making a visible effort. "Niece, do not grieve for me. Truly, I long to die. I have been falsely accused of the vilest of crimes, and I have lost everything that mattered to me: my husband, my daughter, my brother, my crown, my friends, and my good name. Five men have died on my account. My father has abandoned me. I dare not imagine my mother's grief. There is nothing left to live for." She sighed. "I cannot bear to think that Elizabeth is now branded a bastard. Be good to her, Kate. Look after her for me. She is your cousin."

"But will I be allowed to go back and serve her?" Kate asked, supposing—in view of what Lady Boleyn had said—that the entire family would now be out of favor.

"Of course you will," Anne said firmly. "The King will wish it."

Something in her voice made Kate pause. Why would he want the niece of his disgraced wife to attend on his daughter—unless, of course, that daughter was now disgraced, too. But what kind of father would treat his innocent child so cruelly?

Chapter 3

1536

KATE WAS RELIEVED WHEN FATHER THIRLWALL, THE QUEEN'S confessor, came that evening to offer her spiritual comfort in her last hours, for they had all been sitting desolately, trying to make conversation, but horribly aware of what was to happen in the morning. That had been brought home to them by the distant hammering and sawing of wood, echoing across the silent spaces of the Tower. They were building the scaffold on which Anne was to die.

Kate could not sleep that night. By the time morning came, she felt deathly, yet made herself get up and put on her good black gown and the hood that matched it. None of the other young ladies spoke as they readied themselves. They all looked terrified. And they were only to be onlookers. Anne was going to have her head cut off. How much more terrified must she be feeling?

"She's at prayer," said Lady Kingston, when they entered the dining chamber. Bread, cheese, ale, and cold cuts of meat had been laid out on the table, but no one wanted to eat anything. "She's been up all night," she added. "The Archbishop has been and gone. He heard her last confession and said Mass. She asked my husband to be present when she took the Sacrament. She wanted him to hear her declare her innocence before God. She swore, on the damnation of her soul, that she has never offended against the King."

A brief surge of hope fluttered in Kate's breast. It was unthinkable that anyone would lie when they were facing death and the divine judgment to follow. If the Archbishop repeated Anne's words to the King, would his Grace realize that it had all been a dreadful mistake and send a reprieve? She asked Lady Kingston what she thought.

"No," she said. "Put that notion away. Twenty-seven peers judged her guilty. There will be no reprieve."

At half past eight, the ladies were all summoned to the Queen's bedchamber to make her ready for her last public appearance. They found her pale but composed.

"I am determined to make a good death," she told them. "No one shall say that I faltered at the end. It will be over in an instant, and then I will be lifted up out of this miserable world and know eternal joy."

Kate's hands were trembling as she laced up her aunt's gown. She could not see for tears, so Lady Boleyn had to help her before taking her aside. "Pull yourself together, Niece," she muttered. "We must all be strong for her."

Kingston had gone to see to the final preparations for the execution, but at nine o'clock, the appointed hour, it was Lady Kingston who opened the door.

"I am sorry, Madam, but your execution has had to be postponed until noon."

"No!" Anne gasped. "It cannot be! Why?"

"My husband has just received orders to have foreigners conveyed out of the Tower, and he has had to send for the Sheriff of London to see that this is done. He cannot help it, Madam. He knows you will be upset by the delay."

"Indeed, I am! Pray send him to me when he has a moment free."

Kingston came soon afterward. At the sight of him, Anne became agitated and panicky.

"Master Kingston, I hear that I shall not die before noon, and

I am very sorry for it, for I thought then to be dead and past my pain."

"There should be no pain, Madam," he reassured her. "It is so subtle a blow."

Kate shuddered. No pain? Who was he trying to fool? And how did he know?

"I have heard you say that the executioner is very good, and I have a little neck," Anne said. She put her hands around it and laughed nervously.

"I have seen many men and women executed," he told her, "and they have all been in great sorrow, but this method of execution is instantaneous, and I can see that your Grace has much joy and pleasure in death."

"There is nothing left for me in this world," she told him. "I do long to die, but my poor flesh shrinks from it, so I am heartily glad it will be over quickly."

"It will be," he said, and reached out to squeeze her hand.

Kate saw her eyes fill with tears and felt like crying herself.

"I should be grateful if no one would trouble me when I make my devotions this morning," Anne said, blinking the tears back furiously.

She summoned her confessor and disappeared with him into the closet she used as an oratory. Kate and the others exchanged anguished looks. The delay, they knew, would be torture for Anne. She would need to sustain her fragile courage for a little longer. It was dreadful for them all.

Anne was calm when she emerged, and summoned the ladies to attend her, but no sooner were they seated than Kingston arrived. "I am so very sorry, Madam. Your execution has now had to be postponed until nine o'clock tomorrow morning."

Kate could barely believe her ears. They couldn't do this to her, they couldn't!

"Oh, Master Kingston, I am deeply sorry to hear that," Anne lamented. "I beg of you, for the honor of God, to make urgent suit to the King that, since I am in a good state and disposed for death, I might be dispatched immediately. I was prepared to die, and I fear that the delay might weaken my resolve."

Kingston looked deeply distressed. "Madam, I am powerless to change the arrangements. I can only exhort you to pray for the strength to endure longer."

KATE MARVELED AT her aunt's strong will and her deep faith, which sustained her through those terrible final hours. Repeatedly, she sought fortitude in prayer. Her maids found it impossible to stop bursting into tears, and it was Anne who ended up consoling them.

"Death is not a thing to be regretted by Christians," she reminded them. "Remember, I shall be quit of all unhappiness."

It seemed strange to be doing all the normal things—taking meals, or picking at them, going to the stool chamber, sipping wine—when the dread and momentous event of the morrow approached ever nearer. Kate spent much of her time trying to comfort Mary Norris, yet it was hard to find means of consoling her, for the loss of a beloved father in such a horrible way was a dreadful thing. She did not know whether she should be mournful or try to stay cheerful to keep everyone's spirits up; and it was almost impossible to be cheerful when you were dying inside. But after dinner, as they all sat together around the table sewing, Anne did her best to make witty conversation. She even attempted a jest.

"Those bragging, clever people who invent names for kings and queens will not be hard put to it to invent one for me! They will call me Queen Anne Lackhead!" She laughed heartily, and they tried to join in.

Somehow, they got through the evening. As darkness fell, Anne sat down at the table, read her prayer book for a while, then began scribbling. Kate wondered what she was writing, for her farewell letters had been completed and sealed two nights before.

At length, Anne looked up. "I have decided that it is best to be at peace with the world before I die. I have written to your mother and begged her forgiveness for my harshness toward her," she told Kate.

"Madam, she will be deeply touched," Kate said. "I know that she would be here with you if she could."

"Alas, by the time she would get here . . ." Anne left the sentence unfinished.

IN THE MORNING, they dressed her in a beautiful robe of gray damask. Beneath it, she was wearing a low-necked red kirtle she had worn on the night before her arrest. Lady Boleyn placed a short white ermine cape around her shoulders.

"In case it is chilly outside," she said, looking emotional. "Lady Kingston and I will not be attending you. The young ladies are to have that honor."

Kate knew real terror then. It was really going to happen. Nothing in her short life had prepared her for this.

It was as well that Lady Boleyn was binding up Anne's hair, piling the plaits high above her neck, and placing a gable hood on her head, as Kate could not have done it; she was so paralyzed by fear.

"Do I look presentable?" Anne asked. "I am told that the people are being allowed into the Tower to watch."

"You look every inch the Queen!" Lady Boleyn told her.

After receiving the Sacrament, Anne toyed with her breakfast, nibbling on a piece of manchet bread to please her ladies, but it was clear that she had no appetite. Kate noticed that she kept having to visit the privy.

At eight o'clock, Kingston appeared at the door.

"Madam, the hour approaches," he said. "You should make ready."

"Acquit yourself of your charge," Anne told him, "for I have long been prepared."

He cleared his throat. "Madam, a word of advice. When you are asked to kneel, you must stay upright and not move at all, for your own sake. Do you understand me? The executioner is skilled, but if you move, the stroke may go awry."

Kate felt sick. The other young ladies had turned pale.

"I will stay still," Anne said. She sounded as if she was struggling to control herself.

"We must go now," he told her.

Lady Boleyn hugged her tightly. "God be with you!" she said fervently.

As Kate, Nan, and the two Marys followed Anne and Kingston down the stairs, all four of them were crying. Kate felt a surge of bitter anger against the King who had condemned her aunt to this terrible death.

"Your Grace does not deserve this!" she blurted out.

Anne neither turned around nor answered. They had reached the door that opened to the Inmost Ward, and she was staring at the two hundred Yeomen of the King's Guard, who were waiting there to escort her to her execution. Kate had not anticipated that the proceedings would be conducted with such ceremony. She and her companions, still struggling to control their emotions, walked behind Anne and Kingston as the mournful procession began its slow march toward the Coldharbour Gate. As they passed through its massive twin towers, a huge crowd came into view and a great murmur rose from the people when they saw Anne coming toward them.

At the sight of the high scaffold beyond them, hung with black cloth, Kate and her companions began weeping afresh. This was real, it was really happening. The guards parted ranks to let them through and positioned themselves around and behind the scaffold.

Kingston assisted Anne up the steps, and the four maids followed, Kate grabbing the wooden rail, fearful lest her knees give way. As Anne stood in the center, where Kingston directed, they moved to a far corner, their skirts sweeping the sawdust. Several men were waiting on the scaffold, all wearing everyday clothes. Was one of them the executioner, or was he yet to arrive? There was no sign of a sword anywhere.

Kate froze as she glimpsed, lying on the grass below, a wooden chest, the kind in which arrows were kept. They were going to bury the Queen in that? It did not look long enough to hold a human body. Had they not even made provision for a coffin? She stood there, seething.

At Kingston's nod, Anne addressed the crowd. "Good Christian people, I am come here to die, according to the law, for by the law I am judged to die, and therefore I will speak nothing against it. I come here only to die, and to yield myself humbly to the will of the King, my lord. And if I did ever offend the King's Grace, surely with my death I do now atone. I come here to accuse no man, nor to speak anything of that of which I am accused. I pray and beseech you all, good friends, to pray for the life of the King, who is one of the best princes on the face of the earth, who has always treated me so well that better could not be found, wherefore I submit to death with a good will, humbly asking pardon of all the world. If any person will meddle with my cause, I require them to judge the best. Thus, I take my leave of the world, and of you, and I heartily desire you all to pray for me."

Kingston signed for Kate and the other maids to come forward and disrobe their mistress, but they were all blinded by tears and shaking so violently that Anne had to help them remove her cape, her robe, and her hood.

"Pray for me!" she exhorted them. "I beg your pardon for any harshness I have shown toward you, for you have always showed yourselves diligent in my service, and now you are present at my last hour and mortal agony; as in good fortune you were faithful to me, so even at this, my miserable death, you do not forsake me. And as I cannot reward you for your true service to me, I pray you take comfort for my loss. Be not sorry to see me die. Forget me not, and always be faithful to the King's Grace and to her whom with happier fortune you may look to have as your queen and mistress. And always esteem your honor far beyond your life; and in your prayers to the Lord Jesus forget not to pray for my soul."

Kate knew that she would never forget those words, especially that last wise piece of advice. After all, what was life without honor?

A big, brawny man in dark clothes stepped forward and knelt before Anne. As he spoke, in heavily accented English, Kate realized it was the executioner—the Sword of Calais. Her heart began pounding. She could not begin to imagine what Anne was feeling.

"Madam," he said, "I crave your Majesty's pardon, for I am ordered to do my duty."

"I give it willingly," Anne told him.

"Madam, I beg you to kneel and say your prayers," he instructed.

Kate felt faint. This was the moment. She watched as Nan gave Anne a linen coif, saw Anne pull it over her head with shaking fingers, tucking in her hair to leave her neck bare. She stared as her aunt knelt in the sawdust, arranging her skirts modestly about her feet, and heard her ask for a little time to say her prayers.

"O Christ, receive my spirit!" she prayed, over and over again. Below her the Lord Mayor cried, "All kneel in respect for the passing of a soul!" The crowd fell to its knees, but Kingston indicated that Kate, Nan, and the Marys should stay standing.

"Jesu, have pity on my soul! My God, have pity on my soul!" Anne was saying, her voice hoarse. "To Jesus Christ I commend my soul!"

"Please to move out of the way, mademoiselles," the executioner murmured, stretching out his arm to show the maids where they could safely stand. They shuffled across, bursting out again into sobs, and knelt down, leaning on the side beams of the scaffold. Kate bent her head forward, shutting her eyes tightly. She could not bear to watch what was about to happen, but she could hear everything, things no young girl—or anyone else—should ever hear.

"Strike now!" Anne cried. "O Lord God, have pity on my soul! To Christ I commend my soul!"

Kate heard the executioner say, "Bring me the sword!" There was a movement in the direction of the scaffold steps and then a sharp whoosh followed by a most dreadful crunching sound and a muffled thud. A terrible silence descended, broken by the booming of cannon fire from Tower Wharf, announcing the Queen's death to the world.

"Dear Jesus," Mary Zouche gasped, "she's moving!"

Without thinking, Kate opened her eyes and beheld her aunt's body slumped sideways on the scaffold and the head lying in a pool of blood. She could not look away. It was a sight she knew she would carry with her to her grave.

There was no sign of movement.

"I saw her eyes and lips move," Mary insisted.

"So did I," said Nan, who was looking green.

"I can't bear to look," Kate whispered. She drew out her clean kerchief and threw it over Anne's head.

The spectators, in a subdued mood, were melting away. All the men except Kingston had left the scaffold. He came over to Kate and the rest.

"You may prepare her for burial now." He handed them a folded sheet. "Use this for a shroud. There is a chest there." He pointed to it. "There was no time to obtain a coffin. You can carry it into the chapel and await one of the chaplains."

The four girls stared at each other, horrified. Kate could not have borne to touch a dead body that had died naturally, let alone one that had been broken by a bloody death.

"We must do it," Mary Norris told them. "We must see that she is decently laid to rest. We cannot let any man touch her. We must force ourselves to do this heavy duty."

Kingston nodded and picked up Anne's discarded outer clothes, which they had left hanging over the rail of the scaffold.

"These will be distributed among the Tower officials as perquisites," he told them. "It is customary after executions. Of course, they will sell them. I will arrange for her jewels to be collected from her chamber."

Kate was suddenly burning with anger against the King, who had sent her aunt—a defenseless woman—to a violent, bloody death, the horror of which would stay with her forever. It was he who was to blame for her own present misery, he who had robbed her of the innocence of childhood. Truly, he must be the most dreadful man who had ever lived! If he had been present, she wouldn't have been able to answer for what she might have said to him; in fact, she could have killed him. She hated him with all her being.

The four of them struggled to lift up the bleeding body from the blood-soaked sawdust and down the scaffold steps, where they laid it on the grass. Mary bent and picked up the severed head, still covered with Kate's kerchief, and carried it to the arrow chest. Steeling herself, Kate helped the others to wrap Anne's corpse in the sheet, lift it up, and place it in the chest with the head beside it, as reverently as they could. Then, with some difficulty, for they were weak with effort and anguish, they carried the chest into the chapel of St. Peter ad Vincula nearby.

There, they were informed that the burial could not go ahead because the grave had yet to be dug. They sat desolately in the chapel for over an hour, waiting for someone to come. It seemed that the time would never end. At long last, two men arrived and set to work in the chancel, making a lot of noise and jests. Kate flushed with indignation. Had they no respect?

Finally, they were finished, and as they departed, the bell struck noon. Kate found it hard to believe that it was four hours since they had followed Anne down the stairs of the Queen's lodgings.

Father Thirlwall arrived a few minutes later.

"I fear that as it is now afternoon, it is too late to say Mass, but I will say prayers over her," he told them, leading them up to the chancel. Before the altar, the paving stones had been lifted, exposing the earth just inches beneath. A shallow grave had been dug there. The girls sobbed woefully during the committal, hardly able to believe that the living, breathing, healthy woman they had dressed that morning was no more. It seemed such an ignominious end for one who had been queen of England.

When the chaplain had gone, they looked at each other.

"I feel like a sheep without a shepherd," Nan said.

"Well, we are unlikely to feel like that for long, as I'll wager that the King will soon marry Mistress Seymour," Mary Zouche told her.

Kate followed the others out into the sunshine. Already workmen were dismantling the scaffold. Soon there would be nothing left to show what had taken place on that spot.

She wondered what she should do. There was no one to tell her. She supposed she would be going back to Elizabeth's household, but that was uncertain. To her knowledge, no arrangements had been made.

But here was Lady Kingston, walking across Tower Green toward them.

Her voice was brisk. "Mistress Carey, the King has commanded that you travel to Hunsdon House to wait on the Lady Elizabeth.

You will not address her as princess, as she has been deprived of that title, being deemed baseborn. A litter and escort will be arranged."

Kate could have cried with relief. Not only was she not returning to a court hostile to the Boleyns, but she was also going to the peace of the Hertfordshire countryside where, if God was good to her, she would be able to forget the horrors she had seen. Hunsdon was one of the royal nursery palaces and she loved it there.

"The rest of you are to go to your homes, for the Queen's household has been disbanded," Lady Kingston continued. "You too will be provided with escorts." She regarded them with sympathy. "Poor things, this has been a terrible day for you. Can I offer you something to eat?"

Kate had just noticed spatters of Anne's blood on the hem of her gown. She felt a wave of nausea. "I thank you, Lady Kingston, but I could not eat anything," she said, trying not to cry.

Chapter 4

1536

It was a relief to have changed out of her blood-bespattered gown and be away from the Tower. Kate prayed she would never have to go there again. She was longing for the peace of Hunsdon, although she felt a certain trepidation at the thought of what might await her there. What in Heaven would they tell Elizabeth about her mother? And would the change in her status be made cruelly obvious?

As the litter was drawn through London in the afternoon sunshine, Kate was appalled to witness the great joy the people were expressing at Anne's fall. She had known that her aunt was unpopular, yet she had never realized just how hated she was. It seemed that they were ready to believe anything of her. Some were saying that her death was a judgment on her for supplanting good Queen Katherine.

Kate supposed that this was how it would be now. Anne and the Boleyns would be reviled, and no one would want to know them. She was glad that her surname was Carey. She prayed that people would not make the connection.

. . .

AS THE COUNTRYSIDE passed by, Kate fretted about how Elizabeth would react to the loss of the mother she had very rarely seen. She had been cared for by a wet nurse, then by the motherly Lady Bryan. Anne had been merely an occasional visitor and a sender of costly gifts; she had never been a constant presence in Elizabeth's life. Now if the child had been deprived of Lady Bryan, or her beloved governess, Kat Champernowne, Kate would have been more worried. She resolved to give her little cousin all the love she could, and one day, she promised herself, she would tell her the truth about her mother.

When she arrived at Hunsdon, she found men unloading Elizabeth's baggage train in the courtyard. The child, she was informed, had just been carried up to the nursery by Lady Bryan. As she mounted the stairs, Kate saw that the house was a bustle of servants, all hastening to get settled in. Evidently there had been no diminution in Elizabeth's establishment. Maybe the King had a conscience after all.

At the top of the stairs, Kate ran into her great-uncle, Sir John Shelton, the governor of the household. He smiled at her and patted her shoulder. "It's good to see you, Kate. Terrible business, the affair of the Queen. I can't imagine what it was like for you in the Tower."

"It was grim, Uncle," she replied, not wanting even to think about it. "How is the Lady Elizabeth?"

"She is well," he said.

"Does she know yet?"

"No, Kate. We have had no orders, save instructions that she is not to be called princess and a command to dismiss a few servants. Otherwise, nothing has changed, so we are still treating her with the same deference as before. She is his Grace's daughter, after all."

"Will you tell her what has happened?"

Sir John looked horrified. "Not I! We must await the King's pleasure. Come, she has been asking for you and will be pleased to see you."

They entered the nursery and Elizabeth ran to Kate, throwing her arms around her. Her fair-skinned, freckled face was alight with excitement, and long tendrils of burnished red hair were escaping from the embroidered white coif tied beneath her chin.

"Kate! Kate! Have you brought me a present?"

Kate knelt and kissed her. "No, but I will get you one soon."

"Now, my Lady Elizabeth," said Kat Champernowne. She was a plump brunette with a gentle Devon accent, rounded cheeks, a turned-up nose, a warm heart, and a wealth of learning. "Let Kate catch her breath. She has only just arrived. Let us go and comb your hair. You've got it in such a mess." She led the child into the bedchamber.

At that moment, the Lady Mary, the King's elder daughter, appeared. Kate knew that Elizabeth would be pleased to see her. It was a marvel that Mary loved her so much, for Elizabeth's mother had been the cause of years of misery for herself and her own mother, the late Queen Katherine, culminating in banishment and humiliation; and yet Mary lavished all her frustrated maternal instincts on the child. Kate could only admire such open-heartedness.

She felt sorry for Mary, who had been bastardized and deprived of her status as princess, and banished from her father's presence because she had stood up for her beloved mother. In doing so, she had lost any chance of making the great marriage she should have had. Instead, she had been sent to wait on Elizabeth, and been unkindly treated by the servants Queen Anne had put about her. Kate hated the King even more for what he had done to his daughters. How could he have been so cruel?

Kate had vivid memories of Mary's anguished outburst of grief when she learned that her mother had died. That had been back in January. There were whispers that she had been poisoned by her enemies, but Kate could not believe that Aunt Anne would have been so ruthless. No wonder Mary often looked sad and haunted, and older than her twenty years. Her rich attire could not mask her skinny body. She had a snub nose and a downturned mouth, and although her hair was red like Elizabeth's, it was thin and frizzy.

Today, Mary was holding herself like a queen. Hard upon Anne's fall, her status had risen almost overnight. Everyone fell silent and dipped their heads in hurried reverences.

Elizabeth toddled in from the bedchamber, followed by Kat.

"My Lady Elizabeth," Mary greeted her.

Elizabeth turned to Sir John. "Why, Governor, how is it that yesterday I was called my Lady Princess, and today just Lady Elizabeth?"

Kate held her breath. The child not only had an advanced grasp of language, but also of understanding. Sir John was clearly caught off guard. He pulled at his beard, frowned, and hesitated, while Elizabeth stood before him, her imperious gaze demanding a response.

"The King your father has ordered it," he said at last.

"Why?" asked the child, her dark eyes narrowing.

"The King's orders must always be obeyed," he declared.

Kate saw the little face cloud over, but Elizabeth was not letting him off so easily. Just then, Lady Bryan entered the room, carrying a pile of fresh laundry. The little girl tugged at her skirts and repeated her question.

Tears welled up in the old woman's eyes. Kate felt like weeping, too. "You have a new title, my Lady Elizabeth," the governess said, in her most reassuring voice. "The King's Highness has decreed it."

"But why?" persisted the child.

"I'm sure the King has very good reasons," answered Lady Bryan, in a tone that forbade further discussion. "Now, where are those dolls you were playing with earlier?"

"I put them to bed," Elizabeth pouted.

"In the morning? The very idea!" exclaimed her governess. "Look, I've got some pretty silks in my basket, and some Holland cloth. Go and fetch your best doll, and I'll help you to make a gown for her."

Elizabeth looked mutinous, as if she would have liked to press the matter further, but knew that answers would not be forthcoming. Kate knew that the best thing for her was distraction.

She followed Elizabeth into the bedchamber as the child went reluctantly to the miniature cradle by her bed, and sank down beside her. "Let me help you dress her." Her heart was heavy, for she knew that the evil moment had only been postponed.

. . .

WITHIN ELEVEN DAYS, the news reached Hatfield that the King had married Jane Seymour.

"He didn't waste any time!" Lady Bryan muttered. "Still, I suppose he needs an heir, for with both his daughters declared bastards, he has none. And he's not getting any younger."

"There's some who say he has not the vigor to sire children," said Lady Troy, one of Elizabeth's gentlewomen, who was helping the governess to tidy the nursery.

"Hush! You must not speak of such things," Lady Bryan hissed, looking about her nervously. Lady Troy made a face, as if to imply that whether one should say them or not, they could well be true.

Kate could only feel profound sympathy for poor Queen Jane. What must it feel like, being married to a man who had just had his previous wife's head cut off? But the hapless woman had probably had no choice. Kate had never met her, but people were saying that she was very pale in complexion and no beauty.

There had been no further word from the King or Cromwell, no instructions as to how Elizabeth was to be treated. The nursery staff were speculating that his Grace could not bear to set eyes on her.

"He *is* on his honeymoon," Lady Bryan pointed out. "Not many men think of their children at such a time. He knows she is well looked after."

SOON AFTERWARD, A letter from Calais arrived for Kate. She recognized her mother's handwriting. Mother had never been a good correspondent and had written only infrequently over the past two years. Now she had received Aunt Anne's letter; she had heard of her death. Kate had expected her to be comforted by Anne's message of forgiveness, yet Mother sounded distraught, demanding a detailed account of what had happened. She seemed more preoccupied with the grounds on which Anne's marriage had been annulled than with anything else, although she was keen to be reassured that her sister had not suffered unduly, and overflowing with guilt on account of the unkindness between them, and the fact that she had had no opportunity to make her peace. "Pray for us both!" she urged Kate. "At least you were with her."

There were no words of comfort for Kate. Mother seemed not to have understood the horrors she had witnessed. If only they could meet; maybe it would be possible now that Anne was gone. Then Kate might look for more support from Mother. She brushed away a tear. She must be charitable. Mother was doubtless shocked by the news and incapable of thinking of others. And yet there remained a small, niggling feeling that Mother rarely considered anyone's needs but her own.

Kate replied that no one knew why the marriage had been annulled. She reassured her mother that Anne had spoken kindly of her toward the end, and that she too had wished that they were reconciled. She ended her letter by asking when Mother and Will were coming home, for their exchange of letters had made her realize that she needed her mother at this time. But Mother replied that she did not know when they would return to England; Will was serving in the garrison and could not be spared. Besides, she was happy to stay where she was for now, given the circumstances.

Kate perceived in that reply her mother's innate selfishness. There had been no suggestion that she herself might cross the sea to Calais and join them. She cried herself to sleep that night.

ELIZABETH'S HOUSEHOLD WAS at Hatfield in July when the Lady Mary paid her little half sister another visit. As she trotted into the courtyard on a white palfrey, followed by four gentlemen, two ladies-in-waiting, and a female fool, Elizabeth raced out of the front door and danced up and down in her excitement to see her. Mary dismounted and stooped to kiss her. She looked even more sad and haunted than she had before Queen Anne's fall, and no wonder. She had probably thought that the removal of her stepmother would soften the King's heart toward her—but no. The word was that he had just forced her to sign a declaration that his marriage to her mother had been unlawful, which must have gone against everything she held sacred.

"Make obeisance to my Lady Mary," Lady Bryan commanded, and Elizabeth sketched a wobbly curtsey.

"My, you have grown, sweeting!" Mary exclaimed in her gruff voice, stroking Elizabeth's hair and straightening her silver pendant. "You're nearly three now, aren't you?"

Mary embraced Lady Bryan, who had been her lady mistress too when she was little. "How lovely to see you."

Elizabeth was tugging at her sleeve, demanding her attention again. Mary smiled at her. "I have brought you gifts, Sister." She beckoned to a lady-in-waiting, who carried over a wooden box. Inside, wrapped in velvet, was a rosary of amber beads and a jeweled crucifix. "For your chapel," Mary said, pointing to the latter.

"Pretty," said Elizabeth, touching the beads.

"How does my sister, Lady Bryan?" Mary rose to her feet. "And you yourself? It is good to see you again, but I would it were in happier circumstances."

"I too, your Grace. We are well enough, both of us, I thank you," Lady Bryan answered, leading the way into the house.

Kate saw Elizabeth watching them and wondered if she had picked up on Mary's words, for she looked troubled. Kate grasped her hand and took her indoors. "After dinner, we shall go to see the puppies in the stables," she promised.

While roast goose was being served with appropriate ceremony to Mary in the great hall, Elizabeth was sent to the nursery to have her dinner. Mary told her avid listeners that she had seen the new Queen. "Queen Jane is a delightful, kind lady, not at all like her predecessor," she said, with a grimace. "The King summoned me to Hackney to meet them both. It was the first time I had seen him in many years. They were both very kind to me. I know that I have Queen Jane to thank for my reconciliation with my father." Her eyes misted with tears.

He should never have become estranged from you, Kate thought angrily.

"Tell me, does Elizabeth know about her mother's death?" Mary asked.

"No, my lady, we have had no instructions," Sir John said, passing the salt.

"But she must be told."

"Yes, but what shall we tell her—and who is to do it?" Lady Bryan looked distressed.

"I will speak with her," Mary said. "I'll do it this afternoon."

"That will be a weight off our minds." Lady Bryan nodded. "I thank you most heartily."

Mary laid down her knife and shook her head sadly. "I hardly know how I am going to tell her, Margaret," she said miserably, looking to her former governess for support.

Lady Bryan rested a comforting hand on hers. "I wouldn't be too explicit if I were you, Madam."

"Oh, no," agreed Mary fervently. "Do you think she will understand?"

"There is much she understands," Lady Bryan replied. "My little lady is more than ordinarily precocious, as Kate here knows well. As sharp as nails, that child, and clever with it."

"But a child for all that," Mary said, "so I will break it to her as gently as I can, and may our Holy Mother and all the saints help me."

Seeing her so distressed, Lady Bryan sought to steer the conversation away from the subject, but while she and Sir John chattered on about household matters and the state of the weather, Mary toyed with her food, having little appetite for it.

AS SOON AS dinner was finished, Elizabeth was brought back. Kate did not envy Mary her task, and dread mounted as she played with Elizabeth. Mary sat with Lady Bryan, watching them. Kate's heart twisted at the thought of the innocent, unsuspecting child learning the terrible truth about her mother. Her world would never be the same again. How would she take it?

Mary stood up. "I will speak to her now. I have brought my fool to afford a diversion later, if need be," she said.

Elizabeth had been inspecting her new beads, but now her ears pricked up. She liked fools. Their antics made her laugh.

"Come and walk with me in the park," Mary said, taking her by the hand and leading her to the front door. "Lady Bryan, Kate, you can come with us and bring some of the maids." She smiled, then murmured in Kate's ear, "Keep your distance, but within sight in case you are needed."

"Yes, your Grace," Kate said, wondering why she kept being picked for difficult duties and wishing that Mary had chosen one of her own ladies. But Mary had remarked earlier how attached Elizabeth was to Kate, and really the child should have someone she loved nearby when the news was broken to her. And Kate, more than anyone, knew how to distract her.

They walked in the sun-browned park. The day star was blazing down, there was barely the stir of a breeze, and Kate was sweltering in her long-sleeved silk gown. It was as well that she had made Elizabeth wear her wide-brimmed straw hat to protect her face from the sunshine and the glare, while poor Mary, wearing a smart French hood with a band under the chin, was suffering decorously. Her lips were pursed, and she looked unhappy.

At Lady Bryan's nod, Kate and the others sat on the grass as Mary and Elizabeth wandered a little way off. Kate could not hear what they were saying, but she saw Mary caress the long red curls that were escaping from the sun hat. Then suddenly, she sank to her knees and hugged her sister tightly. Elizabeth struggled free. She did not like to be squeezed like that; she was a self-contained child. Yet Mary clearly did not notice, for she was weeping. Kate noticed Lady Bryan watching them intently.

Mary dabbed her eyes with a white kerchief, rose, and drew Elizabeth to a stone seat placed in the shade of an oak tree to afford those who rested there a grand view of the redbrick palace of Hunsdon spread out beyond the formal gardens. She lifted the child onto it and began speaking in earnest. Lady Bryan and Kate exchanged concerned looks.

After a few minutes, Elizabeth suddenly slid off the bench and ran to Lady Bryan, burying her face in her skirts and bursting into violent tears.

"Mother! Mother! Where is my mother? I want her!" she wailed piteously, her small body trembling. "I want her! Get her!"

Both Lady Bryan and the Lady Mary knelt down, doing their best to comfort the stricken child, while Kate reached across and stroked her red curls; but she would not be consoled. "Where is my mother?" she wailed.

"She is dead, my lamb," wept Lady Bryan. "She is with God."

At this, Elizabeth began to scream. "I want her! I want her!"

"You must pray for her," faltered Mary.

But Elizabeth was beyond speech, howling her heart out.

BACK AT THE house, Kate heard Lady Bryan asking Mary what she had told Elizabeth.

"I simply said that her mother had done some very bad things and that she had been punished for them. I said that she was dead and at peace. Elizabeth knows what death is. She said, 'She won't come to see me again, then?' I told her no, but that our father still loves her, as do I, you, her ladies, and so many other people. I said she must pray for her mother, and she said she would. Then she ran from me."

"Of course, you did not raise the issue of her bastardy," Lady Bryan stated.

"No. She is too young to understand it. Let us spare her that burden until she is older," Mary said, her voice bitter.

They were all very kind to Elizabeth in the days that followed. Kate devised new games to play, Lady Bryan found her special tasks to do in the house, the cook served her favorite foods, her sister's female fool made merry jests and capered before her at mealtimes, brandishing her jingling bells, but it was Mary whom she wanted. Mary spent hours playing with her, rescuing her from the tedium of the well-meaning Sir John's dull stories.

"What shall it be tonight, my lady? 'Patient Grizelda' or 'Theseus and the Minotaur'?" he had asked.

"I had Theseus yesterday, *again,*" declared Elizabeth, sighing. "Read 'Patient Grizelda.' " Kat Champernowne was making faces at Kate.

"Listen carefully," Sir John said, opening the book. "This is a fitting tale for a little girl such as yourself, who might profit by its example of an obedient wife."

"The Lady Mary reads stories much better than you do," his

audience pronounced, fidgeting, before he had completed the first page. "So does Kate!"

"Allow me," Mary said with a smile, taking the book. Sir John withdrew gratefully.

THERE WERE NO further storms of tears. With the resilience of childhood, Elizabeth allowed herself to be diverted and, although subdued, responded to the comfort afforded her by others.

"Praised be God," Lady Bryan said, "the worst moment is surely over."

Chapter 5

1536

ELIZABETH HAD A GROWTH SPURT THAT SUMMER. BY AUgust, her clothes were too tight and too short, and Lady Bryan had to beg Cromwell for new ones.

"I've still had no word from the court," she said to Kat Champernowne, exasperated. "I know only of her demotion from princess by hearsay! I know not how to order her, nor myself, nor any of her servants. Look at these smocks! Nothing she has fits her. I'm beginning to wonder if his Grace remembers that he has a daughter. Well, I shall go on treating her as befits the daughter of a king. I shall just have to beg Master Cromwell to be good to my little lady and all of us here."

Kate felt sorry for her. She knew that the dear lady feared she would be dismissed. But she did not have to fret for long, for in August her fears were allayed.

That was when the thing Kate had long been dreading came to pass. The King's daughters were summoned back to Hunsdon, where he intended to visit them. Kate quailed at the thought. She did not think she could bear to see that unspeakable, blood-soaked monster. She feared she might try to scratch his eyes out or give him a piece of her mind. She knew that, in truth, she would do no such thing, but still she did not want to be anywhere near him.

When the royal harbingers brought word of his approach, Kate forced herself to line up in the courtyard with the rest of the household. And there he was, trotting in on his horse, his steely gaze raking over them all, as if seeking out some sign of disloyalty. Kate sank in an obeisance along with everyone else, unwilling to look him in the face, and suddenly, as his retinue clattered into the courtyard behind him, the quiet, ordered world of the nursery household exploded into color, gaiety, and noise. The King was always surrounded by brilliantly dressed gentlemen and ladies—who made much of Elizabeth—and attended by hordes of ministers, officers, and servants. There was no sign of Queen Jane, much to Kate's disappointment. Her presence would have made the occasion more bearable.

When he dismounted, he greeted Mary with a hearty kiss, saluted Lady Bryan quite amiably, and asked to have Elizabeth brought down to see him. In the vast hall of the palace, everyone waited for Mistress Champernowne to bring her from the nursery. Kate stood behind the others, clenching her hands and trying to look invisible. If the King noticed her, she would not answer for what she might say or do.

When the nurse set Elizabeth on the floor, to Kate's horror, the child ran straight to her, carrying the doll they had been playing with earlier. "Grizelda is better now!" she told her.

"Your Grace, the King your father awaits you," Kate muttered, keeping her eyes downcast and giving the little girl a gentle push toward him. She heard Henry roar with laughter as she ran over to him and curtseyed. When Kate raised her eyes, he was looking directly at her. "By St. George, you two cousins are alike," he observed.

Kate realized that he was referring to her and Elizabeth. She lowered her eyes, feeling herself flush, and dropped a curtsey.

"I wish Kate was my sister," Elizabeth piped up. "Mary is too old!"

There was a long pause as Mary reddened and looked distressed.

"Your Grace, Mistress Kate *is* like a sister to the Lady Elizabeth," Lady Bryan said.

"Then we have chosen her well as a companion for our daughter," the King said stiffly. "Come now, Bessy, let us walk in the garden." Kate watched as he lifted the child up, kissed her, and carried her out of the house, his fawning entourage following. Then she fled upstairs and lay down on her bed. When one of the maids came to tell her that dinner was about to be served in the hall, she said she was feeling sick and could not eat.

All she wanted to do was escape. The house seemed tainted by the King's threatening presence. As soon as she judged that he and everyone else would be at their meats, she hastened down the stair that led to the privy garden, flitted along the paths, and slipped through the wooden door in the wall that led to the hunting park. Keeping close to the wall, she ran as fast as she could to a place where she could not be seen from the hall windows and made her way through the trees. She had often brought Elizabeth here to play hide-and-seek, but today she was just glad to be able to sink down and rest against a trunk, breathing in the clear, unsullied air. She would not be disturbed here, and she could stay until after the King had left.

She had not reckoned on Elizabeth. After an hour spent luxuriating in the peace and solitude, she heard voices approaching, and then Elizabeth, saying, "And this is where Kate brings me to play."

"Does she indeed?" It was the King, and the crunching of grass told Kate that he was approaching fast.

What should she do? Pretend to be asleep? Get to her feet, curtsey, and excuse her absence by saying that she had had a headache and needed fresh air? She closed her eyes, praying they would not see her, or would leave her be.

"It seems that Kate is waiting for you, sweeting," she was dismayed to hear the King say.

"But she's asleep," the child said. "She's not well."

"I think she's pretending!" he chuckled. "Am I right, Mistress Carey?"

Kate opened her eyes to see his huge, glittering figure looming over her.

"She's awake! She's awake!" Elizabeth was dancing up and down.

"Your Grace!" Kate made it look as if they had roused her from sleep. She struggled to her feet and strove to speak without betraying her hatred. "I was feeling unwell and very tired."

"No matter." He grinned. "I trust you are feeling better." He extended a pudgy hand and patted her shoulder. She tried not to flinch. "As it happens, I have been wanting to speak with you. I know you have recently given me good service in difficult circumstances, and I wish to thank you."

Difficult circumstances? Had he any idea of the agony he had put her through, or the horror of it all, which she knew had scarred her for life?

"I thank your Grace," she mumbled, knowing that her tone was cold and offhand.

He ignored that. What had she expected—that he would show some Christian compassion for her?

"The greatest service you can give is to continue to befriend Elizabeth," he said. "I want her young ears protected from the infamous bruits that are circulating."

Kate knew what he was talking about. The household was alive with gossip about the late Queen's crimes, much of it concerning Elizabeth's paternity. It was being said that she was the child of Henry Norris or the lowly musician Mark Smeaton, or even, God forbid, Uncle George, which was ridiculous. And then there was fervid speculation about the grounds on which Anne's marriage had been annulled. No one had any idea what they were.

"It is my pleasure," the King was saying, "that Elizabeth shall keep to her chamber for a time and not go out. That way, she will be protected from what people are saying."

"But I don't want to!" Elizabeth pouted.

"You must do as your father's Grace commands," Kate said, stepping back a pace so as to distance herself farther from the King. But he stepped forward and bent to her ear.

"Her mother is not to be mentioned. The subject is too shameful. Lady Bryan has her orders. I am telling you too, Kate, because you are close to Elizabeth."

"Of course, Sir," Kate murmured, trying not to recoil from him. Her heart bled for Elizabeth, who had stooped to pick daisies. She would grow up with the awareness that there was a dark and dreadful secret about her mother's fate. And Kate knew what that was like. She had still not fathomed the mystery about her own mother's past.

"There is no need to be afraid of me, Kate," the King was saying, looking down at her tenderly from his great height. "I have ever had an affection for you, since you were born. I thought highly of your father. You may think me harsh in confining Elizabeth to her chamber, but you must understand that I am determined to keep her in innocence about what happened to her mother for as long as possible."

He had misunderstood her response to him. If he thought to cozen her, he must think again. Why he had a particular affection for her she could not conceive. Many noble courtiers had daughters, and there was always rampant competition for marriages or court posts for them. Why had she been singled out and given one of the most sought-after positions of all? Unless, of course, those pats on the arm betokened something utterly disgusting. No, he could not fancy her! She was twelve years old!

"You will remember what I have said," he enjoined her. "Her mother is not to be mentioned to her."

"I understand, Sir," Kate said. "Now, if I may take her in, it is time for the Lady Elizabeth's dancing lesson."

He nodded, his steely blue eyes still fixed on her. She curtseyed, took Elizabeth's hand, and almost ran with her to the palace. In an hour or so, the King and his colorful train would be gone, and they could all breathe again.

ELIZABETH LOVED TO sit with Kate and look at the vivid pictures in one of the beautifully illuminated books the King had provided. They both enjoyed making music; the child had a precocious talent, and Kate herself was becoming increasingly proficient on the lute, the virginals, and the recorder. Sometimes, they would sort through embroidery silks, and Lady Bryan would let the child pick the colors herself. Then she would teach Elizabeth how to make rows of different stitches, with Kate doing the same. Elizabeth learned quickly, as she learned everything. Already, she knew her alphabet, and her numbers up to one hundred, and in chapel she was striving to understand the Latin rubric of the Mass.

"What is Father Parker saying?" she would pipe up, ever inquisitive, and Lady Bryan would put a finger to her lips and explain patiently, murmuring in a low voice. Afterward, Elizabeth would pester the chaplain, urging him to teach her the words and phrases that so intrigued her. She had only to hear a thing said once and she had it by heart.

When the embroidering palled—after all, Elizabeth was only in her third year, and her quick, darting mind was always flitting to the next thing—Lady Bryan would see to it that her day was filled with distractions: a walk with Kate in the great wide park of Hatfield, a visit to the stables to see her dappled pony, and a spell in the kitchens to watch the cook making marchpane, which she was allowed to sample after it had cooled; the child had an inordinately sweet tooth. Then a story—nothing too somber, but perhaps that old tale of Master Chaucer's about Chanticleer the cock, which always made Elizabeth laugh out loud; and after this, a light supper of pottage and bread, then prayers and bedtime.

Once Elizabeth was settled in her comfortable bed, with its feather mattress, crisp heavy linen, rich velvet counterpane and curtains, and the arms of England embroidered on its tester, Lady Bryan would sign the cross on her forehead and then leave her to go to sleep, settling herself with a book in a high-backed chair by the fire, a candle flickering at her side. Most nights Kate slept on the pallet by Elizabeth's bed-foot. Soon Lady Bryan would be slumbering, her book abandoned on her lap. Elizabeth, however, would lie wide awake, her fertile mind too active for sleep, and then she would lean over the end of the mattress and prod Kate with an insistent finger. "Get into bed with me! We can look at the pictures again!"

And so Kate would clamber in beside her and turn the pages in the flickering candlelight until finally, mercifully, the child fell into slumber. Then she herself would try to sleep. It did not come easily now, for when she was tired, she had no defenses against the ghastly images that came unbidden to haunt her. That sickening thud as the executioner did his work, the blood, the sight of Anne's severed head lying in the sawdust . . . Would she never forget these horrors?

WHEN THE KING came again, even Kate had to concede that he was a loving father to Elizabeth. It was raining, so he sat beside the fire in the parlor with his daughter on his knee, while Kate and Kat sat sewing at the table.

"Are they keeping you hard at your books and your prayers, or do they let you out to play as often as they should?" the King asked, winking conspiratorially at Elizabeth, who laughed.

"I play a lot, Sir," she said, "and I love that doll you sent me. But I do learn my letters and my catechism."

"Well and good, well and good," he said, bouncing her on his strong muscular thighs. Then he let her rest with her cheek against his doublet, which was encrusted with gems and goldsmiths' work, with his bristly red beard tickling the top of her forehead.

"I will tell you something, Bessy," he said. "When I was a young king, I did not wish to be at my prayers or attending to state affairs; I wanted to enjoy life. So can you guess what I did? I would sneak out of the palace by a back stair and go hunting, and my councillors would never know I had gone."

"Didn't you get into trouble?" Elizabeth was wide-eyed.

"Hah!" he roared. "I am the King. They would never have dared!"

"Can you do what you like when you are king?" she asked.

"Of course I can," he replied. "People have to do my will." There was an edge to his voice.

"Then," she told him, "I am going to be king when I grow up."

Stealing a glance at his face in the brief silence that followed, Kate saw that he was angry. Suddenly, he was a man of steel, cold of visage and tight-mouthed. Without a word, he set Elizabeth none too gently on the floor, and drew himself up to his towering height, a big bulk of a man, powerful and daunting.

"You can never be a king," he told her, in a voice as quiet as it was menacing. "You must pray that the Queen bears a son to rule after me. Take her to the nursery, Mistress Champernowne."

Kat rose and hurried to do his bidding, and Kate followed her and Elizabeth out of the room. The child's lips were trembling. "It's all right, sweeting," she said. "Maybe we should have told you that girls cannot be kings."

"Men say it is against Nature and the law of God for a woman to rule," Kat said, setting Elizabeth down on the nursery floor. "To me, that's mere foolishness, but I would not for the world say that to his Grace's face!"

Less than an hour passed before the King sent for Elizabeth again. When they took her back to the parlor, they found him as cheery and as boisterous as if nothing had upset him.

THAT EVENING, KATE was kneeling on the floor of the long gallery playing skittles with Elizabeth and Lady Troy.

Without warning, the child turned a troubled face to her.

"Is Queen Jane beautiful?" she asked, making Kate start.

"I have heard say that she is very fair," Kate said.

"My mother was beautiful," Elizabeth said in a small voice.

Kate did not know how to answer. She was mindful of the King's command not to mention Anne to Elizabeth. But she had to say something, for this was the first time that Elizabeth had mentioned her since that dreadful day in the park.

The child was looking up at her with eyes that seemed old in her young face.

"What did my mother do that was bad?" she asked.

"She was unfaithful to the King," Kate said, picking her words with care. "They said that she was accused of plotting to kill him." She looked anxiously at her little cousin, waiting for the storm to break. It didn't. Elizabeth was in command of herself.

THAT SUMMER, ELIZABETH was summoned to court, accompanied by Lady Bryan, and when she returned from there to Hatfield, she was full of how kind Queen Jane had been to her and how magnificent Hampton Court Palace was.

"It's got a huge high roof, even taller than the one here, and it's all painted in nice colors!" she recounted, hopping from foot to foot. "I didn't want to come home, and the King my father said he was sorry to see me go, but he had to go somewhere with the Queen. The French ambassador said I was a charming child."

"Well, you can be when you put your mind to it!" Kate teased, grinning.

"I *am* charming!" Elizabeth insisted. She was so vain. Already, she carried herself like the queen she would never now be.

She knelt on the carpet next to Kate. "Get out the skittles," she commanded.

Kate made a face at her. "And what do we say?"

"Please!" Elizabeth shouted. As Kate rose, she said, "I miss my father, but I don't miss Queen Jane very much. She's not my real mother."

"You will grow to love her," Kate told her. "Just wait until you get to know her better."

"Kat says that she has to have a son," Elizabeth said.

Heavens, couldn't Kat keep her mouth shut?

"The King your father needs a son to succeed him on the throne, so of course he is hoping to have one," Kate said carefully.

"How does he get one?" Elizabeth asked.

Kate thought quickly as she laid the box of skittles on the floor and pulled back the rug. "He has to wait until God sends one."

That seemed to satisfy the child, who was distracted by the imminent prospect of a game.

AS AUGUST PASSED, Elizabeth kept asking when she was next going to court, or when her father would visit her.

"His Majesty is away hunting," said Sir John Shelton.

"His Majesty is much occupied with plans for the Queen's coronation."

"There is plague abroad. The coronation has been postponed, and no one is allowed to visit the court for fear of the pestilence."

Kate did not doubt that all these things were true—everyone was frightened of the plague—but she felt they did not excuse that monster for not taking the time to see his daughter.

One autumn day, Sir John appeared in the long gallery, where Kate was helping Lady Bryan to make herb-scented sachets for the linen chests. Elizabeth was with them, rampaging about on the hobby horse the Queen had sent for her third birthday. "There is a great rebellion in the north," Sir John said. "They are calling it the Pilgrimage of Grace. The Catholics are determined to halt the King's religious reforms and save the monasteries from closure."

Lady Bryan glanced at Elizabeth, but she was riding up and down the gallery, progressing from a walk to a trot to a canter and then a gallop. She was not interested in the conversation between her elders. It was as well, because Sir John seemed deeply concerned.

"This is the most serious threat to the King. He might lose his throne."

"Never!" decreed Lady Bryan.

"Don't be too sure. He has sent troops north to deal with the rebels, but I fear they will be vastly outnumbered. There's no knowing what could happen." He lowered his voice. "If the King is overthrown by these insurgents, who will they choose to succeed him? His daughters are both declared bastards."

"Shush!" hissed Lady Bryan. "That's treason you're speaking. It's forbidden even to imagine the King's death."

"I wasn't envisaging that, of course," Sir John said hastily, coloring.

Kate bent her head to her sewing. She was aware that the King had broken with the wicked Pope in Rome and made himself Supreme Head of the Church of England, and that momentous changes were afoot in the realm. The Boleyns had been hot for reform of the Church, although no one had explained to her exactly what that meant, apart from the fact that there were people who held opinions that were different from the Church's teachings, which got them into trouble. Lady Bryan said that some were wicked heretics whose minds had been poisoned by a terrible man called Martin Luther, and that they deserved to be burned at the stake for trying to infect others with their lies. Kate thought that was a horrible punishment for anyone, whatever they had done.

She felt nervous about the rebellion, but it was a long way away, and surely the King's army would put a stop to it. She knew about his closing down some abbeys and priories, and Aunt Anne had said that several were not worth saving, while others were hotbeds of Popery, and yet Lady Bryan was of the opinion that the monks and nuns did much good work, looking after the poor and the sick, and teaching children—and who would do that if the King closed all the monasteries down? Yet she never said this in front of Elizabeth or Sir John.

Kate did not know what to think. Grown-ups were always going on about religious change, and most of it went over her head. She loved God, said her prayers, and kept the commandments, and that was enough, she felt.

Of course, the rebellion meant nothing to Elizabeth until she was allowed to participate in the celebrations to mark the crushing of it in December.

"And we are to go to Whitehall, and then to Greenwich for Christmas!" beamed Lady Bryan, holding Elizabeth's hand as they watched the bonfire that had been lit in honor of the occasion. The villagers of Hatfield were capering around it, hands linked, and the ale was flowing freely. The child's eyes shone, and she skipped for joy in her excitement.

Kate was looking forward to going to court, too, for the revelry, until Sir John informed her that she was to go home to Hever Castle for the season. "We cannot take the whole household to court," he said.

Kate was appalled at the prospect of a cheerless Christmas in the company of Grandfather, Grandmother, and Great-Grandmother, and Elizabeth was appalled at being separated from Kate. She jumped up and down in a fury, demanding that Kate go with her, but Lady Bryan was having no such nonsense and commanded her to obey her governor. Elizabeth subsided, looking mutinous.

Chapter 6

1536–37

When kate traveled the great north road south to London and thence to Kent, wrapped in furs in a chariot and escorted by Sir John's retainers, it was bitterly cold. She felt chilled inside, too, wondering what reception she would receive at Hever. For undoubtedly, Grandfather would be home, since he could not possibly be welcome at court now, and then there would be Great-Grandmother, who was in her right mind most days, but sometimes prone to seeing things no one else could see, which was deeply unsettling.

When the litter clattered across the drawbridge at Hever and into the courtyard, men came running out to help with the horses and the luggage. The steward greeted Kate.

"Welcome, Mistress Carey. My lady is waiting for you in the great chamber."

"Is my grandfather not at home?" she asked, handing him her cloak as they entered the castle.

"He is at court, Mistress."

That surprised her. Or perhaps it shouldn't have. Had he managed to turn things to his advantage by condemning two of his children to death?

"Is my grandmother here?"

"She is away visiting my Lord of Norfolk. But my Lady Boleyn is in the parlor."

Great-Grandmother rose shakily from her seat by the roaring fire when Kate appeared. "My dear sweet Kate," she said, holding out her arms. "I have missed seeing you and Harry these three years. You, your mother, and your grandparents are all who are left to me now. Have you eaten?"

Kate pressed her face against the paper-thin cheek.

"I am hungry, my lady," she admitted.

After they had been served a light lunch of broth and bread, Great-Grandmother insisted on going for a walk in the frost-rimed gardens. When Kate wondered if she would be cold (certainly, she herself would be), the old lady sniffed. "I'm eighty-two, child, and I'm made of sterner stuff than that. Fetch your cloak."

Even in winter, the gardens at Hever were glorious, and they were surrounded by the beautiful, undulating Kentish countryside. Great-Grandmother kept up a steady pace, but she suddenly stopped by the bare rosebushes. "Everywhere I look," she said, "there are reminders of those who are gone. I see my grandchildren playing on the grass, Thomas waiting on the drawbridge to welcome the King, and Anne peering through a window at him—she knew well how to play Henry and tie him in knots. It is hard to believe that she and George are dead now, and that I, who by the law of Nature should have died first, am still here."

Kate felt the tears welling.

"I know what they say about your grandfather," the old lady went on, "that he was complicit in destroying his children. God alone knows what it cost him to sit in judgment on them and declare them both guilty—and of the most disgusting crimes. But your grandmother was ill; he had to think of her. He really didn't have a choice. Had he refused, he might have been brought down with Anne and George, and then where would she have been? Mark me, Kate, he came home a broken man. They were both broken, paralyzed with grief and horror. I remember Elizabeth sitting in her chair, rocking in her misery, and her hysterical cries when word came that the dread sentence had been carried out. Thomas uttered no word of protest or sorrow, but you had only to look at him to know that he was suffering. They've not been the same since, either of them. They barely speak to each other, and she's not the woman she was."

She sighed and walked on, the black veil of her gable hood flapping in the wind. "But Thomas is a survivor. He might have lost his office of Lord Privy Seal to Lord Cromwell, but he did manage to retain his place on the King's Council. He was determined to claw his way back into royal favor, and it didn't take much, for I believe that the King genuinely likes him—and finds him useful. Thomas has even made an effort to be courteous to that pallid little bitch who stole Anne's crown."

She stomped on, seemingly ignorant of the cold. Kate drew her cloak tighter around her and shivered. They were walking along the banks of the River Eden now.

"This is where the King used to bring her when he came a-courting," the old woman said wistfully. "She held him off, you know—until he decided he wanted to marry her and realized he couldn't risk getting her with child first. Think of the scandal!"

She turned to Kate, who had caught up with her.

"Well, there was scandal enough without that. Maybe it would have been to her advantage to get pregnant then. She might have borne the son they both wanted. In the end, she failed in that one crucial thing, so she was brought down. I am in no doubt that they concocted a case against her. The granddaughter I knew had her faults, but she was not that much of a monster—and neither was George. As to what was said about them—no one in their right mind would credit it. But I mustn't think about it, or I'll end up going over and over it all in my mind and torturing myself by wondering what it was like for her at the end, flesh of my flesh. You said they didn't even give her a proper burial. I can't forgive that, or the King for marrying again only eleven days after her death. And I can't forgive George's unspeakable wife, for it was she who claimed that he and Anne committed incest. That word is bitter gall on my tongue."

Kate, who had only a vague idea what incest was, could see that she was near to tears, her stout-hearted great-grandmother who rarely showed any sign of gentleness. "It has been a terrible business," she commiserated, inwardly warding off the grief that threatened to overwhelm her when she remembered what had befallen her family.

"Aye, and it was a most unkind thing to send you to the Tower to be with her at the end, although I am glad that someone from the family was there."

"That's what my mother said when she wrote to me afterward," Kate told her.

"I will not have *her* mentioned!" Great-Grandmother snapped. "Three grandchildren I had, and the only one left to me is the one who let the family down."

Kate felt her hackles rising, but she held her tongue. Great-Grandmother had never had any time for Mother, and that wasn't going to change.

"But Lady Rochford is a thousand times worse!" the old lady was spluttering, as they made their way back to the castle. "It was she who testified against your uncle. Can anyone blame your grandfather for refusing to have her under his roof? I have not forgotten him exploding with rage when the King asked him to provide for her. I saw his pen jab the page as he asked Cromwell to inform the King that he did so only for his Highness's pleasure. But he made sure that that filthy whore didn't get her hands on the widow's jointure settled on her at her marriage. And I'm determined she won't have it in my lifetime either! What galls me is that she was welcomed back to court to serve the Seymour woman. I have no doubt that it was a reward for services rendered in bringing down her husband and her Queen."

Kate forbore to comment. After learning what Lady Rochford had done, she had come to loathe her, having always felt that there was something dark in her.

Gratefully, for her fingers felt like icicles, she followed her great-grandmother into the castle, where she was thankful to see that the fire in the great chamber had been stoked up. Sitting on the stool by the old lady's high-backed chair, she took up her sewing.

"This is a sad house now," Great-Grandmother said. "I have ever found beauty here, and an inner peace of sorts, with quietness in abundance. Yet now there will always remain the taint of these late dark deeds." She paused and sighed. "I see Anne from time to time, and I wish I didn't, but I don't tell many people that. Nor do I speak much of my awful gift, or that I kept seeing a sword over her head. The gift is a curse, and it's got me into trouble several times. In one of his unkind moods, your grandfather once called me a witch. But witches practice their craft willingly. My visions come unbidden, and I have never been able to control them."

Kate listened, astonished. She had always been told that Great-Grandmother was mad, but she hadn't quite understood why, for the old woman had often seemed as sane as she herself was. Yet on several occasions she had come upon her talking to someone who wasn't there. But this didn't seem like madness; it sounded like a curse—or a haunting. She shivered to think that Anne's wraith might be walking at Hever.

"The visions are coming more frequently now," Great-Grandmother was saying. "I see Hever, but not the Hever I know. The castle looks decayed and ruinous. Sheep graze where the gardens should be. Then—and maybe I am dreaming—I see a man in strange dark attire, with a pugnacious face and a mustache, very upright and correct. And then my vision of the castle returns once more, only this time it is surrounded by crowds of people all trying to get in, and the gardens are restored, but looking so different, and there is a lake, where now are fields.

"I seem to drift through the courtyard, where I see that the windows have been replaced. Our kitchen has been transformed into a fine hall, the well hidden under a wooden floor. Fine wood carvings are everywhere, and there are portraits on the walls. I recognize the King, and there are two bad likenesses of Anne and your mother on either side of the fireplace. In our great hall, a fire crackles in the large fireplace and tapestries grace the walls. The tables are laid as if for a sumptuous banquet, but the dais has gone and there is no high table for the family. On the wall hangs a little painting of the hall as I know it. It is very strange!"

Kate was open-mouthed, spellbound.

"I'm having more visions as I get older, but I keep them to myself. I saw your uncle George doing something so abominable to his wife that I can't bear to think about it. But there's another vision that comes increasingly these days. I see a young woman with red hair wearing a crown, and I wonder who it could be. It surely cannot be Elizabeth. How can a bastard be crowned queen?" She shook her head. "I hope Henry's being a good father to her and seeing that she is well cared for. She needs stability after losing her mother so tragically, poor mite. I wish I could see her and be a proper great-grandmother to her. But she is far beyond my reach."

Kate nodded sadly. No, Elizabeth would never be queen; nor would Mary, who also had red hair. When she looked again, the old lady had fallen asleep.

IT WAS A quiet Christmas, but properly observed. The Yule log was carried in on Christmas Eve and set alight in the hall fireplace. Kate helped the servants to gather holly, ivy, and bay to decorate the windowsills. The waits came from Edenbridge to sing carols, and there was roast goose and plum pudding for Christmas dinner. Kate longed to be at Greenwich Palace with Elizabeth, enjoying the festivities.

At New Year, Great-Grandmother gave her a silver locket, and Kate returned the gesture with some handkerchiefs she had embroidered. On Twelfth Night, a feast was served for the estate tenants, and Cook baked the traditional cake. Kate found the bean in her slice and was Queen of the Bean for the evening, with the freedom to choose the games and set forfeits. For the first time in her visit, she was truly enjoying herself. Yet she was glad to leave the next day and make her way north to Hatfield, where Elizabeth, now returned from court, would be awaiting her.

When she arrived there, snow lay on the ground and Elizabeth was out in it. Lady Bryan stood shivering as the child threw snowballs, giggling excitedly. When she saw Kate, she ran to her and demanded to be lifted up.

"I had a lovely time!" she said. "The Thames froze over and after we had been to St. Paul's Cathedral, I rode across it to Greenwich on horseback, on my father's lap! The people were cheering and calling out, 'God save King Harry!' And they called out, 'God save Elizabeth!' too. They love me! It was a wonderful day." She struggled to get down, clapped her hands, and danced through the snow.

Lady Bryan smiled, shaking her head in mock despair. "She is far too excited. My Lady Elizabeth, come in and eat your supper, and let Kate catch her breath. She has had a long journey."

Kate was glad to be back. She hummed a tune as she unpacked, then hurried down to the hall, which was filled with the enticing aroma of roast beef. Her mouth watered.

After supper, she sat by the fire with Elizabeth, who regaled her with more stories of her time at court. "We went outside to see the mummers' play about St. George. I didn't like the dragon because it roared a lot, but St. George killed it. The best bit was when he rescued the princess and kissed her hand. She was very beautiful, with golden hair. And then I was allowed to stay up and have candied fruits in the privy chamber!"

"She ate so many that she felt sick afterward!" Lady Bryan murmured, her head bent to her hemming. Kate smiled. Elizabeth's sweet tooth would be her undoing one day. Presently, the child fell asleep, dreaming no doubt of the marvelous revels at court, and Kate carried her off to bed.

AS WINTER TURNED to spring and spring to summer, Kate determinedly made herself avoid thinking about Aunt Anne and that dreadful time in the Tower, or the King. There were still moments when the sense of tragedy threatened to overwhelm her, but they were becoming fewer and fewer. At thirteen, life was beckoning. Her body was flowering into womanhood and the admiring stares of young men were flattering. Not that she saw many at Hatfield or Hunsdon, yet there were some visitors, and some lads in church, whose good looks made her heart race a little. It was of the future that she thought most, a future that she hoped might bring marriage and babies.

She had stayed in touch with her mother, although Mother was not the most enthusiastic of letter writers. Weeks could go by without hearing from her, and then she would receive a long scrawl in which Mother told her every detail of her own life but rarely asked about hers. It did not look as if Mother and Will would be coming home any time soon.

Kate made sure to write to her brother, Harry, who was living at Syon Abbey with his tutors. It troubled her that they had grown apart, having lived separate lives for so long, and she felt it was important to strengthen the ties of blood between them. But Harry proved to be even worse than their mother at keeping in touch, and in the end, Kate gave up.

As autumn descended on the land, Elizabeth's household was abuzz with excited speculation. Would it be a prince or a princess? For Queen Jane had quickened in the late spring and soon her child would be born—a child whose legitimacy could never be questioned—and an heir to England, God willing.

"WAKE UP, KATE, we have just received the most wonderful tidings!" exclaimed Lady Bryan, shaking her by the shoulder. Kate rubbed her eyes, then opened them to see the governess beaming happily in the October sunlight streaming in through the latticed window.

"England has a prince!" Lady Bryan cried. "Queen Jane has borne the King a son! Oh, this is a great day, for the King's Majesty—and for us all!"

Elizabeth was thrilled when they woke her to tell her the news. "A baby brother? At last, I will have someone to play with!"

"His name is Edward," Lady Bryan told her, "and he was born at Hampton Court two days ago on the twelfth of October, the eve of St. Edward the Confessor, a most auspicious day. Now we must make haste, my little lady, because we are summoned to court without delay. The King wishes you to play your part at the christening."

"Ohh!" Elizabeth was scrambling out of bed, bursting with excitement. "What am I to do?"

"You are to take part in the procession."

"Is that an important part?" asked the child.

"Very important indeed," said Lady Bryan firmly, smiling at Kate. "Now, we must get you ready quickly!"

Once more, Kate was told that she must stay behind. It was not fair, she felt. She never got to go to court. Not that she wanted to see that devil the King, but she would dearly have loved to see the splendors of Hampton Court and the pageantry of the christening.

But no.

"Because of the plague, the King is limiting numbers," Sir John told her.

"The plague has died down!" she protested.

"His Majesty is clearly taking no chances. His heir will be too precious to him. And I will not defy his orders."

Kate tried to suppress her disappointment as she waved off an excited Elizabeth and watched the little procession disappear toward the Great North Road.

IT WAS ONLY days later that she heard the bells tolling. Kat looked up from her book.

"I wonder who that's for," she said, going to the window. Kate joined her. There was nothing to be seen. The house was a long way from the church.

A rider appeared, cantering up the drive. He wore the King's livery. Kate and Kat raced into the hall, almost colliding with Sir John Shelton.

"Bad news, I fear," he remarked.

Kate felt a shiver of fear. Not the Prince, she prayed. *Don't let it be the Prince.*

The messenger was shown in and bowed. "Sir John, I bring heavy tidings. Our good mistress the Queen has died in childbed. The King orders that the Lady Elizabeth's household go into mourning for three months. Lord Cromwell will see that you are reimbursed for the outlay."

Kate felt the news like a blow. How cruel of Fate to snatch Jane away in the hour of her triumph and to deprive the newborn Prince of his mother!

"That is indeed tragic news, especially when the kingdom is rejoicing," said Sir John, crossing himself. "I will order black cloth immediately."

Kate was in tears at the thought of the poor royal baby left motherless, and imagining how Elizabeth was taking the news. At just four years old, she had experienced far too much tragedy and loss.

The child arrived home a few days later in a very subdued mood, wearing a black damask gown and a white hood. "I asked God to save the Queen," she said, as she stood watching Kate unpack her clothes. "I prayed very hard, but He didn't hear me." Her lower lip trembled. "Lady Bryan said she is in Heaven now. I am sorry she is dead. She was very kind to me. I will miss her." Tears were threatening, but she did not give in to them.

Kate stroked her hair. "I expect the King, your father, is very sad."

"He went to Windsor. I did not see him. Lady Bryan said we had to go home. I saw her, Kate." The tears were falling now. "I went with Mary to the chapel and I saw her lying there in her robes with her crown on her head and lots of jewels. We had to kneel down for Mass, and then we went up to her. There was a nasty smell, which I didn't like. Mary lifted me up to kiss the Queen's hand, but it was cold like stone. I wanted her to wake up so that everyone would be happy once more and my father would come back. But I knew really that she would never wake up again."

She buried her face in her hands. Kate knelt down and hugged her.

Lady Bryan bustled in and stopped short when she saw them. She shook her head. "It's been a difficult time for her. I'm glad to get her home. Now, for some distraction, I think."

She opened Elizabeth's toy chest.

"Come, my lamb, find something to play with and run along while we finish in here." The child stood, gathered up her beloved skittles, and left the bedchamber.

"It would have helped if the King her father had stayed to comfort her," Lady Bryan said, "but he was much stricken with grief and could not abide to be in the same house as the Queen's body."

Thinking only of himself, as usual, Kate thought angrily.

"I heard that he was framing his mind patiently to bearing his loss. It is said he has also framed his mind to taking another wife."

Kate stared at her. "A fourth wife? And Queen Jane not even in her grave?"

"The situation calls for pragmatism, even at such a time. The life of the Prince is all that stands between stability and chaos in this realm, and many children die young. For the sake of all our futures, the King needs other sons, and he himself has clearly recognized this. And, of course, there are advantages to be gained through a new marriage alliance."

Kate nodded slowly. "I do see that. But the Prince is in good health?"

"Praised be God, he is a lusty child, by all accounts. And so he should be, for the King is guarding his health rigorously. He has commanded that the walls, floors, and ceilings of the Prince's chamber be washed down thrice daily, and that anyone who has been in contact with any infection is not to approach his Highness."

"Poor little babe," Kate murmured. "Is he to come to Hatfield?"

"Oh no, he will have his own household. Elizabeth isn't happy about that, but let us hope she will see him sometimes. We must do everything we can to make her forget this tragedy."

THERE WAS MUCH speculation in the household as to whom the King would marry; it was often the sole topic of conversation at dinner—when Elizabeth was not present, of course. Everyone was agog to hear what Sir John had to report when he returned from his latest visit to court.

"It was to have been a French princess," he related, carving the roast beef, "but the French weren't of a mind to it. Apparently, his Majesty told their ambassador that the thing touched him too near, and that he needed to see the lady before any contract was signed." Sir John shook his head. "He asked that suitable French ladies be brought to Calais so that he could meet them and get to know them a little before choosing. The ambassador was furious! He said that the great ladies of France were not to be paraded like prize animals in a market. And then he dared to suggest"—Sir John lowered his voice, with an eye on Kate—"that his Majesty might like to mount them one after the other and keep the one he found most agreeable."

Lady Bryan gasped; her cheeks had flushed rosy pink.

"Aye, you may well blush, my lady," said Sir John, "and the King did, too. Never have I seen him so embarrassed. He is now looking to Cleves . . ."

Kate was blushing as well. But where was Cleves?

Chapter 7

1537–38

In October, at Lady Bryan's summons, Kate took Elizabeth down to the great hall at Hatfield. Lady Bryan was waiting for them with Kat and Lady Troy. She stroked Elizabeth's cheek.

"Lady Troy is to be your new mistress," she announced.

"My new mistress?" Elizabeth was startled. "But *you* are my lady mistress."

Lady Bryan took a deep breath. "Not anymore, dear child, I'm afraid. I am to be governess to the Prince, and rule over his new household. That is why Lady Troy is to take over."

Elizabeth stood there silently for a long pause. Kate could see that this was unwelcome news, and no wonder, because for as long as Elizabeth could remember, Lady Bryan had looked after her. In all but blood, she had been a mother to her, the person who had cared for her, nurtured her, comforted her, and disciplined her. All her life, Lady Bryan had been there, and now she would be there no more. It must be incomprehensible to such a young child.

"Has my father commanded it?" Elizabeth asked.

"He has, my dear," Lady Bryan said gently.

"It must be a mistake," declared Elizabeth. "Lady Troy can look after the Prince. You must stay here." There was another silence.

"The Prince needs an experienced lady of rank to be his lady mistress," Lady Bryan said. "Long before you were born, I had care of your sister, the Lady Mary. Then I transferred to your service. Now I am commanded to Hampton Court to look after the Prince."

There was pride in her voice as she said it, and Kate feared it must be plain to Elizabeth that this was not just the King's doing, but Lady Bryan's own wish. Her brother was more important than she was—she was old enough to know it—and for Lady Bryan this was promotion, and a great honor.

For once, Elizabeth looked defeated. She was intelligent enough to know that it would be futile to protest further, and that she must accept the situation. But clearly she was hurting inside and realizing that her small world would never, ever be the same. Once again, her universe had shifted, as it had done violently when she had learned of the awful fate of her mother and, to a lesser extent, when Queen Jane had died.

She did not make a fuss. She went up to Lady Troy and hugged her, then bowed her head regally when she sketched a curtsey.

"It will be an honor to serve you, my Lady Elizabeth," Lady Troy said. Elizabeth gave her a small smile. Lady Bryan beamed, too.

The tears threatened to spill two days later, as the little girl waved Lady Bryan goodbye, standing in the doorway of the great hall. She looked desolate. But Kat was there for her. And I will be, too, for as long as God wills it, Kate told herself, although she would also greatly miss Lady Bryan, who had been a reassuring, steadfast presence in her own life, like a second mother.

As soon as Lady Bryan's litter had disappeared in a cloud of dust, Lady Troy turned to Elizabeth and smiled kindly.

"Let's all walk in the gardens," she said brightly. "It's such a fine day. Why don't you fetch a ball. We can play some games, if it pleases you, my lady."

Elizabeth looked at her in wonder. Lady Bryan had never suggested such a thing, and imagining that stately lady, skirts and sleeves flying, throwing or kicking a ball, was so hilarious that Kate could not suppress a giggle as she ran to find the ball. And the game was so much fun, with the four of them, including Kat, laughing and panting as they raced across the greensward, chucking the ball at each other and failing, more often than not, to catch it. Kat had astonishing energy for one of her years; she was not even above crawling through the rosebushes to retrieve the prize, much to Elizabeth's astonishment.

Out of breath and still in high spirits, they sank onto a bench in a sunny arbor.

"Champernowne's a funny name," Elizabeth observed, kicking her feet.

"It's an old Devon name," said Kat, "and mine is an old family. Did you know that we are cousins, related by marriage, my Lady Elizabeth?"

"Are we?" asked Elizabeth, looking delighted. "How?"

"Through your lady mother's family," Kat said carefully.

Elizabeth seemed surprised, but she said nothing. For a long time now, she had not mentioned Anne Boleyn. Nor had Kate, Kat, Lady Troy, Lady Bryan, or any other members of her household spoken of her since that dreadful day when Elizabeth had been told she had been put to death.

Kat changed the subject. It was highly sensitive, and she had her own strong views about Anne Boleyn, her kinswoman, and about the man who had sent her to her death, views she voiced only in private to Kate. Kate knew she was determined that one day, Elizabeth should find out the truth, and if that was to happen, Anne's must not be a forbidden name.

"Come," Lady Troy said, "it will soon be dinnertime."

SHORTLY AFTERWARD, THE Lady Mary took Elizabeth to stay with her at Hunsdon, a dozen miles away, and this time Kate was chosen to accompany her, with Lady Troy and Kat. Mary seemed to think that Elizabeth was missing Lady Bryan very much, but Kate knew that, although this was sometimes the case, the little girl found Lady Troy far more jolly. It was true what their elders said: children *were* resilient.

Life at Hunsdon was boring. There was little there for a four-year-old to enjoy. Mary did play with Elizabeth, but she also expected her to attend frequent interminable services in the chapel, and to spend long hours at her private devotions. Elizabeth fidgeted with impatience as the devout Mary knelt, a still, rapt figure, at her side, and Kat would frantically press a finger to her lips to keep the child quiet, while Kate tried to stifle a giggle.

As they processed out of the chapel after Mass one day, Elizabeth asked, "Why do they ring those bells?"

Mary looked shocked.

"Have you not been taught, Sister, that the bells signal the elevation of the Host?" she asked, frowning.

"Father Parker says it's wrong to have bells at Mass," Elizabeth said, quite innocently.

Mary pursed her lips. "It is very wicked of him to say such things," she said firmly. "The bells signify the holiest moment in the Mass. Come with me."

Kate and Kat followed as she led the child back into the empty chapel, to the altar rails.

"When the priest holds up the bread and the wine before the people," she explained, "he does it to show that a miracle has taken place, for during Mass, as Our Lord promised at the Last Supper, the gifts of bread and wine become His very body and blood, given for us for the redemption of our sins."

Elizabeth looked doubtfully at the altar with its white damask cloth, rich frontal, and golden crucifix.

"But how can that be?" she asked. "They are still bread and wine. I have tasted them."

Mary looked shocked. "But that is the miracle!" she exclaimed. "When they are consecrated, they still look like bread and wine, but they have become the real body and blood of Jesus Christ. I'm surprised that Father Parker has not explained this to you. It is at the core of our Faith."

Kate was praying that Elizabeth would forbear from telling Mary that Father Parker had said something rather different, and thankfully the little girl held her tongue, perhaps sensing that Mary would be cross if she told the truth.

Mary turned to Lady Troy. "I am horrified that the child is so ignorant," she reproved. "Were you not aware? Father Parker appears to have failed signally in his duty. Pray assure me that Elizabeth at least knows her catechism and the Lord's Prayer."

"She does, Madam," Lady Troy said. "And I am sorry if we have been remiss, truly sorry. I genuinely believed that the chaplain had instructed her fully."

"Not fully enough, I fear," Mary rejoined. "You must speak to him urgently upon your return. In the meantime, my own chaplain will school her rigorously in what she should know. She has no mother, and I feel responsible. I am determined to see that she is guided in the right way. For now, I suggest you keep her at her prayers, for the good of her soul."

"Yes, Madam," said the lady mistress meekly, dipping a curtsey. But when Mary and Lady Troy had gone, Kat kept Elizabeth at her devotions for only a few minutes.

"I think we will have a story," she said, "one about a saint, as it is Sunday. I will tell you of St. Ursula. It is a special story for you because you were born in the Virgins' Chamber at Greenwich, which is hung with tapestries telling the story of St. Ursula and her eleven thousand virgins."

Elizabeth knelt by the hearth next to Kate. She loved stories.

Kat began. "St. Ursula was a princess, and her father arranged a marriage for her, but she wished to remain a virgin, so he and her betrothed agreed to allow her three years in which to enjoy her virgin state."

"What's a virgin?" Elizabeth asked.

"A lady who is unmarried, pure and virtuous," Kat told her. "St. Ursula spent that time sailing the seven seas with ten other noble virgins, and each of them had with them a thousand maidens."

"It must have been a very crowded ship!" observed Elizabeth.

Kat smiled. "Indeed, it must. But after they made a pilgrimage to Rome and had lots of adventures, their vessel was blown by strong winds up the Rhine to Germany, where in those days the people were wicked pagans and did not believe in God. Discovering that St. Ursula and the eleven thousand virgins with her were Christians, they tried to make them give up their faith, and when they refused, they put them all to death."

Elizabeth was quiet for a moment, and Kate wondered if she was remembering that she had heard those words before. "All of them?" she asked, after a few moments.

"All." Kat paused. "Hundreds of years later, their bones were found and they were made saints by the Holy Church."

"How were they put to death?"

Kate held her breath as she realized why Kat was telling this story. It was one she herself shrank from hearing because of the terrible memories it called to mind, and she wondered if Kat was right to tell Elizabeth the truth when she was still so young. And yet, she reasoned, it was better that Elizabeth learn it from her, than from someone who believed in Anne's guilt.

"One by one, they were made to kneel, then their heads were cut off with a sword."

"That's horrible," said the child, making a face.

"Ah, but they didn't feel a thing. It was very quick," Kat reassured her.

Elizabeth turned a tragic face up to her governess. Kat stroked her hair and gazed into the girl's dark eyes.

"Is that—is that what they did to my mother?" Elizabeth asked.

"It was, child," Kat said, still stroking her hair. "Poor soul, she died very bravely. And she suffered no pain, for it was all over in a trice."

Elizabeth was silent again. "She did bad things," she muttered in a low voice.

"No, she did not!" Kat said firmly. "It was said that she had been unfaithful to the King, and that she had plotted to kill him. But I am absolutely sure that those accusations were made up by her enemies in order to get rid of her, and that they made such a clever case against her that your father the King believed it."

"Who were they?" Elizabeth asked.

She's wise as an owl, Kate thought.

"Some who were about the King at the time." Kate was relieved that Kat didn't mention the name of Master Secretary Cromwell, for Cromwell was still the King's chief adviser and already, she feared, Kat had said too much.

"So they were telling lies!" Elizabeth had already had the importance of telling the truth drummed into her.

"The peers of the realm found Queen Anne guilty. But there were many who said that it was all just an excuse to get rid of her."

Elizabeth was unsatisfied. "So, you don't think my mother did those bad things?" she persisted.

"No, I do not," Kat whispered. "But I would get into terrible trouble for saying that, so you must never repeat my words. My lady, your mother was innocent, of that I am convinced. Never forget it."

"I won't," Elizabeth declared solemnly. "But it was wrong to put her to death when she hadn't done anything."

"Sometimes, child, justice is not well served and kings, who have the power of life and death, have to make harsh choices. I am sure that his Grace your father felt he was doing the right thing at the time. You must not blame him."

Kate almost snorted. She absolutely blamed the King—yet she also understood that Elizabeth needed to love and trust her father.

"I wish I could tell him he was wrong," said the child, but then, seeing the look of fear on Kat's face, hastened to reassure her. "But I promise I won't."

"Bless you, child," Kat breathed. "Come, now, let's go and play ball. I'm sure we've allowed long enough for your prayers!"

KATE WAS RELIEVED when they returned to Hatfield. The atmosphere there was so much lighter than at Hunsdon. It had been like staying in a nunnery!

At supper that evening, Sir John regaled them with the latest news from court.

"His Majesty's suit has been rejected by the Duchess of Milan. Her portrait had so captivated him that he cast off his mourning garments and asked for her hand. But you will not believe her reply. She said, 'Tell his Majesty that if I had two heads, one would be at his disposal.' "

Everyone gasped.

"Well, I never!" Kat said. "She has some daring—and impertinence! And he the greatest match to be had in all Europe!"

Kate had her own view on that, but she kept it to herself.

"There are other princesses," Sir John said. "I hear he is once more considering the Princess of Cleves."

"Well, I'll believe it when it happens," Kat said.

Chapter 8

1539

IN MARCH, KATE RECEIVED ANOTHER LETTER FROM CALAIS. It was from her mother, informing her that Grandfather was dead. She knew she should have felt sorrow, yet her overwhelming reaction was one of relief, that she would never have to see that horrid old man again. She had felt a similar lack of grief at Grandmother's passing the previous year, except that her main response then had been one of indifference. Mother didn't seem too sad either, although she was unhappy at the prospect of losing Hever, which had become Crown property. Yet the King had been persuaded to allow Great-Grandmother to live out her days there, which Mother stressed was very magnanimous of him. And we're supposed to be grateful, Kate thought bitterly, donning a black dress that she intended to wear for just a week in deference to convention.

FROM THAT SPRING onward, Elizabeth's household was abuzz with talk of the King's coming marriage to the Princess of Cleves. Elizabeth herself was excited at the prospect of a new stepmother, whom she imagined would send her lots of toys and pretty dresses and invite her often to court, which she clearly regarded as a magical place. But it was Kate who, to her own astonishment, was to go there. In November, she received from Lord Sandys, the Lord Chamberlain, a summons to Whitehall Palace, informing her that she had been appointed to serve the new Queen as a maid-of-honor.

She could hardly believe it. Such positions were notoriously hard to come by—Lady Bryan had once said that there was always furious competition for them, and that it was necessary to have a powerful patron to secure one for you.

"So why me?" she asked Kat, as they sorted through her clothes, choosing items that were suitable as court dress.

"Maybe Lady Bryan recommended you," Kat suggested. "Or your great-uncle, the Duke of Norfolk."

"That's hardly likely. He's never taken any notice of me, and he had no time for my mother. Besides, he's done his best to distance himself from the Boleyns since Queen Anne fell." Kate slumped down on the bed, a fine lawn smock in her hands. "I don't want to go to court, Kat. I like being here with Elizabeth."

"Nonsense!" Kat retorted. "The court is the way to preferment. In your case, a good marriage. The new Queen will help you to find a husband."

"But . . . Oh, I can't explain it, Kat, but I think of the court as a threatening place where bad things can happen. My mother says that it's full of backbiters and self-seekers who wouldn't hesitate to destroy anyone in their path."

Kat made a face. "That's a rather pessimistic view. I hardly think that a young maid like you is going to attract those types. Now be grateful for your good luck. You're going to enjoy yourself. Think of all those handsome young gallants who'll be courting you!"

"They won't when they find that I have no dowry." Despite her good intentions, Mother's annuity had been spent on the necessities that Grandfather had refused to supply, and it had abruptly ceased when she married Will Stafford.

"But you are high in royal favor—you serve Elizabeth."

"Is that enough?" Kate wondered. She stood up and peered into her mirror. As usual, her soft, rosy face with full lips, a straight nose, and winged brows stared back at her. Yes, she was pretty, she thought, with her wavy red hair—so like Elizabeth's—and a graceful figure, but would men find her attractive without a dowry?

"I just don't want to leave Elizabeth," she said, turning back to Kat. "I love her, and I know she will miss me. She's already lost Lady Bryan."

"I will look after her," Kat promised.

Elizabeth was most put out when Kate gently broke the news that she was leaving to serve the new Queen, and stamped her little foot. "But I want you here!"

"Now then!" Kat admonished. "You should be happy for Kate's good fortune, my lady. And if you're very good, you will be going to court too for Christmas—and you will see Kate there and meet the Queen."

Elizabeth perked up instantly. "And can I wear my green velvet cloak and my dress with the pearls on?"

"Of course," Kat said, as she exchanged smiles with Kate.

"I shall miss you, Kate," Elizabeth said.

"But we can write to each other. You write beautiful letters." At six, Elizabeth could already manage an elegant italic hand.

"And you'll have me, poppet," Kat said, bending down and hugging the child.

SAYING GOODBYE WAS difficult. Elizabeth clung to Kate and had to be pried away, while Kate was in tears as she climbed into the litter in the courtyard at Hatfield.

"I'll see you very soon!" she called as, with a jolt, the horses pulled it away. She wished she were staying, for she was filled with trepidation at the thought of what lay ahead. Would the new Queen like her? Would she give satisfaction? And how could she stay out of the way of the wolves at court?

All too soon, her escort was telling her that they were approaching Whitehall. Pulling aside the leather curtain, she watched as the guards let them through a crenellated gatehouse with checkered brickwork and an oriel window, which straddled the highway that ran parallel to the River Thames. Adorning the gatehouse were royal emblems and terra-cotta busts of Roman emperors. Beyond lay spacious gardens and orchards. The palace itself was huge, its walls checkered in black and white. When Kate alighted and an usher led her to the Queen's apartments, her jaw dropped at the magnificence of the royal lodgings, which rambled around so many courtyards that she feared she would constantly be getting lost. All the state chambers had high bay windows overlooking the River Thames, ceilings exquisitely battened in gold and wainscots of carved wood representing a thousand beautiful figures. The windows blazed with heraldic glass and the walls were hung with royal portraits, among them several of the King.

In the corner of the Queen's spacious privy chamber arose a spiral stair, which led to a dorter in which there were six tester beds. A woman rose as Kate was ushered in. She was tall and dignified, with a manner that hinted she would brook no nonsense.

"Welcome, Mistress Carey. I am Mrs. Stonor, the Mother of the Maids, and I will be in charge of you young ladies. You may take this bed here"—she pointed to the one in the corner—"and stow away your gear in this chest. There's a peg on the wall for your cloak."

As they waited for Kate's baggage to be brought up, Mrs. Stonor kept staring at her, making her feel uncomfortable. She felt she must break the silence.

"When does the Queen arrive?"

"She will be here before Christmas. She has a long journey from Cleves."

Kate still had no idea where Cleves was.

"You will have little to do until she arrives," Mrs. Stonor said, still scrutinizing her. "Your fellow maids will be arriving soon, so I hope you will make friends. You can then enjoy the pleasures of the court, but I need not tell you that you must always have a care for your honor." She paused. "I served your aunt, Mistress Carey. I was with her in the Tower."

"I was there, too, but I fear I do not remember you," Kate told her. She was remembering Anne saying that, up until her trial, they had set women about her she could never love—and now she could understand why, for she herself had not taken to Mrs. Stonor at all. Anne had said that those women had spied on her. She could well imagine Mrs. Stonor doing that.

"We do not speak of her at court," that lady informed her. "Just be aware of that."

Kate was wondering if people would look at her and realize that Anne had been her aunt. She hoped they wouldn't, for she wanted to remain as anonymous as possible and not draw attention to herself.

She unpacked her things, longing to be back at Hatfield. With nothing to do here, the weeks of waiting were going to drag. She hoped to elude the forbidding Mrs. Stonor, yet feared that might be difficult. Oh, how she wished she had not been made to come to court.

A week later, she was still trying to find her way around the palace, but feeling more positive, for the five other maids-of-honor had arrived. She liked blond, buxom Anne Bassett, whose comely face would attract attention anywhere. Dorothy Bray was also beautiful, and even the somewhat older Ursula Stourton had a pretty face. Kate was especially pleased to see Mary Norris, who had been with her all through those dreadful days in the Tower. The one maid she disliked was one of her cousins, Norfolk's niece, Katheryn Howard, who had a pert manner and a tinkling laugh. She seemed too bold for her own good and flirted merrily with the young gentlemen of the court.

All the maids got their fair share of attention, though, and Kate was pursued by two weak-chinned gallants who seemed to think they were God's gift to womankind, but she became adept at avoiding them. At fifteen, she was secretly longing for a comely young man to pay court to her, yet there had been few opportunities while serving Elizabeth. There had been no offer for her hand, and since Grandfather's death, neither was there anyone left to find a husband for her, for Mother was still in Calais. Yet somewhere at court there might be some gentleman who found her pleasing and would be ready to make suit to her.

With this hope in her heart, her days passed in card playing, music making, archery, practicing dance steps, and laughing and giggling with the other girls. Soon, she began to realize that she was enjoying herself.

Katheryn Howard she could blithely ignore, and indeed Katheryn made no effort to be friends, but there was one dark presence at court who made Kate's flesh shrink. The maids had little to do with the great ladies of the Queen's household, but she had seen among them her uncle's widow, Lady Rochford. The family had never forgiven her for falsely testifying to Lord Rochford committing incest with Queen Anne. Mother, in her letters, still called her "that she-devil." Although Lady Rochford had smiled at her, Kate was determined to give her no openings to make friendly overtures. She loathed the woman with all her heart. She was evil.

Another encounter left Kate feeling even more unsettled. She was racing down a gallery one day, eager to be out of doors with her new friends, who were to meet her at the bowling alley where the young gentlemen congregated—when suddenly, the door at the other end opened and the King marched through, attended by several men clad in black. Skidding to a quivering halt, Kate sank down in a curtsey, lowering her eyes.

Two velvet-slippered feet came to a halt before her. "Rise, Mistress Carey," said a high masculine voice, and Kate stood. The King towered above her, a massive man in his fur-lined gown and damask doublet and bases. He was dripping with jewels and his codpiece was the largest she had ever seen. But what she noticed most, as she dared to meet his gaze, was the way he was staring at her—in almost the same way that Mrs. Stonor had stared at her. He seemed somewhat discomposed.

"Welcome to court, Mistress Carey," he said at length. "I trust you are happily settled in."

"Yes, thank you, your Grace," she murmured.

His eyes were still boring into her. He looked so gross, so old and fat, and he smelled of something rotten beneath the perfumes and the scent of clean linen. She pitied the poor Queen, who had no idea what awaited her in England.

"Well, run along," he said, and patted her arm.

She hastened away, trembling, because he had patted her once before, and she had wondered then if he had some ungentlemanly intent toward her; now she wondered anew, and with more reason, for she was older and the curves of womanhood were upon her. Her flesh crawled at the thought.

Emerging into the gardens, she was seized by a terrible certainty. He had brought her to court to satisfy his wicked lust, and

Mrs. Stonor, and probably others, knew about it! It made sense. She had heard tales about his lust for women, so it was all too believable. He had cast an eye on her at Hatfield and set his mark at her. The coming of the new Queen had afforded him the ideal opportunity to bring her to court.

Horrified, she sat down on a stone bench, her heart beating like a drum. No, it could not be! She could never descend to . . . to . . . She couldn't bear to think exactly what he might want from her, but the other day, Katheryn Howard had said that some men were like animals with women, which Kate found alarming. No. No! The prospect was too horrible. But how did one refuse the King?

As she rose and set off for the bowling alley, she resolved to keep out of his way from now on. She would not be one of those women the gossips loved to sneer at.

WHITEHALL PALACE WAS thronged with people when Elizabeth and her small train arrived for Christmas. An air of happy anticipation filled the air, inspired by the coming festivities and the imminent arrival of the Queen.

"I can't wait to meet my new stepmother," Elizabeth declared, after Kate had greeted her, Lady Troy, and Kat at the gatehouse and they were led by the Lord Chamberlain to the apartment overlooking the Thames that had been made ready for Elizabeth.

"Well, my lady, you will have to be patient because, from what I've heard, she is still in Calais waiting for a fair wind," said Kat.

"There are so many beautiful ladies at court!" Elizabeth was staring as passing courtiers made their obeisances to her, as the King's daughter. She was entranced by their rich gowns, their bejeweled hoods, their air of sophistication.

"The King your father will have invited them in honor of the new Queen," Kat explained.

"I hope she is beautiful," Elizabeth said, "and kind, too."

"I'm sure she will be." Kat smiled.

Kate retired to the maidens' chamber when Kat took Elizabeth downstairs to pay her respects to the King. When they returned, an hour later, she grabbed her cloak and went out with them for a walk in the frost-rimed gardens.

"The Prince is coming tomorrow," Elizabeth announced. "I can't wait! I don't see him often, but I think of him a lot. And I have made him another shirt." She pulled a wry face, for she hated sewing.

"That was a true labor of love," Kate remarked.

"It was a martyrdom!" Kat grimaced, making them laugh.

"I saw the Queen's picture," Elizabeth said. "My father showed me this little box carved like a rose, and inside was the picture. She is beautiful!"

"Well, she will be here soon," Kat said. "But perhaps not in time for Christmas, if the weather doesn't improve."

THE NEXT DAY, Kate attended Elizabeth and the Lady Mary when they went to greet their brother. The future King was now a solemn two-year-old whom they found seated on the floor of his opulent nursery, surrounded by building blocks, a miniature wooden dagger and shield, a gold rattle, a spinning top, a hobby horse, and a pretty white poodle. His nurse, Mistress Penn, a homely woman with a white apron tied over her dove-gray gown, rose as the royal ladies entered, and bobbed. Elizabeth curtseyed low to the Prince, who looked up and fixed his ice-blue gaze on her. Beneath his wide-brimmed feathered hat and bonnet, his straight fringe was very fair, his round cheeks rosy, his mouth cherry red, and his chin tapered to a determined point. Mistress Penn lifted him onto her lap.

"Say welcome to your sisters, my Lady Mary and my Lady Elizabeth," she instructed.

"Welcome, Lady Mary, Lady Lisbeth," lisped the infant. He did not smile.

"I have a gift for you, Brother," said Elizabeth, holding out the finely stitched cambric shirt. Edward stretched out a fat hand to take it from her, studied it for a moment, lost interest, and handed it to his nurse.

"I am sure he will look very fine in it, my lady." Mistress Penn smiled.

"May I hold him?" Elizabeth asked, seating herself beside the nurse and making a lap. The nurse lifted the infant carefully, and he settled contentedly into Elizabeth's arms.

"My Lord Prince is heavy, aren't you, Brother?"

He raised steely blue eyes to her. Their father looked out of them.

"Aren't you going to smile for me?" prompted Elizabeth, pulling a face. There was a faint reaction, no more.

"He'll soon find his tongue, my lady." The nurse smiled.

Gently, Elizabeth tickled the Prince's sides. He jumped in her arms, and finally she coaxed a chuckle out of him.

"You've done well, my lady," Mistress Penn remarked. "He's a solemn boy and rarely smiles."

Edward was now beaming at Elizabeth. She beamed back and rubbed noses with him.

"May I hold him now?" asked Mary. The nurse passed Edward to her, and Mary seated him on her knee, crooning to him, caressing him, and hugging him tightly. The child bore this for a few moments before struggling to get down. He toddled over to his playthings, picked up the hobby horse, and began careering round the room on it, chasing an imaginary quarry.

"When the Queen arrives," Elizabeth said, "I hope we will all be able to live together at court."

Mary looked doubtful. "We must wait on the will of our father and our new stepmother," she said.

Just then, Edward drew to a halt in front of them.

"Bow!" he piped imperiously. His sisters looked at him in surprise, and hesitated.

"Bow!" he repeated. "I'm going to be the King, like my father!"

Mary and Elizabeth rose, suppressing their smiles, and swept deep curtseys before him.

"You too!" he commanded Kate, who hastened to obey.

"Rise," he ordered them, in perfect imitation of King Henry. "Now you may go."

Mrs. Penn was shaking her head, trying not to laugh.

. . .

MOTHER WAS COMING home. Kate read her letter in disbelief, standing by the window in the maidens' chamber with the cold December breeze rattling the panes. Will Stafford had been highly commended to the King for his service in Calais and had been awarded the coveted post of Gentleman Pensioner; he would be a member of the King's elite guard. Mother sounded very pleased about that and delighted at the prospect of seeing Kate. They would be returning in the Princess Anna's retinue, when the weather permitted them to cross the English Channel.

The other maids were clustering around, curious to know what was in the letter. Some were pleased to hear that her mother was coming home, but a few were giving each other snide glances.

"I wonder she dare show her face here!" Katheryn Howard sniffed.

"I'm sure that old scandal is long forgotten," Kate snapped, stung by the remark, and walked away.

As she ran downstairs, she was thinking that it would be good to see Mother again. She had missed her throughout the six years they had been separated, and was ready to forget the self-centeredness that had sometimes left her weeping. But maybe Mother had changed. Who knew what miracles God could work? Kate was pleased that she would be returning to England in prosperity, having been exiled in disgrace. And maybe, just maybe, she would be able to set about finding Kate a husband, a handsome young man who would love her as well as Will loved Mother. For although Kate was enjoying the attentions of the gallants at court, no one so far had shown any serious interest in her. But soon, things might be very different!

CHRISTMAS PASSED IN a whirl of festivities, with everyone eagerly awaiting the Queen's arrival. Soon, the New Year's Eve revels were in full swing. The great hall at Whitehall was packed with people, musicians were playing, and servants were passing about the room, topping up goblets. Sitting with the maids-of-honor, Kate was enjoying herself, but Elizabeth was in ecstasies. The Lord of Misrule had demanded a forfeit of her, and she was commanded to kiss the ten most handsome gentlemen in the room. Everyone, her father included, roared with mirth as she selected first this man, then that, and, with eyes screwed shut, offered a puckered-up mouth to each. In the end, she was so helpless with laughter that she had to abandon the play for a space, holding her aching sides till she got her breath back.

"What of me?" cried the King with mock indignation. "Am I not the handsomest man in the room?" Still breathless, Elizabeth ran to him and planted a big kiss on his lips. The courtiers clapped and cheered.

It was then that an usher entered and whispered in the King's ear. Henry smiled broadly, drew himself to his majestic height, and raised his hand for silence. "Great news, my lords and ladies! The Queen has arrived safely in this kingdom and is even now at Rochester. What say you? Shall we await her formal reception before we behold our bride, or shall we ride to Rochester now, in the guise of an ardent suitor, to nourish love?"

The company, flushed with wine, shouted their approval of the latter plan, and soon everyone was hastening to the palace landing stage to wave goodbye to the King and the gentlemen who were to accompany him.

As he hauled himself into the barge, swathed in furs, he clapped his bonnet down firmly on his head and waved to his watching courtiers. "We will see you all very soon, and then we will repair to Greenwich for the wedding. Farewell!"

"God speed, your Grace!" the courtiers cried.

Chapter 9

1540

NO ONE KNEW WHEN THE KING WOULD RETURN, SO THE Lord Chamberlain announced that the New Year's Day revels would proceed as planned without him. Kate spent much of the day with Elizabeth and Kat, kneeling before the fire and labeling the gifts they would distribute that night.

It was late in the afternoon, and already dark outside, when Elizabeth clapped her hand to her mouth. "I forgot! I promised the Lady Mary that I would join her in chapel for Vespers," she exclaimed.

"Don't worry," said Kat, looking at the clock. "If we hasten now, we won't be late." She fetched Elizabeth's cloak and gloves, helped her to put them on, then escorted her down to the courtyard. Kate watched them from the window as they hurried over to the chapel opposite. Then she heard shouts from the direction of the river. She ran to the Thames side of the palace and looked out. The royal barge was moored at the jetty and the King was alighting. Kate peered through the latticed panes to get a view of the new Queen, but she was nowhere to be seen. Instead, she could tell from the King's thunderous expression that he was not a happy bridegroom.

Cromwell was hastening to the landing stage. Kate saw his

smile falter and die. Holding her breath, she silently eased the window open so that she could hear what they were saying.

Henry glared at his chief minister. "We missed you on our return, Master Secretary," he rapped, in a voice that must have carried across the river.

"I crave your Majesty's pardon," Cromwell answered smoothly. "I was preparing for the feast. I was unaware until a few moments ago that your Majesty had returned." He must have raced like the wind to the jetty, Kate realized.

"We returned, Master Secretary, because there was nothing to stay in Rochester for." The King's voice was icy.

"Was the Queen not there?" asked Cromwell.

"Oh, she was there, Master Secretary, she was there."

"That is a relief, Sire," babbled Cromwell. "And how does your Majesty like the Queen?"

His master leaned forward menacingly. "I like her not. I like her not! She is not so attractive as you and others described, not at all! And if I had known as much before as I know now, she would never have come into this realm!" He looked like a lion about to pounce on its prey. "What remedy, Master Cromwell? What remedy?"

Cromwell looked winded. "Sire, the contract has been signed and agreed. There might be difficulties . . ." Looking at his master's face, he added quickly, "But I will look at it carefully and see if there is a way out."

"You had better find one," said the King. "You got me into this pass, and you are going to get me out of it!"

Cromwell scuttled off like a whipped cur and the King, glowering, stumped off toward his apartments.

He was still frowning that evening when he arrived for the feast and spoke a few terse words to Cromwell, who was waiting nervously by the door. He sat down heavily in his chair of estate on the dais, enormous in his jeweled doublet, a feathered hat perched on his balding, graying head, quite obviously fuming as his narrow eyes raked over his courtiers. The presence chamber was quiet; instead of the usual hum of conversation, there were muffled coughs, a few sniffs and stifled whispers. Elizabeth, sitting at the end of the high table, was looking at her father with a puzzled expression.

Sitting some way away, between Mary Norris and Katheryn Howard, Kate wondered where the new Queen was. If the King didn't like her, would he send her home? She was hoping he would, because then she could leave court and go back to Hatfield with Elizabeth.

The King nodded at the minstrels. They began to play, and the courtiers resumed their conversations in a subdued fashion. Elizabeth started to fidget. She would be wanting the dancing to begin. Kate felt sorry for her, because this was not the happy revelry she had anticipated, and now she might not be getting a new stepmother after all. Kate wondered what it was about the Queen that had so angered the King. Poor woman, she could have no idea of what lay ahead for her. She resolved to be kind to her and remember that she was a stranger in a strange land—and that she would have to share a bed with that horror.

THE NEXT MORNING, as the court prepared to move to Greenwich for the coming royal wedding, Mrs. Stonor summoned the maids to the Queen's presence chamber.

"You must make ready for a journey," she told them. "You are to travel down to Dartford to greet your new mistress, and then you will ride with her to Shooter's Hill at Blackheath, where she will formally be welcomed to England. You will wear the crimson velvet gowns you have been given and take warm cloaks and gloves. And I want not a hair out of place!"

Kate and the others hurried to change, lacing each other into the sumptuous gowns and donning the French hoods with pearl trims that matched the biliments on their necklines. Then they packed changes of body linen and fresh clothing into a chest and hastened down to the courtyard where the chariot that was to take them to Dartford was waiting. Nearby stood richer chariots, into which the ladies-in-waiting were clambering. Kate shrank back when she saw Lady Rochford, for she wanted nothing to do with her. But the chief lady-of-honor, the King's beautiful, auburn-haired niece, Lady Margaret Douglas, threw the maids a smile to warm the chill of the day. Norfolk's daughter, the Duchess of Richmond, widow of the King's bastard son, nodded amiably at them, although the smile inexplicably faded when her eyes rested on Kate. Doubtless Norfolk's antipathy toward Mother had rubbed off on her.

Katheryn Howard had brought a hot brick wrapped in flannel to warm her feet during the journey. "How far is it?" she asked Mrs. Stonor, as they settled themselves on the cushioned seats.

"Less than twenty miles," the Mistress of the Maids replied. "We'll be there by nightfall."

THEIR ACCOMMODATION IN Dartford was an abandoned priory that had been closed by the King last year.

"His Grace is going to have it demolished," Mrs. Stonor informed them. "He intends to build a fine palace here, as a stopping place on the road to Dover." As Kate alighted, feeling stiff and chilled to the marrow, she saw a traceried cloister with a great church still standing beyond the gatehouse. Dartford, she had learned, had been a great nunnery in its day. She felt a pang for the sisters who had been cast out, forced to go back into the world and fend for themselves. And they were by no means alone. Nearly every abbey and priory in England had been closed down in the past four years. Very few remained.

They were accommodated in the nuns' former guesthouse, which had been made comfortable with tapestries, cushions, and feather beds. A hearty stew was served to them at supper, followed by a delicious junket. Then they all fell into their beds, aware that they had an early start on the morrow.

Kate lay awake wondering if her mother and Will would be in the Queen's train tomorrow. She was excited at the prospect of seeing them, and praying that her duties would allow her an opportunity for a private reunion.

She fell asleep with a smile on her lips.

. . .

BUFFETED BY ICY winds, Kate waited outside the town of Dartford with the ladies-in-waiting. At last, they saw the Queen approaching in a magnificent golden chariot, attended by a long train of foreigners in strange attire. There was no sign of Mother or Will, but it was like looking for needles in a haystack.

When Uncle Norfolk, as premier peer of the realm, presented to the Queen the chief officers of her household, Kate saw that she was not pretty. Her face was pleasant, however, and she had a warm smile, although her hair was hidden under a hideous bejeweled headdress. She looked as if she was trying hard to make a good impression. But her gown was outlandish! It had no train, just a round skirt, which would never do at court.

The Archbishop of Canterbury and the Duke of Suffolk were now presenting the ladies and maids-of-honor. As each approached to kiss her hand, they curtseyed deeply. When it was Kate's turn, she finally understood exactly why the King was not pleased with his bride, for as she bent to press her lips to Anna's extended fingers, she caught a whiff of a nasty stench, like unwashed linen and monthly clouts. It was all she could do not to recoil.

"These ladies will be waiting permanently on your Grace," she heard Norfolk inform Anna as he led her through the priory gatehouse to her lodging. "For the time being, they will serve alongside your German and Flemish attendants."

Kate followed with the other maids. Once Anna reached her lodging, she dismissed them, saying that she wished to rest and that her German ladies could attend her. Kate was glad of the chance to slip away. She ran down to the cloister, where members of the Queen's retinue were milling about, seeking their accommodation, and it was there that she ran into Mother.

"Kate!" she exclaimed joyfully, throwing her arms around her, then drawing back to look at her face. "My, my, how you have grown up! When I left, you were a little girl of nine, and now you are a young woman, and a very comely one!"

Kate smiled, trying not to show how dismayed she was to find Mother looking so much older than she recalled. She was plumper, with a double chin; wisps of graying hair were escaping from her hood and there were fine lines around her eyes. But she was still essentially the mother Kate remembered, and when Will, looking as handsome and manly as ever, came up to greet Kate and hugged Mother warmly, Kate saw her eyes light up, making her look almost beautiful.

The three of them sat on a stone bench and talked. There was so much to say.

"I'm going to stay at Hever," Mother said. "I can still do that while your great-grandmother lives, although I hear that she is failing. Will is for the court, but there's no place for me there, unlike when I was married to your father and could share his lodging."

"You may be sure that I will be looking out for you, Kate," Will said. He had a strong, reassuring presence. Kate realized anew why Mother had fallen for him.

They chatted all afternoon. It felt good to be with Mother again, and in much happier circumstances than when she had last seen her. And Mother seemed less self-centered. She wanted to know all about life in Elizabeth's household, and how Kate was finding the court.

"I did not want to leave you and Harry, but I had little choice. We had only cramped lodgings in Calais with no room for children," she said. "I heard that Harry is doing well at Syon, and I knew you would be well looked after in Elizabeth's establishment."

"Oh, I was," Kate said. "I do miss it, for we are close cousins and love each other very much."

Mother gave her a searching look, but then she smiled. "I am glad to hear it."

"I am well content, Mother," Kate said.

"And you have even more reason to be so. Will is happy to provide you with a dowry, so we can now set about finding you a husband."

Kate was deeply touched. "That is most kind of you, Will," she said, her eyes filling with tears.

"I've always wanted to be a father to you, Kate," he said warmly.

"Who do you think would make a suitable husband?" Mother asked him.

"I don't know—Kate will have seen the gallants at court. She's the one to ask." He winked at Kate.

"We don't want some titled fellow who has no money. Or a fortune hunter, for your portion is not massive. But the Queen can help, I'm sure."

Kate wasn't so sure about that. Even if the King did go ahead with the marriage, Anna wouldn't know anyone at court.

"I want a husband I can love," she said. "I'm sure you both will understand that."

Mother and Will smiled at each other. "Most certainly we do," Mother said. It was obvious that a happy marriage and the love of a good man had done wonders for her.

THAT EVENING, QUEEN Anna invited her new ladies and maids to sit with her in the room serving as her privy chamber. She bade them be seated, the ladies on stools, the maids kneeling on the floor. With a homely-looking Flemish lady acting as interpreter, she managed to speak to each of them.

Kate noticed again that the Duchess of Richmond was cool toward her. She had been long enough at court to know that there were two rival parties there: those who clung to the old religious ways and would really have preferred to have the Pope back as head of the Church of England; and those who were eager for religious reform and, in some cases, even suspected of having embraced Martin Luther's Protestant teachings, which was dangerous because those convicted of heresy risked being burned at the stake. Truth to tell, Kate found such matters above her head. But the Duchess was a Howard, and the Howards were the premier Catholic family in the land, while the Queen represented the King's alliance with the Protestant princes of Germany, even though she herself was a Catholic. No wonder Mary Howard seemed not to like the Queen!

Kate was drawn to the Duchess of Suffolk, a lively, headstrong young woman of decidedly reformist views, who was popular with all. By contrast, the Countess of Rutland was haughty, and then, of course, there was Lady Rochford, from whom Kate contrived to sit as far as possible. She didn't like Lady Edgcumbe either, for she had an off-putting superior air. She caught sight of the pair of them, whispering and nodding knowingly in her direction.

Katheryn Howard, of course, must always draw attention to herself, dimpling prettily when spoken to. She looked like a little girl, with her tiny hands and feet, and Kate could see that Anna was drawn to her. And then Anna's face alighted on Kate, and she was staring at her in the unsettling way that others had done. Kate felt herself flushing.

At nine o'clock, Anna rose and indicated that she wished to retire. They were all aware that they must be up early for her official reception at Blackheath. Kate went to bed gladly. It had been a long day, and tomorrow would be even more momentous.

KATE WAS UP and ready before dawn, when the members of Anna's household had to leave. They were to ride ahead and be ready for her at Blackheath. Before her departure, she bade farewell to her mother, who was riding south to Hever, and to Will, who was for Greenwich, to attend the King. Their reunion had been all too brief, and she was sad to see them go, not knowing when they would be able to meet again.

The maids were at the back of the procession, and it was bitterly cold in their chariot. By the time they reached Bexley, Kate's fingers and toes were numb, and they still had a long way to go. By noon, when the Queen was due to arrive, they would be like icicles. But Mrs. Stonor seemed impervious to the temperature; she was more concerned that the maids were looking presentable.

When they descended Shooter's Hill, they saw the stunning silken pavilion that had been set up for their new mistress. Inside, to their delight, they found a lighted brazier, around which they crowded, trying to thaw out. But Mrs. Stonor would have them prepare the gorgeous robes in which they would help to clothe Anna when she arrived, and then they must assist the grooms set out on a long trestle table the many dishes that had been prepared for the banquet. Kate's mouth was watering so much that she sneaked a marchpane comfit into it, praying that Mrs. Stonor would not see her. Then, like the others, she darted back to the brazier to get warm again before dashing back to the kitchen tent that had been set up behind Anna's.

Like everyone else, she kept peering out of the entrance to the pavilion to see what was going on outside. She gasped as she saw the hordes of people gathering on the green expanse of Blackheath. Mrs. Stonor pointed out the Lord Mayor and Corporation of London, in their red gowns. It seemed that the entire nobility of England was here too, and there must have been at least five thousand horses. The broad heath was thronged with hundreds of knights, soldiers, and liveried servants, and crowds of ordinary citizens. And all eyes were upon Shooter's Hill, whence Anna would come.

At noon, the trumpets sounded. As the Queen's procession appeared, her household assembled in front of the pavilion, drawn up according to rank, so Kate found herself standing with her fellow maids to the side of the chief officers. They saw Anna approach, riding in her gilded chariot and followed by twelve of her German ladies, all wearing round gowns with heavy gold chains around their necks. Then came the rest of her retinue from Cleves, including a hundred dignitaries on horseback. Behind them rode the dukes of Norfolk and Suffolk, the Archbishop of Canterbury and other bishops, and the lords and ladies who had joined Anna on her journey through Kent.

At the foot of the hill, the chariot halted outside the pavilion. The Queen's Chamberlain, the Earl of Rutland, bowed before her, then Lady Margaret Douglas welcomed her, accompanied by the Duchess of Richmond and another of the King's nieces, the brisk-mannered Marchioness of Dorset. Anna alighted from her chariot and Kate sank into a deep obeisance as the entire household saluted and greeted her.

"I give you all hearty thanks," she said in English. Then she turned to her chief ladies and kissed them all in turn.

Her almoner made a long speech in Latin, then formally presented to her all those sworn to serve her, which took some considerable time, as each knelt in turn to kiss her hand. Like everyone else, Kate was shivering when the presentations ended, but they had to endure the cold for a few minutes more to hear one of Anna's German officers reply on her behalf to her almoner. Only then could they all enter the pavilion, where more braziers had been lit. Everyone descended hungrily on the banquet, and Kate piled her plate high, ignoring Mrs. Stonor's frown.

After Anna had eaten, the maids helped the ladies to change her into a gorgeous taffeta gown of cloth of gold, cut like the others in the Dutch fashion. The mother of the German maids insisted on replaiting Anna's hair herself, then placed a sheer linen caul over it, and on top of that another of the ugly headdresses, this one being surmounted by a coronet of black velvet.

When she was ready, Anna stood in the pavilion to await the arrival of the King, with her ladies around her. She was trembling, especially when the Earl of Rutland came to say that his Majesty would be arriving soon. Kate felt sorry for her.

Moments later, in the distance, the trumpets sounded again. "Your Grace, it is time," Rutland told her. "The King is about half a mile away. You are to meet him as he approaches."

A richly caparisoned palfrey was waiting for Anna, its reins held by Sir John Dudley, her Master of Horse. Kate saw her look at it in dismay. But she mounted with ease and grasped the reins as she set off with her footmen about her. In front of her rode a great company of gentlemen, and after her came her ladies, mounted in order of rank on palfreys. Kate loved to ride, and she enjoyed being the recipient of admiring looks as the maids passed through the ranks of gentlemen on either side of the road that led to Greenwich Palace. Ahead, she could see the royal trumpeters approaching, and, behind them, marching toward her in orderly rank, a company of spearmen, each wearing a dark velvet doublet and a gold medallion of office on a chain round the neck.

"Your Grace, that is the King's elite guard, the Gentlemen Pensioners," Sir John said. Kate looked for Will, and saw him toward the back of the troop, his eyes fixed straight ahead.

Anna's procession halted to allow the King's Guard to pass. Among the Gentlemen Pensioners, a young man caught Kate's eye. He was long-legged with strong features, a Roman nose, and a neatly trimmed chestnut beard—and he was looking at her with undisguised interest. Her heart gave a flutter and she realized that she was blushing, but then he had gone, and the King's party was approaching.

Henry looked magnificent on his splendid courser trapped in rich cloth of gold, although Kate refused to feel overawed or impressed. Nevertheless, he glittered, godlike, in the weak January sunlight, and the crowds gaped in awe as he passed. To left and right, he turned a princely countenance, raising his hand in greeting. Kate could not see Anna's face and could only guess what she might be feeling.

The ranks of gentlemen parted, leaving a clear path between the King and his bride. Henry spurred his horse and, doffing his cap, came to greet her, looking surprisingly pleased to see her.

"My Lady Anna, welcome to England!" he cried, so that all could hear, and bowed in the saddle, whereupon Anna bowed, too.

"Your Majesty, I am both honored and joyful to be here," she replied. Still the King was smiling at her most kindly. Suddenly, he reined in his horse beside hers, leaned over, and embraced her, to a burst of loud cheers.

"See how my subjects welcome you, Madam!" he said.

Anna returned his smile. "Sir, I mind to be a good and loving mistress to them, and a humble and loving wife to your Majesty," she said loudly, in English. "I thank you, and all the good people here, for this wonderful welcome."

While they were exchanging pleasantries, everyone else was taking their places amid the great concourse of people gathered on Blackheath. Kate looked for the young man who had been gazing at her so appreciatively, but the Gentlemen Pensioners and the King's Guard were now turning around and riding off toward Greenwich, and she had no choice but to follow the bridal pair as they made their way to the pavilion, amid great cheering.

There, the royal couple and their retinues demolished the replenished banquet, but soon it was time to leave for Greenwich. Outside stood an empty litter, hung and upholstered with cloth of gold and crimson velvet. Kate heard the King tell Anna that it was a gift for her, heard her thank him warmly.

With the trumpets going before, the royal couple passed through the assembled ranks of knights and esquires, preceded and followed by their entourages. In the chariot behind Anna's sat six German ladies and gentlewomen, whose fair faces and ornate gowns drew appreciative cheers from some Englishmen watching. Then came the chariots bearing Anna's English ladies, who were feeling a touch resentful at having to take second place. "But the foreign ladies will be going home soon," Mrs. Stonor said.

When they arrived at Greenwich Palace, they were saluted by guns positioned on top of the massive central tower. It dominated the facade facing the river, a long range of apartments boasting a costly expanse of glass in a row of fine bay windows. Passing through the gatehouse at the bottom of the tower, the ladies and maids entered the inner courtyard, where the King and Anna dismounted and he lovingly embraced and kissed her in front of their cheering, clapping retinues.

As he led her through the magnificent great hall, Kate, following with the rest, noticed the guards lined up like statues along the walls, but they were in a different livery to the Gentlemen Pensioners and the intriguing young man was nowhere to be seen. She could not rid him from her mind. Among the many splendors of the day, he stood out the most vividly, and she felt almost breathless at the thought of him. He was somewhere in this court and maybe, if she was lucky, she would see him again soon.

THE QUEEN'S APARTMENTS were as magnificent as the rest of the palace, with every surface painted and gilded. Kate and the other maids gaped, fascinated, at ceilings decorated with gilded bosses, hearths lined with expensive Seville tiles, and window alcoves tiled in green and yellow. Again, Anna thanked Henry for his goodness to her, then he left to deal, he told her, with matters of state.

The German ladies, headed by a formidable matron called Mother Lowe, were poised to change their mistress into another gown for the feast that had been prepared, but Margaret Douglas quickly sidestepped them and commanded Kate and her companions to fetch it from the bedchamber. As they dressed her, Anna seemed distracted, while Mother Lowe and her cohorts were positively simmering. Yet the English ladies took no notice and pressed on with their duties.

Anna looked regal in her gown of rich green velvet, and all eyes were on her as she arrived in the King's presence chamber, followed by her long train of ladies and maids. The banquet was sumptuous, and Kate tucked in with gusto, despite having eaten her fill at Blackheath earlier. That was the best thing about the court—the food was excellent and plentiful. Afterward, they accompanied Anna back to her apartments, where they helped her change into a taffeta gown, then returned to the presence chamber, where Kate had been told there would be dancing. She was excited at the prospect, as she took up her place with the others at the side of the dais where Anna was sitting with the King.

One by one, the maids were invited to dance, and Kate was feeling conspicuous standing there alone when she noticed that *he* was there. He was seated by a table and gazing in her direction. She saw him get to his feet. He was coming toward her!

"Would you do me the honor of dancing with me, Mistress Carey?" he asked. "Francis Knollys at your service." His eyes were green, something she had never seen before, and they were looking at her appreciatively.

"I should be delighted, Sir," she replied, and gave him her hand. He led her out onto the floor and bowed, as the consort of musicians in the corner struck up another tune.

He was not a good dancer, but he was trying hard, and all the time his eyes were on her. He was not her ideal of manly beauty, but there was something special about him, and her heart began to beat faster. When their fingers touched, she felt a frisson of pleasure.

"You know my name," she said.

"Yes. One of the other maids told me," he replied. "Have you been at court long?"

"I only arrived before Christmas. I was in the Lady Elizabeth's service before that, as a companion."

"You must be in high favor, then." His gaze was admiring.

"She is my first cousin."

Francis paused. "Then your aunt was—"

"Yes. I attended her in the Tower." He won't like me so much now, she thought. It seemed best to change the subject. "Tell me about yourself."

Francis smiled, and it was as if the sun had come out again. "Nothing so impressive! I'm twenty-six and I come from a gentry family. My father served King Henry VII and was rewarded with lands, but he died when I was seven, leaving me some wealth. I went to the University of Oxford and then a friend at court recommended me for the post of Gentleman Pensioner. Last year I was chosen as one of those sent to greet the Princess Anna when she arrived in England. How old are you, Mistress Carey?"

"I will be sixteen in the spring," she told him, thinking already that he would be highly eligible as a husband. Could he be the one she had been waiting for? But she was running ahead of herself!

The music stopped and Francis bowed once more. "Will you dance with me again, Mistress Carey?"

"Yes, I will, Master Knollys." She smiled. "And please call me Kate."

"I will—Kate!" he promised. "As long as you call me Francis." They embarked on a stately pavane, then broke into a lively galliard. The floor was crowded and they could hardly hear themselves speak.

"Let's go up to the gallery," Francis suggested. "We can talk there."

Delightedly, Kate let him lead her up the spiral stair. In the gallery overlooking the hall, they sat on an old dusty bench where they could peer unseen through the balusters at the dancers below.

"Do you have any brothers and sisters?" she asked.

"Two sisters called Mary and Jane, and an annoying brother called Henry." Francis grinned. "I love him really! And you?"

"I also have a brother called Henry, but I never see him because he was educated at Syon and now lives at Woburn Abbey. The King sold his wardship to Sir Francis Bryan, who sent him there to complete his studies. He's younger than me."

"And your father and mother?"

"My father died of the sweating sickness when I was four. My mother remarried and lived in Calais for some years, where my stepfather served in the garrison. His name is William Stafford."

"I know him!" Francis exclaimed. "I met him and some of his fellows in a tavern when I was in Calais awaiting the Queen's arrival, and now we serve the King together as Gentlemen Pensioners. A good man, thoughtful and deep. He is as hot for religious reform as I am." He suddenly looked serious.

"Most of my family are," Kate said.

"And where do you stand?" he asked intently.

"Oh, I am, too!" she answered fervently, wanting him to think well of her.

"Then we are happily met, Kate!"

The way he was looking at her made her feel as if butterflies were fluttering in her stomach. She was hoping he would take her hand, but then she spied Mrs. Stonor glaring up at her through the balustrade and knew, with a sinking feeling, that she was in trouble, especially when she saw that Anna had left.

She shot to her feet. "I'm sorry, but I have to go. The Mistress of the Maids is looking for me. I have to attend the Queen!"

Francis rose, looking crestfallen. "May I look for you again?"

"Yes, of course." She darted a quick smile at him and hastened away.

At the foot of the stairs, Mrs. Stonor was waiting for her with a face like a thunderstorm. "What do you think you are doing, Kate Carey? It is most improper for a maid-of-honor to be alone with a young gentleman. It reflects badly on you, your family, me, and most of all the Queen! Have you no regard for your honor?"

"I most certainly do," Kate retorted, stung by her words. "We were only talking, and we were not alone. You could see us!"

It was true. Mrs. Stonor pursed her lips. "You are young and innocent of the ways of men. Young gentlemen are not to be trusted. They take every advantage they can. Never let me see you running off like that again. Now hurry. The Queen is waiting!"

Grabbing Kate by the arm, she hauled her out of the hall.

Chapter 10

1540

"DOES ANYONE KNOW WHEN I AM TO BE MARRIED?" ANNA asked in her husky voice, as her women dressed her the next morning. One of her Flemish ladies, Susanna Gilman, translated.

"We have not been told, your Grace," Margaret Douglas said, exchanging glances with Mary Howard behind Anna's back. Kate, standing near them, holding Anna's headdress, was aware that something was wrong, and it was obvious that the other ladies knew it, too.

"The King has not mentioned the wedding, so I do not know when I should be ready." Kate could hear the concern in Anna's voice.

When she was dressed, the maids returned to the dorter while Anna received her German dignitaries. They did not see her again that day, for Mother Lowe, the German Mistress of the Maids, kept all the English attendants at bay.

"Something's wrong," Mary Norris said.

"The King doesn't like her," Katheryn Howard declared. "He'll send her home, I'll wager."

"He was most affectionate and courteous to her yesterday," Kate reminded her, thinking that the humiliation of rejection could not be worse for the Queen than marrying that loathsome monster.

"Oh, he was putting on an act," Katheryn retorted. "But he won't put his neck in the noose when it comes to bedding her!"

Kate didn't like such lewdness. It was disrespectful.

THE NEXT DAY, Anna could eat little of the choice fare served to her at dinner. Mother Lowe was fussing over her like a mother hen and again waved the English ladies and maids away.

"You will be called for when you are needed," she said firmly.

They weren't needed until it was time to prepare Anna for bed.

"I am to be married on Tuesday in the Chapel Royal here," she told them. "It will be the Feast of the Epiphany."

Kate wished she sounded happier about it. But then, who *would* sound happy if they were marrying someone as gross and cruel as King Henry? If she were in Anna's place, she would be dwelling on the fates of his three previous wives: one divorced and exiled, one beheaded, and one dead in childbed through, it was said, lack of care. In fact, she would be planning to run away.

ON EPIPHANY EVE, before the Twelfth Night feast, the King accompanied Anna to Mass. Kate was among those in attendance as they processed through the court, smiling to left and right at the press of courtiers lining the walls. The King was as courteous as ever. After Mass, he escorted Anna to her presence chamber, and there presented her with a long document on which, he said, were listed the many properties that made up her dower.

"It is a most generous settlement," she said, curtseying. "I thank your Grace, from my heart."

"It is no more than your due," he told her. "My Queen must be seen to live in the comfort and magnificence befitting her rank." He bowed. "Make ready, Madam. We will be wed in the morning. I will send my lords to escort you to the Chapel Royal at eight o'clock."

. . .

THE LADIES WERE telling Anna how beautiful she looked in her wedding gown. Even though it was made in the Dutch style with a round skirt, Kate had to admire the cloth of gold worked in a pattern of large flowers and stitched with great Orient pearls. As became a virgin bride, the Queen wore her fair hair loose beneath a coronal of gold set with brilliant gems. In her hair, and pinned to her gown, Mother Lowe had placed sprigs of rosemary. "Rosemary symbolizes love, faithfulness, and fruitfulness," she'd said in her guttural English. The great ladies of the household came forward with gold chains and a jeweled crucifix, which Mother Lowe insisted on hanging around Anna's neck herself, and a belt adorned with gold and stones to be fastened at her waist. Kate could not help staring at her when she was ready. She looked every inch a queen.

The maids were all wearing cloth of silver, the tissue so light that their skirts floated about them. But it was no proof against the chill of the January morning, and Kate wondered how she would get through the ceremonies without freezing to death. Above her low square neckline, her breasts were covered in goose pimples. Yet the gown did make her look grown up and alluring, and she was praying that Francis would be attending the King, so that he could see her in it. Surely, he would be present at the coming festivities, and she hoped they could snatch time with each other without arousing the wrath of Mrs. Stonor.

Baron Oberstein, a nobleman of Cleves, was to give Anna away. It was still dark when they found him waiting for Anna in her presence chamber at seven o'clock sharp, with Grand Master Hochsteden, another German officer. Preceded by Lord Cromwell, with Oberstein, Hochsteden, and a rather drunk Earl of Essex escorting her, Anna walked to the Chapel Royal, followed by her women.

Kate felt the familiar revulsion at the sight of the King standing at the entrance to the chapel, dazzlingly dressed in cloth of gold embossed with great flowers of silver, a coat of crimson satin slashed, embroidered, and tied with great diamonds, and a rich collar about his neck. Anna made three low curtseys and he doffed his cap, bowing courteously. His face was impassive; Kate found it impossible to detect his mood. He held out his hand to Anna and led her into the crowded chapel, where Archbishop Cranmer was waiting for them.

During the ceremony, the ladies and maids stood two-by-two in the nave. Kate looked around surreptitiously for Francis, but in vain. And he was nowhere to be seen when the trumpets sounded and the bridal pair left the chapel, and it was time for Anna to go back to her apartments. An hour later, everyone returned to the chapel, where the Mass of Epiphany was celebrated with great solemnity. And still there was no Francis.

After Mass ended, there was another fanfare, as the King and Queen went in procession to his presence chamber, where they dined together as the entire court looked on, with the chief lords and officers of state standing in attendance. Anna was seated on a smaller chair beside the King's throne, beneath the intricately embroidered canopy of estate, with the royal arms of England blazoned large in the center. Her ladies and maids stood behind her. Kate was thankful that a hearty fire was roaring up the chimney, for she had been feeling cold to the bone. As the meal was served with great formality, and eaten mostly in silence, her eyes roved along the ranks of Gentlemen Pensioners lined up against the tapestried walls—and then she saw him, and he was looking at her. Her heart leaped, especially when he gave an almost imperceptible smile. She could have feasted her eyes on him all day.

Too soon, the dinner was over, and Anna retired to her apartments, where her ladies and maids clustered around, congratulating her and saying how well she had acquitted herself.

"No one could take their eyes off you, Madam!" Margaret Douglas exclaimed.

"And you bore yourself so handsomely; every eye was upon you!" Susanna Gilman enthused.

All Kate could think of was that dinner would soon be served. She was ravenous, for there had been no time to break their fast before the wedding.

While Anna rested in the afternoon, the maids hung up their

silver gowns on pegs and took the opportunity to make up some sleep. But Kate lay awake. She could not stop thinking about Francis. He must be there for the evening's celebrations. Bursting with impatience, she helped to dress Anna and yawned her way through Vespers. Then she had to sit through supper with the household while the King and Queen dined in private. The waiting seemed interminable.

At long last, the maids were summoned to attend Anna when she processed with the King to the presence chamber, where privileged courtiers had gathered to partake of a banquet of sweetmeats. The royal couple sat on their chairs of estate, and everyone gathered around them to watch the entertainment. Standing by the dais, Kate caught sight of Elizabeth among the company, guzzling from a heaped plate. They caught each other's eye and grinned. Then she suddenly became aware of Francis standing by her side.

"It is a pleasure to see you again, Kate," he said. He was smiling warmly at her. "You look very becoming in that gown."

Kate blushed, suddenly aware of how low-cut it was. "I am pleased to see *you,*" she murmured.

There was no more time for talking because the players were assembling.

"Your Majesties, my lords and ladies, we present for you *The Masque of Hymen,*" announced the Master of the Revels. Kate liked tales of the old Greek and Roman gods, but she had never seen anything like this. Her eyes widened at the sight of lords and ladies dancing together in the most revealing costumes, and she blushed at the bawdy jests, many of which she didn't entirely understand. Francis, standing at her side, had reddened, too.

"I hope you are not offended," he whispered in her ear.

"I hardly know what to be offended about!" Kate giggled. He looked relieved.

But the King's expression was thunderous, and his fair skin had flushed a deep red. His demeanor was certainly not that of an ardent bridegroom, and Anna looked terrified, as well she might, for no one could be in any doubt that he was in a very bad temper indeed. Contrary to his normal fashion, he did not applaud the masquers once, and consequently they played to a silent court.

Hymen was trembling as he addressed his Majesty, reminding him of the joys to be had in the marriage bed. Kate looked at Elizabeth, who surely couldn't understand much of what he was saying, but she was engrossed, doubtless by the gorgeous costumes and scenery.

After the masque had ended, the players came across to the audience with outstretched hands, and pulled people to their feet, enticing them to dance. As the King extended his hand to Anna, a swarthy older man with an eyepatch approached Kate and asked her to join him. Before she could answer, Francis stepped in.

"Mistress Carey has promised me this one," he said, and took her hand, twirling her into the throng. "That is Sir Francis Bryan, Lady Bryan's son, and he has a bad reputation as a libertine. If you value your honor, do not dance with him."

"Oh! He is my brother's guardian," Kate told him. In some of his rare letters, Harry had mentioned him.

"Be that as it may, no woman is safe from him," Francis said firmly.

She felt a little put out at his telling her what to do; after all, he had no claim on her. Then it dawned on her that he was not just being protective—he was jealous!

As they danced, his eyes held hers, and she felt as if she would melt inside. Was this feeling love? How did you know if you were in love? And how did you know if a young man was just playing with you? She wished that Mother were here so that she could ask her.

When the music stopped, the King's jester, Will Somers, tried to raise a smile by telling some jokes, but Henry still sat there with a face like doom, eyes narrowed. Taking advantage of his fool's immunity, Somers rashly plunged on.

"Are we keeping you from your sport, Harry? Go to it, man, delay no longer! Take your sweet bride to bed and swive her lustily!"

The King banged his fist on the table, and everyone jumped. "Enough!" he snarled. "Hold your tongue, Fool. Remember, the Queen and the ladies are present."

He waved Somers away and signaled to the musicians once more.

"Play!" he commanded.

The music began, a lilting melody with a lively drumbeat. Henry surveyed his courtiers with a jaundiced eye.

"What ails you all?" he barked. "Up, up, dance!"

Several gentlemen rose hastily, bowed to their partners, and led them to the floor. Elizabeth was tapping her foot in time to the music, obviously longing for someone to ask her to dance. Kate saw the King turn to the Queen.

"Will you do me the honor, Madam?" he asked.

Anna looked perplexed. "If it pleases your Majesty," she said, accepting his hand, "although I fear I am not skilled in dancing."

"Then I will teach you," he said.

The courtiers drew back as they stepped off the dais, and the music ceased. "We will dance a pavane—the King's Pavane!" Henry cried, and the musicians struck up another tune, slower this time.

"You take one step to two beats," the King said. "You move sideways, and then forward. It is a very slow and stately dance, and most apt for special occasions."

Anna soon got the measure of it, and before the music came to a close, she was moving about the floor with ease. At the end, she curtseyed low as the King bowed to her, and they returned to the dais amid loud cheering. Kate was deeply impressed. Anna had done well. Surely the King would come to her now?

"We will retire now," Henry announced. The music ceased and the whole court rose to its feet. The King was leaving. It was time to prepare the Queen for her wedding night.

"I must go!" Kate told Francis.

"I too! But I will look for you tomorrow."

She tripped away, her heart singing.

She was not needed. Mother Lowe and her cohorts made it clear that they alone were going to attend their mistress, and anyway, it was not proper for young maids to be present on such an occasion. Gratefully, Kate made her way to bed, where she could lie and indulge in blissful thoughts of Francis.

. . .

SHE DID NOT see Anna the next day, for it was customary for a queen to remain in seclusion after her wedding night, and again Mother Lowe was guarding the bedchamber door like a watchful basilisk. Kate spent the afternoon with Francis, watching an archery contest, in which he was engrossed. She wished he could show himself as engrossed in her, but then all the other young gentlemen were there, laughing and laying wagers. So she sat there, wrapped in her cloak, a little way off from the other maids, and tried to look interested, though all she was really seeing was his noble profile, his green eyes, and the delightful way his hair curled down his neck.

But when the match was finished, she had his whole attention and they talked about their childhoods and their time at court. Francis's early years had been far happier than hers, yet he too had lost his father when he was young. It made for a common bond between them. And all the while they were talking, Kate was aware of his eyes on her, ardent and admiring. He made her feel beautiful and special. The time raced by, and she hated having to say farewell when it was time to return to her duties. She would be counting the hours until she could see him again.

THE NEXT DAY, the Queen summoned her English ladies and maids to join her for a walk in Greenwich Park. Her German and Flemish women were not invited, so perhaps she had sensed that there was some resentment at the favor she showed to them. It was a sunny day but cold, and Kate was glad to be wrapped up in her fur-lined cloak.

At the top of the hill behind the palace, there was a crumbling old tower that looked deserted. As they approached, they encountered four young German gentlemen, out hawking on horseback. As they bowed in the saddle to the Queen, Kate saw Anna's eyes light up at the sight of one of them, a beautiful fellow with blue eyes, high cheekbones, and tousled curls.[1] He smiled back, and in

---

1 You can read more about this gentleman in my novel *Anna of Kleve: Queen of Secrets.*

that moment, Kate knew that there was something between them. With that realization came alarm, because she knew, better than most, what happened to queens who were suspected of loving someone other than the King. Fortunately, Anna did not linger. She exchanged a few pleasantries and walked on.

THE YULETIDE CELEBRATIONS were over, and Kat brought Elizabeth to say goodbye to Kate.

"I wish you were coming with me," the child said. At six, she was very forward for her age. "I like Mary, but it would be much more fun to have you as my sister."

Kate felt tears welling up. She would dearly have loved to be leaving with Elizabeth, and was touched by her young cousin's affection for her.

"I wish I could come, too," she said, hugging her. "I hope you will be back at court soon." She kissed her, and then curtseyed, remembering that this was a king's daughter, and watched Elizabeth go, her heart sinking.

AS THE DAYS passed, Kate became aware that the Queen was unhappy and on edge. The court was full of whispers about the King's dislike for her. It was even being said that he had not lain with her properly. Kate refused to engage with the rumormongers out of loyalty to her mistress, yet she felt anxious on her behalf. What must it be like to be a stranger in a foreign land, and to be married to a terrifying man who did not want her?

Kate was sure that Anna had heard the gossip, for the Queen was making a visible effort to win the King's love, or at least his approval. She was doing her best to learn English. She had cast off her ugly German clothes and put on English ones, in which she looked most becoming. She appeared thus attired at a tournament to celebrate her marriage, and Kate was pleased to see the King looking at her admiringly. It was going to be all right, she told herself.

Anna's life soon settled into a pattern. She spent hours sitting in her privy chamber, plying her needle, or gambling with cards or dice with her ladies and maids. Kate found the long days cooped up there a trial, wishing she could be out seeing Francis, yet he too had his duties and had to spend long hours on watch outside the King's apartments, so their opportunities to be together were few. But at least Francis was eager to see her when they were both free. During that idyllic month at Greenwich before they left for London, they would walk in the gardens, watch sporting contests, or just sit in a gallery talking and getting to know each other better. Kate knew that they were growing closer. She found herself counting down the minutes until their next meeting. When Francis held her hand, her heartbeat quickened. And when the gallery was deserted and he bent forward and kissed her, she was in bliss.

"I like you very much," he murmured, those green eyes fixed on hers. "Dare I hope that you like me, too?"

She was ready to shout to the world that she loved him, for she knew it now, without a doubt, yet she restrained herself, for it was his part to speak of love first.

"You know I do," she replied, trying to convey with her eyes how deep the feeling went.

He kissed her again. "I've been thinking, Kate . . ."

At that moment, a crowd of courtiers burst into the gallery and gathered by a window, talking and jesting. Francis smiled and fell silent, and Kate could have stamped her foot in frustration. Soon, it was time for her to return to the Queen, so she did not find out what he had been thinking. She wondered if he had been about to declare himself. Nothing would have been more welcome to her.

Chapter 11

1540

Cheering crowds lined the banks of the River Thames in February when Anna came to London from Greenwich in her state barge. Kate and the other maids were in the vessel that followed. Francis would be in the one that preceded Anna's, with Will and the other Gentlemen Pensioners, although Kate couldn't see him. The river was full of craft, many decorated with pennants, shields, and cloth of gold. The entire nobility appeared to have taken to the water, and every ship seemed to be firing salutes at once. The noise was deafening, the air thick with gunpowder.

The Tower of London loomed ahead, its stark silhouette shadowing the City. Kate could hardly bear to look at it, remembering the grim events she had witnessed there not four years ago. The horror was still with her, and she could not but imagine how Aunt Anne had felt when she was brought here from Greenwich to the Tower. Had she shrunk in terror from the sight of the fortress, fearing that she might never leave it? The thought unsettled her, making her aware that here she was, a member of the court of the devil who had sent his Queen to that gruesome death, a king who was probably the most dangerous man in the world—at whose whim she, or any of those around her, could be cast down. It was a terrifying thought, and for a few moments she wished herself far away from London.

Suddenly, as they neared the great fortress, the air was rent by another crack of guns as the cannon on the wharf shot off a thousand chambers of ordnance in salute. The noise was louder than thunder, and they all clapped their hands to their ears.

Thankfully, the Tower was soon behind them, along with her morbid thoughts, and now they were skimming the rapids under London Bridge. To the right was the City of London itself, with great houses and gardens lining the shore, and numerous church spires rising behind. Kate could hear the bells pealing joyfully above the roar of the crowds. The boat rounded a bend in the river, and the great abbey of Westminster came into view, and in front of it the huge palace of Whitehall, sprawling along the shore.

The barges pulled in by Westminster Stairs, where the King was waiting for Anna. She alighted to rousing applause from the onlookers, and curtseyed to her husband, who led her through the great gatehouse into Whitehall Palace.

"Is that it?" Mary Norris whispered. "Queen Anne went in procession through the City, and there were pageants and a welcome by the Lord Mayor."

"I should imagine that all that has been deferred until her coronation," Mrs. Stonor said. "But that's three months away."

Anna's rooms overlooked the river and the privy garden beneath her windows. She looked pleased to be here, on the doorstep of London. Kate hoped that all was now well between her and the King. It must be, if she was soon to be crowned.

Her mind at rest on that score, Kate hastened to find Francis. She saw him on guard, lined up with his fellows against the wall of the Great Watching Chamber. How tall and fine he was in his livery! Had she ever thought him unhandsome? He now looked to her like the most beautiful creature on earth, and all other men paled beside him, even the swaggering Thomas Culpeper, one of the King's gentlemen, who was hot in pursuit of Katheryn Howard.

Kate moved over to where Francis was standing. He was gazing straight ahead, but she saw his lips twitch when she casually brushed her fingers over his hand.

"Not now," he muttered under his breath, but she knew he was trying not to smile.

She ceased tormenting him and left. She knew when his period of duty ended.

There was a round fishpond in the gardens. At the appointed hour, she sat there waiting for him as long as she dared, until she really could not put off going to the Queen any longer; even so, she earned herself a telling-off from Mrs. Stonor. Having helped to dress Anna for Vespers and dinner, she snatched her cloak and hurried back to the fishpond, thrilled to find Francis waiting for her. He stood up and kissed her soundly, his tongue probing her mouth. As he folded her in his arms, she felt his codpiece harden. It called to mind something lewd that Katheryn Howard had said, amid giggles.

"You shouldn't be doing that," she said, feeling compelled to say something lest he thought she was forgetful of her honor.

"I can't help it," he protested. "I think you know how I feel about you, Kate."

Her heart sang. Any moment now, he would speak of love.

They sat down, his arm about her shoulders, and she leaned into his body. "I like you very much," he said, his eyes deep pools in the darkness. "I wish I could say more."

Why don't you? she wanted to ask. Was it that he was not in a position to support a wife? Or—the thought chilled her even more than the night air—was he promised to someone else?

After that, he seemed a little withdrawn, which made her wonder if she had offended him in some way. But he kissed her good night heartily enough, and with that she had to be content—until the next time they met. She cried herself to sleep, knowing that her great love for him meant that he had the power to hurt her very badly, even unwittingly.

The next day, she detained Mary Norris in the dorter and told her what Francis had said and how his mood had changed. "What do you make of it all?" she asked miserably.

Mary, who was a sensible young woman and very wise, smiled at her. "I'd say that he's in love with you and hasn't the courage to admit it. I've noticed that men don't like talking about such matters."

"So you think he loves me?" Kate craved reassurance.

"Of course he does! Just give him time."

"I will, I will! But I must see him. I must know that he is not offended with me in any way."

"Then you should contrive a chance meeting, and I will go with you so that he does not suspect anything."

"Mary, you are a marvel!" Kate cried, and kissed her.

"I am more than happy to aid the course of true love." Mary grinned.

They took care to be in the gallery that led to the King's apartments at the time when Francis would be arriving for his spell of duty. Together, they stood studying one of the framed maps that hung on the wall, as if their lives depended on it.

"Kate!" Francis was behind them. "How good to see you. And Mistress Norris, well met." He sketched a quick bow, seeming as happy and normal as ever. "I wish I could stay, but I cannot be late. I will see you later, Kate, in our usual place."

The fishpond. Shaded and relatively secluded, it was the perfect setting for their trysts.

"He's a fine fellow," Mary observed, watching his departing back. "You could do a lot worse."

"I don't think I could do any better!" Kate retorted. He would declare himself soon. She knew it!

HE WAS WAITING for her when she arrived. He kissed her hand. Any moment now, he might be on his knees!

"I have to go away for a short while," he said, dashing her hopes most cruelly. "The King has granted me leave."

"Where?" she managed to ask.

"Home, to Greys Court. I have affairs to sort out there, for I have been too much absent, and my mother should not be burdened with them."

She could not help herself. "Will you be away long?"

"Let me think. Two days' hard riding to Oxfordshire and two days back, and leisure for business—about ten days. I really don't want to leave you, but duty calls and there is much to do."

"When do you go?" she asked, wishing with all her heart that he would say he was going to miss her.

"Tomorrow, sweetheart. But we can see each other tonight, if you can get away."

Of course she could get away. She would have got away even if the King himself had forbidden it. His Majesty was to dine with the Queen, and the maids would not be needed until Anna was ready to go to bed. And Francis had called her sweetheart! That was enough to reassure her of his feelings for her.

"You will scarcely notice my absence," he assured her.

No, the time would drag mercilessly, she knew, but she did not contradict him. She wanted him to take away only lovely thoughts of her.

She sped back to the Queen's apartments to robe Anna for the evening. Vespers and dinner seemed interminable. What was she doing here when she could be with Francis? But, at last, she was free and racing down the stairs to the garden door. When she saw him waiting for her, her heart leaped. She loved him so much that, for a moment, she was tempted to cast her honor to the wind and tell him so. That would be a memory to take with him! But she restrained herself, because she instinctively knew he would think the less of her for it—and no man wanted a brazen hussy for a wife.

But he himself was ardent, more so than ever this evening. It was as if the imminent prospect of separation had added piquancy to their loving. He kissed her more deeply than ever, held her as if he could never let her go, and his hand once strayed around her side to her breast, until she gently removed it.

"I'm sorry, I'm sorry," he breathed. "You're so beautiful. I can't help myself."

"No matter," she whispered. "I liked it. But we shouldn't—it's wrong."

For answer, he buried his face in her neck and sought her lips passionately.

"I will miss you, Kate," he said, breathless.

"And I you," she told him. And then they were kissing again, and it was unbearably sweet, and she did not know how she would ever let him go.

THE DAYS SEEMED endless, as she had known they would. She found herself repeatedly lauding the praises of Francis to Mary or confiding her anxiety that he would have cooled toward her when he returned. Sometimes she found herself humming a song from *The Masque of Hymen,* which they had both liked and had sung to each other afterward. It made her feel close to Francis when he was so far away.

She wondered what business he had to conduct. The running of estates was a mystery to her. But one day, she hoped, she would learn from him, and learn so well that she would be a good wife to him. She imagined herself as mistress of Greys Court, running a great household with a brood of children around her—even though she had never seen the place and only knew what Francis had told her of it.

But then she recalled how he had said that he wished he could say more to her.

What was holding him back? She tortured herself with fears that he was betrothed to another, earning herself more than one reprimand from Mrs. Stonor for daydreaming.

"That's the second time I've had to remind you to fetch the Queen's rose water!" the Mistress of the Maids said sternly. "Why, girl, whatever's the matter?"

Kate's eyes had filled with tears. She wondered if she could trust Mrs. Stonor. She really wanted to speak to her mother, but the Mother of the Maids might be someone she could confide in. She gulped. "Mrs. Stonor, I love a young man, one of the Gentlemen Pensioners, but he has taken leave to go home and attend to estate business. I don't know what he has to do, but I fear he is promised to someone else."

Mrs. Stonor shook her head. Her stern face relaxed. "Sit down and calm yourself! Who is this young man?"

"Francis Knollys."

"I know him. He is of good family. Is he in love with you?"

"I'm sure he is, but he hasn't said so. He said he likes me very much, and he wished he could say more. That's why I fear he is bound to another."

To her astonishment, Mrs. Stonor took her hand. "Francis Knollys's father amassed much wealth for his good service to the King and the late King, which his son has inherited. He is a well-set-up young man. Too many of the young bloods at court are younger sons with no prospects and nothing to offer a young lady. By my reckoning, he has gone home to set his affairs in such order that he will be in an excellent position to propose marriage."

Kate felt as if a load had been lifted off her shoulders. "You really think so?"

"I do. And I believe him to be an honorable young man, so I do not think he would have led you on if he was betrothed to someone else. The very idea! You young girls do let your fancies run away with you. Still, I was young once and I remember what being in love was like. But, Mistress Carey, you are forgetting something very important." She drew back and regarded Kate severely. "This matter is one for the Queen herself, because while you are in her service, she is responsible for you, and anything you do reflects on her. Now, I do not think for a minute that she can disapprove of your choice of suitor, but she must be kept informed. I will talk to her."

THAT VERY AFTERNOON, Kate was summoned to the Queen's chamber. Mrs. Stonor was present, and Susanna Gilman was there as interpreter.

Anna smiled at Kate. "Mrs. Stonor says you have a suitor and that he is a good man. I will talk to the King about him, but you may receive him with my blessing."

Kate thanked her profusely and withdrew, not a little perturbed. Had she been too premature in mentioning Francis to Mrs. Stonor? What if he was not thinking of marrying her? And if the King said anything to him, or asked what his intentions were toward her, what would Francis think of her? She cringed at the idea of his thinking her too forward or presuming too much. Oh, she had been a fool, thinking to solve one worry, yet unwittingly creating another!

Why, she asked herself, as she hurried down to the gardens, did the King have to be involved? She had been at court long enough to know that no noble marriage could take place without his approval—yet she was not noble! Her father had been plain Mr. Carey. What interest could the King have in her? It could be because she was Elizabeth's cousin and close companion. But when she thought back on what the Queen had said, she realized that Anna might just have been intending to seek his opinion of Francis. Yes, that must be it.

She sat for a while by the fishpond, wishing that Francis were there with her, and dreaming of his kisses and his strong arms around her. She was hugging these thoughts to herself when Anne Bassett appeared.

"There you are, Kate!" she said. "I've been looking for you. There's to be dancing in the presence chamber tonight. We're to attend the Queen."

Kate sighed. If only Francis could be there. It would not be the same without him. But she went upstairs with Anne all the same and spent quite a happy hour in the maidens' dorter trying on some cream velvet gowns and gold damask French hoods provided by the Lord Chamberlain for the maids-of-honor. Thus arrayed, she joined the others following the King and Queen to the presence chamber. The musicians began playing and, at the King's nod, gentlemen began leading ladies out to dance.

A well-dressed young man presented himself before Kate and bowed. "Richard Beard at your service, Mistress Carey. Will you dance with me?"

He was not as tall as Francis and his hair was dark, but he had a handsome face and kind eyes. Why should I not enjoy myself? Kate thought. *My heart belongs to Francis, but he is not here, and I know I am not being disloyal to him. It is only a dance, after all.*

As they partnered each other in a lively galliard, he told her that he served in the King's Privy Chamber and that he had been a member of the embassy sent to Germany the previous year to arrange the King's marriage. He wanted to know all about Kate, and she found herself warming to him.

When the dance ended, he asked for another, and they set off again. He was regarding her admiringly and she could not but respond to the flattery. Had she not been in love with Francis, she would have liked Richard Beard as a suitor. But the man she loved was Francis. She had eyes for no other.

"I should tell you," she said, when the music stopped and he asked her to step out with him for the third time, "that a gentleman has been paying court to me and I am in hope that we shall be wed."

Richard looked genuinely disappointed. "He is a lucky man," he said at length. "I would not trespass on his territory. But would you be happy just to spend the evening with me, for good company? I would not expect anything more."

"Of course." She smiled. And it was a very pleasant evening.

SHE MET HIM again, by chance, at the bowling alley a week later. She was expecting Francis to return to court any day now, but she was pleased when Richard came over and sought her out as she stood with Mary Norris watching the contest.

"Well met, Mistress Carey." He smiled. "Is your suitor not returned yet?" He looked hopeful.

"He will be here very soon," she told him, thinking that if Francis broke her heart, she at least had someone she could turn to. But Francis wouldn't break her heart—he was a better man than that. Oh, how she wished he were here!

"We were just leaving," she said, ignoring Mary's bewildered expression. "We have to wait on the Queen." She left Richard there, looking crestfallen. It was a thousand pities that she had had to rebuff such a nice man, but she would not be disloyal to Francis.

When she got back to the maidens' dorter, she found a letter on her bed. Recognizing Francis's handwriting, she ripped the seal away. He was coming back to her! He would see her this very evening when he arrived at Whitehall.

The hours did not pass quickly enough. After the Queen had

finished supper, Kate hurriedly donned the cream gown that had looked so well on her at the dance, and ran down to the gatehouse, through which Francis must surely come riding. She waited there an hour and more, until she was thoroughly chilled to the bone, for it was a cold evening. Yet she had forborne to wear a cloak because she wanted him to see how pretty her figure looked in the velvet gown.

And there he was, leading his horse through the archway. When he saw her, he immediately handed the reins to his groom and ran to her, throwing his arms around her.

"My darling!" he exclaimed, with a fervor he had never before shown. "How I have missed you!"

"I have missed you, too!" she breathed, lost in the wonder of the moment.

He kissed her hard on the mouth and smiled. "I must see to my gear." He unloaded his saddlebags and bade his groom take the horse to the stables to be fed and watered. Then he took Kate's hand and led her into the palace. "Meet me by the fishpond in half an hour," he said, squeezing her fingers.

SHE TOOK HER cloak with her this time. As if on wings, she made her way to the gardens, where she saw Francis waiting for her. He seized her hands, kissed her hungrily, then drew her down beside him on the bench.

"What have you been doing while I've been away?" he asked.

"Not very much." She told him all there was to tell. "And a young gentleman from the privy chamber paid court to me, but I made it clear I wasn't interested," she added.

Francis nodded, looking relieved. "That was as well, because you know what I'm going to say to you now." He slid down on one knee. "Kate, will you marry me?"

She was taken aback. Of course she wanted to marry him, but she had thought that he would declare his love for her before asking her to wed him, and she needed to hear him say that he did love her before giving him her answer.

He was gazing up at her imploringly. "I like you very much," he said. "I think we get on well together and I want you to be my wife. I went home because I wanted to put my affairs in order and ascertain that I could provide for you properly before asking you."

I like you very much. We get on well together. These were not the romantic outpourings of love she had looked for. She knew that marriages were made not so much for love as for advantage, yet she had hoped that hers would be different. And Francis had given every impression that he did love her, so why didn't he say so? Had it been a ploy to win her? And yet what could she bring him, apart from herself? She had her dowry, thanks to Will, but it wasn't large, and her family connections were of no advantage at all.

He was waiting, looking at her with a mixture of puzzlement and eagerness.

"Tell me I may hope?" he urged.

"You have given me much to think about," she said slowly. "I will think on it, I promise. And when I am ready, I will tell you my answer."

He rose and sat next to her. "Don't keep me in suspense for too long, please. It would mean so much to me if you were to say yes." He bent and kissed her cheek.

She stood up and smiled at him. "I *will* think about it." Then she left him and ran back to the palace.

OVER THE NEXT fortnight, Francis seized every opportunity to see her. Every time, he asked her if she had made up her mind. He was like a man possessed, yet still he did not speak of love, and she was resolved not to accept his proposal until he did.

There came a day when she was sitting with Mary Norris in a gallery, playing her lute. She had not yet told Mary about Francis's proposal of marriage; she did not want her thinking that he was lacking as a suitor.

Suddenly, he was there. He must have been looking for her. He sat down with them and listened to the tune she was playing.

"That's one of the King's compositions," he said.

Kate ceased playing. She would never have played it if she had known that. She began to strum another piece, to which Mary began singing along.

When they had finished, Francis clapped. Then he fixed his eyes on Kate. "Have you thought yet?" he asked urgently, regardless of Mary's presence.

"Let's talk later," she replied, aware that her friend was staring at them.

"It's all right, I need to go anyway," Mary said, and hurried away.

"You embarrassed her," Kate reproved.

"You're driving me mad, making me wait so long for an answer," Francis said plaintively. "It's been two weeks now, and I need to know where I stand."

"So do I!" Kate cried. "Before I can accept you, there has to be something more."

He looked bewildered. "What do you mean?"

"I need more from you!" She would not mention the word "love."

He pulled her to her feet and wrapped his arms around her. "Kate, I think the world of you. I'm offering you love and devotion. Isn't that enough for you?"

She paused, nonplussed by his nearness and the effect it was having on her. Though he hadn't said, "I love you," he had spoken of love. That, surely, must be proof that he did love her.

"Please say you'll marry me," he said.

"All right—yes!" she breathed, dizzily happy.

"Thank God, thank God," he gasped, reaching out a hand to support himself against the wall. He looked as if he were about to faint. "I can't tell you what this means to me. I love you so much!" And then they were in each other's arms again, kissing as if their lives depended on it.

"TELL ME WHO I should approach to ask for your hand," Francis said later, when they had calmed down and the gallery was growing dim. Any moment now, servants would come to light the torches in the wall sconces.

Kate thought about it. "My mother? Will? No, the Queen. That would be best."

"I will ask the Queen," Francis said. "I will go to her now and crave an audience."

Kate followed him as he sped through the palace. At the door to Anna's apartments, the guards let them in, and an usher went to inquire if the Queen would be pleased to receive Francis. The answer came back that she would.

When he came out, five minutes later, he looked puzzled.

"What is it?" Kate asked. *Surely Anna would not have said no?*

"She has not the power to give her consent. Your marriage is a matter for the King alone. His Grace has commanded it. Therefore, I must try to see him."

"But why? Why is the King so interested in my marriage?" Kate was struck by the notion that something was being kept from her, but she could not fathom what it could be. She looked questioningly at Francis.

"I have no idea, and I did not press the Queen, for her English is poor. I will try to see the King now, but God only knows if he'll be free. There are always hordes of petitioners clamoring for his attention."

KATE SPENT THE day in the doldrums, worrying that the King had plans for her and would forbid Francis to marry her. Moping about the Queen's chamber, she could settle to nothing and was constantly looking toward the door or straining her ears for some sign of his return. Oh, when would he come?

It was six o'clock before he returned to her, and he was smiling.

"I caught his Grace in a merry mood, thank goodness, for it is rare these days. He says we may wed, with his blessing. He also said that he will attend the wedding. It is a great honor."

Kate was stunned. "Oh, Francis! That is wonderful news!" The only thing marring it was the prospect of that gross monster being there on her special day. She wished she could feel as elated about it as Francis clearly did. But then he could not know the depths to which the King had descended. He had not been there during those terrible days in the Tower, nor could Kate speak of them, for the horror went too deep. All she wanted was to forget the experience. One day, when she knew Francis better, she would tell him about it—but she wasn't ready for that yet.

"Meet me in the gallery after supper," he said, kissing her cheek. "We have a wedding to plan!"

"Wait!" she cried. "Surely you should write and ask my mother for her permission? And my stepfather, who is providing me with a dowry."

"Of course," Francis agreed. "I will go and see Master Stafford now. He knew of my hopes and looked kindly upon them. I am sure that he and your mother will be pleased. I will write to her this evening."

Kate wrote, too, fretting a little in case she and Francis should have approached Mother first. She told her how much she loved him and how suitable he was in every way, and begged her to give them her blessing. It was three days before she received a delighted reply, but before then, Will had come to see her. Hugging her like a bear, he told her that she couldn't have made a better choice.

"Where shall it be?" Kate wondered, sitting by the pond that evening.

"We could always get wed at the church at Rotherfield Greys, near my home," Francis suggested. "But the King might grant us leave to marry in one of the chapels royal, since he is to attend. I can ask him. Would you like that?"

"I'd rather get married at Rotherfield Greys," Kate said, thinking that there would be less chance of the King attending.

Francis looked disappointed.

"But if you prefer to marry at court, then I am content," she added quickly.

He brightened. "I will ask his Grace. I long for us to be wed, so let us not wait long. Shall I see if he will permit us to marry at the end of April? That will give us time to make ready."

"All right," Kate said, although if she had her way, she would marry Francis tomorrow. But late April was not far off. As Francis took her in his arms and kissed her deeply in the way she loved, all she could think of was that, in a few short weeks, she would be his entirely.

Chapter 12

1540

Early in March, the court left Whitehall for Hampton Court. Kate had seen Greenwich and Whitehall, and thought them splendid, but she gaped at her first sight of the great redbrick palace as it came into view ahead above the Thames, nestling on the riverbank amid vast acres of parkland. Hampton Court was magnificent! And when she and the other attendants followed the King and Queen through the King's apartments, she drew in her breath at the splendor of the paneling, the rich friezes of putti, the walls glittering with the gold and silver threads in hangings of cloth of gold and velvet, the jewel-colored heraldic glass, and the opulent Turkey carpets.

Kate had learned that Cardinal Wolsey, who had been the King's chief minister for many years, had built Hampton Court, but felt obliged to make the grand gesture of giving it to his envious master. It had done him no good, for he had fallen from favor after failing to obtain an annulment of the King's marriage to Queen Katherine. His story was a salutary example of what happened to those who flew too high; like Icarus, the sun melted their wings and they fell. And yet this court was full of men jostling for advancement and riches, none of them apparently concerned about the perils these might bring. Kate hated the self-seeking, the ruthlessness, and the jealousies that she saw all around her. It was one reason why she hated being at court. But then, of course, there was Francis . . .

As she and the other attendants followed the royal couple to the Queen's lodgings, she heard the King say that he had made many improvements, and that he had had Anna's rooms decorated in the antique style by a German craftsman, especially for her. Anna looked suitably overwhelmed by the gesture.

The maidens' chamber overlooked a spacious courtyard with a cloister, but they had no time to stow away their things as they had to unpack the Queen's chests. Kate was itching to be out in the gardens or the park. She wanted to explore them with Francis. There must be many secluded places where they could be together.

WHEN EASTER CAME, they were still at Hampton Court. Spring was flowering, and Kate went about with a light heart and a light step. So what if there was some murky secret in the past? She was in love, and it could be of no importance to her now.

She and Francis took delight in the awakening gardens. They snatched as much time together as possible, wandering along by the river or watching the games in the tennis play. It made her feel proud, to be squired about by such a tall, attractive man.

In the afternoons, she had to attend the Queen, who liked to walk with her ladies in the ornate gardens that bordered the Thames. Her favorite seat was in the little banqueting house near the ornamental fishponds. There were several such banqueting houses in the grounds of the palace, and Kate and Francis made good use of them in the evenings, when they were the haunt of lovers.

The King had granted permission for them to be married in one of the royal chapels. The date was set for 26 April, and when April came in, Kate found herself feeling deeply excited, for the waiting would soon be over, and then she would be Francis's entirely and know all about the mysteries of married life. The maids often gossiped and giggled about it, and she knew that you had to get naked and let your husband have his way with you, as indeed you must obey him in all things. Katheryn Howard would have enlightened her further, of course, but even if Kate had wanted to probe for information, she seemed preoccupied these days and was often away from court, at the Howards' mansion across the river at Lambeth. Kate wondered if she was still seeing Thomas Culpeper. She hoped not, for rumor had it that he had raped a country girl and managed to obtain the King's pardon. Kate would not have wanted anything to do with a man like that.

Everyone else was talking about the coming coronation, and the jousts and pastimes that would mark it. But Anna was becoming worried.

"No preparations are being made," she told her ladies at dinner one day. "Whitsun is only about six weeks away. Surely arrangements should have been set in train by now?"

It was true. Kate wondered what was going on.

"Such things can be organized at short notice," the Duchess of Suffolk said cheerfully.

"Have the invitations been sent out?" the Duchess of Richmond asked.

Anna had no idea.

Surely, Kate thought, she was worrying in vain. At the first, it had seemed that the King was not pleased with his bride, but he was always most courteous to her—and he was visiting her chamber at night, and doubtless doing that thing that no one liked to mention. Of course there would be a coronation! Even that monster would not publicly humiliate his Queen by denying her one now!

THE OTHER GREAT topic of conversation among the ladies was the closure of the last of the great abbeys, which had all surrendered themselves to the King's commissioners.

"I never thought to see this day," Margaret Douglas mourned, viciously jabbing her embroidery tambour with her needle. "At the outset, the King intended only to dissolve the smaller religious houses."

"Good riddance to them all, I say," chimed in Lady Suffolk.

"Hotbeds of Popery, all of them." Most of the ladies were nodding their agreement. Margaret, a devout Catholic, seemed poised to retort, but kept silent. It was tantamount to treason to criticize the King. For all that he upheld the Catholic faith and its rituals, and was effectively Pope in his own realm, he had appropriated the Church's riches for his own coffers, and was now selling off, or granting, monastic land to noblemen loyal to the Crown. Will had said that he was effectively buying their support for his reforms.

"But the sick and the poor go destitute, since they can no longer receive succor from the monasteries," Margaret persisted.

Kate felt she had little to contribute to the conversation. She had not given much thought to the tumultuous events that were happening around her. What she had heard was that a lot of monks and nuns had broken their vows and been living sinful lives. Yet as she listened, she began to feel sorry for some of them, because it seemed they were not all bad. What of those who had true vocations and had been turned out of the abbeys? They had all been given pensions, she learned, but some of the ladies were saying that they did not amount to much and could not compensate those who had truly forsaken the world and were now cast away. It was awful that no one dared to speak up for them. Queen Anna thought it appeared as if the King was encouraging Lutheranism.

"The reformists are flourishing," she said. "Even Lord Cromwell is one."

Kate did not fully understand what that meant. When she saw Francis later that day, and they were sitting by the fishpond, she asked him about it.

His face grew serious. "I am for reform. We reformists want the Church reformed from within; we are not heretics. But as for Lord Cromwell, there is talk in the court." He lowered his voice. "He is tottering. You are acquainted with Dr. Gardiner, the Bishop of Winchester? He is a staunch Catholic and hates all reformers, Cromwell in particular. Cromwell had him dismissed from the Council, but now he is back, and in favor with the King, a sure sign that Cromwell's influence is not what it was."

"But he is the most important man in the court!"

"Aye, but those who rise high have farther to fall. Remember

Cardinal Wolsey? We must hope that Cromwell does not go the same way."

Kate nodded. "Yet what of the monasteries? They were houses of prayer and they helped people."

He pulled Kate close to him. "They were corrupt, most of them, like the whole Roman Church. I would not sully your ears by repeating the practices that were discovered by the King's commissioners. The King was right to close them down."

"But some monks and nuns led holy lives, surely."

"A few," Francis said begrudgingly. "But those houses were bastions of Popery, and therefore disloyal to the King. A man cannot serve two masters."

"I thought they were meant to serve God!" Kate retorted, with spirit.

"If only they had. But they preferred to serve Mammon."

"My family have always been for reform," she told him. "My grandfather, my aunt Anne, and my uncle of Rochford were hot for it; they thought monks and nuns were lax and unholy. I heard someone say that my uncle was more Lutheran than Martin Luther himself. He could have been burned for it."

"Ah, but no one was sent to the stake in Queen Anne's time," Francis reminded her. "She had a beneficial influence on our King."

"She was no Lutheran," Kate told him.

"Would it have been a bad thing if she was?" Francis was looking into her eyes, his expression serious.

She was shocked, darting her eyes around the gardens to see if anyone could possibly have heard him. This was another thing she hated about the court. You had to watch what you said all the time. The penalties for having a loose tongue did not bear thinking about.

"You should not say such things," she whispered. "It's heresy, and you know what happens to heretics!"

Francis regarded her seriously. "I will say no more, to set your mind at rest. But one day, when the world is different, as it shall be, we will be able to speak of these matters freely. Until then, I will do nothing to risk your happiness. Just forget I said it."

"You know it will be hard to do that!" She gripped his forearms, seized by alarm. "Francis, promise me, as you love me, never to say to anyone else what you have just said to me!"

He hesitated.

"I mean it," she said. "And if you cannot, I release you from our betrothal."

She could see in his face that he was taking this seriously and understood that she really meant it. "I promise," he said at once. "I will not jeopardize your happiness—or mine."

"It doesn't matter what we think privately. But the world—and the King—will come down hard on those who support heresy, and I would not lose you for anything in Heaven or earth."

"Calm down, sweetheart," Francis murmured, cuddling her. "I will not speak of this again to anyone. I swear it. Now let us talk of other matters."

OF COURSE, SHE couldn't forget what he had said. She knew he had spoken truth, and that he was, at the very least, sympathetic to the teachings of Luther. Her betrothed was, in the eyes of the law, a heretic. It was foolish and dangerous, and she could not bear to think of what might happen to him if anyone found out. She wished he hadn't said anything. One chance remark, perhaps when he was in his cups, and he could be in the direst trouble. But then, Francis rarely drank wine or ale. He was abstemious in his habits. And he was not stupid; he was discreet. You rarely heard him voicing his views on anything, and that was probably the wisest course in a court full of backbiters. He had probably only opened himself to her because she was going to be his wife, someone he could confide in. Well, she would never betray him, whatever he did. She loved him too much.

IN THE SECOND week of April, the court moved back to Whitehall, so that the King could be present when Parliament opened. Kate was sad to be leaving beautiful Hampton Court and hoped that they would return soon. She hoped too that Elizabeth would visit the court shortly. She missed her little cousin and often wished herself back at Hatfield. The only thing she really liked about the court was Francis.

One day, sitting with a book in a shady arbor in the gardens, she looked up to see Will Stafford coming her way. She smiled and stood up to grasp his hands.

"Will!" she said. "It is a pleasure to see you."

He hugged her, and they sat down. She had been wishing that she could see more of this kindly, handsome man with his reassuring presence. It was obvious why her mother had risked much to marry him. Yet until now, their paths had rarely crossed. It was good to have the opportunity to talk to him.

"Your mother asked me to see you. She sends her love. But I'm sorry to tell you that your great-grandmother has died. She passed away peacefully in her sleep."

Kate allowed herself a few moments for the news to sink in. She had not been close to the sharp, enigmatic old lady, and knew she would not mourn her greatly, yet what did make her sad was the awareness that the Boleyns had all gone now—all except Mother, and herself.

"Was Mother with her?"

Will patted her hand. "Yes. And she is asking for you. The Crown's officers will be at Hever soon, for the castle now reverts to the King. He should have had it last year, when your father died, but Archbishop Cranmer prevailed on him to let old Lady Boleyn live out her days there. But he will now want what is his, and before they make an inventory, your mother wants you to go there to help her remove the things you don't want them to take."

Kate sighed. She did not want to go back to Hever. There were too many unhappy memories there.

"I should not really be telling you this," Will said, "for it is against my oath of service to the King. Anything that you or your mother take, you will effectively be stealing. But I know there are things that the King most definitely will not want, and also items of personal importance. Do you think you can get away? It will have to be soon, as there is not much time."

Still Kate shrank from agreeing, but reminded herself that this was Will, who had been nothing but kind to her. "The Queen is entertaining the ambassador of Cleves to dinner. They will be at least an hour. I will ask her as soon as she is free." She sighed again.

"You don't seem keen to go to Hever," Will said.

"To be honest, I'm not. There are painful memories there—of *her.*"

"Your aunt? That's understandable. It must have been awful for you, being with her in the Tower."

"It was horrible. I have nightmares about it even now." Her voice broke. "What they did to her was terrible, brutal, and pity her though I do, I don't like to be reminded. All my memories of her are tainted by what I witnessed."

Will put a fatherly arm around her.

"I'm glad you've got Francis to take your mind off it. He thinks the sun rises and sets with you, you know. He's a fine young man—you could not have done better. At least you are not starting your married life under a cloud as I did."

"No, that was unfair."

"It's why I have very mixed feelings about your aunt." He grew thoughtful. "I remember her coronation. I was one of the knights and gentlemen summoned to be servitors at the great feast that followed in Westminster Hall, and that was where I met your mother. I was smitten from the first, and she with me."

Kate was listening avidly. It was the first time anyone had spoken in any detail to her of that great scandal, for she had been just ten when her mother and Will were forced into exile.

"At first, I thought she'd think me too young for her, but when I begged her to marry me, she said yes without hesitation. No one had set much store by her; I think I gave her back her self-esteem."

That was a heartwarming thought.

"It's a mystery to me why no one ever set much store by her," Kate said. "Why? She was prettier than Aunt Anne, and kinder, and she was the elder sister."

Will seemed reluctant to answer. He opened his mouth, then shut it.

Here it was again, that sense that something that had happened in the past was being withheld from her. But then Will spoke.

"I think her family all thought she should have done better for herself after making that promising first marriage. But your mother is that rare person. She didn't care about marrying for money or advantage. She chose me. We fell in love, and our feelings for each other were strong enough to override any fears we had about the consequences of our secret marriage or the hardships we might endure, although I did wonder how well she would adapt to being the wife of a humble soldier." He smiled. "I need not have worried. We were in bliss together. We still are, and I miss being with her."

"But why did people object? You are from a great family," Kate said.

"The Staffords? I am related to them only through two marriages that were made centuries ago. My father was a knight, but my grandfather was hanged as a traitor by the late King Henry because he supported King Richard. My father labored long and hard to recover royal favor, until finally our present sovereign lord reversed his father's attainder and restored some of his lands. I am his Grace's third cousin through his grandmother's family, the Wydevilles." Kate found it extraordinary that Will was blood-kin to the King. She had never realized that. But then so many people at court were related to each other in some way.

Will sighed. "For all this, and my loyalty and good service, I had little to recommend me to your mother or her family. I was not even a knight at this time, and I had but three manors to my name. And that name was doubly tainted by treason, for my distant relation was the Duke of Buckingham, who was beheaded some years ago for conspiring to seize the throne. Since then, the King has looked with suspicion on the Staffords, especially since they supported Queen Katherine. So what appeal did a landless nobody, a simple soldier, have for the mighty Boleyns?"

"They are mighty no longer," Kate reminded him.

"They are not, but they were six years ago. Your aunt was Queen and possessed of great influence. Your grandfather and your uncle were in high favor at court. I was no match for the Queen's sister. Your mother could have contrived to marry more advantageously and thereby extend the Boleyn influence and standing—but she dared to marry merely for love, which most people of rank deemed an offense against God, good order and all, and foolish in the extreme. Furthermore, she had not even had the courtesy to ask her father, her sister, or the King for permission to remarry, but went ahead regardless of her family's interests and the King's likely displeasure. But it was Anne who was the most furious, for she considered herself the head of the family and was enraged that she had not been consulted. Mary put off telling her for ages because she was frightened of her, and ended up appearing at court visibly with child, which set tongues wagging, I can tell you. And Anne and your grandfather immediately prevailed on the King to expel her."

"You must both have been petrified," Kate said, appalled at the lack of feeling Anne had shown. Since those days in the Tower, she had thought of her aunt as a tragic heroine because of the manner of her death, yet now she remembered that there had been quite another side to her.

"It was dreadful. Many harsh words were spoken. I do believe that Anne was jealous. Mary had hopes of a child, when she had just suffered a miscarriage—and she also had a husband who loved her. The King, by contrast, was growing tired of Anne, and was openly dallying with his latest mistress. So there was Anne, the darling of her family, applauded by them all for becoming queen of England, but deeply unhappy; and there was her despised sister, proudly proclaiming her happiness and carrying a child, having flouted all the rules of society."

"I'm beginning to understand why you both left England," Kate said.

"I hope so. We didn't want you to think ill of us, leaving you behind. You were happily and advantageously settled in Elizabeth's household, and we were convinced that Anne's wrath would not extend to you, since Elizabeth was so attached to you. Once I got your mother away, we both felt better. She was glad to escape the miserable bondage of her widowhood and her dependence on her begrudging father. And two years later, we were glad to be out of England, apart from not being able to be there to spare you the ordeal you were made to suffer. I would have moved Heaven and earth to prevent that. But we didn't know what was happening, still less about your part in it. When your mother found out, it was too late, and she was glad at least that Anne had one of her kinsfolk with her. She doesn't speak of that time. It's too painful."

Kate sat silently for a few moments, digesting everything Will had said.

A bell struck and he rose. "Well, Kate, I have to be back on duty. I'm pleased that we've had a chance to talk."

"And I'm pleased that you and my mother rode out the storm and were able to be together," she said. "I pray that Francis and I will know such happiness."

"You have everything in your favor," Will said. "We were poor. The King cut off Mary's royal pension, and we had only my soldier's pay and the rents from my manors to support ourselves. But we loved each other, so that didn't matter, and we weren't in poverty, whatever your mother says!" He smiled, shaking his head.

"You both deserved to be happy. And I'm glad to have you for my stepfather." Kate stood on tiptoe and kissed his cheek. He grinned and patted her shoulder.

"I'm always at your service, Kate. If ever you need me, you know where to find me."

He made to walk away, but she clutched his sleeve. "What happened to the baby?"

"It died," he said, a shadow clouding his face.

"I am so sorry," she told him.

ALL THROUGH DINNER, Kate kept thinking of what Will had told her. Until now, she had thought of her mother as a weak woman, but in the light of what she now knew, that was hardly fair because in defying her family and making a marriage of which she must have known they would disapprove, and in defending it passionately in the face of formidable opposition, Mother had shown strength of character. And while others had forced her to pay the price, she had successfully seized her chance of happiness and freedom. Kate realized that until she herself had fallen in love with

Francis, she hadn't fully understood why her mother chose to marry Will despite knowing how difficult it would be.

"A penny for your thoughts," Mary Norris said, interrupting Kate's reverie.

"Oh, I do apologize," she said, cutting her meat into delicate slices. "I was thinking of my mother. She wants me to visit her at Hever Castle."

"We all know why she won't show her face at court!" Katheryn Howard smirked.

Kate would not rise to the bait. "That scandal is long behind her now. And Queen Anne forgave her at the last."

"I'm not talking about that scandal!" Katheryn laughed. The other maids giggled.

"Then what *are* you talking about?" Kate riposted.

Katheryn stole a glance at Mrs. Stonor, who sat at the head of the table. That lady was regarding her sternly. "I won't have malicious gossip, Mistress Howard," she reproved.

Katheryn subsided, leaving Kate in a turmoil. What was this other scandal?

When dinner was over, Mary followed her to the Queen's chamber. "Take no notice of what Katheryn said," she soothed. "She loves to gossip—and she embroiders everything."

Kate turned to her. "Do you know what she was talking about?"

"I have no idea," Mary said, looking away. Kate was sure she was lying.

Chapter 13

1540

The queen readily gave Kate permission to leave court, but it was with some reluctance that she packed her saddlebags and set off, attended by a groom. It had been hard saying goodbye to Francis, for she was sad to leave him and clung to him tightly before they parted.

She stayed at an inn near Croydon the first night, then they rode south via Edenbridge until they came to the gates of Hever.

The castle was in chaos. Men in royal livery were carrying out furniture, pictures, plate, and numerous other things, and loading them onto waiting carts. And there was Mother, in the midst of them, wringing her hands and looking very distressed.

"They're taking everything!" she wailed, embracing Kate. "Even our family portraits. What would the King want with those? They've removed all the plates and cutlery—we won't even have a cup to our name! Oh, Kate, this is terrible!"

Kate went in search of the steward, who was in his office, talking to one of the royal officials.

"My mother is very upset," she said. "Can't you leave us some necessities?"

The officer looked embarrassed. "I'm sorry, Mistress, but I have my orders. Everything is to be removed."

"But what shall we do?"

"You must leave by nightfall."

Mother came in, beside herself. "I've told them not to touch my gowns! I brought them here from Calais."

"I'll see that they are left for you," the man said. "I am so sorry to inconvenience you ladies. I am only doing my job. And if it helps, there are good inns at Chiddingstone or Penshurst, where you could lodge tonight."

"I thank you, but we will go to Henden Manor, my house at Ide Hill." She turned to Kate. "It was part of my inheritance from my father, and the King has just granted us leave to take possession of it. I inherited half of the Boleyn estate; the other half is the King's. Your uncle Rochford, Grandfather's only surviving son, died without heirs, so Anne and I were left as co-heiresses. Her share went to her daughter, the Lady Elizabeth, which is why the King has claimed it. And I, fortunately, am not left destitute. I visited Henden when I first arrived. It is a fine house and Will and I will make it our home—for now. But I have my eyes on a greater property, which I will tell you about later."

They went outside and watched the men loading the last of their former possessions.

"It is as if they are taking all my memories away," Mother said, her gray eyes filling with tears.

"Did you manage to save anything?" Kate asked.

"A few small items. They are in my chest. But they wouldn't let me take the portraits of my parents. Not that I would have hung them anywhere." Her voice was bitter.

Suddenly, Kate had a thought. There was a small round portrait of Aunt Anne in her bedchamber, which she wanted to save for Elizabeth, for it was important that the child learn the truth about her mother. "Wait here!" she said, and darted across the drawbridge and into the castle. It looked so bare, stripped of its furnishings. Just an empty shell. No one would ever have known that one of the highest families in the land had lived here, or that a king had once come a-courting. But there was no time for reflection. She dashed upstairs, nearly colliding with an officer coming down, a bundle of curtains in his arms.

"I need to use the privy," she said as she pushed past, leaving him no doubt wondering why she hadn't used the one downstairs. But she was worried that she would be too late. She wasn't. The portrait was still on the wall. She shoved it under her cloak and made her way back to her mother.

"I've got my portrait of Aunt Anne," she told her.

Mother looked concerned. "Are you sure no one saw you take it? Stealing the King's property would be seen as a heinous offense."

"No, there was no one upstairs. Besides, he won't want it. He probably hates to be reminded of her."

"He doesn't like to be reminded of any of his past loves," Mother said.

"Surely he honors the memory of Queen Jane?"

There was a pause. "Aye. But no one else. Well, we had best be on our way," Mother said briskly.

They asked the men to load their chests onto a cart, then mounted their horses and turned away. They had not gone more than a few yards when Mother reined in her horse and looked back. "This is the final time a Boleyn will leave Hever. We are the last of the family. We will not come this way again."

Kate was remembering Great-Grandmother's strange predictions about Hever. Had she seen in her visions the castle as it would be under the new owners, whoever they would be? Well, Kate was unlikely to find out. She would not return here, even if she was invited.

They passed through the gatehouse and dismounted by the village church. "I have a mind to say farewell to your grandfather one last time," Mother said. They walked up the aisle to where a large tomb stood beside the altar. On it lay a fine brass showing the late Earl of Wiltshire in the robes of the Order of the Garter.

"It doesn't look a bit like him," Mother said, and Kate had to agree. "I don't grieve for him," she went on. "I'm glad he's gone, for he made my life a purgatory. Is that very wicked of me?"

"No," Kate said. "I didn't like him either. He frightened me because he was always so critical of me and Harry, and we knew he didn't want us at Hever."

"No," Mother said, gazing down at the brass. "He served only his own interests, and I think he saw me as his one failure—before Anne's fall, of course. It's hard to believe he voted her guilty. It was his own neck he was thinking of. Your grandmother never forgave him, even though he said he had done it to spare her the loss of a husband as well as her children."

"I'm not surprised she felt like that." Kate turned to her mother. "He was cruel. How could the death of my father make you a failure? It wasn't your fault that you were widowed. It must have been a terrible loss."

Mother looked uneasy. "It was, not least because your father looked to rise even higher at court. But God deemed otherwise. And Grandfather did not want the responsibility of providing for us. I suppose I should have been glad that the King made him, but it was a mixed blessing. Anyway, that's all in the past now. I shall not come here again."

They walked outside, into the spring sunshine.

"Why isn't Grandmother buried here?" Kate asked.

Mother made a face. "Would you like to lie alongside that man for all eternity? No, she did not. Instead, she chose to be buried with the Howards at Lambeth."

"Did *she* turn against you for marrying Will?" There was so much of her family history that Kate did not know.

"They all did. I don't remember my mother ever saying a kind word to support me. I did not see either of them again after I left for Calais, so I never made my peace with them. That does not bother me. But I am glad that Anne spoke kindly of me at the end, as I was glad of the letter she sent me. It was as if I was dead to the rest of them."

Kate was beginning to feel a little hurt that Mother had not yet asked about her imminent wedding. Yet what could she have expected, with Mother so preoccupied with her own troubles? And this was a challenging day. But as they strode back to the lychgate where their horses were tethered, Mother finally took her hand. "I'm so sorry, Kate. Here I am, fretting about everything, and I haven't even mentioned your marriage. I am truly happy for you, and longing to meet Francis. Will speaks so highly of him—he sounds the perfect husband for you."

"Oh, he is!" Kate cried, squeezing her mother's hand, and proceeded to tell her all about him.

Mother smiled properly for the first time that day. "I rejoice to see that you are very much in love, and I am glad of it. You deserve it, dear girl."

They mounted and trotted off in the direction the cart had taken.

"Mother, all I ask is that Francis and I enjoy the kind of happiness you have with Will. I want us to stay in love all our lives together. You have, haven't you?"

Mother smiled. "Love is a precious thing and needs nurturing. The love you have is a good basis for the future, but sometimes you must work to keep it alive. And that first 'in-love' feeling deepens over time; marriage is not all about passion. It's kindness and tenderness that matter. Be good to each other; be patient. That's the best advice I can give you."

"It sounds like good counsel," Kate said, looking around her at the hedgerows abundant with spring flowers, the broad fields, the tunnel of trees through which they were riding, and the azure sky above. Oh, it was glorious to be alive! The world away from the court was a wonderful place, and it would be perfect if only Francis were here to share it with her.

HENDEN MANOR WAS a large timbered house with a Wealden tiled roof, set in the middle of a glorious hunting park. Kate did not feel bad about leaving her mother there, for the place was so welcoming and peaceful, and Mother was eager to arrange it the way she wanted.

"It will do until I can gain possession of Rochford Hall," she said. "It lies in Essex, and it came to the Boleyns through your great-grandmother, but her kinsman, the Earl of Ormond, has laid claim to her inheritance. Nevertheless, I am determined to fight for it, because she was her father's sole heiress, so it is rightfully mine. It's so frustrating, because the income from her lands would bring me and Will great wealth."

"But you have other property from Grandfather?" Kate asked, gazing through the latticed window at the moat.

"Yes. The King has also confirmed to us Southborough, all the lands in Hever except the castle, and Brasted. We shall have a reasonable living from the rents."

Mother suddenly turned to Kate. "I'm proud of you, Daughter. You have grown up to be wise and beautiful, and virtuous. There is no spite in you, as there was in me and my sister. You are devoid of guile, warm and willing, and you deserve to be happy with Francis. Go back to him and be happy."

"You will come to the wedding, of course?"

Mother hesitated. "If you want me to be there." She didn't sound very happy about it.

"Of course I do! And you surely want to see me wed?"

"Oh, yes." Mother embraced her. "It's just that I don't like going to court. It holds too many memories for me . . . Of your father."

"I understand," Kate assured her. "But please come!"

"Very well. I will be there."

NOT LONG AFTER Kate's return to Whitehall, Francis's mother, Lady Lee, came up from Aylesbury to London for the wedding, and they had dinner in the George Inn at Southwark, where she was staying. Kate had been nervous about meeting her, but her future mother-in-law was kindness personified, and a great lady in every sense. She was wearing black, for her second husband had died the previous year, yet she was cheerful and embraced Francis warmly.

"Well, you have chosen a fine young maiden!" she said, looking Kate up and down. "I am very happy for you both."

Kate had been glad to hear that Lady Lee would not be living with them at Greys Court after their marriage, for she had the dower house in Buckinghamshire; yet now that she had met her, she felt rather sorry about that, for she inwardly found the prospect of running a large household daunting, and now realized that the older woman would have been the perfect one to teach her. She spent the dinner asking for her advice, which Lady Lee very willingly gave.

"You will love Greys Court, my dear," she said. "I was very happy there. And I know that the servants will be pleased to have a mistress of the house living there again." She rose, with a rustle of silks, and straightened her widow's wimple. "Well, I realize you must both get back to your duties, and I need to go to my room to rest. I always take a short sleep in the afternoons. I will see you in the chapel!" She bent forward and kissed Kate warmly.

"You've done well, my son!" she told a beaming Francis.

THE END OF April was in sight—and the wedding. Kate was busy with preparations. The Queen's tailor was making her a gown of pink damask with wide skirts and a low bodice edged with pearls. She would be wearing her hair loose, as became a virgin bride, with a chaplet of flowers. Mary Norris and Anne Bassett were to be her bridesmaids.

She had asked Will to give her away, and he had readily consented. The King had insisted on hosting a private reception for her and Francis and their guests, in one of the little banqueting houses in the palace grounds, and she had grudgingly had to accept because it clearly meant so much to Francis—and one did not refuse the King.

Being so busy, Kate lamented not having much time to spend with Francis, yet they did manage to snatch some time together, and when they were alone, he became increasingly amorous. His hand would stray to her breast or her thigh, but she always pushed it away.

"We will soon be wed!" he protested one evening, as they sat on the parapet of the fishpond.

"It will not be long," she told him. "Have patience!"

"But I ache to make you mine," he murmured, kissing her.

"And I yearn to be yours, but it would be wrong to do it now, and you would not respect me for it."

"I would, my love, I promise!"

"No, Francis. I would not feel right about it. Never think that I do not love you; but I love my honor, too."

"I would do nothing against your honor, my love. But just let me touch you . . . Let me see you!" His fingers caressed her breast where it swelled from her bodice. The sensation was exquisite, undeniable. Then he delved farther, beyond the thick biliment of embroidery, and found her nipple, kissing her vigorously all the time. She knew she should stop him, but it was almost impossible not to give way to the wondrous sensations coursing through her whole being. With a great effort, she stood up, and would have moved away, but Francis only gripped her the tighter, letting go of her breast and pressing her body tightly to his. She could again feel the hardness beneath his codpiece as he bent to nuzzle her neck, and then it caught her at the core, and she knew what Katheryn Howard had meant when she had once spoken of a point of no return. Her reaction was so strong that she thought for a moment she might die of it or forget herself entirely. She jerked away, breathless, before she lost control completely.

"I must go!" she cried. "We should not be alone like this."

"Darling!" Francis was beside himself and breathing heavily. "I am so sorry. I did not mean you any harm. But you are so beautiful, and I was quite overcome. I hardly know how I will wait for us to be wed."

"I want it, too," she whispered. How much she wanted it, right now, she could not express to him. "But we must avoid any occasions for temptation. It is not long to wait. Only a few days."

He stepped forward and kissed her, more gently this time. "I shall be counting them," he murmured.

KATE HAD BEEN hoping that Elizabeth would visit the court, but there was no sign of that happening. It occurred to her that she could go to Hatfield to see her, yet she did not like to ask for more leave as she felt she had presumed on Queen Anna's kindness too often. But she would shortly be leaving her service anyway, for Francis wanted her to live at Greys Court after their marriage.

Anna had been most understanding. She had also given them a covered silver-gilt cup as a wedding gift. Surely, she would not mind sparing Kate to visit Elizabeth?

Anna didn't. "Go to her," she said. "She will be happy to see you." She even provided a groom to escort Kate.

They rode northward, through London and into Hertfordshire. Spring was flowering and the countryside was coming to life. Lambs gamboled in the fields as they passed, and the hedgerows were bursting with flowers of myriad colors. Kate was missing Francis already—how she would have loved to share all this beauty with him—but she was also looking forward to seeing Elizabeth's face when she appeared at Hatfield.

She found the little girl in the garden, picking flowers with Kat. Catching sight of Kate, Elizabeth ran to her and threw her arms around her waist.

"Kate! Kate! I have missed you so much! Have you come back for good?"

"Alas, no," Kate told her, stroking her red tresses and looking down at the sharp little face, turned up beseechingly to hers. "But I have some good news. I am to be wed and leave court, and I wanted to see you before I go."

Elizabeth recoiled. "Wed? Who to?"

"To Francis Knollys, one of your father's Gentlemen Pensioners."

"Like Will Stafford?"

"Yes." Kate was astonished that Elizabeth knew Will. "Where did you meet Will?"

"At Christmas. He's my uncle. Why should I not meet him?"

Kat came up and embraced Kate. "I was thrilled to receive your letter telling me your news. I am so pleased for you."

"Well, *I'm* not!" Elizabeth snorted, flouncing away.

Kate hastened after her. "Sweeting, what's the matter? How have I offended you?"

Elizabeth swung round. "Because you should come back here when you leave the Queen's service! You don't love me anymore! You love this Francis now."

"That's nonsense," Kate said. "Love is boundless. You can love different people in different ways, and I assure you, little cousin, that I love you just as much as I ever did, and I always will."

The child continued to stare at her dubiously.

"You should be happy for Kate," Kat said. "She shouldn't be subjected to this performance."

For answer, Elizabeth turned and ran into the house.

Kat sighed. "I suppose that a child of middling six cannot comprehend the feelings of a young woman. For all that you are close cousins, the age gap is too great."

Kate felt unhappy. "I will go and talk to her."

She found Elizabeth hiding under the table in the still room. "Come out!"

"Kat's cross with me," the little girl said.

"Well, you were very silly." Kate got down on her knees. "When you are older, you will understand that all women want to find a good husband, a man they can love and respect. And I have found one in Francis. I pray that you will one day be as lucky."

"But I'm going to marry a great prince!" Elizabeth boasted.

"Prince or plowman, what matters is that he is kind and that you love each other. As I love Francis." She was determined to bring the conversation back to him, and to make Elizabeth repent of her animosity. But Elizabeth said nothing.

"Cousin, I wish you would be happy for me," she persisted. "When I am married, we will write to each other often, and I will only be a two- or three-day ride away, so I can come and visit you, yes?"

The child nodded.

"We will see each other much more than we have during my time at court."

"Yes." She was thawing.

"And you'll like Francis, I know! He will be another cousin to love you." Goodness, she was having to labor hard!

"I wish I could be a bridesmaid," Elizabeth said.

Kate gave up. "I wish you could, but it will only be a small wedding."

"Did you bring me a present?"

"I've told you before, my Lady Elizabeth, that it's rude to ask for presents," Kate said sternly.

"But I love them!"

"We all do," Kate agreed. "But people like to give surprises. And no one should ever demand a present. It makes you look greedy." She didn't think even this child, with her advanced command of vocabulary, would understand the word "mercenary," which would have been more appropriate. "As it happens, I have brought you a present. Something very special. But first, I have to speak to Kat. Wait here!"

She came upon Kat in the great hall, discussing her charge's meals with the cook and Lady Troy. When they were done, she took Kat aside and told her about what had happened at Hever. "I managed to save a small portrait of Queen Anne for Elizabeth," she said, lowering her voice. "Will it be all right to give it to her?"

"The King would frown on it, I'm sure," Kat said, making a face, "for I understand that Anne's name is not spoken at court. But Elizabeth already has a portrait of her mother. We found it in the attic, and she keeps it behind her bed. You can rest assured, Kate, that I'm making certain she knows the truth, that that poor lady was innocent of all those dreadful crimes and greatly wronged."

"So shall I give her the picture?"

"By all means. She will be delighted. But she'll have to hide it."

BACK IN THE still room, Elizabeth unwrapped the parcel and stared at her mother's face, her mouth a perfect O. "I am like her," she said, "but my hair isn't brown. Was she very beautiful?"

"Yes, she was," Kate lied. She had not found her aunt very attractive and could not understand what the King had seen in her. But then, Anne had been thirty-six, approaching middle age, when she died—and looked it; she was no longer the young woman who had captivated a king. Years of strife and troubles had taken their toll. Certainly, she looked more alluring in her portrait.

Elizabeth laid it down on the table and threw her arms around

Kate. "Thank you, dear cousin!" she cried, having one of her mercurial changes of mood. "It's a lovely present!"

She ran upstairs to her bedchamber to stash it away with the other portrait, then hurried back, clutching her cloak. "Let's walk in the park! Then we can go to the stables and I can show you the new foal!"

Kate followed in Elizabeth's wake, glad to see her happy again, and pleased that she had got over her jealousy. But as they walked along the path, another change of humor came over the little girl.

"I wish my mother was alive," she said suddenly, once they were away from the palace.

"Of course you do," Kate said, feeling for her.

"You're lucky! You have your mother. My father killed my mother."

She cast a challenging glance at Kate. "People told him lies about her and made him believe them. He was tricked!"

"I believe he was," Kate said carefully. She must take care not to criticize the King in any way, because you never knew what a young child might repeat.

"But your mother was very naughty," Elizabeth said, giving her that look again. Her words came like a slap in the face.

"Naughty? What do you mean?" Kate spoke fiercely, and her cousin looked away.

"I don't know. I heard Lady Troy say it to Kat. She said . . ." She thought for a moment. "She said that she was no better than she should be."

Kate had heard Mary Norris say the same about Katheryn Howard, who was careless of her reputation and had been flirting—some said sleeping—with Thomas Culpeper. It was not a nice thing to say about someone.

"Is that all she said?"

"Yes. They saw me and they shut up." Elizabeth skipped ahead. "But it doesn't matter. It's probably nothing."

Kate, shaken to her core, was not so sure. Had Lady Troy been referring to Mother's marriage to Will? But Mother had been held in low esteem by the family long before that, and what Kate had just heard made sense of all the other strange things she'd heard that had hinted at some secret that must be kept hidden. If Mother had been naughty, as Elizabeth put it, it would explain Grandfather's attitude toward her, and the family's desire to keep her away from the court. They would not have let her bring shame on them. But what had Mother actually done to deserve such ostracism? Had she been unfaithful to Father? It was an uncomfortable thought, and it was not the kind of thing Kate could mention to Mother. She could only hope that Elizabeth had misheard what Lady Troy had said.

Chapter 14

1540

On the morning of her wedding, Kate was shaking with nerves. As her mother, Mrs. Stonor, and the maids-of-honor dressed her in the beautiful pink gown and placed the floral chaplet on her head, she stood there trembling, feeling as if she were going to her execution, rather than her marriage. And it was all because that devil would be there. How she wished that she were getting wed at Rotherfield Greys. A small gathering in a country church would have been idyllic.

The late-April sunshine was streaming through the windows as her little procession made its way to the Chapel Royal. At the door, Will, tall and resplendent in his livery, was waiting to greet her. As he offered her his arm, and Mother and the others passed on into the chapel, trumpets suddenly sounded and the King arrived, leaning heavily on a stick and attended by several gentlemen. Kate sank into a curtsey and Will bowed low.

"Now, here's a pretty bride!" the King said, chucking Kate under the chin and raising her. She recoiled from the stench of his bandaged leg, but managed a smile. "Why, I do believe you are nervous," he said, grinning. "No need, no need, child. There's nothing to fear." He looked at Will. "If I may have the honor, Stafford?" He held out his arm toward Kate, and Will melted away.

She took it warily, aware that this was a great honor, yet not wishing to be anywhere near this horrible, cruel man. The trumpets sounded again, and he marched her into the chapel. She would never forget the look on her mother's face when she saw them; it was one of amazement—and dismay. In that moment, she realized that Mother felt the same way about him as she did.

When she joined Francis by the altar, all her nervousness fell away and her heart sang. The way he was looking at her told her that he found her beautiful. It was such a relief when the King placed her hand in her betrothed's and withdrew to the royal pew in the gallery above. Then she and Francis knelt before Archbishop Cranmer and were made man and wife. As Kate looked into her new husband's shining green eyes, she felt that God was smiling upon their union.

THE RECEPTION IN the banqueting house was sumptuous. A vast array of comfits and sweetmeats had been laid out—the royal chefs had done them proud—and the wine was flowing freely. The King raised his goblet in a toast to the bride and groom, then departed. After that, Kate began to relax and enjoy her day.

Her mother-in-law kissed her. "Welcome to the family, my dear. You look beautiful, as a bride should." She tapped her son on the chest. "Francis, I'll say it again—you are a very lucky young man."

"I think we're both lucky, Lady Lee." Kate smiled.

"Call me Lettice, dear. I should like that."

"I will, thank you—Lettice!" Kate promised.

People were crowding around, offering their congratulations and their gifts.

"We'll have enough plate to start a dinner service!" Kate laughed, as she thanked yet another well-wisher.

"Well, we have a handsome house to put it in," Francis said. "I can't wait to show it to you." It had been agreed that they would set off the following morning. Tonight, they would stay in Francis's lodging, two rooms only, but comfortable, he had assured her, his eyes alight with desire. She was half longing, half dreading the moment. She feared she might die of embarrassment. Would it hurt? But hold, she inwardly admonished herself. This was Francis, who would never hurt her, and she had already felt a hint of the pleasure to come. Smiling, she made her way back to the buffet table and piled her plate high.

By the time the food was eaten, and people began to drift away, it was afternoon. Kate sought out her mother and Will.

"We're going to walk in the gardens to get some air," she told them. "We're leaving for Oxfordshire in the morning. I just wanted to say goodbye."

They both hugged her.

"Be happy!" her mother said, tears in her eyes. "Be as happy as we have been."

"Oh, I don't doubt that they will be." Will grinned.

ALONE AT LAST, Kate and Francis walked arm in arm along the river path overlooking the Thames. Ahead of them, they could see the myriad spires of London.

"I will be glad to get down to the country, even if it's only for a week," Francis said.

"It's a shame that you have to return to court so soon," Kate fretted. "We must make the most of the time."

He drew her into his arms. "We will, I assure you!" She shivered with anticipation.

"Are you hungry?" he asked her.

"A little. Shall we go into supper in the hall?"

"No. I thought we could find an inn. The Bell isn't far."

"That would be lovely." Kate liked the prospect of getting away from the court. She never felt at ease there, not least because she could encounter the King at any moment. And sharing a meal with Francis, just the two of them, held huge appeal.

They left Whitehall Palace and hastened along King Street to Bell Yard, where the ancient tavern stood. Francis asked for a private room, and the innkeeper showed them to a tiny chamber, hardly bigger than a closet, with a table for two. He brought pewter goblets, a flagon of wine, knives, and napkins, returning soon afterward with steaming plates piled high with buttery roast capon, vegetables, and manchet loaves.

"The food's very good here," Francis said. "They get a lot of business from the court."

It was indeed delicious, as was the wine, which went straight to Kate's head.

"Steady!" Francis chuckled, as she crashed her goblet on the table. "I don't want to have to carry you back!"

The intimate space, his nearness to her, and the starry night outside the tiny window were all having their effect. When he reached for her, pulled her onto his lap, and started to kiss her, slowly and with undisguised intent, she wanted him to go on and on . . .

"I think we should return," he said, releasing her and helping her up. "I'll just pay the bill."

They walked back, his arm around her. Wordlessly, but with warm, meaningful glances, he led her to his lodging, which was sparsely furnished and very neat. The tester bed was made up with clean sheets and a thick counterpane, and looked inviting. Kate stood there, not knowing what to do. She shivered.

"Are you cold?" Francis asked. "We're not supposed to light fires at court after Easter, but I do have some kindling left. Let me light a fire. It will soon warm up." She sat on the bed while he knelt at the hearth. Then, as the flames began to take, he poured them more wine and joined her on the bed. Soon, their goblets were empty, the room was warm, and he turned to her and took her in his arms again, kissing her heartily.

"There is nothing to fear, sweetheart," he murmured. She wondered if he had done this before. She felt a tingling in her loins, the beginnings of excitement, and gave herself up to his caresses. When he began unlacing her gown, fumbling with hasty fingers, she did not resist. Before long, they were both naked—and, to her amazement, there was no shame, only wonder. Then they were lying together, limbs entwined, and she knew what it was to have a man inside her, to feel a short hiatus of pain followed by that sweet surge of pleasure. And it seemed to her, yet again, that God had smiled down on their marriage and blessed it.

. . .

IN THE MORNING, she woke to find Francis smiling at her, eager to make her his again. Now he was more adventurous, moving her into different positions and kissing her all over. "My beautiful wife!" he breathed. "You are a pearl, a pure mirror of womanhood. I love you so much. You will be my strength and my stay, I know it."

She had never known such joy, such pleasure, and it all came so naturally. She knew now why the poets wrote of love and why men and women did mad things in the pursuit of it. Had she thought herself happy before now? She had not known what bliss awaited.

They could not tarry in bed for too long, much as they desired to, because they had to be on their way. They had a two-day ride ahead of them and needed to make Windsor by nightfall. Dragging themselves away from each other, they hurriedly dressed. Kate took great pride in binding up her hair, as was expected of a married woman, and putting on a new French hood. From now on, she must cover her hair daily.

Francis went off to bid farewell to the King, while Kate sought the Queen.

"May God go with you," Anna said, squeezing her hands. Kate felt a pang of concern for her, for Mary Norris had confided to her that Katheryn Howard was the King's latest amorous interest, which explained why she was so rarely at court these days. Kate could understand why the King was after her, but why she would want him . . . Well, he was the King, and she was a Howard, and Anne Boleyn had had Howard blood. Was that Katheryn's game? And did the King know what kind of life she had led? More to the point, at this moment, was whether Queen Anna suspected that Katheryn might prove a threat to her future as queen.

"Thank you, Madam," Kate replied, trying not to betray her thoughts. "And thank you for being so kind to me."

Anna bent forward and kissed her, then Kate dipped a curtsey and hurried away to find Francis at the stables. He was smiling.

"There you are, darling. I have good news. The King told me that, when Parliament next meets, he will confirm our title to the manor of Rotherfield Greys."

"That is good news," she said, happy to see him so buoyant.

Once their baggage was loaded onto packhorses, they mounted their steeds and rode west. On the journey, Francis told her more about Greys Court.

"The manor house was built about two hundred years ago, but there was a castle there before," he said, giving her a loving, intimate glance, showing her that he too was thinking about the night they had just shared. "Before us, Greys Court had been owned by the Lovell family, but the last Lord Lovell fought for King Richard at Bosworth and then disappeared, so it was seized by the Crown. The King granted it to my father for an annual rental of a red rose, which is paid every Midsummer Day. It's near Henley, which is a nice town."

"What happened to Lovell?"

"No one knows."

They trotted on, leaving London behind them, and then broke into a canter as the countryside opened up before them.

"Oh, it's so good to be going home with you, my darling!" Francis cried.

KATE THOUGHT THE rolling Chiltern Hills beautiful. And when she saw Greys Court nestling among them, she drew in her breath, for it was a beautiful place, set in downland filled with trees.

About twenty servants were lined up, ready to greet them. Francis's steward, Bilkins, signaled to the men to take care of the horses and unload the luggage. Kate smiled at everyone, aware that they were going to play a large part in her life, and that she would need to rely on them at first, so it was wise to be friendly toward them.

Francis proudly showed her around the property. "That tower there is all that remains of the castle. You can still climb it and get a good view of the gardens and the deer park. The well is just as old, but take care, for it is two hundred feet deep."

On the opposite side of the broad paved courtyard stood a substantial fortified timber-framed house with a jettied upper story, a crenellated parapet, and octagonal towers at each corner. "That is

Greys Court, where we will be living," Francis told Kate. "The Lovells extended it about ninety years ago."

He held open the arched front door and Kate walked into a lofty beamed hall with three tall bay windows, a large fireplace, and trestle tables set up on either side. Above the dais was a big wooden panel painted with the Knollys arms: a white chevron with three red roses on a red ground.

"That is not unlike my coat of arms," Kate said. "I have a black bend sinister with three white roses on a white ground."

"We must have a new coat painted with our joint arms," Francis said, drawing her to him and kissing her.

At one end of the hall, a flight of stairs rose to a minstrels' gallery, which led to a spacious chamber.

"We call this the solar," he told her. "It will be our private chamber. And here is our bedchamber." He opened an inner door to reveal an ornately carved four-poster bed with embroidered white hangings and a crimson velvet counterpane. The curtains at the mullioned window matched the hangings. With its polished oak chests and shining pewter, it was a charming room.

"You can stow your clothes in that chest," Francis said. "And there are pegs on the wall. I hope you like it."

"I love it!" Kate enthused, and flung her arms around him.

"I would make good use of it right now," he muttered, his eyes twinkling into hers, "but the servants will soon be here with our gear. I fear we'll just have to contain ourselves until tonight." His words gave her a deep thrill.

They broke apart and went down the stairs. There was a door at the far end of the hall. "The kitchen and other offices are through there," Francis said. He led Kate through, into the bustle of activity that was the large kitchen; it was hot in there, for a fire was crackling in a vast brick fireplace. Everyone stopped what they were doing and bowed or curtseyed. Now, Kate thought, was the time to establish herself as mistress; she was remembering Grandmother, Lady Bryan, and Lady Troy, and she was determined not to let Lettice Lee down, for she was sure that Lettice had ruled this house well.

She took a deep breath. "It is a pleasure to meet you all. I look forward to getting to know you better, and I hope you will find me an approachable and kind mistress. Now, do not let us interrupt your work. My lord here is just showing me around the house, and I'm sure you have much to do. Thank you all." She smiled at them and was met with smiles in return as they resumed their duties. Then she dimpled at Francis, aware that this was the first time that she had called him "my lord," and saw he was beaming at her. He wasn't a lord, of course, but he was her lord, and she was proud to call him so.

When he had shown her the steward's room, the larders, the boiling house, the buttery, and the pantry, they went outside again and walked beyond the tower to the gardens.

"This area was once the lower courtyard," Francis explained. "The upper courtyard—which we call the Base Court—was created when the house was built." Looking about her, Kate saw several buildings in various states of ruin. "The Lovells let this place rot. My father was going to attempt some restoration, but he died before he could start. It would take a lot of work to put all this range to rights."

"Do you need all these buildings?"

"No. We have everything we need around and behind the Base Court."

"Then I would leave them be. They look mysterious and rather charming."

He smiled at her. "I think you have it there. And leaving them would relieve me of a great burden."

As they returned to the house, Kate asked what was in the turrets.

"Guest chambers, the old nursery, lumber rooms. Over there are the gardens and the fishponds." Francis turned and steered her back toward the stables. "Come, let us ride into the village. I want to show you the church."

It wasn't far to Rotherfield Greys. The village was a cluster of cottages with an inn and the church in their midst. In the cool of the church, Francis showed Kate the tombs of his ancestors. There were Greys and Lovells there, too, previous owners of Greys Court over the centuries. Kate knelt beside him for a few moments of quiet prayer, and was touched to see him so deeply in communion with his Maker, whereas she was too distracted by his nearness. He seemed so devout; she hoped he'd realized he needed to put aside all that dangerous nonsense about Luther's heresies.

When they arrived back at Greys Court, a substantial supper awaited them. They took their seats at the table on the dais, while the household seated themselves at the trestle tables. Kate noted with approval the thick linen tablecloths and napkins, the polished silver and pewter, and admired the salt cellar in the shape of a ship.

"We do things the old-fashioned way here," Francis told her as he rose to carve the roast beef. "We eat in the hall, with our people. But if you would prefer sometimes to dine privately in the solar, pray give the order."

"I will do whatever pleases you, my lord," Kate said. He smiled at her and placed three slices of meat on her plate. She poured some sauce on them and took a mouthful. "That is delicious!" she called across to Matthews, the cook, who bowed his head, blushing.

She spent the meal talking to Bilkins, who would be her right-hand man when Francis wasn't here, and learning more about how the household was run.

"I will take you around tomorrow, Madam, if it pleases you, and show you where everything is. You have no need to worry. The staff are very efficient."

"Nevertheless, I would like to understand how everything is done. And I want all the servants to know that if they have any concerns, they can come to me."

Bilkins's expression suggested that he was asking himself what an ignorant sixteen-year-old girl could know about running a great house. "That is most kind of you, Madam. But I usually deal with any worries the servants have."

"But I would like them to know that they can come to me, too," she said firmly, resolved to assert herself. "Especially the women. There may be matters they do not wish to discuss with a man."

He nodded slowly. "As you wish, Madam." She sensed that she had offended him in trespassing on his territory. But this was her house now; she felt it keenly. It had opened up to her and invited her in, and she had every right to be here and impose her will on it. The only person who could gainsay her was Francis.

And he, perhaps having heard the conversation, although he had seemed to be talking with his huntsman on his other side, turned to them. "You will find my wife wise and capable beyond her years," he told Bilkins. "I am sure that she will be a great help to you." He squeezed her hand beneath the table.

"Of course, Sir," Bilkins said, quelled. Kate smiled at him.

More dishes were served, then jellies and custard. She sat there, dizzy from the strong wine she had drunk, longing to be in bed with Francis so that they could revel in that special joy again. When he caught her yawning, he squeezed her hand again and stood up. "My masters, it grows late and we will retire, for it has been a long day. Madam?"

He held out his hand and Kate gratefully took it; then he led her up to the solar, as the servants began to clear the tables.

A FIRE WAS burning on the hearth in their bedchamber. Hot bricks wrapped in flannel had been placed in the bed, and an ewer of water stood next to a basin on a small table. Kate's night-rail and Francis's nightshirt had been laid out on the bed.

"We don't need those," he said, sweeping them to the floor, and when she went to pick them up to fold them neatly, he caught her in his arms and drew her down on the counterpane, laughing, his hand snaking up her leg. "I just want you as Dame Nature made you," he told her. And then they were pulling each other's clothes off, and Kate found that she no longer cared about folding anything.

Afterward, they climbed between the sheets and lay facing for a long while, holding each other tightly. "I will always love you," Francis whispered. "Oh, my loving wife! I feel so blessed."

"And I do, too," she murmured, caressing his shoulder and then his cheek. "I never knew that marriage could be so joyous."

"And we have all our lives to enjoy each other. I do not think I have ever been so happy. The good Lord has been bountiful to us." He kissed her gently, and then more insistently. "Again!" he said, giving himself up to her once more.

. . .

THEY HAD A few wonderful days together. They rode in the deer park and farther afield; they lay in the woods and made love; they walked in the gardens and made plans for improvements; and they spent quiet, harmonious time in their chamber. Kate would play for Francis, and sometimes they sang together, although she had to admit that he couldn't sing, as he had warned her. They rode to church together to attend Mass, there being no chapel in the house. And then there were the nights, the precious nights, when the hours flew past because they were so engrossed in each other. It was the most glorious of honeymoons.

Yet through it all, Kate was painfully conscious that their time together was running out. She could not help counting the days down. *We have five days, four days, three days, two days . . . Now we have just one day before Francis has to go back to court.* Oh, if only he could stay with her and they could run the estate together . . . But no. He had a strong sense of duty, and the court was his best way to future prosperity and advancement. She had to let him go.

She wondered anxiously how she would fare when he had gone and she alone was in charge of the household. She had dutifully taken the tour with Bilkins, determined to learn all she could about how Greys Court was run, yet she had sensed his resentment at having to defer to someone so young, female, and inexperienced. While Francis was here, he knew his place, but how would he behave toward her after her husband had left? Would the other servants follow his lead? She prayed not, for she had made great efforts to be kind to them, aware nevertheless that there were marks she should not overstep. A distance, as Lady Bryan had once explained, had to be maintained. Your servants were not your friends.

And yet Kate had seen with her own eyes King Henry playing at dice with his Master of the Cellar. He had not concerned himself with keeping a distance, but then, she supposed, he was the sovereign and could honor whom he pleased. So dare she try to make a friend of Thomasina, the diminutive fair maid who acted as her tirewoman, helping her to dress, plaiting her hair, and looking after her clothes? Yes, of course she could, and why not? She was the mistress here. They were much of an age, and there was no one else with whom she could be friends. Most of the servants were male, and the plump old woman who did the laundry was quite shy with her.

"Francis," she asked, on their last evening together, "I need your advice." They were sitting in the solar, having brought up with them a flagon of wine to share. "Would it be appropriate for me to make a friend of Thomasina?"

"I don't see why not," he said, "as long as you don't make a favorite of her or allow her undue influence, which may cause jealousy among the other servants."

"I won't," she said, relieved. "It's just that I know I will be lonely when . . ." She could not stop the tears falling, and in an instant he was on his knees before her, grasping her hands.

"Don't cry, darling. I don't want to leave you—it's hard for me, too. But I have no choice. I promise, I will get home whenever I can, and write often."

"I will write to you, too," she wept, hugging him as if she could never let him go. "And you must send me news of the court." She drew back and managed a smile.

"I will regale you," he said, and kissed her.

THE PARTING WAS difficult, but she did as a loving wife should, standing by the mounting block in the courtyard with the stirrup cup, the entire household drawn up behind her, as Francis mounted his horse.

"God speed you, my lord," she said, willing back the tears and handing him the cup.

"May He watch over you, my dear wife," he replied, downing the wine. Then he wheeled his steed around and trotted away, his baggage cart trundling behind. Kate watched him go until she could see him no more. She reminded herself that he was not going very far away, and that she had things to do.

She turned to the servants, looking at Bilkins as she spoke. "Today, I intend to make an inspection of the house. You need not be troubled, as I will do this by myself and decide if I want to make any changes. Thank you. You may return to your duties."

Bilkins looked as if he was about to say something, but evidently thought better of it. She walked past him and into the hall. She would start in the bedchamber.

She spent the day tidying cupboards and chests, rearranging ornaments, and familiarizing herself with the house. Handling Francis's things made her feel closer to him. She trusted he would be pleased with the small improvements she had made. At least she was now becoming well acquainted with Greys Court.

At dinner, she sat in solitary splendor at the table on the dais and ate roast chicken in a rich sauce. It was very good, and she again sent her compliments to the cook before she escaped back upstairs. Late in the afternoon, her work done, she took off her apron and walked in the gardens, then down to the lower courtyard to take another look at the ruins, which fascinated her. It was easy to imagine them inhabited by ghosts or fairies or even dragons. She decided she would not want to be there after dark.

When she returned to the house, she went to the kitchen and asked if her supper might be served in the solar.

Bilkins frowned. "It's not customary. The master doesn't eat there."

"Well, I would like to." She smiled. "When he is here, we will eat in the hall."

Another little battle won, she reflected, as she went upstairs to wash her hands and drag a small table across to her chair by the hearth. She was missing Francis desperately. When would he be back? She felt so lonely here in this unfamiliar place.

She told herself that she must find something beside the house to keep her occupied. Tonight, after supper, she would play her lute and then go to bed and read the romance she had brought from court. She would find out where she could purchase books around here and buy some more. She would ask the gardener to teach her about herbs, so that she could tend the herb garden and make good use of her still room. And she would set aside a part of each afternoon for writing to Francis. If she kept busy, the time would pass more quickly until his return.

Chapter 15

1540–41

IT WAS THREE LONG MONTHS BEFORE FRANCIS WAS ABLE TO obtain leave. By then, it was July, and Kate had settled into a routine at Greys Court, which was beginning to feel very much like home. She had done her utmost to become involved in the life of the household and to keep her finger on its pulse. She made it her business to know everything that was going on, how the house was provisioned, and how its rhythms worked. She took an interest in the servants, talked to them about their homes, their families, and their problems. She cultivated her budding friendship with Thomasina, who was as attentive as one could wish a maid to be, but never overstepped the invisible line between mistress and servant. She discovered that she could work magic with herbs, and that the scents and cordials she made up, and her suggestions for enhancing receipts, were much appreciated. She took care to ensure that she was never overbearing, stern, or intrusive, but approachable, kind, and fair. Even Bilkins now treated her with grudging respect, and had done so ever since the day when the cook had almost sliced off a finger with the carving knife and Kate had not shrunk from the blood, but sent for the local barber surgeon and, until he came, had herself staunched the flow, while everyone else stood there gaping. Since then, it had become clear that Bilkins had decided to trust her. It made her proud to think that she had proved herself not to be the untried girl he had judged her to be at first. She had, indeed, surprised herself, for she had not known that she had it in her to oversee a great household, or do it so successfully.

And Francis, when he came clattering into the Base Court on a hot day of blazing sunshine, and had embraced her joyfully and led her into the house and upstairs to the solar, was delighted to find everything so neat and gleaming. She was pleased when he saw how the servants, even Bilkins, deferred to her when they sat at supper in the hall. His compliments were music to her ears.

"I have some news that may not surprise you," he said, as they began their meal. "The King has had his marriage to Queen Anna annulled."

"Really?" Kate remembered the King's initial antipathy toward Anna, the gossip about his pursuit of Katheryn Howard, and the fact that there had been no news of the coronation taking place. "On what grounds?"

"Non-consummation." He raised his eyebrows. "Did you know?"

"No. He came to her bed on several occasions and stayed the night."

"You didn't hear the gossip? That he thought himself able to do the act with others, but not with her? And that she had evil smells about her?"

"I didn't hear it. Maybe people thought me too young, being a maid. But she did smell, at first, although I think that someone must have dropped a hint because I never noticed it after she was wed. This must have come as a shock for her." Her anger burned at the way that horror treated his poor wives.

"People are saying that she fainted because she thought she was going to be taken to the Tower and beheaded, like your aunt. But no. The King has been very generous, apparently. He's left her a rich woman."

And she no longer has to endure being married to him. "I expect she is pleased about that."

"I hear that she's taken it very well. She is to be called the King's dearest sister." Francis grinned. "And it seems that his Grace will not be long without a queen. The word is that he will marry Mistress Katheryn Howard. Wagers are being laid as to whether he is sleeping with her."

"I pray he will not marry her, or at least, if he does, that he knows she has led an impure life," Kate said. "You know what store he sets by virtue in a queen. I hope she knows what she's doing."

"She is cousin to Anne Boleyn, so she surely must. Apparently, she's preening! And everybody's fawning on her."

"Well, rather her than me."

Francis laid down his knife and eyed her curiously. "You don't like the King?"

"I must not say so." She looked about her nervously. "Do you?"

"Yes. He has been a good lord to me. And, as you have told me, it seems that you owe your advancement in life to him."

"Do I?"

"Yes. Your being placed in the Lady Elizabeth's household and then with Queen Anna. That's some remarkable show of favor."

"Maybe. But my aunt Anne may have chosen me to serve Elizabeth, and it was probably my uncle of Norfolk who sued for my place with the Queen."

"Neither appointment would have been made without the King's sanction. But tell me, Kate, if Katheryn Howard becomes queen, would you want to go back to court to serve her? I can put in a good word for you."

"Never!" she answered heatedly. "I hate the court, and I don't want to return there. Besides, my life is here now, and I have many duties to perform."

"Very well," Francis said slowly. "But if you were at court, we could see each other more often."

"I know, and I'm tempted, believe me, but I'm not comfortable there. The court is full of menace and backbiting and danger."

Francis took her hand. "I can understand what makes you feel that way, especially in view of what happened to your aunt. I will not press you, and I will try to get home as often as I can."

"Thank you," she said, looking into his eyes and liking what she saw there. Oh, she was a lucky girl to have such a kind husband.

And there was much more to love about him than kindness.

After supper, he raced her upstairs to their bedchamber to celebrate their reunion and tumbled her in the bed until she was breathless and overcome by ecstasy.

The days of his visit passed all too quickly. Then there was another painful parting and Kate's life resumed its humdrum everyday course. She was thankful that Francis wrote frequently to her, and gladly reciprocated, filling her letters with all the trivialities of life at Greys Court, so that he would feel closer to home. It was from him that she learned of the execution of Cromwell, for high treason. She was not surprised. She had thought Cromwell's days numbered when the King divorced Queen Anna, whose marriage he had arranged. But to die so horribly—three strokes of the axe . . . She shuddered as she imagined, too vividly, what that had been like.

In August, Francis informed her that the King had married Katheryn Howard. "She seems very young to be queen, but she has assumed a regal manner, and his Grace can hardly keep his hands off her!" Kate could imagine it. She had heard Katheryn brag often about her many suitors, and it was clear that she knew how to hold a man's interest. But something inside Kate recoiled at the thought of that fat, gross man of nearly fifty in bed with a slip of a girl of nineteen. Yet such an age gap was not uncommon. She knew of several instances where a widower had married a much younger bride in the hope of getting children. She shuddered to think of what that would mean for Katheryn, who would never now know the kind of joy that Kate was experiencing in bed with a virile young husband. She prayed for her, because what must it be like to be wed to a man who had divorced two wives, sent one to the block, and seen another die in childbed? She hoped Katheryn realized what a dangerous path she was treading.

She bristled when Francis wrote that Lady Rochford was one of the ladies chosen to serve the new Queen. The woman was evil and malicious, yet she had done very well for herself since she had ensured that Uncle Rochford had been sent to his death. Kate burned with the injustice of it. She was even more glad now that she had resolved not to return to court. The place was rotten to the core, which was hardly surprising, given the vileness of the King.

But now she had something far more important to think about. When she missed her monthly course in August, hope budded within her. In September, she knew for a certainty that she was with child. Her heart leaped at the thought of presenting Francis with an heir. It would be a boy, she was certain.

He was overjoyed to hear the news. He sent a beautiful letter telling her how clever she was and how much he loved her. He exhorted her to rest and take good care of herself. He had written to his mother to ask if she could recommend a local midwife for when the time came.

Kate wrote to her mother, too, and to Elizabeth, to tell them the joyful news. Mother wrote by return messenger, saying how delighted she was. "Keep safe, my darling daughter," she ended. "You are so precious to me."

Elizabeth's reply was less heartening. "I do hope that you will have a good hour when your baby comes, and that you will not forget your loving cousin." Was there a hint of jealousy in her words? It was so like Elizabeth to be thinking of herself.

When Francis next came home, in October, he handled Kate as gently as if she were made of Venetian glass, and would not enter her.

"But I'm fit and well!" she laughed, pulling him to her in the bed. "I'm not even showing yet."

"No, it would be wrong." She knew him in this mood; he would not be gainsaid. "I will not take any risk. You and our child are precious to me."

He made her lie down in the afternoons, a routine she kept after he had gone back to court. Lettice wrote to say that she knew of a woman in Henley who might be suitable and asked if she herself could come to Greys Court for the birth. Mother, delighted at the prospect of welcoming her first grandchild, was also eager to be there. "It is the custom for a mother to be with her daughter at her confinement. I can be your gossip and keep you diverted."

Kate liked the idea of having them both with her. She did not know much about birthing a child, yet she had heard that it was both painful and dangerous, and was consequently a little fearful.

She wrote back to say yes, please come, and got to work preparing guest rooms in the tower, setting the servants to dusting, airing beds, and washing the windows. Of course, her guests would not be arriving until late January, but she might be too ungainly then to arrange the transformation. Once the rooms were ready, they could be locked up until they were needed.

As the weeks passed and her belly swelled, she continued to feel well and was untroubled by sickness or fatigue, which Lettice had written was normal in the early months. Kate was praying that her robust health augured well for the day when she would be delivered.

AS THE NEW Year of 1541 arrived, and she celebrated quietly with the household of Greys Court, Kate felt lonely and a little anxious. She had been deeply disappointed when Francis could not get leave at Christmas. "I would ask you to court," he had written, "but it would not do for you to be seen here *enceinte.*" She had to smile. He was always so proper, despite being inventive and daring in bed, although he'd usually been shamefaced afterward.

He would get away as soon as he could in the new year, he promised, and was true to his word. When he arrived in a blizzard in early January, he was proud to see Kate's high belly and the nursery she had prepared.

"I've interviewed Mother Ash, who seems very competent and will move in when I take to my chamber in March," she told him over supper in the solar. "She thinks the babe will be born early in April. Our mothers are arriving in March, too. Francis, you will get home for the birth, please? I need you to be here." With the time approaching, she was becoming a little frightened, especially after the priest at the church had urged her to make a will. "Just in case," he had said.

"I will do my very best," Francis promised. "It's easy to catch the King in a good mood these days. He's utterly besotted with the Queen."

"Ah, but is she besotted with him?" Kate countered.

"That's almost treason!" Francis grimaced. "She seems happy. She's always wearing new gowns and jewels, and he indulges her every whim. But there's no sign of her bearing a child."

"I wonder if he can do it."

Francis raised an eyebrow. "There is talk. But who knows? Maybe she has rejuvenated him."

"Ugh." Kate shuddered.

"Why do you hate him so?"

"Because he is cruel and selfish, and because I saw what he did to my aunt. I witnessed it, Francis. How could a man do that to a woman he once loved?"

"Because he believed that she had betrayed him. Twenty-seven peers found her guilty, not to mention the dozens of others who saw the evidence and decided that there was a case to answer."

"And all of them must have known what verdict they were expected to give!" Kate was passionate. "It was hardly a fair trial. I was there! By all that's holy, Francis, tell me you don't believe all the lies about her!"

He shifted uncomfortably in his chair, coloring a little. "I don't want to believe them. No one would want to believe that a woman could do such things."

"She was innocent! I'm telling you. She was foully wronged. Yet no one dare speak in her favor, even you."

"Darling, calm down." He rested his hand on hers across the table. "You should not dwell on such things in your condition. I assure you, if you believe her to have been innocent, then I do, too. I trust your wisdom. But what we think must never be voiced outside these four walls. It is so easy to commit a treasonable offense these days. It's treason even to imagine anything to the detriment of the King, let alone criticize his justice. Be guided by me. I know the court better than you do."

Kate subsided. She just wished that the rest of the world could see King Henry as he really was. But maybe they did. Maybe there were many like her, nurturing their hatred and resentment, but afraid to speak out.

"Do you hear news of Queen Anna these days?" she asked, changing the subject.

"She was at court for the New Year celebrations. She and the King are great friends these days, and she gets on well with Queen Katheryn. The two of them even danced together before the court."

"I liked her. The King made a mistake when he set her aside."

"Well, by all accounts, she's done well for herself."

Kate sighed. "Yes, I heard that she was given Hever Castle. I don't begrudge it to her, for I hated the place, yet it seems strange to have someone else living in my family home."

She reached for the ewer. "More wine?"

Francis nodded. "Thank you. But you should not drink too much, sweetheart."

She made a face. "I do declare, Francis Knollys, that you are like an old mother hen, fussing over a chick!"

"I care for you, Kate. You mean everything to me." His face was serious, intent.

"I know," she capitulated. "And I appreciate it."

She rose and sat on his lap. They stayed there by the fire, arms around each other, lost in contentment.

LATE ON A Sunday afternoon in April, Kate felt the first pangs.

Well, this is bearable, she told herself. *It's nothing!*

The pains continued all evening. Mother Ash prodded around, nodded happily, and said that all was progressing normally. First babies could take a long time. Mother and Lettice agreed. They had taken to each other instantly, united by the common bonds between them, and were both eager to see their grandchild.

But Kate had been upset to see Mother so changed. She had lost flesh and looked more than her forty years. When asked, she said she was well. Kate had not liked to probe further.

Banished to the solar—Mother Ash was mortified at the idea of a man in "her" birthing chamber—Francis kept calling through the door to ask if Kate was all right.

"Of course, Sir. Now go and get some sleep!" was the reply.

Kate did not think she would sleep that night, but she did, and when she awoke in the morning, the pains had subsided, much to her disappointment. She rested all that day, with Mother and Lettice sitting beside the bed, then at suppertime, her womb began to contract again, more strongly this time. By eight o'clock, she did not know what to do with herself, the pangs were so great, and by ten, she was crying out for relief. It was the longest night of her life.

"Hold your breath!" Mother Ash enjoined. "It helps to thrust the infant downward."

"I found that pepper worked," Mother suggested. "Make her sneeze, then the babe will come more quickly. I hate to see her like this."

Kate was thrashing on the bed, almost oblivious to what was being said. They tried pepper, they tried poppy syrup, they continually exhorted her to draw in her breath, and then they heaved her into a groveling position, on all fours. None of it did any good.

In the small hours of the morning, the pains became even fiercer. "I can see the child's head," the midwife announced. "Push now, Madam! Push!"

Kate was beyond heeding her. She was saving her strength for screaming. Every time the agony gripped her, she yelled as loudly as she could, calling upon her mother and Jesus to take the pain away.

"Push!" they cried. "For God's sake, push!"

Somehow, the message got through, and she learned that when she did push, the pain decreased. Galvanized by this knowledge, she pressed her chin hard on her chest and strained with every muscle in her body to expel the child, for at last she remembered that she was birthing her baby.

It was some time before things finally began to happen, and then she felt as if she were being torn asunder as the infant was pulled from her. Exhausted, barely able to move, she waited for the joyous cries of welcome. But there was a brief silence, followed by a burst of activity.

"Let me in! I demand it! I must know what is happening."

Suddenly, Francis was there, standing at the end of the bed, shaking his head.

"What is it?" Kate murmured.

"A boy." But there was no elation in his voice.

"Quick! Quick!" the midwife was saying. "Clear its nose. I'll rub its chest." Kate was on another plane, barely conscious of what was going on. And then she heard, "Yes, yes, he's breathing, he's all right," and a tiny white bundle was thrust on the pillow beside her. She could make out a distinct profile; he had his father's nose.

"Our son," Francis breathed, tears streaming down his face. "My darling, how can I ever thank you sufficiently?"

But Kate was sound asleep.

SHE AWOKE TO bright sunshine streaming through the window. So she was alive. She had survived the birth. And she had borne a son and heir. Pride and relief filled her heart. She tried to raise herself to peer into the cradle by the bed, but felt a sharp knife of pain down below. And here was Mother, lifting the child into her arms.

"Don't try to move too much. You tore during the birth, but only a little. It will heal. The midwife washed you and put on a clean clout and night rail. We're all very proud of you. And he's a gorgeous little boy."

Kate looked down. Her son was a joy to behold, with red down and big blue eyes.

"He looks two months old!" observed Lettice, appearing on the other side of the bed. "All of my newborns resembled wrinkled prunes!"

"He's so tiny," Kate marveled, gazing at him in wonder. "He's a miracle."

She kissed his brow and marked how well swaddled he was. She wanted to call him Francis after his father; he looked like Francis and the name suited him.

Francis himself came to see how she was doing and was delighted to find her propped against the pillows, suckling their son. He bent and kissed her.

"He is to be baptized tomorrow. I would like him to be called Henry in honor of the King, to whom I owe much. Do say that it pleases you, Kate."

It most certainly did not. "I wanted to call him after you," she protested. The last person she wanted to name her precious son for was that monster. How could Francis even think of suggesting it?

"We can save that name for another son, for I have a feeling that we will have many children," he said, beaming. Kate flinched. Had he any idea of what she had just gone through, all thirty-seven hours of it? Trust a man to be so unthinking!

"As you please," she said, her manner offhand.

"It would be politic to call him after the King," he said firmly.

"And I said, as you please." She lowered her eyes to the babe, feeding peacefully, and decided that she should be content with her husband's choice of name because it was, after all, her brother's. In her mind, she would be naming her son for Harry—never for the King. And she would call him Hal.

"Very well. And Kate, I trust you will not suckle him for long."

She was shocked. "Why? It is the most natural thing."

Francis looked awkward. "Ladies of rank do not feed their children. They engage wet nurses, so as to be able to . . . er, conceive again. Ask your mother, and mine. They are both concerned."

Kate felt her temper rising. "Conceive again? For heaven's sake, Francis! I have given you a son, at some cost to myself. Now let me have a rest before I think of childbearing again. I want to feed our son myself."

Francis frowned. "It is not done, Kate. My mother has already let it be known that we are in need of a wet nurse and I hope to engage one soon. As soon as I do, you will let her take up her duty, and you will remember yours to me."

She gaped at him. He had never before spoken sternly to her. But then she remembered that he liked tradition and upheld the ways in which things had long been done in his family. Yet she had little Henry's well-being to fight for. She had lost one battle, and she was not about to lose another.

"No," she declared. "You know me for a dutiful wife, but I also have a duty to my son, and his mother's milk is surely best for him."

"Your duty is to provide me with sons and to help ensure that they are well raised, well educated, and well married. You are not a milch-cow! I will brook no further argument. A wet nurse will be engaged."

He turned and walked to the door. "I will send your mother in. I hope that she will talk some sense into you." Then the door shut behind him, startling the babe, who whimpered and then latched onto the nipple again.

Mother appeared, looking vexed. "What's this nonsense I hear, Kate?"

"I want to feed my son!" Kate answered fiercely.

"Well, it's just not done by women of our rank. And if it was, you might not conceive another child while you are doing it. So put that notion out of your mind. You are not some peasant girl—you have noble and royal blood in you."

"Oh, yes, King Edward I's! I was told it enough when I was a child. But the blood's a bit diluted now, since he lived centuries ago."

"Kate! Don't denigrate your lineage; it's a fine one. And don't think you can win this battle. Your husband is determined, and he is right. I strongly advise you to remember your vow of obedience and be compliant as a wife should."

Kate nuzzled her baby's head sadly. She had hoped for more support from her mother, and she knew she would get none from Lettice.

"Very well," she said, feeling as if she had lost something precious. Yet she did not want to fall out with Francis, whom she had come to love deeply in the year they had been married. It was, she supposed, a wife's part to compromise and make sacrifices.

CIRCUMSTANCES, IT SEEMED, were on her side. Two weeks later, Mother had gone home and Lettice had still not found a wet nurse. It seemed that there was not a single woman for miles who had borne a child and was able to share her milk. So Kate had her way and continued contentedly to suckle her son. And he thrived. Her Hal became a happy, beautiful baby, forward in his milestones and not shy to go to anyone who held out their arms. Her love for him was profound and fierce. It was a different love from that which she felt for her husband, which had recovered from the distressing hiatus it had suffered after Hal's birth. When Francis had seen that she was willing to obey him, he was pleased to put her small rebellion down to her deranged womb, and showed himself as loving as ever. So she forgave him; she could not be angry with him for long.

After four months, a wet nurse was found, but when she handed over her son, Kate felt that she had at least given him a good start in life. Mrs. Clements was kind and respectful, and plainly besotted with her charge. She was good with the nursery maids and the rockers, too, and she got on well with Mrs. Wellgood, the efficient new nurse who ran the nursery. Lettice, satisfied that all was well, said her farewells and departed. Francis was pleased that everything was as it should be, and claimed Kate again as his own as soon as he got leave from the court. Once more, she knew that glorious joy of coming together. Giving birth had not diminished it. In fact, after the long abstinence, she became a more avid lover.

The months passed peacefully. Summer gave way to autumn, and the tranquil routine of the household ticked over smoothly. Hal was smiling, he could turn over, he was sitting up, banging his silver rattle on the table. Every milestone brought fresh delights. Kate had not known she could feel so much love for a child.

She wrote as often as she could to Elizabeth, still feeling that she had somehow let the child down in forsaking her (as Elizabeth saw it) for Francis. She was delighted when Elizabeth wrote back in her beautiful italic hand. It was a chatty letter, witty and erudite for an eight-year-old, and Kate had the feeling that she had been forgiven. She sent a reply, and soon more letters were winging their way between Oxfordshire and Hertfordshire weekly. Kate thought she might visit Elizabeth. Hatfield was not so far away, and she could leave Hal for a few nights, even though it would cause her a pang.

Then, in November, Francis returned with news from court.

"The Queen has been arrested!" he told Kate, as soon as he had kissed her and admired their son, and they were alone in the solar. "She is under house arrest at Hampton Court."

"No!" she cried. History could not be repeating itself. "Why?"

"For misconduct before her marriage and adultery after."

Kate took a moment to digest this. "I can believe the bit about misconduct before, because she was always flirting with young men, and I often wondered if she was sleeping with Tom Culpeper, as she greatly favored him. But adultery? Would she have been so foolish, especially considering what happened to her own cousin, my late aunt? Do you believe it?"

Francis shook his head. "Truly, I don't know what to believe. But the King believes it. He is a broken man. If you could see him, you would pity him, for this trouble has aged him. He had just commanded the whole realm to give thanks for his happiness with the Queen, whom he plainly adored—and then he found out that she was not the pure rose he had believed her to be. He has shut himself away and will not see anyone. That's why the Lord Chamberlain gave me leave."

Kate was kneading her hands in distress. "Pity him? As he pitied my aunt? Oh, yes, we were told that, rather than have her burned, he very kindly decreed that she would be beheaded, *out of pity*! And now it seems he will do the same to yet another wife, and a young one at that. Katheryn is only twenty! It's her I pity, being married to that horrible old man—"

"Kate, stop!" Francis held up his hand. "I must not hear this. I have sworn an oath to be loyal to him. What you are speaking is treason."

"But I feel for her. She must be terrified."

"Yet she has grievously offended her lord and sovereign. If she has committed adultery, then she has also committed treason, because were she to bear her lover a child and pass it off as the King's, the succession would be impugned. It is a very serious matter."

"But *did* she commit adultery? And with whom?"

"Culpeper has been arrested, too, and her secretary, Francis Dereham."

"I have heard her mention him. I think they were sweethearts before she came to court. And before the King began to take an interest in her, which was after I left court, she was talking of marrying Culpeper. There was something going on there, definitely. But I find it hard to believe that she would have gone so far as to commit adultery with either of them—and she cannot die for what she did before her marriage."

Francis sighed, leaning forward to warm his hands by the fire. "That's true. But you're right about Dereham. They were lovers before she came to court. She took him into her service earlier this year, which now looks suspicious in itself, and he began bragging of what had passed between them when she was younger. Will Stafford heard him; he's been questioned by the Council. He told them he knew for a fact that they had fornicated together and that if he had been Dereham, he would never have said anything, lest he died for it, but that he himself felt he must reveal it, for the knowledge had stuck in his craw. And, of course, he was bound by his oath of allegiance to the King to testify to what he knew. He felt it was his moral duty."

Yes, that sounded like Will. He would do his duty, even though it was distasteful to him.

"But there is more to this than that," Francis said, lowering his voice. "Kate, what I am going to tell you must remain absolutely secret between us."

She wondered what was coming and felt a creeping dread.

Francis rose and came to kneel by her chair, murmuring in her ear. "You know that I am all for reform of the Church, and that Will is, too. The Howards are Catholic reactionaries—they would bring back the Pope if they could. The reformists at court, and on the King's Council, have now united to bring them down. They are driving this case against the Queen, and the King is letting them do it. Some hold views that would be seen as heretical. Will and I are with them. We are hoping that, with the Howards' influence removed, the King will come to look more kindly on the new religion. After all, he has already broken with Rome, dissolved the monasteries, and pushed forward radical policies—and all in the interests of purifying the Church in England. Why should he not go further?"

Kate heard him out in mounting panic. She had hoped that his flirtation with heresy had been disposed of some time ago, but now, hearing him more or less confirm that he had embraced the

Protestant doctrines of Martin Luther, she began to tremble for him.

"Francis, it is dangerous to hold such views!" she breathed, clutching his hand. "You could go to the stake for them. By the Mass, I do fear for you, and I beg again you not to speak of your beliefs to anyone." She was crying now, terrified in case it was already too late, and others knew his secret. She could not bear to think of the man she loved, and the body she had come to worship, being consumed in the agony of the flames.

He kissed her reassuringly. "Only Will knows my views, and we spoke of the matter while out hunting in the park at Hampton. There was no one in sight, I promise you."

She exhaled in relief. "Promise me that you will never betray yourself."

"I give you my word: I would do nothing to hurt you and Hal."

They held each other tightly for a few moments. Kate was still trembling with nerves, and still not satisfied.

"Then you are both working to bring down the Queen?" she taxed him.

"No. Will but did his duty. I have said nothing against her. But I cannot deny that I would like to see her overthrown, although not in the way your aunt was."

"Then I pray that you will do nothing against her. Whatever she has done, she is young and foolish, and she does not deserve to die for it."

Francis said nothing.

TWO DAYS LATER, a letter from Will arrived, informing Francis that Kate's unspeakable aunt, Lady Rochford, had been acting as a go-between for the Queen and Culpeper. "She is now in the Tower," Will wrote, "and gossip has it that she has lost her wits."

Kate could feel little pity for her, remembering the false witness she had borne against her own husband and Queen Anne, accusing them of the vilest of crimes and branding their names with an enduring slur. And where Katheryn was young and stupid, Lady

Rochford was a woman of the world and, of all people, should have known better than to abet what she must have known was treason.

December came in under a cloud of gloom. Francis had returned to court and reported that the Howards had spectacularly fallen. The Tower was crammed with them to the bursting point. This did not augur well for the little Queen, but the reformists were gleeful, it seemed. Kate, sitting in the garden and bouncing a gurgling Hal up and down on her knee, was glad to be away from the court. It was a vicious place.

Chapter 16

1541–42

FRANCIS COULD NOT GET HOME FOR CHRISTMAS, SO LETTICE came to visit. Her lively company compensated a little for not having him there to enjoy Hal's first Yuletide, and evidently he too was miserable, for the court was gloomy, with the King making no effort to join in the half-hearted revels staged by his courtiers. "He looks sad and has no inclination to feast with the ladies," Francis reported. "He is putting on more weight and looks very old and gray. We can only hope that his mood will lighten in time. As yet, no one knows what is to become of the Queen, who has been sent to Syon Abbey."

Kate wondered how she would fare there, that bright little butterfly of a girl. What must it be like, waiting daily to learn if you were doomed or not? It must be unbearable.

Her thoughts were much with Elizabeth, who was surely aware of what was going on, and who must feel even more disturbed by it than Kate did. Hopefully, Kat and Lady Troy were diverting her with Christmas pastimes and treats, and Kate would visit her when the weather was more settled, she promised herself.

. . .

FRANCIS RETURNED TO Greys Court late in January. He kissed Kate as warmly as ever and swung Hal high in the air, marveling how he had grown, yet he seemed distracted.

"It's this business of the Queen," he said, as Kate helped him off with his boots. "Parliament is going to proceed against her with a Bill of Attainder."

"What is that?" Kate asked.

"It means that they will look at all the evidence and, if they are satisfied that she is guilty, they will pass an Act of Attainder depriving her of her life and property."

"What, without a trial?" Kate was horrified. "Surely she will be given a chance to defend herself?"

"No. There will be no trial." Francis stretched his feet out toward the hearth. "Alas, I fear it will go ill for her. The reformist lords on the Council seem bent on destroying her."

"No, they could not be so cruel!"

"We shall see. I cannot support them in this. But I don't hold out much hope for her."

WHEN FRANCIS HAD returned to court at the beginning of February, Kate decided to brave the weather and go to Hatfield. Wrapped up warmly in a fur-lined cloak, she climbed into her litter, which was plumped with cushions and hot bricks folded in flannel, and waved goodbye to Hal, who was gazing solemnly at her from the arms of Mistress Wellgood. *Please don't cry,* Kate prayed inwardly. *If you cry, I will not be able to go.* But Hal didn't. He suddenly waved back. The litter trundled away.

Elizabeth was ecstatic when Kate arrived. "Oh, I am so pleased to see you, Cousin!" she cried, dancing across the courtyard.

"She's been watching out for you all day," Kat said, disengaging the girl's fingers and embracing Kate herself.

"Well, I am pleased to see you both, and you, Lady Troy," Kate said, as the older woman came hurrying over.

Supper was waiting for them in the parlor: a rich, steaming dish of beef, fluffy dumplings, crusty bread, and a flagon of ale.

They spoke of the weather, of Elizabeth's remarkable progress at her lessons, of Hal's sweet antics, and of domestic matters. The Queen was not mentioned. Elizabeth was cheerful. After the meal, she raced away to fetch her lute, so that she could play a song she had learned for Kate.

As soon as she was gone, Kate turned to the other ladies. "Does she know? About the Queen, I mean."

"Yes, she does," Lady Troy said heavily.

"I sat her down and told her," added Kat. "And of course I had to explain certain delicate things to her, things I would rather have told her about when she was older. She took it quite well, considering, and she asked if the Queen would be executed. I had to say that I did not know. God knows how she will take it if that happens."

"We will meet that when we come to it," Lady Troy said. "Thank Heaven you are here, Kate. It will be a welcome distraction."

"I'm glad I came," Kate told them. "I was only planning to stay for a couple of days because this is the first time I've been apart from Hal, but I'm sure he will do well enough without me, so I could stay a little longer, if that would help."

"Oh, it would, if you don't mind!" Lady Troy was visibly relieved. "We all feel as if a storm is threatening."

"Then I will send word to Greys Court tonight," Kate promised. "But first, I think the Lady Elizabeth is coming back. We must listen to her playing."

LATER THAT EVENING, Kate sat at Elizabeth's bedside, relating the story of Rumpelstiltskin, an old favorite of hers. When she had finished, she expected the child to ask for another tale to put off the evil moment when she must go to sleep, but instead she gave Kate a searching look.

"I know about the Queen," she said. "Kat told me. She said she was in disgrace because she behaved very wickedly. She was unfaithful to my father with two gentlemen." She frowned. "She told me what being unfaithful meant, that a man puts his crest in a woman, but he's only supposed to do it when he's married, and it's wrong to do it to a lady who isn't his wife. Is that really true—I mean, that he puts the crest in?"

Kate was blushing. "Yes, sweeting. It's what married people do. And it's wrong to do it with anyone else."

"It sounds horrid," Elizabeth pronounced. "I wouldn't do it, even if I was married!"

Kate tried not to smile, despite the seriousness of the moment. "We must remember that nothing has been proved against the Queen. She may be innocent."

"But if she isn't, they might cut off her head." Elizabeth looked distressed. "Like they did to my mother."

"I hope not," Kate soothed. "We must pray for her daily. Now, shall we have another story?"

THE NEXT FEW days were tense and anxious. Elizabeth was restless and on edge. Every time she heard a horseman approaching the house, she ran to the window.

"I don't want it to be a royal messenger," she said.

"Does she know about the Bill of Attainder?" Kate whispered to Kat.

"No. Only that the Queen is under house arrest. I am praying that it won't be bad news."

Kate turned away. She was almost certain that it would be.

THE MESSENGER ARRIVED late one evening when Elizabeth was fast asleep. Lady Troy left the parlor to receive him and returned with a grave face. There was no need to ask her what news he had brought.

Kate hurried away to bed, seized with grief for the vital young woman who had been cruelly slaughtered, and white-hot anger against the devil who had sanctioned it. She had little sympathy to spare for Lady Rochford, who had suffered on the same scaffold, yet still she found what had been done to her appalling. The dread tidings had revived terrible memories of the events of 1536, and she could imagine only too well what had happened in the Tower. She could not sleep for thinking of the blade descending on that pretty neck, severing life—and the blood gushing. She still could not get that horrific image out of her head. And now, thanks to that unspeakable monster, she was being forced to relive the most terrible days of her life. She wished he were dead. Beheading would be too good for him.

In the morning, tired and drawn, she went to the schoolroom, where Elizabeth was seated at a table by the fire, doing writing exercises, her quill pen scratching across the paper. Kat was seated at her desk, writing. They both looked up and greeted her but seemed subdued. Kate wondered if Kat had broken the news to Elizabeth. She caught her eye, and Kat gave an almost imperceptible shake of her head.

Kate hesitated, then took a deep breath.

"I fear I must give you some grave news, Elizabeth," she said.

Elizabeth looked up. Her pointed little face was questioning, apprehensive.

"The Queen was beheaded yesterday morning," Kate said quietly. "She had been found guilty of treason by Parliament."

Elizabeth shuddered, then stood up suddenly, covered her mouth with her hands and fled to the privy in the corner, where Kate could hear her retching. Kat ran in after her.

"Hush, hinny," she soothed, holding her tightly and steering her back into the schoolroom. Elizabeth tried to push her away, but then fell on Kat's shoulder, howling. And as she held the sobbing, shaking child, Kat too broke down and wept. Kate just stood there, numb. Had that butcher not given any thought to how this awful news might affect his daughter? How could he do this to her? Was it not his part to protect her? Anger flared again and she balled her fists, wishing she could give him a piece of her mind.

In the days that followed, they sought to divert Elizabeth from morbid thoughts of death with merry stories, games of hide-and-seek, and even a snowball fight when the snow came. They toasted muffins by the fire, played skittles in the gallery, and sang songs, with Elizabeth picking out the tunes on her lute or her virginals. But they were not entirely successful. One day, when Kat had finished reading a story that ended with a beautiful princess marrying a handsome prince, the child stood up and declared, "I'm never going to get married!"

"Nonsense!" Kat said. "Of course you will."

"I will *never*!" Elizabeth insisted.

"We'll see about that when you get older." Kat smiled.

SOON AFTER HER return to Greys Court, Kate realized that she was with child again. It was too soon, she felt, but it was inevitably a woman's lot. Francis was thrilled, though, at the prospect of an addition to their family.

"Children give one power and status," he said to Kate when next he visited. "Hal will continue our line and help our fortunes to prosper. I hope for more sons, and daughters to seal alliances between families, which extend one's influence. I am pleased to see you looking so well again."

"I feel well," Kate said, thinking that all *she* wanted was to get this one born safely. "I only hope that the birth won't be as difficult as last time, but Mother Ash said that was unlikely. I will engage her again."

As the child grew within her womb, she passed the placid months overseeing the running of the household, interesting herself in estate matters, becoming involved in the life of the local community, and getting to know the families in the village. Before she got too big to walk far, she often strolled along the country lanes with a basket of baked bread and meats, covered with a linen cloth, and some homemade cordial and jellies. She took with her only her maid Thomasina and one of the grooms. It touched her to see the faces of the old and the bedridden light up when she appeared. She would sit with them for a while, listen to their stories, and ask if they needed anything. Sometimes she took Hal to see them. He was toddling now and a terrible chatterbox, but the elderly ladies loved him.

She was aware of Thomasina watching her with admiring eyes. The girl came from a poor but respectable family in Rotherfield

Greys, and knew what it meant to her fellow villagers to be the recipients of small kindnesses from the lady of the manor.

"I never thought to find a place so agreeable to me," she told Kate as they walked back to Greys Court one afternoon.

Kate looked at the earnest little face with its doelike brown eyes and merry lips.

"I never thought to have such an agreeable maid." She smiled.

KATE WROTE TO her mother and Lettice, asking if they would come and be her gossips once more at the forthcoming birth. Mother replied that she hoped to be there, but Lettice had hurt her foot and could not travel. "I am deeply disappointed not to be able to come to you, but you will be in my prayers," she wrote.

Francis had been elected Member of Parliament for Horsham, so he was dividing his time between the court, Sussex, and Westminster, which meant that he could not often snatch time to get home. He was absent when Kate went into labor in late October. This time, it was an easy travail. She woke early in the morning with what she thought to be indigestion. It was only when she got up to use the privy that she realized that the pains of an upset stomach would not be coming every few minutes—and really, she should have known better, for by Mother Ash's reckoning, she was well overdue.

She sent a panicking Thomasina for the midwife, who came hurrying up the stairs and performed a quick examination. "You're ready to push, Madam!" she declared.

It was not like the last time. Fully aware on this occasion, Kate was able to push her baby into the world quite easily. Soon, she was holding her daughter in her arms. She called her Mary, after her mother. Francis had already agreed.

Mother had been unable to come to Oxfordshire for the birth after all. She had been indisposed with what she said in her letter was colic and could not travel. Kate hoped that she was all right. Being newly delivered, and with a babe and an unruly boy to look after, she could not get down to Kent, much as she would have liked to. So she had to content herself with letters. She wrote regularly to Elizabeth, too, and was glad to hear that her cousin was excelling at her studies. Elizabeth was full of her achievements—she was never one for hiding her light beneath a bushel. It was nice to hear her speak highly of Will, whom she had seen on her visits to court. Kate hoped that one day, Elizabeth would get to meet Mother, the aunt who had been banished from her life. She knew she could trust Will to bring that about, if it were humanly possible.

KATE WAS UP and about again, and little Mary—the sweetest babe anyone could wish for—was thriving in the care of Mrs. Clements and Mrs. Wellgood, when Francis paid a fleeting visit.

Swooping the babe up in his arms, he gave her his blessing and kissed her. "Such a pretty little maid!" he exclaimed. "She'll be breaking a few hearts one day, you'll see." He smiled at Kate over the baby's head, then leaned forward and kissed her. "You have done me proud, my dearest." Hal was capering around his father, demanding his attention. Francis passed Mary to Kate and swung him in the air. "Hello, little man! Have you been a good boy?"

"I'm the best boy!" Hal shouted, squealing with glee.

Kate made a face. "He's a devil!"

Francis laughed. "He's a boy! What did you expect?"

Later, as they lingered over the supper table in the solar, an ewer of wine and a platter of comfits between them, Francis looked a little awkward.

"I wanted to talk to you about Christmas," he said. "His Grace is in much better spirits these days and seems no longer to be grieving for the loss of the Queen. He has said that the court will be merry again at Yuletide, and is planning to feast the ladies. It's a new habit of his, to invite the wives and daughters of his courtiers to a celebration and play host. He even inspects the tables beforehand."

Kate could feel the tension rising. She knew what was coming.

Francis hesitated. "He wants you to be there."

She recoiled. "Me? Why?"

"He asks after you from time to time. He makes it his business to know what is happening in the lives of those who serve him. This week, he said that you must come to court for the feast because it is a long time since he has seen you. Please say you will come."

Kate was appalled. "Why must I?"

"Because, effectively, the King has commanded it."

"So I have no choice?"

"Not really. And I do not wish to offend the King."

She bridled. "Francis, I am not long out of childbed, and it is Mary's first Christmas. Hal is of an age to miss me terribly, and I don't want to spend the season away from them."

He smiled at her. "You will be with them at Christmas. The feast is to be held on Holy Innocents' Day, so you can leave here on St. Stephen's Day and be back in time for New Year. And my mother will be coming to stay. She can keep the children entertained while you are gone, although I doubt that Mary will need much entertaining."

Kate sat there, miserable. Francis got up and knelt by her chair, taking her hand.

"Darling, I know you have little cause to love the King, but he is the King, and I look to him for advancement, which I trust will come before long. And he is prepared to be a good lord to you, too. We must not bite the hand that feeds us. And there will be many other ladies at the feast." He looked at her pleadingly.

No, she didn't have a choice. "Very well," she said.

THE COURT WAS crowded, and the halls, galleries, and state apartments were festooned with evergreens and infused with the heady seasonal scent of bay, juniper, cloves, and oranges. Francis led Kate to his lodging, where a fire was lit and Will was waiting to greet her, and they shared a flagon of ale. She wanted to know if her mother was better.

"I've written several times," she told him, "but she never tells me anything about her health."

"She is well, I'm sure," he said. "She complains about various aches and pains, but I think a lot of it is in her mind. Don't worry. If I was concerned, I would tell you."

Kate had to leave him then, to change out of her traveling clothes and put on the new gown Francis had paid for. It was black with a low bodice and a crimson damask kirtle, and she felt very elegant in it, thankful that her figure had quickly returned to its normal shape.

Looking in Francis's small mirror, she put on her hood. She had grown plumper in the face, but she thought it suited her, and that her smile was very becoming. Not bad, she told herself, for an old married woman of eighteen!

Both men looked at her admiringly when she emerged from the bedchamber.

"You look a picture," Will said.

"I am indeed a lucky man," Francis chimed in.

He escorted her to the Great Watching Chamber where the feast was to be held, kissed her hand, and left her at the door. When, feeling nervous, she entered the throng of gorgeously dressed women, she was glad of her new gown, for it looked strikingly simple against some of the gaudy get-ups on display.

There was no one she recognized. The vast space was crowded, and everybody seemed to know everyone else. As she wended her way past chattering groups, she felt very much an outsider and at a disadvantage. She spied Anne Bassett talking to an older woman wearing heavy gold chains, but did not like to interrupt them. Oh, why had she let herself be persuaded to come here? This was not her world. She should be home at beautiful Greys Court, where her heart lay. Her arms ached to hold her children.

She wondered if she could sit down at one of the long tables that had been set for the feast, each at right angles to the dais, where the King's table was laid up beneath the canopy of estate bearing the royal arms of England. But she did not like to do so. For a start, she had no idea where to sit and did not want to give offense by taking a place intended for a lady of higher rank.

She was pondering this dilemma when the trumpets sounded and the ladies melted to the side. As the King passed through their ranks, leaning on his stick, they all curtseyed, and Kate, standing at the end nearest the dais, bent her knee, lowering her eyes and hoping he would not notice her. When she rose and gathered courage to look about her, she saw him standing with a group of ladies, laughing and chatting. The way they gazed adoringly up at him filled her with contempt, for how could he ever believe they found him attractive? He was grossly fat—three men could have fitted inside his gown—and his face looked puffy and old, with veined cheeks and piggy eyes, eyes that were leering lasciviously at the bulging breasts of one of the women. Kate shuddered and moved away, intending to lose herself in the crowd, out of his sight. Oh, why wasn't anybody noticing her? Wasn't there someone she could talk to? And when could she decently slip away? She was tempted to do so now.

But there was no getting away. The press of bodies was so great that it was impossible to push through. Then the King came into view again, conversing with Anne Bassett, who seemed to be flirting with him. It dawned on Kate that Anne and others here might be imagining themselves wearing a crown in the not-too-distant future, for the consort's throne was vacant. But who would be foolish enough to put her neck into such a yoke? Francis had said that it was now treason for a woman to marry the King without confessing to any past amours. He'd joked that his Majesty would be hard pressed to find a court lady who hadn't had any, and that few were queuing up for the honor of his hand. Yet tonight, it seemed there were women who would do anything for power and wealth.

Again, she tried to circulate. She saw the Duchess of Suffolk, who had been friendly to her when they were both in Queen Anna's service, but she was in full flight with some other great ladies, and Kate did not like to interrupt them. She hovered on the edge of their group, hoping that the Duchess would notice her, but then a high-pitched voice said, "Mistress Knollys?"

She turned around to find the King standing before her, grinning down from his lofty height.

"Your Majesty!" She sank into another curtsey, praying that he wasn't expecting her to flirt with him as the others had.

"It is a pleasure to see you at court," he said gently. "We have missed you. Yet we hear that you are very happy at Greys Court and that you now have two healthy children. We should like to see them one day."

Kate was surprised to find him so well informed. "I thank your Grace. Yes, I am most contented in my marriage." The thought of this man with his bloodstained hands meeting her children was anathema to her.

He was peering down at her, scrutinizing her closely, in the way that others had done in the past. It still made her feel uncomfortable. Wilting under the King's gaze, she tried not to flinch or think of the wives he had sent to a bloody death.

"We would like to see you at court more often," he was saying.

"Your Grace does me much honor," she replied, longing for this to be over, and thinking that wild horses wouldn't drag her back here again.

"Hmm. One day, I may pay you a visit. I have a mind to see Greys Court, which I have heard is delightful."

Alarms were sounding in Kate's head. *No!* She did not want him sullying the beauty and tranquility of her home with his revolting presence. It was all she could do to be polite to him for the duration of this too-long conversation. But she could not show her revulsion, for Francis's sake. "We would be happy to welcome your Grace."

"I will look forward to it," he said. Their exchange had dried up, and it was not for Kate to speak first. They stood there for some moments before the King spoke. "Well, Mistress Knollys, I bid you good evening. Enjoy the feast."

He moved on, leaving her standing there, trembling, her cheeks hot, her hands clenched. Never, *never,* would she welcome him at Greys Court. If he sent word that he was coming, she would say that she was ill. Anything to keep him away.

The noise, the clamor, the press of bodies, and the flickering candles were overwhelming. She had to get away. Seeing an opening in the throng, she slipped out of the door, then hurried to Francis's lodging. He looked up at her, astonished.

"Why are you back so soon?"

"I felt faint," she told him, quite truthfully. "It was so hot in there, and I had spoken with the King, so I felt I could leave. I must lie down." She passed into the bedchamber, unlaced her stomacher and flopped down on the bed. Francis followed and lay beside her, cradling her in his arms. "I'm so sorry, sweetheart." He paused. "So you spoke to the King?"

"Yes." She wasn't about to tell him how it had made her feel; it wasn't fair on him, for he had to serve that devil and he was eager for preferment. "He said he was pleased to see me at court, and he said he might visit us at Greys Court one day."

"That's wonderful news!" Francis cried. "It's a great honor. It will cost us, though—entertaining the King is an expensive business. But think of the rewards, Kate!"

Kate's heart plummeted. She had not thought of that. It seemed that, if the moment ever came, she must put on a brave front for her husband's sake. She owed it to him, and she would never forgive herself if she allowed her personal feelings to stand in the way of his future advancement. But how would she bear it, having that vile man in her house?

Chapter 17

1543

MONTHS WENT BY, AND KATE WAS THANKFUL THAT SHE HAD heard no more about the King visiting Greys Court. By April, when the blossom was out and lambs were gamboling in the fields surrounding the park, she knew that she was with child again. This time, she suffered badly from nausea and fatigue, and wrote to her mother, inviting her to come and stay. It would be pleasant to spend some time together with their husbands busy at court, and Mother could take pleasure in her grandchildren. Hal was now two, active from the hour he awoke to the hour he went to bed, and mad about horses and playing with the little wooden sword Will had crafted for him. "You're dead!" he would cry, thrusting it at anyone within range.

Mary was sitting up unaided now and talking, or rather, babbling. With her chubby features and enchanting smile, she was a winning child, always wanting to be carried, holding her little arms up to Kate whenever she saw her. Mistress Wellgood had her hands full, and Kate was grateful for her now, when all she herself seemed to want to do was rest. Fortunately, Bilkins—who was much more amenable these days, having come to respect Kate's judgment—was able to run the household as she wished, without her help.

Mother did not reply for two weeks, and when she did, she sounded distraught. Will was in the Fleet Prison, sent there by the Privy Council for eating meat on Good Friday. Worse still, he had been dismissed from the King's service. "And all for such a small offense," Mother wrote. "It could not have happened at a worse time, for I am not myself these days. I suffer from my old malaise, and I do not need all this worry. I am sorry, but I cannot come to you at present."

Kate's spirits sank. She had counted on Mother being with her at this time, and she was worried about her. How unwell was she?

She wrote to Harry, who was now serving in the King's household, and asked him if there was anything he could do to help. She also dashed off a letter to Francis, explaining the situation and asking if he could put in a good word for Will.

Back came a speedy reply. Will had known that he was breaking the law; Francis had visited him in the Fleet, where he had been gratified to see that he was at least allowed to take the air in the prison garden. "I would willingly intercede with the King for him," he wrote, "for he is very sorry for what he did, and he is concerned about your mother, but I do believe that it would come better from you, for his Grace manifests a certain tenderness toward you and often asks after your health."

Why? Kate asked herself. *Why me? Why couldn't he manifest tenderness toward someone else?* But she had to put Will's interests first, for her mother's sake alone. Reluctantly, she sat down and wrote to the King in the most groveling terms she could think of, begging him to show mercy to one who had long served him so devotedly and was bound to him by ties of love and loyalty.

Later that day, she received a reply from Harry. He was only a lowly usher, he explained, and had no influence with the King. But he was concerned about Mother and was going to visit her at Hever. He would let Kate know how he found her.

A week later, Kate was delighted to hear from Francis that Will had been freed from prison and was back in his old post at court. Hard on the heels of that letter came a short one bearing the royal seal, in which the King informed her that he had been graciously pleased to grant her plea, for the love he bore her. She shuddered at that, hoping that he would not want anything from her in return.

That was not the limit of his bounty. In May, Will wrote to Kate, letting her know that the King had at last granted him and her mother Rochford Hall and other lands once owned by her family. It was wonderful news, he added, but it had come at a bad time, for Mother was unwell and not strong enough to cope with moving into Rochford Hall just now. Could Kate possibly come to visit her at Henden Manor? It would be like a physick to her.

Kate's immediate instinct was to go. She longed to be with Mother at this time. Harry had been to see her twice now, and he was worried about her. He told Kate she needed to judge for herself how serious this illness was, for he was no physician, and Mother would love to see her. Kate understood what he was trying to tell her and was thankful that she was not so nauseous or tired now that she was coming to the end of her third month. And the weather was fine, so the journey would not be arduous. Mistress Wellgood was more than capable of looking after the children, and Kate could with confidence leave Bilkins in charge of Greys Court.

She wrote to Francis, telling him that she was going to be away, and why, and that she hoped to return home soon, but could not say when. Then she set her maids to packing everything she would need and departed in her litter for Kent, accompanied by Thomasina and two grooms.

It was a long journey, long enough for several good gossips with Thomasina, whom she was coming to value as a friend and confidante. Without being sneaky or unkind, Thomasina willingly told Kate all about her fellow servants, their quirks of character, their loves, their feuds, and their grumbles. She spoke of her family, how her father had been a small landholder who had relied on his grazing rights on the local common, but had lost them when the land had been enclosed and turned over to sheep.

"We had been comfortable until then," Thomasina related, "but now it is a struggle to live, for I have many brothers and sisters, and there's too many other men in the same situation as my father, all of them seeking work."

Kate had not realized until then how badly the widespread of common land could affect people's lives. But the practice had been going on across the land for decades. She promised herself that she would speak to Francis to see what could be done.

They journeyed in slow stages, stopping overnight at inns in Maidenhead, Windsor, Staines, and Kingston, then at a hostelry near Nonsuch Palace, and so on to Croydon, Westerham, and south into Kent. Kate spent the whole time worrying about her mother, praying that she would be better when she saw her, and that she would not be too late if her worst fears were realized.

WILL RECEIVED HER at Henden Manor.

"I didn't expect to see you here," she said, as they exchanged kisses, "but I am glad to."

"I have been granted compassionate leave while your mother is sick," he told her, a catch in his voice.

"Is she very ill?" she asked, dreading the answer.

"I fear so," he said, his kind eyes misting. "She will be thrilled to see you. I can't thank you sufficiently for coming all this way."

"I was worried about her. I had to come." Kate found herself fighting back tears. She could not credit that her mother might die, could not bear the thought of losing her. How Will must be feeling she could not imagine.

Lying in her cheerful beamed bedchamber with its pretty embroidered hangings and latticed windows, Mother looked like a wraith of her former self. Whatever her malady was, it was eating her up. It was obvious that there was no hope.

Trying not to show how distressed she was feeling, Kate sat by the bed and took her mother's thin hand. "It does my heart good to see you."

"Oh, my daughter, I cannot believe that you are here!" The skeletal fingers gripped hers. "I'm feeling better already." She eased herself upward in the bed, then sank back against the piled-up pillows. "Will, my love, fetch Kate some refreshment. She must be hungry after traveling so far. And I think I will have a little of that mutton broth, if there's any left. I could manage it now."

"Of course," Will said, and left the room.

Mother gripped Kate's hand again. "Oh, it is a joy to see you. I prayed that you would come. Now you are here—and just look at you! Blooming with health, with another little one on the way. How are the children?"

They fell to talking about family matters and—when Will came back with the broth and a servant bringing wine and cakes for Kate—news of the court.

"It's wonderful that the King has granted you Rochford Hall," Kate said.

"Yes." Mother had taken a few spoonfuls and now looked as if she was about to drift into sleep. "He owes it to me."

Kate exchanged looks with Will. "Does he?"

"It's hers by right," he replied. There was a silence, in which they both looked down on Mother. She had dozed off. "I'll take you to your chamber, Kate. You can talk to her in the morning."

With a heavy heart, Kate followed him to a comfortably furnished guest room. Leaving Thomasina to unpack, she joined him downstairs in the parlor, where a table had been set for two and laden with pewter platters of food.

"This is where we've always eaten together," he said, his voice breaking. He bowed his head, his shoulders heaving. Kate hastened to him and put an arm around his shoulders. "I doubt we will ever sit here together again," he sobbed. She knelt, and they wept together. By the time they had dried their tears, the roast meats had cooled, but neither of them was hungry.

IN THE MORNING, when Kate came to see her, Mother fell to reminiscing about her marriage to Kate's father.

"Do you remember him?" she asked, her long graying hair spread out on the pillows.

"Not very well," Kate replied.

"He was a comely young man, and on his way up at court when the sweating sickness took him. He was not thirty-three."

"Did you love each other very much?" Kate ventured.

"Not at first because your grandfather arranged the marriage, but I grew to love him, and I sorrowed greatly when he died. But

I must confess that I was never in love with him as I am with Will." Her tired eyes lit up and she looked almost young again. "Oh, what a scandal we caused! It was our own fault, and we shouldn't have been so hasty nor so bold, but we were young and love overcame reason. I saw so much honesty in Will, and I loved him as well as he did me. He rescued me from the bondage of my life at Hever—you remember what it was like—and I was so glad to be free of it. I could not say him nay."

"I can understand it," Kate sympathized, thinking that she had heard this story before, and realizing how precious these memories were to her mother. "I saw for myself how unhappy you were, and how unkind Grandfather was."

"He had such a low opinion of me," Mother said bitterly. "I was living all the time in the shadow of my successful sister, who also thought me of little account. Do you blame me for seizing my chance of happiness? I had grown sick of my family treating me as a disgrace to them. I thought I might as well give them cause!" She sounded more spirited than at any time since Kate had arrived. "But I was loved for myself, and that meant more to me than anything," she went on wistfully. "Will was younger than me, but he fell in love with me before I did with him. Being so loved gave me the courage to defy those who had treated me so miserably and expected me to do their bidding."

She smiled, and her face was transformed. "We met at my sister's coronation, and the attraction was instant. I seized my chance to enjoy a little dalliance, and I went on enjoying it whenever I could escape my father's vigilance. It lent spice to our love; it was the excitement of forbidden fruit. Of course, it was much more than that. We knew almost from the start that what we had was precious."

Kate found it easy to imagine how simple it would have been, in the chaotic world of the court, to indulge in clandestine meetings.

"It needed only two witnesses and a helpful priest to make us one," Mother said, a hint of mischief in her voice. "The sense of liberation was heady. Many thought I erred in marrying, but I've never regretted it. The world had set little store by me, and Will set so much that I knew I could do no better than to marry him and live a poor, honest life with him."

"Did you realize how angry everyone would be?" Kate asked.

Mother shifted a little in the bed, wincing. "I should have, but I didn't think and I didn't care. And I'm sure that what really rankled with Anne was that while I might have had a man of higher birth, I could never have had one who loved me so well—whereas she . . . Well, she was not happily married to the King. That was what ate at her, I have no doubt. There was always jealousy between us."

Kate could well believe it. There had clearly been jealousy on both sides.

"She persuaded the King that I was not to be forgiven. I wrote to Master Cromwell, begging for his help in bringing about a reconciliation, but to no avail. By then, we were really poor, for my father had cut me off, so we went to Calais. Will had to go back, for he was serving in the garrison, and I decided I'd be happy being a simple soldier's wife. And I was. Honestly, Kate, I would rather have begged for my bread with Will than be the greatest queen in Christendom. And I told Cromwell so. I hope he told Anne!"

She slumped back on the pillows, clearly exhausted by the effort of talking. "I'm glad you know all about it now, and why I married Will, who has been the best of husbands."

"I know that," Kate said, thinking how sad it was that all this had happened just nine years ago, and that neither Mother nor Will could have anticipated that their time in blissful wedlock would have been so short.

The bony fingers clutched at her hand. "There is more to tell," Mother murmured, "for I would unburden my conscience. But now I must sleep. Come back this afternoon."

Kate kissed her forehead, then closed the door quietly behind her. She went to her room to rest but feared that sleep would elude her. She was fretting about what her mother wanted to say to her and why she needed to unburden her conscience. Was she about to find out why she had long felt that there was some secret in her past—or her mother's past? And did she really want to know what it was?

. . .

AT DINNER, SHE told Will what Mother had said. "Do you know what it could be?" she asked.

He clearly did, for he looked uncomfortable. "I think you should wait for her to tell you."

"You're worrying me now," she told him.

"I didn't mean to," he replied. It wasn't the reassuring answer she had wanted.

She dropped the subject, knowing there was no point in pressing him further.

IN THE AFTERNOON, she wrote to Elizabeth, telling her that she was in Kent. Soon, she thought, they would share the common bond that comes through losing your mother. At that, she left the letter unfinished, lay down on her bed, and wept. And then she felt it, the tiniest flutter deep in her belly. She had experienced it before. It was the child stirring. New life. The Lord giveth and the Lord taketh away. And, as Mother herself used to say, when He closes one door, He opens another.

She slid to her knees, thankful for this timely sign. It was as if a hand were reaching out to her in her deep need for comfort. "Blessed be the name of the Lord," she whispered, folding her hands in prayer.

MOTHER SPOKE OF her childhood in Norfolk as they sat together, and Kate began to wonder if her mind had been wandering earlier, but then the sick woman took her hand.

"There is something I have to tell you. I wish I had told you earlier, but I feared that you would despise me, just as the rest of our family have despised me."

"Why?" Kate asked. "I would never do that. You are my mother and I honor you. I always will."

Mother looked pained. "You may not when you hear what I

have to say." She took a deep breath. "I will be blunt. The King is your real father."

Kate's jaw dropped. She could not believe what she was hearing. Her instinctive response was denial. "No! Not that monster! He cannot be!"

Mother regarded her nervously, tears welling in her eyes. "It is the truth."

Kate was rigid with horror. She suddenly felt faint and the room spun around her.

"Kate?" Mother cried. And Kate could not answer, for she was frightened that she was going to die, so strange did she feel. Mother called with all her strength for Will. He must have been waiting nearby, for he was there in an instant.

"I've told her. She looks as if she might pass out," Mother sobbed.

"Lean forward, Kate," Will said, gently yet firmly pressing Kate's head toward her knees. "Deep breaths. Calm down. Think of the babe."

Kate obeyed, and gradually the world began to right itself. "Say it isn't true," she cried weakly, sitting up.

"I fear it is," he said. "Tell her about it, Mary. She deserves to know the truth."

Mother took her hand again. "Three years after I married your father, Kate, the King showed an interest in me. He was younger then, and very handsome, but I did not want to compromise my honor or my marriage by giving in to his demands. You see . . . Oh, this is difficult. Will, leave us, please. You know it all anyway."

Will nodded and left. Mother gave a loud sigh. "When I was very young, I was a maid-of-honor at the court of France. I went there in the train of the King's sister when she went to marry King Louis. I was fifteen. When Louis died and she returned to England, King François that now is came to the throne and I transferred to the service of his Queen, Claude. But the King was a lecherous man and forced me to be his mistress."

Kate was appalled. Poor Mother, poor, poor Mother . . . What a dreadful thing had been done to her.

"Kate, don't look so shocked and don't hold it against me,"

Mother cried. "I had no choice. I was young and innocent, and he was the King. He would not take no for an answer. He seduced me, used me, and then lost interest. And I lost my reputation. People called me horrible names. Your grandfather heard about it for he was abroad on an embassy for King Henry. He took me away from that court and banished me to the country. Five years later, when the scandal had died down, he arranged for me to marry your father."

She squeezed Kate's hand. Kate squeezed back. She was finding it almost impossible to take all this in, still warding off the terrible knowledge that she had been sired by that devil; yet she knew she could not blame her poor mother. "It was not your fault," she said firmly. "The sin was the French King's. He took advantage of you, and that's despicable."

"Oh, I am so glad you understand," Mother cried. "And now you can see why I was loath to succumb to King Henry's advances, even though they were made in a far more courtly fashion. But there was nothing courtly about the way he too forced himself on me."

Kate could well believe it. She would have believed anything of that horror, and she would not, *could not,* think of him as her father. "You were raped by him, too?"

"I suppose I was. But Kate, here is the thing I feel dreadful about. I was reluctant, but he was so handsome and virile that I enjoyed it. And I let him take me again and again after that." Her cheeks had flushed scarlet.

"Did my father know?"

"I don't think he ever realized. The King is nothing if not discreet, for he is the most prudish of men. When he gives way to lust, he is ashamed of it afterward, for he likes to think of himself as the epitome of knightly virtue." She laughed mirthlessly. "He made me feel that I was enjoying his special favor. I believed all the gallant things he said to me. And then I found that I was with child. That child was you. The dates were right, and I knew you were his the moment you were born. You looked so like him. And your father didn't see it, or gave no sign that he did."

"But the King. Did he—does he—know?"

"I told him. As soon as he knew, he withdrew his love from me, and that was the end of it. He's like that. He will not touch a woman when she is with child. That was when he strayed from his wives."

Kate felt anger rising. "But he had a responsibility."

Mother slowly shook her head. "In law, no. I thought he would acknowledge you and make provision for you—a good marriage, a dowry. Yet he told me he would not court scandal, especially since I was a married woman. Owning up to a bastard born in adultery, and the betrayal of a gentlemen who was close to him, would have undermined his kingly reputation and his view of himself as a virtuous prince with a conscience. And he said he had no need to acknowledge my babe, for there is a presumption in law that any issue born to a married woman is the child of her husband."

"That was an easy way out for him," Kate said bitterly. "But he still had a moral responsibility."

"And he has honored it," Mother said. "There were grants to your father and grandfather; nothing that they could not have deserved on their own merits, but timely, and generous. And after I was widowed, I was granted an annuity. Who do you think preferred you to the Lady Elizabeth's household and then Queen Anna's? It was the King, who also attended your wedding and insisted on giving you away. And Will tells me he often asks of you and shows concern for your health and happiness."

Kate got up and went to the window. In the garden below, Will was seated on a bench, deep in thought. She had always looked up to him, but now she saw what a remarkable man he was, for he had dared to take the mother of the King's child to wife, not caring about the consequences.

"You can begin to understand now why my family despised me," Mother said weakly from the bed. Kate turned around and sat beside her, taking her hand.

"That was unkind of them," she observed. "And unfair. If they despised anyone, it should have been the man who put you in that situation—and the French King for destroying your reputation to begin with."

Mother smiled. "Ah, but the Boleyns were all about self-interest.

They cared less for the loss of my reputation than for my failure to exact more by way of reward or compensation from the King. I was the reason why Anne, in her turn, refused to become his mistress. She would not let herself be left with a baby and no money or grand marriage in sight. She aimed for the crown, almost from the first. I may sound bitter, but all I can feel for her now is pity, for much good it did her. I was the family failure, but I was also the sister who ended up happily married. I had riches far beyond everything she had. She never truly forgave me for it."

The effort of talking had exhausted Mother. She closed her eyes and Kate stood up.

"I will leave you to sleep," she whispered. "There is no more need to worry. Be of good cheer."

The eyes opened. "Come back later, child. I have more to say."

More? What more could there be? Kate was reeling. She had had shocks enough today, and she still needed to ingest them.

She walked back to her chamber and peered into her mirror. Yes, she could see the resemblance, which had always eluded her. It was in the eyes, the arched brows, and the determined chin, even the shape of her face and her red hair. She was the King her father to the life. Others had seen the likeness, too, she was sure; that was why people had stared at her, why that monster had eyed her closely. She shuddered. She did not want anyone to know that she was connected to him by blood, did not want to admit to herself that she was his. She wanted to go on believing that Mother had made a mistake and that William Carey had been her true father. How she envied her brother, Harry, for he would never have to question the roots of his existence, whereas she . . .

Her letter to Elizabeth lay on the table, where she had abandoned it. Elizabeth, whom she now knew was not just her cousin, but her half sister. No wonder there had always been a close bond between them. And she, Kate, was half sister too to the Lady Mary and Prince Edward. Royal blood ran in her veins, blood going all the way back to the Norman Conquest and beyond. Blood that she had unwittingly passed on to her children—and to the little one who lay in her womb. It was incredible, and some would be glad of it, but it was a burden she did not want. In fact, it horrified her. She could not bear to think of that gross lump of lard doing with Mother what she and Francis did in joy, could not accept that that was the reason for her being. And, she vowed, none but those closest to her should ever know the truth; she and her children must never be the objects of scandal, and Mother's secret must be preserved at all costs.

But who could be trusted to keep that secret? She knew she could rely on the King to stay silent, but apart from Mother and Will, she could think of only Francis. She could tell him. In fact, she could not wait to unburden herself to him. But should she tell her children when they were old enough? Had they a right to know? Or was it best to leave them in blissful ignorance? Oh, the ramifications of Mother's dreadful revelation were going to be endless . . .

She sat down, took up her pen, and wondered what to say to Elizabeth, beyond the usual domestic news and asking after everyone at Hatfield. Had Elizabeth any idea that they were sisters? Dare Kate ever tell her and explain why she loved her so dearly? Much as she wanted to keep her secret, a part of her yearned for the bond between them to be acknowledged by Elizabeth. But now was not the time. The child was too young. And it was not Kate's place to tell her.

SHE RETURNED TO her mother's room after supper, when the trees outside the open window were silhouetted against a glorious sunset. She closed the window, for the evening air was growing cooler, and sat down by the bed. Mother opened her eyes and smiled at her uncertainly. "I hope you don't think badly of me," she whispered.

"Not at all," Kate said fiercely. "I will not have anyone despise you. The fault was not yours, and it grieves me that you have carried the burden of this knowledge for all these years and felt unable to tell me, who loves you so much!" She felt the tears stinging.

"Will said the same," Mother told her. "But I feared to upset you, for I know you have no love for the King. Yet now that I know my time on this earth is short—no, do not try to contradict me, for it is the truth—I feel that you have a right to know."

Kate stood up and embraced her, weeping, shocked at how light and skeletal her body was. "There is nothing to worry about, dearest Mother. All I want is to be with you at this time. Be at peace."

"I cannot until I have told you everything," Mother said, letting her go. "Sit down. Let me collect my thoughts. My mind is hazy these days. It is the poppy syrup they give me for the pain."

"Is there much pain?" Kate was all concern.

"Not too much," Mother replied. It was plain that she was lying. "Now, where was I? Oh, yes. I am sure you have wondered about the grounds on which Anne's marriage to the King was annulled. Well, it was because of his affair with me, because it placed him within the forbidden degrees of affinity to Anne, which meant that any union between them was as incestuous as he believed his marriage to Queen Katherine, his brother's widow, to have been. In fact, it was more so, because I had borne him a child, whereas the Queen never had any children with Prince Arthur. I am sure this was another reason why the King never acknowledged you, as he did Henry Fitzroy, his bastard by Bessie Blount; because you, my child, are the living impediment to his union with Anne. If that had got out, it would have fatally compromised the nullity suit he was pursuing in Rome, which turned upon the fact that Katherine had been his brother's wife and was therefore forbidden to him."

"So he knew that Anne was also forbidden to him—and yet he still married her?" The sheer hypocrisy of it was breathtaking.

"Yes, he knew. But he was mad for Anne. Nothing else mattered. Anne told me that he sent secretly to Rome and obtained a dispensation that allowed him to marry anyone related to him in the first degree—which meant he could have wed his sister or even his mother. But it was worthless, since the Pope had not annulled his marriage to Queen Katherine—and never did. So when it came to getting rid of Anne, he was able, quite rightly, to plead an impediment to their union. Before that, however, it was essential that word of his affair with me did not become common knowledge. And it didn't; only a few knew of it, although there must have been whispers. Now you can see why my family kept me in the background. They didn't want to risk anyone who might have had suspicions putting two and two together and making four. Thus, when I caused a scandal by marrying Will, Anne was all the more outraged because she feared that others might find out that there had been even greater cause for scandal. It's hard to keep secrets in a court."

She fell silent, leaving Kate to reflect on just how unscrupulous the King really was. All that talk of conscience, that pretense of virtue. Yet she was not surprised. What really mattered to her was that she had not inherited any of his faults or his wickedness. It was disconcerting to know that bad blood might be flowing in her veins.

"I had my own reasons for wanting to maintain discretion," Mother said. "I did not want to embarrass your father or risk his being branded a cuckold, and later I did not want his memory to be stained with any slur. So I insisted on naming you after Queen Katherine, thinking that would deflect any speculation or gossip. And I hope that you, too, Kate, will honor my memory and that of your father by keeping our secret."

"I assure you I will," Kate vowed.

IN BED THAT night, she lay sleepless. So much that had seemed mysterious in the past had now become clear, but she was shocked and in turmoil, struggling to come to terms with her new identity. She felt guilty about having royal Tudor blood and appalled at being the daughter of a man who treated women so badly. Truth to tell, she even found herself wishing to distance herself from her own family, whose ambitions had led them to collude in such a great deception.

She wondered, with a slight chill, if the King saw her as a threat to his lawful heir. The awful dawning awareness that she was effectively as much a bastard as Elizabeth and the Lady Mary was, in a curious way, some comfort, because bastards were unable to inherit anything from their parents. And yet she had heard people speak of Henry Fitzroy and how at one time, desperate to have a son to succeed him, the King had contemplated making him his heir by an Act of Parliament. If that had happened, Fitzroy would have taken precedence over the Lady Mary, whose legitimacy had not then been questioned. No, Kate told herself, I could never be seen as a threat. I'm only a girl, like Mary and Elizabeth. And yet, she had to ask herself, what if Prince Edward died? What then? She would have as much right to the crown as either of her half sisters. Thank God they did not know who she really was, for then they might perceive her as a threat. It was better by far to keep that a secret. Much as she would have liked to share the precious bond of sisterhood with her beloved Elizabeth, she must never know.

AS HER MOTHER grew weaker, Kate stayed on. She could not in all conscience leave her. Informed of the situation, Bilkins wrote to say that all was well at Greys Court and that the children were thriving in the care of Mistress Wellgood. She need not worry.

Resolved to stay until the end, Kate took upon herself the tender nursing tasks that were all she could now do for her mother. She and Will sat with her, reading aloud or reciting prayers. They were comfortable together, bonded by their shared sadness. Kate realized that she had come to think of this strong, caring man as a father figure.

The news that the King was to take a sixth queen, Katharine Parr, the widowed Lady Latimer, made little impact on them. Kate hoped that this wife would fare better than the others, but that would be a triumph of hope over experience. The court seemed very far away. Their world had narrowed down to the sickroom in this quiet corner of Kent.

One evening, as the light was dying and Mother lay wakeful, Will knelt down by the bed, slid across a wooden panel, and drew out something wrapped in gold cloth.

"This is my Bible," he told Kate.

She stared at it. It was the same as the Great Bible that the King had ordered to be placed in every church these four years past.

Prior to that, it had been illegal even to read the Bible in English, let alone possess a copy.

"Your mother and I have derived great comfort and pleasure from it," Will told her. Kate looked at Mother, lying in the bed, and saw her close her eyes, with a slight smile on her face. "It is a wonderful thing for ordinary folk to be able to read the Scriptures for themselves and not have to rely on a priest to interpret them from the Latin. Some priests hardly know any Latin!"

He placed the book on the bed, opened it, and began to read the story of the Sermon on the Mount. "When He saw the people, He went up into a mountain and when He was set, His disciples came to Him and He opened his mouth and taught them, saying: blessed are the poor in spirit, for theirs is the kingdom of Heaven. Blessed are they that mourn, for they shall be comforted. Blessed are the meek, for they shall inherit the earth. Blessed are they which hunger and thirst for righteousness, for they shall be filled. Blessed are ye merciful, for they shall obtain mercy. Blessed are the pure in heart, for they shall see God."

He paused and looked down at Mother. His eyes met Kate's and filled with tears.

"She has gone to her Maker," he said. "It is a blessed release."

Kate took the dead hand and burst into sobs. "Oh, Mother, oh, dear Mother!" She feasted her eyes on the still face, pale as the pillow, wishing to imprint it on her soul forever. "I shall pray for her," she wept.

"No," Will said. "There is no need. She and I believed that our Lord Jesus is the sole mediator between God and man, and that praying for the dead is unnecessary, for He alone will determine the fate of a soul."

Kate was astonished. "But should we not have Masses said for her?"

"No. That would be disrespectful to our Lord, whose judgment is perfect."

She had never heard anyone express such a view, and she was sure that it couldn't be right. Yet she didn't like to say so. "Is that really what my mother believed?"

"Yes, Kate. Like me, she was a convert to the reformed faith. I am trusting you not to reveal this to anyone, as it could go badly for me if it were discovered that I am what some term a heretic. And you know what they do to heretics."

"I do. And I would never betray you." She loved him too much, even though she was startled to hear that Mother had secretly embraced the Protestant faith.

"Your husband is one of our number," he said gently.

She nodded. "I know."

"It is my constant prayer that one day, Kate, we will be able to worship God in our own way, free from the threat of persecution. But for now, we must compromise and follow the ways laid down for us by the Church and the State. Your dear mother will have a Christian burial, even if it is not in the form she would have liked. But we all pray to the same God, whose nature is always to be merciful. I take comfort in that."

THEY LAID HER to rest in the parish church of St. Mary the Virgin at nearby Sundridge. There were no fanfares, just a simple committal service. Will had said that he would not raise an elaborate tomb or have a brass placed on the grave. "A stone will suffice," he said. "God knows where she lies, and she will forever be in my heart. Besides, her inheritance is your brother's to do with as he wishes. He may wish to erect a memorial."

Kate knew that Will's only bequest from Mother was the manor of Abinger in Surrey, where he was going to base himself as soon as he had set everything in order at Henden. But he was departing for France at the end of the month at the head of a hundred foot soldiers, to begin four months' military service. It would divert him from his grief, he told Kate.

Kate doubted that Mother would have wished for an imposing monument. She would have wanted to be buried in peaceful obscurity, as she had lived her last years—and, indeed, much of her life. She had been lucky, for she had found true happiness, which was more than many people could say, and she had died greatly beloved.

. . .

AFTER A TEARFUL parting from Will, Kate set off for home. Having learned that Elizabeth was at Hatfield, she thought she might make a detour there to visit her. She felt the need to do so, even though she knew she could not tell her what she had learned from Mother. She reflected sadly that she now knew how painful it was to lose a mother, and felt she had come to a new understanding of Elizabeth's tragic past.

She was still reeling from the news that the King was her father. The horror she had felt had not diminished. The only father she wanted now was Will, who exemplified to her all that a father should be. Not in a million years could that monster ever compare with him. The worst thing was how her sense of herself had changed. She could not forget that there must be something of the King in her. Heaven forfend that she was anything like him! She had resolved to suppress any character traits that resembled his. None should ever have cause to say that she was her father's daughter.

PART TWO

Dangers

1543–58

Chapter 18

1543

Elizabeth greeted her ecstatically. She was nearly ten now, tall for her age and slender, her features sharper, her red hair very long. But her demeanor changed when Kate told her about Mother's death.

"That's awful," she said, twisting her hands nervously. "I'm very sorry for you."

Kate knew that she was thinking of her own mother. "It is a terrible loss to bear," she said.

"I know," said Elizabeth. Her voice shook. Kate's heart went out to her. This was her sister, bound to her by a close tie of blood. And her own mother had died a peaceful death, not bloodily on a scaffold.

They embraced each other, both of them emotional, and then Kat and Lady Troy came in, fresh from a walk in the park. Both gave Kate their kindest condolences and called for refreshments for her. She spent the afternoon looking at Elizabeth's schoolwork, which the child was proud to show her, and marveling at how erudite she was.

"I was never as clever as you," Kate told her. "I found it easy to master foreign tongues, but the classic works of antiquity bored me, although I loved the myths and legends."

"Oh, but they're not boring!" Elizabeth cried. "You should read Cicero. He is a master of eloquence, an advocate for liberty."

"That's as may be," Kate retorted, "but give me a good romance any day!" They were back to their old easy friendship. Kate now felt less awareness that Elizabeth was a king's daughter, for she was reluctantly coming to accept that she herself was one, too—and she longed to tell her the truth. Indeed, she ventured perilously close to it.

"Do you miss your sister Mary?" she asked one day, a week into her visit.

"Yes. I don't see her very often, but she is nice to me."

"That's what sisters are for."

"I know, but you're nicer."

Kate bit her tongue. Dare she say more? But Elizabeth said it for her.

"I wish that you were my sister," she said wistfully.

Kate nearly blurted the truth out then, but restrained herself just in time. "I wish I were, too," she said.

"You look like me," Elizabeth told her.

This was getting uncomfortably close to the truth. "That's because we are cousins."

"Do I look like my mother?"

"Yes, although you have your father's coloring and his nose. But otherwise, you are very like her."

Elizabeth was regarding Kate intently. "Our mothers had dark hair, so how come you have red hair like me?"

"My father had red hair, like yours," Kate said, thinking rapidly. It was a lie. In a portrait that hung at Henden Manor, William Carey had dark hair. She prayed that Elizabeth would never see it.

She changed the subject, feeling that she had trespassed too far into dangerous territory.

"Shall we walk in the gardens after supper?" she asked.

"I would like that," Elizabeth replied. "And then we could make music together." She had seemingly forgotten that Kate was in mourning.

. . .

BY THE TIME Greys Court came into view, Kate had been away for two months and was longing to get home. She had sent ahead to notify Bilkins of her arrival, but was delighted to see Francis come running out of the house to welcome her as her little cavalcade came to rest in the Base Court. Behind him scampered Hal, who seemed to have grown taller, and then came Mistress Wellgood, baby Mary in her arms, and the rest of the household.

It was good to feel Francis's strong arms around her again as he embraced and kissed her, then led her into the house. "You look blooming," he told her. "I have been so concerned about you, and I was deeply sorry to hear of your mother's passing. She was a kind lady, and I shall miss her."

"Yes, it has been a difficult time, more difficult than you can imagine," Kate said, bending down to hug an excited Hal, then taking the babe from the nurse and showering kisses on her. "How I have missed you all! Have you children been well behaved for Mistress Wellgood?"

"They have, Madam," the nurse said. "Well, Hal has been passably good and this one's been a little angel. How are you keeping?"

"I am well, in the circumstances," Kate said. "But now I need to rest. It has been a long journey."

Francis followed her up to the solar.

"What did you mean about having more of a difficult time than I could imagine?" he asked gently, taking her in his arms and kissing her as soon as they were alone.

"I will tell you, but first, I must lie down, for I feel weary after the long ride. You can be my tirewoman." They smiled at each other. He had been her tirewoman on many intimate occasions.

He untied her sleeves, then bent and unlaced her bodice. She stepped out of her gown, laid it over a bench, then went through to the bedchamber and lay down on the bed in her white lawn smock. "The babe has quickened," she said, laying her hand on her belly. "There! Touch and you will feel it."

Francis placed his hand where she indicated. He broke into a smile. "Yes, I feel it, darling. He's a lusty one!"

"It may be a she . . ."

"I don't mind. Sometimes I think that one lusty son is more than enough!" He grinned.

"I'm so glad you're here," she said, squeezing his hand.

"Bilkins sent to advise me of your coming. I was due some leave and raced home like the wind."

"That's as well," she said, remembering what she had to say to him and feeling her mood darken. "Lie beside me. Hold me."

"Hey, what's wrong, sweetheart? This isn't like you," Francis murmured, lying down on the bed and taking her in his arms.

She began to weep. "It's all been too much. Losing Mother, after supporting her through her last weeks. It was harrowing at times and desperately sad. I hated to see her so ill, and I felt very deeply for Will. He has borne his grief bravely and is dealing with it by returning to France to go soldiering. But I was disturbed when he told me that he and Mother had embraced the Protestant faith—and that he knew you had, too. I am amazed that you would all run that risk."

"Is that why you're upset? Well, my darling, sometimes principles are more important than anything else."

"Even risking my happiness and the children's?"

Francis gazed into her eyes. "Kate, you are my wife, closer to me than anyone. Have I ever betrayed my love for you? Have I given you cause to think me a heretic?"

"Once. That was enough. And it would be enough for the King to proceed against you."

"I remember what I said then, but it could be explained in other ways. I could have defended myself. And for your sake, I would have denied my faith had I been examined. No, Kate, I will not abandon my beliefs. They are too much a part of me. But for as long as it remains dangerous to hold them, I will hide them behind a cloak of conformity. Does that put your mind at rest?"

"Somewhat." She kissed him, forcibly aware of how much he meant to her. "Actually, that was not what was upsetting me most." She took a deep breath, remembering that she had longed to unburden herself to Francis, although now that the moment had come, she was balking at doing so. "Before she died, my mother told me something so horrible and shocking that it made me question everything I am."

"By God, what was it?" Francis's eyes had widened in alarm.

"She told me that I am the King's daughter."

He drew in his breath and was silent for a long moment. Then he said, "To be honest, I have wondered. When we became betrothed, one of the Gentlemen Pensioners jested that I had landed a royal bride. I thought he meant your being Queen Anne's niece, but when I said that we weren't going to make anything of that connection, for obvious reasons, he said he hadn't meant that, but that there had been talk about your mother. I looked at you and thought I could see a resemblance to his Grace, but I couldn't be certain. I thought it remarkable that you had been selected for such high offices in the royal households. But Kate, you have to believe that I did not choose you because I thought you were his daughter. I chose you because I fell for you and thought you would be the perfect wife for me."

"I know that," she assured him, becoming distressed. "But what I am is no cause for rejoicing. I hate and detest the idea of being his child. I loathe him! I cannot bear to think that he is my father."

"Hush!" he soothed, holding her tighter. "You must not always think the worst of him."

"No?" She was vehement. "You were not there when they cut my aunt's head off, by his order, or when he sent a silly young girl to a bloody death. You have no idea of the horror of it. Think of all those he has sent the same way, the hundreds he has killed. Think of his cruelty—"

"Kate, enough! I am his servant. I have told you I must not hear such things. What you are speaking is treason. It is treason to question his justice."

"Justice? It was butchery!"

She sat up, marched into the solar, and pulled on her nightrobe, seething. Francis followed her.

"Sweetheart, I know why you are upset, but—hard as it sounds—they were all punished according to law."

"Katheryn Howard had no trial! She was condemned unheard

by Parliament. And my aunt's trial was a travesty. I was there. Don't give me the law!"

"Kate, calm down." He grasped her shoulders. "Think of the child."

"You don't think of it when you vex me so! The next thing you will be telling me is that Anne was guilty as charged."

There was an awful pause. Francis let her go and sat down by the empty hearth. "I did not say that."

"But you believe it." She sank down opposite him.

"The evidence against her was strong."

"Evidence? Half of it was lies! They used lies as a pretext to get rid of her."

"Kate, darling, are you sure? You were very young when you attended her in the Tower, and clearly very distressed. Is it possible that you misunderstood?"

"I know what I heard, and I know what she told me!" Kate cried, fierce in her indignation. "She swore on the damnation of her soul that she had never offended against the King with her body. I was there at her last confession."

Francis was silent. "Is that what she said? Kate, I remember the gossip at court. She was thought to be pursuing Sir Henry Norris. She may not have offended with her body, but did she do so with her heart? In the King's eyes, that would be treason, too, because it was alleged against her that she plotted with her lovers to assassinate him so that she could marry one of them and rule during Elizabeth's minority."

"And you believe such calumnies?"

"She was convicted for it."

"She was innocent! Why won't you believe me? Are you so in thrall to the King?"

Francis sighed. When he spoke again, he sounded irritated. "Kate, you sometimes seem to forget that I serve the King and that our prosperity depends on his bounty and favor. I have taken an oath of loyalty to him. I am sure you would not wish to be married to a man who breaks his oath. I believe you when you say that your aunt was innocent; it's just that it didn't seem like it at the time. But let us not quarrel. I can understand why this news has upset you, but your royal blood hasn't been such a bad thing, if you think about it. No, hear me out!"

Kate had opened her mouth to protest but subsided resentfully.

"It led to your enjoying a happy life in the household of the Lady Elizabeth and gaining preferment to that of the Lady Anna of Cleves. The King had a compelling reason for bestowing you well in marriage, and it is thanks to him that we have each other. And darling . . ." He leaned forward and reached out his hand to her. "I love you no more and no less for it. To me, you are still the same Kate and always will be. I'm not going to look at you and think of you as the King's daughter. I will go on loving you as you, the woman I married." He took her hand. "I love you as you are, my sweet wife."

Her heart melted at that. In an instant, Francis had given her back herself, made her realize that whoever her father was, she had not fundamentally changed. And as nobody else was in on the secret, she could go on behaving as if she were indeed William Carey's daughter; she did not have to own the King as her father. Of course, she was still distressed that he was, but she would not let the knowledge rule her life. Francis had just given her the strength to do it.

"Thank you," she said, taking his hand, tears running down her cheeks. "You have made me feel a lot better. And I will not ask you to break your oath of loyalty to the King. We will not touch on the subject again."

"There must be no barriers between us," he said, frowning.

"Only discretion." She smiled bravely.

KATE WAS SEVEN months pregnant when, in September, Francis wrote from Windsor Castle that the King would be doing them the honor of paying them a visit in a week's time. "His Grace is minded to go hunting with a small party of gentlemen. He does not wish us to go to any trouble to entertain him."

Kate snorted when she read that. Everyone honored with such a visit went to a great deal of trouble, often at ruinous cost; in this instance, the burden would fall on her—and she had very little time to prepare. She sent for Bilkins and the cook.

"What food does one offer the King?" she asked them. Their

faces registered both horror and excitement when she revealed that his Majesty was coming to Greys Court.

Of course, she felt only horror. She didn't want that devil desecrating her home, didn't want him pawing at her children or tainting the air with the stench of his diseased leg. Yet she could not let Francis down. He would be expecting her to play the perfect hostess. There was nothing for it but to do so—and do it to her utmost.

She set everyone to work dusting, polishing, and scrubbing. She had a bed made up for her and Francis in the finest of the tower rooms, where the children would sleep with them, and ordered the servants to air the solar and make up the bed with the best linen for the King. She prepared guest accommodation and hoped there would be enough space for the royal attendants. Fortunately, Francis said, the King would be traveling with just his riding household, the select few he took with him on hunting expeditions.

She sat for ages with the cook and drew up lists of dishes, ticking those she thought the King would enjoy best. Fortunately, Francis had told her what his Grace liked to eat—and it was the hunting season, so there would be fresh venison, one of his favorites. And all of this for that horror. She could not bear to think about it.

Everything was ready when the royal harbingers came ahead of the King's party to check that all was in order. They nodded approvingly at the rooms made ready for the monarch and his entourage, told Kate that they would only be staying for one night, fitted a complicated lock to the solar door, and set up a cloth of estate and a rich x-framed chair on the dais in the hall. Then they went away to inform their master that all was ready for him.

The next day, Kate was on high alert, looking out of the windows constantly to catch a glimpse of the approaching royal hunting party. She was wearing a new gown of green damask with the stomacher unlaced over the high mound of her belly. Her oversleeves were of fur, her kirtle of cream satin with a matching French hood. She had ordered new clothes for the children, too. Little Hal, now rising two and a half, was racing around in a doublet and gown of crimson velvet that looked perilously near to being ripped, while baby Mary was the perfect little lady in pink, a color that complemented her red curls. Determined to have everything looking perfect, for Francis's sake, Kate tried not to curb their excitement too much—sweet Mary hardly understood what she was excited about—or make them sit still and await the King's arrival. She did not want any tantrums.

When the hunting horns sounded in the distance, she hurried them into the courtyard, summoning her household to join them. Standing by the mounting block, holding her children by the hand, she watched as the King and his gentlemen rode up the hill toward her. To her joy, Francis was with them, elegant and handsome in his livery. When they drew near, she sank into a curtsey.

"Mistress Knollys!" the King boomed. "It is a pleasure to see you again. Rise!"

She stood up. "Your Majesty does us great honor in visiting our humble house."

Men stepped forward to help their sovereign heave his heavy bulk from his horse.

"We thank you for your hospitality," he said, a little breathless.

Francis dismounted and joined them. "If your Grace would come this way . . ."

He led his master into the great hall, where one of the trestle tables had been laid with starched white linen and covered with an array of tempting dishes, the centerpiece being a whole side of venison in a giant pasty. The King surveyed it with approval as servants came forward with bowls of rose water and towels so that he and the other guests could wash before dinner.

"Your Grace has arrived just in good time," Kate told him. "Dinner is ready, if it is your pleasure."

"Indeed it is, Mistress Knollys." His gaze was fixed on Hal and Mary, who were standing by their mother's skirts, clearly overawed by this huge, glittering man. "And these are your children?"

Kate drew in her breath. He was their grandfather, but she did not want him touching them, contaminating their innocent purity with his bloodstained hands. "Yes, your Grace. Henry and Mary." They had been well schooled: Hal bowed nervously, while Mary stared in awe at the huge, towering figure of the King. "Their nurse is about to take them to the nursery to dine." She motioned to Mistress Wellgood, who—well primed—led them away.

"Charming, charming," the King said. "They are a handsome pair, and well behaved, too."

"We are very proud of them, Sir," Francis said, as they escorted him to his chair of estate. They were well-chosen words, calculated to flatter the old monster without acknowledging his connection to them.

During the dinner, Kate sat on the King's right hand, as his hostess, and Francis on his left. The other gentlemen occupied one trestle table, within speaking distance. Kate felt tense as she sat there, trying to act normally. Thomasina, seated at the other trestle tables with the rest of the household, was watching her sympathetically; she evidently knew her mistress well enough to detect when she was ill at ease, and she must be wondering why. Kate could never tell her the truth, though. Let her think that she was overwhelmed by the demands of the occasion.

To Kate's relief, the conversation was flowing easily; she had to admit that the King was practiced at putting people at their ease and knowledgeable, it seemed, about every subject under the sun. He began by discussing the day's hunting and the weather, then spoke of his new Queen, with whom he was clearly well pleased, and moved on to talk about education, asking what plans Francis had for the children. That led to discourses on literature, science, mathematics, and music. Kate was sometimes out of her depth but had no problem with music.

"It is my great love," she told the King, still wondering how she could be sitting here chatting in such a friendly fashion to the man who had butchered her aunt, her cousin Queen Katheryn—and many others. *What hypocrisy!* She hated herself for it.

"My wife is an accomplished musician, Sir," Francis was saying.

"I myself am no mean musician, and a composer as well," the King told her.

He had been drinking heavily. She wondered if he had been nervous about visiting her. It was not such a ridiculous notion, surely? In his position, most men would have felt embarrassed or guilty. But he was the King, so maybe he considered himself above all that, as he plainly considered himself above most human sensibilities.

In his cups, he grew garrulous, rambling on about how he had purged the Church of England of all Popery and how he was rooting out heretics. Kate tensed, never daring to look at Francis. Not by the slightest glance must they betray that the subject held any special significance for them.

The King smiled greedily when a huge apple tart was placed on the table before him, with a great jug of creamy custard.

"I do love my puddings!" he declared. "Do you know, Mistress Knollys, there is a goodwife who comes to my court and makes me the most superb puddings. I gave her a house in Aldgate as a mark of my appreciation. But this looks set to rival any of hers."

He accepted an enormous slice of tart and tucked in greedily. Then he leaned across to Kate. "It's delicious, my dear."

She tried not to recoil or show that she detested him coming so close to her. But he waxed confidential.

"I am sorry to hear of the death of your mother," he said, through a mouthful of apple mush. "I heard from Master Stafford that she was ill."

"It was a terrible time," Kate said, "and I miss her dreadfully."

"I understand," he said, showing an unexpected tenderness. "I lost my mother when I was eleven. I don't think I've ever stopped mourning her."

"I am sorry for your Grace." She had no wish to engage in a heart-to-heart conversation with him.

He hesitated, then took another sip of wine. "You were with your mother when she died?"

"Yes, Sir."

"Did she talk about the past? I mean, about her sister . . . or anything else?"

Kate froze. She could not believe he had referred to Anne, and she suspected he was fishing to find out if Mother had told her that she was his daughter. She was suddenly seized with a sense of devilment.

"We spoke of many things, Sir," she said. "Mostly about my father." It was no less than the truth!

"Hmm," he grunted, the blue eyes narrowing. "And what did she say about him?"

"She said that he would probably have risen at court had he not died of the sweating sickness. She asked me what I remembered of him." She paused, then found that she could not resist baiting him a little. "She told me about her time at the French court and at your Grace's court."

She sensed him tensing beside her. Behind him, Francis was trying to catch her eye, frowning. She ignored him and smiled at the King. "She also told me about the scandal her marriage caused."

He nodded. He was on safer ground here. "It was a bad business. Yet I came in the end to realize that she had chosen well. Stafford is a good fellow. We miss him at court."

"He is in great grief," Kate said. "He has gone to Calais to forget. But it will be hard for him. I know I can never forget her."

The King said nothing.

Kate grew bold. He was not getting off that lightly. "My mother let me into many secrets, Sir. I now know much more about my family background."

He threw her a sharp look, and she realized that it would be unwise to provoke him further. "Sometimes, it is better not to know things, better to let the past stay buried," he muttered. He could not have been clearer. But he now knew she had learned who she was, even if he had no intention of acknowledging her. He had merely been trying to find out if she did know.

Kate was barely holding herself together. She feared that, if she spoke, he would know how angry she was at his words. What kind of man could deny his own child? Her opinion of him had plummeted lower than ever.

She stood up. Excusing herself with a curtsey, she left the hall and hurried upstairs to her bedchamber, closing the door behind her. Then she leaned against it, breathing heavily, and sank down to the floor, unable to control the flood of hot, bitter tears. And there she sat, trying to make sense of her thoughts. What had she expected? That he would acknowledge her as his daughter? And if she had tried to wring that from him only to make him feel guilt, why was she disappointed that he had not admitted it, especially since she did not want to be his child! No, she was not really disappointed. She was relieved.

Getting to her feet, she smoothed her skirts, straightened her hood, and went back downstairs.

THE KING SPENT most of the afternoon resting in his room. Suppressing her inner turmoil, for she now feared that her boldness might have consequences for Francis, Kate supervised the clearing away of the feast and the preparation of supper, which was not—fortunately—as elaborate, just a simple repast of cold meats, cheeses, and salad, with pears stewed in red wine to follow. Then she spent some time playing with her children. Francis found her kneeling on the nursery floor with them, building a tower with toy bricks.

"They're all in the hall, playing cards; those who aren't in attendance on his Grace, that is," he told her, sitting down and ruffling Hal's hair. "Kate, what were you thinking of, discussing your mother with the King?"

"He brought up the subject." She put a brick in Mary's hand and showed her where to stack it.

"But you were baiting him. I heard you."

"No," she lied. "I but told him the truth. It was he who was baiting me, trying to find out if I knew he was my father. So I gave him every opportunity to admit it."

Francis was shaking his head.

"He wouldn't!" she spat. "God, how I hate him!"

"Keep your voice down!" Francis hissed. "Let's just get through tonight and the morning, and then he'll be gone."

"Forever, I hope," Kate muttered.

SUPPER PASSED WITHOUT incident. The King expressed himself delighted with the plentiful choice fare on offer, and the conversation turned to deteriorating relations with France. Kate tried to look interested, but talk of foreign politics bored her, and she was finding it almost impossible to join in because she felt so tense. She was glad when the meal was over and the men fell to dicing and shovelboard.

She sat by the fire, utterly exhausted. She was in her seventh month and entertaining the King had proved a strenuous effort, while she was weary of having to keep up the pretense that she was dazzled by the privilege of having him as her guest. Watching the flames dancing on the hearth, she felt strongly that he owed her something in return for all the suffering he had caused her and her family.

The next thing she knew, Francis was shaking her awake. "His Grace is about to retire to bed."

She struggled to her senses and stood up. "Tell Bilkins to have an ewer of water placed in the solar." She turned to the King, who had just risen from the table. "I bid your Grace good night. If there is anything you need, we will be pleased to supply it."

"We thank you for your hospitality, Mistress Knollys," he said, taking her hand and kissing it. The touch of his lips made her skin crawl. "Good night."

At last, she and Francis were alone. She was swaying on her feet, and he had to assist her to their temporary bedchamber, where he helped her to undress and tucked her up in bed. She was asleep before he joined her.

IN THE MORNING, the King was in a buoyant mood, anticipating a good day's hunting ahead. He complimented Kate on the roast beef and manchet loaves he was served for breakfast, washing them down with good ale. And then—the moment she had longed for—he was on his way. She stood with Francis in the Base Court as he mounted his horse.

He looked down upon them. "I thank you both for your warm welcome. Knollys, I will see you back at court next week. And Mistress Knollys, I thank you for your hospitality. I wish you a good hour when the time comes."

They thanked him, made their reverences, and watched until he and his companions had disappeared from their sight. Francis squeezed Kate's hand. "You did well," he murmured, leading her back into the house. "He was pleased."

"I hope I never have to see him again," she muttered under her breath.

. . .

AUTUMN DREW IN with golden days and cold nights, and in November, the child came. She was a pretty little thing with downy red hair, like her siblings—Tudor red hair, Kate kept reminding herself—and a strong will. They called her Laetitia, after Francis's delighted mother, who had attended her once again, but very soon she too became known as Lettice.

Kate had greatly missed having her own mother at the birth. She was sad that she would never meet this grandchild, never see her or her siblings grow up. But her mother-in-law was as loving and stalwart as ever, and comforted Kate whenever grief overwhelmed her, as it did when she was suffering the emotional aftermath of delivering a child. The birth, like the last one, had been easy, yet this time it took a little longer to recuperate. Lettice took over the ordering of the household and saw to the engaging of a wet nurse. She was very ably assisted by Thomasina, whose devotion to Kate had been immeasurably strengthened in recent months. Francis had leased some land to Thomasina's father at a peppercorn rent, a gesture that had lifted a great burden from her family.

When she was able to sit up, Kate wrote to Elizabeth. She told her about her new little cousin and said that she missed her very much and longed to see her. She was up and about again when the reply came. Elizabeth was well and engrossed in her studies. She had spent time at court with the new Queen, whom she praised highly. She wished that Kate could visit her at Hatfield, or that she herself could come to Greys Court. They must arrange something in the New Year. In the meantime, she wished Kate a very merry Christmas and promised to remember the children in her prayers.

Kate smiled wistfully when she read the letter. She would have loved to go to Hatfield and feel like a young girl again, but she was needed at home. She promised herself that she would go next summer, when she was confident that little Lettice was thriving and that she herself could be spared for a week or so.

Chapter 19

1544–45

THERE WAS A GOLDEN HAZE OVER THE FLAT HERTFORDSHIRE countryside when Kate, Thomasina, and a groom approached Hatfield House in August. Trotting into the courtyard, she saw Elizabeth waving to her from a window. She waved back, but the girl had gone. She reappeared seconds later, hurrying toward Kate with her long red hair flying and her damask sleeves and skirts billowing in the wind.

"Kate, dear cousin! I am so pleased to see you!"

Kate dismounted and pulled her into an embrace. This was her sister, even if Elizabeth did not know it. She had never felt so close to her. "I am so thrilled that the Queen allowed me to come, with the plague being rife."

"It's safe here," Elizabeth told her. "I've been moving about with her, from house to house, trying to escape the contagion, but it's dying down now, so she let me come back to Hatfield."

"Is there any news of his Majesty?" He was in France making war on the French, and Francis was with him. Kate had not known a moment's peace of mind since he had left. She'd not had a letter for a week. The latest she had heard was that the King had laid siege to Boulogne.

Elizabeth's eyes lit up. "Have you not heard? Boulogne has fallen! My father entered the city in triumph."

"Oh, that *is* good news! Were—were there many casualties?"

"I think not. You are worried about Francis, I see. Well, I have not heard anything, and they say that no news is good news. Try not to worry."

"I will," Kate promised, trying not to smile, for Elizabeth sounded like her mother-in-law, not a girl rising eleven.

They entered the palace and found Kat and Lady Troy sewing in the parlor, its windows open to the breezy air. They jumped up and hugged Kate, thrilled to see her, then detained her by asking after the children, when Elizabeth was clearly agitated to be off on her own with her visitor. When the others finally let Kate go, Elizabeth grabbed her hand and took her up to the guest chamber that had been prepared for her. And there, on the wall, was the little portrait of Aunt Anne that Kate had rescued from Hever.

"I had that put there specially for you," Elizabeth said. "And Will gave me that one to go with it."

Kate stared at the other portrait on the wall. It was Mother, but a younger Mother, in all her youthful beauty. Tears welled up.

"Will gave it to you? Will Stafford?"

"Yes. He visited me here last year, before he went to Calais. We had several long talks. He wanted me to know about my mother and yours, and the Boleyn family. He said your mother had wanted that."

Kate had to bite her tongue. Could Will have told Elizabeth that she was her sister? She nearly blurted it out herself, but held back lest Elizabeth take it as presumption on her part. She longed for her to know the truth, for the close bond between them to be cemented by their shared knowledge. But something told her that she might be venturing on dangerous ground. What if the King found out she had given away his secret? She decided to wait and see if Elizabeth said something herself.

When Kate had settled in and her maid had unpacked, she and Elizabeth wandered through the gardens, admiring the flowers and catching up on their news.

"I haven't told you the best thing of all," Elizabeth said. "Parliament has passed a new Act of Succession naming Mary and me as heirs to the throne after Prince Edward."

"That's wonderful news," Kate exclaimed, painfully aware that Elizabeth's restoration to royal status would preclude herself from ever being her equal. Yet she was pleased for her. It must have been hard to be deprived of her birthright and her legitimacy.

"Of course, neither Mary nor I have been declared true born," Elizabeth said airily, tripping along the gravel path. "I doubt my father will ever change his mind on that. But at least we have been restored to the succession, and I believe we have Queen Katharine to thank for that. Oh, she is a wonderful stepmother!" She chattered on, extolling the Queen's virtues, her learning, and her warm heart.

"Yet she isn't in the new painting my father commissioned when the Act was passed. He had Queen Jane painted in it instead, because she is Edward's mother. I'm in it, too, and Mary. I wore my 'A' pendant that was my mother's. Mary gave it to me. She was given my mother's jewels, you know. It's one of my prized possessions—because *she* wore it."

Kate was touched to hear Elizabeth speak so warmly of her mother. It was heartening to know that she had come to have such a positive view of her. She was amazed that she was prepared to wear that pendant publicly, seemingly not caring whether she offended her father. But clearly, she had not, for he must have seen the picture and noticed the pendant. Kate surmised that Kat had nurtured this sympathetic opinion of Anne, yet she also suspected that Will had contributed during those talks Elizabeth had mentioned. Mother would have wanted her niece to know the truth.

THE FORTNIGHT AT Hatfield passed quickly. Kate enjoyed herself hugely, although she missed her children and Francis was never far from her mind. Elizabeth was stimulating company and always eager to go on to the next diversion. They were never idle. One day it was a picnic in the park, another a game of hide-and-seek in the rambling old palace. Often, they rode out, for Elizabeth loved riding and was already an expert horsewoman. On wet days, they made music or practiced dance steps. Not once, in all that time, did Elizabeth give any hint that she knew Kate was anything more than a dear cousin. Disappointed, Kate concluded that Will had not said anything.

All too soon for Elizabeth, it was time for Kate to go home. The girl threw her arms around her as she made ready to leave. "I wish you could stay!"

"So do I, dear cousin, but my children need me."

"*I* need you!" It was not the first time that Elizabeth had shown she considered her needs more important than those of the children, and she had never quite got over her initial jealousy of Francis; indeed, Kate often felt awkward mentioning his name.

"I will see you again soon," she said firmly. "You must come to Greys Court."

"I will," Elizabeth said. "But I'd rather you came here."

"I'll do my best," Kate capitulated, sighing inwardly. "When you are married and have children, you will understand that it is hard to be parted from them."

"Oh, no, I won't!" Elizabeth retorted. "I will never marry."

Kate would have liked to talk about that, but her groom was waiting and the horses were becoming restive. "We'll see," she said lightly, and kissed Elizabeth, only to find herself enveloped in a fierce hug.

"God keep you, dear coz," Elizabeth said, sounding as if she might burst into tears.

"May He keep you, too," Kate said, gently disengaging herself and walking away.

WHEN FRANCIS CAME home, dirty and travel-sore, two weeks after Kate, he was full of the triumph at Boulogne and the part he had played in it. He was clearly exhilarated by the experience of battle.

"Mark me, this victory will be celebrated for centuries to come," he predicted as he lay in bed with Kate following their joyful reunion. She had never known him to be so ardent. It was as if his success had fired up every masculine instinct.

"And you were a part of it," she said, lying in the crook of his arm, her hand on his chest.

"We all were. The King was rejuvenated by it. His bad leg seemed of no account. By God, Kate, this is the beginning. France will soon be ours, you'll see!"

"I hope I will. And Husband, I have news of my own. Have you not noticed that my belly is a little rounded?" She kissed him as understanding dawned.

"Oh, my darling!" he said, and drew her back into his arms. "But we shouldn't . . . you should have told me . . . We might have harmed the babe . . ."

"Nonsense!" Kate giggled. "I had a very interesting conversation with your mother while you were away. She said it could not hurt the babe—it had hurt none of hers, and she'd heard other women say the same."

Francis drew back. "You were discussing such things with my mother? I—I don't think I want to know! I don't like to think of her in that context."

"You're lucky not to have to. I've had no choice but to think of my mother in that context, as you put it. I've had to try very, very hard not to imagine her with the King."

"Oh, God." Francis was laughing and she could not but join in.

"But he was much younger then, slimmer and handsome, I've heard," she said. Not yet the monster he would become. "It's the present Queen I pity. I'll wager that she struggles to breathe!" They both fell to chuckling, and then to lovemaking, but it was gentler this time and there was much kindness between them. Kate fell asleep happy, glad to have her beloved husband home.

BUT HE WAS not home for long. All too soon, he had to return to his duties at court. Kate moped around the house, feeling bereft and wondering if their married life was always going to be a series of long separations. She hated Francis being away, hated not being able to share the important little things with him, like the children's developments and life's everyday pleasures; and she hated sleeping in an empty bed. At night, she had to ward off dark memories and an irrational fear that this time, giving birth would hold more perils than it had before, something she had kept to herself, not wanting to worry him when he could not be with her. By day, she kept busy, ordering her household. She was twenty now, and something of an expert. Bilkins deferred to her, while she relied on him to keep things running smoothly. She set high standards: the house must always be looking its best in case unexpected visitors arrived—and because she liked to live in a clean and tidy environment. Mistress Wellgood agreed; she had the children in a comfortable but firm routine, and they were thriving on it.

Francis sent good news. The King had appointed him Master of the Horse to Prince Edward, who turned seven that October and was already a competent rider. It was a position of high trust, demonstrating Henry's confidence in him. Kate was proud of her husband—but alas, his new duties kept him away from home for even longer periods.

The King invited Kate to court for Christmas, but she was able to excuse herself by pleading the weariness of pregnancy, knowing that he, of all people, well understood the need for a woman to look after herself at such a time. But Francis had no such excuse: he had to be there, so Kate and Lettice did their best to make the season a merry one for the children. There were games and sweetmeats, and great excitement when a band of mummers put on a play of St. George in the Base Court. Wrapped in furs, their cheeks rosy in the cold air, Hal and Mary jumped up and down and laughed uproariously at their antics, and even one-year-old Lettice joined in, though she was far too young to appreciate the humor. Despite Francis's absence, it was a good Christmas.

MOTHER ASH PREDICTED that Kate's baby would be born in the middle of March 1545, and the King graciously granted Francis leave to come home. It was wonderful to have him with her as she neared her time, and she cherished the evenings they spent together in front of the fire in the solar.

On his second night home, they dined there. Francis seemed pensive.

"Something odd happened just before I left court," he said. "I was on guard in the watching chamber when I heard screams coming from the Queen's apartments. Then one of the King's physicians came hurrying past and went through to the privy chamber. Next thing we knew, his Grace himself appeared, leaning on the doctor's arm, and was helped to the gallery. After the doors closed behind them, I saw no more, but in a while the screaming stopped. The next day, I was attending the King when he and the Queen were walking in his privy garden. Suddenly, the Lord Chancellor appeared with a detachment of soldiers, and I was amazed to hear him say that he had come to arrest her Grace. But the King began shouting at him to go away. I have never seen a man look so terrified."

"What was it all about?" Kate wondered.

"I think the two incidents were related. Probably the Queen had offended in some way but had managed to obtain the King's forgiveness. Someone, however, forgot to rescind the order for her arrest."

"What a knife-edge she must live on. I wonder what she did wrong."

Francis lowered his voice. "There have been rumors that she and her ladies have secretly converted to the Protestant faith. Her close friend the Duchess of Suffolk is said to be particularly hot for it, if gossip is to be believed. There's talk that her lodging has been searched for forbidden books." His mouth set in a grim line. "It's the Catholic conservatives at court who are driving this persecution—chiefly the Lord Chancellor and Dr. Gardiner, the Bishop of Winchester. I'll wager that they are behind this plot to bring down the Queen, so that they can push another good little Catholic girl into the King's path. I'm glad they were foiled—*if* it was them."

Kate shivered. "It's frightening, the lengths some people will go to. They're ruthless. But to target the Queen? Francis, be careful. You dare not put a foot wrong."

"Oh, I am careful, never you worry." He took her hand. "I keep no books with me, I go to Mass with everyone else, and I take care not to let slip anything that might give me away. I hold my faith in my heart. God knows the truth of it." He paused and regarded her gravely. "Kate, have you ever considered converting?"

She froze. "No—although since my mother died, I have sometimes thought about it. If things were different, I would want to find out more, but I am too fearful of the consequences."

"I understand. Growing up in the Boleyn family, you must have heard much about the need for religious reform."

"They were all ardent reformists, but I was ten when I left Hever, and too young for anyone to discuss reform with me, although I overheard conversations. And looking back, they were actually devout Catholics. Will said they wanted the Church reformed from within. It was he who embraced the Protestant faith. Mother followed him, as I would look to follow you if the times were not so dangerous."

Francis was silent for a moment, sipping his wine. He leaned forward and whispered in Kate's ear. "This is treason, and I shouldn't say it, but I know that I can trust you. The King cannot live long. He is old before his time and infirm. The Prince is being educated by Cambridge men, reformists all—and more than that, I'll wager—and he, being young, will be susceptible to their teachings. The reformist party at court is growing stronger, which is why the Catholic faction is acting so viciously. Queen Jane's brother, Lord Hertford, is in high favor, and he is zealous for reform. In my view, England will turn Protestant when the King dies. And then, dear heart, I shall instruct you in the true faith."

Kate kissed him. "I should like that. Forgive me for being fainthearted now. And be assured that what you say to me in this room stays in this room."

THEIR CHILD WAS born a week later. It was another fine, healthy boy, and they named him William, for Francis's late father and Will Stafford.

"It's a shame Will cannot be here for the baptism," Kate said, lying in bed with her son in her arms, as Francis gazed proudly at them. Will was now serving in Scotland with Lord Hertford's army.

"He's likely to be away for some time." Francis sighed.

"This war has been going on for too long," Kate complained, kissing little William's downy head.

"That is because the King will not give up on his determination to wed the young Queen of Scots to Prince Edward and bring Scotland under English rule. The Scots, of course, don't like it—and they are suffering for their defiance. Hertford has laid waste much of the south. But they have fought back. After they won that great battle last month, some have been saying that the King has no hope now of winning Scotland. Yet he will not withdraw. He expects Hertford to reverse our losses."

"Why can't each ruler be content with his own?" Kate wondered.

Francis shook his head. "Oh, my little pacifist—how naïve you are. Kings, like other men, are territorial. The more they have, the more they want, and the monarchs of England have long wanted to lay hold of Scotland. To his Grace, this is a God-sent opportunity."

Kate sighed. "I hope you won't have to go to war again."

He hesitated. "I hope not, too." She knew he was just saying it for her sake. She had seen how the siege of Boulogne had affected him, seen the gleam in his eye and the spur to his manhood. If the call to arms came, he would go gladly, she knew it.

KATE READ THE letter avidly. She had not seen her brother, Harry, for years. He was twenty now, and a stranger to her, for they had been parted in childhood and had led separate lives since. She had done her best to keep in touch, but Harry was not a good letter writer and there were long gaps in communication, so she was pleased when he wrote to her that spring to tell her that the King had found him a wife. Her name was Anne Morgan, she was sixteen years old, and her father was a Welsh knight. Kate and Francis were invited to the wedding, which was to take place at court on 21 May.

Francis wrote to say that he couldn't attend, breaking the news that he was shortly to go to Scotland and serve Lord Hertford. He urged Kate to represent them both, but she told him she was still adjusting to new motherhood and did not want to leave baby William. In truth, she shrank from the prospect of going to court and encountering the King, much as she wanted to see her brother married.

Back came a firm reply. "You must go," Francis commanded. "Mistress Wellgood can look after the children, and you told me only last week that William has taken lustily to his wet nurse. I have seen your brother, and I know he will be very disappointed if you are not at his wedding." He added, as if for encouragement, "The King is ill. He has had a burning fever for several days, and the malady has attacked his bad leg. He has remained behind closed doors, and we are all sworn to secrecy about the true state of his health, but there is much speculation, as you can imagine."

He was saying that it was safe to go to court.

Reluctantly, Kate had Thomasina pack her traveling chest, then set off for Whitehall Palace, sad that Francis would have left for Scotland by the time she got there. She was consumed with a mounting sense of dread, knowing that he would be exposing himself to danger and that she would be spending the next weeks or, God forbid, months worrying about him.

He had left the key to his lodging with her brother. When she neared Whitehall, she sent one of her grooms ahead to find Harry, and they were waiting for her at the gatehouse. She hardly recognized the tall, thin-faced, dark-haired young man who was standing there. Gone was the boy she remembered; he had hardened into manhood, and in features he favored the Boleyns.

"Sister! You are most welcome!" They embraced awkwardly. "You have changed!" Harry said, leading her to Francis's lodging. "I hear you have four children now. I pray that Anne and I will be blessed with as many."

"I hope so, too, and that you will both visit us at Greys Court and meet the little ones."

"We'll see," he replied. His manner was brusque and a little off-putting. There was no warmth in him. And when a servant, hurrying along a gallery on some urgent errand, careered into him, he responded with an angry expletive that Francis would never have used in front of a lady.

"Fuck the fool," he muttered, stalking onward. "No respect for his betters."

Kate said nothing. She was wondering why she felt no close affinity with this brother of hers, and if she could ever love him as a sister should.

He unlocked the door to Francis's rooms and cast his eye around. "Passably tidy."

"Tidy enough for me," Kate retorted, as her grooms set down her chest in the next room and disappeared. She wondered if little Anne Morgan had seen the irascible side of her bridegroom, and if she had the character to soften him a little.

"I am looking forward to meeting Anne," she said, moving into the bedchamber. Harry followed.

"She's a pretty girl, and biddable," he said, sprawling in the only chair and watching her maid unpack, his eyes lingering on her bottom. "I'd been hoping for a better match, one that was commensurate with my status as a royal ward, and I also looked to the King for a handsome wedding gift to boost my income, but he has given me no special grants or favors. I could have done with something, for I have only a modest income."

His voice was peevish. Kate tried, and failed, to see anything of their mother in him beyond the dark hair. All she could see was Grandfather.

"But what of the lands you inherited from Father?" she asked.

"I can't take possession of them until I come of age next spring," he said.

"But that's not long to wait. And Anne will surely bring you a good dowry?"

"No," he sighed. "She has three sisters. Their portions are small."

"Then why are you marrying her?" She could not resist asking the question.

"Because the King wills it. I've heard rumors that I am his son.

This should put paid to them. If I was his son, I should have been found a rich heiress. But I am not. Mother told me that I am not."

Kate wondered for a moment if Mother had told him that he was brother to the King's daughter. She doubted it, for surely, in his present mood, he would have mentioned it. And yes, if he had been the King's son, he would have been making a better marriage. Henry Fitzroy, the bastard son the King had acknowledged, had been given two royal dukedoms and the Duke of Norfolk's daughter to wife. She wondered why he hadn't noticed how like the King she herself looked, but then he was probably too wrapped up in himself to consider her.

"Sometimes, it is better to live in obscurity than to be connected to royalty," she said.

Harry gave a dismissive gesture. "Not if one wants to get on in the world."

"Just think of our family. They were high in royal favor—but their fall was calamitous."

"Our aunt had a talent for making enemies, and our mother was a fool."

Kate was shocked. "You should not speak of her like that."

"Oh, come, Sister, she had a poor reputation. She was the King's mistress for a time, didn't you know? She got nothing out of it because she was stupid and had no ambition."

Kate could have shaken him. "You should have more respect. She loved you."

"And she abandoned us to marry a nobody and then had to flee abroad because of the scandal."

"She abandoned no one! We were well looked after. The King was your guardian!"

They were sparring again, as they had when they were little.

He shrugged. "I didn't come here to argue with you, Sister. You must forgive me if I am in a bad mood. I am feeling hard done by."

"There are some who have worse cause for complaint," she retorted. "Think of your little bride, how she must be feeling, far from home and marrying a stranger who quite obviously doesn't want her. Be kind to her, Harry. You will reap the benefits."

He scowled at her. "I will do my best." The scowl softened. "It is good to see you. And that's a fine gown your maid is hanging up."

It was a dusty-green velvet edged with embroidered biliments, one of the best gowns Kate had.

"Don't change the subject!" she reproved. "Be kind to Anne. And be grateful that you enjoy royal favor. You are young yet, and if you give good service, it will bring you rewards."

"I am fortunate that the King knows me for a loyal man and trusts me. I am with him often."

"I have heard that he is ill."

"Yes, but he is on the mend. He will not be at the wedding tomorrow, though. He does not like to be seen in public when he has these attacks. I have seen him go black in the face because of the pain."

"I am sorry to hear it." Kate did not feel sorry. God, she felt, was visiting His anger on the wicked man who had sent so many to their deaths. "So you plan to live the life of a courtier?"

"I want to serve my King, and I want to rise high. I'd like to do some soldiering as well."

Why did all men want to put their lives at risk? Were they naturally combative? Kate knew she would never completely understand them.

"You know, Sister, you much resemble our cousin, the Lady Elizabeth." Kate stiffened, waiting for Harry to remark on her likeness to the King, but he didn't. "I've seen her several times when she's been at court. She's shown herself very friendly to me. It's good to know that she cares for her mother's kin."

"I am close to her," Kate told him. "As you know, I served for years as her companion when she was growing up. I don't see her as often as I would like to these days, but we write to each other. Which reminds me, you should write to me more often! I like to know what you're doing."

He gave her a wry grin. "I know, I know. I will try to be better at keeping in touch."

. . .

THE WEDDING WAS a quiet affair, with only a small gathering in the Chapel Royal. Kate was glad that she had come. The Morgans were a pleasant couple, clearly overawed by the splendor of the court, but touchingly proud of their daughter, a round-faced maid with a mass of dark curls. She looked terrified when her father placed her hand in Harry's, but Harry had caught Kate's eye and suddenly smiled down at his bride.

Afterward, wine and comfits were served, and then the wedding party repaired to the Bell Inn, where Harry had commandeered a private room, and everyone tucked into a hearty dinner. Anne was looking happier by then, and Kate saw Harry lean over and kiss her affectionately on the cheek. Anne smiled back and he kissed her again, on the mouth this time, to the cheers of some of his friends. She began to hope then that all would be well and that his antipathy to the marriage the previous day would soon be a thing of the past.

SHE LEFT FOR home the following morning. Francis was very much on her mind. He would be well on the way to Scotland by now, each mile taking him farther and farther from her. She was glad that Will was with him. Will had paid a brief visit to Greys Court after his return south, and been much taken with his tiny namesake, yet he, like Francis, had been eager to resume military life. Kate was beginning to understand that men's worlds did not revolve around the hearth and the home, or even love itself. Important as these were to Francis, he needed to be out doing things and being active in his own sphere.

That summer, he wrote home of the savagery and slaughter of Hertford's advance across the southern lowlands of Scotland. Kate suspected that he had withheld the worst details from her. Fifteen towns and all the crops had been burned. She could not imagine the devastation.

Francis was away all summer; from his letters, she detected that he was in a buoyant mood. In September, he informed her that Will had distinguished himself by seizing for the King two great

Scottish ships, for which Hertford had knighted him. Kate could not help thinking of how proud Mother would have been. She would have loved being addressed as Lady Stafford.

When the campaigning season ended in the autumn, Francis arrived home unharmed, and Kate thanked God devoutly for his safe return. Yet she could see that he was troubled.

"We've lost Scotland," he said dejectedly, the children crowding around him as he tried to talk to Kate. "I don't think we will ever reverse our losses. But I fear that the King will not give up. He means to bring the Scots to heel."

Kate shuddered, for this meant that Francis might have to go north again next year. It was bad enough when he was away for long periods at court, but when he was a-soldiering, it was misery for her.

Chapter 20

1546–47

It was now March, and Kate had not seen Francis since the end of January, when they had spent an idyllic few days together with the children, and she had pretended that he didn't have to return to court. Those days had born fruit. When April came in, she knew she was with child again.

This time, she was not so well, and both Mistress Wellgood and Lettice, who came hurrying to Greys Court to help her, urged her to rest, shooing the children away and admonishing them not to play so noisily. Kate took advantage of their kindness and spent hours each day lying on her bed, giving in to fatigue and fighting off nausea.

Francis wrote often, as did Will, and there was even the occasional letter from Harry. In the summer, she learned that Harry had pulled strings and got himself elected Member of Parliament for Buckingham. He, Francis, and Will would sit in Parliament together. It was better than fighting wars.

As autumn drew in, Francis wrote more frequently of the King's ill health. Reading between the lines, Kate wondered if the old horror would live much longer. Heaven grant that his son was of a different character entirely. But he was only nine, so others would rule for him until he came of age. She hoped that the Queen would be given the regency. Francis, Will, and Harry were all full of praise for her, especially since she shared their religious convictions. But the King was not dead yet.

In the middle of October, after a difficult pregnancy that had set her to worrying that she might not survive the birth, she brought into the world, with the minimum of pain and fuss, another son. Francis was ecstatic, and commanded that the boy be named Edward after the Prince. Lying back on the pillows, the infant in her arms and her four other children snuggled around her, Kate felt truly blessed. The court, and indeed the world itself, seemed very far away.

THE COURT WAS closed that Christmas. The King was secluded at Whitehall with his doctors and senior councillors, and the Queen and everyone else had been sent to Greenwich Palace. With time on his hands, Francis came home, to Kate's great joy, and they were able to have a family celebration.

After the New Year of 1547 had been rung in, he began fretting about whether he should return to court. Will, who had stayed there, sent a letter telling him that the King was still shut away at Whitehall and no one knew what was happening. Even the Queen had been refused admission to see him. There was no need for Francis to go.

He went anyway. Two weeks later, a letter bearing his seal arrived at Greys Court. Suspecting that it might contain news of some moment, Kate took it to her closet to read.

The King was dead.

She felt nothing. She reminded herself that he had been her father and that convention demanded that she ought to feel some grief. But she had loathed him, and she could only think that the world would now be a better place without him. Nevertheless, she sent to the priest at the parish church to have the bells toll, one chime for each of the fifty-five years of the King's life, and instructed the household chaplain to say a Mass for the soul of the departed. She put on a black gown and wore it for a week.

She wrote to Francis, asking after the new King, who had lost a doting father and was very young to be burdened by the cares of state. Francis, who was busy preparing for his ceremonial role at the coming coronation, snatched time to reply that he thought the boy was more than equal to it. "Already, they are calling him the English Josiah. He is said to be zealous for the reformed faith. Although we had hoped it would be the Queen, Hertford is now Lord Protector, and he and others are coming out as Protestants. My darling wife, I do believe that the day of our delivery is at hand."

Kate's heart leaped, if not for herself, then for her husband. She rejoiced that he could now worship God according to his conscience—he, Will, Harry, and others of like opinions. When next he came home, full of the coronation, the celebratory jousts in which he had acquitted himself well, and Hertford advancing himself to the dukedom of Somerset, he told her in confidence that Parliament was going to turn England into a Protestant realm.

"You must take instruction, my darling," he told her over dinner in the solar that evening. "I hope you will feel able to come with me on this journey."

"I would like that," she said. "Will you teach me?"

They retired to the fireside and Francis fetched his English Bible. "This, Kate, is all that a devout Christian needs to inspire his faith. It is the Word of God, enshrined in Scripture. The Gospel must be your guide. This is what true evangelism means. Take some time each day to read it." He placed it in her hands. "There will be no need to lock it away now."

"But what of our chaplain? What if he sees me reading it?"

"I will speak to Father Paul. He, like all other priests, must obey the new laws. Now we come to what is called the Sacrament of the Mass. What do you believe about it?"

"That when consecrated by the priest, the bread and wine become the body and blood of Christ. I know that is what Protestants deny."

Francis nodded approvingly. "Yes, we see it as symbolic. We do not believe in the miracle of transubstantiation. And this has been the great controversy. Many Protestants have died in the flames for denying that so-called miracle. It is an essential tenet of our faith.

The Eucharist and baptism are the only sacraments we acknowledge."

"But there are seven sacraments," Kate protested.

"And the rest are superstition," Francis said gently. "Like the worship of the Virgin Mary and the saints. There is no command in Scripture to worship them—for Protestants, it is idolatry."

"But the Virgin understands the needs and concerns of women . . . and the saints are like my family."

Francis sighed, then leaned forward and took her hand. "God Himself understands all of us, both men and women. We do not need the Virgin and the saints to intercede with Him for us. Protestants pray directly to God, who knows our needs and our frailties. We have no truck with relics or shrines or pilgrimages. Our faith is rooted in Scripture."

Kate let go of his hand and sat back, thinking. She was not sure she liked this new religion. It seemed to deny much that she believed in or found comforting. She could barely imagine a world without the Virgin Mary; her own name saint, St. Katherine; or the many holy saints whose shrines seemed to be everywhere. Was all that to be swept away, with so much else that she held dear?

"You do not look convinced," Francis said with a wry smile.

"I fear I am not. I thought myself well educated, but I have never heard such radical ideas."

"They are not so radical when you think about them. And maybe you should not think upon them too much, but just accept them as truth. St. Paul wrote that women should keep silent in church, and if they wish to learn anything, they should ask their husbands at home. You have asked, and I have told you what I believe to be right. But I do not expect you to follow my beliefs unthinkingly, darling. I hope that you will come to them yourself. But ultimately, it is you who have to make up your mind which path you want to follow."

Kate heard him out in silence. This would take a lot of thinking about, and there was no one else with whom she could discuss it, no one who would give her an objective view. She wondered if anyone was ever objective about religion. Under one king, you had to worship as you were told, and now, under another, you had to do it a different way. Even if she clung to the old faith, would it be safe to do so?

"I will give it much thought," she promised. "If I can come with you, I will."

Francis smiled at her. "Read the Scriptures while I am away. You will find the answers you seek there, I am sure of it. Then we will talk when I am next home. Now, my sweet wife, let us to bed, for I have a mind to kiss you!"

She took his outstretched hand and followed him into the bedchamber.

SHE KEPT HER promise. The long afternoons after he left found her sitting by the fire, the Bible on her lap, avidly devouring it. It was wonderful to be able to read the Scriptures for herself and not have to rely on a priest to read them aloud in Latin and interpret them for her. Slowly, she began to appreciate that the Word of God was the most precious gift to mankind and that the Protestants were right in believing that it was through faith alone that souls were saved. Once you accepted this, it was possible to see the trappings of the Catholic faith as mere superstition. In reaching this conclusion, she surprised herself.

Once, she tried to discuss the matter with Father Paul, the chaplain, but he shied away, looking deeply troubled.

"It is what your master believes," she said, "and what I believe, too." It was true, she realized. "A new world is coming, and it behooves us all to embrace the true faith."

"Alas, I must not gainsay what your husband has taught you," he said, "but I urge you to question the reasons for your conversion. Are you sure you are not just moving with the times?"

"Please allow me more intelligence," she reproved him. "I have made up my own mind, as my lord bade me do."

And, she reflected, it was a blessing to have the freedom to do that, without fear of bloody or fiery reprisals. She did not write to tell Francis of her decision. She wanted to see his reaction when next he came home. How pleased he would be!

He did not come home for some weeks. By then, from his letters, it was clear that his presence at court was going to be required more often than before. Already, his zeal for the Protestant religion had impressed the young King, who had said that he was glad to have men like him sitting in Parliament.

Kate was pleased that Francis was high in favor but depressed at the prospect of extended separations. She longed to have a husband living at home. But she had been born of noble stock; this was the life for which she had been raised. And at court, Francis could do much to promote true religion. His was the hour. The conservatives of the late reign had been consigned to yesterday. A new order was unfolding.

Chapter 21

1547

Kate had written to Elizabeth to express her sympathy to her over her—their—father's death. She wondered—and hoped—if Elizabeth would now acknowledge their sisterhood. But when the letter came, it was addressed to her "dear cousin." Maybe, Kate told herself, she did not know that they were more closely related. She wondered if it was now safe to tell Elizabeth. But would she be believed? And would it look like presumption? No, she decided, it was best to say nothing. The bond between them was close anyway. She must be grateful for that.

She was thrilled when Elizabeth invited her to stay at Hatfield. She found her hostess very grown up for a thirteen-year-old, but looking somber in her black mourning gown, against which she made a habit of displaying her long slender hands. She was very vain and very witty, and Kate could not help reveling in her company. It had ever been so.

"I will not be here very long," Elizabeth told her over dinner on that first evening. "I am going to live with the Queen at Chelsea in the palace my father left her."

"Is she very distressed by her great loss?" Kate asked, unfolding her napkin.

"She is philosophical. She has great faith."

"That is a blessing. And you? How is it with you, my lady?"

"I am telling myself that he is in Heaven. That is a comfort to me. And I will do all in my power to keep his memory alive."

Kate was aware that the late King's death had left Elizabeth second in line to the throne after the Lady Mary. Elizabeth's status was now the highest it had been since her mother's fall. She was a very important young woman.

"Of course, he was my father," she said, tears filling her eyes. "I do miss him very much."

"I am sure. I am so sorry." Kate reached out a hand and took hers. "I lost my father when I was very young."

"But you barely knew him." Elizabeth's was clearly going to be the greater tragedy.

Kate swallowed the truth. "You're right, I didn't; I have only vague memories of him. I am thankful that I have a loving stepfather in Will Stafford."

"Stafford? Of course. He is a good man. Yet a stepfather cannot replace a real father. I am grateful to have known mine for so long. And I do not think I would tolerate a stepfather well." It sounded like a reproof, as if Kate was somehow wrong to feel filial love for a man who had not sired her. If only you knew! she thought.

"Lacking my own father, I am lucky to be loved as a daughter by such a man," she said.

Elizabeth did not answer. She's jealous! Kate realized. It was time to change the subject.

"King Edward has made a good start," she said.

"Indeed, he has." Elizabeth brightened. "I rejoice that England is turning Protestant. I believe that my father would in time have embraced the new religion. He knew that opinions were changing. Why else would he have had my brother educated by Cambridge reformers?" She helped herself to roast pork. "And you, Coz? Where do you stand in this great debate?"

"I am for the reformed faith," Kate said proudly, "as is Francis."

"So I have heard. It is as well. Soon, the old faith will be outlawed, and the Mass will be banned. This will go hard with my sister, Mary, for she is staunch for the old religion. Yet I am glad of it. It will be an end to superstition and idolatry. And yet . . ." Elizabeth grew thoughtful. "We both know what it is like to have to keep our true beliefs a secret. I would never persecute anyone for their faith, if I became—" She fell abruptly silent, but Kate knew what she had been going to say. *If I became queen.* It would be strange if she had not given the matter some thought.

Their eyes met.

"It was just an idle fantasy," Elizabeth said, blushing. "Edward is healthy. He will marry and have children. And Mary goes before me in the succession. I will never be queen of this realm. Instead, I shall live a fine life as a country gentlewoman in this English Eden. My father left me great wealth, you know. I intend to enjoy it. And in time I will become the favorite aunt of Edward's children. And I shall have suitors, lots of them—but I will never marry!"

Kate was surprised to hear her say this now. She had imagined that it had been the sentiment of a frightened child, and that Elizabeth would have grown out of it.

"I am sure you will change your mind when the right suitor comes along," she said, grinning.

"No, I do not wish to marry."

"But why? All women wish to marry. It is our destiny."

Elizabeth had flushed a deep pink. "I cannot tell you my reasons. I could not confide them to my twin soul." She sounded quite distressed. Kate wondered what people had been saying to her about marriage. But of course, nothing could paint a darker picture of it than the example of her own family. To this young girl, marriage must be equated with infidelity, incest, divorce, bloody beheadings, and death in childbed. And yet, she, Kate, had seen much more of all that than, thankfully, Elizabeth ever had. She had witnessed the shocking reality; and it was her family, too. Yet she had not been put off wedlock. She had a blissfully happy marriage with Francis.

Elizabeth was young. She had not known love. She would learn.

Kate dropped the subject and asked if there was any court gossip.

Elizabeth looked gloomy. "None, now that there are no ladies at court to cause scandal. In fact, I hear that all the talk is of politics and religion. Not that I lack an interest in those matters, but there are far more interesting things in life."

They finished their meal, then played backgammon and cards. It was like old times. Kate forgot she was a matron of twenty-three with five children; she felt like a young girl again.

Her peace was shattered when, as Elizabeth was gathering up the cards, she casually announced that Protector Somerset had decided to revive the war with Scotland. "He is to go north with an army later this year."

"No!" Kate cried.

Elizabeth stared at her. "Why should you object? My father envisaged England and Scotland being united through Edward's marriage to the Queen of Scots. It's a brilliant plan, and it would put a stop to the eternal warfare between our two kingdoms."

"The Scots don't want such a union."

"They are too short-sighted."

"We would not want them to invade us and try to take our realm."

Elizabeth's steely gaze was just like her father's. "That smacks of treason, Kate. I recall that your husband distinguished himself in the last campaign."

"Yes, and I really don't want him putting himself at risk again!" Kate burst out. "That's the real reason why I hate this war. Forget treason! It's because I cannot live for weeks at a stretch in terror for the man I love."

She wished she had said nothing at all, for Elizabeth was giving her a cool appraisal. How could she be expected to know what it was to love, or to fear for the life of the beloved? She was thirteen, for Heaven's sake! And yet she had the air of one who was all-knowing, all-seeing.

"Forgive me," Kate said, "I forgot myself. Of course, I support the King in this war. I do see the wisdom of it. You must excuse my womanly frailty."

"All is forgiven," Elizabeth said lightly. "I know that neither you nor your husband would ever forget your duty to his Majesty."

In her relief that the slight contretemps between them had

been defused, Kate was barely aware that in all their talk that evening, Elizabeth had not once mentioned Francis by name. Always, she had said "your husband." It dawned on her later, lying in bed, that the girl was as jealous of Francis as ever, and that she still resented him for taking Kate away from her, as she perceived it. And not once had she asked about the children.

The next morning, as they parted, Kate invited Elizabeth to spend a few days at Greys Court.

"It would be a pleasure," Elizabeth said, smiling, "but I am not sure when I can get away. Let us see how things settle down at Chelsea."

Kate's sixth sense told her that Elizabeth would never come to Greys Court. Maybe she did not wish to see Kate enjoying all the blessings of a happy marriage and family life that she herself professed not to want.

"I hope you will be very happy at Chelsea," she said.

"I know I will!" Elizabeth's face had lit up. "My stepmother the Queen is a wonderful woman."

They embraced, and Kate rode away, wishing that things could return to how they had once been between them. That could never be, given Elizabeth's elevated status to her, but deep affection still lay between them. They had promised to keep in touch by letter, and Elizabeth had said that she would invite Kate to Chelsea.

As her little procession moved westward, Kate felt her spirits rising. She could not wait to resume her real life and be reunited with her children. And soon, hopefully, Francis would be home again.

HARRY HAD REACHED twenty-one. There had been a celebration in his lodging at court. Francis had gone, and it sounded as if they had all got rather drunk.

"Will is back at court," he had written. "He joined us. You'd think that a knighthood and being elected to Parliament might have gone to his head, but he's still the same old Will, dependable and kind as ever."

Harry, he added, was moving into Rochford Hall, which

Mother had left to him, knowing that Kate was well set up at Greys Court. He was shortly to take up residence there with Anne, who was with child already. Kate thought she might go and visit them, but Rochford was a long way from Oxfordshire. Maybe later in the summer.

There were rumblings of war all through the spring, but Kate was hoping that they would come to nothing. She saw little enough of Francis as it was, without his going all the way to Scotland, with all the worry that entailed.

When he came to Greys Court in May, he brought startling news.

"The Queen Dowager has remarried!" He threw his riding cloak across the settle in the solar.

"Already?" Kate was shocked.

"She's been married since March." Francis's expression was disapproving.

"But King Henry only died at the end of January . . ."

"Indeed. But that rogue Thomas Seymour, or Lord Sudeley as we must now call him, apparently laid such siege to her virtue that she was compelled to accept his suit. His brother the Protector is furious. The Queen seemed such a sensible woman. I cannot understand why she has acted so rashly."

Kate could have told him why. What woman, having endured marriage with that terrifying, obese monster, would not have sought love at the first opportunity? But she kept quiet. Looked at dispassionately, the Queen had behaved foolishly. Surely, she could have held Seymour off for a little while? Or maybe he was too handsome and ardent for her to resist him!

"The councillors are up in arms," Francis was saying, taking his seat by the hearth. "She could have jeopardized the succession. Had she become pregnant immediately, there would have been the possibility that it was by the late King."

Kate sniffed. "Hardly, given what I've heard of the state of his health toward the end. But *is* she with child?"

"Not that I know of. So the word is that the Protector has forgiven them. He had to, because somehow Seymour tricked the young King into giving the marriage his blessing."

Kate had a sudden thought. "What of Elizabeth? In March, she went to live with the Queen at Chelsea."

"She's still there. The word is that the Lady Mary urged her to move in with her because she was worried about the poor moral influence of the Queen's example. But Elizabeth refused to budge. She's shrewd, that one. She knows that Mary will never give up her faith or her Mass, and that it's wise not to be associated with her."

"And she is enjoying life at Chelsea. She has said so in her letters. And she has said nothing about the Queen remarrying."

"Maybe she did not know."

Kate knelt at Francis's feet and leaned her head against his leg. "She wants me to visit her at Chelsea."

"No, my dear. You shall not go. Or not until this scandal has died down. But you could invite the Lady Elizabeth to visit you here. It would be most suitable at this time."

"I am not sure that she would come, but I will write and ask."

The answer was a polite no. Elizabeth was engrossed in her studies. She mentioned that she had been joined at Chelsea by Seymour's ward, her cousin Lady Jane Grey. "He looks to marry her to the King," she wrote, "and they will be well suited, for she is as zealous for the true faith as he is, and as studious. But I wish she was more congenial company. I wish you were here. It would please me greatly if you could come to Chelsea."

Kate sighed. Elizabeth wanted their friendship to be on her own terms. She wanted no rivals for Kate's attention.

She was disappointed. She would have loved to show Elizabeth Greys Court and have her share in her life here, if only for a short while. She would have gone to Chelsea, had Francis allowed it. But he was right. She could not let herself be tainted by scandal. She wrote back, saying that she too was busy, but hoped to visit at a later date. In the meantime, they could write to each other.

SEPTEMBER FOUND KATE at Greys Court, fretting herself silly because Francis had gone to Scotland with the Lord Protector's army. She was pregnant again and feeling very vulnerable. What would become of her and the children if Francis was killed? Hal, now a boisterous six-year-old, would inherit, but she would have to be in charge until he attained his majority. With that in mind, even though she shrank from the thought, she immersed herself more fully in estate business, learning from Bilkins and others how Francis's lands were administered. They were plainly impressed by her grasp of things and were not too proud or hidebound to make light of her questions or her decisions. She was determined that Francis should feel that he could leave everything in her hands during his long absences—or when he was here no more. Tears welled up at the thought, but she resolutely refused to shed them. Too many people relied on her; she could not show weakness now.

In October, she received a letter from Francis, addressed to "My Lady Knollys." What could that mean? Excitedly, she tore off the seal and read that the English had won a great victory at Pinkie Cleugh, near Musselburgh, and crushed the Scots. Afterward, at the camp at Roxburgh, the Lord Protector had knighted Francis in reward for his bravery during the battle. Her heart leaped. He was safe, her beloved, honored as he deserved, and surely, he would be home soon. She went about singing.

When he did arrive, later that month, she gathered their children and the whole household in the Base Court to welcome him, herself presenting the stirrup cup.

"Sir Francis!" she said, looking lovingly up at him.

"Lady Knollys!" He grinned, then downed the wine in one gulp, slid from the saddle, and enveloped her in a bear hug, as everyone cheered and the children danced excitedly around them. He smelled of sweat and the open road and himself, and she drank him in greedily.

Much later, when they lay together, drowsy after lovemaking, she told him how proud she was of him. "You have come home a hero," she whispered, "and now you will be even more in favor—and gain in prosperity."

"That is as well," he grinned, "since I have a growing family to support. Last year, if God had taken me to His mercy, I would not have left four nobles in yearly revenue. Our boys would have had to take to crime and risk the gallows for lack of living! No, my sweet, I am jesting. I am sure that, if I had died then, I would have left them such an example of a happy, yet poor, life that they would have been content to live within their means." He kissed her. "That is the price of having a large family."

"Well, if you will be so lusty . . ." she teased.

Chapter 22

1553

KATE WATCHED FROM THE SOLAR WINDOW AS THE HORSEman rode into the Base Court. It was Francis's messenger, come no doubt with the latest news from court. It was a warm March day, but she shivered uneasily, for the young King's health seemed to be in decline, and both she and Francis were worried about what would happen if he died. For his next heir was the Lady Mary, a fanatical Catholic who had spent the past six years fighting for the right to have Mass celebrated in her house. Again and again, she had defied the law that banned it; she had even told her brother, who saw himself as a second Solomon where religion was concerned, that he was too young at fifteen to have an opinion. That, Francis said, had not gone down well.

Kate dreaded to think what would happen if Mary came to the throne. She herself had embraced the Protestant faith with a fervor she would never have thought possible, while Francis was more zealous for the Gospel than ever. Their household was run on strict Protestant lines, their children well educated in the faith. Kate could not bear the idea of Mary upsetting the new order and turning the clock back to an age of idolatry and superstition. Surely the people would never stand for it?

The babe in her belly stirred, like a butterfly. It had quickened only this past week. She wondered what the future would hold for it. Patting her stomach, she went downstairs to the great hall to receive the messenger. Her eight surviving children were all seated at one of the trestle tables with their tutor, the sun shining upon them through the tall windows. Rising twelve, Hal was by far the liveliest of the brood, but protective toward his younger siblings. A year younger, Mary was quite the little lady, demurely bent to her scribing. Kate and Francis had agreed that their daughters should have a similar education to their sons, although Francis was concerned that the girls especially should be brought up to godliness. "Experience has shown me that, for lack of an orderly moral upbringing," he had said, "young women fall into all kinds of foul crimes. I have seen the daughters of eminent courtiers who are no better than they should be, and I am not having my little maids losing their reputations."

Yet he was not strict with them; he doted on them too much. Kate was the one who did the disciplining, and it was the spirited, headstrong nine-year-old Lettice who needed it most. With her beauty, her red curls, and her mischievous nature, she was a little temptress and knew just how to get what she wanted. That, of course, led to squabbles among the children, for the younger ones didn't stand a chance. William, Edward, and Robert usually banded together against their overbearing sister, while three-year-old Elizabeth—to whom the Lady Elizabeth was godmother—was no match for her at all. Only the baby, Richard, remained oblivious to the power struggles. Yet the children loved each other, that much was obvious. When they got into trouble, they pulled together.

Having received the messenger, taken the letter he brought, and sent him to the kitchens for some food, Kate sat in one of the window embrasures and read it. Francis sent his dear love, as ever. The King was no worse. She sighed with relief to hear that. There was the usual court gossip—Francis knew she liked to be kept abreast of it—and news of Will, who had remarried some years ago and found true happiness, and William Cecil, the clever statesman whom Francis had befriended.

The noise from the children's table distracted Kate. She looked across at them; they were laughing at one of Hal's jokes. As so often, she thought of the child who would never laugh again, little Maud, who had been born the year after Pinkie Cleugh, lived for only two months, and been buried in the parish church. Part of Kate's heart was buried with her. She knew she would never be whole again.

The laughter grew uproarious. Kate frowned at the young tutor, Dr. Palmer, who had come to them from Magdalen College, Oxford, where he had been a fellow and reader in logic—until the college authorities had got wind of his uncompromising Catholic views, of which he had made no secret; indeed, he had spoken so harshly against Protestant scholars that his name had been struck off the list of fellows. He had then met Francis in Oxford and, against all the odds, Francis had taken to him.

"I like his courtesy," he had told Kate. "He's cheerful, pleasantly spoken without affectation, affable, even childlike, yet quick-witted and reasoned in argument. I do not think he has a deceitful bone in his body. I told him that we needed a tutor for the children, since the last one had proved so ineffectual, but that I would not offer him the post unless he embraced the true faith, for I would not have a Catholic in my household. He said he would think it over and meet with me again."

Dr. Palmer had converted. Like Kate, he quickly became an ardent Protestant. There was no need to worry about his sincerity. The children had taken to him happily and were making good progress under his tuition. Kate liked him, although she wondered occasionally about his unconventional approach. Sometimes—like today—he was a little lax on discipline; he wasn't one of those tutors who whipped out the rod or the birch at the slightest transgression. The children's grandmother, who had visited Greys Court recently, made it clear that she would have expected a firmer hand. But Kate was generally content with Dr. Palmer's methods; she preferred the carrot approach to learning, rather than the stick.

She got up and walked over to her children. There was a sudden hush.

"Settle down," she said firmly. "Don't give Dr. Palmer any trouble." She smiled at him and walked through to the kitchen, where the cook was planning a feast in honor of Will and his wife, Dorothy, who were arriving with Francis in two days' time for a short stay. Kate was looking forward to seeing her guests; she was delighted that Will had found someone to love after being a widower for two long years, and she had grown to like Dorothy immensely.

She was happy in her life, glad that the King was still unmarried and that there was no place for women in his court. Thankfully, he did not go in for feasting ladies, unlike his father. She still hated the court, even as she understood that, for Francis, it was the way to advancement. He had survived the momentous changes that had occurred when the Duke of Northumberland ousted Protector Somerset from power and seized the reins of government in the young King's name, then had Somerset beheaded. Francis had advanced considerably in the last six years. His strong Protestant convictions had continued to impress King Edward and Northumberland, and he was constantly required at court, which Kate hated, yet had come to terms with. He served not only as a Gentleman Pensioner, but also as the King's standard bearer—and he still sat in Parliament. He seemed to spend much of his time conferring with William Cecil and others on religious policy—he loved nothing more than a good debate—or, being still fit and active at nearly forty, playing a prominent part in the many tournaments held for Edward's pleasure. Both, it seemed, were a sure route to preferment.

When Francis was at home, he was active throughout the shire, and very popular. He was Justice of the Peace for Oxfordshire, constable of Wallingford Castle, and steward of Ewelme, a palace that King Edward had given to his sister Elizabeth.

It was a busy life he led, but Kate was content to stay at home and devote her time to raising her family and running her household. They had two residences now: Greys Court and Caversham Manor, a lovely, moated house near Reading with nearly three thousand acres of land, which Francis had leased from the Crown. They now divided their time between both houses, which was easy, as they were only six miles apart. Kate was constantly giving thanks to God for bestowing such manifold blessings on her.

After leaving the kitchens, she walked to the herb garden with a list the cook had given her and began to pick the selected plants, the air around her redolent with their scent. The smell of rosemary evoked the last time she had been in a herb garden, which was when she had visited Elizabeth last autumn at Ewelme. Elizabeth had never come to Greys Court or Caversham, despite repeated invitations, so when Kate learned that Edward had given her Ewelme, she was thrilled to think that her unacknowledged sister would be residing so near to her. But Elizabeth had not returned to Ewelme since then, evidently preferring her other houses, and Francis was worried that, if she stayed away too long, it would fall into disrepair. He urged Kate to warn her of that, but Kate did not like to appear to be putting pressure on her to visit. As she had long known, their friendship was to be played out on Elizabeth's terms. Nevertheless, they were still close, still very much in touch by letter, and the affection between them was as warm as ever. Their shared faith had brought them even closer. Yet not once had Elizabeth ever hinted that she knew they were sisters. She had, however, expressed her approval of Francis's staunch devotion to the Protestant faith, and that, Kate knew, was praise indeed, given Elizabeth's usual antipathy toward him.

As she knelt there with her scissors and trug, Kate felt glad that Elizabeth had recovered her good reputation. She had had a hard time after Queen Katharine died in childbed. The following year, when her widower, Lord Seymour, was arrested for treason, it emerged that the handsome, ambitious rogue had made inappropriate advances to Elizabeth at Chelsea, under the poor Queen's very nose, she deeming them innocent—or so it was said. There had been scandalized gossip about morning romps in Elizabeth's bedchamber—scandalous because she was second in line to the throne and to seduce or marry her without royal permission was high treason. That rogue had taken advantage of her when she was not yet fourteen, and Kate was convinced that she had been drawn to him, unable to prevent herself responding to his advances. In recent years, she had tried to talk about what happened with Elizabeth, but Elizabeth would never be drawn on her feelings for Seymour.

It had ended, of course, in tears and worse. Kate had received a distressed letter from her cousin, telling her that the Queen had sent her away from her household, having come upon her in Seymour's arms. To make matters worse, Katharine Parr had been pregnant at the time. Elizabeth had been sent to Cheshunt, to the home of Kat's sister Joan, who was married to Sir Anthony Denny. Elizabeth had not wanted to go there, and she had been distraught at the thought of losing the love of her stepmother. All of this Kate learned from several frantic letters.

After Seymour's arrest in 1549, Elizabeth, still only fifteen, had been mercilessly interrogated by the King's Council in the hope that she would further incriminate him by admitting that he had unlawfully plotted to marry her. Kat and Thomas Parry, Elizabeth's comptroller, were imprisoned in the Tower and questioned, too. Terrified though she was, Elizabeth had held her own, displaying her unique, instinctive mental dexterity. Kate had not heard from her at this time. Later, Elizabeth explained that she had been too frightened to commit anything, however innocuous, to paper lest it be misconstrued and used against her.

She had given nothing away; she had been unable to save Seymour from the terrible consequences of his misdeeds, but she saved herself. And then she had reinvented herself as a virtuous Protestant princess in order to salvage her tarnished reputation. On the few occasions when Kate had seen her, right up to the previous autumn, she had been soberly dressed in black and white, with little jewelry. The fabrics, however, were sumptuous, and the black dyes costly, and Elizabeth had plainly been aware that she looked striking in such elegant attire, which set off her long red hair and slender hands to perfection. At nineteen, she was not beautiful: she had the thin face of the Boleyns and her father's Roman nose; but she was witty and vivacious, and men were undeniably drawn to her. Yet she showed no particular favor to any of them, for she was still determined never to marry. Kate was beginning to believe that she meant it.

TWO DAYS LATER, Kate kept going to the window in hopes of seeing Francis and their guests approaching. It was nearing dinnertime when they arrived and she found herself swept into her husband's strong embrace.

"Oh, Kate, it is so good to see you!" he breathed in her ear, then kissed her heartily on the mouth. "Come and greet our guests."

Kate turned and saw Dorothy alighting from a litter; and there was Will, the same as ever, offering her his hand and looking down on her with the utmost tenderness. When he saw Kate walking toward them, he gave a shout and kissed her fully on the lips.

"Kate, always a joy to see you," he declared.

Kate kissed them both on the cheek. Her stepmother was still only thirty-one, fourteen years younger than Will, and very pretty. Will had decided that he wanted an heir, like all landed men, and therefore had thought it best to take a young bride, yet no one had thought he would find someone as charming as Dorothy, with her pointed little face, wide-set eyes, and dark curls.

"Dot!" Kate greeted her. "You are most welcome!"

She led them into the great hall, where the children greeted them enthusiastically, vying with each other for their father's attention. She showed them to the guest chamber in the tower, where an ewer of water, a basin, and towels of fine Holland cloth had been set out for them.

"Dinner is about to be served," she told them. "Come down when you are ready." From the way Will was looking at Dot, she thought that might not be for some time, but they appeared only a few moments later, hand in hand.

Dinner was a lively affair, and as dish after dish of choice meats was served, Kate enjoyed herself hugely. It was wonderful to have Francis home and to feel the sweet pinch of his hand on her knee beneath the tablecloth; and it was good to see Will looking so happy and enjoying a lively debate on religion with Dr. Palmer. Life was marvelous—and it would remain marvelous if the King lived.

Will and Dot were eager to speak of the charms of their four-month-old son, Edward.

"We named him after the King," Dot said.

"How is the King?" Kate asked.

Francis and Will exchanged glances. "Not well," Francis said.

"But I cannot tell you much more because he has not been seen in public recently. No one knows what is happening. Northumberland says nothing."

Kate shivered, despite the warmth of the fire and the convivial company. She had never met the Duke of Northumberland, but knew he was a firm ruler, and a militant Protestant. Francis had told Kate that he had vigorously opposed the Lady Mary having her Masses; it sounded as if he had made her life a misery with his threats. But why was he keeping silent about the King's health? That sounded ominous.

"Do you think his Majesty is very ill?" Kate asked, looking anxiously at Francis.

"I fear so. If he were not, we would know about it."

"We must brace ourselves for change," Will said. "That will be nothing new to me. I found favor under Somerset, but when he fell, I made speed to get into the good graces of Northumberland. It was he who gave me an annuity in recognition of my good service to the late King Henry, and he has entrusted me with special missions." A shamefaced look came over his face. "I regretted what happened to Somerset, but I agreed with Northumberland that he had misgoverned England. For his overweening ambition, his vainglory, his rash wars, his enriching himself with the King's treasure, and doing all by his own authority, he deserved to be brought down. And then, of course, there were those charges of treason."

Kate and Francis said nothing. Kate knew that her husband did not share Will's views of Somerset, although he supported Northumberland. He had told her that Will had felt it his duty to report to Northumberland compromising words uttered by a servant in defense of Somerset.

"But this will be a different kind of change," Francis said at length. "Somerset and Northumberland have promoted the new religion. Mary is a devout Catholic. Do you see her tolerating what she must see as heresy?"

"I barely know her," Will said gloomily.

"She has fought doggedly for the right to have her Mass. That must tell us something. But the question we must ponder first is, will this kingdom accept a woman as its sovereign lady?"

"It's not natural," Will muttered. "Saving your presence, ladies, women are not born to rule."

"No, they are meant to be subject to their husbands, as they are the weaker sex," Francis said, picking up the ewer of wine and refilling their goblets. "How does wielding dominion over men ride with that? What if a queen regnant marries? Is her husband to be subject to her?"

"I say again, it is against nature," Will opined. "Yet, according to law, Mary is next in line."

"That's as may be, yet she is still, by law, a bastard. Some may take issue with that."

"We can only hope so." Will was shaking his head. "But don't hold out too much hope. There will be those who will stand up for her right."

"She'll have to contend with Northumberland first. I can't see him recognizing her as queen. It will be the end of his career."

"And the end of him!" Will said grimly.

Kate changed the subject; she had had enough of this depressing discussion and did not want the happy atmosphere to be marred. "Would anyone like some cakes? I made them this morning." She handed them around, then turned to Dot. "I have always found it serendipitous that you are a Stafford, too."

"Indeed!" Will chimed in, brightening. "I married above myself, for she is from the grand side of the family. She has royal blood!"

Kate wondered if this was a blessing or a curse.

"Yes." Dot hesitated. "You all know that my mother was born Ursula Pole."

A hush descended again. They knew about the noble families of the realm, and so they were aware that Dot's was a lineage trebly tainted by bloodshed. For Ursula Pole was the granddaughter of the late Duke of Buckingham, a descendant of King Edward III who had been executed for treason more than thirty years ago. Her mother had been Margaret Pole, Countess of Salisbury, a niece of King Edward IV and King Richard III and therefore also of the old Plantagenet royal blood. In 1541, the Countess, at a ripe old age, had been executed by King Henry simply because he saw her as a threat to his throne. Going back further, *her* father, the Duke of Clarence, had been attainted for treason and executed, some said by drowning in a butt of Malmsey wine. But what came most forcibly to Kate's mind was the manner of the aged Countess of Salisbury's dying, since the headsman had been inept and had butchered her horribly on the block. And Dot would then have been, what, fifteen—old enough to know the terrible truth of it.

She quickly turned the conversation to pleasanter things. "Are you gentlemen going hawking this afternoon?"

"Yes, darling, we will. What will you and Dot do?"

"We will spend some time with the children. Yes, you rascals!" Her gaze raked the trestle table where her offspring were enjoying the cakes. "We can play hide-and-seek, or Mother Bird. This hall is big enough for that. And then your aunt Dot and I would like some time to ourselves." She smiled at Dot.

IT WAS A lovely afternoon, and she and Dot ended up in the still room, crushing early flowers for potpourri to scent the rooms. A convivial supper followed, after which Kate played her lute for their guests, with Francis looking on admiringly. It was obvious what was on his mind. The years had not dimmed his ardor. Outwardly, he was an upright, moral man, puritanical in his views, but in bed, he had no inhibitions.

Later that night, after they had held each other close and lain quiet for a while, he spoke. "I like Dot, and Will is clearly happy with her, but I do wonder why he married her. He gained no material advantage from it. She has dangerous family connections, and I gather she brought no dowry to speak of."

"Does that surprise you?" Kate murmured. "She is one of fourteen and has four sisters to be provided for. That will be a fine burden on her father's purse."

"Mine will be burdened too if we have many more daughters!" Francis chuckled.

Kate laughed. "Will fell in love with her. That's why he chose her, just as you chose me. I brought you no great advantages."

"You have brought me everything," Francis said, growing serious. He cupped her face in his hands and kissed her. "I would choose no other, were I to start again."

"And I would still choose you," she whispered, when he released her.

"To return to Dot," he resumed, "what really puzzles me is that Will, a staunch Protestant if ever there was one, chose a bride from one of England's foremost Catholic families, with all its perilous connections."

"But Dot is not a Catholic. She made that very clear this afternoon. She's as staunch for the Gospel as Will is. No, he married her for love, as he married my mother. One can only admire him for spurning material gains for love."

Francis nodded. "I'm sure you're right. But we might also ask what Dot saw in him to begin with. He told me today that he had incurred increasing debts. Last year, at his request, the King agreed to exchange his royal pension for a large cash sum, so that he could clear them. And he confided that his career at court is in jeopardy because in November, he got into a fight with one of the guards and ended up being thrown into the Fleet Prison to cool his heels. He was released pretty quickly, but he is convinced that the episode cost him the Privy Council's respect and confidence."

Kate was dismayed to hear this. "I did not know he had such a hot temper."

"Apparently, the guard said something disparaging about your mother."

"Well, then, I am glad he defended her honor! And I am sure that he will rehabilitate himself in the Council's eyes. He's a good man, Francis. I can see what Dot saw in him."

"I can, too, darling. I feel privileged to have him as a friend. He looks out for me, as my father would have done if he had lived. And I look out for him too, of course." His voice was drifting off, and when Kate looked at his beloved face in the candlelight, she saw that he slept.

THE NEXT AFTERNOON found Kate and Dot sitting by the solar fire with their embroidery tambours. Dot drifted off to sleep, lulled by the warmth and another good dinner, and Kate was about to give way to the impulse too when she heard men's voices below the window, which she had opened slightly to prevent the room from becoming stuffy.

"Sobriety is your name!" Will said in a teasing voice. "You are the lamp and torch of truth. But being committed to reform does not mean that you have to lead a cheerless life."

"I'm not always sober," Francis protested. "I enjoy a drink as much as any man, and good food."

"But look at you, always dressed in black!"

"That's because I like it, and Kate likes me in it, too." It was true. There was something about a man in black that Kate found most enticing.

This was proving to be an interesting conversation, and she tiptoed to the window to hear it more clearly. The men were sitting on a stone bench just below her, so she drew back behind the curtains. It crossed her mind that eavesdroppers were said to hear no good of themselves, but she was too curious to move away.

"She's a good girl, is Kate. And she has made you an excellent wife." Will's tone was fond.

"She is my constant blessing," Francis said, as tears sprang to Kate's eyes. "She unburdens me of many cares and keeps my house, my estate, and my private accounts in good order. She is one of the most intelligent women I have ever known and always offers me sound advice. She gives it to all who ask, even the Lady Elizabeth. They write regularly, you know. And Kate is a steadying influence on our children, who would probably be little ruffians without it. They are a handful, and yet she has time and patience for them all. We both try to set them a good moral example. Kate oversees the education of our daughters and makes sure that that hothead Palmer treats them the same as the boys."

"You afford them the same education?"

"Broadly. I want my daughters to be literate and to write in an elegant hand. I've asked Palmer to give them some instruction in languages. Of course, the boys will go to Eton when the time comes, and I like to think that they will go on to Oxford, to Magdalen College if possible."

Kate smiled, thrilled by Francis's praise. They had discussed their hopes for the children many times, and it pleased her greatly that he consulted her on such matters.

"I would like my children to have a similar education," Will said.

"The key is to find a good tutor. But your Edward is young yet."

"Aye, but he will soon grow. By the way, I hear that Harry Carey has finally sold Rochford Hall."

"Yes, to Lord Rich. I don't think Harry ever liked the place. He spent all that money on refurbishments, too. Still, he got a good price for it. I gather he's been at Hatfield, ingratiating himself with the Lady Elizabeth. She seems to hold him in high favor. She stood godmother to his daughter Philadelphia."

Their voices grew fainter. They were walking away toward the ruins. Kate sat down, giving thanks to God for sending her such a good husband.

Chapter 23

1553

THE FIRST THING SHE DID AFTER HER GUESTS HAD DEPARTED and Francis had returned to court was sit down to write to Elizabeth. She would rather have talked with her face-to-face, for she was full of fear about what might happen if King Edward died and would have loved to hear Elizabeth's views on the matter. But she dared not commit her thoughts to paper. For one thing, it was treason to predict or even imagine the death of the King. For another, that event would bring Elizabeth one step closer to the throne; she would be heir presumptive, and Kate did not want her thinking that she was fishing for special favor. Yet Edward's passing would affect Elizabeth in much the same way as it would affect every other English Protestant. She must have given the matter some thought. She might be harboring the same fears. If only they could meet!

Kate could go to Hatfield, of course. But Elizabeth was mercurial. There was no telling if she would want to talk about the future and she often kept her own counsel, not liking to share her inmost thoughts. No, Kate would write instead. For some reason, she did not want to be away from home at this time.

She sat there for a while thinking of what to say. Then she

began her letter, asking after Elizabeth's health and telling her about Will and Dot's visit, for Elizabeth was fond of Will and always liked to hear news of him. She asked if Elizabeth had heard anything of the King's health or the rumors that he was very ill. "I hope with all my heart that they are untrue," she added, "and I hope that your Grace will be able to reassure me on that point from your own comfortable knowledge."

A week later, she had a reply. "The King my brother is well," Elizabeth had written. "I had it from my lord of Northumberland himself. Whether it be true or not I cannot tell, but I have asked my good friend William Cecil to advise me. I will write again when I know more."

Kate hoped fervently that Northumberland had spoken truth. Why should he lie to Elizabeth, a good Protestant like himself? She felt a little reassured when Elizabeth's second letter arrived, informing her that Edward was indeed well. He had just suffered an ague and there was nothing to worry about. Cecil would keep them informed, though. He was reliable, perceptive, and discreet, a good friend to them all.

Resolutely banishing her fears from her mind, Kate sat down at the table by the solar window with pen and paper. She had long had in mind a project to keep her occupied during the evenings when Francis was absent; it was something for her daughters. She wanted to compile a collection of psalms and meditations that she had found moving and uplifting in the hope of inspiring them and other women to prayer, and to study the Scriptures. There was no time like the present.

She took up her quill, dipped it in the inkpot, and wrote the title. *A Heavenly Recreation, or comforts to the soul.* It occurred to her that if the worst did happen and Mary came to the throne and restored Catholicism, she might have to hide her work, and the English Bible. But she would not think about that now. She would meet that problem when it arose—if it ever did.

KATE THOUGHT LITTLE of it when Francis wrote in May to say that one of Northumberland's younger sons, Guildford, had married Lady Jane Grey. Once, there had been talk that the King himself would marry his cousin Jane, but Francis had told Kate that Edward was hoping for a political alliance and a French princess with a great dowry. In his opinion, his Majesty would have done better with Jane, a good Protestant girl with royal blood, rather than a Catholic bride who could only mean trouble.

Kate's fears resurfaced only afterward, when Francis, in his next letter, confided that King Edward had not been seen in public for weeks. "Something is definitely amiss." He sounded worried. Her hand placed protectively on her growing belly, Kate looked out of the window to where her children were playing a noisy game of tag in the Base Court. At that moment, a cloud overshadowed the sun. It seemed symbolic of the shadow over their lives. What sort of world would her dear ones inhabit if the King died? She watched them, running about, carefree, unaware of the threat to their happiness, and was seized with a fierce resolve to shelter them from change and suffering. Whatever happened, she would raise them in the true faith and protect them from any consequences.

Early in July, Francis came home. His face was grave. As soon as he had greeted his children and his household, he led Kate up to the solar.

"What has happened?" she asked.

He took her into his arms. "I am worried, worried for our future. The King is dying, I am convinced of it. He did not leave his apartments for weeks, and then, two days ago, he appeared at a window at Greenwich. Word had been put about that he would be there, and a crowd had gathered. Will and I joined it and we saw him. Kate, he looked ghastly, like a corpse. I hardly recognized him. His days are numbered, I have no doubt. Northumberland is going around the court looking as if he has not a care in the world, when he should be worried, for Mary is no friend to him and his future looks dismal. I'll wager he is plotting something."

Kate held him tightly, facing up to the bad news. Whatever the political and religious implications, her brother—her unacknowledged brother—was dying, at just fifteen years old. Tears welled up in her eyes. "Where is the Lady Mary?"

"At one of her country houses, I believe."

"Do you think Northumberland will move against her or try to oust her from the succession?"

"I would not put it past him to do both."

Kate broke away and began pacing up and down. "I would not wish her any ill, but that might be the best thing that could happen. Do you think we ought to warn Elizabeth what is going on?"

Francis came up behind her and folded his arms around her waist. "I think that we should keep our counsel and see what happens."

"Yes, but if Mary is set aside, then Elizabeth will be queen, by law."

"I am sure that William Cecil will be keeping her informed. We should not get involved."

Kate twisted around to face him. "But I am her friend. I am her sister, though she may not know it. Will it not look odd if I say nothing?"

Francis frowned. "If you know nothing, and you really don't, then there is no need to say anything."

She defied him. She wrote secretly to Elizabeth, telling her how the King had looked at the window at Greenwich, and asking if she had had any news. There was no reply.

SOME DAYS LATER, after Francis had returned to court, he sent Kate extraordinary news. The King was dead, God rest him—and Lady Jane Grey had been proclaimed queen!

The people, he wrote, had been astonished, standing in dumbfounded silence when the heralds announced the news and when Jane arrived at the Tower of London in state to take up residence there before her coronation. No one knew who this stranger was. Nor did anyone know the whereabouts of the Lady Mary. It was being said at court that Northumberland had sent his son, Lord Robert Dudley, to find her. Francis did not like to speculate on what would happen if he did. He would write again when he knew more. In the meantime, Kate should ask the priest to proclaim Jane queen from his pulpit.

She stood there in shock, the letter in her hand. This was not the outcome she had hoped for. It should have been Elizabeth who was proclaimed queen, not the unknown Jane. And she felt overcome by a deep sadness for Edward, dead so young.

She wasted no time in riding down to the church to tell the priest, Father Michael, what had happened, but he was adamant that he would not proclaim Jane.

"The Lady Mary is the lawful heir," he insisted. "I'm sorry, my lady, but until I know by what legal process she has been disinherited, I will not risk a charge of treason by proclaiming someone else."

Kate saw that he had a point. She rode back to Greys Court, feeling somehow disburdened, and wondering how the future would unfold. If God was good, they would have a Protestant monarch—Queen Jane!

FRANCIS CAME HOME. She had not expected him. He arrived late at night, when most of the household were in bed. Kate was still up, working on her book. Being absorbed in that helped to ward off her fears. When he appeared in the doorway, she jumped up and ran to him, pressing him to her.

"Oh, what a wonderful surprise!"

He bent to kiss her, but then she saw his face. He looked drawn.

"I have left my post," he told her. "I was at the Tower, guarding Queen Jane, but everyone is slipping away and abandoning her."

He sat down by the empty hearth, utterly weary. "You have not heard the news? Mary set up her standard at Framlingham Castle, and the people came flocking. Shire after shire has declared for her, and she has been proclaimed in towns across the realm. Jane is finished. Even her parents have slunk away. The councillors are ready to turn their coats and protest their loyalty. Mary is marching on London." He hung his head.

Kate stood beside him, quaking. "It is the end," she whispered. "The end of our lives as we know them. The end of your career at court—unless you convert back to the Catholic faith."

"That I will never do," Francis declared. "I shall stay at home and be a country gentleman. The yield and rents from our estates will support us. And, my darling, I will enjoy having the time to spend with you and the children. I have been parted from you for far too long."

Kate's spirits suddenly lifted. Her mother had often said that when God closed one door, He opened another, and now it seemed that some good would come out of this dreadful change.

"I could ask for nothing more," she said, leaning into Francis and resting her head on his shoulder. "Yet I cannot but think of all the poor souls who will be lost for want of the freedom to worship as they please. Oh, Francis, what shall we do? How will we continue to practice our faith?"

"We shall go on as normal," he said firmly. "We must pray that Mary exercises tolerance. She is coming to the throne on a tide of public acclaim. She is much loved. She will not want to jeopardize that. Let us see what transpires. It may not be as bad as we fear."

AGAIN, KATE WROTE to Elizabeth. Aware that she was now next in line to the throne, she couched her letter in more deferential terms, yet kept it affectionate. She hoped that her dearest cousin was well; she expressed her deepest condolences on the death of the King, and said that she rejoiced in Mary's accession, and hoped that she would see Elizabeth soon.

It was weeks before she received a reply. When she did, she saw that it was dated at Whitehall. Elizabeth apologized for the delay. She explained that, as soon as she had heard of Mary's triumph, she had ridden to greet her as she approached London and accompanied her when she entered the City in triumph. "Northumberland tried to flee, but he is taken," she added. "All the Dudleys are in the Tower, as are the Lady Jane and her husband."

Soon afterward, they heard from Cecil that Northumberland had been beheaded. There was no word of what would happen to Jane. Francis, who had not returned to court or been summoned there, read out Cecil's letter to Kate: "The Queen has made a good beginning. She is determined to rule well and has a remarkable capacity for conscientious hard work. She attends as many Council meetings as possible and writes many official letters in her own hand. She is bountiful to those who come to her with petitions or grievances and rarely turns anyone away. Yet I fear that, being a woman, she will be incapable of governing effectively."

He laid it on the table. "I agree with Cecil. Women are not fit to rule. A woman is never feared or respected as a man is, whatever her rank. In time of war, it is entirely impossible for a woman to govern satisfactorily. All she can do is shoulder responsibility for mistakes committed by others. And this woman has no training for queenship. She is a political innocent. I see trouble ahead."

Kate could not help feeling a little indignant at his words. She could agree that Mary was not fit to be queen, yet look at what she herself and a lot of other women could—and did—do! They ran estates and households, brought up children, ordered servants, and supported their husbands. Why should they not be respected as much as men were? And was it really impossible for a woman to govern? Were kingdoms not unlike households? She sat there simmering quietly.

Life with Francis at home was not proving to be as idyllic as Kate had envisaged. He was restless, bored, and edgy. She suspected that he had been hoping for a summons to resume his duties at court, for had not the Queen forgiven the entire Privy Council for its disloyalty in supporting Jane? Yet Francis was probably too much of a firebrand. He had never shied from making his views known, sometimes vociferously.

Kate kept busy, feeling as if she were treading on hot plowshares. She made sure that the children did not bother their father when he was in one of his low moods and did everything she could to cheer him. But she instinctively knew that his life here was not enough for him. He was used to being at the very center of events, and he was feeling deprived.

That August, Will came to see them, bringing Dot. He was still at court, serving as a Gentleman Pensioner.

"I am waiting to see what transpires," he said, accepting a goblet of wine from Kate.

"Has Queen Mary made any statement on religion?" Francis asked.

"No, but Mass is being said in the royal chapels."

Francis made a disgusted sound.

"I know," Will said, "but the word is that the Queen means to be tolerant, although many councillors and courtiers are now rushing to declare their error in converting to the new religion and are going about sporting rosaries and crucifixes. You never saw such a lot of time-servers. But Francis, not everyone is so hypocritical. You should come back to court. Your post hasn't been filled. No one will force you to attend Mass."

Francis looked torn.

"Will speaks sense," Kate said. "You've been moping around here. I'll be glad to get you out from under my feet."

Francis assumed a hurt mien. "And I thought you wanted to have me at home."

"I do, but not when you're behaving like an angry bear." Kate laughed. "Besides, at court you'll be able to see which way the wind is blowing. At the slightest sign of trouble, you could resign."

Her husband was nodding. "You're both right. I shall return."

"I'm glad to hear it." Will grinned, clapping Francis on the back.

AS THEY SAT down for dinner, Kate asked Will if he had seen Elizabeth.

"She is one of the reasons I'm here. She is still at court. She's very popular, and when the Queen appears in public, she is often with her, occupying the place of honor at her side, while Mary holds her hand affectionately."

Kate was glad that Dr. Palmer was away visiting his family. She would not have included him in this conversation. "Has Elizabeth attended Mass?" she wanted to know.

"Not yet, as far as I'm aware, but I'm sure she has no wish to alienate the Queen."

"She'll not want to lose her Protestant supporters either," Francis said.

"If only she would answer my letters," Kate said. "I've sent three but received no reply."

Will smiled at her. "That is not surprising. In her position, it would be unwise to commit anything but the most innocuous news to paper. But before I left court last week, I encountered her in a gallery, and she pushed this into my hand. I think she had been waiting for me." He handed Kate a dog-eared piece of paper, folded up small. It bore just the name "Kate." She opened it up and saw the alphabet written beside lines of symbols that made no sense.

"She said I was to give you this also," Will added. It looked like a letter, written in those strange symbols.

Francis was looking over Kate's shoulder. "It's a cipher. We need to decode the letter."

"Let me do it," Dot said. "I used to make up codes with my brothers. I find them fascinating. But I'll need pen and paper."

"Let's eat first," Kate said, even though she was itching to find out what Elizabeth had written.

"A capital idea!" Francis replied.

After dinner, they all retreated to Francis's study, where Dorothy sat at the table and began deciphering the letter.

Kate read it avidly.

"Keep the code in a secret place," Elizabeth had written. "Burn this letter when you have read it, and any others I send you. I cannot write openly, for these are dangerous times for those of our faith. My sister is putting pressure on me to embrace the Catholic religion and is not pleased when I refuse. She says it is unthinkable that her heir should be a Protestant. I fear that she is becoming antagonistic toward me. Ours can never be an easy sisterhood because the past will always lie like a sword between us. Our religious differences can only make matters worse. But I have to stay at court, under her eye. I will write more when I can. I think of you often and long for the old days at Hatfield. When I send to you next, my messenger will give you the password *Semper eadem.*"

Always the same. Elizabeth's personal motto had long been familiar to Kate.

Much troubled, Kate passed the letter around. "I don't like what this portends," she murmured.

Will looked up. "I can see why Mary wants her heir to be a Catholic, but that surely doesn't mean she expects us all to convert back to the old faith."

"I fear this is what carpenters call the thin end of the wedge," Francis observed darkly. "If Mary starts with small things, she may look for bigger ones."

"I still say that we should wait and see," Will insisted. "Come back to court, my friend. Forewarned is forearmed!"

FRANCIS HAD BEEN back in his post for a week when Elizabeth's messenger arrived, a young man who wore no livery yet muttered the correct password and gave Kate a letter with a plain seal before remounting his horse and departing.

Kate took the letter up to the solar and read it with grave misgivings. The Queen was showing Elizabeth marked hostility because of her obstinacy over religion. The French ambassador, Monsieur de Noailles, had begun to court Elizabeth's favor. He was no friend to the Queen because of her devotion to the Emperor Charles V, France's enemy, and was doing everything in his power to discountenance her. "I believe he is trying to set me up as a rival for the crown," Elizabeth had written, "but I am not such a fool that I cannot see that the King of France will not lift a finger to put me on the throne, not when he wants to secure the succession for his daughter-in-law, the Queen of Scots. He means to incite me to rebellion against my sister, or wishes me to set myself up at the head of an opposing faction. His purpose is to keep Mary too occupied to consider supporting the Emperor against the French. Well, dear cousin, I will keep my counsel. You shall hear from me again soon."

Kate screwed up the letter and sat down, pensive. She hoped that Elizabeth would be circumspect. It would not do to anger the Queen further. She could not help fretting about what they would all do if Mary enforced the old religion. What would happen to them if they defied the law? How could they circumvent it?

. . .

KATE'S BABY WAS born at the end of August, with Lettice and Thomasina in attendance. She named her new son Francis, but soon took to calling him Frank to distinguish him from his father. It was an easy confinement and she was soon up and about.

Life's daily round continued as if there were no threats hovering over it. Kate constantly wondered how Francis was faring at court. She was missing him, but glad that he was in a good position to sense danger, if there was any. When he wrote to say that the Queen had smiled upon him as she passed by, Kate began to relax. She was pleased to hear that Mary was resisting all persuasions to have Lady Jane Grey beheaded, yet a little disconcerted to learn that Elizabeth was showing favor to the French ambassador, which didn't sound like the best way to appease her sister.

In his next letter, Francis jubilantly reported that some councillors had let it be known that although the Queen intended to restore the Mass and be reconciled to the Pope, it was not her intention to compel or constrain the consciences of others. All she wished was for the Protestants in her realm to be brought to the truth by God, or through the offices of godly, learned preachers. "It does seem that we will be able to continue openly in our faith," Francis wrote.

Kate prayed he was right. She could not bear to think of a world in which her precious children had to keep their faith secret. She had always been proud of bearing Francis a large family, but with the kingdom in ferment and their faith—and even their lives—under threat, she had become convinced, when she was carrying Frank, that this was not a good time to bring any more souls into the world. She was worried enough about the children she had already.

Yet, looking down at her little son nestled in the crook of her arm, she could not wish him unborn. Her heart swelled with love for him, and a fierce desire to protect him rose within her.

WHEN FRANCIS NEXT came home, he was still in a positive mood, convinced that things were not going to be as bad as he and Kate had both feared.

His optimism proved to be ill-founded. Later in August, when he was back at court, he wrote that the Queen had issued a proclamation affirming her own devotion to the Catholic faith and her hope that her subjects would embrace it as fervently. However, she would not compel any of her subjects to abandon the new religion until a new determination was made with the consent of Parliament. In the meantime, however, the clergy were forbidden to preach.

"She has removed our most powerful weapon," Francis lamented. "Already, the old faith is gaining ground. In London, altars are being set up again and crucifixes put upon them. Yet there are many Protestants who are prepared to resist any attempt to enforce the old faith, and some have been bold enough to disrupt the celebration of Mass. The more zealous of our brethren have been rioting and demonstrating in London, and one even hurled a dagger at a priest who was saying Mass in St. Paul's Cathedral. I pray you, darling, inform Father Michael at Rotherfield Greys that it is my pleasure that there be no changes."

But the priest was not happy when Kate passed on the message. "I will comply for now," he conceded, "but if a new law is passed requiring us all to turn Catholic again, I shall obey it."

"Very well. I understand your position." Kate left him, feeling despondent. She had thought him staunch and had been dismayed to find out that he did not share her optimism that all would be well.

When she returned to Greys Court, she told Dr. Palmer what the priest had said.

"He should have obeyed his patron!" he declared hotly. "Someone has to make a stand for the true faith."

"Alas, Father Michael is not the man to take a stand," Kate said sadly. "He will bend with the wind."

Francis had informed her that Parliament would meet in October after the coronation. He was hoping that it would not pass any radical laws relating to religion. That was Kate's daily prayer, too.

In September, she learned that some Protestant priests were defying the royal edict banning preaching. "Several have been arrested," Francis told her. "A few bishops have been deprived of their sees and imprisoned. Archbishop Cranmer is in the Tower for daring to criticize the Mass. Printers have had their presses confiscated. Many now fear that the old laws against heresy will be revived."

Kate dropped the letter, gripped by terror. Under King Henry, heretics had been burned at the stake. She began to tremble, fearing that it could happen again—and if it did, what would she and Francis do? She could not bear to imagine what it must be like to be chained to a stake with faggots piled up around you; to see the flames leaping up, searing your flesh, starting at your feet, and gradually consuming you. The agony and the horror were beyond comprehension. And it could happen! Shaking, she picked up the letter and stumbled to the cupboard. Taking out the ewer of wine from the evening before, she splashed some into a goblet, draining it in one gulp in a vain attempt to distance herself from her fears.

Through the open casement, she could hear her children playing, and felt faint at the thought of what would happen to them if . . . if . . . No, she could not even contemplate it. But if the heresy laws were revived, what would she and Francis do? They could not abjure their faith! So where could they run to for safety?

She took up the letter again, forcing herself to read on.

"Some of our people have already left for safe havens overseas," Francis had written. "They have gone illegally, since the government will not issue them the necessary safe-conducts, although no effort is being made to stop them from going. Will thinks that the more subversive among them are being encouraged to seek exile. My lady, we have to think about what we should do. It might not be wise to wait to see what laws Parliament enacts. We should think about going abroad now, before it is too late. The important thing is that we are safe. I will never put you or the children at risk—yet I will not endanger our immortal souls."

Kate dashed off a reply, urging him to action now, for their children's sake. "I care not where we go."

"Say nothing to anyone," Francis replied. "I will resign my post and come home."

. . .

"DID ANYONE COMMENT on your resigning?" Kate asked, as soon as the children had been borne off to bed by their nurses and she and Francis were alone in the solar, an untouched chess set on the table between them. She was fearful that he had drawn attention to himself or that it might be thought that he was disloyal.

"No. I saw the Lord Chamberlain and gave back my insignia and my weapons. He said very little." Ah, but it would have been noted by many that you had gone, Kate thought, and some would wonder why.

"No doubt the Queen will be relieved to be rid of a terrible Protestant," Francis said wryly.

"It is no joking matter," she reproved him.

"No, you are right." He reached across and took her hand. "I have been talking to William Cecil. He is as concerned as we are about the future, and about the increasing numbers of Protestants who are choosing exile. He wants me to go to Geneva to meet with John Calvin."

Kate was startled. Calvin was a great French theologian and preacher, seen as the successor to Martin Luther. There were copies of his works in Francis's study; she had read some herself. She had taken greatly to heart one thing he had written: "No man is excluded from calling upon God, the gate of salvation is set open unto all men: neither is there any other thing which keeps us back from entering in, save only our own unbelief." It had somehow strengthened her faith. Yet she was not sure that she agreed with some of Calvin's more extreme beliefs. She could not believe in predestination—that, at the beginning of time, God had selected a few souls who would achieve salvation, and that there was nothing anyone not so chosen could do during their mortal life to alter their eternal fate. Nor did she like what she had heard of his well-known severity toward those who disagreed with him. Yet there was no doubting his sincerity or the force of his character. If anyone could help them, he could. But seeking his help would mean a long parting from Francis. It seemed that their life together was forever destined to be interrupted in one way or another. Nevertheless, she could see that Francis was keen to go.

"Do you think that Calvin would receive us all?" she asked.

"That is not the immediate purpose of my going to see him, darling," he replied. "Cecil wants me to enlist his help in establishing communities for English exiles where they would be best welcomed. Naturally, I will be meeting with as many exiles as I can, and I shall look for a possible refuge for us. I'm going to take Hal with me. He's twelve now and it's time he saw something of the world."

Kate was about to protest but suddenly realized that it would be good for Hal to fly the nest a little. A boy of his age should be allowed to spread his wings. And he would be safer abroad with his father than in England.

ON THE NIGHT before Francis left, he and Kate came together with renewed passion, wanting to make the most of their time together, for they might be apart for some months. It was utterly beautiful, a union of souls as well as bodies, and Kate could not help weeping afterward, suffused with joy and grief. Who knew how long it would be before they could lie together again?

She clung to Francis when they said farewell in the hall, and hugged Hal tightly. He wriggled away, eager to be gone. Adventure and the high seas beckoned; he was longing to join the world of men.

"I will write often," Francis assured her. "Will has promised to keep you informed of events at court. At the slightest sign of trouble, send me word."

"I will," she promised.

He led them out to the Base Court, where the household was gathered to say farewell to their master. He kissed Kate hard on the lips, then mounted his horse. She passed him the stirrup cup, her heart almost breaking, but she was resolved to show a brave face. His mission was a necessary one; it was her part to send him off with a smile. She stood calmly as she watched him and Hal disappearing into the distance, then hurried into the house and made herself busy.

Chapter 24

1553

KATE MISSED FRANCIS AND HAL TERRIBLY, YET SHE WAS GLAD that Will would be keeping in contact with her, although she feared that he might be in danger at court. But he assured her in his first letter that it was safer for him to be where he could keep his ear to the ground.

She was not convinced, and she became less so when Elizabeth wrote to say that the Queen had been showing increasing anger at her failure to attend Mass. "I have been subjected to mounting pressure to conform, and I have been censured by the Council to my face for ignoring the Queen's wishes. I fear I gave them a very rude response. My sister is also trying to make me cast off my plain clothes and wear magnificent gowns like her own. Fear not, dear cousin, I shall dissemble in these matters." Kate smiled at that. No one knew better how to dissemble than Elizabeth.

She deciphered the next page so that she could read on. "It is rumored that the Emperor has offered his son, Prince Philip of Spain, as a husband for the Queen. The French ambassador is in a frenzy and doing his utmost to enlist the support of those who are vehemently opposed to her Majesty taking a foreign consort. He has the right of it, I fear. Once the Spaniards have a foothold here, England will become a satellite of the Empire. They would assuredly introduce the Inquisition and there would be great persecution, as has been seen in Spain."

Kate shivered, praying that it was just a rumor. Yet there must be more to it to have the French ambassador in such a state. He had his spies (as Elizabeth had told her) and was well informed. Elizabeth certainly seemed to be very well informed about him, which suggested that she was too friendly with him for comfort, and that she was trying to store up credit with France. Kate wished she would not dabble with him; it was foolhardy to antagonize the Queen further. She boldly stated as much in her reply.

When next Elizabeth wrote, it was to say that she had come to the conclusion that some kind of compromise was called for. Much as she wished to remain a focus of hope for her sister's Protestant subjects, she dared not risk incurring the Queen's wrath by openly adhering to the reformed faith. She had therefore requested an audience. Mary had kept her waiting for two days before agreeing to see her. Then it became very clear that the Imperial ambassador had been poisoning the Queen's mind with his suspicions of Elizabeth. "She said she knew it was being said that the Papists were having their turn, but that I would remedy all in time. She said that was not going to happen and that I must conform to her wishes. In faith, I do not know how much longer I can put off going to Mass."

Kate wondered about that, too. Parliament was due to sit shortly, and she was fearful of what might ensue. Will was, too, judging by the tone of his letters. When he visited her unexpectedly in late October, she ran out into the Base Court to greet him, bursting with questions. One look at his face warned her that he did not bring good news.

She did her duty as hostess, sending grooms to take the horses, ushering Will up to the warmth of the solar, taking his cloak, and serving him ale, then dispatching Thomasina to the kitchen to order a hearty supper. Only when they were alone did she sit down, clenching her hands in her lap. "What has happened?"

"As we expected, Parliament has repealed the late King's religious laws," he told her. "It means that things now stand as they were at the end of King Henry's reign. The Queen is Supreme

Head of the Church, and the Church is Catholic. A new Act has restored all the sacraments, images, and holy days we have rejected. There was little opposition." He snorted in disgust. "Parliament stopped short, however, of providing for a reconciliation with Rome. Many lords and landholders are concerned that they will have to give back the church properties they acquired when the monasteries were dissolved. But the new Act forbids any criticism of the Mass and bans priests from marrying. Cranmer's *Book of Common Prayer* is suppressed."

"No, this cannot be." Kate was wringing her hands in distress. "That beautiful liturgy . . . I have found such consolation in it."

"Well, church services will be in Latin again," Will said.

"Has Parliament revived the heresy laws?" Kate asked nervously.

"No, there has been no word on that. But this latest legislation is bad enough. Most people are accepting of the new laws, but some Protestants are in an uproar. Churches have been vandalized and priests attacked. There has been a flood of propaganda tracts. But none of it will have any effect, I fear. The Queen is determined to have her way."

"What will we do?" Kate cried.

"We shall conform outwardly and practice our faith in private," Will said, stony-faced. "God will understand. It is what is in our hearts that matters."

Kate nodded. "I agree."

Will hesitated. "I've discussed the situation at length with Dot. If life here becomes intolerable, we shall go abroad. Protestants are welcome in Switzerland and parts of Germany."

"But if you go . . ." Kate stopped herself. She hated the thought of life without Francis *and* Will, yet it was selfish to expect Will to stay in danger when he had his wife and son to consider.

"It is worth thinking about," he said. "Francis would approve, if things got too perilous here."

Kate had been thinking of little else. "I want us all to be safe, but I'd hate to leave England," she told him. "The thought of being away from Greys Court and all I hold dear is a horrid one. And with eight children, it wouldn't be easy." She fell silent, tears streaming down her cheeks.

He rose, bent down, and put a fatherly arm around her. "But you would be with Francis—and safe. And you could worship God as you please. Take heart, though, for it may not come to that. The Queen has not signaled any intention of persecuting Protestants."

"Is it not persecution enough effectively to outlaw their religion?" Kate burst out.

"We should be grateful that she is not sending them to the stake—or not yet." Will's face was grim. "At the first intimation of that, I'm leaving."

"Let us hope that God grants her Majesty tolerance and mercy," Kate said fervently.

THAT NIGHT, LYING in her lonely bed, she was wakeful, her fears overwhelming her. It was upsetting to hear that there had been so little resistance to the new laws, except for those few hotheads on the streets. Maybe most people had conformed to the late King Edward's edicts only for form's sake; maybe they had secretly been hankering for a return to the old ways. But what of those, like herself, Francis, and their friends, who had devoutly embraced the new religion? What of her children, and Dr. Palmer, whom she had now instructed to be circumspect when teaching them about the Scriptures? Could not the Queen understand that there were different ways to God? Could she not pause to learn a little more about Protestant beliefs?

It was no use wishing. Mary had not hesitated to put pressure on Elizabeth, whose views she must know to be sincere. Did it not occur to her that her sister—and many other educated people—had come to their beliefs through reasoning? Thinking of sisters, Mary probably had no idea that she had another one who had never been acknowledged. Nor did she have any idea of how bad an impact her policies were having on that sister. But, given that she had not hesitated to hound Elizabeth, would she have cared anyway?

. . .

WILL HAD ONLY been gone two days when Kate received a letter from him. The Council was opposing the Spanish marriage, which was good news. Some wanted the Queen to marry Edward Courtenay, a young aristocrat who had royal blood, being descended from the Plantagenets. Others thought that Courtenay should marry Elizabeth, who was said to have shown him marked favor. "I do not think that either the Queen or Elizabeth will marry him," Will opined. "He is deep in the pocket of the French ambassador and the two of them have done nothing but stir up trouble."

Kate did not think that Elizabeth would marry Courtenay either, however much favor she showed him. Elizabeth had consistently reiterated that she did not wish to marry at all, and Kate now believed her.

Elizabeth did not mention Courtenay in her next letter. She said she had asked permission to withdraw from court, but the Queen had refused it. "She wants to keep an eye on all my doings. I fear there are some who would have me in the Tower. They will have to find good cause first." She sounded bullish, but Kate could imagine how difficult and nerve-racking her position must be, with different parties pulling her in all directions.

She wrote back, keeping the tone of her letter light and filling it with news of the children and trivial domestic matters. She had resolved not to refer to anything contentious in writing. You never knew who might decipher the letter.

IN NOVEMBER, WILL managed another brief visit.

"You would not believe how violently the people have reacted to the announcement of the Queen's betrothal to the Prince of Spain," he said, over a quiet supper of quail in verjuice. "They hate Spaniards and fear, quite rightly, that England will become subject to the Spanish Inquisition. The Queen has made the mistake of underestimating the temper of her subjects and their suspicion of all foreigners."

"In this case, they are right to be suspicious, I am sure," Kate said, helping him to more meat.

"Yes, they are. They resent Spanish monopolies in trade with America. And they have heard terrible tales of the tortures of the Inquisition. Their officers come for people in the night, you know, and haul them off to prison. They are allowed no counsel and are subject to relentless interrogation. Those who will not recant their heresy are burned in those public spectacles they call Acts of Faith. Prince Philip is a champion of the Inquisition. Up to now, people have accepted the Queen's religious changes relatively peacefully, apart from a few zealots. But now they are vociferous in opposing them. Overnight, it has become patriotic to be Protestant!"

"But surely the Queen is aware of the protests?"

Will downed his wine. "She is, but the Spanish ambassador has apparently told her that she must eliminate all opposition to the marriage. He is never far from her elbow, and she listens to him more than to anyone else. It's been bruited that he has urged her to put Elizabeth in the Tower. I do not see her going that far, but she never shows any friendship toward her these days."

"Elizabeth said that in her last letter. She believes that the Queen still resents the injuries inflicted on her mother by Queen Anne. She says that she herself is so out of favor that no one dares visit her without Mary's permission. She has solicited leave to retire to her estates, but the Queen refuses to grant it."

"She will not let her out of her sight. I tell you, Kate, she fears her, fears her youth, her popularity, and her power to draw people to her. Mary enjoyed great popularity when she seized the throne, yet she has thrown it away by agreeing to this marriage—and now ought to wonder why people look to Elizabeth."

"Elizabeth may prove to be our savior," Kate observed.

Will looked skeptical. "Given the position she is in, I wouldn't hope for too much."

LETTERS FROM FRANCIS arrived only sporadically after taking ages to reach Greys Court, so usually contained only old news. He and Hal were making slow but steady progress, despite the roads being muddy and the inns inferior.

"I miss you, my darling," he had written. "I am counting the days until we meet again. Send my blessings to the children. May God keep you, my dearest wife."

Kate wrote back, hoping her messenger would reach him. It was frustrating, not knowing where he was or how long it would be before she next heard from him. She found herself living for his letters. They were all of him she had for now. It was like being half alive.

Francis's mother was worrying about him, too. In her frequent letters, she begged Kate to urge him to come home and embrace once more the faith of his childhood, outwardly at least. "It will be better for you all," she wrote, "and for me."

Kate kept explaining that Francis would not compromise his principles. "And I support him in that," she added. "Do not fear for him. At the slightest hint of danger, we will escape abroad."

IN THE MIDDLE of November, Kate wrote to tell Francis that Lady Jane Grey and her husband had been tried for treason and condemned to death.

"It is believed that the Queen does not intend to have the sentences carried out," Will had reported. "She seems resolved to be merciful. I imagine that they will remain in the Tower at her pleasure."

That was one small blessing, and late that month, there was another when Mary finally allowed Elizabeth to leave court and go to the palace at Ashridge, north of London. In a coded letter sent from there, Elizabeth told Kate she was glad to be away.

The Queen made a show of affection on parting. I petitioned her not to believe anyone who spread evil reports of me without giving me a chance to prove the false and malicious nature of such slanders. She assured me she would not, and presented me with two ropes of pearls and a sable hood. Since then, her councillors have warned me that if I refuse to follow the path of duty,

I will bitterly repent it. As God is my witness, I would never conspire against the Queen. I have brought priests with me so that Mass can be celebrated here. But do not be deceived. I will never deviate in my heart from the true faith, but I must do all in my power to please the Queen. I know they have placed spies in my household and that my every move is watched. My man Bridges who comes to you has a sick mother in Oxford. He visits her as cover for delivering my letters to you, but if you do not hear from me, you will know that he has come under suspicion and that it is difficult for me to get word to you.

May God keep you, dear cousin, and send you a very merry Christmas.

KATE FELT DISMAL and tense as she prepared for Yuletide. Sad that Francis would not be there to share it, she had invited Will and Dot, but Will wrote to say that he could not get away because the Queen's marriage treaty was to be signed early in the New Year and he was needed at court, where security was being ramped up.

Kate was feeling dejected on Christmas Eve, telling herself that she must not mope because she had the children to think of. She was thrilled, therefore, when a messenger arrived after dinner with a letter from Francis. It was the best Yuletide gift he could have sent her, although it had clearly been written some weeks ago.

He and Hal were well and in good spirits. They had reached Geneva in late November and met Calvin that very day. He had welcomed them most civilly and conversed with them for a long time. On parting, he had praised Francis for his devotion to the faith, but observed that Hal merited even higher praise for his youthful piety and zeal. Kate's heart almost burst with pride. She had done her best to bring up her children in the true religion, and it was now clear that, with Hal, she had succeeded. She prayed that he would stay faithful.

Calvin wanted to help the exiles. He had agreed to set up a colony for them in Geneva. He had also written a letter of introduction for Francis to give to a fellow reformer, Pierre Viret, who was at Lausanne and could help. But refuge would only be granted to those who had suffered religious persecution, which Kate thought fair enough. His mission accomplished, Francis hoped to be on his way home soon.

Kate's heart was full to bursting—he might be here any day! She threw herself into the festivities, making the most of the season for the children and her household. There were no Masses, just a simple communion service and a sermon on Christmas morning. It was no secret within the household that the master and mistress were still observing the rites of the new religion, but Kate did wonder what would happen if someone felt driven to report them? Thinking of Elizabeth's letter, she began to wonder how many of the servants could be trusted. Some might feel torn by divided loyalties.

Lying wakeful at night, she realized that she and her family were not really safe, even at Greys Court. Too many people knew that they followed their faith in private. Anyone might talk.

The answer came with the dawn. She would ask the family chaplain to conduct services in the solar, just for her and the children. She would go to church with her household to show that she had resolved to conform to the new law. She could always explain away the chaplain's presence in the house by saying that he was staying on to assist Dr. Palmer with the children's lessons.

She relaxed a little. She would be very careful.

Chapter 25

1554

JANUARY WAS BARELY A WEEK OLD WHEN WILL REPORTED that the Queen had signed her marriage treaty. Two weeks later, he wrote that there had been a rising in protest against it in Devon, speedily suppressed by government troops. Friends on the Council had told him in confidence that they had proof that a conspiracy was afoot and that there might be risings in other parts of the realm. All leave was canceled. He did not know when he would be able to visit Greys Court again.

After this news, Kate was almost distraught to receive a letter from Francis saying that he was staying on in Geneva to help make everything ready for the English exiles. He did not know when he would be home. "At the slightest hint of trouble, write to me," he had exhorted her. "If you feel you are in danger, come to me with the children. In the meantime, I thank you from my heart for continuing to look to my interests in Oxfordshire." Kate was glad of the responsibility and the myriad tasks that kept her busy. They took her mind off their separation. Bilkins, impressed, told her that she was now quite capable of running her lord's estates unaided. But Thomasina was worrying about her doing too much.

"I don't mind being busy," Kate said. "I just want life to revert to normal and to be free of all my cares."

"You've got to look after yourself, Mistress," Thomasina urged.

"I will," Kate promised, and hastened away to the still room, where she was going to teach Mary and Lettice how to make marmalade.

By late January, Kate had learned of a serious threat from Kent, where Sir Thomas Wyatt had raised his standard at Maidstone and issued a proclamation protesting against the Spanish marriage. His army, Will wrote, was five thousand strong and he was riding for London unopposed because the authorities had been unable to muster any support in the region. "God be praised that you are all in Oxfordshire," he added. "There is enough cause for panic here at Whitehall. But the Queen is steadfast. I will write as often as I can. Do not be afraid. You are not in danger."

He was true to his word. By and by, Kate learned of the terror in London as the citizens braced themselves for the rebels' onslaught. She feared for Will. As a member of the sovereign's personal guard, he would be in the front line if Whitehall Palace came under attack. She could not bear to think about it, could not sleep for worrying.

At least Francis was safely abroad. It was the first time she had felt glad that he was out of England.

She wrote to Elizabeth at Ashridge but received no reply. Then Will informed her that the Queen had had her sister's portrait taken down from her gallery. It seemed that she was suspected of being involved in the conspiracy. She had gone to Donnington in Berkshire and was pleading sickness as an excuse for not obeying Mary's summons to court.

Wyatt had been proclaimed a traitor for having raised evil-disposed persons to compass the Queen's destruction and restore Lady Jane Grey to the throne. Privately, Kate wished him success; it would be the best outcome for the Protestants. Yet she did not wish any ill to Mary.

Will wrote that the octogenarian Duke of Norfolk had marched an army into Kent to deal with Wyatt and his rebels. But hundreds of his men had deserted to the enemy and the rest had fled. Will had seen Norfolk's remaining troops staggering wearily back into London, a sight he had found most demoralizing. "I must warn you, Kate, that the kingdom is facing a very serious crisis, because nothing now stands between Wyatt and London." His words made Kate fearful for Will. Dashing off a reply, she begged him to keep safe.

When he wrote that the councillors were urging the Queen to leave London for the safety of Windsor, but that she had refused, Kate could have screamed with frustration. *Go! Go!* she wanted to say. It was clear that panic was mounting in London. "Apparently, we Gentlemen Pensioners and the Yeomen of the Guard are not enough for her Majesty," Will grumbled. "She has complained to the Council that they have failed to provide her with a bodyguard. In fact, they've been hard at work recruiting men, although many are untrained and useless. Some lords want the Queen to ask the Emperor for military aid, but she will not have him thinking she is unable to deal with the situation lest he doubts the wisdom of sending his son here. You can imagine the reaction if an Imperial army arrived on England's shores. It would confirm the people's worst suspicions. Therefore, she has ordered that London be fortified, and is resolved to remain at Whitehall. She believes she can count on the citizens' loyalty." Kate wondered if she was being overoptimistic. Since her accession, the Queen had lost a lot of her popularity.

She could settle to nothing. Every day, she kept interrupting her tasks to look out for Will's messenger, and snapped at the children because she had a bad headache from tension. But there was no news. The lack of it was driving her to distraction. What was happening in London? Why didn't Will write? Dear God, was it because he couldn't write? Her mind took a dive into Hell. She loved this dear, kind man like a father.

It was a week before she heard from him, and the relief was profound. "Wyatt is taken," he had written. "He was halted at Southwark because the citizens had destroyed London Bridge to prevent him from crossing the Thames. In the City, there was much noise and tumult as the people donned armor, shut shops, and kept guard over their doors. The Queen went to the Guildhall and gave a stirring speech, which turned the hearts of many. Here at Whitehall, we also put on our armor and took up our places in the Queen's presence chamber, weapons at the ready. The palace was packed and her ladies were weeping and wailing. She remained calm and urged us all to place our trust in God."

Kate devoured the rest avidly, reading about Wyatt crossing the Thames at Kingston and marching on Tyburn, outside the city walls. She could envisage the pandemonium at court that Will described so vividly, and had to admire the courage of the Queen in staying at Whitehall. The rebel march had continued unchecked until it was confronted at St. James's Park by a force of cavalry led by the Earl of Pembroke. After a brief skirmish in which many of his troops deserted, Wyatt had led a small band of his men away to Charing Cross, where there was another scuffle. Will had heard the gunfire at Whitehall. Finding Ludgate closed to him, Wyatt had turned to retreat, but his way was barred by Pembroke's company. He had too few supporters to resist such a large force, so had given himself up. "The rebellion has collapsed and he is in the Tower," Will concluded. "The Queen says that God has worked another miracle."

It felt like that to Kate, even though a part of her had wanted the rising to succeed. She was utterly thankful that Will was unscathed.

He came to see her three weeks later, in a somber mood. "Lady Jane Grey and her husband have been executed," he told her, sinking into his fireside seat.

"But the Queen was going to show mercy!" she cried, appalled.

"Indeed, she was. But her councillors and the Spanish ambassador were all thoroughly frightened by the rebellion and told her that she must harden her heart and show her subjects that she is not to be intimidated. Now she wants the law to strike terror into all who venture to do evil. The worst of it is that she has said she will not tolerate heresy in her realm, since it can only lead to seditious plots against her. The Spanish ambassador is urging her to proceed firmly against all heretics."

Kate had to sit down. "Should we leave England?" she asked tremulously.

"Not yet. But we must be vigilant and ready to go at any time. I have already made plans for Dot and I to leave, should the need arise, but I am probably being overcautious. The government has other things to think about than persecuting Protestants." He sighed.

Kate sat there, stunned. What would she do if Will left England? In Francis's absence, he was her rock. She would be bereft. And she would be cut off from the court and all that was happening there. She feared being so alone and isolated.

"These are dangerous times," Will was saying. "The leaders of the revolt are to be executed as an example to other would-be rebels. The Duke of Suffolk is set to go to the block for rising in favor of his daughter Jane, and great pressure was put on the Queen to rid herself of Jane, as she would have remained a focus for rebellion. I'm told it was intimated to her that Prince Philip would not come to England while Jane lived. She reluctantly capitulated."

"That poor girl," Kate mourned. "She could not have been more than seventeen, and her husband was not much older. How dreadful to die at such a young age." She could well imagine their terror at facing the block. It brought back horrible memories.

Will drew her into his arms. "They say she died bravely, strong in her faith."

"That is small consolation," Kate said, as a tear trickled down her cheek.

"I know," he murmured, gentling her like a child. "The new religion has lost one of its best advocates."

"But there remains the Lady Elizabeth," she said, breaking away. "Is there any word of her? She has not replied to my letters."

Will frowned. "I fear that the news is not good. I hesitated to tell you. Queen Mary believes that the Lady Elizabeth was involved in the rebellion, and some of the councillors have been sent to arrest her for questioning."

Kate was aghast. "Do you think it's true?"

"Honestly, I don't know. She is a great dissembler—and she would have had good cause to rebel."

"I think she is too clever for that," Kate said, trying to console herself.

"But Lord Chancellor Gardiner and the Spanish ambassador are convinced of it and putting pressure on the Queen to deal with

Elizabeth as she dealt with Lady Jane. They say she is a traitor and a threat to the Crown."

"I won't believe it," Kate declared, trembling at the thought of what might happen to Elizabeth.

"I pray for her sake that you are correct, but on no account should you write to her. You cannot risk being deemed guilty by association. You are known to be a devout Protestant. Conclusions might be drawn that you were involved with Wyatt, too."

Kate was indignant, fighting back tears. "I am so worried for her, all alone and probably very frightened. She is but twenty. She is without any support and comfort. I wish I could help to succor her in some way."

Will placed his hands firmly on her shoulders. "Daughter, you must not even try. That young lady can well take care of herself."

Kate fervently hoped so. She turned away and sat down. "Have you seen my brother?" she asked. "I have been wondering how he is faring, for he was a convert to the new religion, but I dare not write and ask him."

"I've seen him," Will told her. "He is concerned for his family and his future and has resolved to obey the new laws. The Queen has appointed him her carver and apparently thinks well of him. He has six children now."

"Does he ask about me?" Kate asked.

"He does. He hopes that you are being pragmatic in this present situation."

"I will pray for him," Kate vowed. "Whichever route we choose to take to Heaven, he is still my brother."

WHEN WILL NEXT wrote from court, it was to say that Elizabeth was at Whitehall. She had not been sent to the Tower, although her apartments were heavily guarded and she was being closely examined by the Council. Kate froze when she read that and prayed that Elizabeth would clear herself. Yet, as she knew all too well, had known since she had spent those dreadful days in the Tower with her aunt, people believed what they wanted to believe. To them, that was truth.

"Be grateful you are far from London," Will continued. "Many rebels have been hanged—more than a hundred, I think. Their bodies hang from gibbets at every street corner; they are ghastly spectacles and the stench is appalling. There are severed heads and dismembered limbs on spikes above the city gates. Yet the Queen has also been merciful. Hundreds have been pardoned."

Sickened by what she had read, Kate hoped that Mary's merciful impulses would extend to Elizabeth.

At least the rebellion was over. But now the way was clear for Prince Philip to come to England. Kate shuddered at the prospect of what his arrival might portend.

APRIL CAME IN with a flowering of blossom, yet still Francis was detained in Geneva, and Kate was finding their separation unbearable. He had been gone for seven months now, and it seemed like seven years. When, oh, when would she see him and Hal again? Many times, she resolved to pack up and cross the sea to join him. There was no need, as yet, and it would be foolhardy to unsettle the children. He and Hal were well. She must not worry. He missed her and longed for her presence, but they should both be prepared to make sacrifices for the higher good. She must stay steadfast and strong, and offer up her loneliness and suffering to God. He would comfort her.

She tried, she really tried. She could only admire Francis's dedication to the faith and his determination to do the right thing. Yet it was impossible to quell her yearning for his presence, for his strong arms around her and the joy of their nights together. The only thing to do was to keep occupied. Heaven knew, she had a thousand and one things claiming her attention, not least her children, who were all growing up sturdily and needed a firm hand. Sometimes, their nurses despaired of them, especially the headstrong Lettice, the beauty of the family. Yet when they were with Kate, they behaved themselves, so she tried to spend as much time as possible with them. It tugged at her heartstrings to see the likeness of Francis in them. If only he could be here with them all.

In the middle of April, Will reported that he had been to Tower

Hill to see Wyatt executed. "There was speculation that he would say that Elizabeth was involved in his uprising. But on the scaffold, he refused to incriminate her. It seems there is now no case against her, yet she is still being interrogated at Whitehall. I fear they are determined to find something. My friends on the Council tell me she has confessed nothing, so they are debating what to do with her. Some lords favor keeping her under house arrest in the country, but no one wants the responsibility of housing so dangerous a person under his roof. The Queen is to leave London for Oxford shortly, so they think it essential that Elizabeth be placed in safe custody in a place where she can wreak no mischief. They are talking about sending her to the Tower."

Kate was bursting with anger. How could they treat Elizabeth like this when they had no evidence against her? Jealousy was at the root of it, she was sure, and Mary's fear of her sister. She was so agitated that she could settle to nothing. By the evening, she had developed a punishing headache and took herself to bed with an infusion of lavender, sage, marjoram, and rue.

In his next letter, Will broke the news that Elizabeth was in the Tower. She had tried to delay her departure, then refused to enter the fortress; they had almost had to drag her inside. Now she was imprisoned in the old Queen's Lodgings, where her mother had spent her final days. Kate remembered them only too well. All that gilded antick decoration—it had seemed to make a mockery of the tragedy that had unfolded within. She could not imagine what Elizabeth might be feeling. It seemed an unnecessary refinement of cruelty to incarcerate her in those rooms. She must be haunted by the knowledge of what had happened eighteen years ago, when Queen Anne had stepped out of that lodging for the last time—and was no doubt terrified that she herself was doomed to suffer the same fate. Think of it! Every footfall outside, every knock, every visit from the Constable of the Tower, might herald her end. How Kate longed to comfort her. Yet Will was right: she must make no attempt to contact her. It could be construed as treason.

. . .

WHEN WILL VISITED that month, he told her that the councillors were treating Elizabeth considerately, and that many feared to show themselves as harsh toward her as the Queen wished.

"They think Mary will not live long," he said, lowering his voice and bending close to Kate's ear as they sat on the stone bench in the garden, taking advantage of the mild spring evening. "She is thirty-eight, old to be contemplating marriage and motherhood, and might die in childbed. They are conscious that Elizabeth is her heir. How will she deal with those who hounded her to confess something she had not done?"

"I am glad of their consideration," Kate said. "I cannot bear to think of her shut up in the Tower, alone and friendless."

"Let us hope that she will not be there for much longer," Will said. He sighed. "There is more bad news, I fear. Parliament is sitting again. The Queen has formally renounced the title Supreme Head of the Church, which means that England is once again to be under the authority of the Pope. I am disappointed that there have been few protests. It appears that many people are happy to see the clock put back. It can only be a matter of time before the government proceeds against us Protestants. I dread to think of what will happen when Prince Philip comes."

"I dread that, too."

"Kate, I—I must tell you . . ."

She could read in his face what he was about to say. "You are leaving."

"I am," he confessed. "I am going to Geneva and taking Dot, our children, and our servants with me. I will be traveling under the name 'Lord Rochford'—I know, I have no right to the title, but it was in the family. I wrote to Dr. Calvin, and he has replied that I am welcome there and that I can be of use in administering the affairs of Geneva."

Kate was near to tears, but she kept smiling. She could not beg Will to stay for her sake. He had his family to think of. There were four children now, and another on the way, he had proudly informed her, yet not without some concern. Of course he must keep them safe.

"When do you leave?" she asked, keeping her voice even.

"Alas, daughter, in three days' time. Believe me, I do not want to leave you here without a protector."

"I can look after myself, and to my children's safety," she assured him. "Besides, Francis will probably be home soon." She knew this to be a vain hope. "Go with my blessing, dear Will. Let us pray that we shall meet again soon, in happier times."

SHE MISSED HIM more than she had anticipated. She did not like being cut off from the court. There was no one there she knew well, so she had to rely on the priest and the local carter for news of what was happening in the outside world—and it was sparse, without the inside knowledge to which she had become accustomed.

The carter, who came every week with goods to sell, had heard in a tavern that the Lady Elizabeth had been taken from the Tower to Woodstock Palace, where she was now under house arrest.

"They can't find nothing against her," he announced, "but they be determined to keep her in prison. They's frightened of her, mark my words."

Kate thanked him and paid for her purchases, her mind spinning. Elizabeth was in Oxfordshire—but she might as well have been on the moon. Woodstock was thirty miles away; even if Kate attempted the journey, she knew, with a leaden heart, that she would not be allowed to see her. Yet it was a blessed relief to know that she was no longer in the Tower—and was presumably out of danger. She thought about trying to get a message to her, but could not devise a means.

In July, it was announced from the pulpit that the Queen had married Philip of Spain at Winchester Cathedral with great magnificence. Philip was now king. As the weeks went by, Kate waited tensely to hear whether any new laws on religion had been passed. She pumped the garrulous carter for news, but he told her that, as far as he knew, Parliament wasn't sitting.

"Her's been on her honeymoon," he added wisely. "Not that he'll have much joy of her, I'll bet." He gave a lascivious wink.

"Them say the baker's daughter in her gown be better'n Queen Mary without her crown!" He went away, cackling at his own wit.

ON A SUNNY afternoon in September, Kate was playing Mother Bird with the children in the Base Court. They were all laughing, and in the rumble-tumble of the game, her hood had come off and her long red hair was flying free. She felt like a girl again, not a respectable married woman of thirty.

"Look, Mother, horsemen!" Mary cried, pointing into the distance.

Kate looked. There were four of them, riding up the hill toward the house. She looked again. It couldn't be, could it? *Heaven be praised, it was!* Suddenly, she was gathering up her skirts and running full pelt to meet them.

"Francis! Francis, my darling! Hal, my boy!" she cried.

Francis reined in his horse and jumped from the saddle. "My beloved!" he breathed, crushing her to him in full view of everyone, for the servants had come running out of the house. "I have longed for this moment!" He kissed her heartily on the mouth.

"Oh, I have missed you," she sobbed, when he had paused for air. Her eyes devoured his face, his dear face. He was here; she could not quite believe it. Never had she loved him so much. And he had not changed.

Unlike the tall boy who waited for her embrace. Hal had shot up; she could see the future man in him. With a cry, she pressed him to her heart. "My darling son!"

The children crowded around them, greeting their father. The nurse brought little Frank, now a chubby one-year-old with angelic looks.

"My, how you have grown!" Francis marveled. "Oh, it is good to see you all. It is wonderful to be home."

He and Kate led the way into the house, where Bilkins bowed to his master. "Sir Francis, you will find all in order. Your good lady has seen to that." Praise indeed!

Kate smiled at him. "Pray send to the kitchen to see if there are any cold cuts that can be served to my lord. And bring wine. We must drink a toast. We have much to celebrate!"

Over supper, which was served in the hall with the children, Dr. Palmer, the chaplain, and the upper servants present, Francis and Hal regaled everyone with tales of their travels. Later, when they were alone in the solar, Francis spoke warmly to Kate of Calvin and the reformers they had met, and talked enthusiastically about the growing community of English Protestant exiles who had found a comfortable refuge in Geneva, thanks to the arrangements and accommodation that he and Calvin had put in place for them. He had seen Will and Dot, and they were happily settled. He made it sound like a little paradise.

"If need be, darling, we will go there," he said. "We will be made welcome. But for now, all I want to do is take you to bed . . ."

THE RENEWED PASSION between them bore fruit. By Christmas, Kate knew that she was with child again. Her joy was tempered with anxiety, for Francis had just learned from a friend at court that Cardinal Pole, the butchered Lady Salisbury's son, had been appointed archbishop of Canterbury in place of the disgraced and deposed Archbishop Cranmer—and that he had received England back into the obedience of Rome. The other news was that the Queen was with child. There had been a thanksgiving service in St. Paul's Cathedral for the quickening of it.

"None of this augurs well for us," Francis said, sitting down on the bed beside Kate, who was resting for the afternoon to see if it might alleviate some of the nausea and fatigue she was suffering.

"Should we go abroad?" she asked nervously.

"I fear the time is coming when we might have seriously to consider it," he replied.

"But how can I go feeling like this?" Kate asked plaintively. "I cannot ride in my condition, and I feel sick at the thought of a long journey in a jolting litter."

"We need not leave just yet. Let us hope that if we do decide we have to, you will be feeling better. Let us pray it will not come to it." His voice, Kate thought, lacked conviction.

When he had gone, she lay there fretting. England was now officially Catholic and there was no place for Protestants. If the Queen bore a son, nothing was likely to change for the foreseeable future. Kate found herself almost hoping that Mary and her babe would not survive the birth, then pulled herself up quickly. What was she thinking of? How could she wish that on another mother? And on her own sister, at that? Even though she had never felt the connection to Mary that she had to Elizabeth, she was still conscious of the blood tie. No, all she could do was pray that God would soften the Queen's heart—or find a way for His chosen to worship as they thought best.

KATE WAS GRATEFUL that Francis had friends at court who could keep him informed of what was happening. At first, the news was a little encouraging.

"Things may not be as bad as we feared," he declared, waving a letter at Kate as she sat at the table in the solar making a kissing ball out of evergreens to hang in the hall. It would be Christmas in three weeks' time, and the children were outside in the Base Court building a snowman. Lettice, who had been longing to see Francis since his safe return from Geneva, was on her way to spend the season with them. "I think the Queen has discovered that she cannot put the clock back in every respect. Saints' days are no longer to be celebrated, and the monasteries will not reopen, which was a big sticking point for those who feared that a return to Rome might see them deprived of their property. Chantries and shrines will remain closed, and so-called relics of the saints will not be put back into churches."

"I am pleased to hear it! I had thought that all that superstition and idolatry had been done away with."

"Well, it seems that the Queen wants to focus on the spiritual values of her Church."

"If only she could respect the spiritual values of ours!" Kate wove some red ribbon through the greenery.

"If only she could leave us alone!" Francis sighed. "That would be the best outcome."

He watched her working and smiled. "I look forward to putting that to good use," he said, kissing the top of her head. Then he sat down by the fire, leaving her with a beautiful warm feeling. If only things could continue this way. Life was so good, now that they were together.

"Let's try to stay here in England for as long as we can," she said.

"We will," he agreed.

THEY HAD ENJOYED three days of optimism when Francis received another letter. He came upstairs and broke the wax seal. Kate watched him reading, saw his face turn ashen.

"What is it?" she asked nervously. "Is something wrong?"

He looked at her, apparently unable to speak. When he did find his voice, it came out as a croak. "Parliament has revived the laws against heresy. It is clear that the Queen is determined to eradicate the Protestant religion." He swallowed, as if his throat had closed up.

"Oh, my dearest, what shall we do?" Kate cried, bursting into tears.

"I wish I knew," Francis muttered hoarsely.

"What does it say?"

"It is our worst fear. The Queen means to make an example of heretics to deter others from embracing their beliefs. King Philip is behind this, I am sure, and Cardinal Pole and Lord Chancellor Gardiner. The bishops have been given the power to investigate cases of suspected heresy, and the Church will hand over those found guilty to the secular authorities for burning. The property of a convicted heretic would then revert to the Crown." His voice tailed away.

Kate felt sick. This could not be happening. Their children, themselves, this house, their lives together, all the dear, familiar things around them—and the little one who slept beneath her girdle: these could not be under threat, surely?

But they were, they were. She clung to Francis, weeping. "What shall we do? What shall we do?"

"We go on as normal," he murmured, gentling her. "We go to Mass with everyone else, but we continue to have our own services in private."

"What of the children? Little ones don't know how to guard their tongues!"

Francis was silent for a moment. "Much as it grieves me to say it, I think we dare not risk them giving us away."

"You mean we should exclude them from our private services and bring them up as Catholics?" Kate was a little shocked.

"It is safest that way. It is better than risking the penalty for heresy, darling. I am not sure I am of the stuff of which martyrs are made." Francis's voice shook.

Kate could not bear to think about what death by burning might be like. It was too horrific to contemplate. "I know I am not," she said, shuddering. "I never thought that the Queen was a cruel person. I only met her a few times when I was younger, and she was kind. Everyone loved her. How could she have changed?"

"It may be that all those years of fighting for her Mass under King Edward hardened her heart. And we should not discount King Philip's influence. She is said to be besotted with him."

"And I thought she was a merciful princess," Kate said bitterly.

Francis looked at the letter again, then turned it over. "No signature, and I don't recognize the handwriting. The seal was plain. Whoever sent this wanted to be anonymous, and they wanted to warn us of the danger. I can only ask God to bless them for it."

Kate caught at his sleeve. "Francis, if we are arrested, and they know that we are Protestants, can we save ourselves by recanting?"

"If we are sincere, yes. But if we lapse afterward, then there will be no second chance. Kate, let's not torment ourselves with thoughts of being arrested. We will make sure we are careful, so that we are never forced into the position where we have to recant. Have faith, my darling. And if things look perilous, we *will* go abroad."

THEY PUT ON brave faces for the children and made sure that Christmas was as merry as ever, for who knew where they would be celebrating it next year?

They took their family to church, attended Mass, and conformed to the new laws.

Once a week, in the darkness of night, they had the chaplain conduct a Protestant service for themselves alone. The subterfuge took its toll on them, and both were racked with guilt at betraying their convictions. They could only console themselves by saying, as their chaplain did, that God would understand.

Chapter 26

1555

THE AUTHORITIES DID NOT WASTE ANY TIME IN IMPLEMENTING the new law. In the middle of February came news of the first burnings.

"The Lord Chancellor has condemned five persons to death for heresy," Francis announced, his expression somber.

Kate looked up from her account book, alarmed. "Who were they?"

"The Bishop of Gloucester and a married priest called John Rogers. I had the news from my anonymous friend at court, and he did not tell me any other names. He mentioned Rogers because he was the first to suffer. When they took him to Smithfield, the mood of the crowd was angry and there were loud protests, especially when it became clear that the poor wretch would not be allowed to say goodbye to his wife and children."

"God have pity!" Kate wept, thinking how Francis would feel if he were in Rogers's place and had been denied that last crumb of comfort before facing the agony of the flames.

Francis's jaw was clenched as he read the letter to himself. "I will not tell you more, darling. My friend's account of the burning of Bishop Hooper at Gloucester is too terrible to relate, especially to a lady in your condition."

"No, tell me!" Kate insisted.

Francis shook his head. "It will horrify you, and it might upset the babe." He went into the bedchamber and she heard a cupboard door close.

"Do not dwell on these things," he said, coming back into the solar. "I do not want you distressed at this time. But you had to know that the burnings had started. Forewarned is forearmed."

When he had gone downstairs to meet with a tenant who was seeking to have repairs to his cottage put in hand, Kate could not contain her morbid curiosity. She needed to know what had happened at Bishop Hooper's execution. It was like the tales of ghosts and witches that had both fascinated and terrified her as a child: she had insisted on being told, even though she knew she would have nightmares later. And so it was now. She must know how a man could endure such suffering—and how awful it could be.

She knew where the key to the cupboard was kept. It was at the bottom of the chest in which Francis kept his clothes. She retrieved it and opened the door, then read the letter.

She immediately wished she hadn't. She wished she had heeded Francis. For the details were truly hideous. They had hung a bag of gunpowder around the Bishop's neck to ensure a quick end, but it did not explode and he burned for three-quarters of an hour, pitifully begging the crowd to fan the flames in order to end his agony. There was more, but she had to stop reading lest she vomited.

And this could happen to her, and it could happen to Francis.

AS THE WEEKS passed, they received more reports of the persecution. Kate and Francis were heartened to hear that there had been a public outcry. Many men and women had been brave enough to speak out against the burnings, and large numbers had been clamped in the pillory for slandering the Queen's justice.

Francis was grimly jubilant. "It is clear that, far from converting our people to the Roman faith, these burnings have hardened their resolve and inflamed their anger against the Queen. The bravery of those who have died has obviously been an inspiration to many; already, they are seen as martyrs with beliefs worth dying for."

But the Queen, it seemed, as time went by, was taking no notice. Kate shivered when she learned that, aside from preachers, most of those who had been sent to the stake were craftsmen, farm laborers, or poor, ignorant folk who either could not recite the Lord's Prayer or did not know what the sacraments were.

"I have no doubt that some parish priests are being overzealous in apprehending people and sending them before their bishops," Francis fumed. "And now they are ordering more guards to be present at the burnings to stop the people attempting to aid or comfort the victims. And to think that this is England! We might as well be in Spain!"

"This must be costing the Queen the love of many of her subjects," Kate said, as she moved around him, making their bed.

"Yes, not everyone likes to see Protestants made martyrs, even if they don't agree with their beliefs. I must confess, Kate, that I have wished for a bad outcome to the Queen's pregnancy—may God forgive me—and I know I am not alone in looking to the Lady Elizabeth as our deliverer. I'll say it again: she is our only hope."

"But for her to succeed to the throne, the Queen has to die." Their eyes met. They were speaking treason, for it was against the law even to imagine the death of the sovereign. "I too have had such thoughts," Kate whispered, looking about nervously in case the walls had ears.

She paused for a moment, letting the counterpane drop. She had missed her correspondence with Elizabeth. Every day, she had thought about her and wondered how she was faring at Woodstock. No one seemed to have any news of her, and it would have been foolhardy to write to her.

They learned in Easter week that the King and Queen had gone to Hampton Court to await the birth of their child. Security around them was tight, for there had been demonstrations against the burnings and the Spaniards, who were hated in England. No one seemed certain when the royal baby was expected; some said May, others June. But already, Mary had gone into seclusion, which must mean that the birth was imminent.

Kate estimated that she herself had about two months to go.

Every time she felt her infant move, she was seized with anxiety, wishing she were not bringing new life into a world where so many dangers lurked and people could do unspeakable things to each other in the name of religion. She had got out the swaddling bands and wrapping cloths she had used for her previous babies and had them laundered in readiness for the young master, as the servants liked to call her bump. She was stitching a new bedcover for the cradle, and planned to make herself two smocks of the finest Holland cloth for her lying-in. The babe was heavy in her belly and half of her wanted this pregnancy to be over, while the rest of her felt a powerful urge to keep the child safely inside her for as long as possible.

She was troubled by a terrible story she had heard some of the congregation at church discussing. Whether it was true or not, she did not know, but it was keeping her awake at night. They had spoken of a pregnant woman condemned to the stake, whose baby had burst from her body as she was burning and been thrown into the fire by the guards. She could not get it out of her mind. Sometimes, she thought it would be better for her sanity to convert back to the Catholic faith and be done with it. Yet she could not, in her heart, abjure her religion. It was a part of her now. And she knew that Francis, for all his outward conformity, would never convert. They must be more careful than ever.

She finished making the bed and saw her husband look up from his letter and smile.

"The Lady Elizabeth is back at court. I suspect she has been summoned as a hostage for King Philip's safety. If Mary dies, his future will depend on Elizabeth. Apparently, people are already speculating that he will marry her."

"I doubt she will have him—or any man," Kate said, sitting down on the opposite side of the hearth.

"Pure maidenly modesty," he observed dismissively.

"Don't be too sure. She has never wavered from that opinion since she was eight."

"Well, she may have to. If she ever does become queen, she will have to marry." He looked again at the letter. "She was brought to court secretly because she is still under the Queen's displeasure, but she is staying in apartments near to those of King Philip. What do you make of that?"

"Maybe it signifies his favor toward her. I hope so."

"It is strange for him to be her advocate!"

"Perhaps he thinks he can turn her."

"It sounds as if she is still under house arrest, for she is not allowed to leave her rooms, although she is permitted to receive visitors."

"You don't think . . ." An idea had just occurred to Kate. "If I went to court, I might be able to see her."

"No!" Francis looked alarmed. "It says here that most people are staying away, so if you did, you would be drawing attention to yourself. And it would not be seemly for you to appear at court in your advanced condition. Besides, you have no business to be there."

Kate subsided, feeling frustrated. "Could I write to her?"

"Not yet. Let us see how the wind is blowing."

WHEN, IN LATE May, a letter arrived from one of Francis's former colleagues in the Gentlemen Pensioners, they learned that Elizabeth had had a private meeting with King Philip. No one knew what had passed between them, but Elizabeth was now at liberty and in high favor with him, although it was said that the Queen was not so warm toward her, and that Elizabeth was keeping largely to her rooms. So far, there was no sign of the royal baby arriving. Prayers were being offered up for the Queen's safe deliverance. So much depended on it.

"It does indeed," Francis commented, his face set in stone.

IT WAS AN unseasonably cold, rainy summer. In the muddy fields, the corn failed to ripen, presaging a bad harvest and the prospect of famine during the winter months. Old folks were saying that the like had not been seen for fifty years.

"It is a judgment of God upon the Queen for the persecution," Kate said bitterly.

"God would not be so cruel," Francis reproved her.

"But He governs the weather, does He not?" Kate retorted.

"You should not speak so flippantly of Him," he admonished. "He works in mysterious ways, and maybe His hand is to be seen in what is happening in London."

The mood there was ugly. They knew this from the reports of their friends. The machinery of government had come to a standstill as a result of the Queen's prolonged confinement. The people were still expressing their anger at the sickening spectacles at Smithfield. Scurrilous placards attacking Mary had been posted in the streets, and rumors abounded that she had died in childbirth and that the hated Spaniards had concealed her death for nefarious reasons of their own, or that she was not pregnant at all, but mortally ill. There were also wild claims that Edward VI was about to emerge from seclusion and return to the throne. Many were speaking with deep affection of the Lady Elizabeth, and a printed prayer to be said at her accession was being circulated. Hope sprang anew in Kate's heart. It was late June now, and still the heir to England had not made an appearance—and maybe he never would. She could not think why there should be this delay. Maybe the rumors were correct, and the Queen was ill. Yet at this late stage of pregnancy, as she knew herself, the signs were unmistakable.

Over the next week, they avidly devoured the letters they received, reading them together.

"Thank God we are away from London!" Francis exclaimed. So angry was the mood of the people that the Council had sent troops to keep order in the capital. At court, the atmosphere was tense. With so many people packed into Hampton Court Palace, the air was becoming fetid and tempers short. The animosity between the English and Spanish courtiers was tangible, and fights and squabbles erupted at the slightest provocation. There was even bloodshed. The worst moment had come when a mob of hundreds of young Englishmen had marched on Hampton Court and camped menacingly outside the main gates, swords at the ready to slay any Spaniard who dared to venture forth. The palace guards had driven them away, but the resultant fighting had left six men dead. Everything was in suspense and dependent upon the Queen's safe delivery. But that, Kate thought, was looking less and less likely each day. By her reckoning, Mary had been pregnant for eleven months, way beyond the normal course of nature.

"I am beginning to believe that she is not with child after all," she confided to Francis in bed one night, lying there with her own infant lustily kicking her.

His voice came out of the darkness. "If that is the case, then the monarchy cannot but suffer ridicule and loss of face. It seems that the Queen's enemies agree with you, though. They think she is practicing an elaborate deception, possibly to keep Philip at her side for as long as possible, since he is keen to go and fight his wars against the French."

"I don't know the Queen, but from what I have heard from others, she is not capable of such a deception. No, I think there is something very wrong with her. As a woman, I sympathize, for I can imagine what she is going through. She must long for the waiting to be over."

"I heard that the royal physicians claimed to be two months out in their calculations, and that the child is still not due."

"But the pregnancy was announced in November! That's nearly nine months ago."

"Then you're right, there has to be something wrong."

JULY CAME IN, as wet and dismal as June. Their friends at Hampton Court wrote that the palace was now stinking and filthy, and people were scared of plague breaking out. More ominously, despite reports that the Queen had muddled her dates and the birth might not now occur until August or September, few still believed that there would be a child. The Queen, despite remaining in confinement, had resumed attending to official business. She had been seen taking the air in the gardens, looking her former slender self.

In London, some Protestants were saying she had declared that the baby would not be born until every heretic in the kingdom had been burned.

"That's plain silly," Francis scoffed.

"I think that her baby was born dead, and that she fears to announce it," Kate said.

"You may be right. At her age, I doubt she will ever bear an heir," Francis opined. "Then the way will be clear for Elizabeth."

THEY RECEIVED A letter from Will. He had written several times to tell them about the new life he and Dot had made for themselves in Geneva, where they had been welcomed into the life of the English community. Now he wrote that they were not to worry, but there had been an uprising against Calvin's rule, and although it had been speedily suppressed, he himself had nearly been killed in the fighting; but he was all right, barring a few scratches.

"He shouldn't be fighting at his age," Kate muttered.

"He's only forty-seven," Francis reminded her. "And he's fit and strong after all those years of soldiering."

"But he's very dear to me!"

He took her in his arms. "If you women ruled the world, there would be no wars!"

THERE HAD BEEN no further news from court when Kate went into labor. Painful though it was, at least her child was on time, unlike the Queen's. Then she forgot about making comparisons and focused on the pressing task of bringing it into the world.

"A fair maid!" the midwife announced.

"Praise be!" cried Lettice, who had come, as usual, to be with Kate for the birth.

Kate lay back, exhausted. "May God protect her," she murmured.

Francis was thrilled. "Our eleventh child! What would you like to call her, darling?"

She took the baby from him and kissed her. "I would like to give this little one a name that conveys our solidarity with the Lady Elizabeth. We already have her namesake, little Beth, so we could call this one Anne, after her mother. The Lady Elizabeth will get the message, if she hears." And she would hear, she vowed. Soon, she would write to her. Surely there was no reason not to now?

"I like the name," Francis beamed, nodding at his mother. "Anne it is."

THE NEWS FROM court was odd. No child had been born—at least, there had been no mention of one. The Queen had emerged from seclusion, looking as slim as ever, yet sad and drawn. No explanation had been offered. She and the King had moved to Oatlands Palace.

"I'll wager the babe died at birth," Kate said, still lying in, with tiny Anne sleeping in the cradle beside her. "The Queen will not lose face by admitting it because people will say she is incapable of bearing an heir, and that will give heart to the Protestants."

"Maybe she *is* incapable," Francis said, looking hopeful. "And as the King is now leaving these shores and going to war, there'll be no other child for some time."

"And she is not getting any younger. She's, what, thirty-nine? And not in the best of health, we've heard."

"Well, I, for one, am praying that the King stays away for a long time," Francis declared. "I'm glad he's leaving, and I hope he takes all his Spaniards with him. My nameless correspondent writes that Elizabeth's succession is now seen as a near certainty, and that the King has made sure that she is treated with the respect due to the heir presumptive."

"Then may I now write to her?" Kate asked.

"I don't see why not." Francis smiled. "I don't need to tell you to be circumspect."

KATE SAT UP in bed, her little writing desk balanced on her lap, and waited for inspiration. There, she had it!

"Madam, my dearest cousin," she wrote, "it is long since I heard from you, and I could tarry no longer to ask after your health. I am so glad to hear that you are at liberty and living in your own house." She told Elizabeth of the arrival of baby Anne and other news, taking care to keep her tone light. "We do very well here at Greys Court. I think often of the happy days at Hatfield when we were young. I do very much hope to see you again one day soon, which would be the greatest joy to me. In the meantime, I shall pray for your health and happiness and ask God to have you in His protection. Your loving cousin, Kate."

To her delight, Elizabeth wrote back. She said she had been overjoyed to receive Kate's letter and wanted nothing more than to see her. She had thought of her constantly during her recent tribulations and looked forward to embracing her again and talking with her. She herself was returning to court shortly to bid farewell to the King. When she moved to Hatfield afterward, would Kate come and visit her?

Kate had hoped that Elizabeth would visit *her,* but she should have known better, for Elizabeth's old jealousy of Kate's other life was clearly lively, and probably always would be. She wrote back to say that she would gladly come, if Elizabeth would let her know when she was going to be at Hatfield. In truth, she could not wait to see her.

IN THE AUTUMN, Hal, now a strapping fourteen, was sent to Magdalen College School at Oxford, as Dr. Palmer had recommended, it being his old *alma mater.* Even though she was surrounded by the clamor of her other children, and Hal had already been away for a year in Geneva, Kate missed her firstborn. At night, she would lay her cheek on his pillow and breathe in the scent of him. By day, she kept busy. Yet she accepted that he had to go out into the world of men—and a good education was the key to success in adult life.

When he left, she had hugged him tight—but not too tightly, because he was clearly uncomfortable with it, being at that difficult age—and begged him not to betray by any hint or gesture that he and his family were secret Protestants. "It's for the safety of all of us!" she emphasized.

For the fires of Smithfield and elsewhere were still burning. Dozens of people had suffered for their faith. More English Protestants were now fleeing to Geneva, and also to the Protestant cities of Frankfurt, Zürich, and Strasbourg. The Duchess of Suffolk had fled, too. Will had informed Francis that so many English Protestants had sought refuge in Geneva that an English congregation had been set up. He and Dot had become members. Dot, he added, was expecting another child, to their great joy.

Again, Kate and Francis discussed in earnest whether they should flee England, but Francis was of the opinion that, as they had been conforming to the law for many months, and had given no one any occasion to inform on them, they should stay at home. Kate had not wanted to go anyway—she could not imagine leaving Greys Court—so she concurred eagerly. Yet she remained anxious, for herself and for her loved ones. It was as if they were walking on the edge of a precipice and one false step could send them plunging to their doom. She lived with this fear every hour of every day. Each time she looked at her children, she was overcome with dread. At times, she could barely eat.

Late in September England suffered torrential rain and floods. Men and beasts drowned, houses were flooded, the harvest was ruined, and the damage to farming and trade was immense. Francis and Kate found it a challenge to succor their tenants, who feared starvation in the winter months, and laid in as many stocks of grain and hard cheeses as they could. Great barrels brimming with oats, herbs, vegetables, and beans for making pottage were stored in the barns. For days, the house was filled with the pungent smells of smoking meat and boiling apples.

Other storm clouds were on the horizon. In October, the Protestant bishops Hugh Latimer and Nicholas Ridley were burned in Oxford. The children's tutor, Dr. Palmer, had been present. His face was grim when he returned and saw Francis and Kate. "It is not a story for your tender ears, Madam," he said. "Maybe I could speak with the master alone?"

"Tell me!" Kate demanded. "I am not a child."

He capitulated, looking unhappy. Kate suspected that he needed to share his horror with someone. "The stake was in the town ditch. As they were chained to it, Latimer bade Ridley be of good comfort and play the man, for they were lighting such a candle, by God's grace, in England, as he trusted would never be put out."

The words brought tears to Kate's eyes. It was marvelous, nay, incredible, that someone could be so brave in such circumstances.

"Latimer died quickly," Palmer continued, "but Ridley's sufferings were immense, for he burned for three-quarters of an hour."

"I think we have heard enough," Francis said, looking anxiously at Kate, who was feeling sick. "Thank you, Palmer." The tutor bowed and handed him a crumpled piece of paper, then departed wordlessly.

Francis led Kate into the parlor and sat her down by the fire. Then he smoothed out the paper, which seemed to be some kind of pamphlet. "If you believe this, Bishop Ridley is not the only martyr to endure great agony," he muttered. "It says that this wet weather has resulted in prolonged torture for several poor souls sentenced to be burned. It claims that the public outcry against the burnings has intensified, and that there have often been violent demonstrations at executions. The Catholic religion has become synonymous with brutality, and many long to see Elizabeth on the throne, for she will surely call a halt to the burnings and send the Spaniards back where they belong." He looked at Kate, his face ashen. "This is treason, no less. Imagine what could have happened had this pamphlet got into the wrong hands. To commit such sedition to paper—words fail me. And Palmer is a fool to have bought it, and kept it on his person. He could have put us all in danger. I shall have to impress on him that, whatever I was in the past, I am now the Queen's loyal subject and obey her laws. And this"—he screwed up the pamphlet—"can be burned." He tossed it into the flames. As Kate watched, she was imagining being in the heart of the fire.

ELIZABETH ROSE FROM her chair in the great chamber and held out her hands. "No, Kate, do not kneel to me! You are my own dear cousin, and I am delighted to see you."

She had written to Kate earlier in October to say she was at Hatfield, and looking forward to seeing her. When he'd kissed her goodbye, Francis had urged Kate not to stay too long, and she knew he was worried lest anything untoward happened while they were apart.

Kate went into Elizabeth's arms, a little awed by this tall, slim woman in her high-necked black gown trimmed with fur and the severe French hood crowning her red hair. There was about her a new maturity and a certain distancing—inevitable, Kate supposed, given what Elizabeth had gone through.

"I have missed you!" she cried, as they embraced. "It has been far too long. I cannot tell you how much I have worried about you."

"I had a terrible time," Elizabeth told her, shuddering. "When I was in the Tower, I lived in dread every day that they were going to come and lead me out to the scaffold. You cannot imagine what it was like in there."

"I know what it's like," Kate reminded her. "I attended your sainted mother in those very rooms."

"Yes." Elizabeth paused, looking pained. "And you have named your daughter for her. I am deeply touched. Come, sit down." She showed Kate to a chair by the fire, opposite her own, and summoned a servant to fetch some hot spiced wine.

As they sat sipping their drinks, they caught up on their news—or, rather, they caught up on Elizabeth's news.

"It was King Philip who had me set at liberty," she told Kate. "He wants my favor and—well, I believe he likes me. The Queen was not happy. I don't think she will ever trust me again, or believe that I took no part in Wyatt's rebellion, although I swear to you, Kate, that I did not. When I was given the freedom of the court, she made it plain that she did not delight greatly in my presence, but only suffered it for Philip's sake. It must have galled her to do as he asked and treat me with kindness and respect. By God, she could barely conceal her animosity! She hates me, even though she puts on a civil face. We talk about agreeable subjects only. I dare not mention the King, as she is so jealous of the favor he shows me."

Elizabeth's face was flushed, and Kate wondered if her head had been turned by Philip's attentions.

"He is thinking of the future," Elizabeth said, as if she had read her mind. "I may not say more."

It was obvious what she was thinking, but to voice it would have been folly.

"Would you want him?" Kate whispered, aware that walls sometimes had ears.

"I mean him to think that I do!" Her cousin laughed. "But I have been taking care to behave with circumspection. I even attended Mass daily with the Queen in those last weeks when I was at court. I tell you, Kate, it has been a relief to escape into the country. I find myself liking the quiet life. I have leisure to continue my studies, to walk and ride and do as I please without a thousand eyes watching me."

"Being at court must have been a great strain," Kate commiserated, wondering when Elizabeth was going to ask about *her* life. She longed to unburden her fears to her. But her hostess was too full of her own affairs.

"The Emperor has offered his nephew Ferdinand as a husband for me," she snorted. "I don't think the King is keen on the match. He has something quite different in mind for me!"

Kate thought it wiser not to comment.

"But he has gone to fight his war against the French, so I am at the Queen's mercy. She was deeply grieved when they said farewell. She loves him hopelessly. After he left, it seemed like a court in perpetual mourning. That was another reason why I was glad to get away."

"The Queen won't bear a son if the King is abroad—and England needs an heir," Kate observed, sipping her wine.

"England has her heir—me! And there will be no other. No one thinks Mary will bear a child. She is too old. And I have my doubts that Philip will return. What is there to return for?"

"Is he not hot to stamp out the Protestant religion?"

Elizabeth laughed mirthlessly. "You might think so, but in truth he is trying to curb the Queen's zeal, since he is being blamed for the burnings. But it is she who is set on them. She believes that the hearts of the people have been hardened by heresy and that more examples must be made to bring them to their senses. She wants all Protestants eradicated. No one can gainsay her."

"Is this not a terrible persecution?" Kate muttered.

"We must not say so." Elizabeth's face was set.

"I never thought that England, our dear, merry England, would turn out to be such a dangerous place."

Elizabeth looked at Kate sharply. "You are not thinking of leaving?"

"If things get too perilous, yes, we are. Francis has already been to Geneva to arrange a welcome for our English exiles."

"Don't let him talk you into it," Elizabeth said, bristling. "Now that we are restored to each other, I could not bear to lose you. You have no idea how much I missed you during those horrible months when I was shut away."

Kate was aware of the emotional blackmail. "If we are ever in danger, we will have to go."

"Then I pray you will never be!" Elizabeth said fervently. "You are so dear to me—do not forget it!"

IN DECEMBER, FRANCIS returned from the village looking worried. "I met Father Michael," he told Kate, warming his hands by the fire. "He told me that Parliament has passed an Act confiscating the estates of those who choose exile."

Kate stared into the flames, appalled. "Then we cannot flee abroad if the need arises."

"If we did, we would lose everything."

"All we can do is pray that we never come under suspicion."

"Heaven knows, we conform outwardly, for all the world to see."

"Then let us hope we will be safe." Kate was not convinced. When she looked at her children, all of them excitedly getting ready for Christmas, she felt deep shivers of fear. What would the future hold for them? Would they truly be safe?"

Chapter 27

1556

At the end of May, Kate looked out of an upstairs window and saw a messenger approaching, then heard Bilkins thank him for the letters he brought. Always fearing the worst these days, especially since the burning of Archbishop Cranmer in March, she hurried downstairs to Francis's study. She found him weeping, a letter in his hand.

"Our dear friend Will is dead," he sobbed. "He passed away in Geneva. To make matters worse, Dot has fallen out with Calvin and taken her children to Basel, where she wrote me this letter."

"How did it happen?" Kate asked, shocked and deeply saddened to realize that she would never see her staunch, reassuring stepfather again. For more than twenty years he had been there in the background of her life, a steady, supportive presence, and it was hard to believe that he had gone forever.

"A rheum on the chest, she says." Francis wiped away a tear with the back of his hand. "I tell you, Kate, that one of the brightest lights of our faith has gone out. He will be sadly missed."

"Why did Dot fall out with Calvin?"

"He took custody of her third son, John, and forbade her to leave Geneva with him. She had to appeal to Will's brother, Sir Robert Stafford, who threatened to invoke aid from the French if

Calvin did not let them go. Calvin backed down. I suspect he wanted to keep young John with him to remind people of his faithful father and bring him up to follow in his footsteps."

"But Dot will do that anyway. I am glad she got away."

"She has little money and must rely on the charity of strangers. The Privy Council ordered that no money was to be sent abroad to Will."

"How vindictive of them! They are forcing them to choose between a horrible death and impoverished exile." Kate was suddenly vehement.

"We can thank the Queen for that!"

"How terrible to die abroad, far from the land you love. Mother would be turning in her grave. He will never lie beside her now."

"I dare say not." Francis rubbed away another tear. "Let us pray that we do not have to follow him into exile."

Kate gazed out of the window at the frosted trees and shrubbery surrounding the courtyard. She could not contemplate leaving Greys Court. The prospect was unbearable, especially now, when she suspected that she was with child yet again.

FRANCIS WAS WORRIED about Dr. Palmer. The children's tutor had obtained an illegal copy of one of Calvin's works and made little secret of it. He was growing ever more outspoken in his views and was now as vehement a Protestant as he had before been a Catholic. He refused to attend Mass and made a point of walking out whenever any rite offended him in church.

Kate was becoming frightened to have such a man in charge of her children. Who knew what might happen? The older ones had been schooled to discretion, but the younger ones might blurt out anything their tutor said, and then where would they all be?

She and Francis discussed the matter, and he dismissed Dr. Palmer from his duties, although he assured him that he would continue to pay his stipend. He used his influence to help him obtain the post of master in Reading School. On the day Palmer left, Kate exhaled in relief. The man was too garrulous and opinionated; he had been a danger to them all.

Not long afterward, Francis came to her looking worried. "That fool Palmer is his own worst enemy. One of his colleagues has written to me to say that he was unpopular at Reading from the start, and that he gave his enemies cause to search his study. I suspect he had made his opinions known. They found anti-Catholic writings and threatened to inform against him unless he left the school at once. He has gone to stay with his mother at Eynsham."

"Let us pray he stays there!" Kate said tartly, and returned to checking her accounts, feeling anxious lest Palmer's foolishness rebounded on them in some way.

It was July before they heard of him again. The Mayor of Reading was a friend of Francis, and they had the news from him. Apparently, Palmer's mother had refused to give him shelter on account of his heretical opinions. He had hurried back to Reading to remove his papers and demand arrears of pay due to him, but had been arrested and brought before the mayor, who sent him to be examined by the authorities in Newbury. He'd refused to recant and had been burned at a stake set up in the town's sandpits the next day.

Kate shivered, sickened. It grieved her that a man who had once lived under their roof had met such a terrible end. "This comes far too close to home!"

"Indeed, it does," Francis said, his face grave, "especially as my name came up during Palmer's examination. It was alleged that he had incited my servants to murder and sowed sedition."

"Murder?" Kate was horrified. "What murder?"

"I have no idea, but I will find out. What worries me more is the implication that he sowed sedition in my household."

"But *you* have done nothing wrong! You dismissed him! Therein rests your defense, if any man accuses you."

"No, Kate, I have done nothing wrong, but the fact that my name was raised is troubling. Darling, I fear that the net around Protestants is tightening. I hate to say it, but I think the time has come for us to go abroad."

She gaped at him, appalled. "But they can prove nothing against us. You weren't implicated in his heresy."

Francis gripped her shoulders. "My love, some are using this persecution to settle old scores and rivalries. Others are being burned simply for being ignorant. I heard of a case where one poor soul was condemned because he could not say the Lord's Prayer. In such a climate, no one is safe. Now attention has been drawn to us. We must think of the children."

Kate stared at him, appalled. "No. We cannot leave. I cannot bear the thought. And anyway, how will we flee abroad with ten children and no home to go to? It's madness, Francis!"

"I have prepared a way for us, darling," he insisted. "I will go ahead and find us accommodation."

"And how am I to travel with the children? Tell me that?" Tears were streaming down Kate's face. "Travel can be dangerous; the journey will take weeks, and I am plagued by nausea. Are we just to uproot the children from the only life they know, and with Hal set to go up to university at Oxford in the autumn?"

He regarded her sadly. "Kate, I know you will not like this, but we cannot take them all. We will find places for the older ones here and take the younger ones with us."

"No!" she cried, aghast. "I will not be parted from any of my children! It is madness. They might not be safe from persecution. They could be used against us, as hostages for our return, because once we flee, we will make our position very clear. Francis, I have ever been an obedient wife, but I swear I will defy you on this point! I will not go!"

Seeing her so fierce, Francis gave a deep sigh. "I hope you know what you're doing, Kate. Because if the authorities come for us, it will be too late to flee, and what then will become of the children? Would you have their lives blighted by the memory of their parents dying a horrible death? I dare not even tell them what has happened to Dr. Palmer."

She sank down on a stool, weeping. "No! But to leave all that is dear and familiar, when we may not have to? Let us just wait a while. If Dr. Palmer had implicated us, you would have been arrested by now, surely?"

"You have a point there," he conceded. "Very well, we will stay on here for now. But if there is the slightest possibility of our being in danger, we must go. I want your promise on that."

"Very well," Kate said. She was full of misgivings.

. . .

THE NEXT WEEKS were tense. They remained alert and permanently on edge.

Nothing happened. Hal, now a tall, broad-backed fifteen-year-old, went cheerfully up to Oxford. Waving him goodbye, Kate wondered if she would ever see him again. She had impressed on him the necessity to attend Mass and never to betray his true beliefs, and he had solemnly promised her that he would obey. It was hard letting him go, harder than it had been when he went away to school.

In November, it was announced in church that Lord Chancellor Gardiner had died. He was known to have been a moderating influence on the Queen, and Kate and Francis were fearful that the persecution of Protestants would now escalate.

"We cannot risk staying in England," he declared that night, as they lay in bed in each other's arms.

"Please, Husband, let us wait and see. Entrusting ourselves to the mercies of the seas and the compassion of strange nations will involve great risk. We would be cast adrift, relying on the charity of foreigners. And if we leave, this house and all your property will be confiscated."

"Even that will be preferable to being burned alive," he said, holding her tightly. "I am telling you, darling, we must leave, and soon. We dare not tempt Fate by staying. I will go ahead, as I said, and find us somewhere to live. You can find places for our older children, then follow with the little ones."

Kate burst into tears. The prospect of leaving Greys Court, and England itself, and being parted from her children, and from Francis for the time being, was overwhelmingly awful. It tore at the very core of her being. Now she understood what her mother had been through when she had had to abandon her children for exile in Calais. She felt so desperate that she feared she might miscarry.

"It is a heartbreaking decision to make," she sobbed.

"That is why I am making it for us," Francis said firmly.

. . .

IN THE MORNING, they gathered together their children, all except the baby, Anne, and explained what was going to happen. They emphasized the danger and the necessity for maintaining discretion and showing fortitude.

"Mother is going to stay here with you until the baby is born, and then she will bring some of you to join me," Francis told them. "But you, Mary, Lettice, Will, and Ned, must stay here, as we cannot take you all. Rest assured that we will find good places for you. It will be no different from what would happen if things were normal; as you know, most gently born children are sent to noble households to learn manners and the skills that will befit them for their paths in life."

Mary and Lettice were crying. The boys were biting their lips, trying to play the man. Beth and little Frank clung to Kate's skirts, bewildered by what was going on.

"You will be well looked after," Kate promised. "I would not send you anywhere I deem unsuitable. And the rest of you will be going on an exciting journey." Her voice shook as she said it. "Now, we need you all to be brave and grown up for us. It may be that our parting and our sojourn abroad will not last long. I shall pray daily that we all will soon be reunited."

"We will be brave for you, Mother," Mary declared, drying her tears.

"Yes, we will!" the others chorused.

THERE WAS NO time to waste. Francis packed up as much luggage as his sumpter mule could easily carry, and took enough money to live on until Kate joined him. She was to bring the rest of the coin they had in their treasure chest, along with her jewelry and some plate, which they could sell if they needed to.

"When it is time, get the servants to crate everything up and take it ahead to Maldon," he instructed. "It is better to go across country and take ship from there, than to go through London to Dover. It will be a longer sea crossing, but there is far less chance of your departure being noticed. And take the plain horse litter, the one without our coat of arms."

"Will I find a ship easily?" Kate asked, in deep trepidation because this coming voyage into the unknown seemed an immense undertaking.

"At Maldon? I am sure you will. And you can pay good money. That always helps."

"I will settle our affairs here and then shut up the house," Kate said, trying to stay practical in order to ward off her feelings of dread. They only had one more night together before Francis left. God only knew when they would lie together again.

When they finally retired to bed, she clung to him, wishing that she was not so great with child. She could feel it in her belly, moving between them.

"I wish we could be properly together," she whispered, longing for him.

"There are more ways than one of being together," he murmured, and began to stroke her breasts. They began pleasuring each other, and when her climax came, her womb contracted so violently that she thought the babe would be expelled immediately. But the feeling subsided. In its place came the dear, familiar rush of love for this man who was everything to her, and she held him tightly, not wanting the feeling ever to end.

IN THE MORNING, she stood by the mounting block as Francis climbed astride his horse and handed up to him the stirrup cup. She had to summon all her self-control to keep the smile on her face and be brave for him; she did not want him taking away a memory of her weeping. When he gazed down at her, she could see that he too was struggling to control his emotions. There were tears in his eyes. But he raised a firm hand in farewell to the children and the assembled servants.

"God be with you all!" he cried. Then his gaze moved to Kate. "And with you, my dearest wife."

As she watched him ride away, she thought she would die of misery.

. . .

THERE WAS SO much to do that she had to concentrate on practicalities and was glad of the distraction. The nights were the worst. She missed Francis desperately and felt very alone and vulnerable. Any time soon, the authorities might get to hear of his departure. She prayed he would take ship before that happened. But what would become of her and the children if they descended on Greys Court and threw them all out—and she eight months gone with child? She shivered at the thought, catching her breath at the possibility that she might be arrested for heresy. It made her want to gather up her brood and flee now.

She fought against letting her imagination run riot. Probably, she told herself, she and Francis had overestimated the danger. But it was better to be safe than sorry.

She now faced the pressing task of finding places for the older children. It went against all her instincts to send them away, yet she knew it must be done. Gradually, the arrangements were made. Hal would reside at the university in the holidays; she had arranged that with his tutor. Mary, Lettice, Will, and Ned were to stay with her brother, Harry, and his wife, who had children of much the same age. Kate had invited Harry to Greys Court, and he had come to discuss the arrangements. She was thankful that he'd brought Anne with him because she was warm and friendly, whereas he had become something of a martinet. As for his language . . . Yet Kate knew that she could rely on him to care for her children. He had at least spoken kindly to her of that.

It would break her heart to part with them all. That Christmas was the saddest she had ever known, with Francis absent and no word yet from him, and the older children about to leave home. His mother came to stay again, much to Kate's comfort, but she seemed distracted and somehow diminished, which Kate put down to her anxiety about Francis and their uncertain future, which she was unable to hide. Kate worried about what it was doing to her. How she herself kept up a semblance of good cheer was beyond comprehension, but she did. She owed it to her offspring to be strong.

Chapter 28

1557

IN JANUARY, THE HOUSE SEEMED VERY QUIET, DESPITE THE presence of five young children. Yet they were subdued. They did not want to be parted from their older siblings, and were aware that a new life was ahead of them in a strange land, far from their beloved home. Kate could have wept for them.

Her daughter was born on a freezing winter morning, when icicles hung from the gable above her window. She slipped into the world easily, a mewling little thing who hardly had the strength to take suck and died that night, unbaptized. Nevertheless, Kate persuaded Father Michael to bury her in the churchyard.

She was not present, of course, for she was lying in, drained emotionally and physically, grieving for her lost infant and painfully aware that when she emerged from her confinement, she would probably have to leave England immediately. But she could not go until she had heard from Francis. That had been the plan.

They brought her the letter on the day she got out of bed for the first time and sat, well wrapped, in her chair by the fireside. Her heart leaped when she saw that it was from her husband and she devoured his words avidly.

He had reached Basel in December and visited Dot, who was coping bravely with widowhood, much to his admiration. Then he had gone on to Frankfurt and become a member of the Calvinist congregation there. That had been just before Christmas. He had returned to Basel, liking it better, and he thought that Kate would like it, too. "I have found us a good lodging," he had written. "Come now, if you are recovered from your confinement, and join me. I long to see you. I feel as if I have been banished for the truth of the Gospel."

Her instinct was to run to him, but she could not leave until she had been churched and released back into society, and that was a week away. The days could not pass quickly enough.

She wished she could see Elizabeth, but Elizabeth was back at court—and hating it, according to her last letter. Sitting up in bed, trying not to look at the space beside her where the empty cradle had stood, Kate wrote to her, using the private cipher they had agreed between them, and told her why she had to go away. "I long to be with Francis," she confided, then realized that such a declaration of devotion might make Elizabeth jealous. But no, let it stand, she told herself. Her cousin must accept that she loved her husband. He was not a subject to be skirted around. To balance things, she told Elizabeth that she was very distressed at the prospect of being parted from her.

She had just been churched when a reply came, with a packet of money enclosed. Far from being jealous, Elizabeth clearly sought to comfort her.

"You should temper your sorrow for your long journey with joy in the knowledge that you will be returning shortly," she had written. Kate stared at that. Did Elizabeth know something others didn't? Was the Queen ill? Or was Mary having a change of heart about persecuting Protestants?

Think of this pilgrimage rather as proof of your friends' love than the leaving of your country. Length of time and distance of place cannot separate the love of friends nor deprive any of your goodwill. There is an old saying, when bale is lowest, boot is nearest; thus, when your need is greatest, you shall find my friendship equal to it. Others may make promises, but I will do as much in words and deeds. My power is but small, yet my love is as great as those whose gifts tell their friendships' tale. Your messenger shall not return empty. Lethe's flood has no course here, for I will keep you in good memory. And to conclude there is a word I hardly can say, yet am driven by need to write—it is "farewell," for which I grieve deeply.

Your loving cousin and friend, Cor Rotto.

KATE HAD TO smile through her tears. It was typical of Elizabeth to insert classical allusions into a letter. Yet her description, in Italian, of herself as "Broken Heart" betrayed her deep distress. It was one of the most affectionate letters Elizabeth had ever written to her. It attested to their enduring friendship, which had become closer thanks to the shared bond of religion that tied them in these dark days. It was heartening to reread Elizabeth's assurance that she would wait with joy for Kate's speedy return, for it hinted at her hopes that her sister's rule would not last for much longer.

She wrote back, expressing her thanks, and seized the opportunity to ask Elizabeth if she would take Mary and Lettice into her household, knowing that they would be able to continue their education under her auspices, since Elizabeth's renowned tutor, Roger Ascham, had returned to her service. Moreover, when Elizabeth became queen, as surely she would one day, she might well advance those who had served her well and help them to make good marriages.

Back came the response: the Lady Elizabeth would be delighted to receive Mary and Lettice. Enclosed was a note in cipher. "It is my hope that, by means of your daughters, we will be able to keep in touch."

The two girls, Mary, fourteen, and Lettice, thirteen—and already a beauty with her flaming red hair and perfect features—had heard a lot over the years about their mother's happy days with Elizabeth and were delighted by this new turn of events.

"It will be much better than going to Uncle Harry's," Lettice declared.

"It will," Mary agreed. "He frightens me."

Kate frowned. "Don't speak of your uncle like that." Yet she had to admit that her brother was stern and irascible. It was a mercy they did not meet, save for rare uncomfortable visits, for he had become puritanical as he grew older. And yet, Kate reminded herself, he had agreed to take her children in, and for that she was deeply grateful.

"He doesn't frighten me!" retorted Lettice, ever the spirited one. "But I am thrilled to be going to the Lady Elizabeth."

Kate was glad for her, and for Mary. It would help to ease their parting. As for Will and Ned, she consoled herself with the knowledge that Harry was mostly at court, in the Queen's service, and that they would be subject to the gentler rule of his wife, Anne.

SOON, EVERYTHING SHE and her little ones would need had been packed and sent on to Maldon to await her coming. Fighting back tears, Kate bade farewell to her older children and swallowed the lump in her throat as she watched them leave home. Now all there was left to do was lock up the house and pay off Bilkins and the servants, who were all desperately sad at being laid off.

"But I hope to be back in England before too long, and then I will summon you all back, if you have not found places elsewhere," she told them, noticing that Bilkins had tears in his eyes. "You have served me well and I cannot express my thanks sufficiently. May God go with you."

They all knew why she was leaving and had been sworn to secrecy. She knew she could trust them; they had been with the family for a long time and if they were going to report her, they would have done so long ago.

Just as she was preparing to depart, and Thomasina and the two nursery maids she was taking with her were bundling the children into their cloaks and gloves, a carter turned up at the front door with wares to sell and a letter for her. She looked over the tray of cheap toys on offer and impulsively bought some wooden animals and three rag books to keep the children amused on the journey, since most of their other playthings had been packed. Then she opened the letter.

It was an official notice from the Treasury, informing her that, since Sir Francis Knollys had gone into voluntary exile and was a notorious heretic, his manor of Caversham had been reassigned to the Countess of Warwick.

No. This could not be. Wildly, she looked around her at Greys Court, slumbering in the winter sunshine. If Caversham had gone, it too would be taken away. She might be looking at it for the last time. This notice made it clear that she was leaving England not a moment too soon. It was known that Francis was a Protestant, and suspicion might well fall on her if she tarried. Swallowing her grief—for it felt like a bereavement—she turned her back on Greys Court and climbed into the waiting litter.

IT TOOK THEM ten days to reach Maldon. They covered only ten miles each day because Frank and Beth had to keep getting out to be sick, thanks to the rutted roads and the jerking motion of their carriage. Kate dared not seek hospitality at the houses of people of their acquaintance lest they inform the authorities where she was, and the inns they stayed in were sometimes insalubrious, yet costly nonetheless. Thanks to another bad harvest, the food served to them was sparse and unappetizing. Yet at night, she slept like the dead, not caring that the lumpy bed she shared with her five children might be infested with bugs.

It was a relief to reach Maldon and find that Thomas, the burly groom she had sent ahead with their baggage, had found a ship and stowed everything on board for her. He had also paid for their passage and was ready to escort them on their long journey.

SHE HAD NEVER felt so sick. The heaving of the boat was a living purgatory and at times she longed to die. She spent all her time in their cabin, her head down on her forearm, unable to move. She thanked God that Thomasina was a good sailor and could take care of the children, who were suffering, too.

If only they could get some fresh air! Kate longed to be out on deck, but the ship's master believed it unlucky to have women on board, and commanded that they keep to their quarters. These were clean and commodious, at least to begin with, but she could eat none of the food brought to them, wholesome though it was.

At last—at last, dear God—they saw land out of the tiny window. The master informed them that they would soon be making port at Sluys. After five days at sea, they disembarked on a dark January evening, and Kate found herself barely able to stand. Thomas hurried away to get the litter, the baggage cart, and the horses off the ship, then the bedraggled little party waited as he went off to find them lodgings, still wobbling on his sea legs. He returned to say that he had commandeered rooms at an old inn, and they gratefully made their way there, Kate carrying little Anne and the other children clinging to the hands of Thomasina and their nurses.

It was a relief to sleep in a bed that didn't move about so unpredictably that you thought you might be thrown off. Kate found her appetite again and they all enjoyed huge helpings of a rich Flemish stew. It gave them heart to embark on the long journey ahead. According to Francis, Basel was six hundred miles away. It seemed an unimaginable distance, but they were to cover it in slow, easy stages.

At dawn, they set off.

GHENT, BRUSSELS, LUXEMBOURG, Metz . . . Soon, one city looked much like another. Kate would have liked to stop to see the sights, yet she remained aware of the need to press on, while the awareness that Francis would be waiting for them at the end of the long trek gave a spur to her determination. Fifty days until she would see him, forty, thirty . . . Soon they were at Nancy, then Colmar. Her spirits rose with every mile they crossed. Resolutely, she refused to think of Greys Court. What mattered was that they were all safe. She still feared for the children she had left behind, yet she knew they were in good hands.

They had been traveling for exactly sixty days when they sighted the towers and spires of Basel in the distance. Kate's heart soared as they crossed the bridge over the River Rhine, which led to the city. Somewhere, amid all those tall houses with red roofs, Francis was waiting. The children could barely contain themselves at the thought of seeing their father, and Kate was no less excited.

"The house is on the marketplace," she told Thomas. "Can you ride ahead and find it?" She was praying that Francis would be in.

It was a joy to see Protestant churches and people going in and out without fear of persecution. There were Protestant tracts on the booksellers' stalls, and many of the citizens were wearing the sober attire decreed by Calvin. Kate was glad that she had put on her best black gown and hood. She wanted to fit in here—and she also wanted to look her best for Francis.

Thomas appeared ahead, waving, and ran back to them, taking up the reins of the litter and shouting at the cart horses to follow. Kate hoped there would be a yard at the house where they could keep their vehicles.

The marketplace was packed with booths and people, and their progress around it was slow. At last, Kate found herself standing outside a tall white house with timber beams, shuttered windows, and a tiled roof. It was clean and well kept. She could hardly believe that she was here at last. Journey's end. It was a miracle!

She alighted from the litter, telling her excited children to remain where they were for the moment. Her heart pounding, she walked up to the door and rapped on the knocker. And then Francis opened the door.

When he saw her, his face was transformed, radiant.

"Darling Kate!" he breathed and swept her into his arms before she could draw breath. It was glorious to have him hold her once more and she clung on as if she would never let him go again, returning his kisses with equal ardor. The children had burst out of the litter and were crowding around them. "Father! Father!" they were crying, overjoyed to see him. He bent down and hugged them all, and when he stood up, he was weeping unashamedly.

"We are safe, darling, we are safe!" he said hoarsely.

"Yes," Kate replied, "we have done the right thing." But in her mind, she wondered, as she had been wondering throughout the journey, when she had had a lot of time to think. Had it been the right thing to leave their older children in England? In doing so, had they placed too great a burden on their young minds? It would take only one false word to land them in disaster. Yet she was sure she had drummed into them the necessity for circumspection—and with that she must content herself, or she would go mad.

FRANCIS LED THEM indoors.

"I'm renting the ground floor only. We have five rooms and a kitchen. It will be a tight fit with the children and the servants, but we'll manage. I need to conserve what money I have, since we don't yet know what will happen to my lands in England."

"I have brought plenty of money," Kate told him. She would not mention the loss of Caversham, not yet.

"You darling girl!" He embraced her again.

The main room of their lodging was sparsely furnished with a settle, a table, a cupboard, and several stools, but it was cluttered with Francis's stuff—bags, books, writing materials, mugs, plates, even a recorder. Three beds had been crammed into the room designated for the children.

"Anne will have to sleep in the middle, in case she falls out," Kate observed. "At least there is a chest for their clothes."

The bedchamber she was to share with Francis had a carved tester bed, unmade, of course, for he had no domestic skills.

"Do you have anyone to keep house?" she inquired.

"A woman comes in daily to cook and clean."

She made a face. "She's not much of a cleaner, is she?" They laughed.

"Her cooking's not much better either." Francis grinned.

"I'll see to her," Kate vowed. "Or I'll hire someone else."

"You always were brilliant at running a household, darling." He kissed her. "I can't tell you how glad I am you are here. Or how wonderful it will be to worship freely together."

Happiness shot through her. They were together. That mattered more than anything. Still she did not tell him about the loss of Caversham. Nothing must spoil their reunion.

Chapter 29

1557

THE JOY THAT OVERWHELMED THEM IN BED THAT NIGHT was unparallelled. They melted into each other and quenched the longing that had built up over months. Kate had never known such delight.

The morning found her waking with a smile on her face, and there was Francis, pulling her into his arms again, ready for more lovemaking. But they could hear the children laughing and shrieking next door, and a clattering from the kitchen that announced the arrival of the servant.

"I can't relax with all this going on," Kate muttered, and got up, leaving Francis protesting.

"Come back!" he moaned, reaching out his arms.

"Later!" She smiled, pulling on her robe. "Although I would far rather not be tearing myself away from you!"

She was glad to see the nurses up and about, seeing to the children, but when she walked into the kitchen, she was horrified to see a squalid mess. And there, banging about, was a slatternly woman wearing a dirty apron that had once perhaps been white, and smelling of something Kate preferred not to think about. As for her fingernails . . .

She said something in German, of which Kate had only the

rudiments. Kate ignored her. "I am Mistress Knollys. Is there a well? We need fresh water. *Wasser!*"

"*Dort!*" replied the slattern, pointing to the door.

"*Sie!*" Kate hissed, pointing to her, indicating that she should fetch it.

With a surly look, the woman picked up a grimy bucket.

Horrified, Kate mimed a scrubbing motion. The help shrugged and ambled toward the door.

"Get out!" Kate cried, losing her temper.

Francis had come up behind her. "Are you dismissing her?"

"Of course I am. Look at the state of this kitchen!"

He addressed the woman. "*Ilse, austeigen! Jetzt! Komm nicht zurück!*"

She dropped the bucket with a clang, gave him a filthy look, and stalked out. "I told her not to come back," Francis said.

"Good. Will there be any cooked food in the market?"

"Yes. I'll send Thomas out for some."

"Thank goodness. We can have it for breakfast. Then I'll set to work in here."

Replete with roast chicken and pumpernickel bread, Kate put on her oldest dress and tackled the kitchen with Thomasina, bidding the nursemaids help them. By dinnertime, it was scrubbed clean, and a fire was crackling merrily beneath the cookpot on the hearth. Thomas had brought back meat and vegetables, and they had a hearty stew for their meal. In the afternoon, Kate turned her attention to the other rooms, which needed a good clean, and soon the whole apartment was looking like a new pin. There was fresh linen on the beds and the pewter tableware shone.

Francis observed the transformation with awe. "You're a marvel, Kate."

"It's a good thing I came," she said, with mock tartness. "You'd have just gone on living in squalor, wouldn't you?"

"I had other things on my mind," he protested.

"I'll wager you didn't even notice! Anyway, we need a new servant."

"You might try the marketplace."

Kate was there first thing the next morning. There were fewer stalls today, but Francis had been right: there was a booth where people were advertising themselves for hire. Among them was a plump woman with apple cheeks and plaits tightly coiled around each ear. Her clothes were clean and she smelled wholesome. Her name was Eva and she could do cooking and cleaning. This Kate learned from the man who ran the booth, who spoke a little English. A quarterly wage was agreed, plus his fee, and Kate took Eva home with her. Eva was so pleased to have been hired by the gracious English lady, and to find herself working in an orderly house, that she was willing to do whatever was asked of her—and she did it well.

Soon, the household settled into a pleasant routine. Kate, Francis, and the children took their meals together in the parlor, while the servants ate at the kitchen table. Kate would sometimes help out with the cooking, and even the shopping; it was so convenient having the market just across the street.

In the mornings, she gave lessons to her children, and Francis would spend an hour teaching Beth, Robert, and Richard. When the nurses took the little ones out in the afternoon, Kate would embroider or make music, while Francis wrote long letters to Calvin and other reformers. That April, he enrolled as a student of the University of Basel and made friends with a learned Englishman called John Foxe, who had published Protestant tracts in King Edward's reign and had to flee when Queen Mary revived the heresy laws. He and Francis shared the same strong views about religion, and he was a regular dinner guest at Kate's table. One day, he told her, he was going to write a book about the sufferings of the Englishmen who were being martyred for their faith.

Francis had been greatly saddened to hear of the confiscation of Caversham, but there had, as yet, been no news of Greys Court. His attorney, Master Thomas Stafford, was keeping an eye on the house, but any day, Francis and Kate expected to be informed that the Crown had seized it. They were both delighted to hear, however, that the Countess of Warwick had given Caversham to Master Stafford to hold for his master. Kate was deeply touched by such a generous gesture, but then the Countess was the daughter of the late Protector Somerset, and daughter-in-law to the ill-fated Northumberland, so must secretly be harboring Protestant sympathies.

The news from England, though, was not good. The fires of Smithfield were blazing as hotly as ever. Following the bad weather that had ruined last year's harvest, the land had been visited by an epidemic of influenza. In one of her infrequent, coded letters, Elizabeth wrote that many regarded these tribulations as the judgment of God upon Mary.

Kate dared not write to Elizabeth too often, in case her letters were intercepted, which might draw attention to the fact that her daughters were living under Elizabeth's roof. At their age, they would be considered old enough to be examined on their beliefs, and that was the last thing she wanted to happen to them, especially—as Elizabeth had assured her, more than once—now that they had settled happily into their new lives. She missed them so much and was poignantly aware that they were of an age when girls growing to womanhood needed their mothers. She missed the boys, too, but had heard from Anne, her sister-in-law, that they were well and attending diligently to their studies and the military exercises in which Harry was drilling them.

And then, one morning in late April, Francis called her in from the kitchen and bade her sit on the settle. His face was grave.

"Kate, we are not as safe as we thought. I heard at church that Queen Mary is sending agents to hunt down Protestant exiles."

Kate's hand flew to her mouth. "Why?"

"Because doubtless she wants to make an example of them. There have been rumors, but no certain report until now. Today, I learned of the death of the late King Edward's tutor, Sir John Cheke, and what happened to him after he went into exile. Last year, he traveled from Strasbourg to Brussels to receive his wife, lately come to join him. He had also been promised a safe-conduct to meet with Lord Paget and Sir John Mason, his wife's stepfather. All went well, but when he traveled on to Antwerp, he was seized on the orders of King Philip, and taken, as it were, in a whirlwind over the sea, not knowing where he was going until he found himself in the Tower of London. It's almost certain that Paget and Mason plotted his arrest. The poor man was pulled from his horse and clapped into a cart with his legs, arms, and body tied to it."

"But that's awful!" Kate cried, feeling as if the earth were giving way beneath her.

"In the Tower, Sir John was visited by priests who tried to convert him and told him that nothing less than a full recantation would satisfy the Queen. If he failed to make one, he would be sent to the stake. In the end, he submitted, and was made to read out his recantation in public. After that, he was required to be present when Protestants were condemned to be burned, and this so affected his heart that he died. Kate, this could happen to us."

Kate was striving to be sensible. "Could it? It has happened to one man, and he was abducted nowhere near here."

"Yes, but there has been talk among the exiles here. Some have disappeared, and no one knows what has become of them. Others think they are being watched. I think we should be vigilant."

Reluctantly, Kate agreed. She could have wept, because it had been so wonderful and liberating to feel safe in Basel, and now she did not feel safe any longer. She told herself that they were probably worrying unnecessarily, yet she could not convince herself of it.

She kept looking about her every time she left the house. She insisted that the nursemaids accompany the children wherever they went and keep their eyes open for anyone suspicious. She set Thomas to keep watch over the house. Francis took to taking a pistol with him when he went abroad.

One day, when Kate was in the market, she noticed a man lounging by a fish stall. It was his attire that drew her attention, because he was swathed in a heavy black cloak and had a felt hat pulled down low over his face. He looked odd, because it was a warm day and no one else was wrapped up like that. She thought he was looking her way but couldn't be sure. Surreptitiously keeping him in sight, she walked past several stalls to see if he followed, but he did not. Harmless, then. She really should not be seeing abductors around every corner!

But he was there two days later, when she went out with Eva to buy fruit. He was still there when they had shopped around the market and retraced their steps. The next day, when the family left the house to walk to church, she saw him standing on the opposite corner, and then her blood really did run cold.

"Don't look now, but I fear that that man over there is shadowing me," she muttered to Francis.

He stole a quick glance. "By Heaven, I've seen him, too. He was in the *bierkeller* yesterday afternoon when I dropped in for a drink. I thought it strange that he was all bundled up on a spring day."

"Well, he's been there twice in the market this week, and I think he was watching me."

Francis frowned. "Shall I challenge him?"

"No. He will deny any sinister intention—and he may just live locally. But let us be watchful."

OVER THE NEXT few days, Kate saw the man again from a window; he appeared to be watching the house. Francis saw him talking to a fellow with an eyepatch; they were standing at the edge of the square. Then he appeared near the church again.

"I don't like this," Francis admitted, after they had walked past him. "We must keep the children indoors. Heaven forbid, one of them could be taken hostage for our sakes."

When they returned home, a letter was waiting for Kate. She tore it open, recognizing Elizabeth's code. Taking it into the bedchamber, she sat down and began to decipher it.

Elizabeth had sent it a month ago. It was brief and to the point: "My dear cousin, I have it on good evidence that a plot is afoot to kidnap you and your husband and spirit you back to England. If that happens, I could not answer for your safety. Be vigilant."

Trembling, Kate showed Francis her transcript of the letter. "We have to leave," she said. "We dare not risk staying here."

"You are right," he concurred, greatly alarmed. "I have friends in Frankfurt who will help us. We shall go there. It is nearer to England, if we hear that the situation has changed at home."

"How wonderful it would be if that happened," Kate said

plaintively. "It is the news I long for. But we should leave tonight." She could feel panic rising. "We must think of the children." The need to protect them was overwhelming.

THAT EVENING, THEY broke the news to the servants. Eva wept because she had family in Basel and did not want to live over three hundred miles to the north. One of the nursemaids wept because her sweetheart in Basel had just asked her to marry him; she would not be leaving. Only Thomasina, the other nursemaid, Meg, and Thomas would be accompanying the Knollyses.

The children were excited at the prospect of what was described to them as an adventure by night, and obediently helped to gather together their things. Kate forbore to tell them that they would be on the road for over a month. She would leave that until later.

Fortunately, the cart and the litter were stored behind high gates in a yard that abutted the house, so no one could see the servants loading the travelers' belongings onto the cart. With all the lights in the house extinguished, Kate hoped it seemed that the whole household was asleep. They would not light lanterns until they were well clear of the city; until then, they would find their way by moonlight, taking the back roads. She wondered fearfully if the cloaked man was there, watching, as she wrapped her children up warmly, despite the mild night, and bade them keep silent.

As a nearby clock struck midnight, Francis peered out of the front door. The market square seemed deserted. There was no sign of the man in black. He and Thomas opened the gates to the yard, wincing as the wood creaked, and Thomas went to fetch the horses from the stable. He would drive the baggage cart and Francis would drive the litter containing Kate, the children, and the maids. As the men harnessed the animals, Kate ushered her brood into the litter, holding a finger to her lips to remind them that they had to be very quiet.

She could not stop inwardly thanking Elizabeth, who had proved a true friend to her and who might well have saved their lives by warning them of the danger in which they stood—which they were not out of yet. She was so tense that her whole body felt taut as a bowstring. As the litter moved off, her heart was beating like a drum.

The streets of Basel were quiet. They did not encounter a single soul until they reached the city gates, where the guards demanded to know where they were headed.

"We are going to visit my sick mother in Colmar," Francis explained. "We had an urgent summons this afternoon. I fear we may have to stay some time, hence the baggage."

They were waved through, and then they were on their way. No one was following. Kate and Thomasina sat holding hands, both extremely tense, until they were satisfied that they had safely got away and were able to relax and go to sleep, snuggled up with the children.

FRANKFURT WAS BUSTLING and prosperous, dominated by the cathedral on its high hill and crammed with tall houses with steep roofs. It was a city of merchants from all nations, and Kate was glad to hear some English voices. Many were weavers; others worked in the book trade. She was delighted to learn that there was an annual book fair, which was clearly a big event, for people spoke of it with pride. Hopefully, she would be able to get some books there. She had hated being obliged to leave hers in England, but they had been too heavy to bring with her.

They had found a lodging in the house of a fellow exile, John Weller, a wealthy London merchant. Francis had been corresponding with him for a year or more, and he made them all very welcome. He did not seem to mind that his home was overcrowded. He and his wife, Susan, had five sons and a number of servants, so space was at a premium. But John Weller was a large, jovial man who relished having English gentry under his roof. He was delighted to learn that Kate was the niece of Anne Boleyn.

"Ah, there was a lady who was a great friend to the Gospel. She was sorely wronged," he observed over dinner that first night, when the children were in bed.

"She was indeed," Kate agreed. She could imagine Weller's reaction were he ever to discover that King Henry's own daughter had sheltered in his house.

Francis was interested to know more about his connection with a Scottish Calvinist exile called John Knox.

"Oh, yes, Sir Francis, I knew him when he was in Frankfurt last year. But his views were extreme; he'd even criticized the Emperor in one of his pamphlets. He had to go to Geneva to escape the attention of the authorities. I heard that he had returned to Scotland and that he was preaching Calvinist doctrines in Edinburgh. He's a fiery man with strong opinions, not a comfortable man."

"I wish him luck in Scotland," Francis said drily. "It's under the heel of the French and the Catholic faith is entrenched there, and looks to remain so with the young Queen of Scots married to the Dauphin and living in France."

"With her mother acting as regent in Scotland!"

"Aye. The British Isles are in the grip of two obstinate, backward-looking women."

"But the situation in England may change," Kate said. "That is what we are hoping for."

"We all want to go home," Susan chimed in. "I have heard that Queen Mary is not in the best of health."

"I would never pray for someone to die," Kate said, "but I am sorely tempted. Think of the suffering she has caused, the lives she has ruined. Because of her, I am forced to live apart from five of my children. I worry about them every day. If it wasn't for your generous charity, I don't know what would become of us."

"Think nothing of it," boomed their host. "You are welcome to stay here for as long as you like."

"It is a shame that you missed the Duchess of Suffolk," Susan said. "She and her family stayed here earlier this month on their way to Poland, where she has been offered a refuge. Queen Mary's agents were after her, for she had defied an order to return to England, and she was lucky to escape."

Francis and Kate exchanged a long look. It seemed that no one was safe, anywhere.

"Do you think we will be troubled while we are here?" Kate asked nervously.

"By English bullies? They'll have to get past me first," Master Weller said defiantly. "No, you'll be safe with us."

Kate sincerely hoped so. She was weary of looking over her shoulder all the time and she wanted her children to lead normal lives.

"No one knows we are here," Francis said. "I want it to stay that way. Kate, when you write to friends in England, especially the lady at Hatfield, don't reveal our whereabouts."

"I won't," Kate promised, thinking that she would write to Elizabeth and the children, but tell them that, for safety, they couldn't write to her. It was going to be hard, not hearing from them, but it was for the best.

Chapter 30

1557–58

THEY DECIDED TO USE FALSE NAMES. FRANCIS WAS MASTER Edward Smith and Kate was his wife, Anne. The names were chosen with the deliberate intention of being unmemorable. Kate was enjoying the sense of anonymity this new life in Frankfurt afforded her. She was settling into it better than she had expected to, and the children and the servants were adapting well.

Soon, there would be a new baby. The joyful reunion had quickly borne fruit, and the child would arrive in the New Year, by Kate's reckoning. She'd be rising thirty-four by then, old to be venturing on another pregnancy, and yet she had delivered all the others without too much trouble, so felt confident that she would sail through this confinement, too. And she felt more positive this time, for although this little one might be born with an uncertain future, it would be born in safety.

In England, new laws were making it increasingly difficult for the exiles to obtain any income, but there were ways. Francis wrote to his attorney, Master Stafford, directing him to send all monies to Master Weller's bank in nearby Offenbach, whence they could be forwarded to him. The new arrangement worked, and the family were able to pay their way and live comfortably, despite the cramped conditions. It was limiting for Kate and Francis to have their youngest children sleeping in their bedchamber, but it was another trial that had to be borne. They were lucky to have been taken in by such kind people.

Kate liked Frankfurt. She loved the tall, timbered houses festooned with flowers at the windows, the cheery *bierkellers,* the colorful shops. The Wellers' home was near the river, on the banks of which she liked to take the children for walks.

In the autumn, Kate and Francis visited the book fair, marveling at the huge array of printed books and manuscripts on display. There were many Protestant tracts for sale, and Francis bought quite a collection, while Kate indulged herself with a few romances and a volume of poetry, which were among the few books in English for sale. Most were in German, which she was trying to learn, yet was still defeated by that language's complicated declensions. Thankfully, Francis was becoming fluent, having spent hours mastering them.

It still seemed incredible to be able to practice their faith openly and bring up their children in it. If only things could be different in England. But the news from home was not encouraging. The persecution was raging as fiercely as ever, and it was reported that Queen Mary was due to bear a child in March. Kate's spirits sank when she heard that.

"It could spell the end of all our hopes," she said to Francis, as they helped to clear the dinner table.

"Take heart, darling. Remember what happened last time. I do not believe that she can bear a child. She is too old."

"But what if she does?"

"Let's meet that when we come to it." And he took her in his arms, gentling her.

It would be a good life, Kate thought, were it not for the fact that they were exiles longing for home. In December, they were admitted as full members of the Protestant congregation of Frankfurt. Francis was active in the church and Kate was admired for her devotion to the faith. Each Sunday, they attended with their children and their servants, all dressed in sober black and white, sitting in a row listening attentively to the sermon and saying their prayers devoutly.

But the bustle and spirit of Frankfurt still could not make up for what she so missed—the beauty of the changing English seasons, the peace of Greys Court, and the laughter of the children they had left behind.

JANUARY 1558 BEGAN with the saddest of news. They received a letter from Francis's brother via the bank, informing him that their mother had died. The news hit Francis hard.

"I wish I had seen her one last time and been able to say farewell," he said bitterly, tears in his eyes. "By God, I'd like to damn Mary to Hell for the trouble and grief she has caused us!" It was a rare outburst because he was not a man given to extremes of emotion, but he was in the grip of grief and Kate understood only too well how he felt. She too mourned for Lettice and wept at the realization that she would never see her again.

They did not quite know what to think when, a week later, they learned that the French had captured Calais, England's only remaining territory in France.

"As a true Englishman, I am horrified," Francis said, frowning as he stared at the newsletter that had lately arrived from Antwerp. "Yet this is what comes of the Queen taking a foreign consort, for he has dragged our country into his continental wars when she is already bankrupt. This is one reason why there was such an outcry against the marriage. People could foresee what might come of it."

"Do you think they will rise against the Queen?" Kate asked.

"We need another Thomas Wyatt," he said grimly. "I cannot think that this will boost Mary's popularity."

"If she has any left!" Kate said sharply. "Yet she is to bear a child in March. And if it lives, this misrule and persecution will go on. Can God not see how our land is suffering? Why does He not do something?"

"We must not question His will or judgment," Francis reproved. "Remember, the mills of God grind slowly, but they grind exceedingly small. The day of reckoning will come, mark me."

"It cannot come soon enough!" Kate said.

Late that month, her baby came, a healthy boy whom they called Thomas.

"Let us hope that he grows up in a world in which he will be free to practice his faith," Francis said, looking down on the tiny face that was the mirror of his own.

"Amen to that," Kate said fervently.

ONE DAY IN March, Francis steered Kate toward the tiny window of a jeweler's shop.

"I want to buy you a gift for your birthday," he said.

"There's no need," she protested, "but I appreciate the thought. Shouldn't we conserve our money? There's no knowing how long we'll be here."

"No, darling. You've been a true helpmeet to me and a wonderful mother to the children. I want to buy you something special. I can afford it."

Touched by his love for her, Kate capitulated. Looking at the display, she saw a locket in chased gold—not too ostentatious, for it would not do for people to think them wealthy or that their tastes were too worldly.

They went into the shop to find a customer already being served. As they were waiting, a man in a black furred gown of fine quality followed them in. Kate heard Francis catch his breath.

"Francis Knollys!" the newcomer exclaimed. "Fancy finding you here in Frankfurt. I have been looking for you for months. You left some unfinished business in England and her Majesty appointed me to search for you, so that it might be resolved. Pray come with me now. My friends are waiting outside."

Kate froze. Who was this man? She had never seen him before, yet he reminded her of the man in black she had seen in Basel, although he was of heavier build.

Francis had gone very pale. "Come, my dear," he said, "I do not know this person nor am I about to go with him." He grabbed her hand and pulled her from the shop, then they ran together to the nearest alley, dived down it, and emerged at the other end.

Kate heard footsteps behind them and men's voices shouting, "Halt! Stop!" Terror gripped her.

Francis plunged on to the left and they ran, weaving through passersby as if the hounds of Hell were at their heels. Kate feared her heart would burst, but Francis urged her on until they came to a convent.

"In here!" he said. They dived through the gates and into the portress's lodge. An elderly nun peered through a grille.

Francis pleaded with her, speaking German, while Kate waited in terror, aware that their pursuers might burst in at any moment. But the nun nodded and said something she did not understand.

A bolt slid back. "She says we can hide in the parlor," Francis said. "*Danke, danke, meine Schwester!*"

The door opened, then the good nun locked it behind them, smiling encouragingly. She showed them into a sparsely furnished room with a plain crucifix on the wall, then spoke again.

"She is going to fetch Mother Abbess," Francis translated.

The Abbess came presently, a stout woman with a starched wimple and rosy cheeks. Fortunately, she spoke some English. She told them that no one else had come knocking and that there was no one loitering in the street—certainly no one with a description resembling the man in the shop.

"It is probably safe to leave," she said, "but you should go in disguise. I bring you habits. Wait here."

She came back quickly with a nun's habit and veil for Kate and a cowled priest's robe for Francis, two pairs of sandals, and a sack, then left them to change. They stripped, bundled up their clothes in the sack, and put on their disguises, pulling down the veil and the cowl to hide their faces. Then, grinning nervously at each other's appearance, they put on the rough sandals.

"I may not agree with their Romish beliefs, but I must say that in future, I will have a hearty respect for nuns," Kate said. "They have been our saviors this day. We can never fully thank or repay them for their kindness."

"I will make a donation, when it is safe to do so," Francis vowed.

They returned to the lodge, where they thanked the portress warmly for her kindness and urged her to express their gratitude to the Abbess on their behalf. Then they emerged into the street, cautiously looking about them. There was no one suspicious in sight, so they made their way back to the Wellers' house, keeping their heads down as they went.

Weller was dumbstruck when he saw them. "Have you converted back?" he asked, only half jestingly.

"No, of course not," Francis said. "And this is no joke." He explained what had happened. "Alas, we cannot stay here. Frankfurt is no longer safe for us. We have to leave, and soon."

Kate felt tears welling up. It was horrible being a fugitive again, and even more horrible having to uproot the children. She had liked living in this house, had grown fond of her hosts, and hated this feeling of being hunted. It was frightening. But yes, they had to leave.

"I have a friend in Strasbourg, a good Protestant called Johann Hummel," Weller told them. "He lives alone in a big house and has sheltered English exiles in the past. I will write you a letter of introduction."

While he was doing this, they gathered their belongings, stowed them once more on the cart, and told the children and the servants that they had to go on yet another journey.

"To a lovely town called Strasbourg," Kate said. "You will like it there."

"But I like it here," Robert said.

"So do I," chimed in Richard. "Why do we have to leave?"

"Because your father has business there." Kate had no intention of scaring them by telling the truth. They were too young to understand and, anyway, why burden their young minds with it?

They left, as before, in the dead of night. Kate's heart thudded so loudly that she thought the guards on watch at the gates might hear it, and it did not stop thudding until Frankfurt was safely behind them. Another twenty days on the road lay ahead. Kate felt weary at the thought. At this rate, their money would run out, what with the cost of inns, and food being so expensive. But John

Weller was arranging for their funds to be transferred to a bank in Strasbourg, so there should be money waiting for them when they got there.

BY THE TIME Kate saw the walls of Strasbourg ahead in the middle of April, they were exhausted and demoralized. It seemed they were destined to flee from place to place ad infinitum. It wasn't fair to the children, or to themselves. She prayed that they would be left unmolested here until it was safe for them to go back to England.

Like Frankfurt, the city was clustered around a hill on which stood a massive cathedral. The houses, again, were tall and timbered, and there was an abundance of flowers everywhere. Strasbourg had an unmistakable air of prosperity.

They found Meister Hummel's house without difficulty. It was near the river and had a long balcony above a ground-floor terrace. With some trepidation, Francis knocked on the door. Asking a stranger to accommodate two people, six young children, and three servants seemed very much like cheeky presumption, but they had no choice.

A woman in a neat apron and cap showed them into the hall. It had a black-and-white-checkered floor, ornate woodwork, and latticed windows. A small, white-haired man rose from a tall chair by the fire.

"Master Smith," he said, beaming at them. "I have been expecting you."

THEY SETTLED IN quickly. Meister Hummel lived on the ground floor only. "I can no longer manage the stairs because of my stiff legs," he explained. "You can have the run of the rest of the house. Gerda does all the cooking and cleaning."

"Oh, but I will help her," Kate hastened to assure him. "We can't have her waiting on us."

"I am sure she will appreciate that." He smiled.

Upstairs, they found the best accommodation they had had

since leaving England. The bedchambers were spacious and theirs led onto the balcony, which afforded a pleasant view. There were fine feather beds, oak furniture, and tapestries. Meister Hummel was clearly a very rich man.

Yet they had to bear in mind that he was elderly, and Kate was continually admonishing the children to keep quiet and stop racing around. Francis, busy with his correspondence and visits from leading Protestants, and growing ever more frustrated with their situation, was increasingly testy, both with her and the little ones. It saddened Kate that she felt only relief when he went off on the first of what proved to be a series of calls to be paid on his fellow reformers, several of whom lived quite some distance from Strasbourg. She longed for an end to their exile, for life to be as it used to be. That was her constant prayer.

By the summer, it was apparent that no heir would be born to the Queen. Philip had once more left her and gone off to fight his wars, and there were reports that Mary's health was failing. Kate and Francis kept a constant ear open for further news. Almost, she could smell the scent of autumn at Greys Court. Soon, soon, God willing, they would be back there and reunited with their other children. How she had missed them!

She wished she could feel sorrow for Queen Mary, whose hopes of motherhood had been twice thwarted and who had been abandoned by her husband. But Mary was no longer the sad, slight, kind girl Kate remembered from her days at court. No, she had become her father's daughter, single-minded, cruel, and vengeful. It was hard to believe that she and Kate were half sisters. Kate could only be grateful that she herself had more of her mother in her. She would rather be a Boleyn than a Tudor any day!

PART THREE

The Secret

1558–69

Chapter 31

1558–59

On the third Sunday in November, Kate and Francis went to church with their family. They were settling down to listen to the sermon when the minister mounted the steps to the pulpit and said, in both French and English, that he had an announcement to make.

"I have just received news from England of the death of Queen Mary and the accession of Queen Elizabeth to the throne. Those of you who are in exile here because of your faith will no doubt rejoice because the new Queen is known to be a friend of the Gospel . . ."

Kate hardly heard the rest. The news had come like a thunderbolt, and suddenly she and Francis were embracing for joy and hugging their children. Elsewhere in the church, there was similar rejoicing as the minister and the rest of the congregation looked on, smiling.

After the service had ended, they hurried back to Meister Hummel's house and told him of their liberation. He clapped them on the back, called for eau-de-vie to celebrate, and insisted on giving them money toward the cost of their journey home, ignoring their protests.

Immediately, Kate began packing up their belongings, getting the children to help. She kept out their warmest clothing because they would be traveling in winter and prayed that the roads would not be too muddy or ill-kept.

Francis was to go ahead because they had no idea what would be awaiting them in England or if they even had a home to go to. He set off the very next morning, leaving Kate to follow on in the litter with the children, with Thomas bringing the luggage in the cart.

"As soon as I get to London, I will wait on Queen Elizabeth and pay my respects," Francis said, as he mounted his horse. It was good to see him with a vigorous sense of purpose at last, now that they could look forward to a better, happier, and safer future with all their children around them.

"Pray give her my love and duty and say that I am longing to see her," Kate urged.

"You may depend on it," he declared, and gave her his most engaging smile. "Farewell, my darling, until we meet again in England."

"God go with you!" she cried. She stood there watching until his horse had disappeared around the corner at the end of the street, then hurried inside to finish her packing. With nearly four hundred miles to cover this side of the English Channel, and more than a hundred to go before they reached Greys Court, with a sea crossing in between, they would be traveling for at least forty days, so they would not be back in time for Christmas, but no matter! They were going home, and that was more important than anything.

THEY HAD AGREED that Kate would cross to England from the port of Boulogne, since they were unsure of the situation in Calais. Francis would send any letters from England to an old inn called l'Etoile near the cathedral, where they would be waiting for Kate. He had left precise instructions on how to find it.

Kate could not wait to reach Boulogne, for the journey was long and arduous with the six children and only Thomas and the maids to help. The weather blew wet and windy, and it was cold. They spent their days huddled together in the litter, swathed in cloaks, bumping over the rutted roads. Many a time Kate had to ask Thomas to stop because one of the children needed to be sick. Some hostelries were acceptably clean, but others were squalid, yet they still had to pay exorbitant prices for poor accommodation and indifferent food. Yet each day brought them closer to their destination, and that gave Kate heart to carry on.

At last, in early January, they reached Boulogne, where they could see the sea. Beyond lay home—a deeply comforting thought. They found l'Etoile without difficulty and Kate was thrilled to find a letter from Francis awaiting her, which had only recently arrived. As soon as they were settled in, she eagerly broke the seal and devoured the news.

There had been no need to worry. Greys Court was still theirs, and Master Stafford had kept it in good order, for which Francis had been able to reward him, as Caversham and the income from his lands had been restored to him. The Queen had welcomed him warmly to court. For his experience, his understanding, his truth, and his love for the Protestant religion, she had immediately made him a Privy Councillor and Vice Chamberlain; he would be assisting the Chamberlain, Lord Howard of Effingham, to run the royal household. And on 3 January, Elizabeth, having said that she was resolved to promote those who had served her at Hatfield, had appointed Kate a Lady of the Privy Chamber. Kate was to come to court as soon as was convenient to take up her new post. Lettice had been made a Gentlewoman of the Privy Chamber on the same date. "She is quite the young lady now," Francis had written, "and reckoned one of the best-looking ladies of the court."

Kate read the letter with mixed feelings. Such instantaneous advancement and favor was wonderful, and to be singled out for such prestigious posts was a signal honor, but she was wondering just how much of her time would be spent waiting on the Queen, and how much would be left to spend with her family, for she did so much want to be with them, especially those from whom she had been cruelly parted for nearly the past two years. She prayed that Elizabeth would not be too demanding.

In a postscript on the back of the letter, Francis had written that he had visited Hal at Oxford and was pleased to report that he was doing well, and that he had seen Kate's brother, Harry, at court. Will and Ned were thriving so well in his household that he was tempted to leave them there, if Kate agreed.

Every instinct cried out against it, for she had joyously envisaged their all living together as a family again. Yet now her babes were growing up and settled elsewhere, one at court and two in their uncle's household, and there was little she could do about it, since Lettice especially had been advanced beyond most parents' dreams and was in the best position to attract a good marriage, while it was the custom for boys of gentle birth to be brought up away from home, not tied to their mother's apron strings. The bitter fact had to be faced: things had changed, and they would never be the same again.

TEARS STREAMED DOWN Kate's face when the coast of England emerged from the sea mist ahead of them. Glimpsing it through the cabin window, she knew a moment of exaltation. No matter what had become of her family, this was her land, a land from which the black clouds of fear and persecution had been miraculously lifted. God had spoken. He had ushered in a new age, one in which the souls of the righteous would be free.

Her heart sang again when she saw Greys Court in the distance. She could hardly believe that they were home. When she entered the house, ushering her children before her, she was delighted to see everything as she had left it, and that the place was clean and swept. At Francis's request, Master Stafford had reengaged Bilkins and most of the former servants, who were all lined up outside the house to greet her—Bilkins was in tears, she was touched to see—and he had appointed a tutor, Master Ingham, for Beth, Robert, Richard, and Frank, and a nursemaid, Edith, who would help Thomasina with Anne and Thomas. Both were waiting in the hall to be introduced to their charges, and Kate was glad to relinquish the children to their care, for she was weary and had much to organize. The older ones were excited to be back at

Greys Court, but the younger ones stared around in awe, for they had yet to recognize it as home.

Kate did not have very long with them. Elizabeth had sent her a summons demanding her presence at court as soon as possible. "We long to see you," she had written. It was her use of the royal plural that really brought home to Kate how their roles had changed. Elizabeth was no longer just her cousin, her secret sister; she was now her Queen and must be obeyed.

There was nothing for it. She must set things in order here, leave the house and her young family under the capable rule of Bilkins, and get to court without delay. God grant that she had a good journey and that the roads were clear and not mired with mud.

WHEN, AFTER MAKING excellent time, she arrived at Whitehall Palace, Kate was informed that the Queen would see her at once. An usher conducted her through the presence chamber, which was crowded with petitioners, and then, under their envious eyes, took her through the door that only the highly privileged entered, which led to the privy chamber beyond.

Elizabeth was waiting for her in an apartment painted all over with green foliage and pink flowers, in the midst of which was a throne upholstered in scarlet beneath a cloth of estate in the same rich material. Rush matting covered the floor, on which sat three ladies in rich gowns. One was Kat, who smiled at Kate delightedly.

Elizabeth, slender in a high-necked gown that showed off to advantage her red-gold hair, rose from the throne, holding out her arms. "My dearest cousin, you are most welcome! We have longed to see you!" There sat upon her a new air of authority and confidence; she carried her queenship as if she had been born to it. Already, it had set her apart from ordinary mortals.

"Your Majesty." Kate swept a deep curtsey, then felt the Queen's hands raising her and pulling her into an embrace.

"I do not know how I have borne your absence," she said, kissing her cheeks. "I have worried about you every day. I cannot tell you how overjoyed I am to behold you safe and well."

"It is thanks in part to your Majesty's warning that I am here," Kate told her, "for if you had not alerted us to the danger we faced in Basel, God alone knows where we might be now."

"Well, you are here, and I am glad to have been of service," Elizabeth said. "And I never want to be parted from you again. You mean everything to me."

Gratified as she was to have been afforded such a warm welcome and reassured that her cousin's love for her had not diminished, Kate felt a tremor of unease. Elizabeth was Queen now; her word, nay, her every wish, was law, and not to be gainsaid. How would she herself ever make it clear to her that she did not want to be always at court, and that she had a life of her own and a family who needed her?

"I hope you are pleased to be serving me as a Lady of the Privy Chamber," Elizabeth said.

"I am overwhelmed to have been so honored," Kate said. "I cannot thank your Majesty enough."

"You are one of only four such ladies." The Queen beckoned to the others, who rose and embraced Kate. "Kat you know, of course. She is Chief Gentlewoman of the Privy Chamber and my new Mistress of the Maids."

"It is so good to see you, Kate." Kat dimpled, looking plumper and more rosy-cheeked than ever. Kate hugged her again, aware that Kat now outranked her, although, knowing the woman as she did, she could not imagine her throwing her weight about.

"You'll remember Blanche," Elizabeth continued, prodding forward a homely body in a black gown and hood. Blanche Parry was the Queen's old nurse, who had taught her Welsh, her native language. "And this is Lady Carew, who gave me such stout support after Wyatt's rebellion, when I was under suspicion." The hazel-haired lady dipped a bob, smiling.

"Your duties, Kate, will include looking after gifts given to me and my pet parrot and monkey. Above all, I have chosen you four because, of all those who were clamoring for places, you are the only ones I want as my daily companions. Dearest Kate, I am determined that, having lost you once, I will never let you leave my side again."

Kate blenched inwardly, hearing this again. What did it mean? Was she to take it literally? No, surely not!

She could not leave it at that. "Your Majesty's affection and favor mean the world to me," she said. "I will be happy to serve you and give you all the time I have, aside from that I will need to spend attending to the needs of my beloved husband and our children."

There was an awkward silence. Elizabeth was frowning. "Kate, dear cousin, I do not think you can be aware of the magnitude of the signal honor I have bestowed on you. Your husband serves me here at court and he has been assigned one of the largest lodgings I have at my disposal. You surely have nurses and tutors to care for your children? It does not seem to be a problem for my other ladies."

Kate hesitated. How could she tell Elizabeth, who had always said she had no desire for marriage and children, how deeply she loved hers? She would never understand.

"They do have nurses and tutors, your Majesty, but they love their mother much more and hate to be separated from her."

It was the wrong thing to say to a woman who had been separated from her own mother in the cruelest way imaginable. "Are my needs not greater?" Elizabeth demanded to know. "You said you would always love me, that I would come first with you."

But that, Kate forbore to point out, had been long years ago, when they were very young.

Aware that she was denying her most visceral instincts, she forced herself to smile. "I will always be here when your Majesty needs me."

Elizabeth's good humor was instantly restored. "Your love is the most precious thing in the world to me," she declared. "I love you above all other women in the world."

Kate had a sinking feeling that the burden of that love would prove very heavy indeed.

KAT LED KATE to the lodging they were to share. It was near the Queen's own bedchamber and magnificently appointed, with two large rooms and their own privy. "I hope you'll be comfortable here," she said.

"I am sure I will," Kate assured her, eyeing the wide tester bed with its plump bolster and scarlet velvet counterpane. She laid her cloak across the carved chest at its foot and poured water from the ewer into a silver basin, then splashed her face with it. She felt weary at the prospect of her future—and trapped. This was not what she had envisaged at all.

"It is the Queen's pleasure that her ladies wear black or white," Kate said. "Then she herself can stand out all the more in her rich gowns."

"I have plenty of black and white clothing," Kate said. "I have very little in other colors."

"Good. And the Queen has granted you some items from the Royal Wardrobe," Kat told her, pointing to two black velvet gowns hanging on pegs attached to the wall. Most women would have killed for such tokens of favor.

"We ladies all dine together in the Great Chamber. We have a table reserved exclusively for our use. Her Majesty takes dinner and supper with eight of her women, so when summoned, we eat with her. We take it in turns to sleep on the pallet bed in her bedchamber."

Kat sank down on a stool. "I can see that you are unhappy about having to live at court. The Queen is a possessive mistress, and selfish. It is what comes of being at the center of attention all her life. She cannot comprehend that her ladies have lives of their own. She has made it clear that she does not approve of her maids marrying, even though it is her duty to find them husbands. She lectures them frequently on the subject."

"She has always resented Francis," Kate confided. "She has hardly ever uttered his name."

"Yet she has advanced him handsomely, and probably for your sake."

"But what good will all this preferment do us if we never see each other, never spend time with our children?" Kate cried, and burst into tears. "If my husband has a double lodging, I should be staying with him, not here or with the Queen!"

Kat looked at her sadly. "My husband is Master of the Jewel House, yet I hardly ever see him, even though he too is at court."

"It was not for this that I came home," Kate wept.

"I suppose we should think ourselves lucky," Kat reflected, patting her hand. "Her Majesty dismissed all the late Queen's Catholic ladies and replaced them with women like us who have reformist sympathies. There was fierce competition for places, I tell you! Be grateful that some of your kinswomen are here: your daughter Lettice is a maid-of-honor alongside your nieces, Katherine and Philadelphia Carey. Your sister-in-law, Mistress Carey, is a lady-in-waiting."

"And I long to see them, especially my daughter," Kate cried. "Yet I want us all to be at Greys Court together, not here."

Kat rose. "Until you stop yearning for that, my dear, your life will be a misery. Make time to see your husband when you can. And be grateful that, among all the noble ladies here, you have earned Lady Fortune's grace, for you are in high favor with our noble Queen, who holds you in the greatest esteem. That is a blessing not to be sniffed at."

BUT IT WAS a blessing she did not want, Kate agonized, as she went in search of her daughter. She found the maids where Kat had directed her, playing tag in the privy garden, so bundled up in furs against the January cold that they looked like bears. Then one turned and saw her, and she found herself looking into the face of Lettice—a Lettice grown older and more beautiful than she could ever have dreamed. Her little babe was exquisite: slanted, almond eyes, fair skin, and full lips of cherry red; copper curls were escaping from her hood.

"Mother!" she cried, and flung her arms around Kate. "They said you might arrive today! I can't believe you're here."

Then they were hugging and kissing and laughing all at once, only—joy of joys—to be joined by Mary, here at court in the train of the Duchess of Suffolk, who had returned to England as soon as she heard of the Queen's accession, and Kate's nieces, narrow-faced replicas of her brother, both now serving the Queen despite their youth. As she stood chatting with her daughters, Kate watched her nieces romping excitedly. They were like boisterous colts, bounding and skipping about, with no care to the decorum required of them. But when Kat appeared, she merely cast an indulgent eye on them and smiled. "As long as they behave when they're with the Queen, I let them enjoy being children," she murmured to Kate.

Kate withdrew with her daughters to an arbor in a sheltered corner.

"Are you happy?" she asked.

"Oh, yes," Lettice replied, "especially now that you're here."

AFTER A GLORIOUS hour spent catching up on news and drinking in the sight of her girls, here in the flesh and so, so beautiful, Kate parted from them and went to find Francis. He had sent her a note detailing the location of his lodging and she found it easily, but it was deserted. He must be busy at his duties. She could not linger, as the Queen might need her, so she hurried back to the royal apartments, promising herself that she would return later. But no. After supper, which was served with great ceremony in the privy chamber, Elizabeth smiled at Kate.

"Attend me in my closet, dearest cousin. We have much time to make up."

Frustrated at being kept apart from Francis, Kate followed the Queen into a small room hung with rich tapestries. A Turkish carpet covered the floor and a fire burned merrily in the hearth. Elizabeth indicated that Kate should take the chair opposite hers.

"Your Majesty is too kind," Kate murmured.

"Not 'your Majesty' while we are alone, dear cousin. Call me Bess," Elizabeth bade her. "We are kin, are we not?"

Their eyes met. Did Kate detect a gleam of recognition that they were more than cousins? She could not be sure. Now that she was back with Elizabeth once again, all her feelings of kinship and affection had surged back, and she longed to share this closest bond with her.

They talked deep into the night, of Elizabeth's troubles during Mary's reign, and then of Kate's exile. As the time sped by, Kate became increasingly anxious to be gone, for Francis must be wondering where she was. But Elizabeth showed no sign of wishing to retire.

"I have a great task before me," she said, as a clock struck one. "There are urgent matters of state that must be debated in my first Parliament. Foremost is the question of religion. I am determined to make the Protestant faith the established religion of this realm."

"I rejoice to hear it, as will your true subjects," Kate applauded.

"You know, I studied nothing but divinity until I came to the throne, and I am convinced that our faith is the way to God. But when it comes down to it, Kate, there is only one Jesus Christ. The rest is a dispute over trifles."

Kate was impressed to hear Elizabeth expressing such an enlightened view.

"Unlike my sister, I am no fanatic," the Queen went on, "and I hate fanaticism in others, of whatever persuasion. For me, the arguments of theologians and divines are as ropes of sand or sea-slime leading to the moon. I see many who are overbold with God Almighty, making too many subtle interpretations of His will, as lawyers do with human testaments. If I were not certain that mine were the true way to God's will, God forbid that I should prescribe it to my subjects." She leaned forward, her thin face alight with purpose. "You know, Kate, I differ very little from Catholics in my beliefs, as I believe that God is in the Sacrament of the Eucharist. But I abhor the darkness and filth of Popery."

"Amen to that," Kate said, shuddering at the memory of the horrors of the late Queen's reign. "I do believe, Bess, that the people of England will always equate Catholicism with persecution."

"Indeed, they will! And, really, what should it matter to a ruler if their subjects choose to go to the Devil in their own way. I would rather spare those who disagree with me, because I would enjoy having theological arguments with them. My sister could never see things that way."

"Her late Majesty took her faith to extremes," Kate ventured, glancing surreptitiously at the clock.

"And some say *I* have no religion at all!" Elizabeth laughed.

"Yet I read the Bible regularly, and I always set the Last Judgment before my eyes and rule as I shall answer for to a higher Judge."

"No one could be more sincere."

"And yet men make such complications about religion! Take transubstantiation. In my view, Christ took the bread and broke it, and what His words made it, that I believe, and in that spirit I take it. Yes, Kate, I am determined to tread a middle road. My watchwords will be caution, compromise, and moderation, for I do not wish to offend my Catholic allies in Europe. The truth is that I need them. They see me as a bastard, a heretic, and a usurper. To them, the true heir to my throne is the Queen of Scots, the Dauphine of France. And yet the Act of Succession passed under my father bars her from it. Besides, she is a foreigner, born out of this realm. Yet she is a Catholic, and that counts for all with some people!"

"Bess, will you outlaw the Catholic religion in England?" Kate asked, stifling a yawn. If she did get to bed with Francis, she would be too tired for any passionate reunion.

"Again, I must compromise. For now, both Catholic and Protestant services will continue in the churches. I am hoping that a peace will be concluded with France, because it will frustrate those who support the claim of the Queen of Scots. It is a necessity because she and her husband have begun styling themselves King and Queen of England, if you please!" Elizabeth's eyes blazed with indignation. "So peace with France is a priority, and with Spain, to guard our trade and hopefully obtain protection against the French. I know well that my success in the field of diplomacy depends on my playing off those bitter enemies one against the other."

The clock chimed two.

"Is that the time?" Elizabeth said. "I must go to bed." She rose, picked up a candle, and opened the door to the gallery. Kat was there, slumped on a window seat, fast asleep. "We'll leave her there. You can attend me to bed, Kate."

Kate's heart sank as she followed the Queen to her bedchamber. There was nothing for it; she would be spending the night on the pallet bed at the foot of Elizabeth's. Kate could only pray that Francis would guess what had happened and understand.

She helped Elizabeth to disrobe, unlacing her sleeves and her bodice, laying away the rich gown and kirtle in a chest, then lifting the fine lawn night rail over her sovereign's head before helping her into bed. Then she divested herself of her own clothes, pulled out the pallet bed, which was thankfully made up, doused the candle, and climbed wearily between the cold sheets.

"Good night, Bess," she said.

But Bess, it seemed, was in no mood for sleep. "Kate, there is another matter that Parliament must address, and it is one I dread to broach. Aside from Kat, there is no one I can confide in—except you."

"I am honored that you feel able to talk to me," Kate said, stifling the urge to drift off, although in truth she was now coming wide awake, wondering what was worrying the Queen. "What is the problem?"

"It is the matter of my marriage. The succession, my councillors tell me, depends on it. They say that if I do not marry and produce an heir, I have no clear successor. But Kate, for me, it is not a question of whom I should marry—which they are debating furiously—but of whether I *should* marry."

Kate was startled. "But you must!"

"The word 'must' is not to be used to princes!" Elizabeth reprimanded her.

She hastened to apologize. "I crave your Majesty's forgiveness. I was just so surprised."

"As are my councillors. They think my reluctance stems from maidenly modesty. Hah! If I had been born crested and not cloven, they would never dare say such things to me!"

"But there is surely a need to provide for the succession?"

"Indeed. But how? Remember, I come from a race that is not known for its fruitfulness. The Act of Succession provides that, after me, the crown should pass to the heirs of Father's younger sister, Mary, who was queen of France and then married the Duke of Suffolk. That means her two daughters with the Duke, Frances and Eleanor. Frances has borne three daughters, including the late lamented Lady Jane Grey. That leaves Lady Katherine and Lady Mary Grey."

Kate had never met these cousins and knew next to nothing about them.

"They are both Protestants," Elizabeth was saying, "but I can't abide the sight of Katherine. I suspect that she has dynastic pretensions and that she is plotting with the Spanish ambassador. I do not wish her to succeed me. Nor do I much favor her sister Lady Mary. Some say that their father's treason in supporting Northumberland has rendered their claim to the succession forfeit."

"What of Eleanor?"

"She is dead, and has left a daughter, who is married to Lord Strange. In my sister Queen Mary's time, some people saw her as a likely successor to the throne because, unlike the Grey family, she took no part in Northumberland's treason. Yet I am told that she has no desire for a crown. Even so, I shall insist upon her coming often to court, so that I can keep an eye on her."

The Queen sighed. "That leaves my cousin Lady Margaret Douglas. Her mother, my father's elder sister, Margaret, who married the King of Scots and was grandmother to their present Queen Mary, was excluded from the Act of Succession. At the time it was passed, King Henry was at war with Scotland and his ambition was to marry my brother, Edward, to the Queen of Scots and so unite England and Scotland under English rule. The Scots would have none of it, hence the war, and therefore, when determining who was to succeed him, my father passed over Margaret's heirs. The Lady Margaret is the child of her second marriage to the Earl of Angus, and is married to the Earl of Lennox, with whom she has two sons. But she is a Catholic—and a very ambitious woman. When I was in disgrace in my sister's reign, there was much talk that Queen Mary would name Margaret her heir. So you see, Kate, none of those in line for the crown are worthy of it. And I do confess that I have an abhorrence of naming anyone to succeed me. I have known what it is like to be the heir and the focus of conspiracy and rebellion, and there are threats enough to my security without that. If I acknowledge the right of any of these claimants to succeed, I suspect I will be back in the Tower within a month!"

Kate lay there, feeling tense. It had just become very clear that Elizabeth had no love for most of her female relations, and was suspicious of all of them, because clearly, they were too close to the throne for comfort. Yet understanding this boded ill for the Queen ever acknowledging Kate as her sister. Would she think that Kate had ideas above her station or even dynastic ambitions? She might not believe that, half sister to the monarch though she was, she had no desire to be queen, and she could never claim the throne anyway, for a bastard could not succeed, having no rights of inheritance. In the eyes of the law, she was William Carey's daughter. It was best, she concluded, to leave matters as they were and not hope for too much. It was enough that Elizabeth had someone who loved her unconditionally and posed no threat to her.

"The answer, of course, is for you to marry and bear children," Kate ventured, wishing she was in Francis's arms.

"So everyone keeps telling me! King Philip has already proposed himself as a husband. I told his ambassador that the issue of my marriage will be raised in Parliament. But Kate, that is what I dread! I cannot easily explain my aversion to marriage. I cannot see it as a holy estate. Indeed, it seems to be anything but! I think I shocked one of my bishops when I said that. But there have been so many marital conflicts and disasters in my own family that I cannot see wedlock as a secure state, and I fear to enter it."

Kate guessed that she was referring to her father's disastrous matrimonial career, the disputed marriages of both his sisters, and the tragedy that had been Mary's marriage to Philip.

But then Elizabeth's voice came out of the darkness. "I am terrified that, if I married, my husband might carry out some evil wish. Dear God, Kate, I hate the idea of marriage more every day, for reasons I would not divulge to my twin soul, if I had one."

She had said the same thing before, long ago. "But why?" Kate could not help asking. "The love of a good man for his wife is well worth having. I have found great joy with Francis. I cannot tell you—"

"Francis is not royal! He is not looking for principalities or to wield dominion over you. He is a kind man—that much I have seen. No, Kate, I cannot discuss this, even with you. Let us go to sleep." Without another word, she turned over in the bed.

Kate lay there sleepless for a while. Half of her resented Elizabeth for keeping her from Francis; the other half felt for her, since she was in an impossible position and it seemed that there was no way out of it. Elizabeth would just have to confront her fears.

Chapter 32

1559

THE NEXT MORNING, ELIZABETH ROSE EARLY, DEMANDING that Kate help her to dress, as she planned to go out for a brisk walk around the gardens. "No need to attend me," she said. "Blanche can do that. Go and break your fast."

Relieved to have some time to herself, Kate threw on her clothes and hurried away to Francis's lodging, praying he would be there. And he was! He was still abed, and when he saw her, his face lit up with joy and he stretched out his arms to her.

"My darling wife! How I have longed to hold you . . ."

Their coming together was sublime, a fusion of hearts and bodies that left them smiling at each other delightedly. Lying in her husband's arms, Kate felt perfectly contented, and yet she knew that their time together would be brief.

"I have to go back," she murmured, sitting up, her long hair rippling over her breasts. "The Queen will be needing me."

"Not so soon, surely?" He reached out and clasped her around the waist.

"Yes, so soon!" She told him what Elizabeth had said about never being parted again and the demands she was making on her. "I fear I will have no life of my own, and that we will have to snatch time together—and Heaven knows when we will see our children!" A tear trickled down her face.

Francis drew her into his embrace. "We will find a way. We must be permitted some leave. I have estates and my political duties to attend to; you have the children. The Queen is imperious, I know, but she has been good to us. There is a price to pay for it."

"It is too high a price."

"Let us see how things work out. If it all becomes too much for you, I will speak to her."

"No!" Kate did not want to lose credit with Elizabeth so soon; somehow, she knew that any complaint would not go down well. "You're right. Let us see what transpires. It may not be as bad as I fear."

WHEN SHE RETURNED to the royal lodgings, she found Kat in the privy chamber, seated at her embroidery.

"Is the Queen back?" she asked.

"Not yet. She's gone riding." Kat looked up. "You've been crying, child. Can I help?"

Kate turned away to hide her tears, gazing unseeing out of a window, and poured out her woes. "No one can help me. I have just had to leave my husband, when all I want is to be with him. What I most desire, after years of exile, is just to lead a normal life as a wife and mother."

Kat laid aside her tambour and thought for a while. "Some would kill for a place such as you occupy. The Queen likes to advance her mother's kin, but usually only on their merits. She loves you for yourself. You and your brother are her closest blood relations on the Boleyn side, and I have noticed that she behaves toward you yourself with far more familiarity than she uses to other members of her court. She has welcomed your daughters into her household, which will doubtless lead to them making good marriages. You are all basking in her favor. You are in a very strong position. And she loves you, Kate, more than any other, even me."

Kate sighed. "So you think I should be grateful?"

"I do." Kat resumed her embroidery.

. . .

THAT AFTERNOON, WHILE the Queen was receiving ambassadors, Kate found Francis in the garden, strolling along with William Cecil, who had been appointed the Queen's Secretary of State and was now riding high in royal favor and very influential. Both men bowed to her and Cecil smiled.

"I will leave you with your good lady," he said. "I am sure you will find better things to talk about with her than the troubles in Scotland."

Francis took Kate's arm, and they walked along by the Thames. It was cold, but sunny, and it was good to have some time to themselves. Kate told him what Kat had said.

"She does have a point," he agreed. "We are both privileged to have our positions at court. I like to think that my preferment demonstrates the Queen's faith in me and my abilities, and I want to do my best for her. She has made me one of her leading councillors and I sense that my opinions carry some weight, although I suspect that she thinks my Protestant views too radical."

"She likes moderation in religion. She told me."

"She's going to come up against some opposition there, for many of her subjects hold extreme views, both Catholic and Protestant. But what I can't understand is why she has advanced me so rapidly. Is it because I am a stout Protestant?"

Kate wondered. Francis's promotion had happened very quickly. Prior to that, Elizabeth had hardly ever mentioned him, and she suspected that it was chiefly his connection to her that had secured him the Queen's favor, although she would never voice that opinion to him. Let him believe that he had got so far on his own merits—which, of course, he deserved to do!

"I'm not sure that that is the reason," she replied.

"No, I rather thought not. She's already made it clear that she finds my views extremely annoying. And for my part, I can only deplore her own. Do you know that she worships in private with all the trappings of the Catholic faith?"

"She has always had a love of ritual. Yet I do not doubt the soundness of her beliefs. She is a convinced Protestant."

"That remains to be seen," said Francis. He pulled Kate to him and hugged her. "I cannot help but wonder if you are the cause of my sudden advancement! She makes no secret of that fact that she loves you above all other women in the world."

"Nonsense!" Kate reproved him, anxious not to betray her suspicion that he might be right. "You were advanced on your own merits and for your loyalty."

"And you, my darling. Lady Fortune has been gracious to you. You are in favor with our noble Queen well above the common sort!"

They had reached the far end of the gardens when a bell chimed four.

"Is that the time?" Kate cried. "I must go back."

"Come to me tonight!" Francis bade her.

"I will if I can," she called, as she hurried away.

"YOU'RE LATE!" ELIZABETH reproved, when she arrived breathless in the privy chamber, having run all the way. "Where were you, dearest cousin?"

"I beg your Majesty's pardon. I met my husband while taking the air in the gardens, and I'm sorry to say that I forgot the time."

"Such a lovely man," Blanche Parry said, before Elizabeth could reprimand her. "And such a friend to the Gospel." Kate looked at her gratefully.

"You were supposed to be in attendance on me an hour since," the Queen said peevishly.

"I did not realize it was so late. I apologize again. But Madam, I do love my husband, and the time we spend together is precious. We have had too many partings." She could feel tears welling up.

"Well, be mindful in future," Elizabeth said tartly.

As her mistress turned away, Kate struggled not to cry. It had just been made more than clear to her that the Queen's insistence on her presence would preclude her enjoying any kind of normal existence. She was doomed, it seemed, to a life of eternal frustration. Yes, she could see Francis and Lettice daily, if she could snatch the time, but not the rest of her family. She would have to subordinate her children's needs to those of the Queen, and she did not know how her heart would stand it.

IN THE MIDDLE of January, two days before her coronation, Elizabeth rode in procession through London. When she left the Tower, all dressed in virginal white, in a white litter, Kate and Francis were in the procession, but not together. Wearing crimson and gold, Kate rode with the other ladies-in-waiting who followed the Queen. Not far behind them, similarly garbed, were the maids-of-honor, among them Lettice and her cousin Katherine Carey, Harry's daughter, and, despite her youth, Beth, who had just been appointed to the post, while Mary was also here today.

They lodged at the Tower that night. Kate hated being there. She had shivered as she rode through the Lion Tower entry, unable to shake off her recollections of the horrific event she had witnessed in the fortress nearly twenty-three before. Queen Anne's face as she stood on the scaffold facing her end still haunted her, as did the memory of her aunt's bloody, broken corpse.

Yet it must be a thousand times worse for Elizabeth, who could only imagine her mother's gruesome end. She could not but be thinking of Anne and what she had suffered in this place—and there was a poignant reminder of her the next day, when, making her state entry into London, she passed through a triumphal arch in Gracechurch Street, for above her, as part of one of the pageants mounted in her honor, the citizens had erected life-sized figures of King Henry and Queen Anne, crowned and seated together, with a pomegranate—the symbol of their fortuitous fertility—between them; and above them both towered the figure of Elizabeth herself, in majesty. Kate felt tears well in her eyes at the sight. How proud Anne would have been of her daughter. It was heartening to know that, in her own way, Elizabeth was paying homage to her on the auspicious day of the coronation itself, for the lightweight crown she wore after the ceremony in Westminster Abbey was the one made for her mother to wear at *her* coronation.

During the celebrations that followed, Kate watched Elizabeth as she presided over her court. The Queen was in her element, reveling in all the feasting and the merry pastimes, and flirting with the gallants who clustered around her, showering her with flattery. She watched her older daughters, too, as they made eyes at the ardent young men. They were now around the age she had been when she met Francis, and soon he and she would have to think of finding husbands for them. But for now, she would let them enjoy themselves. Youth, after all, lasted for no time at all.

ELIZABETH HAD NEVER given any sign of bearing a grudge against the father who had signed her mother's death warrant. She often spoke of King Henry with pride. She clearly revered his memory and gloried in his fame. In truth, she regarded him as the victim of a malicious conspiracy against Anne Boleyn. Kate noticed that she rarely referred to her mother.

One afternoon, when Parliament was in session, Elizabeth was closeted a long time with William Cecil and Sir Nicholas Bacon, Lord Keeper of the Great Seal, and emerged in a state of agitation.

"It seems I am to be thwarted in a matter most important to me," she announced, bustling into the privy chamber with a great swishing of skirts. Kate and the other ladies looked up, astonished.

"In one of her first Acts of Parliament, my sister had herself declared legitimate and her mother's marriage lawful. I have just consulted Sir Nicholas Bacon as to whether I too should take steps to legitimize myself, but he has told me that I should let sleeping dogs lie." She sat down, punching one hand into the other. Kate had long known that Elizabeth found the taint of her bastardy hard to bear, not just as a matter of pride, but because of its implications for the security of her throne. But Bacon was right, of course. It was best not to rake up the past. Kate said nothing. The matter was too sensitive, and anything she did say might be taken amiss.

Worse was to come. One Monday in early February, Kate and the other ladies were present when a deputation from the House of Commons came to lay a petition before the Queen. She received them in the presence chamber, seated beneath her canopy of estate emblazoned with the arms of England, with her ladies about her.

The members knelt, with Sir Thomas Gargrave, the Speaker of the Commons, in the forefront, looking nervous, as Kate wondered what sort of petition justified this kind of ceremony.

"Your Majesty," he said, as Elizabeth gazed regally down at him, "Parliament has been debating the succession and the common weal of this realm, and would like respectfully to remind your Grace that it would be better for you and your kingdom if you would take a consort who might relieve you of those labors which are only fit for men."

Kate saw a flash of indignation blaze on Elizabeth's face, but instantly it was gone, to be replaced by a steely glare. She could imagine the impact this petition was having on the Queen; she was herself shocked by it, and the implication that her mistress was unfit to rule.

His voice faltering a little under that basilisk gaze, Sir Thomas pressed valiantly on. "We would also remind your Majesty that, while princes are mortal, commonwealths are immortal. If you remain unmarried and, as it were, a vestal virgin, such a thing would be contrary to the public interests. We ask that you consider taking a husband as soon as possible in order to safeguard the succession."

Elizabeth was plainly astonished at his boldness, but she recovered herself and responded graciously. "In a matter most unpleasing, what does please me is the apparent goodwill of you and my people. I must tell you that I have chosen to stay single, despite being offered marriage by several great princes. Indeed, I consider that I already have a husband and children." Extending her hand, she showed them her coronation ring. "I am already bound to a husband, and that is the kingdom of England. As for children, you and every one of my subjects are my children and kinsmen." She paused and frowned. "I am gratified that you have not gone so far as to name any potential husband, for that would be most unbecoming to the majesty of an absolute princess, and inappropriate for you, who are subjects born."

She was magnificent; she had the deputation both quaking and staring up at her with admiration. But she had not finished with them yet. "I will do as God directs me. I have never been inclined toward matrimony, but I will not rule it out completely. If I do marry, I will not do anything to prejudice the commonwealth, but will choose a husband who would be as careful for the preservation of the realm as I am myself. However, it is possible that it will please Almighty God to frame my mind to live out of the state of marriage."

"But Madam," the Speaker protested, "what of the succession? You have no obvious heir."

That was untrue, Kate knew. Lady Katherine Grey was the lawful heir, but she could not see the Queen ever acknowledging her as such.

"I promise you," Elizabeth was saying, "that this realm will not remain destitute of an heir. If I remain single, I am certain that God will so direct our counsels that you will not need to be in doubt of a successor, who may be more beneficial to the commonwealth than any born of me. In the end, this shall be sufficient for me: that a marble stone shall declare that a queen, having reigned such a time, lived and died a virgin. Go forth and tell that to Parliament."

She swept out, leaving them kneeling there. Following in her wake, Kate was wondering if Elizabeth's attitude was the right one. She had to marry! It was the only way to assure the continuation of her line. And yet she knew something of the reason for the Queen's reluctance. She wondered if her cousin would ever confide fully in her.

Seating herself by the fire in her closet, Elizabeth was ebullient. "What did you all think of my answer answerless?"

There was a silence. Kat patted her mistress on the shoulder before taking her seat. She knows, Kate realized. *She knows more than I do.*

"Is it the right decision?" Blanche asked. "For your realm, I mean."

"Without a doubt." Elizabeth was emphatic. "When a woman marries, her husband expects to wield dominion over her as his wife, which is his right. But think of my sister, who was a sovereign queen, wielding dominion over her people, as I do now. Her marriage was a disaster, because how could King Philip wield dominion over her? It is impossible to be both queen and wife; it can only end in misery."

"But does Parliament understand that?" Kat asked.

"They won't like my response, and neither will Master Cecil, but I have not committed myself. I have left the door open."

Lady Carew, normally the quiet one, leaned forward. "Your Majesty, may I speak my mind?"

"Pray do so."

"If you do not marry, there will be no satisfactory solution to the succession question. Your religious settlement will be at risk."

"For a woman to reject marriage—it is against the laws of nature," Kat put in.

"So men keep telling us," Elizabeth snapped. "They want a masculine succession. Cecil never ceases to tell me of his hope that God will direct me to procure a father for my children. He, indeed most of my councillors, see a female ruler as an unnatural aberration; he makes no secret of the fact that he longs to see a man in control, and that can only be achieved once I am married and preoccupied with what he sees as my proper business of bearing children. He'd have my husband ruling in my name! Now do you see why I am determined to stay single?"

Lady Carew said nothing. There was a silence. At least two of them knew that this was not the only reason why Elizabeth did not want to marry.

"Any son of my body might conspire to overthrow me," the Queen said. "Do you think my councillors would object? No! At best, pressure might be put on me to abdicate in favor of that son. The seeds of conflict would be there from his birth. It is my belief that princes cannot ever like their children, especially those destined to succeed them. I could quote you many notable examples where there was discord and strife between monarchs and their heirs. All things considered, I would prefer, for my part, to leave the matter of my successor to Providence, trusting that, with divine help, a suitable heir will become apparent."

She gestured for Kate to pour her some wine. "There are advantages to my remaining single. My sister's unhappy example exposed the dangers of marrying a foreign prince. Such a husband might offer protection against my enemies, but he might also drain my resources in wars of his own, as Philip did. He might regard England as a subordinate state of his own country, and he might have to spend long periods out of England. I know my subjects—they are insular and hate foreigners. Remember Wyatt's rebellion against Mary's Spanish marriage? They are unlikely to accept another foreign consort."

"You could always marry one of your own subjects," Kat said. "I'll wager that most Englishmen would favor one of our own countrymen in preference to a stranger."

"Cecil doesn't agree, nor does the Duke of Norfolk. They foresee greater advantages from a princely alliance. And I have no desire to marry one of my subjects. It could cause dangerous rivalries at court and in the country. Factions might form, as in the wars between Lancaster and York, and that could lead to civil war. Besides, I will not demean my royal blood by marrying a commoner. Above all, I do not want to lose my freedom, having suffered constraints of one kind or other throughout my life. I have no desire to become the subordinate of any man. I mean to rule by myself, without interference."

She drained her goblet. "I must change for dinner and my afternoon audiences. Kate, attend me."

Kate had been hoping that she could get away to see Francis, but it looked as if she must remain on duty for several hours yet. In the Queen's bedchamber, she picked up the gorgeous pearl-encrusted gown that lay waiting on the bed and helped her mistress to change.

Elizabeth was still justifying her decision. "I am inclined toward a single existence. I have found the celibate life so agreeable that I would rather go into a nunnery, or even suffer death, than be forced to renounce it. I would much prefer to be a beggarwoman and single than a queen and married. If I were a milkmaid with a pail on my arm, I would not forsake that poor and single state to marry the greatest monarch."

"But why do you hate marriage so much, Bess?" Kate asked gently, lifting heavy ropes of pearls over Elizabeth's head.

"I do not hate it. I hold nothing against it, nor do I judge amiss of those who, forced by necessity, cannot live another life. But I am determined not to give way to such fleshly weakness."

Ah, there was the rub. It came to Kate that it was not marriage that Elizabeth feared, but the act of procreation. She had guessed that there was a more fundamental reason for her mistress's aversion to marriage. "It is not fleshly weakness, but a natural instinct implanted by God," she said. "And it can be beautiful when two people love each other." She was thinking with longing of Francis.

"And awful if they don't!" Elizabeth retorted. "Imagine letting a man you hated do that to you!"

"But *you* can choose your husband. You do not have to marry a man you hate."

"I do not have to marry at all!" Elizabeth rounded on her. "Let me tell you, Kate, that certain events in my youth have made it impossible for me to regard marriage with equanimity or to see it as a secure state. Look at the marital problems of my father and my aunts, for example! Because of that, I stand in awe myself to enter into marriage, fearing what might ensue. And you must not say this to anyone, but I am very afraid of the dangers of childbirth. Two of my stepmothers, and my grandmother, died in childbed. My sister suffered the mortifying humiliation of two pregnancies that were not pregnancies. I have seen young brides marry, give birth, and die within the space of a year. My physician has warned me that childbirth might not be easy for me. I'm scared, Kate. I'm very scared."

"But I myself have borne thirteen children, and I am here to tell the tale," Kate said reassuringly, doing up the clasp of her mistress's jeweled girdle. "You are strong and healthy, Bess—you could birth ten children!"

Elizabeth flushed. "I cannot bear the thought!"

"But you are denying yourself some of the greatest joys in life! Looking back, it was as if I was half alive before I had children. Until you have a child of your own, you can never know or understand how powerful that bond is. Your love for that child would overcome any of the problems you envisage."

"I do not love children in general," Elizabeth insisted. "I have no desire to be a mother. I am not like you, Kate. And there is more to life than marriage and children."

Kate would not allow her love for her family to be belittled. "I want nothing more!" she declared. "I say again, until you experience it, you cannot know what you are missing or how powerfully love eclipses everything else."

Elizabeth bridled, and Kate knew she had said too much, overstepped the bounds of their friendship.

"Love does not come into this. It was my supposed love for Lord Seymour that got me into trouble in my brother's reign. And look where love left my mother. No, Kate, this is about politics. I cannot look for love. I know that in Catholic courts fantastic tales of my alleged promiscuity abound. I must be circumspect."

She dismissed Kate soon afterward. Kat and Blanche could attend her at her afternoon audiences, she said.

As Kate sped downstairs, hoping to find Francis, she was thinking that if Elizabeth cared that much for her reputation, she would take the trouble to conceal her partiality for handsome, virile men. She was an outrageous flirt, so it was no wonder that there were rumors about her, rumors of which Kate had recently become aware. Yet she knew that Elizabeth was too much mistress of herself, and too frightened of physical love, to succumb to the temptations of men. Proud and dignified, she was deeply conscious of her exalted status and would never risk her reputation. She did not live in a corner. A thousand eyes could see all that she did. Kate felt certain that she was inviolably chaste. Those rumors were sheer inventions of the malicious, possibly to put off those princes who would have found an alliance with her useful.

BY A STROKE of luck, Kate ran into Francis in a gallery. What with the coronation and the Queen's demands, she had not seen him for days. His face lit up when he saw her.

"Darling! What brings you here?" He took her hand and squeezed it.

"I was looking for you. Can you spare some time?"

"Of course."

"But you were hurrying somewhere."

"It is nothing that cannot wait."

They sat down on a stone window seat. "I have missed seeing you," Francis said.

"I know, I know. I have missed you, too, but the Queen keeps me at her side and it is difficult to get away. Oh, Francis, I am weary of my life here already. I did not come back to England for this."

He shook his head sadly. "I suppose we should be grateful for our good fortune. But could you not tell her that you need more time at home? Say you are unwell, or something . . ."

"That's just it—I can't. She says she depends on me and that I must never leave her. And she confides in me. I know things that she would never tell her councillors, even Cecil."

"What things?" Francis's voice was suddenly serious.

"I can't tell you here." Courtiers and servants might pass along the gallery at any time. "Come into the courtyard."

A door farther along led into a tranquil garden enclosed on all sides by covered walks. The garden was bare now, but Kate imagined that it would look lovely in a few weeks when spring came. Once she was sure that they were alone, she told Francis what Elizabeth had said about remaining unmarried, and why. "I thought you should know."

He frowned. "Indeed, I should and so should her Majesty's Privy Council. This is a matter of national importance. The Queen's marriage is not a matter of personal choice, but of state policy. She must marry. The kingdom needs an heir."

"She is set dead against it, and I worry that she is condemning herself to a lifetime of loneliness and enforced chastity. It seems that the act of procreation frightens her to the extent that she would be unable to give herself to a man."

Francis looked exasperated. "Now you can see why women are not born to rule! A king would just get on with things and do his duty. She should be focusing on whom she should marry, not whether she should! I'll wager that once the right suitor presents himself, she will change her mind about remaining celibate. She loves nothing more than flattery."

Kate wasn't so sure. Francis had not been there when Elizabeth opened her heart.

He pulled her into his embrace. "Let's not spend our precious time talking about the Queen. When are you going to come to bed with me?"

She kissed him full on the lips. "When I can get away at night. Having had the afternoon free, I may be expected to sleep in the Queen's bedchamber."

He groaned. "I ache for you, Kate. I've hardly claimed you since we returned to England. Just for tonight, pretend you're ill and come to me."

"I'll try," she agreed, fearing that Elizabeth was too sharp-witted to be duped.

"If you don't come tonight, darling, I'll be away for the next few days."

"Away?"

"Aye. The Queen has made me steward of the borough of Reading, and she has leased Reading Abbey to us both. I am going to see it and take possession, then see what my duties involve."

"She's said nothing to me, but that's good news! I wish I could come with you."

"Ask her if she can spare you. It would be wonderful if we could go together." Francis's eyes were shining in anticipation.

"I will think of a way," she promised, determined to wrest permission from the Queen.

SHE DID NOT feel so bullish when she stood before Elizabeth later that afternoon. She did not like lying, but after thinking up and rejecting numerous pretexts for craving leave of absence, she had finally settled on one that the Queen was bound to accept.

"Your Majesty, I am sorry to say that I am not well. This morning, I suffered a laxness in the belly, so I consulted a physician in the Strand this afternoon, and he told me that I have a contagious humor and must rest." God forgive me the lie, she prayed inwardly, rubbing her stomach.

Elizabeth looked alarmed. "Contagious? Then you must go home, Kate. Send for your litter at once, and do not return to court until you are better."

"Your Majesty is too kind," Kate said weakly. "By great good fortune, my husband is going to Reading. He can escort me part of the way."

Elizabeth's eyes narrowed. "We can't have him catching this humor. I will arrange for one of the grooms to escort you."

Panic seized Kate. "I thank your Majesty, but I have my own groom, who brought me here. He lodges across the river at Lambeth, where he has family. I will send a messenger to summon him."

Elizabeth still looked suspicious. "Very well, then," she said stiffly. "Do not stay away any longer than you have to, Kate. I shall miss you very much."

Chapter 33

1559

SHE HAD DONE IT. SHE HAD ESCAPED, WITH THOMAS TAKING the reins, and she had got word to Francis of what she was doing. She spent the night at a nice inn in the village of Kensington, and he met her there the following morning. It was a joy to be free, to be going away together. It felt like an adventure.

She briefly wondered if the Queen might send someone to check that she was going home on her own, but there was no sign of anyone, and she did not really think that Elizabeth would go so far; she had many more important things to do.

It was like being newlyweds again. They slept in inns along the way, using false names, lying in each other's arms, and enjoying being just the two of them. The sense of freedom was delicious, heady.

In Reading, which lay only a few miles south of Rotherfield Greys, they made for the site of the ancient abbey.

"I thought it would be in ruins," Francis said, "but Cecil told me that, after the dissolution, King Henry converted the buildings into a royal palace for his own use when on his travels."

"It will be a big house, then," Kate said.

They had not realized it would be quite so big. It was palatial and it was easy to see, without the steward having to explain, that

Abbey House, as it was now called, had been formed from several buildings, notably the gatehouse, the Abbot's Lodging opposite, and part of the range abutting the old cloister, which included a fine old hall, a large chamber that had once served as a refectory, a parlor, a dining room, ten bedchambers, a garret with a large gallery, and several other small rooms, all standing around two courtyards. There was also a garden.

"It will be big enough for all the family," Francis said, gazing around.

"If we can ever gather them together," Kate chimed in wistfully. "And this is all ours?"

"Yes. The Queen has granted it to us."

"But will she let us live here?"

"It is to be my base as her officer in these parts. Greys Court will remain our mean residence. We can use this one as a town house. It's only a day's ride from Windsor and accessible to London by river. There's a large park with good hunting. I'll wager we'll be entertaining the Queen here one day."

Mention of the Queen made Kate feel guilty. She should not be here. She was enjoying her holiday because she had deceived her mistress. And yet, why should she not spend time with her husband? If Elizabeth insisted on keeping them apart and refused to acknowledge the great love between them, they had no choice but to resort to deception.

They snatched a few days at Greys Court. It was an absolute joy to be back at home with the children, to gaze upon their shining faces and feel their arms around her, and to see the lovely old house looking so well kept. Bilkins was doing an admirable job, and both Kate and Francis were grateful. And there was Thomasina, as comfortable a presence as ever, and ready for a good gossip.

On the day before they were due to leave, Kate was violently sick. She feared it was a judgment on her for pretending she was ill, but when it happened again the following morning, it dawned on her that she had missed a monthly course and that she might be with child again. She confided in Francis, and he insisted that she stay on at Greys Court.

"I can't do that," she protested. "I feel bad enough about leaving the Queen on a false pretext."

"Then we will make the journey in slow stages, so as not to tire you," he insisted. "You must take care of yourself, darling."

She basked in his care for her, just as she prayed that she really was pregnant, hugging to herself the comforting thought that, if she was, she would have the perfect excuse to leave court for several months.

WHEN SHE GOT back to court, she found Elizabeth laughing with her brother, Harry, in her privy chamber. He was not only Sir Harry now, having been knighted soon after the Queen's accession, but also Baron Hunsdon and the proud owner of the royal manor of Hunsdon in Hertfordshire, where Kate had stayed with Elizabeth many times when they were young.

The two seemed to be getting on famously. When Kate rose from her curtsey and Elizabeth had greeted her, asking if she was completely recovered, Harry hugged her.

"You look blooming!" he told her.

"I am greatly restored to health," she said hastily, lest the Queen smell a rat. Harry could be plainspoken; he had no tact. He had an honest, stout heart, yet Kate deplored his swearing and the obscenities with which he peppered his speech, although Elizabeth clearly liked them.

"I was about to tell her Majesty about a wooden statue they have at the Tower," he told Kate. "It's dressed up in old King Harry's clothes and if you press a secret mechanism in the floor, his codpiece rises up in all its lusty glory!"

Kate felt herself blushing, but Elizabeth roared with laughter. "That's priceless!" she gasped. "My father would not have approved, though. He was an old prude. By God, Harry, I like a man to be blunt—and I love you two the best in all the world."

It was at moments like these that Kate could forgive Elizabeth for her selfishness. There was a lot to love in her, and to admire. She went into the Queen's embrace, with Harry patting her on the back.

"I'm so glad you are well again and restored to me," Elizabeth murmured.

They settled down to a game of cards. Kate was thinking that it was small wonder that the Queen loved her Carey cousins, since her royal relations were a constant source of anxiety and suspicion, and therefore not to be trusted. But she and Harry posed no dynastic threat; the Queen knew she could count on their love and their loyalty.

She was still hoping that Elizabeth would give some tacit acknowledgment that she knew of the closer bond between herself and Kate. She mentioned it to Francis on one of the rare nights when they managed to go to bed together, lying in the crook of his arm with the candlelight flickering on their entwined bodies.

"Kate, be reasonable," he whispered. "You know that acknowledging the existence of a child born to Henry VIII and your mother would be a major embarrassment to her, and why she has never sought to have Parliament declare her legitimate. It would be politically, and personally, disadvantageous to her to acknowledge you as her father's natural child by your mother."

He sighed and pulled her to him. "I know you crave that closer bond with her, but such a revelation would draw unwelcome attention to her bastard status, and that's the last thing she wants at this time, when she sits insecurely on her throne. Just be grateful that you are very close to her and that she loves you as her cousin."

"But do you think she knows I am more than that?"

"Who can say? She keeps her secrets well."

"I know," Kate fretted. "And maybe I ought to keep my paternity a secret to avoid further sullying my mother's memory. Yet I do just wish that, privately, Elizabeth would give me some hint that she knows we are sisters."

"You're wishing for the moon, darling," Francis said, and kissed her, then rose up on his elbow and doused the candle.

BY MARCH, IT was a certainty that Parliament would establish the Protestant Anglican Church in England. A peace with France was soon to be concluded. The hot topic of the moment was the Queen's marriage.

"I am not going to marry King Philip," she declared to Kate and Kat one evening as they sat up late by the fire drinking hot aleberry. "He doesn't really want a heretic for a wife and, as you know, I have no wish to marry at all."

"So you are not considering the suit of the Emperor Ferdinand?" Kate asked.

"No! He is a pious bigot who is fit only for praying for his own family," the Queen retorted. "But I hear that he is to offer me his younger son, the Archduke Charles. He thinks thereby to bring about my conversion to Catholicism. Hah! But I hear that Charles is not overly religious and that *he* might turn Protestant after the wedding."

"So you might consider him?" Kat pressed.

"I want to keep the Emperor friendly," Elizabeth smirked.

ONE DAY IN late March, while sitting by the fire, engrossed in a history book, Elizabeth looked up mischievously at her ladies. "I have a new suitor."

"Who is it?" they wanted to know.

"The Earl of Arundel," she said, her eyes twinkling.

There was a pause. "So you will consider marrying a subject?" Kat asked.

"Who said anything about marriage?" Elizabeth retorted.

"The Earl of Arundel might well have it in mind," Kate ventured.

"Indeed, he might!" Elizabeth laughed. "I am told he has a good opinion of his chances!"

"But he is too old for your Grace," Lady Carew pointed out.

"He is forty-seven and a widower with married daughters." Elizabeth was twenty-five.

Kate was aghast. "He has no good looks, no manly physique, nor any courtly manners to commend him."

"Lady Knollys speaks truth," Lady Carew agreed. "He is a flighty man of no ability, rather silly and loutish."

"Ah, but what he has to offer me is his wealth," Elizabeth told them. "And he has a family lineage stretching back as far as the Norman conquest."

"Neither is sufficient compensation for his boorish stupidity," Kate said.

"You think I am taking his courtship seriously?" Elizabeth grinned. "I account him a buffoon, even though it pleases me to string him along. And he is not the only subject who would lure me into marriage. Sir William Pickering fancies his chances, too!" At that, the women burst out laughing.

"He's been champing at the bit since December," Blanche said.

"He is rather debonair," Kate put in. "And he did support you, Bess, during the late Queen's reign."

"I seem to recall," added Kat, slyly, "that when he first presented himself at your court, you granted him a private audience that lasted for four or five hours."

Elizabeth's thin face colored. "There was much to talk about. And Blanche was there. I wasn't alone with him."

"I was." Blanche did not look up from her needlework.

"That's as may be, but it's given rise to a lot of talk that you will marry him. People are beginning to seek his favor."

"Pshaw! It was just my way of rewarding an old friend whom I was glad to see again after an absence of so many years."

Kat did not look convinced.

"I have no intention of marrying him," Elizabeth said.

"Well, you'd better tell him that, because it's gone to his head. He's spending a fortune to fund his estate as a future king, giving himself airs and graces and entertaining on a grand scale, just as if he were royal. The London bookmakers are giving odds of twenty-five to a hundred that you will soon wed him."

Elizabeth just laughed. "Well, I won't!"

Kate was thinking that if these matters were not of such great importance, things would be verging on the ridiculous. For Arundel, not to be outdone, was now swaggering about the court. One day, he ran to catch up with her in a gallery and thrust something at her.

"Lady Knollys, for this consideration, please convey my worthiness to the Queen!" he pleaded.

She stared at the glittering brooch in her hand. It must have cost a king's ransom.

"I don't take bribes," she said. "You may rest assured, my lord, that her Majesty knows your merits."

Things reached such a pass that Arundel challenged Pickering to a duel, but Pickering declined to fight, publicly declaring that Arundel was the weaker man. A furious Arundel then went about protesting that if Elizabeth married Pickering, he would sell all his estates and live abroad.

And good riddance to him! Kate thought.

WHEN SHE AND Kat were alone in the Queen's bedchamber, sorting out her jewels into new caskets, Kat said suddenly, "This business with Arundel and Pickering is all a front, you know."

"I do," Kate replied. "What could they offer compared with the Archduke?"

"No, I mean a front to divert people from what is really going on. Have you not noticed that Lord Robert Dudley is often about the Queen?"

Lord Robert, the Queen's Master of Horse? He was the handsome son of the late unlamented Duke of Northumberland, and his saturnine dark looks had many women gazing lustfully after him. "Yes, I have, but only as one of the many gentlemen who frequent her chamber for merry pastimes. Surely you are not saying—"

"Oh, indeed I am." Kat laid away the last of the pearls. "She has seen him in private, too. She visits him in his chamber day and night. I have tried to talk to her about it—but it was like trying to get blood out of a stone. I fear Lord Robert has come so much into favor that he can do whatever he likes with public affairs. She even consults him on politics. I'll wager Master Cecil would have much to say about that! He cannot stand him."

Kate was astounded and hurt that Elizabeth had not seen fit to confide in her.

"But he's married," she said.

"Yes, although his wife has a malady in one of her breasts."

"You mean she is dying?"

"Some say so. There is gossip. I'm clean amazed that you haven't heard it."

So was Kate, but she was so often with the Queen or contriving to spend time with Francis and their daughters that she had no leisure for gossiping with courtiers, unless it was at the gatherings in Elizabeth's chamber—and of course no one had mentioned Lord Robert there, while he himself had not appeared to be paying any more attention to the Queen than the other men present, although they all behaved as if they were dying of love for her.

"I've heard nothing."

"They are saying that she is only waiting for Lady Dudley to die so that she can marry Lord Robert."

"No wonder they are being discreet! But to carry on with a married man . . . So much for all this talk of wanting to preserve her virginity and not wanting to wed. Surely she has not compromised her honor?"

"I doubt it has gone that far, although they've had plenty of opportunities! And he's a very handsome young man. I'd bed him myself if I were twenty years younger!"

"But you, Kat, would not pursue a married man, and neither would I. I can't believe it of the Queen. She dare not risk her reputation!"

Nevertheless, it soon became obvious to Kate that something momentous was going on between Elizabeth and Dudley. Overnight, it seemed, he had risen to great favor. The Queen showed him overt affection, which he no less ardently reciprocated. When they were together, which was increasingly often, he would lay a proprietorial hand on her arm and even kiss her on the mouth.

Kate longed to warn her that such behavior might well have consequences, but Elizabeth made it clear that the subject was not one for discussion. No longer was she confiding in her loving cousin about her suitors; when Kate tried to speak to her about Lord Robert, she was abruptly cut off. Elizabeth was going her own sweet way to Hell.

Francis was appalled when Kate told him of the latest intimacies between the Queen and her paramour. They were sitting up late in Francis's lodging, sharing an ewer of wine, but their pleasure in each other's company had become muted by his urgent concern.

"How far has this gone?" he asked. "The councillors are very worried because the most scurrilous rumors are circulating. He is married, and many are rightly shocked that she should show him such favor. Cecil is furious. He despises Dudley and sees him as a threat to his own power. The Queen consults Dudley on state affairs, yet he is not one of her ministers. Cecil says he has influenced her opinions on matters that are not within his remit."

"She doesn't talk to me about men anymore," Kate said. "She must know that I cannot approve. I'm assuming that the Archduke is now out of the running?"

"No. The Spanish ambassador is still cherishing hopes, but he has not found it easy trying to negotiate anything with her Majesty because she is so changeable. For my part, I fear she will never make up her mind to anything that is good for her."

Kate sighed. The nausea had eased, but she was still quite tired with her advancing pregnancy and had been wondering how soon she could decently crave leave of absence from court. She longed to see her children—no matter how often she wrote to them, letters were no substitute. Their absence was an ache in her heart, a constant, urgent, painful need.

She had not yet told Elizabeth about her condition, and in fact she dreaded doing so, but she would have to say something soon, once her belly became obvious. The sooner the better, she thought, because she was weary of all this rumpus about her mistress's courtships.

"Sometimes she says she wants to marry and that she will only accept a great prince, which puts Lord Robert's nose out of joint, and which he doesn't try to hide. Then she acts as if she is in love with him and keeps him at her side. In truth, I'm sure he has no idea of where he stands with her."

"Is she in love with him?"

"Looking at them together, it seems obvious. His duties bring him into daily contact with her. They ride out together most days since they share a passion for hunting. I can see what attracts her:

he is cultivated, witty, charming, and attractive—stimulating company."

Francis frowned at that. "If I did not know better, I would wonder if you were in love with him yourself." He was only half joking.

"Not I! There is only one man for me, and it is yourself," she assured him. "But I understand why she loves him. She can relax in his company, and they share the same mischievous sense of humor—he knows well how to amuse her. He has the gift of teasing her without giving offense. They have known each other since childhood, and he sold lands to support her during her sister's reign. I think he knows her better than anyone."

"Except you, perhaps. That's as may be, but he is not free and she should not be consorting with him."

"No. And she has abandoned all discretion. She makes no secret of her affection for him and never misses a chance to praise his talents as a horseman or in arranging tournaments and entertainments. She dances galliards with him, leaping high into the air with abandon. Everyone is astonished."

Francis shifted in his chair, looking deeply concerned. "For someone who claims to set a high value on the good opinion of her people, it seems she cares not a jot what they think of her."

"I don't believe she has bedded with Lord Robert. She is attended round the clock by us ladies and her maids-of-honor, and we would know. And she is too canny to risk an illicit pregnancy."

"Great God, think of the scandal! I hope you're right, Kate."

A distant clock sounded. "I must go," Kate said. "It's my turn to sleep in the Queen's chamber."

"Oh, no," Francis groaned. "This is intolerable. Does she not realize that we have a married life?"

"She prefers not to realize," Kate said, kissing him yearningly. "She is jealous. She wants me to herself."

She parted from him with a heavy heart. They never knew, from day to day, when they would be with each other again. At times like these, she hated Elizabeth. But then the Queen would show her some kindness or declare how much she cherished her, and Kate would love her all over again.

. . .

ON ST. GEORGE'S Day, Elizabeth bestowed the Order of the Garter upon Dudley and the three senior peers of the realm, the Duke of Norfolk, the Marquess of Northampton, and the Earl of Rutland. Kate, waiting on Elizabeth with the other ladies, thought it evident from the frosty demeanor of the three great lords that they were furious about the honor being given to Dudley, which was understandable, for they had long offered the Queen good service in various ways, while he was the son and grandson of upstart traitors. His only qualifications for the honor were good looks, superb horsemanship—and the love of his sovereign.

By now, he was freely dispensing patronage to a growing clientele of his supporters at court—sycophants who otherwise would never have given him the time of day. In the privy chamber, his word was law. The councillors, Francis told Kate, were outraged. But Elizabeth fondly tolerated this situation, although she never permitted Dudley to forget who was mistress and who was servant, and was not above reminding him of it in front of others. Many were suspicious of his motives and resentful of his overfamiliarity with her. The nobles reviled him as an upstart, while others thought him a self-seeker who was professing love for the Queen only to further his own ambitions.

Yet Kate could sense that the love between them was genuine on both sides. There was no escaping the warmth and sincerity in Lord Robert's voice when he spoke to Elizabeth or his obvious concern for her well-being. With others, he was haughty and reserved, but in her company, he was affability itself. The strong sexual rapport between them was evident.

"Isn't Lord Robert handsome?" the Queen asked her ladies one day as they watched him playing bowls beneath her window.

They all dutifully agreed.

"I love his courage and his manliness," she went on. "It will please me to tame this charmer and make him my creature, for he is everything that a man should be. His presence uplifts my spirits; I must see him every day."

She was fond of giving nicknames to the men who served her.

Cecil was her "Spirit." She now took to calling Lord Robert her "Eyes." He lapped it up like cream.

Kate suspected that he had one supreme advantage over all Elizabeth's other male admirers. He could not offer her marriage, so she had the best of both worlds. With his wife safely living in the country, the Queen could enjoy all the advantages of male companionship without having to commit herself to marriage, the loss of her independence, or the surrender of her body. As a single woman, she could remain in control of the relationship, whereas if she married, she would be subject to her husband's will. She could also preserve the image of herself she was carefully nurturing, that of "the Virgin Queen." Her courtiers had become fond of playing guessing games to determine if she really deserved the name.

Kate wondered if Lord Robert was entertaining hopes that he would one day marry Elizabeth. If his wife was indeed dying, the time would come when he would be free to offer himself as a consort to the Queen—an irresistible prospect for an ambitious man. For the present, however, he seemed content to bask in her favor and enjoy the benefits it brought. He must know that it was essential to keep it, for without Elizabeth's affection, he would be at the mercy of the noble wolves who were waiting to devour him.

IN MAY, THE Emperor's ambassador, Baron Breuner, arrived in England.

"Not the most crafty person in the world," Elizabeth pronounced. Kate, present at the audiences, watched her run rings around him. When he nervously laid the Archduke Charles's proposal of marriage before her, she betrayed no emotion.

"I thank the Emperor for deeming me worthy of his son," she said, "but I would remind your Excellency that, although my subjects continually exhort me to marry, I have never set my heart upon anyone, nor wished to marry at all—although I might change my mind, for I am but human and not insensible to human emotions and impulses."

Breuner was dismissed, looking crestfallen, and Kate was glad when the Queen retired with her ladies to her chamber, because she was still suffering the fatigue of pregnancy and had an irresistible need to sleep.

She was trying her hardest to stay awake when Elizabeth snapped her fingers and told her to buck up and attend her again in the presence chamber because Bishop de Quadra, the Spanish ambassador, was demanding to see her.

"Breuner's got at him," she muttered, sweeping through the door with Kate in her wake, suppressing a yawn.

"Yes?" she barked, as the Spaniard bowed.

"I understand that your Majesty is concerned about the Archduke Charles's views on religion. My information is that he might be thinking of leaving the Catholic Church."

Kate detected a flicker of interest in Elizabeth's eyes, but the Queen remained dismissive. "That is immaterial. I would rather be a nun than marry without knowing the man, nor do I wish to rely on the faithfulness of a portrait painter. I have heard rumors that the Archduke has an abnormally large head, and I dare not risk accepting a deformed husband."

"That is not the case at all," de Quadra reassured her smoothly, but he was wasting his words.

"Your Excellency, I will never marry unless it be to a worthy man whom I have met and spoken to."

Kate suppressed a smile. It was highly unlikely that any prince would risk coming to England to be inspected and risk the humiliation of being sent away. Royal marriages were never made like that.

Elizabeth knew it, of course. She gave de Quadra a sly glance. "Might I suggest that the Archduke comes here? Would he agree to that?"

"*He* would come out of love for your Majesty, but it is doubtful if the Emperor will send his son on approval. Indeed, Madam, it is a most unusual request."

Elizabeth smiled at him. "I am sure the Emperor will understand my position, as a maiden queen."

THE EMPEROR DID not. He refused to send his son to England. But Breuner persisted.

Elizabeth told Kate and Kat that he had laid the proposal before the Council.

"I'll heed their advice, but only on condition that I will be able to see and know the man who is to be my husband before I accept any offer of marriage."

"Then you'll be wasting your breath," Kat commented tartly.

Elizabeth gave her one of her looks. "In that case, I'll tell Breuner that I will not marry at all for the present, but that God, with whom all things are possible, might change my mind in the future. I hope the Emperor will respect my honesty."

Francis told Kate that the lords were becoming increasingly exasperated with the Queen's mercurial changes of opinion and her "answers answerless," as she delighted in calling them.

"The Emperor will most likely be offended and upset by her attitude," he fretted, taking Kate's hand as they strolled along a gravel path between railed flower beds. "Breuner is in a terrible state, not knowing if there is any point in pursuing this marriage business. In truth, Kate, her Majesty is impossible. One day she blows cold, the next she is paying Breuner every attention, flattering him and even flirting with him. The poor man hardly knows what to think. His chief concern is that she might accept someone else as a husband."

"Prince Erik of Sweden?"

"Who knows? She praised his portrait highly."

"She was very taken with a letter he sent with a passionate declaration of love."

"Yet she has told him that he will have to leave his country to marry her. She said she would not leave hers for any consideration in the world. But it is not realistic for a monarch to abandon his kingdom."

No, it wasn't, and Kate was not surprised when Elizabeth turned Erik down. By then, she was entertaining proposals from the dukes of Saxony and Holstein, spinning things out in her usual way.

But there, in the background all the time, was Lord Robert.

"Baron Breuner is very concerned about the Queen's regard for Lord Robert," Francis murmured one night when, for once—oh, joy—he and Kate lay together. "He is fishing to find out if the councillors believe there is any truth in the rumors that they have bedded together."

"That's odd, because one of his servants approached me today," Kate told him.

The man had been lurking in the gallery when she left the Queen's lodgings to go to dinner.

"Excuse me, my lady," he'd said, looming before her, so that she was obliged to stop. "My master, Baron Breuner, has asked me to ask you about the rumors concerning her Majesty and a certain gentleman."

Kate bristled. "Which gentleman?"

"Lord Robert Dudley. You have heard these rumors, surely?"

"I have heard baseless gossip," she retorted.

"Yet you must agree that your mistress shows her liking for him more markedly than is consistent with her reputation and dignity?"

"Does she?" Kate was cautious. "I know for a certainty that she has never been forgetful of her honor." It was a lie, because she had no idea what went on when the Queen and Dudley were alone together.

She recounted this to Francis.

"You answered well," he said. "In future, you should refuse to listen to such questions."

"I will. I would have done so today, but that man took me off my guard."

Suddenly, there was a fluttering in her belly.

"Ooh," she exclaimed. "Darling, feel that." She guided his hand to the place. "There!"

The fluttering came again, like a trapped butterfly. "The babe has quickened!"

"God be praised!" he declared, kissing her. Then he paused. "You have to tell the Queen."

"I know. She will not like it."

Chapter 34

1559

Kate picked her moment carefully. She waited until Elizabeth was relaxing after supper, a wine cup in her hand, listening to Lady Carew playing the virginals.

"Bess, may I speak with you?" Kate asked, kneeling down beside the Queen's chair.

"That sounds ominous." Elizabeth grinned.

"Not ominous—in fact, happy news." Kate suspected it would be anything but happy to her mistress. "I am with child, and it has quickened. It will be born in October, by my reckoning."

The music stopped abruptly and the room fell silent. Elizabeth exhaled loudly, testily.

"I trust you are not thinking of leaving my service and abandoning me?" she snapped. No word of congratulation, no expression of joy. But Kate had not expected any.

"Not at all, Madam, although I will need to crave leave of absence to go home for the birth."

Elizabeth's lower lip quivered petulantly. "I suppose you will have to," she said ungraciously. "But there's no need for you to leave court yet, not until the end of the summer. Then you can put the child to nurse and come back as soon as you are churched."

Kate wanted to scream at her that it couldn't be like that, that she could not bear to be parted from her newborn so soon, but what was the point? Elizabeth would never understand. She hadn't a maternal bone in her body.

Her heart plummeting, she bent her head to her embroidery so that no one could see the tears in her eyes. She longed to be at home, to gather her children in her arms, and be away from the wearisome intrigues of the court and the Queen's constant demands for her company.

"I HAVE TURNED down the Archduke," Elizabeth announced at the beginning of June, as her ladies were dressing her for the evening.

"Was that wise?" Kat asked.

"I believe so. Admittedly, marriage to him would have enhanced my standing in the eyes of Christendom, but when I looked in my heart, I found that I had no wish to give up my single life. I prefer, with God's help, to abide in it."

Kat pursed her lips. Blanche was shaking her head behind Elizabeth's back, but she was less outspoken than Kat and rarely ventured to criticize her former charge. Kate wished that Elizabeth would set her course and stick to it, and stop playing games. Tomorrow, she would be saying something else.

Shortly afterward, the court moved to Greenwich, to be diverted with entertainments. Kate was glad of the opportunity to spend time with Lettice and Beth, sitting with them at archery contests or gliding along the Thames in the evenings in the Queen's barge, serenaded by minstrels. In July, Lord Robert organized a tournament for the Queen's pleasure, and sat beside her in the royal stand, like a consort. It was followed by a lavish picnic in the park, served in pavilions decked with flowers. He commissioned masques, and he and the Queen went out riding together nearly every day. Francis grumbled that she was neglecting her state duties to be with Dudley.

The pleasant idyll was interrupted by news from France of the death of King Henri, who had been mortally wounded in a joust.

Elizabeth looked worried, as did many courtiers, for Henri had supported the claim of his daughter-in-law, the Queen of Scots, to the English throne, and had even added the royal arms of England to her escutcheon. The peace treaty had preempted him from taking things further, but now he was dead, and a new king reigned, who might try to enforce Mary's claim with more vigor.

"François II is but fifteen," Elizabeth related over dinner with her ladies in her privy chamber. "He's a weakling, but very much under the dominance of his mother, Queen Catherine, and his wife's powerful uncles, the Duke of Guise and the Cardinal of Lorraine, who are all staunch Catholics and virtually rule France. What concerns me is that they are hostile toward me."

"Do you think the French will attempt to seize your throne for the Queen of Scots?" Kate asked.

"It might be worse than that," Elizabeth explained, taking a second custard tart. "Queen Mary's Catholic mother is regent in Scotland, although she is not popular there now and the Calvinists are trying to take over. They are insisting on more radical reforms than we have ever seen in England, or anywhere else, for that matter. But while the Queen Dowager is in power, there is always the risk that Scotland and France will join forces to put the Queen of Scots on my throne."

Kate shivered. If there was a war, her beloved Francis would be called upon to fight, and eighteen-year-old Hal, and possibly even William, who was fourteen now. God, she prayed inwardly, let it not come to that . . .

"The French troops in Scotland," Elizabeth was saying, "are helping to ward off the Calvinist lords, but if the French gain the upper hand there, they might decide to invade England from the north. We can only pray that the reformers prevail. A Protestant Scotland would suit me very well." She dabbed her napkin to her mouth. "For the present, I might reconsider my position on the matter of my marriage. If I could make mischief for the French, and so keep them occupied, I could take a husband who would give the King of France much trouble and do him more harm than he could ever anticipate."

"Does your Majesty have anyone in mind?" Lady Carew asked.

Elizabeth smiled wickedly. "Indeed, I do. The Earl of Arran is a thorn in the side of the French. Until Queen Mary bears a child, he is heir to the Scottish throne, and the Protestant lords in Scotland are in favor of a match between him and myself, since we are both the chief upholders of God's religion in our kingdoms—and our marriage would unite England and Scotland."

It made perfect political sense, but seeing Elizabeth flirting with Lord Robert later that afternoon, Kate doubted she would ever go through with it. Did she intend to make a political marriage and keep a lover on the side? Surely she had more sense than that, with her throne so vulnerable to her enemies.

Arran was eager to wed the Queen. An announcement of the betrothal was expected daily. Was Lord Robert looking as if his nose was about to be put out of joint? Not in the least. He seemed as confident as ever, flashing that devastating smile at Elizabeth at every opportunity. You could almost see her going weak at the knees. But all her talk was of Arran coming to London in August.

To complicate matters, Erik of Sweden was still pressing his suit, and had sent to say that he was coming to England to do his wooing himself. Kate stood with Elizabeth gazing at his portrait. "He is very personable—and Protestant," Elizabeth observed thoughtfully. "I might make a show of considering him—just to make the Scots more eager to conclude a treaty." As if they needed encouraging.

"What I really want," she went on, "is the protection of the Emperor and King Philip against French aggression. Cecil wants me to revive negotiations with the Archduke, and I believe I will do that—and then drag them out for as long as it pleases me."

She was in a high good humor that summer. In July, following the custom of her father, she declared that she would go on a progress; it would be in Kent and Surrey.

"We shall leave on the seventeenth of July," she told her ladies. "We have a week to make ready."

Kate's heart sank. She was six months gone with child, and the last thing she wanted to do was go on a long journey in the heat of summer; she could not ride because of her condition, but litters were uncomfortable, jolting along rutted, dusty roads.

"Bess," she said, knowing that she was venturing into dangerous territory.

Elizabeth turned around. She did not look in a receptive mood.

Kate took a breath. "Begging your pardon, but I fear that, in my condition, I will not be up to going on progress."

The Queen looked her up and down. "You're not ill, are you? You've whelped thirteen, have you not? You must have the strength of an ox. Of course you must come on progress. I've never heard such nonsense."

"Madam, with respect, you have never been pregnant," Kate cried, goaded into rashness by such unkindness.

Elizabeth rounded on her. "But if I were, I would not let it stop me from doing anything. Now buck up and start packing."

How Kate hated her in that moment. As soon as she could get away, which was hours later, she fled to Francis's lodging and, grateful to find him there, wept on his shoulder.

"This is monstrous!" he growled. "*I'll* speak to the Queen." Almost breathing fire, he left her there, trembling. But he was back within a quarter-hour, seething.

"She will not listen," he raged. "She has a heart of ice. I marvel, Kate, that you can ever love her."

Kate had had a chance to calm down. Her anger had dissipated. "She is damaged," she said. "How can she not be when you consider what happened to her mother? And with a father so distant and terrifying? She has a compelling need to be loved—and I am her blood kin. I cannot stay—I must return to her. Thank you, my heart, for speaking up for me."

"I feel emasculated," Francis growled. "It is a husband's duty to protect his wife and cherish her, but that woman is making it impossible."

Kate wound her arms around him. "I know, I know. And you do that so well, when you are let. Neither of us can help it if the Queen prevents you. Now I really must go. I will return later if I can."

Elizabeth was cool to her for the rest of the day. That night, and the next, she kept her with her. It was, Kate thought, a kind of revenge.

. . .

ELTHAM PALACE, DARTFORD, Cobham, Nonsuch Palace . . . The journeys seemed to go on and on. The babe was restless, and Kate suffered heartburn as a result of so much rich food and wine. The lavish entertainments arranged by Arundel—who still fancied his chances as one of the Queen's suitors—lasted for five days and were clearly designed to impress. One banquet went on until three in the morning; by then, Kate was asleep on her chair, and Francis had to carry her to bed.

They both noticed that Elizabeth's relations with Lord Robert were becoming increasingly intense. With their intimacy now more and more obvious, the scandal surrounding their affair escalated. If Dudley had been unpopular before, he was now one of the most hated men in England, the target of widespread envy and resentment among the Queen's subjects both high and low. Meanwhile, his many jealous enemies at court, who affected to believe him capable of any villainy, however foul, delighted in making political capital of his treacherous family background, the implication being that here was another of Northumberland's race fleshed in conspiracy and poised to make his bid to rule England. Kate was astonished to hear even the Queen, in a moment when she was in a pet with him, reminding him that his father and grandfather had been traitors.

William Cecil, whom Kate saw often, as he was frequently with Elizabeth, made no secret of the fact that he resented, distrusted, and feared Dudley. He complained of him often to Francis. When the progress moved to Hampton Court, and Kate snatched an hour one afternoon to walk with her husband by the Thames, he told her why Cecil was so concerned.

"He resents the hold Lord Robert has on the Queen; he distrusts his ability to advise her on political matters, and he fears the consequences of their dalliance. Dudley is a married man, so his relationship with her Majesty can only attract the worst kind of speculation. If his wife dies of her illness, the Queen might marry him, and then—well, goodbye, Cecil! Either way, the throne would be undermined and the public weal threatened. None of the lords can bear to contemplate a future with Dudley in power. That is why Cecil is working in earnest for the Queen's marriage to the Archduke."

"It will never happen," Kate predicted. "What she loves is the game of courtship. It is the breath of life to her. I can never see her giving herself to any man."

"But she's no fool, and surely she realizes what this disastrous affair is doing to her reputation? She professes to care deeply about what her subjects think of her, yet she turns a blind eye to the hatred they show toward Lord Robert."

"I think she is in love, and that it is a kind of madness."

Francis paused and placed his hands on Kate's shoulders, and as she gazed at him, she saw suddenly that he had aged. His face was delineated by fine lines and there were gray hairs in his beard.

"*We* are in love, my darling wife, yet it is not madness, it is true and right," he said, pulling her into his embrace. "The Queen has no right to love Lord Robert. He is vowed to another. Their love is not pure and true like ours."

And that was more or less what Kat said when one day, to the evident consternation of the Queen and the other ladies in attendance, she fell to her knees in the bedchamber. "Bess, with all the love I bear you, and have always borne you, I implore you in God's name to marry and put an end to the disreputable rumors that surround you. You must know that your behavior with Lord Robert Dudley has occasioned much evil speaking, and I care deeply about your good name and reputation."

Elizabeth visibly bridled. "Kat, if I have shown myself gracious to Lord Robert, he has deserved it for his honorable nature and his loyalty. It is beyond me how anybody dare object to our friendship, seeing that I am always surrounded by you ladies, who can at all times see whether there is anything dishonorable between me and him. However," and now her tone turned defiant, "if I ever had the will, or found pleasure in a dishonorable life—from which I pray God to preserve me—I do not know of anyone who can forbid me."

Undaunted, Kat persisted. "But the rumors are very damaging to your reputation, and my deepest fear is that they might alienate your subjects or even provoke a civil war."

"Nonsense!" retorted Elizabeth. "I must commend you for the devotion that has prompted you to speak out, but you must realize that I cannot take a husband without first weighing all the advantages and disadvantages."

"In that case," Kat pressed on, "should you not distance yourself from Lord Robert?"

To Kate's astonishment, tears welled in Elizabeth's eyes, and when she spoke, her voice was full of emotion. "Kat, don't you understand that I need to see him constantly? It is because I have so much sorrow and tribulation in this world and so little joy." It was obvious that she was telling the truth.

THE RUMORS PERSISTED. Soon afterward, during a merry gathering of courtiers in the Queen's chamber, an attractive young gentleman took a seat next to Kate. They sat there for a while, listening to a lute player. Elizabeth was sitting with Dudley, who was holding her hand and occasionally raising it to his lips.

Kat leaned in close to Kate and murmured, "I don't think you've met Master Borth. He is in the suite of Baron Breuner." Kat smiled at the young man.

Master Borth smiled; he had magnificent teeth. "Enchanted to make your acquaintance, Lady Knollys." They conversed for a while, making small talk, and then he grew confidential. "I hear that you are close to the Queen, my lady. She has told my master that she is so beset by duties that she has not had time to think of love." Kate realized he was fishing, no doubt spying for Baron Breuner.

She hesitated, watching Elizabeth flirting with Dudley. For someone who had protested that she had no time for love, she was doing little to dispel the impression that she had already given her heart. Yet Kate would not speak against her. "That is true," she said. "I can swear by all that is holy that her Majesty has never been forgetful of her honor."

Borth's teeth gleamed at her again. "Yet it is surely not without significance that her Majesty shows her liking for Lord Robert more markedly than is consistent with her reputation and dignity?"

"He is one of her most loyal servants," Kate insisted. "They have been friends from childhood. That is at the root of the affection between them. Baron Breuner need have no concerns on that score."

He left her in peace after that, evidently hoping that she was right.

IN AUGUST, KATE was delighted to receive a letter from Dot Stafford, who, it transpired, was now back in England. The Queen herself had sent her money to aid her return from Basel, and had invited her to court to serve as a lady of the bedchamber.

When Dot arrived at Hampton Court soon afterward, Kate embraced her warmly, while Dot made a fuss of her and her enormous belly.

"I am hoping to go home to Greys Court for my confinement soon," Kate told her, as she showed her to the chamber where she would sleep and they began unpacking Dot's belongings. "*When* the Queen says she can spare me, that is."

"But you must be near your time," Dot exclaimed. "You should be resting."

"The Queen does not understand normal feminine matters." Kate sighed.

"You mean the rumors are true? That she does not function as a woman?"

"She is like every other woman, except that she does not like to think of her ladies being married and having children. These are things she would like to happen to herself, I am convinced, but which frighten her. So she is jealous."

"Extraordinary," Dot reflected, hanging up a good black gown on a peg. She was still wearing mourning for Will. "Well, she won't have any need to be jealous of me. I have no intention of remarrying. Will was everything to me and no man could ever replace him. I've rebuilt my life, my children are well cared for, and in coming to court, I know I will never lack for company. I mean to serve the Queen faithfully and do all the good I can for everybody."

"Knowing you as I do, you will do that wonderfully." Kate smiled. She took Dot's hand and they got on with their task while exchanging news of their children.

THAT EVENING, IN the Queen's presence, Kate had a dizzy turn and nearly fainted. Elizabeth stared as Kat helped her to a chair.

"I've told you, Bess, this poor soul has to go home to have her babe," Kat reproved her. She was the only person who could speak so candidly to her mistress and get away with it.

"Very well," Elizabeth sighed. "Kate, when you are feeling better, you may go home."

"Oh, thank you, Bess," Kate breathed, struggling to regain her equilibrium.

"But I expect you to return to court immediately after you are churched," Elizabeth told her.

"Yes, of course," Kate agreed, glad for now just to be going home. She would put off thinking about her return for as long as possible.

"You'll have to arrange an escort, because I can't spare your husband," Elizabeth went on relentlessly. "Anyway, birthing a babe is not a man's business, so you won't miss him."

Kate bit her tongue. She tried to feel pity for the Queen, who had no idea of how sweet it was to have a good husband to cherish her, yet she could only feel anger, fighting back tears at the prospect of being parted from Francis at such a hazardous time. She did her best to hide her feelings and was grateful to reach the privacy of his lodging, where she lay down on the bed and wept. And that was how he found her. Scooping her into his arms, he cradled her until the storm had passed, kissing her gently and murmuring words of love.

"She is not like other women," he said at length. "She has a heart of ice."

"She, more than anyone, should know that childbirth is dangerous. She lost two stepmothers in childbed, and she has lost friends, too. She should understand my fears and my need for your support. At such times, I care nothing for convention—I just want you near me, even if it is only in the same house. Oh, she is cruel, *cruel*!"

Francis harrumphed. "Indeed, she is. She is preventing me from doing my duty by you in your hour of need, and that I find hard to forgive. Once again, I feel emasculated. We are always at her beck and call; she repeatedly ignores the sacred bond between us."

"But what can we do?" Kate cried, meeting his eyes and seeing her anguish mirrored there.

"I will find a way to come home," he said. "You go tomorrow. I will follow, I promise."

Chapter 35

1559

GREYS COURT SLUMBERED IN THE SEPTEMBER SUNSHINE. Never had it looked more inviting than it did now, glimpsed from the window of the litter. Kate could feel herself unraveling, feel the peace seeping into her veins.

And here were her children racing to greet her, closely followed by nurses, tutors, Bilkins, and the rest of the servants, all delighted to see her, all eager to welcome the mistress home.

Gratefully, she sank down in Francis's chair by the hearth in the hall. "Bilkins, I will catch up with you on estate and household business tomorrow, when I have rested after my journey. For now, I would spend time with my young ones." She beckoned them, and they clustered around her, nestling on the floor. It was a pity that Hal, Will, Ned, and Robert were up at Oxford, Ned and Robert having only just entered Magdalen College School, but Richard, Frank, Anne, and Thomas were here, and the older three were plainly thrilled to see her. It grieved her that little Thomas barely knew her. They were growing up fast; she had missed vital periods of their lives, and her heart burned anew with anger against Elizabeth, who had kept her away from them so unkindly. Anne was no longer a toddler, but a lively four-year-old, as boisterous as her brothers. Kate wished that Mary, her sensible eldest daughter, were here. At nearly seventeen, Mary was a young woman already and ripe for marriage and babies. Kate made a mental note to ask Francis to think about finding a husband for her.

She wrote to the Duchess of Suffolk, asking if she could spare Mary to be her gossip during her confinement. The Duchess kindly agreed, and it was Mary to whom Kate turned when it came to preparing for the birth. The only other women at Greys Court were Thomasina and Mistress Bilkins, but Kate did not know her intimately. It went against convention to have an unmarried girl as her gossip, but there was no one she would rather have had by her side. The midwife she engaged raised an eyebrow, but Mary, dear, sweet child, was willing. "Anything for you, Mother," she said.

AS THE DAYS passed and the leaves turned gold, Kate kept a constant lookout for Francis. He had written to say that he was coming home as soon as he could, which left her in a fever of impatience, not knowing when she would see him. But he was as good as his word. When he strode into the hall, to find her discussing wages with Bilkins, Kate leaped to her feet, all ungainly as she was, and flung herself at him. "You came! You came!"

He looked slightly embarrassed at such a display of emotion in front of Bilkins, who hurriedly departed for his office, but then he hugged Kate warmly and kissed her. "Indeed, I did! I told the Queen I had pressing business in Reading. She expects me back next week, but of course that business is going to be prolonged—and prolonged again—if necessary." He kissed Kate again. "How are you, my darling?"

"I am well—all the better for seeing you—and the children will be overjoyed. They are at their lessons now, but when they finish—"

"Then we will not disturb them. I want you to myself for a little while."

"If only I was not great with child . . ."

"Then you'd soon be great with another one," he chuckled.

. . .

THE BABE CAME on 21 October, emerging into the world before Mary's astonished eyes.

"A daughter!" the midwife announced, as the infant emitted outraged squawks. "She's got good lungs on her!"

"Mary," Kate said, elated to have her brief ordeal behind her, "go and fetch your father."

"Madam!" cried the midwife, outraged. "Men have no place in a birthing chamber!" Obviously, the poor woman thought the world had gone mad—in this household at least.

"But I want to show him his daughter myself," Kate declared.

Francis hurried into the room, ignoring the midwife's dark looks, and gazed at the babe lying in the crook of Kate's arm.

"She's you to the life," he said.

"I thought so, too," she agreed. "She's beautiful. And she gave me so little trouble. Mary was a wonder. She held my hand throughout."

"Is that so?" he said, beaming at Mary. "Then, Daughter, you can choose a name for this little one."

Mary smiled delightedly and thought for a moment. "I'd like to call her after you, Mother."

"Then Catherine it is," Francis agreed, "with a C, to differentiate the two. I couldn't have chosen better myself!"

KATE HAD KNOWN that the domestic idyll would not last. Francis hung on at Greys Court for as long as he dared, but he could not stretch his absence until Kate's churching. He stayed until he was satisfied that she was recovering well, then reluctantly set off for London, leaving her bereft.

Once she had been churched, she knew her time with her family was limited. The children begged her to stay, and she did not know how she would bring herself to leave them, especially the tiny infant who tugged most closely at her heartstrings. But the wet nurse and the rockers were engaged and in residence, and she could delay her departure no longer. She felt she would die of misery as the litter carried her away.

Within a day of returning to court, she was bored sick with talk of the Queen's marriage, which was still the chief topic of conversation—will she, won't she, and if so, who? Elizabeth was as enamored with Lord Robert as ever, and insisting that she was not contemplating marriage at present—although, she said, she might change her mind if the Archduke Charles came to England.

Kate was in attendance when Bishop de Quadra angrily pointed out that her Majesty had all but invited the Archduke for inspection and must therefore be serious about wedding him.

"Oh, but I only wish to meet him and get to know him *in case* I decide to marry at some future time," Elizabeth replied airily.

De Quadra withdrew, simmering and puce in the face. "I have been made to look a fool," he muttered to Kate and the other ladies. "I do not pretend to understand her Majesty."

The ladies exchanged glances. They didn't understand her either.

Foul slanders against the Queen were ever more rife, and not only at court.

"Our ambassadors abroad are shocked at what they hear," Francis confided to Kate when they met at the serving hatch one evening to collect their "all-night" refreshments. "They forbear to report the details for they are too offensive to be committed to paper. Of course, they say they know the rumors to be false, but they are unanimous in wishing for the Queen to be more discreet in her dealings with men and marry soon. To be honest, Kate, if she doesn't, what hope is there for the succession?"

"If Dudley were free, she might marry him."

"Don't be too sure of that."

"Then why is she advancing him so generously? He is now Lord Lieutenant and Constable of Windsor Castle. He commandeers influential court posts for his friends and supporters."

Francis led her out into the courtyard, where they could not be overheard. "He is advancing himself, setting himself up as the champion of Protestantism. He would like to see England at the forefront of a religious revolution and a declared enemy of Spain. His views are too radical. Even I would not go so far. We should be thankful that he has no seat on the Council. Already he meddles too much in politics."

"But Francis, many are courting his favor, for they believe he might one day be king. And I do not doubt that, whatever else he is, he is sincere in his beliefs."

Francis did not look convinced, but he let the matter go. Raising a hand, he touched her cheek. "You look sad."

"Can you blame me?" she responded bitterly. "I was dragged back here against my will. I hated leaving the children, especially baby Catherine. I hardly had time to get to know her. I long to hold her. Dear God, if I could resign my post I would, but the Queen will never let me go."

"Have you asked her?"

Kate hesitated. "I fear to anger her. You've seen what she's like in a rage."

He nodded, with feeling. "She treats her councillors like naughty schoolboys at times. One lord said recently that he would prefer to face the King of France in battle than the Queen in a fury. And then, of course, she will come out with some pearl of wisdom and we're all yapping at her feet like puppies. She is the most infuriating woman."

"I know! I meant to tell you that when I got back last week, she asked if I was well, but said nothing about our new baby. It seems unnatural, this constant denial of the normal instincts in women."

"She is jealous," Francis observed.

"No, it goes deeper than that, I think. Anyway, I will try to talk to her."

"I will back you up. But Kate, if you do get to go home, you will see me even less than you do now. What with my parliamentary commitments and now being put forward as spokesman for the Council on questions of politics, I am overwhelmed with demands on my time."

Kate felt like screaming with frustration. "It is not fair, having to choose between spending time with my husband and spending it with my children. I do declare, Francis, that I am going to have this out with the Queen."

He drew in his breath at that. "Very well. But don't anger her too much."

. . .

SHE CHOSE HER moment carefully. Christmas was approaching and Elizabeth was happily planning a continual merry-go-round of balls, banquets, masques, and hunting parties.

One evening, when the women had prepared her for bed, Kate hung back in the bedchamber, taking her time to lay away the gorgeous clothing the Queen had worn earlier. When they were alone, she turned to Elizabeth, who was still seated before her mirror, admiring herself, and began combing her mistress's long red tresses.

"Bess, can I speak freely?" she asked.

"If it's about Lord Robert, no," she said sharply. "I've already had Kat warning me that if I marry him, I will incur so much enmity that I might one evening lie down as the Queen of England and rise the next morning as plain Mistress Elizabeth."

"No, Bess, it is nothing to do with Lord Robert." Kate watched her mistress visibly relax. "It is about me. You know how fond I am of you, beyond the ties of blood. We are cousins, but I would be as a sister to you." She paused to see if that evoked any response. Still she longed for Elizabeth to acknowledge the closer bond between them. For that, she could forgive her a lot.

"But I do look upon you as a sister," the Queen replied. "No woman is dearer to me. Tell me, Kate, what is all this about?"

"I just want to stress that I would never do anything to hurt you—but that you sometimes hurt me, whom you say you love."

There was a seemingly endless pause. Elizabeth's expression was hard to read. "How do I hurt you?" she asked at length.

"You keep me from those I love. I long to serve you, but I have a husband and children, and I rarely get to see them. If only you could be just a little more aware of my needs—"

Elizabeth rounded on her. "You talk of needs? Have you any idea of how lonely it feels to be queen and how much I need to have those I love around me? By God, Kate, I have raised you higher than most other women in this land; many would kill to be in your place. I have raised your husband, too. But what do I get in return? Complaints!"

Kate was trembling. "No, I beg you to listen, Bess—I am truly grateful. It is just that I cannot fathom why you do not understand my need to be with the man I love and our children."

"Oh, I understand perfectly!" Elizabeth was working herself into a temper now. "You are like all the rest, content to subsume yourself in a mere man."

"But that is the life I want, the life I have chosen," Kate said quietly. "I am not a queen like you. Yet there must beat a heart in your royal breast. It beats fervently enough for Lord Robert!" She regretted the words immediately.

Elizabeth gave her a cold stare. "But I do not let my feelings for Lord Robert rule me. I am mindful of my position. I would have expected more of you, Kate. Marriage and children are not everything."

"They are to me!" Kate cried, goaded beyond endurance. "I will not see them belittled. I ask, Bess, that you accept my resignation."

"No! It is refused. Now go away and don't ask me again, since you know what the answer will be."

"But Bess, I am begging you. I am so unhappy, so torn." Kate fell to her knees.

"Why should you not be happy serving your Queen?" Elizabeth spat. "You don't know how privileged you are, and I will not have my love for you count for naught. Now get up and leave me. We'll have no more of this nonsense."

Kate seized her hands. "It's not nonsense," she said gently. "I love you truly, as my Queen and as a sister. The last thing I want to do is hurt or offend you. But please remember that I need to be with my husband and children from time to time, for I love them, too. And if, as I hope, you yourself find a man to love and marry, then you will know how I feel."

She rose.

"You may go," Elizabeth said in a voice of ice, and turned away.

Chapter 36

1560

In the new year, the Queen declared that she was not interested in marrying either the Archduke or Erik of Sweden. Lord Robert took that to mean that he would soon be elevated to the king consort's throne.

"If I live another year, I will be in a very different position from now," he boasted to a gathering of courtiers in the Queen's chamber, while they were waiting for Elizabeth to arrive.

Kat bent toward Kate. "He's laying in a good stock of arms, they say. Every day, he assumes a more masterful part in affairs. He presumes more and more, and there is talk that he means to divorce his wife." But as the weeks passed, and his lordship took no steps to have his marriage dissolved, Kate concluded that it was pure gossip and that Lady Dudley was expected to die soon of her malady.

That spring, Elizabeth granted Kate and Francis the manor of Taunton and leased to them the castle there. She also bestowed on them the stewardship of Syon House. "You may make use of it whenever you wish," she told Kate. Kate was wondering if the Queen was trying to make up for her unkindness. It was a generous gift, but she didn't want to live at Syon House.

"Why ever not?" Francis asked, when they collected the keys and went to inspect it. "It's nearer to London."

"I would always be looking over my shoulder," Kate said, shivering as they stepped into the deserted hall and gazed at its abandoned splendors. There were dead leaves on the checkered floor and spiders' webs festooned the tall windows. The rafters soared darkly overhead. "I would be looking for ghosts," she said.

Francis laughed. "Oh, Kate . . ."

"No!" she protested. "This is not a happy place. Katheryn Howard was imprisoned here before they took her to the Tower to be beheaded. It then belonged to Protector Somerset, who was also beheaded. And it was here that they offered the crown to Lady Jane Grey—and look what happened to her. No, I should never have a quiet night's sleep here."

"As you wish." He shrugged. "But it will be my duty to look after the place—as if my workload were not heavy enough—and it would please me mightily if you could come with me sometimes. It would give us a chance to be alone together, away from the court. And Greys Court is only about thirty miles to the west. You could ride there and back to see the children under cover of visiting Syon."

"Indeed, I could," Kate conceded, warming to the prospect. "It just angers me that we have to resort to such convolutions in order to lead some semblance of a normal life."

"We must make do with what Dame Fortune has decreed for us," he said, taking her into his arms. "Let us not spoil this precious time alone together." He bent and kissed her. "There's a bedchamber in the steward's lodging . . ."

KATE WAS MISSING her children dreadfully; her empty arms longed to cuddle her baby, who would be sitting up now. But Elizabeth was enjoying another glorious summer. Cecil was in Scotland, having negotiated an advantageous peace with the Scots and, freed from the threat of war, the Queen gave herself up to a season of revelry in the company of Lord Robert. At the end of July, they left Greenwich to go on progress, traveling by slow stages along the Thames and staying at great houses along the route. Robert, as Master of the Horse, was much in evidence, but he was also to be seen at Elizabeth's side long after his official duties were done. They rode and hunted nearly every day, and in the evenings, they danced and made music.

"She is a wanton," Francis muttered, standing next to Kate and watching the Queen flirt outrageously. "I hear that she spends whole days closeted alone with him. This fellow is ruining the country with his vanity!"

Kate sighed.

"She has little regard for marriage," Francis growled. "Her conduct is unseemly. And yet, with this new peace, which has seen the Queen of Scots renounce her claim to the English throne, our Queen's prestige has been much enhanced in the eyes of the world. Cecil ought to be well satisfied with what he has achieved."

Kate said nothing. There was no need, for the musicians had struck up another tune and she was hoping that Francis would ask her to dance. But he just stood there, impervious to the irresistible beat of the tabor.

She knew that Elizabeth was not pleased with Cecil. She was furious with him for not demanding the return of Calais from the French and for not forcing them to reimburse the money she had spent fighting them in Scotland. Kate suspected that Dudley was behind her complaints and out to discredit Cecil. The Queen was also angry with Cecil for having written from Edinburgh to express the hope that God would direct her to find a father for her children to ensure the succession. Elizabeth had screwed the letter up into a ball and flung it on the fire.

When, at the end of July, after an absence of two months, Cecil caught up with the court, he doubtless expected to receive a grateful welcome from his sovereign. But Elizabeth was cool and distant. Kate watched his face as her disfavor had its impact on him. Later, Francis told her how worried Cecil was.

"He is most alarmed," he said, as they lay together in his lodging. "He is utterly dismayed by the change in the Queen's attitude toward himself. She has shown no gratitude for his triumph in Edinburgh, and she has refused even to defray all his expenses.

Now, when he needs to consult her on state affairs, he is told that she has gone out riding with Dudley. The signs are that she means to marry the man if he could be freed from his marriage. Cecil is about to fall on his sword. He thinks she is recklessly ruining her reputation and courting disaster."

He extricated himself from Kate's arms and rolled over onto his back. "The sooner the Queen has a husband, the better—but not if it is Lord Robert Dudley. I tell you, Kate, Cecil is very depressed and is seriously considering tendering his resignation. But I pray he reconsiders. No monarch ever had such a devoted servant."

IN AUGUST, KATE begged for leave to go home for a visit, since she had been away for ten months. Her attempts to flit off to Greys Court while visiting Syon House with Francis had been thwarted by the Queen, who had permitted her to go, but insisted that she be back within three days. Again, leave was refused, and she accompanied the court when it moved to Windsor at the end of the month. Elizabeth was in a good mood, having learned that the Scottish Parliament had abolished the authority of the Roman Catholic Church and made the Calvinist form of Protestantism the official religion of Scotland.

The Scots wanted to conclude Arran's marriage alliance with the Queen, but Elizabeth was enjoying herself too greatly with Lord Robert to show much interest. It seemed obvious to many that he was her intended husband.

One afternoon, as she sat playing music with her ladies in the privy garden, she suddenly laid down her lute.

"The malady in Lady Dudley's breast has got worse," she said. "I hear too that she is very downcast, which is hardly surprising in the circumstances."

Kate said nothing. This depression could also have been caused by Amy Dudley's grief about her husband's pursuit of the Queen, or by her belief that he was only waiting for her to die so that he could marry where he pleased.

"Poor lady," Elizabeth said, then picked up her lute again and began talking about the festivities that were planned for her twenty-seventh birthday a few days hence.

But when the great day came, she was preoccupied.

"Kate," she said, "attend me in private." She led the way into the closet she used as an oratory. "Lord Robert's wife is dying. Her suffering is great, so it will be a merciful release."

"I am very sorry for her," Kate murmured, "and for Lord Robert."

Elizabeth gave her a strange look. "This must go no further. The only other person I have told is Bishop de Quadra. He too is enjoined to secrecy. You can imagine the speculation that would arise if this became public knowledge."

Kate could not fathom why the Queen had confided in the Spanish ambassador, of all people. The news would be all over Europe in ten minutes. It was rather odd.

The interlude preyed on her mind until she snatched a few minutes with Francis after supper and he insisted that they go walking in Windsor Great Park.

"Cecil is still in disgrace," he told her. "He is convinced that Lord Robert is trying to deprive him of his place in the Queen's counsels. He fears anyway that her Majesty is conducting herself in such a way that it is impossible for him to continue in her service. He says it is a bad sailor who does not make for port when he sees a storm coming, and he foresees ruin if the Queen continues her intimacy with Lord Robert. He does not believe that her subjects would tolerate their marriage. So he is determined to retire into the country, although he supposes she will send him to the Tower rather than let him go."

Kate could believe it.

Francis was looking about him, frowning. There was no one in sight. "Would that I could retire with him! Yet he has implored me, for the love of God, to remonstrate with the Queen, to persuade her not to throw herself utterly away as she is doing, and to remember what she owes to herself and to her subjects. But Kate, you know how she is. I value my neck too much to risk her displeasure."

"She would just ignore your advice," Kate said.

But Francis was distracted. "By God, I fear for Cecil. He is like a man possessed. He said to me twice that he would be better in Paradise than here. And then he said the strangest thing, warning me that it was in the strictest confidence. He said that they were thinking of destroying Lord Robert's wife. They had given out that she was ill, but Cecil insists she is not ill at all, she is very well and taking care not to be poisoned. He said he trusted that God would never permit such a crime to be committed, or so wretched a conspiracy to prosper."

Kate had gone cold. "Who are *they*?"

"He did not say—and I was too stunned to ask. What shocked me more was that he said the only other person to whom he had confided this was that blabbermouth Bishop de Quadra."

"Bishop de Quadra?" Kate could barely believe this. She told Francis what the Queen had said earlier. "Is Cecil stirring things up?"

"What do you mean?"

"Is he deliberately planting in de Quadra's mind the notion that the Queen and Lord Robert are plotting murder? He must know full well that his words will be reported and then repeated throughout the courts of Christendom. The Queen herself will soon hear of them. Francis, if Cecil is so concerned about Elizabeth risking her reputation, he could not have done more to ruin it completely!"

"He is distraught, darling, and so painfully aware of his peril, that I fear his usual caution has deserted him. I think he is trying to bring the Queen to her senses by whatever means he can. His career is at stake—and the very future of England and the Protestant settlement!"

He put an arm around Kate and steered her back toward the castle.

"It doesn't make sense," she said, greatly perplexed. "If Lady Dudley is not ill, why would the Queen lie about it?" She could not, *would* not, believe that Elizabeth would be a party to murder.

As they began walking up the Lower Ward, something momentous occurred to her. Cecil must be aware that if Lady Dudley met her end by foul play, Lord Robert would be a free man, but the public outcry would be so great that he could never marry the Queen, since most people would believe he had killed his wife. Undoubtedly, Cecil wished, above all else, to prevent Dudley marrying the Queen. Was it possible that Master Secretary, their good friend and one of the most upright men Kate knew, was orchestrating some kind of plot? She did not want to believe it.

KATE'S HEAD WAS spinning with questions. What *was* the truth about Lady Dudley? Was she really as ill as Elizabeth had said? Or was Cecil correct in asserting that she was well? One of them must be lying.

That evening, as she helped the Queen to prepare for bed, she braced herself to ask that which she was burning to know. "Bess, it may be that Lady Dudley is not ill at all, and that you have been misled."

"What?" Elizabeth rounded sharply on her, red curls flying. "Who says so? I know for a fact that she is ill. Lord Robert himself has confided in me."

"It was just gossip I heard in the court." Kate was not going to mention Cecil's name.

"By God, Kate, you are so *silly*!" Elizabeth erupted. "I thought you of all people were above listening to foolish gossip. Would you believe that above the word of your Queen? God's Teeth, I thought you had brains in your head!"

Kate was stunned speechless by this outburst. "It was actually my husband who reported it to me," she blurted out when she could speak. "He heard it in the council chamber. And I do not heed foolish gossip—you should know me better."

"Should? I am your Queen. The word 'should' must not be used to me!"

"I am also your dearest cousin, as you have been pleased to call me—and more than that, if the truth be known." She wished the words unsaid as soon as they had tumbled, almost unbidden, from her lips.

Elizabeth was flushed with fury. "More than that? What do you mean?"

"I think you know," Kate said, trembling.

"I have not the faintest idea of what you mean," Elizabeth snapped.

Her vehemence led Kate to believe that she was lying. "Why will you not acknowledge the bond between us?" she cried, goaded beyond bearing.

Elizabeth's eyes were like glass. "I know of no bond other than our cousinhood. I think, Kate, that you should lie down. You have become a little crazed. It must be this unseasonable heat."

"Yes, I will do that!" Kate flung back, and almost ran from the room, tears streaming down her face. To be rejected so cruelly was torture to her. She made her way out of the Queen's apartments, down the privy stair, through the garden, and onto the terrace, crying uncontrollably. And it was there, by a stroke of great good luck, that she came upon Francis chatting with a group of black-gowned councillors. He broke away when he saw her and came hurrying over. "Whatever is the matter, my dearest?"

"Not here," she sobbed, drawing him away. When they were out of earshot of the others, she told him what had transpired between her and the Queen. He held her close, and she could sense the anger in him.

"For all the outward love her Majesty bears you, she reduces you to tears too often," he seethed. "And now I will probably make you weep more, for I am to be sent abroad very shortly. Diplomatic business."

Kate sat down heavily on a stone bench, oblivious to the waiting councillors. She was immersed in misery. Things could not go on like this. She felt a sudden, overpowering need to get away, to ride like the wind to Greys Court and her children. Baby Catherine would be a year old soon—and she was a stranger to her. She could not bear it.

"I am proud to live in this court," Francis muttered, "but I resent the high price we have to pay for it."

"And yet you will not leave it," she chided him.

He shook his head. "I cannot. I am bound, as you are, by my oath of allegiance. Like you, I resent being held in bondage, yet I value the privilege of serving the Queen. I can humble myself shamelessly to afford our children an example to keep them on the path of righteousness."

"They could not have a better pattern to follow," she said, calmer now, yet still distressed. "I wish I had not pushed matters with the Queen. I am convinced now that she knows the true nature of our kinship but will not admit it."

"She is insecure, darling. She sees threats to her position everywhere. That is why she hates her cousins on her father's side."

"But I am no threat! How can I be? They have claims to the throne, I don't. All I want is her sisterly love."

"You want the impossible," he said sadly.

TWO DAYS LATER, Kate and the other ladies were sewing in a circle in the Queen's chamber, while Elizabeth was playing chess with Lord Robert at a table by the open window, with much laughter and touching of hands. An usher appeared and announced the arrival of Dudley's manservant, Master Bowes.

"Whatever can he want?" Lord Robert asked testily.

"Let him come in and we'll find out!" Elizabeth grinned.

Bowes arrived, cap in hand. He was shaking. Kate began trembling herself, wondering what news he brought.

"Your Majesty, my lord, there has been a terrible calamity. My Lady Dudley is dead. She was found yesterday at Cumnor Place at the foot of a flight of stairs. Her neck was broken."

Kate stared at Elizabeth, whose face had turned white and whose mouth gaped in a speechless "O." Lord Robert looked stricken, genuinely bewildered. "I cannot believe it," he kept saying.

"What a terrible shock," Elizabeth croaked when she found her voice.

Lord Robert stood up. "Summon a courier," he instructed Bowes. "Send him to Cumnor Place to find out more details. And bid him be quick."

As Bowes sped away, Elizabeth sent for Cecil. He listened gravely as she told him what had happened. "Let the news be made public," she said. "Make it clear that the death was accidental."

"But we don't know that!" Dudley rounded on her.

"She must have fallen down a staircase," Elizabeth said firmly. He subsided under her panicked stare.

She turned back to Cecil. "I can well imagine how my subjects will react to the news. An inquest must be held, and quickly."

"I will order it, Madam," Cecil said, effortlessly in charge once more, and doubtless gratified that it was he to whom the Queen had turned in the wake of this tragedy. Kate doubted she would hear any more talk of retirement.

Elizabeth rose. "Robert, you must leave court. You will be suspected of foul play, and I cannot be seen to be associating with you until your name is cleared. You will go to your house at Kew and remain there until the coroner gives his verdict."

Lord Robert looked devastated. Doubtless he was fearful for his future. "I am innocent of her death, I swear it!" he protested.

"*I* know that, Robert, but the world needs to know it, too."

"She was dying," he said helplessly. "If someone killed her, there was no need. By God, I will leave no stone unturned to uncover the truth. If need be, I will see justice done and clear myself of any complicity if such a foul crime was committed. I beg of you, Bess, to make the most rigorous inquiries. The only way to exonerate me lies in finding the real culprit."

"If there is one," Elizabeth said. "Now leave us."

Her use of the royal plural made Dudley blench. It was obvious to everyone that she was distancing herself from him. He left, unwillingness in his posture and his manner. Kate thought she detected a gleam in Cecil's eyes as he watched him go. *Was it triumph?*

A FEW DAYS later the coroner delivered a verdict of accidental death.

"The verdict leaves no room for doubt," Elizabeth announced at supper. "My councillors agree with me." Her relief was palpable. "Lord Robert's name has been cleared, and he is on his way back to Windsor. The matter is now closed. As a mark of respect, the court will observe a month's mourning for Lady Dudley."

Francis was less ebullient when Kate found him in his lodging that evening. "The Queen may have drawn a line under this tragedy, but not everyone is so certain of Dudley's innocence. Some think that the evidence laid before the coroner was insufficient to exonerate him from guilt and that the truth remains to be exposed."

"Elizabeth seems very sure of his innocence."

"That's as may be, but I'll wager that she will never marry him now. People will say she colluded in murder."

"Do *you* think it was murder?" Kate asked, kneeling at his feet and meeting his eyes.

He shook his head. "If you mean, do I think that Lord Robert did away with her, no. He has many faults, but I do not think him capable of killing his wife. Yet there is something suspicious about her death."

"I agree." Kate fell silent, not sure if she wanted to share her suspicions, even with Francis. She didn't want to think about them herself.

"So, what do *you* think?" he prompted gently.

"I have asked myself who has profited from the death of Lady Dudley, and it doesn't appear that Lord Robert has. Rather the opposite, for I suspect that the last thing the Queen wanted to hear was that he was a free man. You know the great aversion she has to marriage."

"Who has profited, then?"

"This is strictly between ourselves," Kate said, leaning in closer and taking a deep breath. "Think about our friend Cecil. He was restored to favor as soon as the news reached court. He wished to prevent a marriage between the Queen and Lord Robert; we both know he feared it would bring disaster on England. He could have foreseen that if Lady Dudley died in dubious circumstances, the finger of suspicion would point to her husband—as indeed it has. He also knew that Elizabeth would be unlikely to risk her popularity and her crown by marrying someone whose reputation was so tainted."

Francis was frowning.

"You don't credit my theory?" she pressed him. "Well, I'm not done yet. I've been thinking this through for days. Remember, Cecil saw Dudley in the ascendant when his own future appeared to be in ruins. He feared not only for his position, but also for the future of England. If the Queen had married Lord Robert, it could have cost her the throne. He tried to warn her that she was plunging headlong into disaster, but she did not listen, and he was afraid that she would marry Dudley and wreck everything he, Cecil, had struggled to achieve. Is it not conceivable that he decided upon a course that, although regrettable, would force her to stop and think?"

Francis was nodding, his face grave.

Kate pressed on. "It is possible that, when he heard Lord Robert and the Queen giving out that Lady Dudley was very ill, he decided to act quickly."

"But he is not a cruel man . . ."

"No, he is not! Yet he could have reasoned that, since she was dying of a painful disease, cutting short her sufferings could only be an act of mercy. It makes sense that, having laid his plans, he told de Quadra it was not true what Elizabeth and Dudley were saying, and that Lady Dudley was quite well. Then, knowing that his words would be reported, he confided that Dudley was plotting to kill her, thus planting the seeds of suspicion before the deed was done. It would have been easy for him to have it carried out. Given the poor woman's perilous state of health, it would have been the work of a moment for a hired assassin to break her neck and then lay her body at the bottom of the stairs. Cecil probably felt that her murder would have been more than justified by its consequences."

"I don't know what to think." Francis sighed. "I will not believe ill of a good friend and colleague, and I doubt we will ever learn the truth. If you are right, which I hope you are not, Cecil is so clever and subtle that he will never give himself away. I agree, he had a compelling motive for doing away with Lady Dudley, and yes, he is the person who has profited most from her death. But being a patriotic man dedicated to the service of the State, he would likely have reasoned that it was his country and his Queen who were the chief beneficiaries."

Kate said nothing. She felt sick, sensing that she had, in some way, let herself down in raising the subject, even with Francis, the only person in whom she could confide these horrible suspicions. It was a terrible thing to accuse a good friend, a man of upright reputation, of murder. She could hardly believe that they were having this conversation.

IN THE MIDDLE of October, the court came out of mourning and speculation mounted as to whether Elizabeth would now marry Lord Robert. The rumors would not be stilled. It was said that she was secretly betrothed to Dudley and even that she was already expecting his child. Time proved these rumors false, but the story of Amy Dudley's death was continually embroidered and embellished. It seemed to Kate that people were always ready to believe the worst.

"My Lord of Sussex is of the opinion that her Majesty should marry Lord Robert," Francis told Kate one evening over supper. "Like the rest of us, he is concerned about the succession and feels that any husband is better than no husband for her. I cannot subscribe to that view. I would hate to have to bow the knee to Dudley as king."

Kate was weary of the subject. She thought all the speculation a waste of time because she did not believe that Elizabeth would marry at all, whatever she said in public. She just liked to keep her suitors dancing on strings she pulled herself.

One afternoon, as they sat around the hearth, Kat took it upon herself gently to remind Elizabeth that it was her duty to marry and provide for the succession. Kate held her breath, anticipating another explosion of rage. But Elizabeth remained calm.

"But Kat, think of the risks I would take in marrying. Unwed, I remain in control and keep the upper hand in any relationship; once married, the roles would be reversed, even though I am a queen. I would lose my independence and my autonomy, and that prospect fills me with horror."

"Even if you married Lord Robert?"

Elizabeth shook her head. "Especially if I marry Lord Robert, who is a subject born. And furthermore, if I do not marry him, it will prove those vile rumors false and distance me from the scandal of his wife's death."

But her words belied her actions. It was plain to everyone that nothing had changed between her and Dudley: far from being defeated by the rumors and gossip, he was as self-confident and proud as before. He seemed to see nothing improper in his courtship of the Queen, which fueled much of the talk that they would marry, which flourished side by side with speculation that a foreign marriage for her Majesty was about to be announced. Elizabeth reveled in being at the center of such intrigues.

A few evenings later, Kate and Francis dined with Cecil and his erudite wife, Mildred. His chambers were tastefully furnished but not showy, and the food was excellent.

Naturally, the conversation led to the ever-present issue of the Queen's marriage. "I grow more confident by the day that there is really little cause for concern," Cecil declared, refilling their goblets. "The Queen's political judgment remains as acute as ever, and although she will not renounce Lord Robert's company, I know for a fact that she will not marry him. She told me so herself—she said she would not marry a subject. I've ceased putting pressure on her to dissociate from him because it only makes her angry and more determined to favor and protect him."

"That's true," Kate said. "Kat's husband recently made derogatory remarks about him, and the Queen lost her temper and banished him from court. Kat was in a terrible state. She wept on Lord Robert's shoulder and begged him to sue for her husband's reinstatement. To his credit, he agreed, and the Queen relented."

"I heard about that," Cecil said.

Naturally, Kate thought. His spies were said to be everywhere.

Mildred laid her hand on her husband's. "I am thankful that the Queen has not allowed her private feelings to undermine her good sense. She has clearly realized that if she abrogates her moral authority as queen, she will lose all respect and credibility, and possibly the throne itself."

"She has acted with good sense," Francis agreed.

Before November was out, the gossip was dying a natural death. Lord Robert remained at the Queen's side, consort in all but name, but Elizabeth was firmly in control. She had his constant presence, his loyalty, and the stimulation of his company. Kate believed that she had never wanted more than that.

AT CHRISTMAS, ELIZABETH granted Francis the lease of Syon House. It was now his to do as he pleased with.

"We shall refurbish it to banish the ghosts and install the children there," he told Kate. "Syon is much closer to London than Greys Court, so we will be able to visit them easily. It can be our nursery house. And we will keep Greys Court as our chief residence."

Kate could suddenly see past the ghosts. She began to warm to Francis's plan, even though a lot of her children had flown the nest, if only for the academic terms. William was at Oxford, Edward, Robert, and Richard at Magdalen College School, and Hal was keen to become a lawyer and, following in his father's footsteps, enter Parliament. Already he was looking for a suitable seat. Frank, now seven, was soon to go to Eton. Mary had returned to wait on the Duchess of Suffolk. Lettice and Beth, of course, were still serving the Queen as maids-of-honor. So it was only Anne, now five, Thomas, two, and baby Catherine, who came to live at Syon, although Kate was grateful to have any of her children closer to her.

Over the following months, she got away to see them whenever she could, which was not as often as she would have liked, but it was good to be able to spend more time with them, especially little Catherine, who was in her second year now and very engaging. Kate had feared that she would not know her mother, but Catherine was an outgoing, loving little soul and came to her without hesitation. She thanked God that the long months of separation had not severed the bond between them.

Chapter 37

1561

THE FOLLOWING SUMMER, KATE BECAME AWARE THAT THE Queen's despised cousin, Lady Katherine Grey, seemed distracted. The slender, fair-haired young woman served Elizabeth in her privy chamber, having been demoted from the bedchamber at the beginning of the reign, so her path crossed often with Kate's.

Kate had her suspicions. If she had not known better—for Lady Katherine was unwed—she could have sworn that the girl was with child. But Elizabeth did not appear to notice, and she was always hot against any hint of a fall from grace. Her ladies must be above reproach: any wantonness reflected badly on her.

In July, the Queen took the court on a progress through East Anglia. By the time they reached Ipswich, Katherine was clearly in some distress.

"Are you thinking what I'm thinking?" Kat muttered in Kate's ear as they watched her wilting in a corner, not joining in the card game that was making the players laugh so much.

"I have been thinking it for some time," Kate whispered.

The next morning, Elizabeth summoned Kate to her closet. "That foolish girl!" she hissed, working herself up into a rage.

"Who?" Kate asked, but she knew the answer.

"Katherine Grey, of course! I've got to tell someone, Kate. I'm at my wits' end with her. The silly fool has only taken it upon herself to contract a secret marriage with the Earl of Hertford, or so she claims. She went to Lord Robert in the night, weeping and wailing. Imagine it, going into a man's bedchamber—what would people think? She told him she was with child and begged him to intercede for my forgiveness. Well, she can beg all she likes."

"She has indeed been foolish!" Kate pretended to be astonished.

"More than that, she has placed the succession in jeopardy, since there is no way of proving that her child is legitimate. The only witness to her so-called marriage has just died. And she thinks I will name her my successor? By God, in having succumbed to her lusts, she has shown herself as too weak to be a suitable heir to the throne. I am wondering if it's all part of some conspiracy against me."

"I don't think she has the brains for that," Kate said soothingly.

"No, but Hertford might be manipulating her." Elizabeth bit her lip.

"Is there any proof of that?"

Elizabeth shook her head. "No. Cecil thinks that this illicit pregnancy is a sign that God is displeased at the prospect of a Grey claimant succeeding to the throne."

"But Bess, *is* it an illicit pregnancy?"

"Of course it is! I don't believe all this nonsense about a secret wedding. It was a piece of mummery at best."

Kate wasn't sure what to believe. She didn't know all the facts. "What will you do?"

"I shall keep her close until we return from the progress. I have a mind to send her to the Tower. Don't look at me like that. She will be well housed, and I shall make sure she has some comforts, and someone to attend her when her time comes."

Unwelcome memories of Anne Boleyn surfaced in Kate's mind. She shuddered. "You will not proceed further against her, once the child is born?"

Elizabeth stared at her. "I am not a monster, Kate. You ought to know that."

"Of course I do. It's just that a court of law might deem her actions treasonable."

"No, I shall stop at imprisonment. By God, these cousins of mine do plague me! There's the Queen of Scots. She's returning to her kingdom now that she is widowed and demanding that I recognize her as my heir. She continues to flaunt my royal arms quartered with her own. Well, she shall not have a safe-conduct through England. She can hazard the perils of the North Sea! And I wish her well of her people. They are all Calvinists now—how will they welcome a Catholic queen? The Protestant lords in power will give her short shrift, I'll wager."

Kate knew Elizabeth well enough to understand that her antagonism toward Mary, and Lady Katherine, was driven by insecurity and jealousy. It was widely known that Mary Stuart was regarded by Catholic Europe as having a better title to the English throne than Elizabeth. And Elizabeth could not hide the fact that she regarded Mary as her rival: younger, and reputedly more beautiful, the widowed Mary had usurped Elizabeth's position as the most desirable match in Europe. And surely, she would soon be looking for a husband. But who? Elizabeth must fear the arrival of a powerful Catholic prince in Scotland, while the close proximity of the Catholic claimant to her throne would pose a continuing threat to her security. Oh, yes, she could understand Elizabeth's concerns.

"You are the only cousin I can trust—you and your brother Harry," Elizabeth said, taking Kate's hand. "I know I am not always kind to you, and that I make too many demands on your time, but never forget that I love you above all other women. And it is a great comfort to me to have a kinswoman who poses no threat to me."

Her emotional declaration—rare indeed—was a measure of how distressed she was about the threats from her dynastic rivals. Kate bent forward and hugged her.

"You are very dear to me, too, Bess," she said, ready in that moment to forgive her a lot.

WHEN THE COURT returned to Whitehall in August, Lady Katherine Grey was imprisoned in the Tower and Lord Hertford was summoned home from a mission abroad to join her there, but housed in a separate cell. They were not allowed to meet or be treated as husband and wife. In September, Katherine gave birth to a son, Edward Seymour.

"By God, this is all I need!" Elizabeth erupted, and stormed off into her bedchamber, slamming the door behind her. The ladies looked at each other.

"She fears that Lady Katherine's ability to produce a son will make her a more attractive prospect as queen in the eyes of the people," Kat said quietly. "A male heir is a real threat to our mistress."

Kate knew it was true. Francis often said that a lot of the councillors resented having a woman reigning over them. No wonder Elizabeth felt insecure.

She went after her. "Forgive the intrusion, Bess, but if you want someone to talk to, I am here. I know how hard this is for you."

Elizabeth turned around, tears on her cheeks. "It is. Katherine is young and fruitful, and I am of barren stock."

"That's not true." Kate was aware that, once more, she was venturing upon dangerous ground.

"Sadly, it is." The Queen sighed. "I am the only one left of all my father's children."

Kate was bursting to contradict her, but this was not the time. "If you married—"

"I've told you, I do not wish to marry!" Elizabeth snapped. "The very idea is anathema to me. There will be no more Tudors after me."

Kate gathered her courage. "Marriage is not so awful, Bess. The act of procreation is a beautiful thing, a tenderness between husband and wife. And children bring joy and fulfillment to a woman. Believe me, I know. I am sure that, if you took a husband—the *right* husband—you would be happy. There would be no more need to worry about the succession or your cousins' ambitions."

"You make it sound so easy," Elizabeth said, her anger abating. "But my fear is too great. My father's tenderness for my mother, and Katheryn Howard, went so deep that he had them both beheaded. And what good is husbandly tenderness when you are dying in agony with the child he gave you? No, I will not take the risk."

"Then I will not trouble you by raising the matter again," Kate said. "I would not anger or upset you. We just have to accept that we are different women with different views on life."

"It is the best way," Elizabeth agreed. "As to Lady Katherine, I will not let her set up her brat as a rival claimant to my throne. I am ordering the Archbishop of Canterbury to chair a commission to investigate the validity of her so-called marriage. Until then, my foolish cousin can stay in the Tower."

IN THE WINTER, Francis asked Kate to bring Lettice to meet him in the Chapel Royal at St. James's Palace, where the court was staying.

"Do you know what it's about?" Lettice asked, as they made their way through the galleries of the redbrick palace. At just eighteen, she had become a stunning beauty with her heavy-lidded eyes, full lips, and cloud of red hair. She had an inner grace and charm that seemed irresistible to both men and women, and was fast becoming one of the ornaments of the court. But Kate did not want her lovely daughter forever in the snares of court life.

She knew what Francis was going to say because they had discussed it. He had been talking of finding a husband for Lettice for some time. She had pointed out that Mary, as their eldest daughter, should be married first, but they both knew that the Duchess of Suffolk did not want to lose her just yet. So he had set about finding the right match for Lettice, and Kate had approved his choice wholeheartedly.

He was waiting for them, beaming, beneath the glorious ceiling that King Henry had installed for Anna of Cleves. Not the most auspicious place to discuss a betrothal, Kate thought.

Francis kissed them both. "I have good news. Lettice, I have found you a noble husband. He is Walter Devereux, Viscount Hereford. You will be a viscountess. I hope you are pleased."

Lettice seemed speechless.

"I think she would like to know more about Lord Hereford

than his lordly credentials," Kate said. "What kind of man he is, for example."

"He is young, Lettice, about two years older than you, and of good Welsh stock."

Kate had to laugh. Men were so obtuse. "We are not buying a horse for breeding! Tell her what he is like as a man!"

"Pleasant and personable. Dark-haired, bearded. I suppose you ladies would think him handsome."

"Can I meet him?" Lettice asked.

"I have asked him to come here. He should arrive in a few minutes."

"You will have seen him around the court," Kate said.

"We've come to a reasonable agreement about the dowry, Lettice. You will be well provided for."

The door opened and Walter Devereux walked in. He was tall and did indeed have dark good looks. Kate suspected that there was a tough side to him beneath the courtesy. But Lettice seemed very taken with him. She blushed prettily when he told her how pleased he was to have found such a beautiful bride.

"We must arrange the wedding!" Francis declared.

ELIZABETH WAS NOT best pleased to learn that she was to lose her maid-of-honor, but she conceded defeat graciously, for was it not her role as their mistress to ensure that her maids made good marriages? And she could hardly disapprove of Viscount Hereford.

The young couple were married in December in the church at Rotherfield Greys. Lettice looked enchanting in her white satin wedding gown sewn with rubies, and Walter made a handsome bridegroom. They were clearly happy with each other, and although Kate shed a tear when they departed for Walter's seat at Chartley in Staffordshire, she felt confident that her precious daughter was in safe hands.

Chapter 38

1562

AT NEW YEAR, KATE WAS TOUCHED WHEN ELIZABETH GAVE her three covered gilt bowls, which weighed more than anyone else's gifts of plate. It was a measure of her love for her. Elizabeth had been very kind when Kate said that she was missing Lettice.

"She'll be having a fine time," she said. "She'll have been presiding over her first Christmas as mistress of Chartley and leading her husband a merry dance in bed, I'll wager! She won't want her mother fussing around, I'm sure!"

Kate hesitated. Lettice was not the only one who had been having a fine time in bed. "I have something to tell you, Bess," she said. They were seated in the Queen's chamber by a roaring fire, while the other ladies were tidying Elizabeth's bedchamber. "I am with child again."

"What? You're nearly thirty-eight! It's almost indecent . . ."

"We were surprised, too, I assure you. I thought I had done with childbearing. Catherine will be three this year."

"So this one will make—how many?" Elizabeth was always forgetting.

"Sixteen, in all. But I lost two some years ago." Her heart still bled for little Maud and that tiny child who had barely breathed.

"So when is the babe due? When will you need to leave court?"

"In May. I want to have this child at Greys Court. With your permission, I should not tarry here beyond Easter. I am told that childbirth becomes more risky as one gets older."

"Hmm."

Kate had known that Elizabeth would make difficulties.

"I really cannot spare you, yet I know you must go home then. But be back as soon as you are churched."

"Thank you, Bess. I am most grateful for your kindness."

It had been quite easy, this time. Freedom beckoned.

FRANCIS WAS AS proud as a peacock that Kate was expecting again. Despite his advancing years and sober exterior, he rejoiced in this latest proof of his virility.

"I have asked Master van der Meulen to paint your portrait to mark this fine achievement," he told Kate. "He did that wonderful full-length of the Queen, and he has just painted your brother. I was lucky to secure him, as he is in much demand. He doesn't come cheaply, though." He made a rueful face.

When Kate finally sat—or rather, stood—for the artist, it was March, and she had a high belly. She wore a rich black gown edged with white fur and gold embroidery over a white damask kirtle, and a white cap on her head. The gown was parted in the front to show her unlaced stomacher. She had donned a pendant of pearls and diamonds and hung an oval tablet from her gold girdle. It was chased with an image of Francis in his livery as a Gentleman Pensioner.

It took a week for Master van der Meulen to finish his preliminary sketches because Kate could not stand for long periods. She had left court by the time he started work on the painting and did not see it finished until Francis brought it to Greys Court on a flying visit in May.

"What do you think?" he asked, pulling off the wrappings.

There was herself to the life. But there too, unmistakably, was her father, King Henry. The likeness was striking.

She wished that Elizabeth could see it. Confronted with the strong resemblance, she could hardly have failed to make the connection. But maybe one day she would see it, although Kate doubted that, in reality, Elizabeth would ever visit Greys Court.

Francis also brought troubling news. "The Archbishop of Canterbury has ruled on Lady Katherine Grey's marriage," he said, as he and Kate sat up late into the evening that first night, with her newly hung portrait looking down at them from above the hearth in the hall. "Sadly for her, the only witness is dead and the priest could not be traced. So the commissioners pronounced the union null and void and its issue illegitimate. For their unlawful copulation, Katherine and Hertford are sentenced to imprisonment in the Tower at the Queen's pleasure. It is fortunate that her Majesty did not demand the full penalty for treason provided for by law."

"But they will suffer punishment enough," Kate observed. "They are cruelly parted, and Lady Katherine can say farewell to her hopes of being designated the heir to the throne."

"Indeed. There is a certain amount of sympathy for her. Many think her marriage was good and valid, and some say that she and Lord Hertford have been too sharply handled. Others say that if the Queen had done her duty by marrying and producing an heir of her own, the proceedings against these young people would have been unnecessary."

"Ooh," Kate said suddenly, as a dull pain forked through her lower back.

"Are you all right, darling?" Francis asked, instantly concerned.

"I think so," she said. But several minutes later, the pain came again, accompanied by a gush of her waters. "It is begun," she told him. "The babe is coming."

HER CHILD WAS born at half past two the following afternoon. It was a girl. Summoned in to see them both, Francis cradled the swaddled infant, looking down upon her lovingly. "I think we should call her Dudley, as a compliment to Lord Robert. It will please the Queen greatly."

"Dudley? But that's a boy's name, surely? Or, rather, a surname."

"Darling, where have you been hiding? It is the fashion to give such names to girls. The Howards called one of their daughters Douglas. Someone else I know called one of their girls Parnell. Dudley suits our little one, do you not agree?"

"If it is your pleasure," Kate said, glad only to have emerged from her travail with a baby safely delivered.

So Dudley it was. The Queen was delighted to hear the news, and the name, and offered to be godmother, a great honor; she sent three more gold basins as a gift for the child, and money as a reward for the midwife. And Elizabeth Tailboys, Countess of Warwick, Lord Robert's sister-in-law, agreed to stand as the other godmother. She was the daughter of Bessie Blount, who had borne King Henry his bastard son, the Duke of Richmond, and when she arrived for the christening, it was plain to see that Bessie had also borne his late Majesty a daughter. We are sisters, Kate thought, amazed. Yet she said nothing. It would not have been appropriate.

Two weeks after the christening, Kate became aware that little Dudley was not thriving. She was small and unenthusiastic about taking her milk. The wet nurse was in despair; none of her efforts made any difference. Kate took a clean cloth dipped in cow's milk and put it to her baby's rosebud lips. At last, the child responded, so she handed her to the nurse to be suckled, then lay there watching until she was satisfied that the babe was getting the nourishment she needed.

Greatly relieved, she found herself desperate for sleep, so that night, the nurse offered to take Dudley into her own bed to keep her warm and feed her when she needed it.

"Yes," Kate agreed. "If she cries, I will come and take her in with me."

In the morning, she and Francis were aroused by the nurse's frantic screams. Barely awake, they leaped out of bed and ran to the nursery. The woman was howling her heart out. She could only point to the bed. And there lay the little babe, white as marble.

"You have killed her!" Francis wailed. "You overlaid her!"

"No!" cried the nurse, beating her breast. "I woke early and was sitting up in the chair, watching over her. She seemed normal.

Then . . ." She gulped. "Then I noticed a change in her breathing—and almost immediately, she wasn't breathing anymore." She broke down again, sobbing.

Kate felt numb. As a mother, she should have seen the danger signs. But last night, she had put her need for sleep first and given her child to a stranger to be warmed and comforted. If she had kept Dudley herself, the child would have departed this life secure in her mother's love. *But I was not there.* The knowledge tortured her. "It's not your fault," she whispered to the nurse. "It is God's will."

She turned to Francis and threw herself against his breast, clinging to him as to a life raft. "Our little girl is dead!" she wailed. "Oh, God, how will I bear it? How will I live?"

He held her wordlessly, bleakly, devastated in his misery. "I am sorry," he said at length, to the nurse, speaking over Kate's head. "Leave now. I will send your money. My wife and I would be alone to take our powerful sorrow together."

THE DAYS PASSED in a fog of misery. Kate carried out her daily tasks, even when she could hardly stand as she rose from her bed in the mornings. The little body was prepared for burial and tied in its shroud. When the day came, it was laid in the vault Francis was having constructed in the aisle of the church. Maud was there, and Kate caught a glimpse of her tiny form, shrunken to skeletal proportions inside its winding sheet. She caught her breath and looked away, clinging to Francis as this other little one was laid to rest. The tears kept coming and coming. This could not be happening. Her empty arms ached for her child. She had nothing to give Anne, Thomas, and Catherine, the three who most needed her. There they stood, solemn in their black garments, bewildered by the tragedy that had befallen them. How hard it had been to explain to Catherine what death meant, and that Dudley was never coming back.

"She is with God now," she'd said. "He is looking after her."

And that was just what the vicar was saying. "Jesus said, 'In my Father's house are many mansions'; there is room for everybody.

You must not worry about Dudley anymore. She is in God's care." His face was filled with compassion.

Kate took that comforting thought away with her.

She functioned. She ran her household. She cried in private, in the arms of Francis, and then Thomasina, when he had to return to court. But her heart was in that vault, with the precious dust that lay therein.

Elizabeth wrote, sending heartfelt condolences. "I desire to give all the comfort I can to you, but was loath to have written at all because the offering of sympathy can be but a fresh occasion for sorrow. Yet I wish to assure you that whatever comfort I can minister to you, I shall not fail to give." It was one of the most moving letters the Queen had ever sent Kate. But the court and all its intrigues seemed far away.

Kate could not stop tormenting herself. Again and again, she went over Dudley's last hours, asking herself if she should have known what was about to happen. She tried to remember the last time she had kissed her baby, the last words she had said to her, but the memories eluded her. What was almost worse was thinking that Dudley had lived in vain. What had it all been for, those months of pregnancy followed by the pain of her birthing? *No!* she told herself. *I will not believe that she had no purpose in this world. Children bring love, and if that is all they do in the short time allowed them, then they have lived worthwhile lives.*

Another letter arrived from the Queen, saying that it would do Kate good to return to court, take her mind off her loss. But Kate could not face returning.

Francis had had to resume his duties. He had been elected Knight of the Shire for Oxfordshire and had to sit in Parliament, too. He found solace in his work, but he had been loath to leave Kate.

"I will be all right," she assured him, and kept herself busy. Music was her salvation. She had always loved it, but after Dudley died, she could not face playing a note. Then one day, she took up her lute and made herself strum it. It was easier than she had anticipated, even if the melody brought tears to her eyes. That day, she realized that she would heal. It would be a slow process, and she was not yet ready for the outside world, but she began to give her attention to her children again and was rewarded by seeing them happy and loving toward her, relieved to have their mother back. God, she told herself, had been good to her. He had sent her sixteen children and taken only three to Himself. She was blessed indeed, for she knew of other mothers of large families who had fewer than half their broods left to them.

Elizabeth bestowed several more grants of property jointly on Francis and Kate, in reward for their good service. It was an inducement to go back to court. Certainly, it was an honor for her, as the Queen's kinswoman (as she was styled in the documents), to be included in grants to her husband. She wondered if it was a tacit recognition of the secret bond between her and Elizabeth, but Francis thought it was largely a reminder of where she ought to be and that the Queen was prepared to be generous to get what she wanted.

It did not matter. Kate still could not face the court. Grief made her feel fragile. She found that she was living as two people. One was outwardly carrying on with life, finding pleasure in things and even laughing; the other was mired in sadness, longing hopelessly for that which she could never have again.

Elizabeth sent increasingly impatient letters demanding that Kate return to court, but Kate repeatedly sent her excuses, pleading that she was not yet herself and that she was struggling to face life. She prayed that her dearest cousin would understand.

The next she heard was that Elizabeth was ill.

"It is smallpox," Kat wrote. "We are all praying for her recovery."

Kate's instinct was to go to Elizabeth, but Francis forbade it. "Are you mad?" he wrote. "Smallpox is highly contagious, and it can kill. At the very least, it can leave you scarred for life. You must think of yourself and the children. The best you can do for the Queen is pray for her."

Kate prayed. She went to the church and told the vicar to ask for the prayers of the congregation. She knelt, alone in the nave that evening, begging God to spare Elizabeth. And all the time, she was aware of those two sleeping angels lying only feet away, and that other little one, at rest in the churchyard. She kissed her hand and laid it on the cold stone that covered them before she began the walk home.

"Your brother has wrought a cure," Kat wrote. "He called in a German physician, and when that physician had given up hope, he made him persevere; Blanche says he showed him the point of a dagger. And now the Queen is recovering. She is weak, but she will soon be well and is planning to depart for Windsor when she is strong enough."

Kate was relieved to hear it. She could not have coped with another bereavement.

IT WAS TRUE what Mother used to say, that when the good Lord closed one door, He opened another. Kate was thrilled to receive a letter from Chartley in which Lettice confided that she was shortly to give birth to her first child. "I wish you could be with me," she had written. "I would give much to have you here. Do come to Chartley for Christmas."

Kate was torn. Francis was expected to be at court for the Yuletide season, but their other children would be at home and looking for her to make Christmas merry for them after all the sadness. Yet Lettice needed her. How would she feel if anything ill befell her and she had not gone to her? It was that which decided her. She would not fail another child.

She explained her position to the nurses and the tutor. Could they make a happy Christmas for the children in her absence? She herself would order the feasts, but could they lay on games and mummings? Yes, of course they could, and willingly. Thomasina immediately began gathering greenery for a kissing ball to hang in the hall. The children could help her to make it.

It pained her to say goodbye to her darlings at such a precious time of year, yet Chartley was calling. She set off two weeks before Christmas to give herself time to cover the hundred and twenty miles to Staffordshire at a steady, undemanding pace.

It was a long journey, and it took her through Oxford, Banbury, and Coventry. Mercifully, the weather was kind, if cold. She spent the nights at inns or great houses, the owners of which were glad to open their doors to the Queen's beloved kinswoman.

Christmas was approaching when Kate sighted Chartley at last. The timbered manor house lay near the massive ruins of the abandoned Chartley Castle, and was adorned with battlements and surrounded by a moat.

Lettice came hastening out to welcome her. It was unsettling to see her daughter, her baby, heavily pregnant. But the girl was radiant with health and happiness. "How are you, Mother? I am so sorry about Dudley. This must have been a terrible year for you."

"It has been hard," Kate admitted, as they went into the hall and servants ran to bring in her luggage. "But it gives me joy to see you, child. Tell me, are you liking married life?"

"Mostly," Lettice said, giving Kate that little-girl sideways glance that had always got her out of trouble when she was younger. "I miss the court—and Walter, er . . . Well, he's a good husband."

Kate was quick to pick up on the pause. "He is attentive?"

"He was. But once he knew I was with child, he backed away."

Kate smiled. "He will return. And you've not got long to wait now."

"I know. The waiting seems endless. Walter is out hunting at the moment, but you will see him when he gets back."

They spent a pleasant Christmas. It was quiet because Lettice did not feel up to entertaining, but Kate relished the peace. The change of scene had done her good. There were no memories of Dudley here, only in her heart, and those she tried to keep buried for her living daughter's sake.

Chapter 39

1563–64

As they exchanged gifts on New Year's day, seated around a crackling fire in the parlor, Kate wondered if Elizabeth was pleased with the fine carpet fringed with silk she had sent her. It was eight months since she had left court and the Queen's letters demanding her return had tailed off. The costly present had been sent to mollify her. She really should go back, she knew. She could not keep wallowing in grief. But first, her daughter needed her.

Lettice's baby came in January. It was a girl whom she called Penelope. Holding the darling little thing, her first grandchild, Kate was struck by her likeness to Dudley. God, it seemed, knew how to fill the empty place in her heart. She felt consumed by love for the child, flesh of her flesh, and when the time came for her to go home, she had to drag herself away and force herself to keep smiling as the litter bore her off. Lettice had promised to visit and that would have to content her. At least the girl had made a speedy recovery and was happy with her baby. And Elizabeth had written to say that she would be godmother, a sure sign that Kate was not out of favor.

When she arrived home at Greys Court, she thought again about returning to court, but she could not face it, not yet. It was wonderful to be back with her children, even though the older boys were away at school or university. She did not want to leave the young ones, did not want to spend another moment apart from them, for she had learned that you could never take them for granted.

When Francis next came home for a visit, Kate showed him the estate and household accounts, and they took a walk around the grounds.

"You have done well," he told her. "I could not run this place so well without you."

"Don't forget Bilkins," she reminded him. "He's not as young as he used to be, but he keeps things going."

"Yes, but I have noticed that he defers to you much more these days."

"Well, I have made it my business to learn about every aspect of household and estate management. I feel it is my duty to know what is going on and what should be happening."

"You're a marvel," he said, bending down and kissing her. "Dame Fortune smiled on me the day I wed you."

In the evening, he told her that the Queen had appointed him governor of Portsmouth.

"I may have to go to France, to Le Havre," he warned her. "Last year, my lord of Warwick was sent to garrison the town and help the Huguenots, the French Protestants who are being oppressed by the government. A while back, they occupied the port of Le Havre. But then they came to terms with the Catholics, and asked Warwick to evacuate Le Havre, whereupon the Queen commanded him to hold it against all comers. He's still there, but the town is under siege by the French. Personally, I think the Queen was wrong. I admire her determination to support the Protestants, but they don't appreciate it. They want Warwick gone."

"So where do you come into this?" Kate did not want to see Francis put into any danger.

"Don't look so worried. One of my duties as governor of Portsmouth will be to see that our garrisons are properly provisioned. I may have to get fresh supplies to Warwick."

"But won't that be at some risk to yourself? Won't the French be patrolling the sea around Le Havre?"

"If they are, we shall evade them. Don't worry, darling. And my services may not be required anyway."

Kate prayed that he was right.

"You've missed all the scandal," he said, changing the subject.

"What scandal?" Kate wanted to know.

"The Queen has been in a bad mood for weeks. Last month, Lady Katherine Grey gave birth to another son in the Tower."

"But I thought she and Lord Hertford were not permitted to see each other?"

"Apparently, the Lieutenant of the Tower was sympathetic. The Queen is absolutely furious. She has given orders that under no circumstances are they to meet again. She had Hertford hauled before the Court of Star Chamber, which found him guilty of having compounded his original offense of having deflowered a virgin of the blood royal by having ravished her a second time. He was heavily fined. The Lieutenant has been dismissed from his post."

"I feel so sorry for them. Imagine how much worse this must be for them if they were lawfully married."

"But they cannot prove it. To be frank, they have both been unbelievably foolish."

"I hope her children have not been taken from her. That would be the worst thing."

"No, they are still with her in the Tower. She is comfortably housed there and has her own servants. She is lucky to have kept her head."

Kate shivered. She doubted that Katherine had had the brains to foresee where her actions might lead her.

IN JUNE, FRANCIS wrote to say that the Queen was sending him to Le Havre with provisions and wages for Warwick's forces. "Fear not," he concluded. "I will be back soon."

It was one of the longest fortnights in Kate's life. She was beside herself with anxiety, not knowing what was happening with him.

Constantly, she was on the alert for a messenger bringing news—or, Heaven forbid, a body broken in warfare. In the end, it was no messenger who came, but Francis himself.

"It was as easy as shelling peas," he told Kate, after she had thrown herself at him in a passionate embrace. "We got the supplies to them. There was no sign of the French at sea. But the army at Le Havre is suffering terrible privations, plague, and sickness; the soldiers are in a weakened state and not likely to hold the town if pressed. I was glad to get away. I pity my lord of Warwick; his is a thankless task."

"I trust the Queen is pleased that your mission was successful," Kate said, as she poured wine into two goblets.

"I think so. You never know with her. She was asking for you, though, wanted to know when you'll be returning to court. I said I did not know, but that I would ask you. She was quite considerate. She said it would do you a power of good to be occupied in her service, for it would take your mind off things."

"I am fully occupied here. I don't want to go back to court."

"I don't think you have a choice," Francis said gently. "The Queen will not be patient forever. And life must go on." Their eyes met. She could see the grief in his, yet he had been braver than she had. He had got on with things, done what he was supposed to do.

"Very well," she said. "I will not risk disfavor falling upon us. I will do my duty."

WHEN SHE FINALLY returned to the court at Greenwich Palace that month, Elizabeth received her warmly with hugs and kisses, and the other ladies seemed genuinely delighted that she was back among them. And there too, to her great pleasure, was Dot Stafford, newly appointed Mistress of the Robes.

"She is a good friend and kinswoman," Elizabeth told her. "I love her for that, and for my Uncle Stafford's sake."

Feeling quite emotional, Kate walked in the gardens with Dot. They had much catching-up to do, exchanging news about their families.

"You know, I still think it is marvelous to have the freedom to worship as I please," Dot said. "I will never forget the terror of Mary's reign. We have a world of blessings in Queen Elizabeth."

"Amen to that," Kate said, wishing that, in her case, they did not come at so high a price. Already, she was missing her children, missing the gentle pace of life at Greys Court, missing the still, small form that lay in the church. No, she would not let herself dwell on that. Dudley was with God, and she herself must move forward.

KATE SOON REALIZED that Elizabeth had not mentioned Lady Katherine Grey. She was preoccupied with the affairs of her other troublesome cousin, the Queen of Scots.

"Mary is negotiating a marriage with Don Carlos, King Philip's son," she told her ladies as they sat in the park enjoying a picnic, which was spread out on a great damask cloth before them. There were roast meats, great wheels of cheese, salads, and new bread, heavily buttered. "I do not see such a marriage as being in England's interests. We don't want the Spanish at our back door. What I would like to see is Mary married to a loyal Englishman."

"But who?" Kat asked.

Elizabeth signed to Kate's daughter Beth to bring more wine and chuckled. "Lord Robert Dudley," she announced. "I have pondered the matter for some time and discovered that I quite like the idea."

It was Kat who found her voice first. "But he is *your* favorite, Bess. You see him every day. There is clearly much love between you. You would miss him if he went to live in Scotland."

And, thought Kate, you are already inordinately jealous of Queen Mary, and this would only make things worse.

"Besides," Kat said, and then paused.

"Yes?" Elizabeth was frowning at her.

"I was going to say that the Queen of Scots might not take kindly to the suggestion that she marry your Master of the Horse," Kat said.

"But you would have had me marry him myself," Elizabeth said quietly.

Kat lowered her eyes. "Is Lord Robert keen?" she asked at length.

"Whether he is or not is immaterial. No, he is not keen. He doesn't want to leave England for a land of barbarians, as he thinks of the Scots, and he doesn't want to leave me, for he still cherishes hopes of marrying me. Yet he will do as I ask. I know I can count on his cooperation."

Kate felt rather sorry for Lord Robert, forced into a situation from which there was no retreat. He must be praying that this was just another of Elizabeth's mercurial whims and that by next week, she would have thought up some other scheme.

THE PLAGUE CAME to London that summer, as it often did when the weather was hot. When a case was reported in the Tower, the Queen left the capital and sent Katherine Grey and Lord Hertford into the country, there to be kept separately under house arrest until she decided what was to be done with them.

Meanwhile, with Warwick at the limits of his endurance, Elizabeth sanctioned the surrender of Le Havre. Early in July, Francis was again sent to Portsmouth with orders for victuals and other provisions for the army. And there he remained throughout that month and for the greater part of August, much to Kate's annoyance. She felt even angrier when he wrote describing the difficulties he was having in sending supplies for the stranded troops. It sounded as if he was facing an impossible task.

In his next letter, he informed her that he was shortly to cross to Le Havre again to convey the Queen's instructions for the withdrawal of her troops. After that, his duties would take him to the Channel Islands and the Isle of Wight. Kate wondered when she would see him again. She had to wait until September, when they managed three days together at Syon House. It was like being newlyweds again.

AT NEW YEAR 1564, Kate received a gift of silk stockings from Katherine Grey, who had never given her anything before. She took them straight to the Queen.

"Hah!" Elizabeth said, fingering the fine silk. "She is hoping to persuade you to intercede for her. In case you are contemplating it, Kate, it will be a waste of breath. She does not deserve your sympathy." She went on gleefully opening her own presents, unwrapping plate, gloves, items of clothing, and jewels.

Kate wished she could take similar pleasure in the exchange of gifts, but she was missing her children, not having been allowed to go home for Christmas. At least Beth was with her, she thought, as she watched her daughter setting out the Queen's gifts on trestle tables.

Life at court resumed its normal course. She found the routine stifling, day after day, and there was little that interested her. She seemed to spend a lot of her time wishing that she was somewhere else.

In March, she and Francis managed to get away to Greys Court to celebrate her fortieth birthday together.

"You look just like the sixteen-year-old maid I married," he complimented her, as they sat in the great hall toasting the occasion, with their children around them.

"Go on with you," she ribbed him, but her heart swelled with joy to know that he saw her that way. And as they went indoors, hand in hand, she understood it, because although his hair was graying and receding, and his face was worn by cares, she could still see in him the young man with whom she had fallen in love.

IN APRIL, QUEEN Mary sent an envoy, Sir James Melville, to the English court to discuss the mooted marriage with Lord Robert. Elizabeth had not given up the idea, but had persisted in pushing it, like a dog with a rag, much to Robert's evident fury. But Kate did not believe she would ever let him go. She kept him as close to her as ever and acted like a woman in love.

Mary, in turn, was playing Cupid.

"She has sent with Sir James a proposal of marriage from Count John Casimir, the son of the Elector Palatine, with his portrait," Elizabeth told Kate one evening, when they were alone. "By God, have you seen him?" She held up the miniature. "He has a face like a squashed turnip. Kate, I need you to speak in confidence to Sir James. Tell him that I will never marry because I know myself incapable of bearing children, and because I will never render myself subject to a man." That rang true, of course, but . . .

Kate had to ask. "Do you know for certain that you cannot bear a child?"

"It would seem so," Elizabeth replied. She was being evasive, as only she knew how to be.

"Then I will tell him."

Kate approached the envoy at a court banquet as they mingled among the guests. Bending to his ear, she gave him the Queen's message. He looked surprised.

"I am sorry to hear it. May I tell my mistress that, failing any issue of her body, she will be named her Majesty's successor?"

"I know nothing of that," Kate said quickly, knowing that to say more would be to venture into perilous waters. Fortunately, Melville did not press her.

THAT SUMMER, KATE was delighted to hear that Lettice had borne a second daughter, whom she had named Dorothy. The promised visit had never happened, so she vowed to herself that she would go to Chartley as soon as she could. But when she approached Elizabeth to ask for leave, she was informed, yet again, that she could not be spared. She could not even get away to Greys Court to bid farewell and good luck to Richard and Frank when they went up to Oxford in September, or to Hal, when he entered Gray's Inn to start his training as a lawyer. But at least Francis and Beth were at court. Thankfully, Francis had not been sent abroad again.

At the end of September, Elizabeth created Dudley Earl of Leicester in a splendid ceremony in the presence chamber at St. James's Palace. She told her ladies that she was raising him to the peerage in order to make him a more fitting husband for Queen Mary. Kate was among the glittering throng of courtiers who witnessed the solemn occasion. The new Earl conducted himself with the utmost gravity and dignity, so Kate was shocked—

and she could see that others were, too—when she saw Elizabeth smilingly tickle his neck as she invested him with the collar of his earldom and his ermine-lined mantle. So much for her repeated assertions that she looked upon him as merely a brother and best friend, as she'd been calling him ever since she had suggested him as a husband for the Queen of Scots.

After the ceremony was over, Kate was standing near the Queen when she spoke with Melville.

"How do you like my new creation?" she asked him.

Melville bowed his head in assent. It was no secret that the Dudley marriage was unpopular in Scotland.

Elizabeth laughed and pointed to a tall, beautiful young man who was acting as her sword-bearer. It was Lord Darnley, the son of her cousin Margaret Douglas and the Earl of Lennox. "I think you prefer yonder long lad!"

Melville gazed distastefully at the effeminate-looking youth. "No woman of spirit would choose such a man. He is more like a woman, for he is beardless and lady-faced."

"Ah, but he is lusty," Elizabeth countered, "and he has a claim to my throne. I do believe that, given the slightest encouragement, he would marry your Queen."

Melville was looking increasingly uncomfortable.

"There is no need to look so worried," Elizabeth trilled. "I will never let Darnley go north to Scotland while my newly created Earl of Leicester is finding favor with Queen Mary. I do assure you that I am sincere in my desire for their marriage."

Was she? Kate asked herself. It was hard to believe, but although Elizabeth often changed her mind on a daily basis, much to the exasperation of Francis, Cecil, and her other councillors, in this matter she had stood constant for months.

IN EARLY DECEMBER, the court moved to Whitehall for Christmas. The weather was bitter and the Thames froze over. Francis and Kate were among the courtiers who played bowls and skittles on the ice, laughing as they skidded all over the place. But then Elizabeth fell ill with a flux, and became so poorly that her ladies were terrified that she might die. There was no more playtime for Kate, who had to take her turn to sit with her mistress.

It was a relief when the Queen raised herself in the bed and said that she felt better. Even so, it was a quiet Christmas because she was still unwell with bad catarrh and a slight fever. She complained of pains in the stomach and all over her body, and spent the long hours reading in her dark, stuffy bedchamber. Kate and the others were obliged to attend her. Kate thought she would go mad at being confined for so long. She barely had a chance to see Francis because Elizabeth was peevish and would not excuse her, even for an hour. The only time she had to herself was in bed at night.

Chapter 40

1565

By new year's day, the queen was better, well enough to take pleasure in her gifts, nodding her appreciation as each one was presented to her by Blanche Parry, who had been made Keeper of the Jewels. Elizabeth paid Kate special thanks for the six handkerchiefs edged with gold, silver, and silk thread that she had made herself.

The ceremony over, Kate at last had time to see Francis. She found him in the White Hall, talking to some of his fellow councillors. He left them and joined her, and they walked around a cloister, looking out on the frosted grass of the lawn.

"It has been too long," Kate said, leaning on his arm. "I could not get away."

"Thank Providence that the Queen is restored to health, and not just for our sake," he said, pulling her closer to him. "We have been very worried about what would happen if she was taken from us. We'd have Katherine Grey and the Queen of Scots pressing their claims. It could lead to war."

"Heaven forbid! But she is well now."

"Aye, and the Scots seem keen at last for their Queen to marry Leicester."

But, inexplicably, Elizabeth had just changed her mind.

"The Queen of Scots has requested that Lord Darnley be sent to Scotland," she announced to her ladies as they sat talking in her privy chamber. She still looked thin and tired after her brush with death, which made her look old beside the fresh young beauty of Beth and her other maids.

"And you are letting him go?" Kat asked, astonished.

"I think I will," she replied.

"I thought you said you would never send him to Scotland," Kate had to say.

"It is just a courtesy visit," Elizabeth replied. "He has business of his father's to attend to."

Kate held her tongue. The Queen was no fool; they all knew perfectly well why he was going. He wanted to marry the Queen of Scots.

Elizabeth smiled. "I have my reasons for allowing him to go."

As she led her ladies in to supper, she murmured in Kate's ear, "If I give Queen Mary enough rope, she will hang herself. He is a nasty, vicious boy who will seize her crown if she lets him."

Kate felt a chill come over her. She had a strong presentiment that something very bad would come of this.

SHE WAS PRESENT when Melville saw the Queen and told her that his mistress planned to marry Lord Darnley. "It was an immediate attraction, Madam. Her Majesty tried to control her feelings, but she has become so enamored of Lord Darnley that she cannot bear to be apart from him."

Elizabeth smiled sweetly. "I am pleased to hear of her happiness. Yet I am not pleased with my subject Lord Darnley, who has gone north to Scotland in direct contravention of my command. He shall be hearing from me about this."

Kate stared at her. Oh, she was playing a clever game, for the truth was very much otherwise. She had fully intended for Darnley to go north, calculating that Mary would find him beguiling, and had effectively set the fox on the hen. Melville looked completely nonplussed, as well he might.

Kate was more preoccupied with the marriage of her eldest son, Hal. Twenty-four that April, he was to wed one of Elizabeth's maids-of-honor, a sweet girl called Margaret, the only child and heiress of the very wealthy Sir Ambrose Cave, Chancellor of the Duchy of Lancaster. Kate knew and liked Sir Ambrose, who chivalrously wore a yellow garter on his arm in honor of the Queen, who had dropped one while dancing.

Elizabeth was fond of Hal, not least, she said, because he was Kate's son. "He is a fine young man," she declared, "and I hold him in the highest esteem. I shall attend his wedding."

It was a great honor, but Kate felt under even more pressure now to ensure that the day would go smoothly. The nuptials were to be solemnized at Durham House on the Strand, and she was anxious that everything would be perfect. But two weeks beforehand, she fell ill with stomach pains and had to take to her bed.

"This malady is the last thing I need," she told Elizabeth when the Queen visited her, bringing a bowl of cherries. "I don't know what's wrong with me. I have a flux and my belly hurts."

"I will send for Dr. Huicke," Elizabeth decided. He was the Queen's own physician. "We must have you well again for the wedding."

Kate felt relieved. With so much yet to arrange, she could not be lying here in bed.

Francis was with her, summoned by the Queen, when the doctor came. He asked her some questions, tested her water, and prescribed some physick. To her huge relief, she was soon up and about. Elizabeth embraced her warmly when she returned to her duties.

"It is thanks to you and Dr. Huicke that I am well again," Kate told her.

THE GREAT DAY came. Kate wore a new gown of ash-colored satin trimmed with gold, with a quilted cap and a white veil.

"You look beautiful," Francis complimented her, as they descended the stairs to the state rooms to check that everything was in place. She smiled and reached for his hand.

Downstairs, the guests were gathering: it was wonderful to see all their children together, for once. There they stood, a shining group in their finery, with family members and numerous courtiers, among them Cecil and Mildred, and Leicester, as they had learned to call him, who was dressed as magnificently as a king. There had been so much competition among foreign ambassadors for invitations that instructions had had to be issued asking them all to refrain from approaching the Queen when she appeared, lest sensitive matters of precedence cause offense to the rest.

Hal looked dashing in his new suit of white satin, and the little bride was a picture of loveliness in her crimson-and-gold gown, with her long straw-colored hair cascading down her back. After Margaret had made her entrance on her father's arm, the Queen arrived, attended by most of the great ladies of the court, and the ceremony began. Kate wiped away a tear to see her son married, remembering him as a little boy in leading strings with an engaging smile and long skirts. It seemed such a short time ago. He was a big, broad-shouldered man now, but the winning smile was still there, and it was a joy to see his new wife looking up at him so radiantly.

After the wedding came the bridal supper with a lavish array of tempting dishes. That was followed by a masque depicting Hymen, the god of marriage. As it was being performed, Kate saw Leicester looking meaningfully at the Queen, but she tapped him with her fan and kept her eyes glued to the players. Afterward, there was dancing, then a thrilling tournament in the grounds, ordered specially by Elizabeth, which was a rare honor. In the evening, the feasting began. The celebrations went on until half past one in the morning, by which time Kate was ready to drop. But the bride and groom had yet to be put to bed, and she was pulled along by the other laughing ladies to prepare her daughter-in-law, while Francis and Sir Ambrose went off to clothe Hal in his nightgown. Amid bawdy jests, the young couple were helped into bed and the guests stifled their mirth as the Queen's chaplain blessed the nuptial couch and prayed that the pair be fruitful.

"To your duty, son Knollys!" roared Sir Ambrose.

"May God be with you both," said Francis, much more on his dignity, firmly ushering the company out of the bedchamber. Yet he quickly shed it when he and Kate were finally alone. Pulling her into his arms, he tumbled her on the bed. "I am remembering our own wedding night," he murmured. "You look as alluring now as you did then . . ."

THE NEXT DAY, when Kate arrived in Elizabeth's bedchamber for the dressing ritual, she found the other ladies there, but not Kat. Elizabeth looked worried.

"Kat is not well. She has taken to her bed."

Kat had been ill a few weeks earlier, but had since recovered, or so it seemed. No one had thought that it was anything serious.

"What's the matter?" Kate asked.

"A fever," Elizabeth said distractedly. "It came on in the night. I've sent for Dr. Huicke."

As soon as she was dressed, Elizabeth went to sit at Kat's bedside.

"She has loved her like a mother," Blanche said, folding the Queen's night rail.

"And Kat has looked after her like a mother," Kate added. "She has been with her for most of her life."

Later that morning, she peered around the door of Kat's chamber. Kat was sleeping, but she was restless. Elizabeth raised a tragic face. "I don't like the look of her. She's burning up." She touched Kat's forehead. "She has too much yellow bile."

"What did Dr. Huicke say?"

"He said that the fever must run its course. He has prescribed her some feverfew, but she will not take it."

Kat seemed a little better that night. "She is sleeping more peacefully and Blanche is sitting with her," Elizabeth said. "I feel I can go to bed now."

Kate was woken the next morning by Blanche shaking her, looking distraught. "I can't wake Kat! I watched over her all night and she was very restless, but within this last hour, her breathing changed and now she lies unmoving. I fear she has gone from us."

Kate struggled out of bed, pulled on her night-robe, and hastened after Blanche. Yes, there lay Kat, peaceful and still. Her eyes were open, but only the whites were showing. The two women closed them, folded her arms over her breast, and said a short prayer for her, then reluctantly departed to break the news to Elizabeth.

"No!" the Queen cried. "It cannot be true! God would not be so cruel as to take her from me."

She insisted on seeing the body, at the sight of which she sank to the floor, wailing. "She was like a mother to me, a loyal friend and devoted servant. She loved me for myself. Life will never be the same again. I have lost a confidante, someone who loved me for myself and dared to reprove me when she thought it necessary. How will I ever forgive myself?" She broke down again.

"Bess, you could not have known that she was going to die," Kate said soothingly, kneeling down beside her and pressing her to her bosom. "We all thought that she was beginning to recover."

Elizabeth just knelt there, sobbing, clutching at Kat's dead hand. When they finally persuaded her to leave, she walked unsteadily back to her bedchamber, weeping bitterly. It was days before she could face dealing with state affairs. She ordered that the court observe mourning and had herself dressed in deepest black, her only jewelry being a locket with Kat's likeness in it.

"You shall replace her," she told Kate. "You shall be my Chief Lady of the Bedchamber."

"I am truly honored," Kate said, although she was grieving for the friend whose shoes she had to fill, and knew that this new post would entail more personal sacrifices on her part. "I hope I shall follow well in such worthy footsteps."

"You know I love you above all others," Elizabeth said, gripping her hand.

"I know that, and I am sensible of the honor you do me."

"I shall entrust you with the safekeeping of all the gifts I receive. And you shall have gifts of your own a-plenty."

Elizabeth was as good as her word. She showed her favor by giving Kate the most expensive presents she had ever given anyone—sumptuous gowns, jewels, a painting by an Italian master. But in the wake of Kat's death, she grew more possessive than ever, wanting Kate at her side all the time, even at night.

"I need you with me," she told her, squeezing her hand. "I've lost Kat, but I have you and I cannot be without you."

Kate felt desperate. How could she try to get away when Elizabeth was grieving and needed her? She could not be so heartless.

She sent a note to Francis, asking him to meet her in the privy garden that evening. Leicester was coming to have supper with the Queen and she could get out of the palace. When she saw him, she hugged him tightly, then told him of her predicament. "There is nothing I can do. We just have to be patient. But when I think of the children, how fast they are growing up, and how precious our time together is, I could weep." Suddenly, she was actually weeping. "I have always thought it a great unkindness in the Queen to be blind to my needs. Yet she is devastated by Kat's death. What can I do?"

Francis held her to him, gentling her. "How long will she be at supper with my Lord of Leicester?"

"Two hours, maybe longer."

"Then come with me to my lodging. Let us be together and shut the world out for that time."

BY AUGUST, ELIZABETH was back in harness, but still mourning Kat deeply, as was Kate, who had not been permitted a single visit home in recent weeks. Then there came a day when the Queen's anger overcame her lethargy.

"Are those Grey sisters always to plague me?" she shouted, crashing into her privy chamber after a council meeting. "It's Crookback Mary this time." Lady Mary was Katherine Grey's younger sister; she was pretty, but with her short stature and the hump on her back, no one had expected her to find a husband, even if the Queen ever permitted her to marry. "She's only gone and wed my Serjeant-Porter, Master Keyes!" Elizabeth seethed. "He's twice as old and twice as tall—and he's no match for *my cousin*!"

Kate was shocked. For Mary Grey to throw herself away on a servant was appalling—had she no sense of her place in this world? And yet she could understand the young woman's frustration at being condemned to a life of spinsterhood.

"How did this come to light?" she asked.

"Lady Mary came and confessed to me. She said they were secretly married one night in his lodging at Whitehall. Neither will reveal the identity of the priest. Well, they are now paying for their foolishness. I've sent Master Keyes to the Fleet Prison, and he has been told that he will only be released if he undertakes never to see Mary again. I tried to get the Bishop of London to declare the marriage unlawful, but he refused. He will pay for that! I've sent Mary to Chequers in Buckinghamshire under house arrest."

Kate felt a surge of sympathy. Elizabeth had been far too harsh. The marriage posed no threat to her. She could not seriously imagine Lady Mary ever plotting to steal her crown, and the man she had married was a commoner of no rank. They had not committed treason. All they had done was fall in love. Elizabeth had certainly overreacted, and the draconian punishments she had meted out to them were an indication of how sensitive she had become regarding the succession.

That issue raised its ugly head again in the summer, when news came that Queen Mary had married Darnley—much to Leicester's evident relief. Elizabeth affected to be furious, but when she heard that the Scottish Protestant lords had risen in rebellion against the marriage, Kate saw her smile fleetingly. This, she realized, was just what the Queen had intended.

Elizabeth fell out with Leicester that August—Kate had no idea what it was about, but she saw that the Queen was determined to have her revenge, watching as she flirted outrageously with one of his friends, Sir Thomas Heneage, a handsome, married courtier. He was a young man of pleasant wit and elegant bearing, who could have been born for the court, but he was no match for Elizabeth's wiles: he was putty in her hands and fawned after her like a puppy. Leicester made no secret of his jealousy, but Kate took little notice, for Walter had brought a very pregnant Lettice to court. She was overjoyed to see her daughter and hear news of her granddaughters.

Lettice's beauty was the subject of many admiring comments. People were still saying that she was one of the best-looking ladies at court. But Kate was not pleased when Leicester began blatantly flirting with her, when clearly it was only in retaliation against the Queen. It was most unseemly, pursuing a married woman who was heavy with her husband's child. Yet Lettice seemed to be enjoying his attentions.

Elizabeth was enraged. After seeing Leicester take Lettice's hand and bring it to his lips—in *her* privy chamber, if you please, in full view of her courtiers—she flew into a temper. "What do you think you are doing, my lord? Have you no respect for your sovereign?"

He glared at her. "I might ask what you think you're doing, playing the coy maiden with that idiot Heneage!"

"Oh, jealous, are we?" she retorted. "God's death, my lord, I have wished you well, but my favor is not so vested in you that others shall not enjoy it, too. And if you think to rule here, think again, for I will have but one mistress and no master."

Leicester visibly quailed before her. Suitably admonished, he shut himself in his apartments for the next few days. But Elizabeth backed down, too. Heneage was sent quietly from the court. Cecil persuaded the angry pair to make it up and Elizabeth summoned Leicester to her presence. When he came out, Kate saw that he had been weeping. But they were now reconciled, and all was sweetness and light between them.

Behind Elizabeth's back, however, Leicester continued to court Lettice.

Francis, who had thought their flirtation to be over, was outraged. "Let him rut on his own turf, not mine," he fumed. "I shall have to speak to him. Where's her husband in this?"

Kate tackled Lettice one day, as they strolled down by the river, out of earshot of the other courtiers. "People are talking about you and my lord of Leicester."

"It's just a flirtation, Mother, nothing more." Lettice smiled her sweet smile. "What more can there be, with me in my condition?"

"I should hope there would be nothing anyway!" Kate retorted, tart. "I will not have it said that my daughter is of loose morals. You are making a public spectacle of yourself."

"It's just a bit of fun, that's all!" Lettice's voice rose in pitch, just as it had when she was little and thwarted of something she wanted.

"What has your husband to say about it?"

"I doubt he has noticed." The slanted eyes became downcast.

Kate was instantly concerned. "Is all well between you?"

"Things could be better. I wish that Walter was more exciting, but he's not unkind. He's just so occupied with estate affairs and military matters. I wish he would spend more time with me."

"I'm sure that a lot of wives feel as you do," Kate said, her heart sinking. "But there are ways in which you can divert him. All men like to be flattered, and he would be pleased to know how much you love him, I'm sure."

Lettice turned troubled eyes to her. "But Mother, I don't. I thought I did at first, but I don't really know what love is."

"You will not find it with Leicester," Kate said sharply. "It is your duty to love your husband, and with time it will become your pleasure, I am sure."

She left it there. It was not her place to interfere between husband and wife, and Lettice did not seem unduly unhappy. The Leicester flirtation would soon be resolved because she and her husband would shortly be leaving court for Herefordshire, in good time for the birth. No real harm had been done.

Observing Leicester, however, Kate sensed a change in him. His relationship with the Queen was evolving; the heady passion of love had mellowed, and with it clearly also his conviction that she would eventually marry him. There was no doubt that he still loved her—he was not entirely self-seeking—but his feelings for her now seemed to be those of a long-wedded husband for his wife. Kate worried, though, that he would look elsewhere for the fulfillment he could not find with her. Well, he would not find it with her daughter!

THAT AUTUMN, WILLIAM and Edward entered the Middle Temple to begin their legal training, while Frank was admitted as a student to Gray's Inn, where Hal was still studying. Kate and Francis were so proud of their sons and pleased that they had all opted for the law.

They spent the season at Windsor, where Elizabeth mostly occupied herself with riding and hunting. She tired everybody out and put her ladies to shame.

"There is more work than pleasure in this for us," Kate complained to Dot, returning from an endless day spent cantering around the Great Park in search of deer.

In the middle of November, she was delighted to hear that Lettice had presented her husband with a son and heir, whom they had named Robert. As soon as she could get away, she promised herself, she would ride north to see her grandson. But that was a big if, for the Queen was as demanding as ever and hated Kate to be away from her. She now spoke very tartly of Lettice, so it was best not to mention her name.

Chapter 41

1566–67

KATE WAS STILL AT COURT FOR THE NEW YEAR CELEBRATIONS. Elizabeth showed her appreciation by giving her a tablet of gold set with diamonds and rubies, and a pearl pendant. The other ladies got gilt pots. There was no doubting whom the Queen loved the best. Five days later, Beth was promoted to the post of Gentlewoman of the Privy Chamber, which meant that Kate would see her more often. Beth was sixteen now, a pretty girl with red curls framing her face and a winning manner. Soon, Francis said, they would have to find her a husband.

In March, there came the most shocking news from Scotland. There had been a lot of gossip about Queen Mary's marriage to Darnley, which had all but broken down. It was no secret that Darnley was jealous of Mary and that he wanted to seize power for himself, despite being hated in Scotland. Nevertheless, she was pregnant with his child. Talk had filtered through to England of her increasing reliance on her Italian secretary, David Rizzio. Some said that he was her lover and had even fathered her baby.

Kate was alone with Elizabeth in her bedchamber when a letter bearing Mary's seal was brought to her. She watched the Queen's frown deepen as she read it, heard her draw in her breath.

Elizabeth turned to her. "Rizzio has been murdered," she said.

"By whom?" Kate was aghast.

"There was a conspiracy," the Queen said. "Some armed lords burst in on Mary as she was dining in private with Rizzio and one of her ladies. Darnley was sitting with them, and he jumped up and joined in with the lords when they jostled the Queen aside and attacked Rizzio, who clung to her skirts, screaming for justice. But he was dragged away and savagely murdered. His body was found pierced with fifty-six dagger wounds. They kept the Queen at bay by pointing a pistol at her belly."

Kate's hand had flown to her mouth. "The poor lady. She must have been terrified."

"Laying violent hands on an anointed sovereign is a shocking thing," observed Elizabeth, shuddering. "And they shut her up in her rooms with Darnley. It took her two days to convince him of the likelihood that they would murder him next. He was frightened witless and blurted out the names of all who had taken part in the killing of Rizzio. Mary is certain that the plot was aimed at her, that the lords had hoped to bring on a miscarriage, that she might die in childbirth, and that Darnley had plotted with them to make him king in her place. As if they would have let him rule, the fool!"

"Is she still a captive?"

"No. She writes that, with the help of the loyal Earl of Bothwell, she and Darnley managed to escape from Holyrood Palace and rode through the night for Bothwell's castle at Dunbar. Her letter is dated there. She is doing her best to raise an army. Kate, I must leave you, for I must see my councillors."

Bit by bit, news filtered south. Queen Mary had raised an army and marched back to Edinburgh, only to find that the conspirators had fled the city. She was now estranged from Darnley and excluding him from all state affairs. "He remains at court; though, heavily watched, I imagine," Elizabeth said, tart.

Kate could not forget that Elizabeth had sent Darnley north. Was this what she had intended? But how could she have predicted that it would happen? She seemed genuinely horrified at how Mary had been treated. She had taken to wearing a miniature of the Scottish Queen suspended from her waist chain. Impassioned, she turned to Kate. "Had I been in Queen Mary's place, I would have taken my husband's dagger and used it to stab him." Kate had no doubt that she would have done it.

She sighed inwardly. Cecil was still hopeful of negotiating a foreign marriage for the Queen, but Mary's experiences would be further proof to Elizabeth of the dangers of wedlock. She would be even more averse to taking a husband after this.

IN APRIL, KATE was unhappy to learn that Francis was being sent to Ireland to control the expenditure of Sir Henry Sidney, the Queen's Lord Deputy, who was trying to repress an Irish rebellion and was much hampered by the interference of influential courtiers at home. Elizabeth had charged Francis to report back on the situation and order Sidney, in her name, to deal promptly with the rebels, to avoid further outlay.

Kate hated it when Francis had to entrust himself to the perils of the sea. She could not sleep for wondering where he was and if he was safe, or imagining storms or the monsters of the deep, in which she did not normally believe. He had told her that he would soon be home, but the days stretched endlessly. When he did come back, to her massive relief, they enjoyed a loving reunion, yet he was clearly troubled.

"Sidney is doing all he can to resolve the situation. He cannot do more, contrary to what the Queen thinks. And tomorrow, I have to tell her that I have commended him for his efforts and told him that no one, least of all her Majesty, would expect him to conduct the campaign on strictly economical lines."

They were lying in each other's arms in their lodging, savoring being close again. It was past midnight, but their peace was suddenly interrupted by some ladies and maids-of-honor, who started shrieking with laughter in the adjoining lodging.

Francis raised himself on one elbow, fuming. "Have they no consideration? They make this racket every night, to my extreme disquiet, though I have often warned them that I will complain to the Queen."

Kate was seized with a sense of mischief. "I have a better idea!

Take off your nightshirt, but put your hose back on." She watched as, looking at her quizzically, he stripped, then pulled up his hose and tied his points.

"Now," she continued, "put on your spectacles and take this." She reached for the copy of Aretino's racy *Dialogues* that they had been reading together earlier. It was a debate between two experienced women about the comparative merits of being a wife, a whore, or a nun; it was explicit, earthy, and not for the fainthearted.

"Go out, knock on their door, and when they answer, pretend you are reading it and enjoying the naughty passages. Let them draw their own conclusions as to your intentions!"

Francis was blushing. "But the world knows I am a faithful husband, and I do not want it bruited that I read Aretino for stimulation."

"They will just think you eccentric, or not quite awake at this late hour," Kate giggled. "I'll wager it will stop them from waking you again. Try it and see!"

He did as she bade him, and she had to admit that he gave a very good impression of a man out on the prowl for sex, like so many of the young court gallants. But then she heard the laughter change to shrieks of dismay, and saw Francis run back into their bedchamber, slamming the door behind him.

"Well, I dare say I posed a sad spectacle and gave them a pitiful fright!" He grinned. "Although I pray that word of this never gets back to the Queen."

"If it does, I'll set her right," Kate said, laughing. "Now take off those hose, dear husband, and come back to bed!"

THAT JUNE, ELIZABETH received word that the Queen of Scots had borne a healthy son and heir, who had been christened James, a name borne by many Scottish kings.

She was pensive that afternoon. Kate and Blanche tried to distract her with cards and music, but her heart was in neither.

"I wonder what gift I should send for the Prince of Scots," she said suddenly.

"Some costly plate?" Blanche suggested.

"A covered cup?" Kate chimed in.

"I will think on it, and on whom I should send to represent me at the baptism. You do both realize that the birth of this child immeasurably strengthens Queen Mary's claim to be my successor. Up until now, her ambitions have been only for herself, but from now on, they will be for her son. I told Melville I was glad to hear the news, but in fact it troubles and saddens me."

"I can understand why it troubles you, Bess, but why feel sad?" Blanche asked.

"Because I am barren."

"But you don't know that," Kate challenged her. She had heard this before.

"I know that I will never have children."

Kate gave up and bent her head to the bonnet she was sewing for her grandson. She knew that nothing she could say would alleviate Elizabeth's fears of marriage and childbirth.

She was glad when August came and the Queen set out from Greenwich for her annual progress. They traveled through Northamptonshire to Stamford, then moved to Oxfordshire and the old palace of Woodstock. Kate was painfully aware that Greys Court lay within a day's ride. When she had suggested that Elizabeth pay her and Francis a visit, the Queen had merely smiled and said there wouldn't be time. Kate was disappointed, for she believed that her mistress would enjoy the peace of Greys Court, and she wanted Elizabeth to see the home she loved, but Francis, who was also accompanying the progress, was relieved that her Majesty had declined.

"It would have ruined us," he said. "When I think of the expense we would have incurred, I shudder."

From Woodstock, the court accompanied the Queen when she rode out in her litter to meet the dons who were waiting to escort her into the City of Oxford, where she received a warm welcome from Leicester, the Chancellor of the University, and from the mayor and aldermen, while the scholars shouted, "*Vivat Regina!*"

She thanked them in Latin, then responded in Greek to a loyal address in that language before attending a service in Christ

Church, where a *Te Deum* was sung. There followed a busy day touring the colleges and listening to public orations, disputations, sermons, lectures, and debates. Then the students acted out a play based on the tale of Palamon and Arcite, which the Queen visibly enjoyed, until the stage collapsed, crushing many people, much to her horror—and Kate's, who could not bear to look, while Francis jumped to obey Elizabeth's order to fetch her own barber-surgeons to help the wounded. Later, they learned that three people had been killed and five injured. The rest of the performance was postponed until the next day, after which Francis received an honorary Master of Arts degree at the hands of Leicester. Then Elizabeth gave a Latin speech she had composed herself, declaring it her wish that learning should prosper. The applause was thunderous. When she left Oxford, the students and university officials ran alongside her litter for two miles beyond the city.

Kate and the rest of the court had been under the impression that Elizabeth would visit Leicester's seat at Kenilworth Castle, and the gossipmongers were certain that it would betoken an imminent announcement of their betrothal

Elizabeth was furious when she heard. "I have no plans to go to Kenilworth," she told her ladies, almost spitting out the words. But the next day, having been closeted for a long time with Leicester the previous evening, she declared that she had changed her mind. So to Kenilworth she went and pronounced herself impressed with all the improvements he had made to the castle. But no announcement followed.

EARLY IN JANUARY 1567, the Queen appointed Francis Treasurer of the Chamber, placing him in charge of payments to England's ambassadors and envoys, and to foreign diplomats. The extra income would be welcome, since he and Kate had so many children to support, but it was a weighty responsibility because the smooth success of Elizabeth's foreign policy would to some extent be dependent on his efficiency. Kate did not doubt that Francis would excel at his new duties. He was shrewd, conscientious, and good with figures.

He got on well with Elizabeth these days, though Kate knew he had a poor opinion of her statesmanship, which he wisely took care to conceal.

"I can only deplore her obstinacy and willfulness," he had confided recently, one night as they sat up late. "I don't fawn on her, like her courtiers do, and I think she likes me for my honesty. I spoke frankly to her the other day. I told her that if she discourages her faithful, godly councillors by not taking their advice when all the passions of her mind are aroused, then I feared that she could not expect them to stand by her."

"And you were talking about . . . ?"

"Her marriage—what else?" he groaned.

TOWARD THE END of February, Kate was sitting with Elizabeth in the closet the Queen used as a study, going over the ladies' and maids' expenses, on which Elizabeth liked to keep a tight rein. They were both swathed in fur-trimmed gowns because the weather was bitterly cold. As Kate got up to add logs to the fire, there was a knock and Cecil came in.

"Your Majesty, you should see this. It is from your agents in Scotland." He handed her a letter and a drawing. "The King of Scots has been murdered."

"What?" Elizabeth rose to her feet.

"The house in which he was lodging was blown up. This letter gives a far more honest account than you will ever receive from the Scots. I will leave you to read it."

He withdrew, and Elizabeth sat down heavily at her desk, looking stunned.

"Should I leave?" Kate asked, shaken herself.

"No, stay. I should be glad of your company," Elizabeth murmured.

They had known that Darnley was ill. The official line had been that it was smallpox, but Cecil's agents had discovered that it was syphilis. Darnley had been taken sick while staying with his father in Glasgow, but they had recently heard that he had returned to

Edinburgh to convalesce in a house at Kirk o' Field, south of the city. At the time, Elizabeth had thought it strange that Darnley would leave the safety of his father's domain for the capital, because the lords who had murdered Rizzio had never forgiven him for betraying them and were likely to be out for his blood. It was strange, too, she observed, that there had been a reconciliation between Mary and Darnley, given that he had not only colluded in her attempted murder, but had also, these past months, been doing his best to blacken her reputation in the eyes of the Pope and Catholic Europe—presumably in the hope of overthrowing her and seizing power himself, which was what he had always wanted. Kate too had thought it odd that Mary would even contemplate taking him back. But back he had gone, and she had been nursing him, apparently devotedly, back to health. Kate had thought her a fool. If any man had treated her that way, she would have let him rot in Hell. But Elizabeth felt that, really, Mary had had no choice but to make the best of things with Darnley.

"She cannot divorce him, because there are no grounds, and she dare not impugn the legitimacy of her child," she had told Kate, as they lingered over the supper table a few weeks earlier, discussing Mary's impossible situation.

"But surely he has committed treason?"

"Undoubtedly, he has, but in law, apparently, the King of Scots is incapable of committing treason, so she cannot be rid of him that way. No, Kate," Elizabeth had insisted, "she must make the best of things, as so many married people do. It's another reason why I shy from marriage. I would never leave myself open to the anguish she has suffered."

But now Darnley was dead. Kate sat silent while Elizabeth read the report and pored over the drawing. She looked up, her expression unreadable.

Kate could not stop herself. "What happened?"

"There was a great explosion at two o'clock in the morning on the tenth of February. It shook the whole city of Edinburgh and reduced the house at Kirk o' Field to a heap of rubble. They found the bodies of Darnley and his valet in the nearby orchard. It looked as if they had been strangled or suffocated, for there were no injuries on them. Possibly the explosion was merely supposed to destroy any evidence of murder."

Elizabeth paused. "He was just twenty, my young kinsman. Some might think he got what he deserved."

"But who was responsible for his death?"

"Wait and listen, for there is more to it. Queen Mary was awakened by the blast. She showed herself shocked and horrified when they told her what had happened and vowed that the murderers would be speedily discovered and punished. She had spent the day with Darnley and only left to attend the wedding of one of her ladies at Holyrood Palace. She has concluded that the killers meant to assassinate her, too. Had she not decided to return to Holyrood, she would probably have died."

Her eyes met Kate's. Kate dared not voice what she was thinking; one could not accuse one sovereign to another.

Elizabeth spoke at last. "Many people had a motive for doing away with Darnley or stood to gain from his death. I know what is in your mind. You think that the prime suspect must be Queen Mary herself. She had long since ceased to love him and had certainly wanted to be rid of him. She regarded him, quite rightly, as a dangerous liability. But then we have to consider the Earl of Bothwell." Elizabeth had once deemed Bothwell the best of the entire Scots nobility because he was the only one who had refused to accept the bribes her agents had pressed on him. "His name has been linked with Mary's, and it's been said that he would attempt anything out of ambition. He might have seen murdering Darnley as the way to gaining a crown for himself."

She rose and began pacing up and down. "Many of the Scots lords hated Darnley, and those who murdered Rizzio had vowed vengeance on him."

"What do you think, Bess?" Kate asked.

"It is far too early to draw any conclusions," Elizabeth replied, sitting down again. "I need to write to Mary and urge her to act now to preserve her honor. She must find the perpetrators and bring them to justice, even if they are near and dear to her."

. . .

KATE DID NOT know what to think. Certainly Queen Mary's departure for the wedding had been timely—and some might see it as suspiciously so. And there was something that didn't ring true about her reconciliation with Darnley. Later that day, over supper in Francis's lodging, Kate asked him what he thought.

"Queen Mary is lucky to be rid of the young fool," he said, "but if she does not immediately pursue and punish the murderers, the finger of suspicion will point at her."

"Do *you* think her guilty of murder?" she asked.

"I have to say that the circumstantial evidence against her is damning. However, it is not proof of her guilt. We must keep open minds."

But Mary seemed paralyzed by indecision and reluctant to act against Bothwell, who was widely believed to be the man who had plotted Darnley's murder. Scotland, by all reports, was in an uproar, but the Queen was doing nothing to satisfy the public's clamor for justice.

Chapter 42

1567

In April, Kate learned from Elizabeth that Darnley's distraught father, the Earl of Lennox, had pressured Mary into allowing him to lodge a private indictment of Bothwell. But while he was permitted to bring only four witnesses to the hearing in Edinburgh, Bothwell had arrived with an intimidating following of four hundred men, whereupon Lennox deemed it wiser not to pursue the case. Without him, it collapsed, and Bothwell was acquitted.

Kate found the next news even more shocking. Bothwell had waylaid and kidnapped Mary when she was traveling to Edinburgh after visiting her son at Stirling Castle, and then borne her off to his castle at Dunbar.

"Cecil's agents say that he ravished her there," Elizabeth revealed over dinner in her chamber, her outrage evident in the angry flush that had spread down to her neckline. "That he should dare to treat his Queen thus! The man should be castrated and hanged!"

Later that day, Francis surprised Kate. "The Council has seen reports that the abduction and so-called rape were done with Queen Mary's consent and foreknowledge. She actually turned down an offer to rescue her. Now it will be impossible for her to refuse to marry Bothwell. He has got what he wanted. And maybe she has, too."

Kate did not know what to think. Elizabeth was incensed and greatly perplexed because Mary, who had still not brought her husband's murderers to justice, was apparently showering favor on the chief suspect. And Bothwell's way was made clear when the Church of Scotland condemned him as an adulterer and granted his wife a divorce. It was not long before news came that Bothwell had married Mary, whom he had led back to Edinburgh, holding her horse's bridle as if she were his captive.

Many thought the Scottish Queen's conduct depraved and were convinced that she had connived with Bothwell to murder Darnley. Even Elizabeth ceased defending the reputation of her sister monarch.

"I can only deplore her behavior," she said, on the day she learned of the marriage. She looked deeply moved; the matter was affecting her profoundly. "I have the greatest misliking of the Queen's doings, and I am ashamed of her. It does not become an anointed sovereign to forget her honor and her dignity thus. It reflects on me; men will use any excuse to say that women should not rule. And in Mary's case, I have to agree with them."

She was so overcome that she started to weep and hurried off to her closet, beckoning Kate to follow her. Staunching her tears, she stared out of the window, and when she spoke, her voice was bitter. "Now you see why I would not marry, or even receive, my Lord of Leicester after his wife was found dead. He was exonerated of all blame, but mud sticks, dear cousin, it sticks. I remembered my dignity as queen. I could not risk being tainted by association, and I put that consideration before my private feelings. But Mary! What has she done, with her husband murdered, and in his grave less than three months? She has married the man who probably murdered him! I do believe she has lost her mind. It is the kindest construction I can put upon her conduct."

"It does beggar belief," Kate agreed, wishing she could put her arms around Elizabeth and comfort her as a sister should, yet knowing instinctively that such a gesture would not be welcome, for Elizabeth was trying to master her emotions.

"To be plain with you, I grieve for her," the Queen said. "She could not have made a worse choice, and in making it, she has all but proclaimed herself guilty, too, and so people will believe, even if she is innocent, which I am coming increasingly to doubt. I shall write to her and show her my opinion plainly."

Kate would not have liked to be the recipient of such a letter.

IT TRANSPIRED THAT Mary's ill-advised marriage had not brought her happiness. Francis told Kate that Cecil had learned that, just two days after the wedding, the Queen of Scots was regretting what she had done. She had said that she wished to die and called for a knife with which to kill herself. Yet, despite her mental anguish, she seemed unable to resist Bothwell's masculine charms.

"It sounds as if she is in thrall to him," Kate said. They were sitting on the grass on the riverbank below the palace, eating cherries from a basket, and basking in the sunshine. Yet that could not banish the darkness of the subject they seemed to be endlessly discussing whenever they saw each other.

"The Scottish lords find the marriage intolerable," Francis told her. "They will not put up with Bothwell as king of Scots. Things are going to end badly."

Kate feared he would be proved right, and she was not surprised to learn that there had been an armed confrontation between Mary and her lords at Carberry Hill outside Edinburgh. Very little blood had been spilled, but at the end of the day, Mary was in the custody of her nobles and Bothwell had fled.

Elizabeth was shaking with rage—and with fear, because what had been done to one anointed queen could easily be done to another. But this was England. The nobles were loyal. They respected and revered their Queen, even when they grew exasperated with her.

"So much for the lords assuring Mary that they intended no harm to the Crown." The Queen's voice was sharp as steel. "They placed her under guard like a common felon. They led her back to Edinburgh, through the packed streets, and her subjects reviled her as an adulteress and murderess. They were screaming, 'Burn the whore! Kill her! Drown her!' " Elizabeth shivered. "There were placards depicting her as a mermaid. What humiliation!"

It was tantamount to calling Mary a prostitute. Kate shuddered with outrage and revulsion that a queen could be treated thus.

"They have imprisoned her in the fortress of Lochleven, which stands on an island in the middle of a lake. She had nothing with her but the clothes she wore. My information is that she is with child." Her voice rose. "I am deeply concerned at the implications of this captivity of a queen by her subjects. Whatever Mary has done—and, I assure you, I can only deplore her behavior and I have little sympathy for her on a personal level—she is still an anointed sovereign, to whom by nature and law her people owe loyalty and obedience. Their treatment of her is setting a dangerous precedent. Therefore, I am determined to fight for her release." She rose, and her voice cracked. "I'm sorry, I can speak of this no more." She hastened from the privy chamber.

"These are indeed dangerous precedents," Blanche said.

Dot nodded. Kate would have run after Elizabeth but decided that she was best left alone. "I think that the Queen of Scots is her own worst enemy," she said.

IT WAS NOW July, and the news that filtered south from Scotland was worse and worse. The Queen of Scots had miscarried of twins and lost so much blood that she was now confined to bed. Despite Elizabeth's efforts to persuade the lords to remember their oaths of allegiance and release her, they took advantage of her weakened condition and forced her to sign an instrument of abdication in favor of her thirteen-month-old son, whom they had quickly crowned King of Scots. Public opinion in Scotland was now violently opposed to Mary, and Elizabeth's intervention was greatly resented. The lords were threatening to break off their alliance with England in favor of a new one with France if she did not support them.

"Of course, it would be logical for Protestant England to be allied with a Protestant government in Edinburgh," Francis pointed out over supper one evening. They had been talking about how happy Hal was in his marriage, and how well the children were doing in their chosen careers, and the talk had drifted, as it usually did, to events in the wider world.

"But isn't that government illegal? By what right do the Scottish lords rule?"

"They have no true right, Kate, but it is usually the victors who make the laws, and they will find some justification for their actions, I'll warrant." He leaned forward and speared some meat on his knife, laying it on her plate. "To be honest, do we want a Catholic queen ruling Scotland? The only reason Elizabeth is defending her is because she is frightened of the implications of her deposition. Truly, Mary is not fit for office. Morally, she is wanting—and that is putting it mildly."

"I agree with you to a point," Kate said. "Yet she has been treated brutally and unfairly."

"It might be no more than she deserves." Francis's tone was disapproving. "At the very least, she has shown appalling judgment all along, especially in marrying Darnley. Look where that has led her!"

Kate paused, hesitating to say what was in her heart. "I think I know who was responsible for that. Our Queen was adamant that Darnley should not go to Scotland—yet she sent him, knowing what kind of man he was."

Francis shook his head. "Even she could not have predicted what would happen. You know I don't think a lot of her statesmanship, but she was not responsible for Mary's decisions."

"But Francis, she knew that Mary would take the bait. Darnley had a claim to the English throne—a better one than hers, as you once told me, she being a foreigner born out of the realm. It was a certainty that Mary would have thought to strengthen her claim by marrying Darnley."

"I grant you that Elizabeth would have foreseen that, but why would she have connived at a marriage that posed such a threat to her own position?"

"Because she knew that Darnley would cause trouble for Mary!"

Francis smiled. "He could equally have caused trouble for Elizabeth. No, Kate, I don't hold our Queen responsible for Mary's troubles. But what I would like to see is her washing her hands of the woman and making friends with the Scottish lords. That would be very much in England's interests."

Kate knew herself bested. She still thought she was right, but Francis liked to assert his superior masculine judgment, and she would not argue with him, for the sake of preserving the harmony between them. Besides, what did affairs in distant Scotland have to do with them?

ELIZABETH SPENT MUCH of the summer fuming against the Scottish lords.

"What warrant have they in Scripture to depose their Prince?" she burst out one day, while composing a letter to her envoys in Scotland. "Or what law have they found in any Christian monarchy which states that subjects may arrest the person of their Prince, detain them captive, and proceed to judge them? No such law is to be found!"

She had been warned that any attempt to rescue Mary would only lead to her being killed. Kate was of the opinion, though, that had Elizabeth not reacted as violently to the lords' treatment of Mary, they might have executed their Queen without further ado. Now relations between Elizabeth and the men who should have been her Protestant allies were so frigid that war seemed a very real possibility.

Her councillors, however, were pressing her to foster friendly relations with the new regime in Scotland.

"We're all very concerned about her Majesty's obsession with bringing the Scots to heel," Francis confided to Kate. "She refuses to recognize the lords' authority, yet she will have to do so soon because they are well entrenched in power and there is little likelihood that Mary will ever be restored to the throne. And to be honest, Kate, although Elizabeth outwardly professes not to approve of the present situation, I don't doubt that, in her heart, she likes it well enough."

Kate suspected that he was right. She had learned over the years that the louder the Queen protested against something, the more she was secretly in favor of it. But Elizabeth continued to vocalize her animosity against the Scottish nobles, standing in the gallery that led to the council chamber and berating her lords for not having thought of a way in which she could revenge the Queen of Scots' imprisonment and deliver her, then shouting that she would declare war on the Scots. When Cecil opened his mouth to defend the lords, Elizabeth rounded on him.

"Master Cecil, any person who is content to see a neighboring prince unlawfully deposed must be less than dutifully minded toward his own sovereign."

Kate saw Cecil wince, but he persisted. "Might I remind your Majesty that if you threaten the Scots with war, they might well carry out their threat to execute Queen Mary."

She subsided at that, but she was in a foul mood for two days afterward.

THAT AUTUMN, KATE was unwell with stomach pains, a fever, and a flux, similar to the symptoms she had had when she was ill before Hal's wedding. The Queen once again summoned Dr. Huicke, but he could only diagnose an imbalance of the humors and prescribe an infusion of chamomile, sage, and mint.

In a few days, Kate felt better, but two weeks later, she suffered a recurrence of the symptoms, and this time the herbs were less efficacious. She did not recover until Christmas, and then she found she had lost her appetite—or rather, she was nervous about eating lest certain foods set off another attack. Francis and Beth were both concerned about her, and though she assured them that she was quite well really and that it was nothing to worry about, inwardly she was fretting about the future. What if her symptoms were the signs of some serious disease? How would her loved ones manage if she died?

What nonsense! she admonished herself. They were all making a fuss about nothing.

Chapter 43

1568

By the spring, Kate was more herself, even if her stomach felt constantly delicate these days. Elizabeth had been more than supportive, ordering special dishes to tempt her and sending her off to bed early, but she had virtually usurped Francis's role as comforter, which rattled him no end. At length, Kate told her that she would feel much better if she could sleep in her own bed, to which Elizabeth reluctantly agreed.

In May came the news that Queen Mary had escaped from Lochleven with the help of her custodian's brother, who had imagined himself in love with her. He had escorted her to Hamilton, southeast of Glasgow, where she had been joined by several lords and an army of six thousand men. Kate, who had been quietly sewing a smock for Lettice's youngest baby, was startled to hear Elizabeth whoop in jubilation as she read the news. Having announced it to her ladies, the Queen immediately sat down to write a message of congratulation to Mary, offering help and support.

It probably never reached her. The next they heard, the Scottish lords had risen in arms and Mary's force had suffered a crushing defeat at Langside. She had fled in panic from the battlefield knowing that all was lost, and made her way into England, announcing that she had come to place herself under Elizabeth's protection and seek military aid so that she could crush her enemies for good.

Elizabeth was horrified when she read that. "Why has she come into England when she could have gone to France, where she has her dower income and can practice her faith?" she wondered fretfully. "I was happy to champion her cause in Scotland, but does she really think I will provide her with an army when she has always shown herself to be ambitious for my crown? Hah!"

She agonized over what she should do with Mary, yet she had to make a decision quickly. The authorities in the north were awaiting instructions as to how to treat their uninvited guest, who had been placed under guard in Carlisle Castle.

That night, Elizabeth kept Kate and Blanche up late, discussing her dilemma. "The best solution would be to bring about a reconciliation between Mary and her lords on terms favorable to England. I would like to send her back to Scotland. She must be restored at once. I shall insist upon it. Cecil says that if we send her back, we will be sending her to her death, yet I cannot furnish her with an army."

"You insisted on her restoration before, Bess, and the Scots took no notice," Blanche pointed out.

"Yes, but what can I do with her? Every option open to me carries its dangers."

"You could send her to France?" Kate suggested.

"That would be folly! We don't want a French army north of the border again."

Elizabeth got up and began pacing, her silk skirts swishing angrily. "I can't leave her at liberty in England. She will be an inspiration to every Catholic malcontent in the kingdom. There are still those of the old faith who regard her as having a better title to the English throne than I do, especially in the north, where the Protestant faith has barely taken root. They've been rejoicing there at her coming to England. She could become a focus for rebellion or treason. By God, I wish she had not come!"

She sat down, shaking her head. "There is only one course open to me, I fear. She must remain in England for now, not in prison, but in honorable custody as my guest, where I can have her under constant observation. Kate, your husband can go north to Carlisle to welcome her in my name and take charge of her."

Kate stifled her dismay. She did not want Francis going so far north to a region where the people were said to be savages, and she knew he would not relish the task, for he heartily disapproved of the Queen of Scots.

"He will escort her to London, then?" she asked.

Elizabeth stared at her. "Oh no! He must tell her that it will be impossible for her to be admitted to my presence because of the great slander of murder that attaches to her name, of which she is not yet purged. Until she has been formally acquitted, I, as an unmarried Queen, cannot receive her or welcome her to my court."

Kate was near to weeping. She could feel her unsettled stomach churning. "Then when will my husband return?"

"Did I not make myself clear? He is to be Queen Mary's host in the north, or rather, her custodian for as long as I need him to keep her there."

To be assigned such an important duty was a great honor for Francis, but Kate thought she might faint. They had often been parted, but the thought of him going so far away from her with no date set for his return was unbearable, and she needed him at this time, when she was fearful for her health and feeling vulnerable. "When does he depart?" she whispered.

"Immediately," Elizabeth said, seemingly unaware of the impact her decision was having on Kate, who was struggling not to cry.

As soon as she was free, Kate ran to Francis's lodging, only to find that he wasn't there. She sat on the bed, twisting the fabric of her kirtle in her hands, keening in misery. How would she bear life without him?

It was nearly midnight when he returned. She knew by his face that he had received his orders. "Oh, Kate . . ." he said, and she went into his arms, drinking in the reality of him, knowing that she would have to live on this memory for perhaps a long time. *Oh, why had the wicked Queen of Scots chosen to come into England?*

"I have begged the Queen to let you come north with me," he said, his voice breaking. "But she refuses to be parted from you."

"How will we bear it?" she cried.

"We will bear it because our love is strong," he soothed her, but his hands were trembling.

They held each other for a long time and then they sat down and spoke of practicalities and finances. The children were well provided for and well looked after. The younger ones could stay with their tutors and nurses at Syon, where Kate could visit them. Bilkins could always be trusted to run Greys Court efficiently, and both Kate and Francis would keep in touch with him by letter, and with the steward at Syon. They had been discussing possible spouses for their older unmarried children, but those plans would have to wait for now.

"You must press the Queen to let you come north to visit me," Francis said. "I will continue to ask her, too. She cannot keep us apart indefinitely." He shook his head. "I do not relish this appointment, and not just because it takes me away from you. You know that I have no good opinion of the Queen of Scots, and I fear her penchant for intrigue. It is a heavy burden her Majesty has laid upon me."

"I do not envy you," Kate commiserated. "But I see that you are the best man for the office, the one who will be the most impervious to her wiles. She is very beautiful, I hear, and she may play on your chivalrous instincts." She was voicing her inmost fears. She trusted Francis, of course she did, for he had never given her cause not to. Yet the Queen of Scots had a reputation; she was clearly an enchantress, one whom even the most moral of men might not be able to resist.

Francis looked horrified. "Darling, she will never arouse any chivalrous instincts in me. Since I met you, I have never looked at another woman. She can work all the wiles she likes on me—it won't get her anywhere."

"I'm sorry, Francis. I do trust you, indeed I do. It's just that I have heard such scandalous things about her." She rested her head on his shoulder, and he put his arm around her.

"She'll have no opportunity for scandal at Carlisle."

Their parting soon afterward was searingly painful. Kate did not know how she kept a smile on her face when she stood by the mounting block in the palace courtyard and gave Francis the customary stirrup cup to hearten him for his long journey.

"The weather is good," she said, when what she really wanted to say was, *Don't go! Don't leave me! I cannot bear to be without you!* Why was it that people said such inane things at times of crisis?

"God be with you, my heart," Francis said, and blew her a kiss as he rode away at the head of his train. He did not look back.

IT WAS A month—a long, miserable month—before she heard from him. In a lengthy, affectionate letter, he told her that he was quite comfortable at Carlisle Castle. "As soon as I arrived, I was admitted to Queen Mary's presence. She keeps royal state here like a queen. To be frank with you, I can see how she entraps men, although you must not worry, for even if I were inclined to stray, I do not find her beautiful. Many have flattered her because of who she is." Kate smiled. Elizabeth would be pleased to hear that. She was inordinately jealous of Mary.

"She asked if the Queen would receive her, but I told her that it would not be possible just yet, not while she was under suspicion for her husband's murder. She did not like that, of course, but I think that plain speaking is the best course. I keep her under constant guard, but she is allowed to go hunting with an escort. All in all, I do not think that my task will be onerous. She is doing her best to be gracious to me. It serves no one well if we are at loggerheads."

Reading the letter was like hearing Francis's dear, familiar voice. And when, at the end, he spoke of how much he missed her and how lonely the nights were, the words blurred and she broke down. Oh, it was cruel, *cruel,* to be separated! She must make Elizabeth understand how much unhappiness it was causing them both.

THAT EVENING, AT supper with the Queen and the other great ladies of her household, Kate related what Francis had written in his letter. Elizabeth smiled when she heard his comments about

Mary not being as beautiful as the flatterers said, so Kate seized her moment.

"Madam, when am I to see my husband again?" she asked.

Elizabeth's smile faded. "When he is no longer needed up north. I thought you understood that, Kate. He is deployed there because it is where he can be most useful to me."

Kate was growing desperate, clenching her teeth in frustration. "But Madam, I love my husband. It is hard, not to say unnatural, to be without him. May I not visit him from time to time?"

Elizabeth remained unmoved. "It is inconvenient at present. We will talk about it some other day."

It was another of her maddening answerless answers. Grief and anger battled in Kate's breast. How could Elizabeth be so inhuman?

She simmered until it was time to prepare the Queen for bed. When Elizabeth was standing there in her night-robe, and the others were leaving, Kate faced her.

"Bess, I am so unhappy. I cannot live without my husband, and I cannot comprehend why you don't understand that, or feel for us."

Elizabeth's cheeks flushed. She looked just like her father. "Kate, in my position, I cannot afford to let my emotions govern me. The decisions I take are for the good of the State. Francis is the best man for his office. His godliness will protect him from the Queen of Scots's machinations. I expect *you* to understand that, sometimes, sacrifices have to be made for the highest good."

Spare me your philosophy! Kate thought angrily. "But I need him here." She hated herself for letting the tears spill. "I am worried about my health."

"I am sorry to have put you in this situation," Elizabeth said, in a kindlier voice. "I am hoping that a solution to the problem of the Queen of Scots will soon present itself. In the meantime, if you feel unwell, talk to me. I have the best physicians in the kingdom."

Kate could do no more. She bade Elizabeth good night and retired tearfully to her lonely bed.

. . .

IT WAS OBVIOUS from his letters that Francis was not happy. He regarded Mary as a threat to the security of the realm, and he was clearly worried that she would escape. "She resents the restrictions on her liberty," he wrote, "and I have to endure her tears and rages. I have informed her Majesty that she is causing me more pains, perils, and grief than she does to any other man."

Kate resolved again to beg Elizabeth to let her go north and be a support to Francis, but when she raised the matter, Elizabeth rounded on her.

"Kate, you must trust my judgment and accept the situation! Your husband is doing an excellent job at Carlisle, as I was certain he would. And I need you here. I do not want to hear any more of your complaints."

Kate shut her mouth. She dared not protest too much.

ANOTHER MONTH PASSED, and still no decision had been reached in respect of Mary's future. Francis had written regularly, and it was beginning to seem, to Kate's dismay, that he was reconciling himself to living in the north. He had apparently enjoyed watching football matches with Mary on the green outside the castle's postern gate. Despite their religious differences, it was apparent that he was beginning to like the Scottish Queen. Kate was not at all happy about that. She had heard too much about Mary's enchantments. Francis had been a faithful husband, but he was a man with needs, and they were not currently being met. Her imagination soared in tortuous twists and turns.

Elizabeth was pleased with his work but concerned to hear that he felt that security at Carlisle was problematic.

"I have decided that he shall take her to Bolton Castle," she declared. "It's farther south, but it's a secure fortress and sufficiently far from both Scotland and London to pose any great security risk."

Mary, however, refused to go. Francis wrote to Kate: "If I had to enumerate the difficulties that we have had to persuade her, instead of a letter I should be writing a book, and that somewhat tragical!"

Yet in July, he did manage to escort Mary to Bolton. Kate hoped that the Queen would assign custody of her to Lord Scrope, the castle's owner, but Elizabeth was having none of it. Francis was to stay where he was. At her lowest moments, Kate began to wonder if Elizabeth was doing this so that she could have Kate all to herself.

Her unease mounted when she learned that her husband was trying to amuse Mary—who spoke French and Scots—by teaching her English, which would necessitate their spending long periods of time together. Why could the woman not use French, the language in which she and Elizabeth corresponded? Yet she need not have worried. In his next letter, which he addressed to her as "you, who are my other self," he wrote that his position was becoming more and more distasteful to him. "I have written to Cecil and demanded my recall. My dearest, pray use your own influence to bring that about, that I may be released from this unwelcome duty."

Kate felt completely reassured after reading that.

She raised the subject when she next saw Elizabeth, which was at a tennis match the following morning.

"Kate, the answer is still no," the Queen said, her eyes on the players. "Do not ask me again."

A few days later, she was complaining that Francis was being overzealous in trying to convert his charge. "It's one thing to make her an Anglican, another to force on her his puritanic views!" she snapped. "It seems he has commended to her the extreme doctrines and forms of Master Calvin. Well, he shall hear from me about that!"

Kate began to hope that she would now recall him. Even his return home in disgrace would be better than this separation. But all Elizabeth did was send him a sharp reprimand and order him to desist from trying to convert Mary. Soon afterward, Francis protested to Kate that Mary had accepted his plain speaking on religion quite contentedly, even if she had taken no notice.

Kate had now come to accept that she could trust her husband with the Scottish enchantress, but she missed him so badly that it was making her ill. Her old abdominal pains had returned and her digestion was uncertain, making it imperative that she be always within reach of a privy. Beth was concerned, yet Elizabeth seemed not to notice. For all her declarations that she loved Kate above all others, she had no idea of how unhappy she was making her.

Kate wrote and vented her frustrations on Francis, who replied that the Queen's behavior seemed contradictory to him, too. Beth had written to him to express her fears about Kate's health, and he wrote that he also was worried, which alarmed her. Had Beth exaggerated her symptoms? Heaven forbid, she did not want him to suffer anxiety on her account.

"I hope you are taking your physick," he wrote.

She had not, she confessed in her reply. Beth had been nagging her about it, too. Belatedly, she downed the foul-tasting stuff, but too late. Toward the end of July, she went down with a raging fever.

Elizabeth was deeply concerned. She summoned the royal physicians and sat waiting with Kate, holding her hand, until they came. She even wrote herself to Francis, informing him of Kate's illness. But she did not recall him.

By early August, the crisis had passed, and Kate was well enough to sit up in bed and read a letter newly arrived from Bolton. "I am very sorry to hear that you are fallen into a fever," Francis had written. "I would to God I were with you, so that I might attend and care for you and bring about your good recovery. I trust you shall shortly overcome this fever and recover good health again. But darling, I fear that when you are in health, you often forget to prevent any sickness by taking your physick, and then you fall sick, and it is too late. I pray for your help, that I may be recalled and return to you, for I have little to do here. I have written to Master Secretary in this behalf."

Reading his words, and sensing his helpless desperation, Kate begged Elizabeth, from her sickbed, to let him come home. But once more, Elizabeth refused.

"It is impossible, Kate. He is needed in the north," she said, and changed the subject, leaving Kate in misery. That night, she cried on Beth's shoulder.

From then on, Francis wrote repeatedly to Elizabeth and Cecil, begging to leave his post and return to London. When Kate was up again, but still feeling weak, Cecil came to see her. "I am sorry for your sickness, and for the Queen's intransigence," he soothed. "Her mind is set—I can do nothing with her. Your husband has written again to say that as you have lately been sick, he believes that light duties and quietness of mind are the only means to preserve your health. He knows you are desirous to go north to be with him if he is not to return to court soon. He has asked me to tell you he thinks it likely that he will be at Bolton for five or six weeks. Between ourselves, Kate, I do not think anyone knows the Queen's mind on that matter. I am aware that Francis has spent a lot of money on doctors and medicines for you—I know the royal physicians do not come cheaply. If he is going to be in the north for longer, he thinks it's imperative for you to join him, for the comfort of your spirits and the healthful exercise of your body in traveling there. He does not want you remaining at court, for until your body be stronger, he doubts that daily attendance on the Queen will improve your health."

Kate agreed. "The best cure will be to see him," she said, tears welling. But nothing changed.

IN SEPTEMBER, KATE received a package from Bolton. It contained a beautiful chain of gold pomander beads strung on gold wire.

"It is a gift from Queen Mary," Francis had written in the enclosed letter. "She asked me to assure you of her friendship and desires to make your acquaintance. She has probably grown weary of hearing me speak of you! See how she corrupts me; she knows that the way to my heart is through you, my darling."

That afternoon, when Elizabeth and her ladies were taking a brisk walk in the park, the Queen setting the pace, she was in a peevish mood. "It seems that your husband is being too lenient with Queen Mary," she said to Kate, who was struggling to keep up. "I fear he has come under her spell."

Kate was riled by her words, which seemed to emanate from pure cattiness. "I know for a fact that my husband is above that," she retorted.

"He is a man like all the rest," Elizabeth replied.

"He is the best of men!" Kate said angrily.

"He accepted a costly pomander from her."

"It was for me!" Kate lifted up the pomander at the end of her girdle for Elizabeth to see.

"Ah. Well, that puts a different complexion on things." There was no apology, of course. "You will be pleased to know, Kate, that I have ordered a commission of inquiry into the murder of Lord Darnley. Mary's innocence must be established before I can receive her at my court. The inquiry will open next month at York. In the meantime, I have ordered my commissioners to press for her restoration."

This was music to Kate's ears. It might mean that Francis could come home.

However, the inquiry at York reached no conclusion in October, and in November it was reopened at Westminster. To the Queen's annoyance—and Kate's intense frustration—it became clear that the Scottish lords' chief objective was to keep Mary out of Scotland. She was not summoned to attend the second inquiry, and was not present, therefore, when the Scottish lords revealed the existence of a casket of letters that they claimed contained incriminating evidence against her and Bothwell, proving her an adulteress and murderess.

Kate could not have cared less. She suffered another attack of fever that month. Elizabeth could not have been kinder, even with everything else she had on her mind—except to give Kate the one thing she truly needed. She sat with Kate daily until she felt better, and they had long discussions about Mary.

Elizabeth confided that she was skeptical about the casket of letters. "It is possible that compromising passages have been inserted into genuine letters. Naturally, Mary has denied having written them. But my Lord of Norfolk has seen them, and he is convinced that they are authentic. He was utterly appalled at their contents and informed me that they are proof of the inordinate love between Mary and Bothwell and her abhorrence of her husband. He says she is a wicked woman."

Kate was not surprised when the commissioners and the Council unanimously accepted the Casket Letters as authentic. But no one seemed to know how to proceed against Mary. The last thing Elizabeth wanted was for an anointed queen to be proclaimed guilty of murder, but she did see the necessity for Mary to accept her deposition and live quietly in England as a private person for the rest of her life, and she told Francis to persuade Mary to agree to this.

Kate was distraught. If Mary remained a prisoner in England, she might never see Francis again. It was too terrible a prospect to contemplate. She feared she might suffer a relapse and die.

IN THE MIDDLE of December, Elizabeth moved to Hampton Court. Kate was feeling well enough to make the journey from Whitehall, but she was glad of Beth's arm to lean on as she climbed into the royal barge. Hopefully, she would be better when Christmas came.

On her arrival, Elizabeth summoned her councillors and nobility to Hampton Court to hear the commission's proceedings read out to them. The peers agreed that these were such foul matters that her Majesty's position was justified.

"Queen Mary's crimes are now so apparent that she can never be received at court," Elizabeth announced. "However, she cannot be declared guilty unless she puts forward a defense—which she has consistently refused to do, unless it is to me in person—which is out of the question. So, for the present, she must stay where she is."

Kate felt sick when she heard that, and Francis was clearly feeling desperate, too. It was a very cold winter and Bolton sounded like a bleak place. "We are utterly unprovided for," he complained.

"We lack firewood and victuals. Cecil is sending some, God be praised. How I miss my home comforts—and my beloved wife."

Kate had been hoping that Lettice and Walter would come to court for Christmas, but they remained at Chartley, marooned by the weather. Kate felt very lonely amid the throngs of courtiers and the gaiety. She would have liked to pay a visit to the children at Syon, as she hadn't been for weeks, but still did not feel up to it. She would not let herself think of happy Christmases of the past when she had been with her loved ones, although they had been few and far between in recent years. All she wanted was to behold Francis's beloved face and be held in his arms.

Two days after Christmas Day, while helping the Queen to dress, she was seized by a terrible pain across her middle. It was so bad that she had to sit down, holding her breath and leaning slightly forward in the hope that it would ease. Once more, Elizabeth summoned Dr. Huicke, who took one look at Kate and ordered her to bed.

"Drink this," he ordered, and she downed some syrup, which made her drowsy, but took the edge off the pain. She lay there, longing for it to subside completely and fearful of what it might import. She was only forty-four and she didn't want to die just yet. There were too many people who needed her.

Chapter 44

1569

BY NEW YEAR, KATE WAS UP AND ABOUT, YET SHE COULD NOT face food and felt very weak.

Informed of her illness, Francis sent a frantic letter. "I have heard that you are gravely ill, my dearest. I have begged to be recalled, or at least to be allowed to visit you."

His request was ignored. Kate could not believe Elizabeth capable of such cruelty.

Francis tried, again and again. "I have assured the Queen and Cecil that I can easily be replaced as Mary's guardian. But all I am told is that her Majesty wants me to keep her in safe custody and prevent her escaping."

Kate herself pleaded with Elizabeth for permission to go north to visit Francis.

"What are you thinking of?" Elizabeth cried. "Traveling in your state of health might prove exceedingly dangerous, and I could not bear to lose you. Staying at court is the wisest course, because you have access to my physicians."

"But I yearn to see him, Bess! If I am not long for this world, it may be my last chance." Kate raised her hands in supplication.

"Don't say that!" Elizabeth snapped. "I will not have such talk. I will not listen to it."

But Kate had looked in her mirror, had seen how she had aged, how ill she looked. She could feel it in her bones: her days were numbered. She *must* see Francis soon.

"I beg of you," she pleaded, weeping. "Let me go to him."

"There is no need for you to go all that way," Elizabeth retorted. "You are making a fuss about nothing. At least wait until you are better."

There was no reasoning with her. She could not face the truth.

FRANCIS SOUNDED AS if he was at his wits' end. "I wrote to Cecil," he informed Kate. "I told him that as her Majesty will not let me look after my wife, hopefully she will comfort her with clemency and courtesy. I rather regret being so outspoken, but Cecil has assured me that you are well amended and that he is doing his best for us."

Well amended? Lying on her bed, the letter at her side, and lacking the strength to pick it up again, Kate wished fervently that she were. But she was better than she had been, so there was hope yet.

In his next letter, Francis expressed his joy that she was well again. "I have been so anxious that I almost wrote somewhat plainly to her Majesty. I only held off when Cecil reported that you were much improved. But I am grieved and disappointed by the Queen's continual denial of my coming to the court last Christmas, and I was on the verge of informing her that you are in a miserable state."

So Francis too, despite being all those miles away, had understood that Elizabeth had been making light of Kate's illness. Like Kate, he could not understand why she was denying her the comfort of her husband's presence. "She has never granted us what we wished for or rewarded us enough for our service," he complained. "For all the outward love she professes to bear you, she makes you often weep on account of her unkindness, and that could pose a great danger to your health. I think we would both be truly happy if we were in disgrace and I was released from my trust, and you from your love for her. Then we might retire to lead a poor life in the country and be done with the court. I am ready to prepare myself, if you like the idea." Kate's heart leaped. He was leaving the decision to her, and she knew without a doubt what she would choose, for they could not go on like this. She would ensure that they would be together again—and free of this burdensome existence.

"Arm yourself against illness by making God your refuge," Francis urged her. He sent his regards to Mildred Cecil and Dot Stafford, who had been keeping him informed of Kate's progress. He said he had sent their daughter Beth some gold for her store box. "I look for the joy of exchanging New Year gifts with you soon. I hope for a favorable reply, my dearest wife. Your loving husband."

Kate knew what he wanted to hear—and longed to say the word. But first, she must get stronger.

SHE TRIED TO eat. She knew the flesh was falling from her. Her gowns hung loose and her cheekbones were gaunt.

"Alas, I fear I am not getting better," she confided to Elizabeth.

"Nonsense! You just need to give yourself time." But there was fear in the Queen's eyes.

There came an evening when Kate was at dinner with the Cecils. She had forced herself to go, knowing that she could not face food. When steaming platters of meat were carried in, she swayed in her chair.

"What is it, Kate?" Cecil leaped up to support her.

"I feel so ill," she muttered. "I must lie down."

Mildred half carried her to her own bed and sat with her, mopping her brow.

"I cannot inconvenience you like this," Kate murmured.

"It is nothing," Mildred soothed, her horsey face creased in concern. "I will read to you, then maybe you will settle."

Kate slept that night in the Cecils' lodging, and in the morning she was carried to her own rooms.

"I am in a doleful state," she told Beth, who was helping her into bed. She felt so ill that she doubted she would ever rise from it. Yet she must write to Francis. It might be her last chance. She asked for her writing desk but was asleep by the time Beth brought it.

Cecil came to see her. "My dear lady, it grieves me to see you so poorly," he said, clearly taken aback at the sight of her looking so ill.

"I fear I am not long for this world," she said, her voice cracked and faint.

"I came to tell you that your husband has written to the Queen, begging her to dismiss him, as he is in great grief at being apart from you. She has promised him that he will soon be rid of Queen Mary, and he has asked me to hasten that."

Kate gripped his hand. "Pray help us, good Cecil. I long to see him. It will be the greatest comfort to me."

But would Francis get here in time, even if the Queen granted his request? She was failing fast, she knew it, burning up with fever again. Even Elizabeth was looking worried. She had Kate moved to a bedchamber near to her own to be nursed, and summoned all her physicians.

"You will lack for nothing that men can devise for your recovery," she told her. "I have asked them to give me news of you every hour. I will sit with you as often as I can." Kate had rarely seen her look so upset.

She kept her word. Day and night she sat with Kate, diverting her with talk or reading to her. She sent the nurse out and herself tended to her, washing her face and helping her to the close stool. It was all very comforting, and it was lovely to have Beth there, too, and dear Mary, whom the Duchess of Suffolk had given leave to attend her—but the person Kate craved to see was her husband.

"You have told Francis how ill I am?" Kate asked, shivering uncontrollably.

"No, I have not," Elizabeth replied. "I did not want to worry him."

It was too much for Kate. She mustered her strength. "But he should know! You just want me all to yourself! How can I love you when you ignore my unhappiness and my earnest requests to be with Francis? For all we know, it may now be too late!"

She watched as Elizabth crumpled before her. "But I love you,

Kate—I love you more than anyone else. I know it is a selfish love, but there is no one else I can be close to. I am not to blame for your illness, yet I am aware that I am the cause of you and your husband being put asunder, for which I am truly sorry." She wiped away a tear. "I have good reason for favoring and loving you above all others." Kate was astonished. Did Elizabeth mean what she thought—and hoped—that she meant? Were the words she had longed to hear about to be said?

Elizabeth took Kate's hand. "I have tried to treat you as a sister. I have loved you as a sister. If I have ever been unkind, I pray you will forgive me."

Kate looked into her eyes and saw more tears in them. It had not been what she wanted to hear, yet in that moment, all her pent-up resentment dissipated. She squeezed the Queen's hand.

"I forgive you," she said.

"You are a good woman, Kate," Elizabeth said, wiping away the tears. "You have been a good servant, and you have lived a blameless life free from scandal, a life of sacrifice and steadfast devotion, of virtuous love and godliness. No reward could ever be sufficient."

It was obvious that Elizabeth thought she would die soon, and evident that she was making her peace with her. It did not frighten Kate, for she had made her peace likewise with God. Death would release her from sickness, pain, and strife. All she regretted now was that she would die before she could be reunited with Francis.

"I think I will sleep," she whispered, wanting to be alone with her thoughts, to think of Francis. It brought him nearer to her. She would have to await him in Heaven, but she knew she would never depart from his heart. He would be distracted with sorrow, for they had enjoyed nearly thirty years as man and wife and were like twin souls. The poor man would be bewildered as to how to care for his family and manage their large household. His situation would be pitiful. And their children, her beloved children, would mourn their mother. Would that she could have lived many more years with them and die an old lady. But God evidently did not desire it. She would have to trust in Him to comfort those she left behind.

. . .

IN HER DREAM, she was with Francis at Greys Court, their children about them, and she was healthy and whole, and the world was glorious. It was cruel to awake to reality the next morning, for she was too weak to move or even speak. It was a wonder she had not died in her sleep.

Elizabeth came in, decked out in a gown encrusted with pearls and gems. "Good day, Kate. I trust you slept well. It is the fifteenth of January, the tenth anniversary of my coronation." Kate was not fooled by the false gaiety in her voice. The Queen looked distraught as she gazed down on her. But she could not summon the strength to speak any words of comfort.

"Kate?" Elizabeth asked, catching her breath. "Kate, my dear sister . . . ?"

It was the last thing Kate heard.

Author's Note

THIS NOVEL CAME INTO BEING BECAUSE I THOUGHT IT would be interesting to explore in fiction the likelihood that Katherine Carey was Henry VIII's daughter. As I discovered when I was researching my biography of her mother, Mary Boleyn, the circumstantial evidence is strong, and I wanted to imagine how clues and rumors could have impacted on Katherine's life. How would she have discovered the truth? And would she have wanted it to be known? Because the truth could have been the touchstone for intrigue and plots against the very throne itself.

Constructing Katherine's story from the available source material, which is sparse in parts, has been an enjoyable challenge and necessitated some educated guesses and creativity. Where evidence exists, I have kept closely to it. What follows is a summary of what we do know.

Mary Boleyn was the sister of Anne Boleyn, Henry VIII's second wife. In 1520, she married a rising courtier, William Carey. Around 1522–23, Mary was briefly Henry VIII's mistress. She bore two children, Katherine (who was almost certainly named for Queen Katherine of Aragon), probably in March or April 1524, and Henry, born on 4 March 1525. Katherine is likely to have been fathered by Henry VIII. Henry did not acknowledge her, and had no need to, for there was a presumption in law that any child born to a married woman was the issue of her husband. It would have taken an Act of Parliament to nullify the legal presumption of paternity, and there was no reason why Henry VIII would have wanted to court scandal by pursuing such a course.

The recent discovery of a Latin dictionary in which Katherine's husband, Sir Francis Knollys, listed the births of their children in order has assisted the debate about her date of birth and paternity. The dictionary provides firsthand evidence that her youngest child, Dudley, was born in May 1562, which tends to corroborate the traditional identification of a portrait of a pregnant Elizabethan lady as Katherine Carey.

This portrait, by Steven van der Meulen, is dated 1562 and is now in the Mellon Collection at the Yale Center for British Art in New Haven, Connecticut. Its provenance tends to support the identification of the sitter as Katherine Carey, as it was in the possession of her descendants until 1974, when it was sold, along with other Knollys family portraits, at Sotheby's. A portrait of Katherine's brother, Henry Carey, Lord Hunsdon, has also been attributed to Steven van der Meulen and dated to 1561–63. Steven van der Meulen painted Elizabeth I and several luminaries of her court, so it is credible that both her Carey relatives commissioned him to execute their portraits.

What is persuasive about the portrait is the sitter's striking facial resemblance to Henry VIII, which impacts immediately on the viewer. This is not, of course, conclusive evidence; it could be entirely coincidental that Katherine looked like the King, for they were distantly related by blood.

There is evidence that Katherine's royal paternity was no secret to some at the Elizabethan court. In 1582, Sir Philip Sidney was amorously pursuing her granddaughter, Penelope Devereux, Lady Rich, whom he addressed as Stella in *Astrophil and Stella,* his famous cycle of poems and songs about lovers. In one, he calls Stella "rich in the riches of a royal heart"; he twice gives her the royal title of "her Grace" and, in a verse that refers to strange tales "broidered with bulls"—a likely reference to the Boleyn arms—speaks of "hiding royal blood full oft in rural vein." He calls her "Princess of Beauty," or "a princess high, whose throne is in the mind," refers to Stella being "so right a princess," or "a queen," and says how her "humbleness grows one with Majesty," which may also possibly be allusions to her royal blood. In fact, the royal theme, and the language of majesty, recurs throughout the cycle. We might infer from this that Sidney knew that Tudor blood ran in Penelope's veins, and although his poem is not prima facie proof of that, given that poetic language can be subject to various interpretations, taken with the other evidence it acquires a certain significance.

Even more compelling evidence that Katherine Carey was the King's child emerged after William Carey died of the sweating sickness in 1528, leaving Mary destitute with two young children. The King forced her reluctant father, Thomas Boleyn, Lord Rochford, to take her under his roof and maintain her, and she returned to Hever Castle. Later that year, at Anne Boleyn's behest, Henry VIII assigned Mary a substantial annuity that had formerly been paid to her late husband, a most generous gesture. Was it made to please Anne? Probably, but it is also possible that the King was making provision for Katherine Carey, now that William Carey was no longer alive to be a surrogate father to a royal bastard. That would account for Henry's openhandedness, which is comparable to the inexplicably large grant he made to another probable bastard daughter, Etheldreda Malte, some eighteen years later. Bolstered by the other circumstantial evidence, this is one of the most compelling arguments for Henry's paternity of Katherine Carey.

Mary Boleyn described her years at Hever Castle with her children as a time when she had been "in bondage." Maybe she stayed for the sake of her daughter, so that she could put money by for her—Katherine would need a dowry one day, and the greater it was, the better chance she would have of making a good match. Fortunately, Thomas Boleyn was often away at court, leaving behind him a household of women: his burdensome daughter Mary; his possibly estranged wife, Elizabeth Howard; his insane and aging mother; and his four-year-old fatherless granddaughter. It cannot have been the happiest of households.

Very little is recorded of Mary during the six years of her widowhood. She was a silent witness to the meteoric career of her sister, Anne, and the ascendancy of her family, but she either preferred to remain in the background, or it was deemed fitting by others that she should do so—and with good reason.

In 1533, Anne Boleyn became queen and gave birth to a daughter, the future Elizabeth I. It is possible that Katherine Carey, who was nine when the Princess was born, joined her little cousin's household, which was set up at the palace of Hatfield, Hertfordshire, in December 1533, and thereafter perambulated between the nursery palaces of the Thames Valley. Being in such early close proximity may in part account for Elizabeth's great affection for Katherine in later life.

Katherine's world was rocked in 1534, when Mary Boleyn married a man deemed a nobody, William Stafford, thereby incurring the anger of the King and Queen, who banished her from court. Apparently, Henry was persuaded to cut off her royal pension, as in a letter to Thomas Cromwell, written three months later, Mary refers to having to beg her bread with her new husband. They were to pass the rest of their married life in relative obscurity and poverty. By 1535, Mary's son, Henry Carey, now ten, had been removed from her care, and was living at Syon Abbey, receiving a good education as Anne Boleyn's ward.

Given that she belonged to a family known for its radical opinions on religious reform, Mary Boleyn probably had similar views, while William Stafford later revealed himself to be so staunch a Protestant that he was prepared to choose exile in Geneva during Mary I's reign rather than stay at home and risk persecution for his beliefs, and there became a friend of the austere reformer, John Calvin. Katherine Carey would also marry a man who was "well affected to the Protestant religion," and they too chose exile.

From 1534 to 1539, Mary Boleyn probably lived in English-held Calais, where William Stafford was a member of the garrison. That would explain the absence of any reference to them in contemporary records at this time and account for how the couple managed to subsist during the time of their disgrace—and it would also explain why there is no mention of Mary in the numerous sources documenting the cataclysmic fall of the Boleyns—and Anne Boleyn's execution—in 1536.

It is possible that Katherine went with the Staffords to Calais, yet given her well-established closeness to the future Elizabeth I, it is likely that she was still in Elizabeth's household, perhaps as a companion, as she is not listed among her servants. In the novel, she is there at the time of Anne Boleyn's fall, and a witness to her little cousin's loss of status, for after the two-year-old Princess was declared a bastard, she was styled the Lady Elizabeth and her household was reduced. Nevertheless, it remained royal, by any standards, and she continued to be served as if she were the King's legitimate daughter.

For more than a century, a tale has circulated that Katherine Carey was one of the four distressed (but unnamed) young ladies who attended Anne Boleyn in the Tower during the four days after her condemnation and accompanied her to the scaffold. The tale appears to derive from Augustus Hare, writing in 1878 of Katherine's tomb in Westminster Abbey, but he does not cite his source, and one hopes that Katherine, at twelve, would have been considered too young for such a grim duty. There is no record of her serving Anne Boleyn, and she is not recorded as a maid-of-honor until 1539. Even so, I have made dramatic use of the legend in this novel. Even if Katherine was not present at her aunt's execution, it would surely have had a terrible impact on her.

In November 1539, when Katherine was fifteen, she was appointed a maid-of-honor to Henry VIII's fourth wife, Anne of Cleves. Her great-uncle, the Duke of Norfolk, had secured similar positions for two of his other great-nieces, Katheryn Howard and Mary Norris, but he had been estranged from Anne Boleyn and probably had no time for her sister, Mary, so it is unlikely that Katherine's appointment owed anything to his influence. However, if Katherine was the King's daughter, then Henry VIII himself may have ordered her appointment. She was not the King's ward, and he was not obliged to make provision for her, although, of course, his interest in his daughter is easily explained. It is perhaps telling that, of all the girls of noble and gentle birth who might have been lucky enough to gain places in the new Queen's household—and the clamor for such places was great—Katherine, who had little merit as the daughter of Henry's former mistress, niece of his executed wife, and scion of the disgraced Boleyns, was one of the few who were chosen. Soon afterward, she was to make a good marriage to an up-and-coming courtier. This all points to Henry doing his duty as a father in providing for her.

Katherine came to court ready to serve the new Queen prior to the latter's arrival in January 1540. On 26 April, aged sixteen, she was married to Sir Francis Knollys, aged perhaps twenty-six, a Gentleman Pensioner of Henry VIII's household and a colleague of William Stafford. No royal grants or gifts marked the marriage, although the King's influence may be perceived in an Act of Parliament that was passed the same year confirming the couple's title to the manor of Rotherfield Greys near Henley in Oxfordshire, previously held by Knollys's father. It was here, at Greys Court, a fourteenth-century manor house and tower with a Tudor house added on, that Katherine and Francis made their home. In 1542, Francis was elected MP for Horsham. The couple's first child was born in 1541 and named after the King.

According to her memorial plaque in Westminster Abbey, Katherine bore Francis Knollys sixteen children—eight boys and eight girls—of whom at least eleven survived infancy. Only fifteen are shown in effigy as kneeling weepers on their parents' magnificent (but empty) tomb at Rotherfield Greys, built by their son William in 1605. There are seven sons on one side, seven daughters on the other, and a swaddled infant lying beside the effigy of its mother. The births of the children—who might have been Henry VIII's grandchildren—were recorded "in order" by Knollys himself in his Latin dictionary, but he listed only fourteen: eight sons and six daughters. The last child he recorded was Dudley, born in 1562, the only one of the brood known to have died young, being "killed" soon after her birth. Almost certainly, she is the infant lying beside the recumbent figure of Katherine Carey at Rotherfield Greys. I have assumed that her elder sister Maud also died young. The missing daughter probably died at birth or was stillborn.

I have speculated that Mary Boleyn died at Henden Manor, Kent, which she had inherited from her father as his co-heiress, and that she was buried in the local parish church of St. Mary the Virgin at Sundridge, Kent. It is sometimes stated that she died at

Rochford Hall in Essex, but she did not come into possession of it until four days before her death, so it's unlikely that she died there.

Under Edward VI, Francis Knollys distinguished himself in the war against the Scots, and for this he was knighted. A staunch Calvinist, he was forced to flee abroad after Mary I began burning Protestants for heresy in 1555; Katherine followed him before June 1557. At least five of their children went with them. When Katherine left England, her "loving cousin" Elizabeth wrote a sad letter of farewell and signed it "*Cor Rotto*" ("Broken Heart"). This is primary evidence that the two women were close and had long since laid the enduring foundations of future friendship. The shared bond of religion had surely brought them closer in the difficult days of Mary's reign, and Elizabeth's assurance that she would wait "with joy" for Katherine's "short return" betrays her hope that her half sister's rule would not last long.

The Knollyses' sojourn in Europe is not well documented, so I have had to be creative in imagining their life there. Queen Mary's agents did kidnap some Protestants and bring them back to England; we have no record of any attempts to capture Katherine or Francis, but I have invented two for dramatic purposes, to illustrate that exile did not necessarily guarantee safety.

On Elizabeth's accession in 1558, the couple deemed it safe to return home. The new Queen had a policy of advancing her Boleyn relatives, but only on their merits; the Careys were her closest blood relations on her mother's side, toward whom she always behaved with far more familiarity than she used to other members of her court. Sir Francis was made a Privy Councillor, Vice-Chamberlain of the Queen's Household, and Governor of Portsmouth. Amid fierce competition for places at court, Katherine was appointed a Lady of the Privy Chamber, alongside her sister-in-law, Anne Morgan, Henry Carey's wife, and of course her Carey nieces. The Knollys children, like their cousins, the young Careys, were welcomed at Elizabeth's court, and several made good careers or marriages there, while some of the daughters waited upon the Queen. They all basked in her favor and may have been substitutes for the grandchildren she never had.

The acknowledged existence of a Carey half sibling would undoubtedly have been a considerable embarrassment to Queen Elizabeth, and could even have compromised the legitimacy of her title to the throne; she had herself been declared illegitimate in 1536, probably on the grounds that her parents' marriage was invalid because Henry VIII's affair with Mary Boleyn had created a canonical bar to his marriage to her sister, Anne, a ruling that had never been reversed. In the eyes of Catholic Europe, the new Queen was a bastard, a heretic, and a usurper. It would therefore have been politically disadvantageous for her openly to acknowledge Katherine as Henry VIII's natural child, living proof of the impediment to Elizabeth's parents' marriage.

Elizabeth "loved Lady Knollys above all other women in the world." Katherine clearly had an attractive personality, being graced with "wit and counsel sound" and "a mind so clean [and] devoid of guile." She received some of the most expensive presents Elizabeth ever gave and was entrusted with the safekeeping of gifts presented to her mistress. However, Elizabeth's love for Katherine was marred by selfishness: she wanted her in constant attendance, regardless of Katherine's own needs or those of her family. She was temperamental and her sharp tongue sometimes made Katherine "weep for unkindness."

To make matters worse, during the first decade of her reign, Elizabeth kept Sir Francis Knollys busy with diplomatic missions. In May 1568, when the deposed Mary, Queen of Scots, fled to England and was placed under house arrest, he was appointed her custodian. Knollys pleaded to be allowed to take his wife with him when he was sent north that year, but Elizabeth refused to be parted from her. In the winter, learning that Katherine had fallen ill with a fever, he begged in vain to be recalled. His repeated requests for leave of absence to visit his ailing wife were also ignored, and he was distraught at Elizabeth's "ungrateful denial of my coming to the court." In his last letter to Katherine, he wrote of how he desired them both to retire from the Queen's service and live "a poor country life"—much as his mother-in-law had done with William Stafford.

In his absence, the ailing Katherine had to make do with being "very often visited by the Queen's comfortable presence." When she felt a little better, she asked Elizabeth if she might travel north to be with her husband, but Elizabeth adamantly refused to allow it, arguing that "the journey might be to her danger or discommodity." She was fearful for Katherine's health, and when her cousin suffered a relapse, she had her nursed in a bedchamber near to her own and sat with her often.

Mary, Queen of Scots, would blame Elizabeth for Katherine's early death at the age of nearly forty-five, claiming that it was the consequence of her husband's enforced absence in the north during the last months of her life. In fact, we do not know the cause of her death, save that she had recurring fevers; some have suggested that years of relentless childbearing had undermined her health. She passed away on 15 January 1569 at Hampton Court while Sir Francis was still at Bolton Castle guarding Mary, Queen of Scots.

Elizabeth collapsed in "passions of grief for the death of her kinswoman and good servant, falling for a while from a prince wanting nothing in this world to private mourning, in which solitary estate, being forgetful of her own health, she took cold, wherewith she was much troubled." As for the bereaved husband, he was "distracted with sorrow" for his great loss. "My case is pitiful," he wrote.

In April 1569, Elizabeth arranged for Katherine to be buried in St. Edmund's Chapel in Westminster Abbey, herself paying handsomely for the funeral—far more than she ever spent on burying other cousins, even those of royal birth. And, perhaps for a very good reason, this was almost a royal funeral. The obsequies were directed by the Duke of Norfolk, as Earl Marshal, and the Earl of Leicester, the Lord Treasurer. The funerary furniture was so valuable that it became the subject of a dispute between the Chapter of Westminster Abbey and the College of Arms. A mural tablet of alabaster, adorned with armorial shields—one of the first of its kind in the abbey—marks Katherine's resting place.

It is often said that Henry VIII's line died out with Elizabeth I. None of his legitimate children left issue, and his acknowledged bastard, Richmond, was childless. But if Katherine Carey was

Henry's daughter, as seems likely, then his direct bloodline survives in numerous direct descendants.

I should like to express my warmest thanks and appreciation to my wonderful commissioning editors, Frances Edwards of Headline in the UK and Susanna Porter of Ballantine in the USA, for their encouragement and support. I owe a huge debt of gratitude to both publishing teams for their expertise and professionalism, and especially to my fabulous editor, Flora Rees, whose sensitive creative input has been invaluable. I would like also to thank my publicist, Alara Delfosse, for the tremendous help she gives me, and to my excellent copy editor, Mary Chamberlain. To my amazing literary agents, Julian Alexander and Ben Clark, and their assistant, Sarah Stamp, I owe more than I can express—you're all stars!

This book is based on research I undertook for my biography of Mary Boleyn, but among the numerous sources I have since consulted, I would specially like warmly to acknowledge Wendy J. Dunn's book, *Henry VIII's True Daughter.*

Special thanks and love go to my family and friends, who have supported me during the writing of this book, especially my lovely daughter, Kate, and her husband, Jason, my cousin Chris, and uncle and aunt John and Jo.

Alison Weir
Carshalton, July 2025

Dramatis Personae

Characters are listed in order of appearance.
The names of fictional characters are in italics.

Katherine (Kate) Carey, daughter of Mary Boleyn and, probably, Henry VIII

The Princess Elizabeth, later Queen Elizabeth I, daughter of Henry VIII and Anne Boleyn

Margaret, Lady Bryan, Elizabeth's Lady Mistress

Henry VIII, King of England

Anne Boleyn, Queen of England, his second wife

Thomas Boleyn, Earl of Wiltshire, Katherine Carey's maternal grandfather

Mary Boleyn, his daughter, sister of Anne Boleyn; Katherine's mother

Henry Carey (Harry), later Lord Hunsdon, Katherine's brother

William Carey, Mary Boleyn's husband; Katherine's legal father

Elizabeth Howard, Countess of Wiltshire, wife of Thomas Boleyn; Katherine's grandmother

Thomas Howard, 2nd Duke of Norfolk, her father; Katherine's great-grandfather

Katherine of Aragon, Queen of England, first wife of Henry VIII

George Boleyn, Viscount Rochford, Katherine's uncle

Jane Parker, Lady Rochford, his wife, Katherine's aunt

Margaret Butler, Lady Boleyn, mother of Thomas Boleyn; Katherine's great-grandmother

William (Will) Stafford, later Sir William Stafford, Mary Boleyn's second husband; Katherine's stepfather

Sir William Kingston, Constable of the Tower of London

Elizabeth Wood, Lady Boleyn, Katherine's great-aunt

Mary Scrope, Lady Kingston, wife of Sir William Kingston

Mary Norris, maid-of-honor

Mary Zouche, maid-of-honor

Nan Cobham, maid-of-honor

Thomas Cromwell, "Master Secretary," the King's chief minister

The Gentleman Jailer of the Tower

Thomas Howard, 3rd Duke of Norfolk, Katherine's great-uncle

Sir Christopher Hales, Attorney General

Sir Henry Norris, Groom of the Stool, father of Mary Norris

Henry Howard, Earl of Surrey, son and heir of Thomas Howard, 3rd Duke of Norfolk

Charles Brandon, Duke of Suffolk, brother-in-law to Henry VIII

Jane Seymour, Queen of England, third wife of Henry VIII

Mrs. Orchard, Anne Boleyn's former nurse

Thomas Cranmer, Archbishop of Canterbury

Father Thirlwall, Anne Boleyn's confessor

The Sheriff of London

The executioner: the "Sword of Calais"

The Lord Mayor of London

Kat Champernowne, later Ashley, Elizabeth's governess, later her Mother of the Maids, Lady of the Privy Chamber, and Chief Lady of the Bedchamber

Sir John Shelton, governor of the Princess Elizabeth's household; Katherine's great-uncle

The Lady Mary, later Mary I, Queen of England, daughter of Henry VIII and Katherine of Aragon

Blanche Milborne, Lady Herbert of Troy, gentlewoman, then Lady Mistress, to the young Elizabeth I

Jane the Fool, Mary's female jester

Mark Smeaton, musician, one of Anne Boleyn's executed alleged lovers

Father Matthew Parker, Elizabeth's chaplain, later Archbishop of Canterbury

Geoffrey Chaucer, author

Pope Clement VII

Martin Luther, founder of the Protestant religion

Prince Edward, later Edward VI, King of England, son of Henry VIII and Jane Seymour

St. Edward the Confessor, King of England

Christina of Denmark, Duchess of Milan

Anna of Cleves, Queen of England, fourth wife of Henry VIII

William, Lord Sandys, the Lord Chamberlain

Mrs. Stonor, Mother of the Maids to Anna of Cleves

Anne Bassett, maid-of-honor

Dorothy Bray, maid-of-honor

Ursula Stourton, maid-of-honor

Katheryn Howard, Queen of England, fifth wife of Henry VIII

Mistress Sybil Penn, nurse to Prince Edward

The Lord of Misrule at Henry VIII's court

Lady Margaret Douglas, Henry VIII's niece

Mary Howard, Duchess of Richmond, daughter of Thomas Howard, 3rd Duke of Norfolk, and widow of Henry Fitzroy, Duke of Richmond, Henry VIII's bastard son

Katherine Willoughby, Duchess of Suffolk, wife of Charles Brandon, Duke of Suffolk

Eleanor Paston, Countess of Rutland

Katherine St. John, Lady Edgcumbe, lady-in-waiting

Thomas Manners, Earl of Rutland, Chamberlain to Anna of Cleves

Frances Brandon, Marchioness of Dorset, later Duchess of Suffolk, daughter of Charles Brandon, Duke of Suffolk, and Mary Tudor, Queen of France, and niece of Henry VIII

Sir John Dudley, Master of the Horse to Anna of Cleves, later Earl of Warwick and Duke of Northumberland

Francis Knollys, later Sir Francis Knollys, Kate's husband

Mother Lowe, Mistress of the German Maids to Anna of Cleves

Sir Robert Knollys, father of Francis Knollys

Henry VII, King of England

Mary, sister of Francis Knollys

Jane, sister of Francis Knollys

Henry, brother of Francis Knollys

Sir Francis Bryan, courtier, son of Margaret, Lady Bryan, and guardian of Henry Carey

Susanna Gilman (née Horenbout), artist, lady-in-waiting

Baron Oberstein, a nobleman of Cleves

Grand Master Hochsteden, a dignitary of Cleves

Henry Bourchier, Earl of Essex

Will Somers, Henry VIII's fool

Thomas Culpeper, courtier

Richard Beard, courtier

Cardinal Wolsey, Henry VIII's former minister

Stephen Gardiner, Bishop of Winchester, later Lord Chancellor

Richard III, King of England

The Widville family, relatives of Henry VIII through his maternal grandmother, Elizabeth Widville, queen of Edward IV

Edward Stafford, Duke of Buckingham

The Stafford family

Thomas Butler, Earl of Ormond

Lettice Peniston, Lady Lee, mother of Francis Knollys

Sir Robert Lee, her late husband

An innkeeper at the Bell Inn, Whitehall

The Lovell family, former owners of Greys Court

Bilkins, steward at Greys Court

The Grey family, owners of Greys Court

Matthews, cook at Greys Court

Thomasina, Katherine's maid

Mother Ash, Katherine's midwife

Henry (Hal) Knollys, Katherine's first son

Edward I, King of England

Mrs. Clements, Katherine's wet nurse

Mrs. Wellgood, nurse to Katherine's children

Francis Dereham, secretary to Katheryn Howard

Mary Knollys, Katherine's first daughter and second child

Thomasina's father

Mary Tudor, Queen of France, later Duchess of Suffolk, sister of Henry VIII

Louis XII, King of France, her husband

François I, King of France

Claude of Valois, Queen of France, his wife

Arthur Tudor, Prince of Wales, older brother of Henry VIII and first husband of Katherine of Aragon

Henry Fitzroy, Duke of Richmond, bastard son of Henry VIII

Bessie Blount, his mother

Katharine Parr, Queen of England, sixth wife of Henry VIII

The goodwife who made puddings for Henry VIII

Elizabeth of York, Queen of England, mother of Henry VIII

Latetitia (Lettice) Knollys, Katherine's second daughter and third child

Thomas Wriothesley, Lord Chancellor

Edward Seymour, Earl of Hertford, later Duke of Somerset and Lord Protector of England; brother of Jane Seymour

William Knollys, Katherine's second son and fourth child

Mary, Queen of Scots

Anne Morgan, wife of Henry Carey

Sir Thomas Morgan, her father

Anne Whitney, Lady Morgan, her mother

Edward (Ned) Knollys, Katherine's third son and fifth child

Father Paul, chaplain to the Knollyses

Thomas Seymour, Lord Sudeley, brother of Jane Seymour and husband of Katharine Parr

Lady Jane Grey, granddaughter of Mary Tudor, Queen of France, and Henry VIII's great-niece

Robert Knollys, Katherine's fourth son and sixth child

Richard Knollys, Katherine's fifth son and seventh child

Elizabeth (Beth) Knollys, Katherine's fourth daughter and seventh child

William Cecil, later Sir William Cecil, statesman, later Secretary of State to Elizabeth I

Maud Knollys, Katherine's third daughter and sixth child

Dr. Julius Palmer, tutor to the Knollys children

Dorothy (Dot) Stafford, second wife of William Stafford

Joan Champernowne, sister of Kat Ashley

Sir Anthony Denny, her husband

Thomas Parry, Elizabeth's comptroller

Edward Stafford, son of William and Dorothy Stafford

Henry, Lord Stafford, father of Dorothy Stafford

Ursula Pole, his wife

Edward III, King of England

Margaret Pole, Countess of Salisbury, niece of Edward IV and Richard III, and mother of Ursula Pole

Edward IV, King of England

George, Duke of Clarence, his brother

Richard, Lord Rich

Philadelphia Carey, daughter of Henry Carey

Lord Guildford Dudley, son of John Dudley, Duke of Northumberland

Lord Robert Dudley, later Master of the Horse and Earl of Leicester, son of John Dudley, Duke of Northumberland

Father Michael, the priest at Rotherfield Greys

Antoine de Noailles, French ambassador

Charles V, Holy Roman Emperor and King of Spain

Henri II, King of France

Francis (Frank) Knollys, Katherine's sixth son and tenth child

Pope Julius III

John Calvin, French theologist and preacher

Philip of Spain, son and heir of the Emperor Charles V; husband of Mary I and King Consort of England, later Philip II, King of Spain

Simon Renard, Imperial ambassador

Edward Courtenay, great-grandson of Edward IV

Pierre Viret, religious reformer

Sir Thomas Wyatt, rebel leader

William Herbert, Earl of Pembroke

Henry Grey, Duke of Suffolk, husband of Frances Brandon and father of Lady Jane Grey

Sir John Gage, Constable of the Tower

Cardinal Reginald Pole, Archbishop of Canterbury, son of Margaret Pole, Countess of Salisbury

John Hooper, Bishop of Gloucester

John Rogers, Protestant martyr

Anne Knollys, Katherine's fifth daughter and eleventh child

Hugh Latimer, Bishop of Worcester

Nicholas Ridley, Bishop of London

Ferdinand of Habsburg, Archduke of Austria, later Ferdinand I, Holy Roman Emperor

Elizabeth, Edward, Ursula, William, John, and Dorothy Stafford, children of William and Dorothy Stafford

Sir Robert Stafford, brother of William Stafford

The Mayor of Reading

Katherine's sixth daughter and twelfth child, unbaptized and unnamed

Roger Ascham, Elizabeth's tutor

Anne Seymour, Countess of Warwick

Thomas, Katherine's groom

Ilse, a slatternly cleaning woman of Basel

Eva, a cleaning woman of Basel

John Foxe, Protestant clergyman, theologian, and author

Master Thomas Stafford, Francis Knollys's attorney

Sir John Cheke, Edward VI's tutor

William, Lord Paget

Mary Hill, Sir John Cheke's wife

Sir John Mason, her stepfather

A man in black

Meg, nursemaid to the Knollys children

John Weller, London merchant, exile in Frankfurt

Susan Weller, his wife

John Knox, Scottish Calvinist reformer

François, Dauphin of France, later François II, King of France, first husband of Mary, Queen of Scots

Marie de Guise, Regent of Scotland, mother of Mary, Queen of Scots

Thomas Knollys, Katherine's seventh son and thirteenth child

Another man in black

The portress at a convent in Frankfurt

The Abbess of the convent in Frankfurt

Johann Hummel, a Protestant of Strasbourg

Gerda, Johann Hummel's servant

William, Lord Howard of Effingham, Lord Chamberlain

Master Ingham, tutor to the Knollys children

Edith, nursemaid to the Knollys children

Blanche Parry, Elizabeth I's former nurse, Lady of the Privy Chamber to Elizabeth I

Elizabeth Bryan, Lady Carew, Lady of the Privy Chamber to Elizabeth I

John Astley, husband of Kat Ashley (who spelled her married name Ashley)

Katherine Carey, daughter of Henry Carey

Eleanor Brandon, Countess of Cumberland, daughter of Mary Tudor, Queen of France and Duchess of Suffolk, and niece of Henry VIII

Lady Katherine Grey, sister of Lady Jane Grey

Lady Mary Grey, sister of Lady Jane Grey

Lady Margaret Clifford, daughter of Eleanor Brandon

Henry Stanley, Lord Strange, her husband

Margaret Tudor, Queen of Scots, sister of Henry VIII and mother of Lady Margaret Douglas

James IV, King of Scots, her first husband

Archibald Douglas, Earl of Angus, second husband of Margaret Tudor and father of Lady Margaret Douglas

Matthew Stewart, Earl of Lennox, husband of Lady Margaret Douglas

Henry Stewart, Lord Darnley, their son, third husband of Mary, Queen of Scots, and King of Scots

Charles Stewart, his brother

Sir Nicholas Bacon, Lord Keeper of the Great Seal

Sir Thomas Gargrave, Speaker of the House of Commons

Thomas Howard, 4th Duke of Norfolk

Charles of Habsburg, Archduke of Austria, son of the Emperor Ferdinand I, and one of Elizabeth I's suitors

Henry Fitzalan, Earl of Arundel, one of Elizabeth I's suitors

Sir William Pickering, one of Elizabeth I's suitors

Amy Robsart, wife of Lord Robert Dudley

William Parr, Marquess of Northampton

Henry Manners, 2nd Earl of Rutland

Baron Breuner, Imperial ambassador

Bishop Alvaro de Quadra, Spanish ambassador

Prince Erik of Sweden, later Erik XIV, King of Sweden, one of Elizabeth I's suitors

Francis I, Duke of Saxony, one of Elizabeth I's suitors

Catherine de' Medici, Dowager Queen of France, mother of François II

Adolf, Duke of Holstein, one of Elizabeth I's suitors

A servant of Baron Breuner

Henri, Duke of Guise, uncle of Mary, Queen of Scots

Charles de Guise, Cardinal of Lorraine, uncle of Mary, Queen of Scots

James Hamilton, Earl of Arran, one of Elizabeth I's suitors

Master Borth, Imperial agent

Mistress Bilkins, wife of the Knollyses' steward

Catherine Knollys, Katherine's seventh daughter and fourteenth child

Master Bowes, Lord Robert Dudley's manservant

A coroner

Thomas Ratcliff, Earl of Sussex

Mildred Cooke, wife of Sir William Cecil

Edward Seymour, Earl of Hertford, husband of Lady Katherine Grey

Edward Seymour, their son

Walter Devereux, Viscount Hereford, husband of Lettice Knollys

Steven van der Meulen, court painter

Dudley Knollys, Katherine's eighth daughter and fifteenth child

Douglas Howard, Lady Sheffield

Elizabeth Tailboys, Countess of Warwick, daughter of Henry VIII and Bessie Blount

German physician

A nurse to Dudley Knollys

Penelope Devereux, daughter of Walter Devereux, Viscount Hereford, and Lettice Knollys

Ambrose Dudley, Earl of Warwick, brother of Robert Dudley, Earl of Leicester

The Lieutenant of the Tower

Thomas Seymour, son of Edward Seymour, Earl of Hertford, and Lady Katherine Grey

Don Carlos, son and heir of Philip II, King of Spain

Sir James Melville, Scottish envoy

Count John Casimir, son of Frederick III, Elector Palatine

Dorothy Devereux, daughter of Walter Devereux, Viscount Hereford, and Lettice Knollys

Margaret Cave, wife of Henry (Hal) Knollys

Sir Ambrose Cave, Chancellor of the Duchy of Lancaster, her father

Dr. Robert Huicke, royal physician

Thomas Keyes, Serjeant-Porter, husband of Lady Mary Grey

Edmund Grindal, Bishop of London

Sir Thomas Heneage, courtier

Robert Devereux, son of Walter Devereux, Viscount Hereford, and Lettice Knollys

David Rizzio, secretary to Mary, Queen of Scots

James Hepburn, Earl of Bothwell, third husband of Mary, Queen of Scots

Sir Henry Sidney, Lord Deputy in Ireland

Prince James, son of Mary, Queen of Scots, and Lord Darnley; later James I, King of England

William Douglas, guardian of Mary, Queen of Scots, at Lochleven Castle

George Douglas, his brother

Henry, Lord Scrope of Bolton

Various lords, ladies, Privy Councillors, gentlemen, knights, officers of the royal household, ladies-in-waiting, maids-of-honor, courtiers, ambassadors, Members of Parliament, bishops, clergymen, clerks, scholars, physicians, yeomen warders, Yeomen of the Guard, Gentlemen Pensioners, soldiers, guards, stewards, servants, grooms, ushers, harbingers, messengers, midwives, nurses, tutors, mummers, executioners, spies, workmen, citizens.

About the Author

ALISON WEIR is the *New York Times* bestselling author of *The King's Pleasure, The Last White Rose,* and the novels in the Six Tudor Queens series: *Katharine Parr, The Sixth Wife; Katheryn Howard, The Scandalous Queen; Anna of Kleve, The Princess in the Portrait; Jane Seymour, The Haunted Queen; Anne Boleyn, A King's Obsession;* and *Katherine of Aragon, The True Queen.* She has also written numerous earlier novels and historical biographies, including her England's Medieval Queens series.

alisonweir.org.uk
facebook.com/AlisonWeirAuthor
X: @AlisonWeirBooks

About the Type

This book was set in Garamond, a typeface originally designed by the Parisian type cutter Claude Garamond (c. 1500–61). This version of Garamond was modeled on a 1592 specimen sheet from the Egenolff-Berner foundry, which was produced from types assumed to have been brought to Frankfurt by the punch cutter Jacques Sabon (c. 1520–80).

Claude Garamond's distinguished romans and italics first appeared in *Opera Ciceronis* in 1543–44. The Garamond types are clear, open, and elegant.